Kaleidoscope

PERSPECTIVE CHANGES IN
FOUR SUSPENSE-FILLED ROMANCES

LAURALEE BLISS
GLORIA BRANDT
DIANN MILLS
KATHLEEN PAUL

BARBOUR
PUBLISHING

Behind the Mask © 1999 by Lauralee Bliss
Yesteryear © 2001 by Gloria Brandt
Love in Pursuit © 2001 by DiAnn Mills
Escape © 1999 by Kathleen Paul

ISBN 1-59310-166-X

Cover design by Corbis

Published by Barbour Publishing, Inc., P.O. Box 719, Uhrichsville, Ohio 44683, www.barbourbooks.com

Our mission is to publish and distribute inspirational products offering exceptional value and biblical encouragement to the masses.

 Member of the
Evangelical Christian
Publishers Association

Printed in the United States of America.
5 4 3 2

Kaleidoscope

Behind the Mask

Lauralee Bliss

To my beloved grandmother and namesake, Laura Schreiber, who so eagerly anticipated this book. I love you, Grandma.

Chapter 1

Gail Shelton despised airline travel. Although she never confessed her fear to anyone, her stomach would twist into painful knots, and a solid lump would form in her throat the moment she boarded an aircraft. Today was no exception. As she walked unsteadily down the passenger tunnel linking the aircraft to the terminal building, she clutched her stomach and swallowed the bile that rose in her throat.

The plane had encountered severe turbulence during its descent through a bank of puffy clouds into Logan International Airport, Boston's thriving air transportation center. Knowing her propensity for air sickness, Gail had pawed through the magazines stuffed inside the pocket of the seat in front of her, searching for the motion sickness bag. She had wanted to keep it close at hand. Next to her had sat an elderly woman, a pair of knitting needles clicking between her fingers, who conversed nonstop about her grandchildren. Beneath the tangle of yarn and needles emerged the beginnings of a blue baby sweater for a new arrival, or so the lady informed her. Gail's mind had buzzed with the woman's incessant chattering until, in desperation, she pulled out an airline magazine and pretended to read the boring articles. The woman had peered over Gail's shoulder at the article on summer gardening and immediately launched into a diatribe on the varieties of flowers and vegetables she raised. Gail sensed her irritation rising to the brink of an explosion. She forced down a sharp reply and continued reading.

After the normal flight time had elapsed, the captain warned his passengers of imminent turbulence as the plane approached Logan. As her seat shook, Gail imagined the plane taking a nosedive into the frothy waves of the Atlantic Ocean, near Boston Harbor. Clutching the armrest in one hand and the motion sickness bag in the other, she wondered if the seats really would serve as flotation devices. Somewhere she had once read that the chance of surviving a crash would be greater if the passenger's seat was located in the tail section of the plane. Aware that her seat was near the nose of the plane, fear formed a hard lump in her stomach. She closed her eyes and began to pray.

At last Gail had felt the plane touch down on the runway. Her stomach lurched into her throat then settled into its place. The plane cruised around the maze of runways to finally rest at the gate where she hoped her sister and brother-in-law would be waiting.

Now as Gail walked briskly down the carpeted passenger causeway, thankful to be done with the dreadful flight, her foot suddenly twisted beneath her. Passengers bumped into her from behind, uttering quick apologies, as Gail looked down to find the heel of her pump resting on the floor. "Great," she muttered, grabbing up the broken heel in disgust. "If anything else goes wrong today, I'm going to tell Dorrie to drive me back to New York and save the visit for some other time."

Hefting her purse and her carry-on, Gail hobbled down to the gate where cushioned chairs were aligned in rows. Passengers sat reading newspapers or books while waiting for the next flight. Gail scanned the countless faces before her but recognized none of them. "I'll bet Dorrie forgot I was coming today," she grumbled, limping along on one high heel.

Finally, she heard a voice shout her name, and strong arms grabbed her up in a hefty embrace. "Oh, I'm so glad to see you!" Dorrie cried, whirling Gail around with the force of her affection.

Gail politely wiggled her way out of the embrace. "Look, it's been a long day, Dorrie."

"C'mon, let's go get your luggage then." Dorrie noticed the pointed object in Gail's hand. "What's that?"

"It used to be part of my shoe," she grumbled, showing her older sister the mismatched shoes and the gaping hole where the heel had once been nailed. "This trip hasn't gone right since the moment I left. Some old lady sitting next to me talked the entire time. Then the plane tossed around so much, I almost threw up the bag of peanuts they gave us as a snack."

Dorrie tugged on Gail's left hand. "C'mon, forget your miseries and show me the rock."

"The rock? Oh, you mean my ring."

"Yes, your ring. We aren't going to baggage claim until I see it."

Gail sheepishly brought forth her hand, only to scowl at the chipped nail on her forefinger, a victim of the storage bin that had contained her carry-on. The huge diamond glittered in the lights of the terminal.

Dorrie whistled. "Whooo-eee, now that's some rock! It's at least two carats— maybe ten, by the size of the thing. Is this guy of yours loaded or what?"

"Keith is a very hard worker," Gail quickly answered, withdrawing her hand from her sister's view. "He makes good money repairing computers now that he's no longer a waiter."

"I'll say he does. Wow! Well, c'mon, Mick's supposed to meet us at the baggage claim after he parks the car."

"Did you bring Jamie?"

Dorrie shot her a grin. "Well, since he is a bit young at ten months to care for himself, I decided to bring him along for the ride."

Gail frowned as she followed her sister through the hordes of people headed for the baggage area. "There you go making fun of me already, and I've only been here ten minutes."

Dorrie hooked her arm through Gail's and gave a squeeze. "I'm not trying to poke fun at you. I was only making a joke. Don't be so serious."

Gail exhaled an exasperated sigh. "If you'd had the kind of day I've had, you'd be serious, too."

"Well, you're here safe and sound, and your nephew can't wait to see his favorite aunt. Plus, I'm dying to hear all the wedding plans. I'm still the matron of honor, right?"

Gail held her carry-on bag up before Dorrie. "I have all the information tucked right in here. Ask me when we get out of this stuffy airport and to a place where I can freshen up. I must look like a wreck." She sniffed her clothing, scrunching up her nose at the odor of plane exhaust. "I've got to change my clothes and put on some perfume after the stench of that airplane."

Dorrie laughed. "Same ol' Gail," she said before adding quickly, "but I wouldn't want you any other way. You did my makeup on my wedding day and taught me everything I needed to know about etiquette. I suppose Mother appreciated the fact that Mick and I finally agreed to have the marriage ceremony inside a church."

"If we had settled on your version of a wedding, the ceremony would've taken place in some backwoods camping area with mosquitoes and flies all over the wedding cake. A church is where people are supposed to get married."

"And we had a great time. I'll never forget it as long as I live."

Gail cast her sister a sideways glance. "I'll bet you won't forget when I tried to catch your bouquet and collided instead with the punch bowl."

Dorrie shrugged as a broad smile crossed her lean features. "Hey, what's a wedding without a few bumbles? You were the star of the show, Gail."

"And so was my yellow bridesmaid's gown with red polka dots, as I remember." Dorrie laughed merrily.

"But if I hadn't crashed into the punch bowl, I wouldn't have met Keith."

Dorrie paused at that moment to clutch her throat, extend her hand, and act out in distress, "Oh, this is simply dreadful! Look at my lemon yellow gown! I look worse than a child with chicken pox! Please, dearest waiter, would you help me? Oh, you are the most wonderful man!"

Gail couldn't help but smile. "He was wonderful—my hero of the night. He helped me to my feet and found a mop to clean up the spill. I'm so glad he doesn't do that job for a living anymore. This computer business is certainly much better."

"I'll say, judging from the size of the rock you're wearing. Well, here we are— baggage claim."

The shrill of a baby in distress halted their conversation. Without a word, Dorrie took off through the crowd, leaving a bewildered Gail to search the sea of faces for her sister. Finally, she noticed the tall form of Dorrie's husband, Mick, standing next to a stroller. He was trying in vain to comfort the screeching ten-month-old. "He sure has a set of lungs on him," Mick was saying as he surrendered the fussy infant into Dorrie's care. "Must come from your side of the family."

"Hey, I don't even know where I'm going and you leave me in the middle of a crowd!" Gail interrupted as she stumbled up, tucking loose strands of curly hair behind her ear.

"Sorry, but this noisy baby needed his mother," Dorrie said, cradling the infant who began sucking on his fist. "Just follow the shrieks and you'll always find Jamie Walters."

"Good to see you again, Gail," Mick said congenially, holding out his hand.

"You can at least give me a hug." Gail approached him with her arms out-stretched. "We're related now. And if it weren't for me, you two would have never met."

"Well, you're right about that," he admitted as they embraced.

"Mick, why don't you help Gail find her luggage on the carousel over there while I entertain Junior," Dorrie suggested.

"You can't miss my bags," Gail added. "They have big red roses on them. I hope they arrived safely, though. I don't trust these airline carriers one bit. That's why I pack an extra outfit and all my cosmetics in my carry-on, just to be on the safe side."

Gail followed Mick as he skillfully negotiated a path through the crowd. They reached the conveyor belt that was carrying passengers' luggage around a large loop. While waiting for her bags to arrive, Gail studied the profile of Mick Walters. She decided he hadn't changed much since the time they all met in New Hampshire almost three years earlier while Dorrie and Gail were vacationing in the White Mountains. He still possessed a brawny, muscular frame and honey-blond hair that swept across his forehead. And those fantastic blue eyes. Gail had tried in vain to make Mick her own during that time, but it was plain to see that Mick had fallen head over heels in love with Dorrie. Dorrie and Mick were a perfect match, sharing a mutual interest in the great outdoors that Gail despised with a passion.

Watching Mick as he scanned the conveyor belt for her flower-adorned bags, she decided that while Mick possessed some interesting traits, she felt fortunate to be engaged to the man of her dreams. Both men were similar in stature, but Keith possessed straight dark-brown hair and chocolate-colored eyes that would stare tenderly into her own. At times he also wore wire-rimmed glasses that gave him a serious appearance. Gail had fallen in love with him the moment he had gallantly arrived on the scene in his crisp white shirt, black vest, and bow tie of a waiter—ready to help her up from the floor after the mishap with the punch bowl during Dorrie and Mick's wedding. At the conclusion of the reception, held near

10

her aunt's home in the Catskill Mountains of New York State, Gail found herself in Keith's company while he cleaned tables. They had made small talk about the evening, after which they agreed to swap phone numbers. To her delight, she discovered that Keith lived with his parents only a short distance from her aunt's home. Several months later, they were reacquainted when Gail returned to visit her aunt. During her stay, Keith invited her out to dinner. On a verandah decorated with ferns and white lights, they sampled a light fare of grilled tuna on a bed of rice pilaf while sharing with each other their hopes and dreams.

"And you're a part of my dreams now," Keith had told her as the lights in the ferns reflected in his dark eyes. "That's why I've come to a decision. I'm going to look for work down in Westchester County."

"You mean near me? Oh, Keith, that's fantastic!"

"It's about time I got away from here and made a new life for myself." His hand found hers. "And I want you in my life."

After Keith landed a computer repair job, they saw each other almost daily. One thing led to another, until six months later when Keith presented her with the diamond that now decorated her left hand.

"Hey, I said is this yours?" A flowered bag hovered in midair before her eyes, next to Mick's puzzled face.

"Oh, uh. . .yes," Gail answered, checking the name tag.

"A lot on your mind?"

"Just remember how it was when you and Dorrie were engaged."

"Okay, I get the message." Mick hefted the two bags. "We're looking forward to hearing all about the wedding plans. I know you did a good job organizing ours. If there's anything Dorrie and I can do to make life easier, let us know."

"Thanks." Gail smiled, remembering the day she called to share the news of her engagement with her older sister. Dorrie was ecstatic that Gail had finally abandoned her numerous relationships to settle down with one special guy. The exclamation of approval over the telephone had ricocheted across the room, prompting smiles by both their mother and father, who had welcomed the announcement with hugs and tears of acceptance.

Oh, how I prayed you would find a special man, Dorrie wrote Gail later in the month. *Our Bible group prays all the time for family members, and you've been on our prayer chain.*

Gail read the remark in the letter without the caustic reaction she normally experienced whenever Dorrie espoused her Christianity. Lately, Gail had been thinking about Dorrie and her walk with God. Seeing how Dorrie and Mick led a happy and fulfilled marriage, Gail desperately wanted her own marriage to pulsate with the same joy.

Now she followed the little family out of the terminal building. Mick carried Gail's bags while Dorrie wheeled the stroller with baby Jamie nestled inside.

11

Gail imagined herself walking side by side with Keith, rolling her own baby stroller along with a new little person cuddled beneath a blanket. The wee face and large eyes would peer out to acknowledge the awesome world revolving around him. Tingles of apprehension shot through her at the idea of caring for a little baby. *No doubt Dorrie will make sure I know all about infant care before this visit ends.*

Once the bags were placed in the trunk and the baby was fastened into his infant car seat, they sped off into the nightmare of tangled traffic that plagued Boston. As Gail watched the buildings of the city shrink in the distance, she recalled a trip that Keith and she had taken to New York City. Amid the tall skyscrapers and the frantic pace of city life, he treated her to dinner and a Broadway play. The lights and music of the play dazzled Gail, but nothing warmed her heart more than when Keith reached for her hand and clasped it in his for most of the production. His touch reached into the depths of her heart, stirring up a wave of love like no one else ever had. Gail certainly had had her share of relationships in the past, but this was different. She knew deep down inside that this was the man she wanted in her life. Not long after the special outing, Keith proposed to her with a similar eagerness for a lifelong relationship.

"I said, how are Mother and Dad?" Dorrie repeated as Gail gazed dreamily out the car window.

"I told you she's a little hard of hearing," Mick said. "I waited five minutes with the baggage before she knew what was going on."

"Oh, love does that to you," Dorrie added. "I remember that after we got engaged, I never heard my boss at the office. He finally got so irritated with me, he broke down and bought a dictation device so he wouldn't have to repeat himself anymore." She turned and yelled to Gail, "So how are Mother and Dad?"

Gail cast her an irritated look. "You don't have to scream, Dorrie. I'm sitting right behind you. I can hear everything."

Dorrie shook her head. "Honey, you ain't hearin' nuthin'. You've got the disease, don't you know? It's that long-lost look of love that comes over us women when we've hooked a man. But to be honest, I think he's the one who's got you— hook, line, and sinker."

Gail twirled the diamond ring around her finger, watching the stone reflect delicately colored patterns as the sunbeams streamed through the car window. For once she agreed with her sister's observation.

"So I'll ask again, how are Mother and Dad?"

"They're doing fine. Mother's worried about the wedding, of course. When I get back from this trip, we'll go shopping for the dress. Dad takes it all in stride."

"He always does," Dorrie agreed. "He's very level-headed."

"Like you."

"Like me?"

"Of course. You're the spitting image of Dad and I'm more like Mother."

Dorrie nodded in agreement. "I can't argue with that. For some reason, Mother could always relate to you."

"And Dad always stuck up for you," Gail hastily answered. When they were younger, Gail often flaunted her relationship with their mother before her older sister. Secretly she was glad Mother favored her, for Dorrie delved into life with a certain vitality that sparked jealousy within Gail. Now that she sat poised to seal a lifetime commitment with the man she loved, past parental relationships and jealous emotions seemed moot points by comparison.

"Look, I don't think it matters," Dorrie said in a soft voice, echoing Gail's sentiment. "As far as I'm concerned, those years have passed. Now it's on to bigger and better things in both our lives."

Gail could not help but agree, thankful that the years of sibling rivalry and heated debates were only memories. Their lives now traveled similar paths and were filled by the two men who loved them and the challenges yet to be faced.

Chapter 2

T his is a much better place than where you lived when you first got married," Gail said as Dorrie gave her the whirlwind tour of their new townhouse. "At least it doesn't look like a bachelor pad."

Dorrie cupped a hand to her mouth and whispered, "Between you and me, I couldn't stand those striped curtains Mick used to hang from the bay window in his old apartment. The first day I saw them, I wanted to rip them to shreds and use what was left for dust cloths."

"What's this I hear?" Mick asked as he sauntered in. His blue eyes sparkled with curiosity as he looked first at Gail, then Dorrie.

"Oh, Mick, Dorrie was just telling me how much she misses your old apartment," Gail teased.

Mick folded his arms and pretended to be irritated, despite the tiny smile hovering at the crook of his mouth. "Right. And I'm sure she told you the curtains were not even fit for lining the bottom of a bird cage."

Gail exchanged a look of surprise with her sister before they both erupted into laughter.

"See? I know what you two are talking about," he murmured good-naturedly as he strode out of the guest room.

Gail turned to where she had laid her suitcases in a row on the bed. She unzipped her first suitcase to reveal a mountain of clothing, all neatly folded into small piles with hardly a wrinkle to be found.

"Do you plan on becoming Jamie's nanny and moving in?" Dorrie asked, pointing a finger at the stack of clothes. "You're only staying for a few days, Gail. You've got enough stuff to last a year!"

"I never know what I'll be doing, so I like to come prepared. Whether I go shopping at the mall or pushing Jamie's stroller outside, I need the right outfit. And of course, the weather here in New England is so unpredictable."

"I hope this Keith character knows the expensive tastes of the dame he's marrying," Dorrie commented, helping Gail hang up her clothes. "I guess it's a good thing he got that new job."

"He loves the clothes I wear," Gail retorted defensively. "He says I'm beautiful. Which reminds me, I must show you the gorgeous bracelet he gave me for Valentine's Day." She reached over to her carry-on bag and inserted a tiny key into the lock. Inside the case she removed a long velvet box. Beneath the lid, buried in matted cotton for protection, lay an exquisite gold bracelet studded with precious diamonds.

Dorrie sucked in her breath like the whirl of a miniature vacuum. "Are those real diamonds?"

"They sure aren't rhinestones! Of course they're real. I just love this bracelet."

"I don't get it. Where does Keith come up with the money to buy this kind of jewelry?"

Gail shrugged as she replaced the treasured piece within the confines of the carry-on. "I told you, he's doing well at his job."

Dorrie's hands flew to her hips. "He can't be doing that well. Didn't you tell me he just started this job?"

"He's been there almost a year. Honestly, Dorrie, he's very thrifty. He saves most of his money, unlike me."

Dorrie narrowed her eyes and twisted her lips. "So what else has he given you, if I might be so bold as to inquire?"

"Nothing much. Just an angora sweater, a pair of pearl earrings—"

"Nothing much!" Dorrie interrupted. "Are you kidding me? Earrings, a bracelet, a sweater—all on top of that ring of yours?"

Gail's face contorted into lines of irritation. "What, are you jealous or something?"

"No, I'm not jealous. I just think that—"

"He's very good to me," Gail snapped, slamming down the lid to the carry-on, an action that underscored the vexation rising up within her. "He would give the shirt off his back if someone needed it." She strode across the room and flung herself on the bed, allowing her head to sink into the feather pillow.

"Have you ever met his family? Are they well off?"

Gail screwed her eyes shut. "I don't know if they are. No, I haven't met them yet. Keith says his parents do a lot of traveling with the business they operate. When I return home, I plan on meeting them."

Out of the corner of her eye, Gail watched Dorrie settle down on the bed next to her. Dorrie pulled her knees up to her chin in a posture of thoughtfulness. "I hope they don't mind all these wedding plans, considering you've never met them."

"Keith tells me they're excited about the plans. They think I'll make a fine daughter-in-law."

Jamie's scream in the next room brought Dorrie instantly to her feet. "Duty calls. Get yourself some rest. We're ordering a pizza tonight. I'll let you know when it arrives."

Gail mumbled her thanks before rolling on her side and shutting her eyes. She thought of Keith and the night he asked her to marry him. Like a movie displayed in slow motion, she dreamt through every sequence leading up to the big moment when he popped the long-anticipated question.

"But what will your parents think?" Gail gasped, staring at the huge diamond set in gold and nestled inside a red velvet box. "I mean, they've never even met me."

"Don't worry about it," he reassured her as he slipped the ring along Gail's manicured finger. "Everyone thinks it's a great idea. We're meant to be together. You and I both know it. That's all that matters."

Gail relaxed when she heard those words. She examined the diamond setting under the light and thought it was the most beautiful ring she had ever seen. To her, the ring signified much more than a promise of commitment. It signified that a man was willing to love her for the rest of her life.

As she sat absorbed by the ring, Keith traced an index finger down her arm until his hand rested on hers. The sensation sent tingles racing up her back. When she turned, his lips met hers with an urgency that lingered. Gail smiled as she reflected on the sweet encounter. When they parted, he urged her to make a night of it, detailing plans for a glorious encounter in a quaint bed and breakfast to celebrate their engagement. Gail only shook her head and said she wanted to wait until the wedding night.

When Keith asked her why she would cling to such ideas in this day and age, she said, "I guess it has to do with my upbringing. Mother and Dad were very strict about relationships. Dates were fine with them, but there was no stepping over the line." Even then Gail recalled the conversation she had had with her mother as they sat together on a rose-print comforter in her parents' bedroom.

"I know you like boys, Gail," Mother had said, "but there's something I need to share with you. I've never spoken about this until now. Your father and I made a commitment when we were young to wait until our wedding night to show the deepest expression of our love to one another. I know it sounds old-fashioned by today's standards, but as my mother told me, intimacy is the one true gift of love you can give to your husband. Don't waste it on some man you will never love. Save yourself for that special night after the wedding when the two of you are together and you see the wedding rings on your hands. It will mean so much more to you that way. Think of it as a special wedding gift for your man that you can't buy for any price."

Gail never forgot those words. Even when Keith applied pressure, suggesting they celebrate their love commitment symbolized by Gail's engagement ring, Gail clung to her belief that she must keep herself pure as a special wedding present.

She snapped open her eyes at the memory of the confused look that crossed his face. He was willing to honor her desire to wait until their wedding night, but Gail sensed he did not understand it.

"Sometimes I wonder myself," Gail murmured, cupping her hands beneath her head. "I know I love Keith, but I just can't take that last step, not after what

Mother shared. And Mother and I have always shared things about our lives. I can't just ignore something she believes in so strongly. Besides, she's right. I like the idea of being a wedding present to Keith. He will be so glad I can give him something special on our wedding day, especially after all that he's given me."

At that moment, Dorrie poked her head into the room. The smell of hot pizza wafted in after her. "Supper's on, Sleepyhead."

Gail jumped out of bed, ran a comb through her mussed hair, and ventured out to the kitchen where Mick was fastening Jamie into his highchair. Bits of oat cereal lay scattered across the chair's tray.

"He can eat cereal now?" Gail watched in disbelief as Jamie attempted to scoop up the cereal with his tiny fist and stuff it into his mouth.

"He eats like food is going out of style," Dorrie commented, producing a small container of pureed meat and sweet potatoes.

"You make your own food?"

"Of course. I don't trust that junk the stores call 'baby food.' Ugh. Have you ever tasted the stuff?"

Gail shook her head as she slid into a chair Mick held out for her, smiling her thanks in his direction.

"I sampled some at a baby shower the church threw for me," Dorrie continued. "We had to taste different jars of baby food, then write down what we thought they were on a scrap of paper. The one who guessed the most jars of food won a prize."

"Did you win?"

"Not by a long shot. After a few bites of the stuff, I gave up and made a vow that my baby would eat only natural food."

"In fact, Dorrie's excellent at making pureed pizza," Mick added.

Gail wriggled her nose at the image of a pizza slice being transformed into a reddish glob inside a food processor. "Ugh! That's disgusting, Mick."

"I agree," Dorrie echoed as she spooned food into Jamie's mouth, ducking the little fist that continued to push cereal in at the same time. "Go ahead and dig in before it gets cold. I'll be through here in no time. Jamie wins the race when it comes to eating."

Mick bowed his head and offered up a simple prayer for the food, adding a quick prayer for Gail and her wedding plans. When he finished, he slid a slice of pizza onto his plate, then pushed the box across the table to Gail.

"Okay, so let's hear the plans for the big day," Dorrie said.

Gail chewed and swallowed several bites before launching into details of the wedding. She explained the features of the church and the banquet hall she had found close to their parents' home. "And the rent's cheap on Dad. It's hard to afford two huge bashes."

"That's wise. I'm sure it was bad luck that our parents had two girls. We have to buy most everything for the wedding, including the reception, the fancy dress you struggle into only once, the veil. . .the list goes on. Have you bought your dress yet?"

Gail shook her head as she wiped her mouth on a napkin before placing it back across her lap. "Not yet. Mother plans on going dress shopping with me when I get back."

"We could go to a few bridal boutiques here in Boston if you want," Dorrie suggested.

Gail snickered. "You and I don't have the same tastes, Dorrie. Why, you'd probably suggest that I wear a pair of white shorts and a T-shirt to match."

Dorrie spun around, holding the spoon containing orange baby food high in midair. "That's not true. I had all the right attire, including a floor-length gown with a train, and even a veil. I looked very nice for our wedding, didn't I, Mick?"

Mick swallowed a large mouthful of pizza before saying, "You were gorgeous, Dorrie."

"There, you see?"

Gail twirled strands of mozzarella around her finger to form a ring. "I want to buy something special with lots of lace, beads, and a train that stretches halfway down the aisle, just like a princess."

"That costs money. I don't think your cashier's job at the department store will pay for something that extravagant."

"Well, Keith said he'd—"

Dorrie plunked the spoon down on the small table in front of Jamie, who tried to paw it up with his fist and stick it into his mouth. "Don't tell me this dude is going to finance your wedding dress as well." Turning to Mick, she ranted on while Gail stared at her in dismay. "You won't believe the cash this guy doles out. He's bought her jewelry, clothes, and who knows what else. It sounds to me like this guy has robbed a bank or something in the last year rather than start a new job."

Gail shot out of her seat and threw her napkin on the table. "How can you even say something like that?" she cried. "I'm tired of you questioning the things Keith has given to me out of the goodness of his heart. Excuse me, but I'm going for a walk."

"Gail, wait a minute," Dorrie pleaded as Gail strode out the door and into the twilight. Gail heard the faint echo of her sister's voice calling for her as she marched down the sidewalk, passing a row of townhouses, until she reached a small park established for the residents of the community. Scalding tears dripped down her cheeks. She now regretted coming on this visit. Before she arrived, Gail was excited about the plans for her wedding. Now her joy was dampened by Dorrie's doubts and questions. Gail wiped a hand across her wet cheek and walked over to a swing, where she plopped herself down. *When will Dorrie ever accept the good that comes my way? Either she's jealous of Keith's generous nature, or she only wants to make my life as miserable as possible.* Gail swung to and fro, burdened by her rash of thoughts. She knew Dorrie would never accept her until she uttered vows of Christianity. "Well, if that's what being a Christian is all about," she muttered, "then I don't want any part of it." She closed her eyes, wishing Keith was there to comfort her. She missed his gentle words and strong arms cradling her in times of distress. How could she make Dorrie and others understand that it was simply Keith's love and affection that prompted his outpouring of generosity and nothing else?

Dorrie appeared from the evening shadows to occupy a neighboring swing. Together they watched the sun set in the distance before she said, "I remember when I fell off a swing back in school. Fell right on my back. I couldn't breathe. It was the scariest sensation in my life. The teacher had me rushed to the emergency room where they said I had the wind knocked out of me." She glanced over at Gail who gazed at the ground beneath the swing. "Guess I should've had the wind knocked out of me before I started saying all those things at the dinner table tonight. I'm sorry about what happened. I only want you to know that I care."

"That's not true," Gail muttered. "You want to control my life. You always have."

"I want what's best for you. Look, I've never met Keith. I just want to make sure he's taking care of you right. Maybe once I get to know him I won't have all these reservations. You know I can't help but be an overprotective sister. I've been that way all my life."

Gail's shoes scuffed up the dirt below the swing. "I know, but I get tired of the lectures and the do's and don'ts. I'm old enough to make my own decisions. I don't need a big sister telling me what to do every waking minute." She lifted her head to see orange and red clouds materialize in the sky, a product of the final rays of the setting sun.

"Okay, you're right. I do get kind of pushy and all. Since this is your big day, you do whatever you want. I'll go along with it without any squabbling. Promise."

Gail cast her a look out of the corner of her eye. "And no more comments about Keith's money?"

"Cross my heart. I'll keep my mouth shut, even though I may need Super Glue to help me."

Gail cracked a small smile and relaxed as her feet scuffed up puffs of dirt. After a moment of reflection, she launched into details of the wedding day, planned for October. Dorrie listened and offered a comment or two but allowed Gail time to air her thoughts.

"It's amazing how much there is to do for one day," Dorrie admitted. "If it will make life any easier for you, I'll help with the invitations. Send me your guest list and I'll even try to have the addresses done in calligraphy by the woman who teaches art in Mick's school."

"That would be nice," Gail agreed, remembering Mick's job as a science teacher in a middle school. "Okay. I ordered them a few weeks ago, so they should be there when I get back to Mother and Dad's."

"Remember, they have to be in the mail about two months before—"

"I know, I know," Gail said impatiently before a yawn erupted on her face.

"I'll bet you're exhausted." Dorrie cupped her hand around Gail's elbow and gently ushered her to her feet. "Let's head back. You can take a nice relaxing shower before you hit the hay."

"Does Jamie still wake up in the middle of the night?" Gail asked as they strolled down the sidewalk toward the townhouse.

"Sometimes. He's pretty good about sleeping through the night. It's not like the early days when he'd bawl for food every three hours. I could hardly drag myself out of bed to feed him. Mick would have to get him and I would nurse him half asleep. Sometimes the baby and I would fall asleep together. I'd wake up in the middle of the night with this warm bundle in my arms and wonder where he came from."

Gail laughed until she lapsed into silence, pondering the notion of motherhood. The idea of caring for a little baby unnerved her. She never particularly liked children to begin with. Dorrie often watched the neighbors' children to earn a little extra money, but Gail refused to do it. Kids scared her in many ways. They were overdemanding, unpredictable, and noisy. With the possibility that she and Keith might have children of their own, she felt a strange anxiety course through her. Her body trembled in response.

"What's the matter?" Dorrie asked.

"K–kids."

"Have you and Keith talked about it?"

Gail shook her head. "That's the least of our worries. There's so much to do right now with the wedding and all. As it is, just the idea of caring for some baby gets me all knotted up inside. I mean, if you make a mistake, that's the end."

"Of course it isn't. Look, every first-time mother claims ignorance in some area of baby care. When I found out I was pregnant, I immediately ran out to the store to look at all the baby things for sale. As I stared at the stuff, most of which I had no idea what it was even used for, I prayed, 'Lord, how am I ever going to manage?' "

"But you like kids. You're a natural around them."

"Right. I changed a diaper a few times, maybe gave one or two bottles, and read stories. Having your own is a whole different ball game. Sometimes when you let them howl themselves to sleep, you wonder if you're doing the right thing or if you're damaging them for life. You wonder if you will know when it's time to buy them the next pair of shoes, or move into another diaper size, or what consistency of food they can eat without choking. That's when you really have to trust God."

Gail raised her hands. "Please, no more. I'll just concentrate on my wedding and worry about mothering some other time."

"I think that's a good idea," Dorrie agreed, giving Gail an affectionate squeeze that sent warmth radiating through her. "One thing at a time."

At this moment, Gail could plainly see her sister's caring attitude. In the past, such displays would have been overshadowed by thoughts of Dorrie's sisterly domination over her or jealousy about Dorrie's accomplishments. Gail realized now that Dorrie's concern for her well-being reflected the Christian commitment she had made long ago.

As Gail readied herself for bed that night, she wondered about Dorrie's Christianity. Many times Dorrie had tried to reach her with the gospel, but Gail batted the idea away as if it were a pesky fly buzzing in her face. She felt religion to be a private matter—something that should be practiced inside a church on Sunday mornings. The idea of living for God every breathing moment seemed hard to swallow. Now she found her feelings changing. Perhaps the idea of a lifetime commitment with Keith opened her heart up to other commitments as well, like the one Dorrie had with God.

Gail had shuffled into the bathroom to remove her makeup when she heard the voices of Dorrie and Mick conversing in the bedroom next door. She had just dampened a cotton pad with makeup remover and rubbed it across her eyelids to clean off the shadow when she heard the word "gang" uttered in the adjacent room. Gail's hand froze. *They must be talking about Mick's work with those gangs in Boston!* She recalled the letters Dorrie had sent to her in the past, explaining Mick's desire to follow in his father's footsteps and reach out to the gangs of inner Boston. Gail shuddered at the thought of confronting such vicious young men, especially after Mick's father suffered a debilitating gunshot wound at the hand of a gang leader. Yet the conversation sparked her curiosity. She pressed an ear to the wall.

"But I thought Corky was no longer involved in the Vultures gang," Dorrie said in a strained voice.

"Corky says he's not. He only wants others in the Vultures to come and hear about God. That's why he's talking to them about joining my Bible study at the soup kitchen."

"Mick, I don't believe that for a minute. Corky hasn't changed. He's still involved with them. Here you spent all your time reaching out to him; you even went to that drug rehab program with him. I spent nights alone nursing a sick baby while you were tending to his needs. Now he's going right back into the mud again. What's the sense in all this?"

"Dorrie, if Corky was back with the gang, why would he call and tell me he wants to reach them with the gospel? He knows I wouldn't approve of him talking to them for any other reason. Corky thinks of me as his big brother."

Dorrie's voice rose as she said, "Maybe he was just tickling your ear or something."

"No, he isn't. I believe he's sincere."

"Oh, Mick, I want to believe in what you're doing out there in the street. I know it's important to reach the gangs with the love of Jesus. You promised your father you'd carry on his ministry. But I'm really afraid right now. Think of what could happen if Corky or one of the other gang members turns on you when you least expect it."

Gail heard Mick sigh. "Dorrie, you're being irrational."

"I'm not irrational! Maybe I'm the one dealing in reality! I happen to care about us. . .about our family. When it was just the two of us, it was different. I could handle the danger of you working the streets, trying to reach those drugged-out guys. But now you have your son to consider, Mick. You have a family. What will happen to us if that new leader of the Vultures, Odysseus, comes after you like the former leader did with your father? It could happen, you know. And I won't be a widow!"

Silence prevailed until Mick's gentle voice broke through the dark cloud hovering over the tiny home. "So you want me to quit? If you want me to, I will. I don't want you getting this upset. If I'm going to continue in this ministry, we have to agree on it together."

Dorrie exhaled a troubled sigh. "No, I don't want you to quit. I'm just worried that something might happen to you. I only want a vacation from my fear. Is that too much to ask?"

Gail could picture Mick's arms curling around the distraught Dorrie, comforting her fears before kissing away the salty tears sliding down her cheeks. Heaving a sigh, Gail quickly scrubbed her teeth, then made off to the bedroom. She buried herself under a blanket as if to hide from the danger concealed within the conversation. "Thank goodness I will never have to deal with things like that in my marriage," she whispered in relief.

Chapter 3

A h, young Quintin, come right in," the butler said, stepping aside to allow him access into the stately home. "Your father is expecting you in the library."

Quintin frowned as he trudged inside. His sneakers scuffed along the Oriental rugs covering the fine wood floors. He never acknowledged the posh interiors that spoke of great wealth—the crystal chandeliers dangling from every room, the wainscoting of the walls, or the oval glass window at the rear of the home that allowed streams of golden sunshine to bathe the hallway. He walked into the library and took a seat on the leather couch. An odor of cigar smoke and brandy met his nostrils. Across from him sat a man in his mid-sixties, a cigar tucked into the corner of his mouth. Dressed in a dinner jacket, the man was sporting a droopy mustache that rested on the butt of the cigar. As he puffed, his feet rested on a cushioned stool, while curls of smoke spiraled toward the ceiling. A glass of brandy sat in a strategic position on the table, close to his fingertips.

The man pulled the cigar out of his mouth and flicked the ash into a tray. "Why didn't you inform me of your engagement?"

Quintin folded his arms across his chest and studied the rows of old books lining the shelf behind the stout figure of his father. The hard voice generated no paternal warmth or concern. This was strictly business.

"I asked you why you didn't tell me."

"Because it's my business, Pop."

The man jammed the cigar back into his mouth. "In case you've forgotten, your business is my business, and an engagement is a highly important matter that should have been discussed with me first."

Quintin kept his gaze fixed on the books of the library, wondering to himself if anyone had ever bothered to pick the books off the shelf, let alone open the dusty covers to read the contents. He could not remember reading any of the classics growing up, nor could he recall his parents reading to him as a child. An overwhelming sense of loss ensued when he pondered the little things he had missed out on while growing up in a wealthy environment.

"Quintin, are you listening to me?"

Ten, eleven, twelve, thirteen, he counted in a row before proceeding to the next shelf. *Fourteen, fifteen, sixteen.*

"Who is this woman you plan to marry?"

Twenty-one, twenty-two, twenty-three— The counting and the older man's interrogation both came to an abrupt end when the butler entered the library carrying a glass of brandy on a silver tray. Quintin was grateful for the interruption. He took the glass and set it on the table.

His father took a sip of his own brandy before placing it beside him. "There are ways of finding out. If you won't tell me, then you force me to put Grant on the case."

Quintin's gaze darted to his father's icy stare that augmented the threat. "Don't you use that buzzard to spy on me," he hissed.

"If you won't tell me what I wish to know, you leave me no choice. I will find out everything. Grant is very good at what he does."

"You call him good? Why, he'd hurt his own mother if the price was right."

"He keeps our operations running smoothly."

"He's a no good—"

"Well, it hasn't hurt you any, has it?" his father spat, straightening in his chair. His teeth smashed the butt of the cigar before he removed the stub with his fingertips. "I see that you've dipped into the accounts, presumably to buy extravagant gifts for your fiancée. And where do you think that kind of money comes from? Men like Grant keep the money flowing. He's good in the business. I'd show him more respect if I were you."

Quintin ground his teeth and looked away. His father began tapping the armrest with a rhythm that disturbed Quintin. The beat reminded him of a countdown to some unknown outcome.

"I assume you will stay and have dinner with me tonight," his father continued. "I had your room prepared. We can discuss this later."

"Actually, I don't plan on staying, Pop. I have a million things to do."

"Such as?"

He grinned before jumping to his feet and jamming his hands into the pockets of his jeans. "Pop, I'm gonna be married. There are plans to be made, things to arrange."

"I don't like your attitude, Quintin. I have not given my permission for this so-called union of yours."

"I'm not asking for your permission, Pop. I'm already engaged, you see."

The older man's lips twisted into a snarl beneath the mustache. "Don't be impertinent with me. You know where things stand. I must know all the facts—who this woman is, who she associates with, what she knows. It could prove dangerous."

"Pop, she doesn't know a thing about us. There's no need to worry."

"And how do you plan on keeping everything from her? There will come a time when she will be exposed to—"

"I don't want her knowing anything. You keep your silence pretty well in your elite circle of friends. They know nothing about what we do. In fact," he added with a hint of sarcasm, "you pride yourself in all the secrecy."

"And I hope my son possesses the same discretion," the older man answered in a guarded voice. "Now, I insist that I meet this young lady as soon as possible. We will set up an appointment."

Set up an appointment. Quintin nearly laughed out loud. *Sounds like a doctor trying to cure a disease that might infect the business.* "Sorry, but I just don't have the time. Now, if you'll excuse me, I have to get going." He turned to leave the library.

"Quintin!"

He ignored the plea. In the dark hall outside the library doors, Quintin bumped into a short man with black, greasy hair and a face pitted from a severe case of acne as an adolescent. A grin on the scarred face revealed a gaping hole in a row of teeth that filled the thin-lipped mouth.

"Watch where you're going," Quintin muttered.

"If I were you, I'd watch where you are going, you young fool," the man retorted.

"Grant, you were born to live in a hole, not among decent people."

"I see only that the big boss's son is headed for trouble. You of all people should know it's unwise to go against your father's wishes."

Quintin narrowed his eyes. "And who are you to tell me what to do? You have a lot of nerve, standing outside the door listening to our conversation. Nothing's private anymore with you slithering around like some snake."

"I'm not your father's right-hand man for nothing."

"That's for sure. Anyone making the kind of money you do is bound to stick close to the source. But I won't have you breathing down my neck."

Grant's hand brushed open his sports jacket, exposing the hilt of a pistol he wore in a leather holster. "I'll say it once more. You would be wise to listen to your pop and do what he says, like an obedient son. Look at it this way. Before a guy enters into a marriage, isn't it normal to have the bride-to-be meet the father of the groom? Won't you bring all kinds of suspicion down on yourself if you refuse? What will your bride say?"

"You're made of slime, you know that? Pure slime."

"I see only that your father's wishes are carried out."

"You see only your own self-interest in this game. If you will excuse me, I'll do as I see fit. Now get out of my way."

"Stubborn fool," Grant muttered, glaring at Quintin with beady black eyes.

Quintin refused to acknowledge the threatening look of his adversary. With his gaze fixed on the exit, he marched down the hall and out the door, breathing a sigh of relief at having escaped the darkness within the mansion. The bright summer flowers, arranged in beds around the circular driveway, did little to ease the anxiety in his heart. If it were not for the strength of love binding him to his fiancée, he would never allow her to enter into this corrupt family of his. Yet he could not fathom life without her. Now with Grant involved, he might have to risk letting her visit his father—to prevent Grant from following her every move.

Quintin climbed into his car and swiftly drove out the tree-lined drive leading to the estate. He checked his rearview mirror often to make certain he wasn't being followed. Many times in his travels he sensed the wily Grant in the dark corners, the man's black eyes glinting, his ears attentive to every whisper. He knew Grant had somehow discovered the news of his engagement and had immediately informed his father. Quintin was thankful, though, that his fiancée had not found herself confronted by the man.

With his father threatening to use Grant as a spy if he did not agree to a meeting, Quintin knew he had no choice. There was never a choice for him when it came to his father's ultimatums. Pop was the boss. Everyone listened to the boss and followed his directions—or suffered the consequences. *Including me,* he thought miserably. *Can I put her through all this, though? Am I being selfish by marrying her, knowing it might place her in harm's way? But I love her so much! I have to marry her. I must never let her know who we are or what we do. If I want her safe and in my arms until death do us part, then I must lock the secret of the family within me and keep it from her forever.*

Quintin drove for awhile, then powered up his cell phone. He withdrew from his pocket a slip of paper upon which he had written a phone number and punched in the digits, eagerly anticipating the sound of her voice. Instead the mechanical whirl of an answering machine met his ear, along with a strange message that ended with the words, "And remember, God cares about you."

Quintin frowned. He hung up without leaving a message. He recalled in numerous conversations with his fiancée that her sister was a deeply religious person. He wondered how she could visit under that kind of pressure. To him there was nothing worse than people spouting off their religion in an attempt to convert others. He would never admit that the reverent messages had convicted him at times. One day he found the Ten Commandments, printed in some small pamphlet, tucked underneath the windshield wiper of his car. He was ready to wad the paper up into a tight ball when he started reading the words. "Thou shalt not kill; Thou shalt not steal; Thou shalt not covet another's belongings; Thou shalt not commit adultery." He sucked in his breath. *How many of those commandments have I broken, let alone my family? Is God angry about all the deceit and disobedience?* Quintin had brushed the thoughts aside as he pitched the convicting paper to the ground, unsure if God even existed.

Now the message on the answering machine prompted him to think again about the existence of God. If there was a supreme being, why did He allow man to commit evil? And if he was supposed to obey all those rules in the Bible, why didn't this God send down a lightning bolt from heaven and strike him dead for disobeying them? Perhaps Quintin had grown to believe himself invincible, like his father had. Quintin knew his pop refused to believe that the authorities, or even God Himself, could catch him in his misdeeds and deal the punishment he rightly deserved. He could have won the award for best actor with his efforts to mask his sins with occasional acts of kindness; actions designed, Quintin knew, to conceal from others what lay buried beneath the surface. Quintin sighed. He was too much like his father in many respects. That fact gnawed at him fiercely.

✳

"I really enjoyed myself," Dorrie announced to Gail as they arrived back at the townhouse, burdened with shopping bags from a trip to the mall. "I'm so glad you convinced me to buy some new outfits."

"Let's face it, Dorrie. After awhile, jeans and T-shirts just don't cut it." Gail hurried into the back bedroom and tossed her bundles on the bed. She could hear Dorrie checking the answering machine in the living room and promptly ran back for a report. "Any messages for me?"

Dorrie shook her head. "Mick called. He's going to be late tonight at the soup kitchen. Then someone else called but didn't leave a message."

Gail frowned. "Oh. I was hoping Keith would call me. I miss him so much."

"I imagine you do." Dorrie set to work opening up an activity board she had purchased for Jamie at a toy store. She placed it down on the carpet and watched the infant boy reach out his tiny hands to investigate the knobs and buttons. "You wouldn't believe the phone bill Mick and I piled up while I lived on Long Island and he lived here in Boston. I had to work overtime just to pay the bill."

"It's nice that Keith lives close by. I don't have to worry about phone calls, unless it's to plan an outing or something. I get to have the real flesh-and-blood guy all to myself."

"Yeah, that must be nice." Dorrie lapsed into quiet thoughtfulness as she picked up the bags and carried them to the master bedroom. Gail followed to help her hang up a new dress and fold some shirts.

"So is Mick going out on the streets tonight?"

Dorrie whirled at the sound of her voice. "You scared me! I didn't know you were there. Yes, Saturday nights are his busiest time. He works in the soup kitchen with a guy named Harry. They serve food that arrives from the area restaurants. Sometimes it's pans of macaroni and cheese, or lasagna, or luncheon meat. I used to help out once in awhile, before I had Jamie. When Mick gets done there, he walks the streets and hands out tracts."

Gail picked up a new blouse from the bed and used a pair of shears to snip off the tags. "I. . .I wasn't trying to be nosy or anything, Dorrie, but I couldn't help overhearing you guys talking the other night. You don't want him working with those gangs anymore, do you?"

Dorrie's arms stiffened into robotic movements as she forced a hanger through the neck of a dress. "Sometimes it's not a question of what I want but what God wants."

"Well, you'll probably faint when you hear this, but I happen to agree with what you said. But I don't think God would want Mick sacrificing you and Jamie for a bunch of weird kids that smoke pot and kill each other."

Dorrie sighed. "It's hard to know what to think. Sometimes I try to rationalize it, but I only end up more confused. I'm trying to trust God for our safety."

"I'm glad I don't have to worry about things like that," Gail remarked. "I couldn't handle it if Keith found himself in danger every night. I mean, if something happened to him, I'd die, too."

Dorrie grew silent as if pondering the statement. Gail sensed that her sister experienced similar thoughts often when Mick was absent. Perhaps she had considered what life would be like for her and little Jamie if a gang member were to shoot Mick—like the bullet fired into his father's brain six years ago. The injury had bound the older man to a life in a wheelchair at an extended-care facility.

Tears welled up in Dorrie's eyes. She turned away to avoid displaying her emotion. "I have thought a lot about it," came the muffled voice as she finished hanging her new clothes inside the closet. "I've spent many sleepless nights worrying about him. I look behind my back often to make sure that none of those gang members are stalking Jamie and me. I know I shouldn't live my life dreading what's around the corner. I guess that's why I want Mick to quit the work so I can just relax for once in my life."

"I think your reactions are very normal," Gail offered. "You love your husband and your son. There's nothing wrong with that."

Dorrie turned at that moment and threw her arms around Gail. "Oh, Gail, I had a feeling we'd grow closer once you were married, but now I can see it's already started. Long ago when we took that camping trip of ours to the White Mountains, I wanted to have a special relationship with you. I guess we both had some maturing left to do before that could happen. Now we're entering stages in our lives where we can help each other."

"I think so, too, Dorrie," Gail agreed, surprised by the tears swimming in her own eyes. "But I know I need to grow up some more. I mean, I still get jealous of you sometimes. I used to think you were out to get me with all that religious talk of yours. But I know, deep down inside, that you really care about me."

Dorrie nodded. "It's like what Mick and I decided to put on our answering machine for people who need to hear the message. We say on the machine that God cares about you. I could not begin to care for you like I should without God's help."

"Yeah," Gail said slowly, knowing deep down her sister's words were true.

"And God does care. Sometimes I need to grasp the whole meaning of that, especially where Mick's mission field is concerned. I need to have a heart for those gang members like God does. Then I wouldn't feel so frightened. You know, most of those poor kids come from broken homes or abusive situations. They have never known the love of a family. They use drugs and alcohol as their escape and then end up committing violent crimes because they have nothing else to do with their lives. It's amazing to think that God really cares about them. He sent Jesus to die for them as He did for all of us, so we can share in God's love. That's the message Mick takes to them—a love that every heart longs to have."

Gail quietly listened. In the old days her pride would have drowned out the religious talk. As she observed Dorrie's vulnerability while searching for comfort within the words, Gail found herself listening instead of reacting. Dorrie was reaching deep into the meaning of her faith, searching for something to grab hold of that might lift her out of her pit of fear. For all of Dorrie's steadfast convictions, it amazed Gail to see how much her sister needed to understand the purposes of God in her life almost as much as Gail did herself.

Later that night, after she had gone to bed, Gail heard the door to the townhouse open and close and the weary footsteps of Mick slowly ascend the stairs. Gail squinted at the lighted numerals on the clock to see the time—midnight. She sighed and was fluffing her pillow when the voices in the next room caught her attention.

"You don't have to worry anymore, Dorrie," Mick said as his shoes hit the wall opposite Gail's room. "I told Harry I'm quitting."

"What?" Dorrie cried, the tone betraying her astonishment.

"God closed the door to this whole ministry. Nobody cares to hear the gospel. I was all set to have the Bible study tonight with these guys Corky promised would come. No one showed."

"Oh, Mick, I'm so sorry."

"They were too busy counting the goods they plan to sell to pay for their drugs. Corky told me all about it, how the Vultures sell all the stuff they steal to some guy who buys them out. Then they have loads of cash for their drugs and booze. He told me about the time the lights went out in Boston—how they had a field day looting the stores, making off with televisions, stereos, the works. He said they made enough cash in one night to buy crack for months. The Vultures have the reputation for being the richest gang in the 'hood,' as Corky put it. And for some reason, God wants me to reach out to them. It's ludicrous."

Gail shivered as she crawled deeper into her blankets.

Mick continued. "I tell you, Dorrie, when I heard that I thought to myself, what's the use? Those guys think they have everything. They don't need God when they can nurse their troubles away with a good snort or a shot of hard liquor."

"Mick, just because no one came to the Bible study doesn't mean you should—"

"Yes, it does," he interrupted. "I'm quittin' this whole thing. I feel bad because I promised Dad I would reach out to that gang, but I can't go on like this."

Gail heard Dorrie exhale a troubled sigh. "I know I'm partially to blame for this. I'm sorry about what I said. I'm trying to give God my anxiety. I don't want my fear leading you away from the path He has planned for you."

"Dorrie, it isn't just you. It's the rejection you feel when someone wads up the tract you give to them in love, then lights a match to it. It's that kid who would rather inject drugs into his veins after hearing the gospel preached than getting right with God."

"Well, what about Corky? Are you giving up on him, too? He could use a Bible study, probably more than anyone right now."

Gail could hear the sneering chuckle rise in Mick's throat. "You never liked Corky anyway, so what does it matter? You always thought he was pretending or something just so he could hang around with the gang."

"Well, I was wrong about that," Dorrie said softly. "Only God knows what's going on in his heart. It's our responsibility to see that he continues to grow in the ways of the Lord. Please, Mick, I'm sorry I haven't supported you."

"Dorrie, I've already told you it's not that. I love you and Jamie. I want us to be a family and do family things together."

"But Mick, you know those kids on the streets. They're looking for a big brother who'll be like family to them. As God helps me, I'll share you with them because I know you can reach their hearts. Corky is proof of that."

"Corky is only one insignificant acorn off a three-year tree of hard work. It isn't enough for me."

"Then I'll ask you one more question. Did God tell you to quit this ministry to be with Jamie and me?"

Gail lay silent in her bed, waiting for what seemed like an eternity for Mick's answer.

"No. God didn't tell me to quit."

"Then we'd better both obey Him and keep going. We're both learning in all this. I think we've reached a crossroads in your work. When you give all this over to God and wait on Him, I think you're going to reap a great harvest. Just don't keep looking to your own power to make these young people come out of their shells and reach out to God. Allow God to work in their hearts. We need to be ready when the opportunity comes."

Mick's voice softened to a mere whisper as Gail strained to hear. "I love you so much, Dorrie. As always, you know the right thing to say at the right time." She heard a soft ruffle of blankets, followed by silence.

Gail lay back on her pillow, her eyes wide, thinking about what had been shared. She wondered what kind of conversations she and Keith would have in the middle of the night. "Well, I'll tell you one thing," Gail muttered, flipping over on her side, "we're going to be a normal couple. We'll go to work, come home, fix dinner, and cuddle in each other's arms. I couldn't possibly live on the edge like Dorrie and Mick. Thank goodness I'll soon be home, safe and sound with the one I love."

Chapter 4

The following evening, Gail kissed her sister, brother-in-law, and nephew good-bye before heading through the security check-in for her flight back to New York. As Dorrie clung to her, whispering farewell and voicing her excitement about the upcoming wedding, Gail sensed the bond that had formed between them. Dorrie seemed eager to help in any way she could and promised to arrive early the week of the wedding to help with any last-minute details.

Gail glanced over her shoulder once more as she boarded the plane and saw the pair wave a final farewell, the baby stroller nestled between them. She wondered what life had in store for her during the next few months. She located her seat adjacent to a small oval window. Through the window she could see the maze of lighted runways. As she sat down, she sensed a renewed eagerness to see Keith. He had finally called her in Boston and expressed a longing to see her. The sound of his rich voice expounding on his love for her had caused goose bumps to break out on her skin. He also mentioned that he had arranged for them to have an intimate dinner at their favorite place after spending a whole day together. Gail felt fortunate to have netted such a thoughtful man. There was no one like him in the entire world. As she leaned her head against a spongy pillow given to her by one of the flight attendants, a delightful thought crossed her mind: Soon she would have him forever.

✳

A taxi dropped off Gail and her bags at the modest ranch home in Westchester County where she lived with her parents. Once inside the front door, her mother immediately informed her of the arrangements she had made for the wedding. "Oh, and I found the perfect dress. You must go with me tomorrow to see it."

Gail gulped. "But Mother, Keith and I are spending the whole day together—we've already planned it. We have so much to talk about. Then we're going out to dinner."

"But there's a special sale going on at this boutique, and you really shouldn't miss out on the fabulous price."

Gail had to admit she was curious about what her mother had discovered in her absence. She decided to call Keith and see if he might be able to meet later that day.

"Gail, I was really counting on us being together all day," he protested. "I even took time off work."

Gail sighed as she played with the engagement ring on her finger. "Oh, I wish there was some way to work around this. Mother says I really must see this dress while it's still on sale. If I like it, I don't dare pass up such a deal. Can't we meet afterward?"

"Well, look—I really need to see you tonight. How about meeting me at Doc's?"

"What, right now?"

"Yes, right now. There's something I have to discuss with you."

"Well, uh. . . ," Gail began, wondering what could be the reason for his insistence. "I just got home, and Mother is—"

"Look, forget about your mother and concentrate on me for a change. Now meet me at Doc's." He then added, "Please."

The receiver clicked in her ear. She winked back the tears that invaded her eyes. Why was Keith so angry? She had never known him to be irritable unless he'd had a run-in with a coworker at the computer company. *That must be it,* Gail decided, *trying not to read too much into the conversation. He's had a bad day at work. It happens to all of us, I guess.*

When Gail announced her plan to meet Keith at Doc's, a cafe down on Main Street, her father cast her a concerned look. "At this time of night? You just got home."

"Yes," her mother interjected. "And we also need to discuss ideas for the flowers and the cake so we can stop by those shops after we go to the wedding boutique."

"Look, I'll be back as soon as I can. It sounded kind of urgent. I need to borrow the car, Dad, if that's all right."

"Just be careful. I don't like the idea of you roaming the streets this late at night. Go straight there and come straight home."

"I will." Gail hurried off to the car, not wishing to be late. She hoped the time with Keith would be more pleasant than the phone conversation they'd just had. Her hands trembled as she steered the car out onto the highway, wondering why he had requested their impromptu meeting. "I only hope he's not having second thoughts about our engagement," Gail said to herself. She swallowed hard, forcing down the anxiety that crept up within her. With a shake of her head, she tossed back a mound of curly hair. "Now who's afraid? Keith said he loved me. He told me so on the phone while I was in Boston. There's nothing to worry about."

She arrived at Doc's and through the window saw Keith sitting at a table in the far corner of the establishment, fidgeting with a cup of coffee. His glasses lay on the table. She watched him draw his fingers across his eyes, then lift the cup of coffee and take a swallow. Gail inhaled a deep breath, checked her appearance in a lighted compact inside her purse, then walked into the shop with her head high and a smile on her face.

Keith's head popped up when the front door creaked, announcing her arrival. He jammed on his wire-rimmed glasses and pulled out a chair for her.

"I. . .I came as soon as I could," Gail managed to say while scanning the strange expression on his face.

His eyes darted to the window. "You didn't see anyone hanging around outside, did you?"

"No." Her muscles tightened at the mere suggestion. "Is something the matter?"

"No, nothing's the matter. I just know there's plenty of weird people out this time of night." He lifted his mug. "You want some coffee?"

Gail shook her head. "I'll never get to sleep if I drink coffee this late in the evening."

"Well, I don't want that to happen. You need your beauty sleep." He cracked a faint smile as he saluted her with his cup, then took a hefty swallow. "I could drink this stuff all night and it would have no effect on me. Even when I drank a gallon of it while pulling an all-nighter studying for an exam, I still fell asleep with my head in my textbook." He leaned back in his chair and folded his arms. "How was your flight from Boston?"

"It was nice. I like flying in the evening. There's no crowds and the Manhattan skyline is beautiful."

"How is your sister and her family?"

"We had a nice time together. Jamie is so cute. I think this was the first time Dorrie and I were actually civil with each other. It seems like all we've done our entire lives is fight over some silly thing. Now she sees that I'm mature, ready to handle marriage and all." Gail felt a sudden shyness at the words. She dropped her head to acknowledge the ring glittering on her left hand, hoping she was mature enough to handle whatever the future held.

Keith focused his gaze on his coffee mug. "Well, that's primarily what I wanted to talk to you about."

Fear rose up within her in response to these words. *Oh no, he is having second thoughts. That's why he was so cross with me on the phone.*

"I think it's time you came home to meet the family."

Gail exhaled a sigh of relief before breaking out into giggles. "Is that all? Oh, Keith, you had me scared to death!"

His head jerked up, sending his wire-rimmed glasses scooting back up his nose. "About what?"

"Well, you get crazy ideas running through your head when the one you love asks for a meeting this late at night. Couldn't you have told me this tomorrow?"

"Well, I wanted to see you. I missed you, you know." His hand reached out and clasped hers tightly.

"I missed you, too. I guess that's reason enough, huh?" She smiled, watching his dark brown eyes soften into a mist that spoke of his feelings for her. "When am I supposed to meet them?"

"I was thinking we could drive up next weekend."

"Okay. That should be fine, as long as I can get someone to switch weekends with me at the store. I can stay with my aunt. She gets lonely in that big house of hers. She'll love the company."

Keith glanced away for a moment. "I hope you like. . .well, my family."

Gail chuckled. "I'm sure I'll love your family, Keith! I love you! I only hope they'll like me."

"Just be your ol' bubbly self and everything will go fine. Don't try to be someone you're not." He grew serious then and picked up his mug to throw the rest of the coffee down his throat.

They conversed for awhile longer, about wedding plans and other things, until Gail noticed the late hour on her watch. "I'd better get home before Dad has a coronary." Keith walked her to the car parked across the street. Before she could drop into the driver's seat, his arms curled around her.

"I really missed you," he said softly. "I'm glad you're back."

"I'm glad to be back, too."

His lips were soft and warm against hers when they kissed. When they parted, a smile lit her face. They embraced once more before she sank down into the driver's seat.

"I'll call you," he promised, waving farewell as she pulled away from the curb and headed down the lighted street.

✳

Keith frowned when he thought of the words he had spoken to Gail that night. *Don't try to be someone you're not.* "Yeah, and what about me?" he mumbled, scuffing his shoe across the pavement. "Gail doesn't even know who I am." He turned and was headed down the sidewalk toward his car when suddenly a deep voice called to him from the shadows of a dark storefront.

"Wise decision."

Keith wheeled to find Grant walking out of the murky shadows toward him, a cigarette in his fingers. His grin displayed the gaping hole created by several missing teeth.

"What are you doing here?" Keith growled. "Quit following me."

Grant only shook his head and mouthed a tsk-tsk as he flicked the ash of his cigarette onto the ground. "You know I can't do that, Quintin. This is what I'm paid for, to make certain you do what's right. And you made a wise decision, involving the boss in your wedding plans."

"I'm telling you right now to beat it. If you so much as show your ugly face around Gail, you'll have me to answer to."

Grant only chuckled as he blew a ring of smoke into the air.

"Just don't press your luck, Bub. I mean it. Stay away from Gail. In fact, stay away from us, period." Keith marched off, only to slow as he reached the corner. A great heaviness fell on him when he considered the consequences of bringing Gail into his corrupt family. "What am I doing?" he wondered aloud. "How can I drag Gail into the middle of all this? How can I enter a marriage relationship with enough baggage to fill the cargo hold of a 747? Do I love her so much that I'm willing to risk my family's involvement in our marriage and our lives?" He paused to consider the question before kicking at a stone that tumbled away into a gutter. There seemed to be no way of escaping his treacherous family. "But there has to be. I won't let Pop take control of our marriage. I can't. There has to be a way out, a quick and easy way for us to be together without his influence in our lives. Then we can get far away from here—from all the corruption and men like Grant."

✳

Gail was surprised by Keith's gloominess as they traveled together to the Catskill Mountains of New York State, home both to her aunt and to Keith's family. She tried to engage him in conversation, describing her trips to several stores to investigate flower arrangements and sample wedding cakes. "I want you to help me decide on the best flowers and cake after we get back," Gail urged, poking him in the arm to elicit a response. "Tell me what kind of cake you like best. Mother and I sampled a carrot cake that was just out of this world. And the flowers. I can't decide if I want roses in my bouquet or white gardenias. The flowers in the florist's shop smelled just heavenly."

Keith shrugged his shoulders. "Aren't flowers and cake something the bride's supposed to worry about?"

"But I thought you might want some input. I mean, this is our wedding, not just mine."

He kept his eyes focused on the road before him as he stirred in the driver's seat. Finally he licked his lips and said, "Gail, to be honest, I just don't know about this."

"What?" she asked. "You've been quiet ever since we started this trip. Is something wrong?"

"Well, I'm kind of having second thoughts about throwing a big shindig and all. In fact, I really think we should just skip all these fancy arrangements and elope."

Gail's eyes widened in alarm. "Elope! Are you kidding? Why?"

"It just seems like you're going through an awful lot of hassle for one day. We know we love each other and want to get married. I don't see the reason behind flowers, cakes, churches, and everything else. Then you have to deal with family, which is another headache."

Gail blinked, surprised by his change of heart. She assumed Keith, to whom she had confided her heartfelt dreams, would realize the importance of having a fancy wedding with all the trimmings. Every night she went to bed thinking of walking down the aisle dressed in a gown sparkling with beads, with a long train that stretched behind her for miles. She pictured the band playing a romantic melody as they danced their first waltz and her feeding Keith a piece of wedding cake lovingly cut with a silver knife. "I don't understand, Keith. Why this sudden change? I thought we agreed to have a nice wedding. The families are expecting it."

"That's the whole point, the family bit. It's hard to explain. I guess I'm just uptight about you visiting my home. You see, I come from a very strict household. They hold to strange ideas and, well, strange customs, I guess you could say. I don't want to see you or your family hurt by anything my family might try to do."

Gail stared at Keith in confusion as a ruddy flush filled his cheeks. Bony white knuckles protruded from his hands as he gripped the steering wheel. "Keith, really, what can be so bad about your family? They're only people, like you and me. If I'm going to be a part of your family, then I should try to knit myself in with them somehow."

"No!" he shouted. "That's the whole point. I don't want you knitting yourself in. I don't want you involved with them in any way, shape, or form."

She blinked in astonishment at the caustic tone of his voice. "Is there something you aren't telling me?"

"No!" he said again in a voice that sent Gail shrinking in her seat. She shifted her attention to the scenery whirling past the car window. She heard a sigh, followed by fingers reaching for her hand. "Look, I'm sorry I lost my cool. I just want you to know that I've reached a decision about us. I feel it would be better for all parties involved if we pull into the next big town and find a justice of the peace to marry us. Then we can go on with our lives in some remote location, away from any family interference."

Gail watched her dream of a fairy-tale wedding slowly disintegrate before her eyes. "B—but Keith, I already put a deposit on the dress, and the veil I want reaches to the. . ." She paused when he steered the car into a rest area.

After parking the car in an isolated spot, he leaned back in his seat. Quietly, almost inaudibly, he said, "Gail, I'll be blunt with you. If we don't elope, then we don't get married. It's that simple."

His words numbed her senses. "B—but why can't we have a wedding?" she wailed. "You haven't told me why! You said this has to do with your family, but—"

"Gail, just trust me, please." He removed his glasses and threw them on top of the dashboard. "I love you enough to do it this way. I've thought about it ever since the night we left Doc's. I knew I had to come to a decision, as painful as this is turning out to be." He reached out a finger to gently dry the tear gliding down her cheek. "I love you more than life itself, but there are certain things I cannot have you involved with, chief of which is my family. I

37

wish you could see that I'm only trying to protect you."

Gail fumbled for her purse, unzipped it, and withdrew a crumpled tissue. "I don't know what to think, Keith. We've known each other for a long time and you've never once mentioned this problem with your family. Now that we're ready to finalize the arrangements, and I'm ready to meet them for the first time, you lay all this on me." She blew her nose. "It just doesn't make sense."

"Gail, do you love me?"

"Of course I do. What a silly question."

"If you love me, then please marry me right now and don't ask any more questions."

Gail stared at her engagement ring, wondering if she was ready to make a commitment to a man who had suddenly turned her life upside down in a matter of a few minutes. Yet her heart knew there was only one answer to give to the one who occupied her thoughts almost every moment of the day. Softly she said, "I'll marry you today, if that's what you want."

"Great!" he exclaimed, straightening in his seat as he turned the key in the ignition. "We'll drive to Poughkeepsie and find a justice of the peace right now."

Gail sat still in her seat, numbed by the abrupt turn of events. She was thankful to see Keith's happiness return, but the situation did little to relieve the turmoil in her own heart. There would be no wedding music, no fancy dress, no well-wishers to congratulate her on her special day, no beautiful arrangement of cheeses and fruits for the reception. There would only be the impersonal ceremony conducted by a justice of the peace, a signature on a piece of paper legalizing their marriage, and all her dreams buried in the dust.

She could hardly hear Keith as he tried to brighten the situation by promising a beautiful honeymoon in the Caribbean, complete with moonlit walks on the beach, a boat ride to a deserted island, and anything her heart desired. Gail tried to gulp down the lump in her throat and listen to his plans, but nothing could remove her disappointment. *My heart's desire was a beautiful wedding like Dorrie's,* she thought sadly. *Now it's gone because of his family. What could possibly be so wrong that we must elope? Maybe his family doesn't want him marrying someone like me.* She paused to consider this reasoning. *Maybe they expected him to marry someone they know and like. I guess Keith believes we must elope to avoid some major blowup.* She cast him a glance out of the corner of her eye and saw the smile on his face. At least Keith wanted to demonstrate his love by marrying her against his family's wishes. She made up her mind to remain positive about the situation, praying that her heart would find healing from this painful blow.

Chapter 5

"Well, it's over." Keith tucked an arm around Gail as they walked down the sidewalk toward the car. "It's official. We're now Mr. and Mrs. Hampton."

"There wasn't much to it," Gail said meekly. The ceremony was just as awful as she knew it would be. The simple affair was presided over by a stern justice who demanded his fee up front before he would conduct the marriage. His secretary stood in as a witness with a blank face of indifference. The office where the ceremony took place smelled of paper and ink. The only plant in the room was a potted fern, decorating an obscure corner. Gail never felt so disappointed in all her life. Since they had not purchased wedding bands beforehand, the secretary hastily fashioned two makeshift rings out of paper clips, which they exchanged at the appropriate time. Keith promised after the ceremony that they would go at once to a jewelry store and buy a pair of rings, but Gail only wanted to leave town as soon as possible.

"Why don't we find ourselves a cozy place to spend our wedding night?" he suggested. "Maybe a nice bed and breakfast. Would you like that?"

Gail shrugged her shoulders as she twirled the paper clip wedding band around her finger. Nothing seemed to matter anymore. The way this day had gone, she would probably have to settle for a night in some cattle barn. Keith could not help but notice her mood and tried his best to alleviate it by promising everything but the stars in exchange for the hasty ceremony.

"I just hope you're happy," she mumbled as they walked past a jewelry store.

"Of course I am. This is the happiest day of my life. I only wish I could make you happy." He glanced back to see the store sign and the ornamental jewelry pieces shining in the windows. "C'mon," he urged, tugging on her hand. "Let's go pick out those wedding bands right now."

"I don't know if I want. . . ," Gail began as they entered the store.

"May I help you?" inquired a matronly woman who stood behind a showcase that displayed a large assortment of silver and gold wedding bands.

"We want to see the most expensive wedding bands you have in stock," Keith informed her, oblivious to the astonished look on Gail's face.

The woman arched an eyebrow. "Do you have the money to request such a thing, young man?"

"Lady, I wouldn't be asking if I didn't." He waved his checkbook in front of her face. "I can sign over any amount I wish. Trust me."

"Keith. . . ," Gail began, but he ignored her.

The woman brought out several different styles of rings to try on, including a set with a price tag of ten thousand dollars. The solid gold bands, decorated with sparkling diamonds, took Gail's breath away.

"We'll take those," Keith said and promptly wrote out the check.

Gail was beside herself as she watched him write out the huge sum before handing the check over to the woman. All at once, the recollection of Dorrie's comments concerning his pricey gifts flashed into her mind. She tried to bury her uneasiness when the woman handed them the expensive purchase in a velvet box.

"There you are," Keith told her. He slipped the ring on her finger, followed by a kiss. "Now do you feel like Mrs. Hampton?"

"I guess so," Gail murmured. The large diamond ring and glittering wedding band on her finger made her entire hand sparkle like expensive cut crystal in the sun. Gail hid her hand beneath the arm Keith offered her and strolled with him down the sidewalk. "Do you mind if I ask you something?"

"Shoot."

"Where did you get that kind of money?"

He paused before he replied, "I saved it."

"You saved ten thousand dollars? Why, it can take years to save up that much money!"

"Don't worry about it. I have it and that's all you need to know." He gave her a squeeze. "Besides, you're worth every penny and more. Look, there's our car. Let's get going and find a place to spend the night."

※

Gail tried to relax at the quaint bed and breakfast they had discovered during their travels, but the events of the day weighed heavily upon her. Keith appeared ready and eager to give of himself in every way, but Gail spurned his affection and curled up instead in an easy chair. She stared out the small window at the glimmering street lights below, numbed by all that had happened.

"Don't you want to be with me?" Keith asked. When she refused to answer, he said, "Look, if I'm not mistaken, you promised me a gift on our wedding night. Remember?"

Salty tears stung her eyes. How could she give a gift when there was no wedding to be had? All the dreams she had stored up these many months had disappeared, replaced by emptiness and sorrow. She sniffed and mumbled, "You promised me a wedding, not some legal ceremony in an office."

Keith stared at her dejected form for a moment before padding across the hardwood floors and kneeling down next to her chair. "Gail, please don't be upset. I wish there was some way I could convince you that we did the right thing."

"I just wish I was better prepared for all this. I wish I hadn't set my sights so high on having a nice wedding. I wish you'd told me earlier about your plans to elope before I went around town with Mother, trying on dresses and eating wedding cake." Her voice began to choke with emotion.

Keith took off his glasses and drew his fingers across his eyelids. "Well, things kind of came up while you were visiting your sister in Boston. There was no way I could tell you any sooner. This is the only way I could think of to avoid family interference and get on with our lives." He tossed the glasses on a nearby table and nuzzled his face in her hair. "Please believe me, Gail. I love you so much. Maybe when things settle down some we can throw a big party for your family and friends. We'll have it in a ritzy hotel somewhere with anything you want. I'll even buy you a beautiful ball gown to make up for the wedding dress. You'll look like a queen." He began to nibble on her earlobe.

Gail giggled. "Stop, that tickles."

"What do you say? Will that make up for all the trouble I caused you?"

She turned and gazed into his dark eyes. His arms curled around her, and she relaxed in their strength. "Well, if you think this is the right thing to do."

"I know it is. Trust me."

She melted under his warm embrace and the lips that paid hers a tender call. For the rest of the evening she forgot about weddings and receptions to enjoy their love.

✳

The shrill ring of the telephone in the middle of the night jarred them both awake. Keith fumbled for the receiver.

"Hello?" Keith sat up in a start, rubbing his weary eyes as he listened. "What? Who is this?" His fingers curled tightly around the receiver. "I'm not playing your game," he hissed. "Get off my back or you're asking for it." He tossed the receiver on the hook and buried himself in the bed once more as if to shield himself from whatever lay in wait outside the walls of the room. Soon he felt a hand shake the quilt and a whisper drifted down from above. He peeled back the cover to find Gail staring at him.

"Who was that on the phone, Keith?"

"Just a prank call. Don't worry about it."

"You tell me not to worry, but I am right now. You knew that person on the phone, didn't you? What did they want?"

Keith only buried himself beneath the quilt. "I said not to worry about it."

"Keith, please don't do this to me," Gail begged, pulling the quilt away from his face. "Don't shut me out now that we've made love and everything. I—I don't know what's going on with us. You always seemed so transparent in the past, but now I don't know. It's like there're walls between us. First it's the secrets about your family, and now it's a mystery call. Please tell me what's going on."

Her pleading voice pulled a cord in his heart. Once more he pushed away the quilt, took her trembling form into his arms, and cradled her close to his chest. His hand gently pushed back the curls from her face. "Shhh, it's going to be all right. Trust me."

"You tell me to trust you," Gail mumbled, pressing her face into his shoulder, "but I don't know why I should. . . ."

"Gail, Gail," he murmured, "I wanted to spare you all this. I really did. I guess I just loved you too much to let you go." He tipped back her chin, staring into brown eyes that appeared so vulnerable and afraid. He kissed her gently. Only when her tears glazed his cheek did he realize the mistake he'd made. *I should have let you go when I could have, for your own good*, he thought. *That would have been a true act of love. But I was selfish and now it's too late.*

A loud knock suddenly sounded on the door. Keith hugged Gail close to him. Again came the thump of a fist, rattling the door on its hinges. He jumped to his feet and raced to the window, searching for an exit from the room. A quick scan of the situation told him the window of the room was far too high. . . . There was no escape. He frantically searched for another idea.

"Get dressed quick," Keith whispered hoarsely. After Gail did so, he took her by the arm and shoved her to the floor. "Now get under the bed and don't make a sound!"

"B—but, Keith, what's going on?"

"Do as I say! And keep quiet."

Gail crawled into the tight space, wedging herself between the bed and the hard floor just as the lock to the door clicked and the door swung open. Two men sauntered in. One of them pocketed a nail file.

"What do you think you're doing?" Keith demanded.

Grant's thick voice blanketed the room. "I'm sorry to disturb you, but have you forgotten about the appointment with your father?" His dark eyes swept Keith as a tiny smile hovered in the crook of his mouth.

"I don't know what you're talking about. Now get out of here!"

"I'm afraid you did make an appointment, and as I said on the phone, I intend to have you keep it."

"You're developing a big nose for trouble, Pal," Keith snapped. "I told you the other day to get lost. Guess you don't understand English."

The other man began kicking over suitcases and scattering personal belongings as he searched the room.

"Both of you get out of here right now, or I'll—"

"Call the police?" Grant interrupted. He snickered. "That would prove interesting. By all means, go ahead. In the meantime, where is your bride this evening?"

"That's none of your business."

Grant sighed and shook his head. "You really are making things difficult. I have a job to do. Your father specifically wanted to meet this fiancée. . .or wife, I should say. Now must I punish the boss's disobedient son for refusing direct orders?"

"Who are you kidding? You can't lay a finger on me and you know it."

"But there are other ways to convince you, wouldn't you say?" At that very moment, Gail was dragged out from underneath the bed by Grant's accomplice. Her enormous eyes appeared like the dark circles of a raccoon's on her pale face. She fell into Keith's arms, shaking like a tree limb in the breeze and heaving with every breath. Keith glanced over the curly ringlets of her hair to see the spark of challenge in Grant's dark eyes. He knew the man was capable of anything if he felt deterred in his work. With great reluctance, Keith ordered Gail to pack.

"But Keith, w—where are we going?"

"Just do it, Gail. Now."

She obeyed with a sniff as the two men watched her place a few meager belongings into a suitcase. Keith threw his own clothes into another bag before tossing it hard into Grant's stomach. "Here," he snorted. "Do something useful and be our bellboy. Just don't expect a tip."

"I will receive my tip after I deliver you and your bride safely to your father."

"I'm sure you will. Just like the postman. Must be a hard life."

"I rather enjoy it. The work proves quite entertaining, chasing a belligerent son from town to town. For one who doesn't wish to be followed, you don't cover your tracks well at all."

"I'm not slick like you. I intend to run my life the way I choose. I don't care who sees it."

"Unfortunately you will have to convince your father of your new independence, won't you?" Grant began to chuckle. "That won't be easy, I can assure you."

Keith opened his mouth to counter the statement, but finding no suitable words, he clamped his mouth shut and turned away.

※

Gail wanted to scream and cry, but fear kept the emotions bottled up within her as she followed Keith and the two men into an awaiting car. Questions assailed her mind as she cowered in the backseat, her hands clinging to Keith's arm for strength. *Who are these men? How do they know Keith? Where are they taking us in the middle of the night?* She tried replacing the confusion with peaceful thoughts as the car took off down the lighted street but found herself in turmoil. All her mindless ideology of the past did nothing to calm the gnawing sensations of fear that whittled away her strength. In the midst of her duress, she thought of Dorrie and her strong Christian commitment. She knew how much Dorrie relied on God during those fearful times that tested her. Without knowledge of what lay ahead, Gail could only cry out in her heart, *Help me, God! I don't know what's happening, but I know You do. Please, help me.*

Despite her fear, Gail soon drifted off into a restless sleep as Keith's hand gently caressed her curly hair. The two men in the front seat did nothing but gaze out the car windows. Occasionally Grant's eyes would survey them in the rearview mirror. Once or twice he opened his mouth as if to say something, but he did not.

After a trip of some ninety minutes' duration, the car slowed before a large gate and a security phone. The abrupt change in motion sent Gail yawning and rubbing her eyes in confusion. "Where are we?" she asked as the strange man behind the wheel spoke swiftly into the phone at the gate.

Keith remained silent. The gate swung open, allowing them entrance into the estate of his father. As a youngster, he used to pride himself in the family wealth, often bragging to playmates about the large white gate and security phone that blocked all but important guests from visiting. Such thoughts of personal greed were repulsive to him as he watched Gail try to understand what was happening to her.

"Home, sweet home," Grant mumbled, climbing out to open their car door.

Gail followed the men through the wide doors of the home and into a beautiful foyer with a dazzling chandelier and large oval window in the rear hallway. "Where are we?" she whispered again to Keith as she beheld the finery of the home. She watched with anxiety when one of the men gestured for Keith to follow while the other tried to escort her into a separate room. Her fingers dug into Keith's arm. "No, I'm not going. Keith, please don't let them take me away from you! Please let me stay with you!"

Keith turned about with his hands inside his jeans pockets, calm and composed in the midst of the sumptuous surroundings. His reaction to this strange situation unnerved her. "It's all right, Gail. We're home."

"Home? This is your home?"

He nodded toward the sitting room. "Right. So just go in there for a bit and wait for me. I'll come back for you."

"I don't understand." Her confusion increased as she was escorted into an elegantly appointed sitting room and the door locked behind her. Her hands trembled as she tried to sit on a sofa. She soon found herself pacing instead. After a time, the decorations in the room beckoned her to investigate. A shelving unit displayed various artifacts from around the world, including tusks, pottery, sculptures, and weaving. On the opposite wall hung a family portrait in a gilded frame. Gail ventured forward to examine the painting. The mother and father sat in armchairs with their two sons standing proudly beside them. The mother was plump yet stately, with rosy cheeks and brown hair. The father wore a huge mustache that draped across his face. Upon closer inspection, she noted that one of the youths in the painting looked something like Keith, with dark hair and eyes and a mischievous smile. The painting was dated 1985. An engraved brass plate read, "The Costello Family."

"The Costello family?" she whispered, shaking her head. Next she inspected the many artifacts lining the shelves. Each item had its own label and serial number. Someone in the family had traveled far and wide to obtain a collection of curiosities from around the globe, then had taken pains to identify and number each piece. Gail shook her head in wonderment. Could all this really belong to Keith's family? If so, why did he choose to conceal this life from her?

The door suddenly burst open, startling her. One of the men who had driven Keith and Gail to this mysterious place now waved his hand. Gail walked along the wooden flooring that creaked ominously beneath her footsteps, until she entered a large library. The odor of tobacco mixed with alcohol permeated the air. Before her sat Keith and a distinguished-looking gentleman with salt-and-pepper hair and sporting a long mustache with curled tips. She drew in a sharp breath. *The man in the painting!*

The older man smiled congenially and pointed out a seat for her with the stub of a cigar. "Come sit down, young lady. I know you have had quite an extraordinary day."

Gail sent a questioning look in Keith's direction. His eyes remained fixed on the books lining the shelves.

"I hear that you two were married today by a justice of the peace."

Gail twisted the rings on her left hand with trembling fingers, wondering why she had ever agreed to Keith's proposal.

The man shifted in his leather chair. "Come now, there's no reason to be afraid. I deeply apologize if the two bodyguards who escorted you here were anything less than cordial. When I discovered my son had not arrived for his scheduled meeting, I worried for his safety and sent my men out to find him. Of course I did not realize you were married."

Gail relaxed a bit after hearing this explanation. *So this man is Keith's father.* She glanced around the room. He's richer than King Midas if he employs bodyguards and lives like this. Gail jumped at the thought of wealth. She squared her shoulders and crossed her legs, trying to appear like a regal daughter-in-law. "Oh, that's all right, Sir. I understand now. At the time it was a little scary."

The man smiled before rekindling his cigar with a match. He puffed for a time, flicked the ash into a tray, then remarked, "I was sorry to hear you did not choose to proceed with a wedding. I'm sure it would have been a glorious affair."

"Yes, well. . ." Gail paused, a flush coming to her face when she recalled earlier being concerned that the patriarch of the family might not wish her to be his new daughter-in-law. "I know I'm not what you all thought I would be and everything. . . . I mean, I'm not from a very noteworthy family. We're just ordinary people, you see, and. . ." She paused when Keith gave her a strange look.

"Nonsense. Notoriety is hardly important. You seem like a very intelligent young lady. And you're quite beautiful as well. I think my son made an excellent choice."

Gail smiled for the first time that day. She felt her confidence soar, fueled by the compliments. "Well, thank you. And you have a lovely home here." A yawn escaped and she clamped a hand over her mouth. "Oh, pardon me. I guess I'm a little tired."

"Well, it is the middle of the night. The maid will show you to the guest room. I will see you again in the morning. Good night."

Gail rose and bid him good night before following the petite maid who stood waiting outside the library doors. Keith followed her up the winding stairway to a room at the end of the hall. The mere sight of the room, with a separate sitting area and private bath, left her breathless.

"Keith, you have such a wonderful home!" Gail exclaimed, bouncing up and down on the bed. "I don't know why you never told me about it. There are so many gorgeous artifacts in that sitting room, not to mention the beautiful statues and the furniture. Your family is so rich!" She slid off the bed to sink her feet into the thick carpet. "This is like living in paradise."

"Stay here awhile and you'll sing a different tune," he muttered before quickly offering her a small smile. "I suppose it is."

She straightened and looked at him expectantly. "So is this the place where you grew up?"

He nodded. "This room used to be Archie's. . .uh. . ."

"Who?"

"It was the boys' room," he said quickly. "It was changed into a guest room after we moved out."

Gail wrinkled her face in confusion. "We? You mean you have a brother?"

A strange expression swept across Keith's face. He rubbed his hands together and shuffled his feet in agitation. "Yeah, I had a brother."

"Where is he? I'd love to meet him. I bet you two squabbled a lot when you were kids, huh? You wouldn't believe the fights Dorrie and I used to have when we were little. When my parents first lived in a small apartment, we had to share a bedroom, and wow, that's when the fireworks began. She wanted things done one way and I wanted them another. And Dorrie is a very messy person. I liked things neat and orderly, but you always knew when Dorrie had come through—it was like a tornado hit the room or something."

Keith's feet continued to shuffle in response to her lively chatter. "Look, Pop and I need to talk for awhile. I'll be in later. Go ahead and get some sleep."

"All right."

They kissed quickly before Keith walked out of the room and stumbled down the stairs. He burst into the library where his father stood, perusing a book. "Why did you do this, Pop? Why did you send those two punks to drag us here in the middle of the night? You scared Gail half to death. Now she'll start questioning everything."

He closed the book with a thump. "Highly unlikely. You saw the look on her face. She believes an overprotective father only wanted to find his lost son. I'm thankful you at least picked yourself a naive girl without a brain."

Keith bristled. He felt his fist clench, and he fought to relax. "Pop, why don't you just leave us alone and let us live our lives in peace. I'm not involved with the business anymore. You're getting along just fine without me."

His father picked up a fresh cigar from the humidor and ran it along his mustache, inhaling the fragrance of the tobacco. "That's where you're wrong, Quin. I need you and soon." He took up a match and lit it. "Grant has informed me that your new wife has a sister living in Boston. It works out perfectly with my plans."

Keith stared in alarm.

"I need you to go to Boston very soon to check on some business for me. Having family in the vicinity will give you an excellent reason to be in the area."

"I told you I don't want to be involved anymore."

His father's eyes glinted like a predator in the darkness as he puffed on the cigar. "You have no choice in the matter. You're in this with me. You always have been and always will be. Don't think for a moment you won't be recognized in New York, San Francisco, Chicago, or half a dozen other cities where we've conducted business. Your name's known in the inner circles, just like mine."

"It's been over a year since I've done anything significant. And about my name—you might as well know that I'm going by a new alias. Gail knows me as Keith Hampton, not Quintin Costello. So don't use my real name while she's here."

The older Costello cracked a smile and gestured at Keith's eyeglasses with his cigar. "And I assume those glasses you wear are to further conceal your identity. You think just like your father. You are crafty but also adept at handling my affairs." He stepped closer, his voice softening. "Quintin, I need you. You're my heir. You must know what to do with the business if something ever happens to me."

"Pop, I don't intend to—"

His father held up a hand, silencing him. "Don't even say it. You are my only heir with both your mother and Archie gone." He choked as he added, "You're all I have left in the world besides this estate, which is far too big for an old man like me."

"Pop...," he began, knowing it was senseless to argue. His father would only continue in his tactic of persuasion by dredging up the pain he carried for the dissolution of his family. He would then wave his hand while acknowledging his vast holdings and claim that he wanted his only son to have his inheritance.

"Don't make me have to spell it out for you," his father continued. "We're both in this for the duration. You made a commitment to remain by my side."

"Yeah, but it's different now, Pop. I'm married. I have new responsibilities."

"I know you're married, much to my displeasure. I warned you about the consequences. I won't let some marriage certificate change what we have agreed to."

"But it does!" Keith retorted, pacing before the sullen master of the household.

"Everything has changed. I don't want Gail involved in any of this."

"She doesn't have to be. Keep her out of it. You know how."

Keith paused before his father. "You mean live a lie. You did the same thing with Mother, and look what happened to her."

A pained expression crossed the man's face. He spat out the cigar into an ash tray. His gnarled fingers groped for the shot glass brimming with brandy that he threw down his throat. "You're blaming me again for that. I've told you time and time again I had nothing to do with it."

"But you drove her to it, Pop. She was never happy. She knew things were going on right underneath her nose. Then after Archie died, she couldn't take it anymore and she. . ." Keith paused, unable to voice the consequence of his mother's depression. All the family's riches and lavish lifestyle were not enough to keep her in the land of the living. His hand flicked away a sudden tear escaping down his cheek. "Anyway, I won't have the same thing happening to Gail. She thinks my mother is alive and well and everything in the family is cool. I don't want her to know what drove Mother over the brink."

He strode out of the library, ignoring the assortment of faces peeking out from various recesses within the grand hallway. His father's spies lurked everywhere, eavesdropping on the discussion. The Costello household was a grand avenue for the corrupt who were eager to make fast money by accommodating Keith's father. Gazing about at the luxurious surroundings, Keith felt sick to his stomach. Something would have to give in all this—but what he didn't know. All he knew for sure was that he could not have Gail caught in the middle.

Keith peeked in the guest room and found Gail asleep. He stroked her soft cheek with his finger. It would be difficult to hide the circumstances of his family's wealth from someone as curious as Gail. Undoubtedly she would find out everything. And if he tried to shield her from it, what then? He bit his lip, recalling his mother's reaction to the family secrets. He could not bear to see Gail driven off the same precipice that had claimed his mother. He closed his eyes, perplexed about what to do in the days ahead.

Chapter 6

Gail awoke the next morning to find her clothes pressed and laid out for her on a nearby chair. Next to her the bed was still made up. She frowned, wondering where Keith had spent the night. As she climbed out of bed, a delicious fragrance greeted her. A beautiful arrangement of long-stemmed red roses in a cut-glass vase sat on the dresser. The heavenly aroma filled her nostrils as she skipped over to the adjoining bath to take a shower.

Despite the terrifying events of the previous evening, it thrilled her to be in the midst of such luxury. She couldn't understand why Keith disliked the beautiful surroundings. Perhaps such wealth lost its allure after a lifetime of exposure to it. For Gail, who had lived her entire life in low- to middle-income housing, the elegance was a treat. As the soothing spray of the shower washed away the anxieties of yesterday, she reminded herself to be bright and cheerful so Keith's father and mother would accept her. She didn't want to do anything that might irritate them, especially knowing that she had married into their wealth.

Scrubbing her arms with a sponge, she suddenly realized that Keith's purchase of ten-thousand-dollar wedding bands did not seem extravagant now that the money situation had become clear. Many times she had dreamt of walking into a store and buying the most expensive item on the shelf. She grew tired of always having to settle for cheap imitations. She stopped scrubbing and smiled. Why, now she could have anything she wanted! She had married into wealth! Gail closed her eyes as the water sprayed her face, imagining the fancy house she and Keith would buy, complete with an in-ground swimming pool and a tennis court. She would hire a personal maid and have her own hair styling salon right inside the house.

Gail stepped out of the shower and quickly toweled herself dry. Today she must look and feel her best. She would put on plenty of makeup to hide the flaws in her skin and eyeshadow to highlight the color of her irises. Sighing in dismay at her wardrobe, she wished she had brought along fancier outfits. After spending about an hour pampering herself and carefully making up her face, Gail opened the door and peeked into the hall. She tiptoed carefully to the top of the stairs. The chandelier in the hallway glimmered as she walked down each step, glancing around the banister for Keith. The maid, dressed in a standard black uniform and white apron, came out into the foyer and offered her a smile.

"Good morning, Miss. Breakfast will be served on the patio. If you will follow me."

Breakfast on the patio! How lovely. Gail walked through glass doors and out onto a brick patio decorated with white wicker furniture. Flowers in large earthen pots bloomed in abundance. Beyond the patio was an in-ground pool filled with crystal blue waters and a cabana for changing. *Just like the home of a famous movie star,* she thought dreamily, sitting down in one of the wicker chairs. The entire back yard was fenced with black wrought iron that, in places, was covered by thick vines. Birds darted above her, chirping their merry morning songs.

"Good morning," a deep voice addressed her. She turned to see Keith and his father walk out to the patio. They drew up wicker chairs opposite her. "And how was your night?" asked Keith's father.

"Oh, just fine, Sir," Gail said, offering the family patriarch her best smile. Glancing over in Keith's direction, she noticed the dark circles under his eyes and the worry lines etched in a distinct pattern around his mouth. It was apparent he had slept poorly. She wondered again where he had spent the night before pushing the thought aside. "I noticed your lovely pool. Do you swim a lot in it, Mr. Hampton?"

"I enjoy a dip now and then. It's refreshing to take a swim when the temperature rises in the afternoon. Perhaps you would like a swim while you are here?"

Gail's eyes sparkled. "I would love it!" Again her gaze darted toward Keith, who sat slumped in his chair with his chin resting in his hand.

Soon the maid arrived to serve breakfast. Bowls filled with fresh fruit and plump blueberry muffins caused Gail to salivate in anticipation. "Coffee?" the woman asked, holding up the crystal pot.

"Oh yes, please. Keith was telling me he can drink coffee any time of day and it has no effect on him."

The father glanced at his son. "Well, he must have inherited the trait from me." He cleared his throat. "In fact, we are very much alike in many respects."

Gail sipped the steaming coffee before asking, "Is your mother sleeping in, Keith?"

At this, Keith jumped as though he'd been stung by a bee. "No. She, uh. . . she. . ."

"She's out of town on business, my dear," the father interrupted. "I'm deeply sorry she isn't here to greet her new daughter-in-law. I'm sure she would find you absolutely delightful."

"I'm sorry, too. What does she do?"

"Oh, she's a. . .um, fashion consultant. Why, I'm certain that at this very moment she is enjoying breakfast at a café in New York City." He chuckled as he raised his china coffee cup.

Keith only bobbed his knees back and forth while looking off in the direction of the high iron fencing surrounding the property.

"Keith mentioned he had a brother, too. Does he live nearby?"

Both father and son exchanged glances before the father said softly, "He was killed in a dreadful accident, my dear."

Gail immediately put down her coffee cup to stare at Keith. "Oh, I'm so sorry. I didn't know."

"That's quite all right. It was a terrible tragedy. He was driving late one night and lost control of his car. He hit a tree head-on."

Gail tried reaching for Keith's hand across the table, but he had tucked his hands beneath his arms as if to shield himself. "Keith, I'm sorry. Here I rambled on about Dorrie last night without even thinking. That was really insensitive of me."

"Don't worry about it, Gail," he said quietly. "You didn't know. It's just, well, hard to talk about."

"Let's switch to another topic, shall we?" his father quickly interjected. "I'm glad you both are here together. I wanted to inform you of a decision I've reached concerning a wedding gift. Quin. . .uh, Keith tells me he would like to take you on an extended honeymoon, young lady. So I've decided to pay all the expenses as my wedding gift to the both of you. Wherever you decide to go, it's on me."

Gail's eyes widened in astonishment. "Really? That sounds wonderful; thank you!"

"You're quite welcome. Discuss it and I will have my travel agency make all the arrangements. In fact, I will even have the butler, Charles, locate some of those travel brochures we keep in a file drawer in the office. Look them over at your leisure."

Gail was about to announce a desire of going to Paris or Rome when Keith announced in a sharp voice, "I already told Gail we're going to the Caribbean."

"But Keith, you heard your father. He said anywhere we want! That means Europe, too, doesn't it?"

The father smiled before reaching into the pocket of his jacket to pull out a cigar. "That's right. Europe, a Mediterranean cruise, Hong Kong, wherever you choose."

"You see? How can we pass up this opportunity? If we can't have a wedding, then at least we can have a beautiful honeymoon."

She was perplexed to see Keith absently pull apart a muffin until it was no more than a mass of crumbs on his plate. He downed his coffee in several gulps before excusing himself to wander off on his own.

❋

Anxiety assailed Keith as he watched the cool manipulation of Anton Costello at work on the love of his life. He remembered the countless days and nights when his father had employed the same tactics on his mother—kind words, smiles, gifts, trips—all the while concealing the true business dealings of the family. Now with Gail exposed to similar techniques, Keith understood all too well the lies his mother had endured for years. During that time he had worshiped his father, who

51

provided the family with everything they desired. No one questioned what Anton Costello did or with whom he associated. Instead, family members became involved in their own activities.

Archie, the older of the two Costello sons, was studious and thoughtful but a weakling, his father would sometimes say with a sneer. Yet Archie found favor with their mother, Treva, who liked his quiet ways. Quintin, or Keith as he now addressed himself, was the more adventuresome of the two. His father loved him for that and found him dependable and trustworthy with the company secrets. When Keith grew older, he remained constantly by his father's side, intrigued by the danger attending the business. His mind assimilated with ease any information his father cared to share. Nothing excited him more than traveling with his father or the other men to the major cities, arranging meetings with their contacts, finding out about shipments, and collecting goods to sell for profit. Most of all he enjoyed the challenge of outwitting the law enforcement agencies that sought to subdue them.

As the business expanded into major cities throughout the United States, his father hired new people to help, including Grant, who was well known in the circles of corruption for his organizational skills and his ability to spy on adversaries. Keith and Grant immediately locked horns, for Keith felt the man eroded Keith's influence within the business. At about the same time, his older brother, Archie, began complaining about all the unlawful activity. He had recently undergone a religious experience—a "brainwashing by lunatics" as Keith called the conversion. Those in the business watched with apprehension as Archie began warning his father to change his ways or reconcile himself with the authorities. The threat alarmed everyone, especially Grant, who had settled into the business well and looked forward to a promotion within the chain of command.

Then one night the family received the disturbing news of Archie's death in an automobile accident. The vehicle had been found against a tree with the front end smashed as though a giant fist had dealt the death blow. Archie had perished instantly. His death sent Keith's mother into a deep depression. She refused to leave her room for days on end. Keith delved into the workings of the business to escape the pain. A few months after Archie's funeral, he and his father left on an extended trip to Europe, leaving his mother in the care of friends. When they arrived home, they were met with more tragedy. Treva Costello had overdosed on a deadly combination of sedatives and alcohol and now fought for life in the intensive care unit of Albany Medical Center. Keith visited his mother only once while she was there. The tubes in her arms and neck sickened him. After several days of struggle, the troubled woman died, grieving over the loss of her eldest son and her life in general.

Keith brushed away a stray tear as he recalled her funeral, held under an overcast sky. Anton Costello had been all business in response to his wife's death and never mourned, as far as Keith could tell. Likewise, Keith had masked the effects of his own grief until just recently, when he began sensing the loss of his mother. Hearing Gail's incessant chatter about her family, it pained him that his mother was no longer alive to share in his life. There were only the harsh demands of a headstrong father who insisted that Keith remain in the business, despite his marriage to Gail.

The soft touch of her hand on his arm sent Keith whirling around to find Gail staring at him, an inquisitive look in her brown eyes. When she inquired about his moodiness, a wall of solid stone rose up within him.

"Guess it's hard remembering Archie and all," Keith mumbled.

Gail leaned her curly head against his chest. He could not help but run his fingers through her hair. The gesture brought comfort to his troubled soul.

"I wish I hadn't talked so much about Dorrie last night."

"It's okay," he said. "Dorrie's your sister."

"Yes, but—"

"Hey, I mean it. After the honeymoon is over, we'll make a trip to Boston and visit her."

"I know she'll like you. And I bet you'll get along great with her husband, Mick. He's built like you—broad shouldered with big muscles." Gail ran a finger across a rippling bicep before slipping her hand around his upper arm. "He's athletic, too, but really into religion like Dorrie. He teaches biology at a middle school, then on weekends he does some pretty dangerous stuff."

Keith was suddenly riveted. "What dangerous stuff?"

"You wouldn't believe it." They walked arm in arm until they reached the far side of the pool. Gail knelt down to pluck out a few stray leaves floating in the warm water. "He works with the gangs right in the heart of Boston. I don't know how he does it. I would be scared stiff."

Keith's eyes widened as he glanced quickly toward the patio to find that his father had left. He knelt beside Gail as she trailed her fingers in the water. "What do you mean he works with the gangs? What does he do?"

"Oh, he helps run a soup kitchen. Then he goes out on the street and talks to gang members about God. Dorrie doesn't want him doing it anymore. She's afraid he'll end up like his father."

"What happened to his father?"

"Some gang leader shot him in the back of the head. Mick's father used to work with a gang called the Vultures. One day they just shot him in an alley. Now he lives in a nursing home because he can't do anything for himself. I've even visited him there. He can't talk or feed himself. Every day the nurses have to dress him and wheel him around. It's really sad. The only good thing is that he does know what's going on. Mick and Dorrie talk to him all the time. He even smiled once when they brought in my little nephew, Jamie, for a visit."

Keith listened carefully as he piled up a mound of white stones that bordered the pool. "And this all happened in Boston?"

She nodded.

"When?"

"About six years ago. It was terrible. I can't believe Mick still wants to go out there and talk to that gang after what they did to his father. He's crazy to take such risks." She came and nuzzled her head against his chest. Instinctively, Keith wrapped his arms around her. "That's why I'm so glad you're not involved with anything dangerous. I simply couldn't take it."

A strange sensation overcame him. He released her and rose to his feet. "Say, let's get our minds off gangs and violence and have a look at those travel brochures, shall we?"

Gail flashed him a look of surprise. "Does this mean I get to choose someplace other than the Caribbean for our honeymoon?"

Keith nodded, watching her eyes light up in excitement. "You heard Pop. It's on him. Might as well take him up on his generosity—for now anyway."

"Oh, goody!" she sighed in delight, skipping alongside him like a young child who had been given a grand Christmas present. "I can't wait!"

Keith hardly felt like celebrating as his mind buzzed with the information concerning Gail's brother-in-law in Boston. He made up his mind to speak with his father about it as soon as he engaged Gail's interest in the travel brochures.

❋

Anton Costello sat calmly at his large mahogany desk, a cigar smoking away in the ashtray. Keith entered and sat in one of the highback leather chairs. His father glanced up upon his arrival and offered a small smile. "Well, have you decided where you would like to go for your honeymoon?"

"Gail is looking over the brochures right now."

"And has she found anything interesting?"

"Everything interests Gail. She'll find it hard to reach a decision." Keith leaned over with his hands clasped together and his elbows resting on his knees. "Pop, I've got something important to tell you."

"Yes, what is it?" Costello asked carelessly, shuffling through the stack of papers littering his desk.

"I just found out something I think you should know. Gail was telling me about her sister and brother-in-law who live in Boston. She told me her brother-in-law's father, who's one of those street preachers, was shot six years ago. He was involved with a gang in Boston."

Keith's father raised his bushy gray eyebrows to acknowledge Keith's concerned face.

"It seems to me I recall some kind of fiasco back about that time in Boston," Keith continued. "It was a gang called the Vandals or something."

"The Vultures," his father corrected, rattling papers as if trying to drown out the discussion. "What of it, Quintin?"

"Well, correct me if I'm wrong, but I remember you putting someone on the hit list about that same time—someone who was interfering with the gang and the business and who needed to be dealt with. Was it that street preacher?"

Anton Costello shrugged indifferently. "I don't keep track of incidents that took place more than five years ago. If the man in question had his nose in our business, it's entirely possible that we put him on the list."

Keith shot out of his seat. "Pop, do you realize what you're saying? One of your people shot a member of Gail's extended family!"

"Calm down, Quintin, and take a seat." He pointed to the chair with the tip of his cigar before plugging it back into his mouth.

"No, I'm not going to sit. Think what you have done to Gail's family! All the heartache, the loss of a loved one. . ."

Costello stared with frosty eyes. "Quintin, you of all people should know that when someone begins to infiltrate our organization, he must be silenced or we risk discovery." He paused, flicking the ash from his cigar before returning it to his mouth. "Yes, I do vaguely recall the incident. There was some unknown individual—I believe he was a street preacher, now that you mention it—who had infiltrated the Vultures gang. He started asking all the wrong questions. He needed to be silenced before he leaked vital information to the police. I believe the gang leader himself took the full rap for the shooting." He added with pride, "Fortunately, none of my men were implicated in the deed. We were very careful."

Keith stared at his father. The man sitting before him was no longer a human being but a block of hard flesh, frozen by years of relentless criminal activity. "I don't believe you're actually saying this! An innocent man is a vegetable in some nursing home because one of your men plugged a bullet into his brain, and all you can do is boast about not being caught?"

Costello rose, snarling, "That preacher was no innocent man, let me tell you. He was a danger to our entire operation in Boston! If he had gone to the cops, you and I would both be rusting behind bars the rest of our lives." He took out the cigar and pointed it at Keith like a weapon. "If I were you, I'd put a stop right now to this lovesick, mercy routine you're infected with and face the hard facts. We're here to run a business and make a profit. Period."

Keith began to pace before the desk. "I don't want any part of this. I mean it. I'm through."

"It's too late to back out now. You're too involved. Don't think for a moment you won't go down with the rest of us if you start getting soft on me. Just remember that everything about you is known on every street corner of every major city. A new name or a pair of glasses won't protect you if any of this leaks out. You know full well that when someone on the outside knows too much, he must be disposed of, plain and simple." Costello stuffed the cigar back into his mouth and sat down.

Keith stared hard at his father. "So tell me, Pop, did this hit list of yours also include family members? Like Archie, maybe? Or Mother?"

The older man's face went white as he spat out the cigar. "Are you out of your mind? How dare you even suggest such a thing!"

Keith spun around and headed for the door.

"Quintin, come back here! I'm not finished with you!"

Keith's hand rested on the doorknob. "Yes, you are. I'm finished with this whole rotten thing. Gail and I will be leaving shortly on that glorious honeymoon you promised us. From now on, you just leave us alone." He left with the door slamming behind him, refusing to acknowledge the shadowy figure standing in a dark recess of the hallway, staring with piercing black eyes.

Chapter 7

When Gail and Keith arrived back in Westchester County, they were besieged with questions from Gail's parents regarding the hasty marriage performed by the justice of the peace. Huge tears gathered in Gail's mother's eyes as she pulled out the wedding dress she had purchased during their absence. Her father sat in a recliner inside the family room, shaking his head in dismay.

"I don't know if I can return this now," Mother lamented to Gail as her finger traced the delicately curved neckline and the fancy beadwork on the bodice of the dress. "This was supposed to be a surprise. I was going to have you try it on and arrange for all the necessary alterations." She stared unhappily at Gail and then Keith. "I don't understand why you eloped after all the plans we'd made."

"It's kind of hard to explain," Gail began with a sideways glance at Keith, hoping for some support. He just stood there, silent, with his hands jammed in his pockets. "Keith's family. . .well. . ."

"I talked Gail into it," Keith finally told them. "I thought it would be the best thing to do, considering my family situation."

Gail's father shot him a look that could have melted ice. "And what's that supposed to mean, young man? We gave our permission for you to marry our daughter on the assumption that there would be a wedding ceremony in a church, officiated by an ordained minister. I cannot understand why you decided to elope."

Her mother continued to sniff and dab her eyes with a tissue. "All the plans. . . everything ruined!"

Her father pointed to the sofa, urging Gail and Keith to sit. "Let's just talk about this rationally, without all the emotion." When they were seated, he continued. "So what is it about your family that is so worrisome, young man?"

"Dad, they're rich," Gail interrupted. "I mean filthy rich, with a mansion, an in-ground pool, a fancy cabana, the works. I think Keith was afraid I wouldn't be accepted into his wealthy family. He didn't want them saying no."

"I love your daughter, Sir," Keith added. "I, well, I couldn't take the chance that my family might interfere with our wedding plans. I. . .I didn't want them spoiling it. Eloping seemed the only logical alternative."

"I see," Gail's father said quietly. "So your parents don't like the idea of their rich son marrying the daughter of a blue-collar worker, is that it?"

"No, Sir, that's not it at all," Keith answered in all earnestness. "I mean now that my father has met Gail, he likes her very much."

"But you pushed my Gail into a commitment before she was ready," Gail's mother added, the bitterness lacing her voice. "You must have known how much this wedding means to her and the rest of our family."

"I do now," he admitted meekly, staring down at his sneakers.

The Sheltons exchanged rueful glances, trying to make sense of it all. "Well, what's done is done," her father finally said. "However, I hope you will at least consider having a decent marriage ceremony in a church, even if you are legally married under the law."

"Well, maybe after the honeymoon, Dad," Gail said. "We're leaving in just a few days."

"A few days!" her mother moaned. "Where?"

Gail squeezed Keith's hand in anticipation. "Oh, we're going to take a fabulous ten-day tour of Europe. It'll be simply wonderful! London, Paris, Stockholm, Amsterdam, and there will be ritzy hotels, fabulous restaurants, and the best shopping in the world! Keith's father offered to pay all the expenses as a wedding gift to us."

Keith aimed a weak smile toward Gail's parents, who only stared at him in disdain. Their eyes burrowed into him as if attempting to uncover his real intentions. At times Keith found himself questioning his own motive. He vowed that all the secrecy was out of love and a concern for Gail. Yet the more he tried to hide the truth about the Costello family from the curious people in his midst, the more he found himself tumbling into a deeper pit. Right now there was nothing else he could do. Lies and deception seemed to be the only way to protect Gail and her family. After the recent conversation with his father, he knew no one, not even Gail, would be safe if she were to discover the truth behind the Costello empire.

Keith straightened in his seat and managed another lopsided smile to hide the turmoil brewing within him. "After all I put Gail through, I thought she would enjoy a relaxing trip to Europe. But once we return, we should have that ceremony you've suggested, Mr. Shelton. I can't promise my family's participation, though. They do whatever they please."

"Well, I suppose I will have to be happy with that," he answered, rising slowly to his feet to offer Keith a handshake. "I only wish you two had confided in us."

"I'm sorry, Dad," Gail told him, running to give him a hug. "Please don't be angry with us. I'm happy, really I am."

"We're not angry," he said, stealing a quick glance at his wife. "We're just disappointed that we couldn't share in your special union."

Both Keith and Gail were thankful when the discussion ended with a minimal amount of conflict. Although there were sad faces, accompanied by a few harsh words, the Sheltons appeared ready to accept the marriage and offer whatever assistance they could to help the newlyweds adjust to their new life.

That afternoon, while her mother offered Gail suggestions concerning her wardrobe for the upcoming honeymoon, Keith ventured downtown to a travel agency to confirm the itinerary for the trip. Once inside, he settled into a chair before a huge desk. On the other side of the desk sat a young girl with red hair and bulky jewelry. She gave him a bright smile as she tapped her red-painted fingernails on a keyboard, entering the information he gave to her.

"Yes, Mr. Hampton, you and your wife are confirmed for Flight 102 leaving for Paris, France, on the fifteenth. Departure time is seven-o-five P.M. from JFK. I have your hotel reservations right here, as well as train tickets for your other destinations in Europe."

Keith tapped his fingers on the desk while waiting for the printer to spit out the information A thought suddenly crossed his mind. He leaned over and asked if a Grant Sotari was also scheduled for the flight.

The girl typed in the name and waited a minute or two as the computer scanned the passenger list. "No, Sir, I don't see his name listed."

Keith thought for another minute, then said, "Try the name Leon Fish."

The girl raised her eyebrows. "Leon Fish? Are you kidding? What kind of a name is that?"

"Just try it, please."

She shrugged and typed in the name. "I can't imagine being born with a name like that. . . . Well, what do you know; there is a Leon Fish on the cabin passenger list."

Keith's heart began to race. He rose to his feet and ran fingers through his hair. *So Grant is going as I suspected he would. That means he'll be tracking us every minute of the trip. Somehow I have to throw him off, but how?* He searched his mind for an idea until his eyes fell on a glossy brochure lying on the desk. He picked it up. "What's this?"

"Oh, the customer who was here before you just booked a weekend trip to Lake Louise next month."

"Lake Louise?"

"Why yes, in the Canadian Rockies, about a hundred miles west of Calgary in Alberta, Canada. The Olympic Winter Games were held in Calgary awhile back—I think in 1988."

Keith opened up the leaflet and briefly reviewed the hotel amenities. "Looks like a nice place."

"Oh, it is. I have relatives who've been there. That's the Chateau Lake Louise you're looking at. It's a premier hotel built on the shore of an alpine lake. The Victoria Glacier is in the background. Of course it's still a little chilly there this time of year, but the hotel itself is quite—"

"Sounds good to me. Book us a week's stay at this, uh. . .Chateau whatever." She arched her eyebrows.

"And you fly in where?" Keith inquired.

"The nearest regional airport is in Calgary, Alberta."

"Then I want a flight to Calgary leaving on the fifteenth, first class—make it an early evening flight out of JFK."

"But excuse me," she interrupted, glancing at the itinerary, "that's the same day you're scheduled to leave for Paris, France."

"The Canada trip is for my friend, Quintin Costello," Keith said hurriedly. "He's jealous because I'm taking this whirlwind tour of Europe. Maybe a trip like this will keep him happy."

"I'm sure it will," she said, typing in the name as Keith spelled it for her.

"And put down his girlfriend. . .uh, Dorrie Shelton."

"Dorrie? Is that her real name?"

"I think so, but you never know about my friend. He gets a new girlfriend every week. Maybe after this trip he'll change his mind and finally marry this one."

"All right, then. I assume you want a rental car for them?"

Keith nodded. "The best you have available. Maximum upgrade."

"Yes, Sir." After a few minutes of typing and scanning the computer readouts, she said, "I have your friend and his girlfriend scheduled to depart at six P.M. from JFK on flight 253, first class, arriving in Calgary at nine-thirty, but of course that's mountain time. Unfortunately since you booked so late, the round-trip flight for two will cost the maximum list price of eleven hundred fifty-two dollars and thirty cents with tax, not counting the rental car for ground transportation and the hotel fees."

"Just total it all up and I'll pay it," Keith said. "Be sure you book a nice room at that hotel, too. Make it the honeymoon suite and maybe they'll even get hitched in time to use it. And another thing, Miss. . . ?"

The girl whirled around in her seat. "Oh, I'm Darcy. Darcy Weeks."

"Ms. Weeks," he said, slipping her a hundred-dollar bill from his wallet, "if some guy comes walking in here with dark hair and a pitted face, asking about these arrangements, I would prefer it if you didn't spill the beans. My friend will try every trick in the book to discover what's going on. The man's quite sly, you know. I've had a hard time keeping secrets from him. Just say you never saw me."

"Wow," Darcy exclaimed, staring at the hundred-dollar bill he offered. "Why, sure! No problem."

"In fact, I'll make it two for your trouble." He added another of the bills to the one sitting in the palm of her hand. "I care about my friend, but he sure doesn't care about himself. Now print up that itinerary quickly so I can get out of here."

"Oh yes, right away." Darcy whirled around in her seat to face the computer and madly typed away as though the money had energized her fingers. Keith sat still, his thoughts churning. He knew Gail would be disappointed at the change of plans, but he must keep one step ahead of Grant in this game or lose much more than he could afford.

❊

"Why do I need Dorrie's birth certificate when I already have my own passport?" Gail wanted to know as she searched a file cabinet in her father's office for the original document. "I'm so glad I decided to go ahead and get my passport a few years back."

"Just trust me, you'll need it."

Gail peered up at Keith with a perturbed expression. "I hate it when you say, 'Just trust me.' That means you're up to something, doesn't it? You're the most mysterious man in the world, Keith Hampton. It's like you're playing a game with me or something."

"Well, this really is a game of sorts. It's like Stratego. Ever play it?"

Gail shook her head.

"I'll have to show you how sometime. I used to play it a lot when I was a kid. The object of the game is to capture your opponent's flag. You hide your pieces and use them to destroy your opponent's men in order to reach his flag."

"It sounds confusing, if you ask me."

"Well, as you go step by step you begin to reveal the pieces you have hidden from your opponent. So you might say I'm slowly revealing pieces of my strategy to you."

"Yes, but I'm not your enemy," Gail teased, her face suddenly turning serious. "At least I didn't think I was."

Keith chuckled as he wrapped his arm around her. "Of course you're not my enemy. I'm thinking of others at this moment. The only way I can capture my enemy's flag and win is to reveal as few of my men as possible at any one time."

Gail shook her head before returning to her search inside the file cabinet. "You're so confusing, Keith. I wish things could just be spelled out simply. Life is too complicated, hanging around with you."

He sighed. "I wish it wasn't so complicated. There are many decisions I've made over the course of my life that I wish I could change. Sometimes I wish I could be born all over again and start my life fresh."

Gail laughed as she withdrew the birth certificate with Dorrie's tiny baby footprints stamped on the back. "Yeah, but you can't. We're only born once, unless you believe in reincarnation or something."

"Reincarnation," he snickered. "Yeah. For all you know, you may have eloped with a guy who once lived as an Arabian prince in another life."

Gail lifted an eyebrow. "It's a good thing Dorrie isn't around to hear you say that. She'd have a fit. The one time I mentioned reincarnation she exploded, informing me that it was a mystic philosophy that people use so they won't have to face the day of judgment. She says that, according to the Bible, you only live once and then comes judgment before the throne of God or something." Both became silent, pondering that inadvertent mention of the Bible.

Later that evening they enjoyed a pleasant dinner at one of their favorite restaurants. While driving back in the car, Keith picked up Gail's hand and held it in his. "I haven't mentioned this to you because of everything going on these last few days. I hope we can soon start acting like a married couple, if you know what I mean."

"I know. I've thought about it, too. I'm feeling better about everything, now that we are going on our honeymoon. I guess it's a little unnerving, being at our parents' homes." She leaned back in her seat. "Why don't we celebrate while we're on our honeymoon? Isn't that what you're supposed to do anyway?"

Keith doubted she would even want to be with him after discovering what he had done to her honeymoon plans. "Gail, I don't want to wait any longer than I have to. I've been really patient and—"

"I know you have. C'mon, though, wouldn't it be more romantic to experience love in Paris?" She giggled at the thought before resting her curly head on his shoulder.

"Paris," he echoed. *I only hope and pray you'll feel the same way about Canada.*

✳

The next day, Keith decided to take a stroll around the neighborhood to sort out any remaining details before leaving for Canada. He grew edgier as the time drew near, wondering how Gail would react to their change in destination. Yet the more he thought about it, the more the plan made sense. Grant would never suspect that they would change their honeymoon destination to some Arctic region in the far north. Surely this plan would outwit his clever opponent and allow him and Gail a welcome breather after the recent upheaval in their lives.

As Keith rounded a corner, he spotted a figure leaning against the side of a building, casually speaking into a cell phone. He darted behind a row of parked cars and crawled along the pavement until he was within earshot of the conversation.

"Yes, Sir, I checked with the travel agency here in town," the voice said. "They are still listed as passengers on the flight to Paris this evening."

Keith's muscles tightened as he recognized Grant's voice.

"No, Sir, I have not seen anything out of the ordinary. Yes, we are also confirmed for the flight. However, you do realize your son will become quite belligerent once he discovers us on the trip." There was a pause. "Yes, but the idea of a bodyguard has never settled well with young Quintin." Another pause. "It will be difficult to change his mind concerning the business, but I understand the seriousness of the situation."

Through a window of the parked car, Keith could see Grant's head nodding up and down as the man's fingers fumbled in a shirt pocket for a cigarette.

62

"Are you certain that's what you want?" Grant asked, tucking the phone beneath his chin as he lit a smoke. "Very well, then. I have yet to fail you, Sir, as you know. I will call you from Paris when we arrive."

Keith ducked behind the auto and watched from the ground as Grant's feet shuffled to and fro. The odor of cigarette smoke floated down on him from above. After a time, the feet clad in dark shoes moved off down the street. Keith closed his eyes and heaved a sigh of relief. The conversation had confirmed one major detail. Had he not changed the itinerary for the honeymoon, both Gail and he would have found themselves at the mercy of his adversary.

Keith rose to his feet and brushed off the gravel from his jeans, preparing to head back to the house when a voice stopped him dead in his tracks.

"So you also like to spy, young Costello?"

Keith jerked around in response. Grant appeared from behind the car with a sardonic grin plastered on his face. Regaining his composure, Keith said quickly, "Unfortunately, spying is a necessary evil when I hear there'll be two unwanted stowaways on board our flight to Paris tonight." He chuckled scornfully. "Really, Grant, I had no idea you were also planning a honeymoon."

Grant stood puffing on his cigarette. He blew rings of smoke into the air before he said, "Agree to remain in the business, young Costello, and I won't have to make the trip."

"Haven't you learned yet that what I do in the business is none of your business?"

"And haven't you learned that whatever interests your father interests me? Your father's primary concern is that your youthful presence remains within our organization. I intend to see that his wish is carried out."

"Let's discuss the options after my honeymoon, like normal, decent people." Keith slapped his forehead. "Whoops, I forgot—you're not normal, are you, Grant? In fact, you're far from normal. I always thought your primary habitation should be the exotic species exhibit at the Bronx Zoo."

Grant flicked cigarette ash on the ground before Keith's sneakers. "While you do have a sharp wit, Quin, you have no smarts. The only way one can succeed in this game is to be smart."

"I intend to succeed. I'm going to win the game by capturing your flag, Buddy." He whirled, ready to saunter away.

"I would not try to challenge me or you will regret it."

Keith turned and walked backward with confidence. "It's too late for that, Bud. This is a challenge. We'll find out soon enough who has the real smarts in this game. See you in Paris." He walked briskly down the sidewalk as the other man stood calmly beside the parked car, smoking the cigarette until the butt fell to the ground and his shoe smashed it flat.

Chapter 8

A re you finally going to tell me about this game of yours?" Gail asked as she checked her makeup in a lighted compact.

Keith's hands tightened around the wheel of the car he had rented for the trip to Kennedy Airport. He frequently glanced in his rearview mirror, looking for any sign that Grant and his associate might be following but found nothing unusual. He made painstaking efforts to conceal their tracks by driving an out-of-the-way route to the largest international airport in the United States. He hoped the effort would pay off.

Keith braked at a stoplight. "Well, I guess I should tell you what I've decided to do before we reach the airport. You must believe that this is for your own good, Gail."

She dropped her compact inside her purse. Her lips curved downward into a frown. "I know what you're going to say. We're not going to Paris, are we?"

Keith flashed her a look of astonishment. "How did you know?"

A muscle twitched in one smooth cheek as she folded her arms and looked out the window. "Because nothing in this relationship has turned out the way I expected. The honeymoon had to be next on the list."

An uneasy Keith noticed Gail's growing agitation. How would she react when he told her their new destination? He began by gently informing her of a place he had found that was devoid of the hassles of hotel transfers and traveling through foreign lands.

"You mean you found someplace better than Europe?"

Beads of sweat gathered along the back of his neck, dampening the collar of his shirt. He steered the car onto the expressway. "Well, not exactly. Look, Gail, I'll be frank with you. Remember those two guys who came stalking us the night we eloped, then drove us to my father's home in the middle of the night?"

"How could I forget? That was the most terrifying night of my life!"

"Well, my father put the same men on the flight to Paris with us."

Gail stared at him, aghast. "Why?"

"Supposedly to act as bodyguards while we are in a foreign country. But I can tell you for a fact, these aren't the kind of characters you can trust in a dark alley. Just because they work for my pop doesn't mean they're well mannered—not by any stretch of the imagination."

"So you changed the plans for the honeymoon because of them?"

"Yes, and that's why I had you locate your sister's birth certificate. You're going as your sister, Dorrie, so you won't need your passport."

"And who are you going as?"

Keith flushed. "Oh, I picked a family name out of the hat. Anyway, I had to throw these two guys off track, so I arranged for an alternate destination. The girl at the travel agency highly recommended it. And I reserved the honeymoon suite. The hotel overlooks this nice lake. I'm sure you'll love it."

"But where's it at?"

"Uh. . ." He paused, glancing once more in his rearview mirror, "well, it's in Canada."

"Canada! You mean Montreal? I've never been to Montreal. You know they speak French in that province. I guess it would be just like going to France."

"Actually, it's in a real scenic part of the country—the Canadian Rockies."

Gail's face wrinkled in confusion. "The Canadian Rockies! Why, that sounds like. . ." Her face contorted into an angry scowl. "No, you couldn't have. Don't tell me you booked us on some vacation in the mountains."

"It sounds real nice."

"I don't care if it sounds nice! I'm not going to any mountain location, no way. Those places are full of bugs and animals. I'll bet the place you've got us staying at is no better than a flea bag."

"Gail, honestly, this is a top-notch hotel with all the extras. Believe me, it's the last place those two guys would think to look for us."

Gail closed her eyes in an attempt to stifle the tears. "Why, Keith? Why did you have to go and ruin my dreams again?"

"Gail, please. I had to do this."

"I know. Just like we had to elope, and we had to ride with those two weird men in the middle of the night. Now we have to change our honeymoon plans. I'm so tired of it all. If I had known you would be someone who doesn't care about my feelings, I wouldn't have married you." She turned in her seat, crossed her arms, and stared out the window.

"Gail, please," he begged again. "This will give us time to be by ourselves without someone watching our every move."

"Can't you call your father and tell him not to send these men of his to Paris? I mean, this is supposed to be our honeymoon, after all. We certainly don't need any bodyguards!"

"Pop does whatever he wants, Gail. I've never been able to change his mind."

"Humph," she snorted bitterly. "Looks to me like you're attached to him by a chain."

Keith winced as the truthful words reverberated in his ears. There could never be a more accurate depiction of what plagued his life at that moment—a long chain that bound him to the will of his father. "You're right. Pop does run my life more than he should. That's why I'm taking these steps to break free of him. He still believes he has to run my life. Maybe the death of my older brother has something to do with it. I'm trying to break free, Gail. Eloping was one giant step in my effort to break the chain. This trip is another."

Gail inhaled a sharp breath, her gaze fixed on the brick apartment buildings comprising the borough of Yonkers in New York City. A train clacked along the tracks paralleling the freeway in an apparent competition with them as they strove to reach their respective destinations first. Keith and Gail were similar in that respect—each endeavoring to fulfill his or her own needs as they traveled the path of life. Gail speculated to herself about Keith's motive for the change. She knew from the start he was not thrilled with a trip to Europe. At one time he had suggested they have their honeymoon in the Caribbean. Now their destination seemed as far from that as the North Pole. Did he really change their plans because of the bodyguards, or was there some other unspoken reason?

"Well, I guess I don't have much choice in the matter," she mumbled. "I only wish I could do something I want for a change."

"When we get there, Gail, you can do whatever you want."

She raised an eyebrow. "Really?"

Keith crossed his chest with two fingers. "I promise. Whatever you want. If you want to spend each day lounging in the hot tub with room service all week or you want to buy out the mall in Calgary, it's your choice."

Gail relaxed as these pleasant images drifted in her mind. Keith did have a wealthy family, after all. She decided that if she couldn't go to Europe, she would at least spend a huge wad of money as payback for the sheer lunacy of being forced to endure a honeymoon in the mountains of Canada.

✳

Gail snuggled next to Keith, her head resting on his shoulder, while he read an airline magazine as they flew toward their Canadian destination. So far he could not have been more pleased with how things were going. Upon their arrival at Kennedy Airport, Gail and he spent most of their time waiting around at the car rental agency until the last possible moment. They appeared like a confused young couple, dashing through check-in, then airline inspections. They reached the departure gate just as the attendant was set to lock the door leading to the aircraft.

"You just made it," she told them with a smile.

Keith had been so busy wading through the crowd in search of their gate, he did not even have time to find out if Grant was following him. Now that they were safely in flight at thirty thousand feet, he spent a few minutes walking up and down the aisle, examining the passengers. To his relief, he found no one resembling the two men sent by his father. Keith returned to his leather seat in first class, silently proclaiming victory over his opponent.

"At least this flight is better," Gail commented, snuggling up to his arm. "I usually get so airsick."

"Is that why you have the motion sickness bag on your lap?" Keith asked with a grin.

"That's why. But I don't think I'll need it. We can use it as a doggie bag for all that great airline food."

Keith rolled his eyes. "Don't say anything more or I may have to borrow the bag."

Gail smiled. A flight attendant strolled by and asked how they were this evening.

"Just fine," Keith told her with confidence.

"We're on our honeymoon," Gail added.

"Congratulations! When was the wedding?"

"Well, uh. . . ," Gail faltered, giving Keith a sideways glance.

"We decided we couldn't wait and eloped," he told her. "When we get back from our honeymoon, we'll throw a big party and invite all the relatives."

The attendant nodded. "A friend of mine did the same thing. Of course, the parents weren't too happy about it, but once they had the party, everyone was fine."

"That's what we're hoping," Keith said before returning his attention to the magazine.

After a few minutes, they were surprised to see the flight attendant return with a huge bottle of champagne, decorated with a bright red ribbon. "This is from the airline with our compliments," she said, proceeding to uncork the bottle.

Gail giggled as she watched the champagne sparkle in the crystal goblets set before them. Keith held up his glass to proclaim a toast. "To the most wonderful woman in the world—and the only one who could put up with all these arrangements and not lose her cool completely."

Gail smiled and sipped the champagne before placing the goblet on the table. "I really shouldn't drink much of this," she confessed. "I can get tipsy pretty fast. Dorrie says I shouldn't drink at all."

"Is that another one of your sister's no-nos from the Christian rule book?" he scoffed.

"Well, she believes drinking causes more harm than good. I've had major problems whenever I drink, so she may be right."

"That's why I never bother associating with Christians. They follow too many rules. There's no freedom at all. Besides, the Bible can be interpreted in so many ways. Who knows what's really right and what's wrong?"

"All I can say is both Dorrie and Mick are pretty committed to what's written in there. And Mick's mother, who also is a Christian, believes like they do. Dorrie says God can show you what the Bible means. She says you can't go by man's interpretation."

Keith opened up the magazine. "I find it way too constricting. Rules, regulations, laws—who needs them?"

Gail stared at him in puzzlement. "But every society needs laws, Keith. Without them, people would be killing and stealing from one another."

Keith flipped a page. "They do that anyway, even with all the laws on the books. If you ask me, I think men make laws just so people can break them and get away with it."

"Well, I'm thankful that we have a judicial system that tries to defend the rights of victims while punishing criminals. I mean, look at Mick's father. Do you think it's right for the person who shot him to walk away without paying for his crime? I mean, Mick's dad was just handing out pamphlets in the street."

"Let me tell you, that preacher was doing a lot more than just handing out pamphlets."

"Huh?"

Keith flushed, realizing his blunder. "What I meant is, he must've done something more than hand out brochures to get that gang all riled up. I think he should've stayed off the street and in his church where he belonged. Then he wouldn't have gotten hurt, right?"

Gail sat in silence, unsure of what she believed.

"Weren't you telling me you're worried about your brother-in-law because he's following in the same footsteps as his father? In fact, even your sister is concerned that something might happen to him. Why take the risk? Be safe and stay off the street."

"Dorrie did mention her fears to me. But she's willing to trust God with Mick's life. I don't understand how she can have that kind of trust. It makes me wonder how someone can believe God for life-and-death situations. Mick feels the same way. He believes that sharing the Bible is worth the risk."

"Those beliefs seem to make people do crazy things, if you ask me. That's what they all are—crazy."

Gail fell silent under his cynicism. Her discomfort persisted even as the plane began its descent into the city of Calgary, Alberta. Keith bubbled over with descriptions of the various trips he had made in his lifetime. Gail listened thoughtfully, all the while questioning the internal makeup of the man sitting beside her. There was something disturbing about him, yet she could not put her finger on what it was.

As the plane touched down, Keith gripped her hand in his, whispering, "We're going to have a great time."

Gail only shrugged. Her moodiness continued as they retrieved their luggage from baggage claim, then proceeded through customs. Only when they stood waiting for a bus to take them to the car rental agency did Keith mention her melancholy.

"You're still mad that we didn't go to Paris, aren't you? Look, I promise I'll make it up to you. Just give me a chance, okay? Please don't turn to stone on me, or neither one of us will have a good time."

Inside the rental car, heading toward the resort high in the mountains, Keith's patience finally ran out. "You're driving me up the wall with this silent routine," he complained. "Is this how you're going to act the entire trip?"

Gail bit her lip and continued to stare out the window.

"Please answer my question!" he shouted.

The tone of his voice sent her head spinning and tears erupted in her eyes.

Keith drove the car off the highway and into an abandoned gravel lot. "All right, we're going to sit here until you tell me what this is all about. I don't care if we're here all night, but I deserve to know why you're acting this way."

Gail remained silent.

His fist banged the steering wheel. "All right, maybe I should have let you traipse off to your beloved Paris. Then you would have witnessed firsthand what I protected you from. You think I'm only looking out for number one. Well, you're dead wrong, Gail. I happen to love you enough to keep you away from two hoodlums who would like nothing better than to use you against me." He thrust his head back against the seat. "The problem is, they aren't here and you're still fighting against me."

"Why would those two men use me against you?" Her voice quivered.

Keith opened his mouth to rattle off an answer, but instead he paused and said, "I'd rather not go into that."

"Well then, now you know why I'm silent. You're like a mystery. During the flight here and at the airport, I've been trying to figure you out. I don't know what makes you tick anymore. I used to think I knew, but ever since I came back from Boston, things have been different between us. When I saw you give the customs officer that birth certificate, it suddenly dawned on me that you're hiding things from me. For instance, your last name isn't Hampton, is it?"

His face flushed. Fingers slowly tightened around the steering wheel. "Are you kidding? Of course it is."

"No, it's Costello, right?"

"Where did you come up with that?"

"Keith, I saw the painting of your family hanging in the sitting room the night we visited your parents' estate. I saw the parents, the two boys, and the name Costello engraved on a plate beneath the portrait. I knew when I met your father that he was the man in the painting, but it didn't occur to me until now that you were one of the boys. Why did you change your name?"

Keith licked his parched lips while sifting his brain for a response. He thought of concocting some story about a long-lost cousin but feared it would backfire like everything else. "Okay, you're right. My last name is Costello. And you might as well know that my first name is not Keith, either."

"What is it?"

"Quintin."

"Quintin?" She pondered this for a moment until she remembered watching him fish out the certificate bearing the name Quintin Costello and hand it to the customs official. "Of course, the name on the birth certificate!"

"My friends used to call me Quin. Quintin sounds like an executive or some congressman."

"Quin. I like that. It fits you better. But why did you change your name to Keith Hampton?"

He exhaled a loud sigh. "Look, can't we drive on to the resort? It's getting late and the rental agency says the hotel's a two-hour drive from Calgary. We'll discuss this some other time."

Gail stole a glance out the window as they proceeded down the highway. Despite the late hour, the sky remained bright with the final rays of the setting sun, offering views of the snowcapped mountain range. Above them loomed a bank of rocky cliffs that stood like a silent sentinel, frosted with snow. "This is a pretty area," she confessed. "It looks like Switzerland."

"Yeah, it does."

"So why did you change your name?"

"You aren't gonna let that drop, are you?" he shot back. "Let's just say the name came with a lot of memories I wanted to leave behind. I thought that by changing my name and getting a different job, I might free myself up a little. You know how you told me that I'm too dependent on my father? Well, the name change was my declaration of independence—my rebellion against the family hierarchy, I guess you could say."

"I've heard of people changing their names," Gail remarked. "I just wish you had told me about it earlier. It makes me wonder what else you're hiding."

Quin sighed. "Remember the game of Stratego? How a player reveals his pieces as the game is played?"

"I know, but—"

"Well, I'll reveal things about myself step by step. For now let's just concentrate on having a good time on our honeymoon and forget about our families, names, and everything else."

"Shall I call you Quin instead of Keith? I mean, that is your real name."

"You can call me whatever you want, so long as we can enjoy our honeymoon. Agreed?"

Gail nodded, allowing his hand to slip over hers and give a tight squeeze. Yet she could not settle the disturbing feeling that there was much more to the man than what she knew. While Gail had never been one to analyze others as her sister did, she could not help but be drawn to the mystery that enshrouded her husband. She decided she must find out everything there was to know about the man named Quintin Costello.

Chapter 9

When they arrived at the Chateau Lake Louise, Gail exhaled a sigh that mirrored her awe. In the atrium of the hotel, built at the turn of the century, they saw paneled walls, thick carpets, and a spiral staircase leading to a dining room and indoor pool. On a brochure they read that the grand hotel had begun as a simple log chalet nestled beside an alpine lake. By 1900, it had become a full-scale hotel renamed Chateau Lake Louise. Gail stood expectantly next to Quin as he confirmed their reservations at the desk. Given the late hour of their arrival, the lobby was empty of the stream of tourists that typically would be seen at the hotel bordering the pristine lake. They followed a bellboy and a rolling cart containing their luggage to the top floor. The young man unlocked the door to reveal a beautifully appointed suite with all the amenities, including a second bottle of champagne resting in a silver bowl. Gail ventured to the balcony of the room overlooking the lake to see the hotel lights glimmering upon the placid waters. Goosebumps rose on her skin as the chilly mountain air shocked her flesh.

"It's cold here," she remarked, rubbing her arms to generate some warmth. "I didn't pack the proper clothing for a place like this."

"We'll go shopping," Quin promised. "The receptionist told me about the shops in Banff, which is about an hour's drive from here. I'll buy you a whole new wardrobe."

Gail unzipped one of her suitcases and donned a sweater before returning to the balcony. She settled into a chair to gaze into the night. Quin soon joined her, two glasses of champagne in his hand.

"Let's drink to our honeymoon," he said, handing her a glass.

Gail clinked his glass and took a tiny sip before placing it on the stone flooring beneath her seat. She cupped her chin in her hand, suddenly apprehensive at the idea of spending a honeymoon with a man who had only just revealed his true identity minutes before they arrived here. While they were married legally by the state, she realized the marriage certificate bore the name of Keith Hampton, not Quintin Costello. He seemed like a stranger rather than the one she loved.

Quin set down his glass, rose, and knelt beside her, gently massaging her shoulders with his fingers. Instead of the gesture relaxing her, she felt her tension increase. *How can I go through with this honeymoon? None of what I've seen these last few days reassures me that he's the man I married.* Gail shot out of the chair at that moment, upsetting the champagne glass at her feet. The smell of alcohol rose to her nostrils, prompting a wave of nausea.

"What's the matter?" he asked.

"I, uh. . . ," she began as he stood and placed his arms around her.

"Just relax," he whispered, nibbling on her earlobe. "We've waited a long time to be alone, and now we have a whole week to discover everything about each other. I can't wait."

Gail turned away from him and leaned against the railing. "I don't know who you are. I thought I married Keith Hampton. Now that I've discovered you're this Costello person, you're like a stranger to me."

He laughed. "Gail, c'mon. I'm still the friendly waiter who helped you up from the floor at your sister's wedding. I haven't changed."

Gail did not find this situation humorous. "That man was Keith. You're not. I. . .I want my old Keith back."

The comment sent a wave of distress rippling across his face. "Gail, I'm right here! I'm the same guy. Look, if it makes you feel any better, continue calling me Keith."

"It's not just the name, it's your family, the painting, the wealthy estate—all the things I never knew about you."

"Sometimes there are things you don't know about a person until after the marriage."

"Well, that's true. I knew nothing until we got married. Now it's like I've given my whole self to some stranger in the street. I don't love a stranger."

Quin threw up his hands before plunking himself down in a chair. "I don't believe this. Now that we're on our honeymoon, alone for the first time since we got married, you decide you don't love me."

Gail sniffed. "I love Keith Hampton, a waiter turned computer repairman. I didn't marry a Quintin Costello who has wealthy parents and strange men following him wherever he goes." She dried the tears on the sleeve of her sweater.

Quin rose from his seat and stroked her arm with his fingers. "Gail, I love you. Don't you think that maybe the mask I've worn is simply a way of protecting you?"

"Sometimes I think I'd rather face the danger than all this secrecy, Keith—I mean Quin." She blew out a frustrated sigh. "You see? I don't even know what to call you! This whole thing has divided us because I don't know the real you."

Quin stood still and silent as a war of conflict raged within him. He realized more than ever his selfishness in keeping Gail while trying to conceal his past. He wanted to protect her from the evil but only succeeded in raising a wall between them. Slowly he blew out the air from his lungs, forming a cloud in the cold mountain air. "Well, since you're so unhappy about marrying an impostor, I'll give you a choice. We can stay here and try to make this work, or we can go home tomorrow and forget this ever happened. I know I've been secretive, but there are reasons for it. I've asked you time and time again to trust me. If you were to find out certain things, it could have severe repercussions." He lifted his eyes to acknowledge the star-strewn sky above them. "I thought I could keep you from all this, but I knew the night we arrived at my father's house that I would never be able to conceal my life from you. Pop tried to conceal his life from my mother, and now she's gone because of it."

"What do you mean?"

"I didn't want you to know the truth about her. I wanted you to think she's alive when she's. . ." He paused as the grief clogged his throat. In a choking voice, he said, "She's dead. She committed suicide."

Gail's mouth fell open. In an instant, she was on her feet.

"It happened about three years ago. I kept her death hidden inside me, afraid to face the pain of it, just like my father."

"So there's only the two of you. . .you and your father?"

He nodded.

"Now I see why your father wants to control you." Gail shook her head as she wrapped her arm around his shoulders. "That's terrible. Why did she do it?"

"She was upset about my brother's death. Mother always loved Archie more than me. When he died in the car accident, she never got over it. There were clashes between her and my father. Pop and I left for a business trip in Europe. When we returned, she was in intensive care at the hospital after overdosing on alcohol and sedatives. I saw her once, but that was it. I never got to tell her good-bye." A tear escaped down his cheek.

"Oh, Keith, I'm so sorry," Gail murmured, hugging him close.

"I know she never loved me, but I wanted her to." His voice cracked as his wet cheeks reflected the light of the lampposts lining the walkway below. "I was mad when she died. I didn't want anyone to know. Now I miss her so much. I wish I could tell her that I understand why she was so sad. I—I wish she could be here for us."

"Oh, Keith," Gail moaned, shaking her head. "I don't know what to say."

Quin wiped the tears from his face. "There's nothing you can say."

"You've been through so much with the loss of your brother and mother. In a way you're very much like Mick. He went through the same kind of tragedy with his father. Dorrie was able to help him when no one else could."

Quin grimaced at the mention of Mick's father and looked away.

"We really need to visit Dorrie and Mick after this trip," Gail said.

"After this trip? I thought you didn't want to stay here."

"I think we should stay and spend this time getting to know one another. We need to be honest and get our lives out in the open. If you are willing to do that, then I think everything will be better between us."

Quin shook his head. "I can't do that."

"What?"

"I can't tell you everything. Don't make me, Gail."

Her face fell. "So I have to live in a marriage full of secrets, is that it? I'm not going to do that. I won't. If we can't be honest with one another, then there's no sense in going on with this relationship." She whirled back to face the night. "I hate this place. It's so cold. It's. . .it's dark and eerie. I'm just not strong enough to deal with any of this."

Quin stood still and silent. Finally he turned and walked back into the suite. "Fine. Then we won't go on. I've just finished telling you of some of the worst pain inside me, and you decide you still want to dump me. Super. I'll make arrangements for us to leave tomorrow." He picked up his suitcase and slammed the door as he went out.

The noise echoed in her ears. Gail threw herself down on the bed. She felt confused and lost, without a sense of direction for her life. How could everything that had seemed so right in the beginning turn out so wrong? Tears dampened her pillow. Dorrie had known there was something wrong with Keith. She had sensed it, but Gail had only pushed her warnings aside. Now she felt trapped with a man she knew nothing about and who was unwilling to tell her anything. She continued to weep until there were no more tears left to shed.

Finally she rose and went to the dresser. She opened a drawer to find a Bible inside. Her hand curved around the book and pulled it out. "Okay, God," she said aloud, her hand shaking. "I'm at the end of the road here. I just don't know what to do. Help me find the answers, please, before I go crazy!" She settled herself on the bed, propped up by several fluffy pillows, and began to read. Scripture after Scripture spoke of God's love for her and His desire for her to understand Him. She remembered that Dorrie had once said that to know the purposes of God, you must be willing to surrender your life to Him. "What does that mean?" she wondered, gazing about the ornate room until her eyes fell on the phone. Dorrie. Dorrie would know. Dorrie would help her understand this awful situation. Despite the late hour, she dialed her sister's number in Boston with trembling fingers.

The groggy voice of Mick answered the ring. In the background, she could hear Dorrie say, "Two A.M.! If it's Corky again, you hang up, Mick. I mean it."

"Mick, it's me, Gail. Please, I need to speak to Dorrie."

"Gail?" came Dorrie's voice. "Honey, what's wrong?" Fresh tears spurted from Gail's eyes at the concern in her sister's voice.

Forty minutes later, Gail was still on the phone, yet now a tremendous peace filled her heart. During the conversation, Gail had acknowledged the emptiness in her life. With Dorrie's help, Gail reached out to the living God and found Him willing to fill the emptiness, to accept her into His family. Now she felt a peace greater than anything she had ever known. With God in her heart, she was able to confess to Dorrie everything she had learned about Quin and his family.

"I don't love him anymore," Gail said. "He lied to me about everything."

"Oh, Gail," came the voice that soothed like balm pouring over her wounded soul. "I know this is hard, but you must think of Quin as someone who needs God. He doesn't understand what he's doing. Before you do anything else, read 1 Corinthians 13. It's the chapter about love. Although you don't feel like you love him right now because of what he's done, read for yourself what God says about love."

"He isn't the man I fell in love with. He's an impostor." She began to cry. "I gave my innocence away to an impostor. . .to a man I don't even know anymore! I can't be married to someone like him."

"You need to find out who you did marry, Gail. You can't go back on the vows you said to him, even if he used a different name. The vows we make are for life. Let God help you love Quin and understand him. Don't try to do it by yourself. You found out tonight that you can't handle it alone. Now that God is in your heart, you are never alone. He will help you. Always remember that."

"I'll try."

"Just enjoy yourself while you're there. Let go and let God, I always say. Remember how I'm trusting God for Mick. You are a babe in Christ right now, but you're going to have to grow up quickly and trust God for Quin. And when you get back home, come see us as soon as possible. I think it would do Quin good to talk to Mick. They share similar stories of pain with their family members."

"I will, Dorrie. Thanks so much."

"You've made me happy as a lark," Dorrie exclaimed. "We'll be praying for you."

"Thanks."

When Gail hung up the phone, she sensed the love of God flowing through her heart. All those questions she had about Dorrie's faith in an unseen God had been answered. After experiencing His love and forgiveness, God reigned in Gail's own life now. As she readied herself for bed, Gail decided that she must help Quin discover this personal Savior and friend himself. She would try to reach out to his heart and, in the process, find a new love for him that only God could supply.

※

Gail slept well in the enormous bed, only to be awakened the next morning by the telephone ringing. She rose up on one elbow and reached for the receiver.

"Hello?"

"It's me."

A smile broke out on her face. "Oh, Quin, you won't believe what happened to me."

"Look, I wanted to let you know that the bellboy will be up in half an hour to collect your luggage. I booked us a flight back to New York that's leaving in four hours. That gives us two hours for the drive back to Calgary and plenty of time to go through customs before boarding."

Gail's face fell as her hands clenched the receiver. "But, Quin, I don't want to leave."

"You'll be home in no time, ready to get on with your life. . . ." He paused. "What did you say?"

"I said I don't want to leave." She glimpsed the bright sunshine streaming through the parted curtains. "It's a new day, Quin. I feel brand new on the inside, just like the gorgeous day outside."

"You seem different this morning. I thought you hated being here. I recall the words very clearly. 'Dark,' 'cold'. . ."

"Not anymore. I love it here."

"What made you change your mind?"

"God," Gail said reverently.

"God," Quin repeated before chuckling in scorn. "How did God perform that miracle? Send the archangel to your room last night?"

The comment drew Gail away from the window. "No. I was really upset about what happened between us. I read the Bible for awhile after you left. Then I talked to Dorrie."

"You mean you called your sister in Boston?"

"Yes, and she told me all about getting saved."

"Getting saved, huh? Saved from what?"

"You know, from your sins and everything."

Quin sighed in exasperation. "Look, Gail, if you're going to fill my head with a lot of religious nonsense, then I'll take that next flight out of here. You know how I feel about Christianity. A lot of do-gooders bent on following a bunch of rules."

"But God is real, Quin. He spoke to me last night."

"He spoke to you." Quin snapped his fingers over the phone. "So just like that you're now religious? Wow, and you complain that you can't figure me out! Look who's hiding things now. So how long have you really believed in this Christianity stuff—the whole time and only now you've decided to tell me?"

"I didn't believe anything until last night," Gail said earnestly. "Dorrie explained it to me. I prayed with her and—"

"And now you're instantly changed. Well, if it's all right with you, why don't we just set this God stuff aside and try to figure out what we're going to do. That is, if you care to be around me anymore."

"Of course I do. I want to stay." She padded across the floor, stretching the telephone cord to the limit so she could view the breathtaking scenery outside the balcony doors. The snowpack in the crevices of the mountains glistened in the morning sunlight. "Have you seen how beautiful it is here?"

"No, I've been on my cell phone calling for flight reservations. I didn't sleep a wink all night, either. The lobby was like a freezer. I'm stiff and my neck has a crick in it or something."

"Then come up here with me. It's nice and warm. There's even a hot tub."

"Excuse me? Am I hearing you right? Just last night you didn't care if you were even with me."

"This is the perfect place for a new beginning, Quin."

She sensed his confusion on the phone. "Well, okay. If you want to stay, I'll cancel the plane reservations."

Gail hung up the phone. She felt like soaring on one of the wispy clouds that drifted across the azure sky. She replaced the receiver, then skipped over to the doors leading to the balcony and opened them. A blast of cold air hit her face. Everything appeared new to her, fresh and alive, reflecting a beauty she had never known in her life. "Oh, thank you, Lord!" she breathed, inhaling the sweet fragrance of the tall ponderosa pine trees dotting the steep mountainsides. "Thank you, Lord, for allowing me to see Your creation with new eyes this morning. Oh, Dorrie, you are so right! You can see God in the mountains!"

Today was a new day, and with God's help, she would make it through.

Chapter 10

You really are different," Quin observed as Gail brushed out her curly hair before the huge mirror. "I mean, you look the same and all, but there's something different. . . ." He couldn't help but notice the change when he had arrived back at the room, suitcase in hand, to find the hot tub filling and Gail greeting him with open arms. He had felt it was like awakening to a new morning after a nightmare. He had pushed the change in her aside to bask in their love but now stared at her in wonder.

"Well, I'm starving," Gail announced. "Do they serve breakfast around here?"

"They're serving a buffet breakfast right now, in the Poppy Room."

Gail threw the brush on the counter. "Great. Let's go. Then maybe we can decide on what to do."

"I figured you'd probably want to go shopping or just lounge around," Quin remarked as they headed for the elevator.

"Are you kidding? I'm not going to waste this gorgeous day. It's too pretty to spend it in a store."

Quin eyed her in puzzlement. Could this be the same woman he married? Gail seemed like a stranger. It was as if she existed on some other level than he did. Now he understood all too well Gail's distress concerning his identity. Inside the spacious dining room, he could not even look out the huge plate-glass window that revealed the blue waters of the alpine lake, framed by the rugged mountains.

"Oh, look at that, Quin!" Gail breathed as she raced over to peer out the window. "Have you ever seen anything so beautiful in all your life?"

"I don't know," he said glumly as they took their seats. After serving themselves from the buffet, he focused his attention on his plate of food. His fork stabbed at the fruit chunks while Gail stared out the window. Finally he threw down his fork and said in all earnestness, "Look, Gail, you don't need to do this for me."

"Do what?"

"Pretend you like this place. I know you don't. You made it clear to me that you would rather be in Europe. There's no sense in hiding the fact behind this facade of yours."

"I'm not hiding anything," she said cheerfully. "I'm just seeing how pretty everything is. It's like I woke up to a whole new world."

"Believe me, it's the same cruddy ol' world out there," he said flatly, stirring cream into his coffee.

"Not when God's in it."

Quin leaned back in his chair and crossed his arms. "Look, Gail, I don't know what's come over you, but I'm begging you to put an end to this. I'm really sorry I didn't tell you who I was from the beginning. Please don't play the same game with me."

She reached out her hand to him. "Quin, I'm not playing a game. This is for real. God came into my heart last night. It's like what we talked about before we left on this trip—about being born again and starting over. I know what that means now. Everything is different. It's like the old me passed away and a new Gail has taken her place."

"Please, I want the old Gail back, even if we weren't getting along."

Gail shook her head as she resumed drinking her coffee. "I don't want that person back again. Never in a million years."

Quin fell silent. Perhaps he deserved this. After all, hadn't he been playing a similar game with Gail? Now it was his turn to be the victim and he didn't like it one bit.

After breakfast, Gail bustled over to the activity desk with Quin trailing far behind. She engaged the receptionist in lively chatter about things to see and do in the area. With a pile of literature in her hand, she found a padded armchair and sat down to sift through all their options. "Listen to this, Quin. You can take horses up to a neat rock formation just behind the chalet. There's an English teahouse up there and everything."

"That's nice," he said, playing with the button on his rugby shirt.

"And look at this." She held up a pamphlet outlining a gondola ride to the summit of a great mountain. "Doesn't the view look beautiful? Let's do that, too."

Quin said nothing. He continued to play with the button until it popped off the shirt. Gail looked over to see the button resting in his hand. "Oh, Quin. Maybe we can find someone to fix it."

"Who cares? I just want someone to fix us."

Gail appeared to ignore his comment and motioned to him with her hand. "C'mon, I want to put on jeans before we go horseback riding."

"I can't even imagine you on a horse," he scoffed.

"I can't either, but that's what makes this so fun! I feel like I can try new things." She paused to consider the statement. "Maybe that's why Mick can do his work without fear. God gives him the strength. We all have fear. It's ingrained in us. But that fear just goes away when God is there."

Quin wondered about her statement as they headed back to their suite. He had never allowed fear to establish a foothold in his life, but now he suddenly felt afraid. He was afraid of Gail and what she had become. Still if she had not changed, there would be no marriage or honeymoon. Thinking of the special time they had shared that morning, was it really so awful that Gail had found peace with God? She had poured out her love to him, and now she was delighted with the destination he had selected for their honeymoon. The consequences appeared positive, but the change in her made him feel unworthy. Perhaps that is why he wanted the old Gail back, whether the marriage suffered or not. He could not face the sin that stained his soul.

❋

Despite his discomfort, Quin enjoyed himself on the excursion into the pristine mountains. The weather was picture perfect as they rode on horseback to a rock formation known as the Bee Hives, perched high atop a cliff above the chateau. There they sampled English hospitality at a quaint log teahouse. Gail seemed more beautiful than ever to Quin, with her radiant smile and shining eyes. After the meal, he sneaked her into the woods behind the teahouse and gave her a kiss.

"You are so lovely," he told her, pushing back her curly hair with his fingers and gazing into her face. "Even if you do get into this God of yours and all, I still love you."

"And I love you."

He raised an eyebrow. "Do you really?"

Gail nodded. "Really. I'm still learning how to do it, of course. It takes time."

They walked hand and hand to the hitching post where the horses were tethered. "I'm amazed how quickly you picked up horseback riding," he commented.

"It was a little scary," she admitted, "but I just kept concentrating on other things, like the woods or the scenery. In no time I was really enjoying the ride. Maybe we can own horses someday."

Quin chuckled and helped her up onto the animal. "That's a new one. My little Gail owning a horse farm."

"It seems unreal, I know. But 'I can do all things through Christ who strengthens me.' I read that verse this morning while you were in the shower."

Quin fell silent as they followed their guide back down the trail. He watched Gail sway to and fro on the horse, her hair flying in the breeze, her face acknowledging her surroundings with a joy he could not understand. *Help me understand what's going on with her,* he found himself thinking. Quin paused when he caught himself praying for the first time in his life. *She's affecting me more than I realize.*

❋

The next day, they drove in the sporty rental car to the quaint village of Banff, where Quin bought Gail an assortment of fashions at the little shops dotting the streets. They ate lunch at the famous Banff Springs Hotel, which appeared like a great castle in the midst of a pine forest. Afterward, they strolled along the green of the famous golf course surrounding the hotel where numerous elk feasted on the succulent grass. Quin tried to think of things to say, but his mind was blank. He found nothing worthy of her interest. Gail, on the other hand, filled his ears with stories of her youth, her days as a cheerleader in high school, and the excursion she took with Dorrie in the mountains.

They paused at a wooden bridge spanning a creek. "I found out during our trip to the White Mountains how different Dorrie and I were," Gail said. "Sometimes I really hated her Christianity. She seemed to know everything, and I felt like a dust speck without a brain. But during these last few weeks, I've come to understand that she really does care about me." Gail glanced up to find Quin staring off into space. "It means something when someone cares for you."

"Yeah, it does."

"I know you mentioned believing your mother didn't care for you."

"No, she didn't."

"But you got along with your father?"

Quin snorted. "Sure, as long as I did whatever he wanted. I thought it was real cool, you know, getting involved with his precious work. Pop prides himself on one thing—his business. He's greedy and he's selfish. I suppose that's where I picked up those traits. He wants things done his way, and he makes his fortune the only way he knows how. I'm trying to get myself out from under it all. That's why I went to such pains to change my name, and wear eyeglasses, and take mundane jobs like a waiter or some kind of computer wizard. I wanted to get out of the whole mess."

Gail narrowed her eyebrows questioningly. "What exactly does your father do?"

Quin picked up a small oval stone and pitched it into the creek. "It's kind of complicated. He's into sales, I guess you could say."

"What does he sell?"

"Expensive merchandise. He gets ahold of it at a cheap price, then sells it off to the highest bidder. He comes away rolling in cash, but that's about it."

"I guess you learned that money isn't everything."

"It's nothing. It buys trips, clothes, even wedding rings. But it doesn't buy love." He turned to Gail. "I can tell it didn't buy your love. At first you seemed to like the presents and the idea of marrying into wealth. But a few nights ago, when you found out I wasn't Keith Hampton, you were willing to throw it all away. What made you change your mind to stick it out with me?"

"Well, Dorrie helped me. She said I made a vow to you, even if it was before the justice of the peace and with a different identity. I made a vow to stay married to you as a person, no matter what. She said I couldn't walk away from something like that. And she told me to read 1 Corinthians 13. It's a chapter all about love. It says that love bears all things and it lasts." Gail brought forth her hand, glittering with the large diamonds embedded in both rings. "I know these rings won't last even though they are beautiful. But the love behind the gift of these rings will. That's all that matters anyway."

"Can love heal the past, too?" he asked softly. "Can it forgive?"

Gail looked into his face to see the pain in his eyes. "Yes," she told him, cupping his cheeks in her hands. "It can." She reached out to kiss him.

Quin was moved by her touch, which eased his aching heart. For the first time, he felt an internal joy. Perhaps a little of the joy that bubbled up within Gail had rubbed off on him. He found the sensation a welcome relief after all he had endured.

※

Gail ran the water in the shower stall of their suite until it was piping hot. She hoped the steam might warm her chilled limbs after a drenching rain had caught her and Quin off guard while they headed back to the car at the Banff Springs golf course. A shower would also refresh her for the evening's activities. Quin had urged her to dress up tonight, for they were going to the best restaurant at the hotel. She felt invigorated by the warm spray that streamed over her face. The day had gone well, despite her apprehension. Quin responded eagerly to the love that Gail ministered with God's help, much like a withering plant in need of moisture. Gail thought about the similarity while the water coursed down her face. Quin's sad features and the stories of his past conjured up the image of a plant dying in a drought. As the water ran through her fingers, she thought of love flowing like the water, reaching into his heart, refreshing him and restoring him to life.

She stepped out of the stall and dried off quickly, then spent time applying her makeup. She took extra care to appear nice for Quin in the hope that it might speak to his heart and strengthen their relationship. After dressing in an ankle-length gown, she sat in a chair and waited for him to return from running a few errands. During her wait, she watched the sun sink behind the glacier. The remaining sunlight cast an orange hue across Lake Louise and the surrounding mountain peaks. A few courageous people were still seen paddling canoes across the chilly water while enjoying the sunset.

After what seemed like an eternity, Quin finally arrived. When she opened the door, the odor of alcohol wafted into the room.

"You were drinking?" Gail asked.

"I had a few drinks before I came back here. Is that a problem?"

"Well, I don't know." Gail tried to mask her disappointment by slipping a hand under his arm. After the encouraging signs during their walk at Banff Springs, she had hoped there might be changes stirring within him.

"By the way, you look ravishing in black."

"Thanks."

Quin glanced at her curiously. "There's something wrong, isn't there?"

Gail pretended to fiddle with the gold clasp of her black clutch purse. "Well, you told me you were going to run a few errands. I didn't know that meant having drinks at the bar."

Quin paused in the hallway before the bank of elevators. His dark eyebrows narrowed. "So now that you're a Christian, that means I have to stop having fun?"

"No, I didn't say that."

"But you're implying it."

"Well, maybe I don't want to see you hurt. You see, I was hurt by alcohol once. I. . ." Gail paused. "I was nearly raped while I was drunk one night. It was terrible. I will never forget it. I learned that drinking only hurts people, Quin. It makes you lose your senses. You do things you wouldn't normally do. It messes up your mind, and I don't want your mind messed up. I love your mind just the way it is."

He cracked a small grin. "Well, thanks. Okay, I won't drink. I didn't know it would upset you so much."

Gail snuggled against his arm, inhaling the spicy scent of his aftershave.

"And don't worry; I didn't just leave to get drunk," he assured her as they walked into an elevator. "I ran my errands."

They arrived in the Edelweiss dining room, where a waiter led them to a small table beside a plate-glass window overlooking the lake. A candle decorated the table, and next to the candle was a huge vase of red roses.

"Oh, they're beautiful, Quin!" Gail gushed. When she took her place across from him, she noticed a small package wrapped in a gold bow, sitting on her dinner plate. "What's this?"

"A wedding gift," he told her. "You gave me yours, so here's mine."

She blushed as she tore the wrapper off and opened a case. Inside was a simple gold locket in the shape of a heart. "Why, it's beautiful!"

"Simple," he told her with a wink. "Not extravagant, not flashy. Just plain simple."

"I love it. Please put it on me." Gail moved to his side of the table and sat on his lap while Quin opened the clasp. As he positioned the necklace around her curved neck, he noticed a brawny man dressed in a leather jacket, sitting alone at a table near theirs. The man appeared to be studying the menu, but every so often his dark eyes would regard Gail and Quin from above the menu he held. Quin gave Gail a swift kiss on her cheek before ushering her back to her seat. Once or twice he turned his head to watch the man at the table nearby. Quin did not recognize him from any past contact. He tried to remove the stranger from his thoughts and concentrate on ordering dinner.

"So what's on the docket for tomorrow?" Quin inquired as he tackled the appetizer brought to him—smoked salmon on a bed of crisp greens.

"I don't really know. I haven't thought that far."

"Maybe we can take a nice long drive," he remarked. "Maybe up the Icefields Parkway to Jasper National Park."

Gail's eyes brightened. "I was reading up a little on it. There's a glacier you can walk on, or you can take a tour in one of those big snow coaches."

"Fine. We'll do that. As I said at the beginning of our honeymoon, whatever Gail wants, Gail gets."

She frowned and laid down her fork. "Quin, you make me sound really selfish. Why don't we do something you want?"

"I am. I'm with you."

"No, really. What would you like to do?"

Quin thought about it, and when he did, he sensed the man staring at them from across the way. A strange feeling, like sharp prickles, ran up and down his back. It was the feeling of being watched. "We'll talk about it later," he said in a whisper.

Their dinners arrived, tastefully garnished with edible flowers and fruit. Gail slowly ate hers, relishing every delicious bite. After a time, she glanced up to see that he had not eaten one bite.

"Why aren't you eating, Quin? Is something wrong?"

He shook his head.

"You really should eat. The food is delicious."

He finally picked up his knife and fork and began cutting up a slice of beef, but he found his appetite had vanished. *Grant.* He watched the man out of the corner of his eye. *Grant finally found out where we went and sent his goon to follow us. Oh, God, what am I going to do?*

Quin jumped from his seat in a start, pulled out a pile of bills to pay for the dinner, and took Gail by the arm. "C'mon, let's go."

"Quin, what is it? Are you sick?"

He said nothing as he walked swiftly from the dining hall and to the back stairs. "Let's. . .uh, let's go to some of those boutiques on the lower level, shall we?"

"Well, if you want. I just don't know why. . ." She paused when they came to a children's boutique. "Oh, look at the cute bears. Some are dressed as Royal Canadian Mounted Police. And look—here's one dressed in red, white, and blue, holding a little American flag in his paw. Aren't they adorable? I'm going to get both for Jamie—one from our trip and one to celebrate July Fourth next month."

Quin remained outside the shop, peering up and down the corridor while Gail bought gifts for baby Jamie—a T-shirt adorned with bighorn sheep as well as the small stuffed bears. At another shop, Gail purchased shirts with designs of mountains stitched on them for Mick and Dorrie, along with several gifts for her parents.

"Do you want to buy your father anything?" Gail asked Quin.

"No. Nothing for Pop. He doesn't need anything, at least anything worth his while."

"I remember seeing all those artifacts in the sitting room. I wonder if maybe he would like something from here for his collection?"

Quin cast her a look. "You don't want to supply that shelf, Gail."

84

"I guess I shouldn't ask you why."

"Right. Don't ask why."

Silent and confused, Gail trailed along as Quin led her back to the honeymoon suite. Once inside, he triple-locked the doors and went out to examine the balcony.

"Quin, what's going on? You're acting really strange."

"Don't worry about it, Gail," he mumbled.

She tossed the purchases into a chair. "Please don't say that. It's the same thing you told me the night those men came to our room at the bed and breakfast. I am worried. You haven't been right since dinner."

He stared over the balcony at several people walking along the pathway below. Some paused to gaze out over the lake adorned with shafts of moonlight shimmering on its placid surface. Others pointed up at the hotel. Quin sucked in his breath, wondering which one of them might be his adversary. He turned to find Gail hovering at his elbow, her brown eyes wide with concern.

"Gail, listen to me. I don't want you going anywhere without me."

"Is there a problem with those men again?"

"There may be. I caught some strange-looking character staring at us at dinner tonight. He didn't look familiar to me, but I'm not going to take any chances. Grant has all kinds of low lifes working for him. That guy maybe one of them."

"You think it may be one of your father's bodyguards?"

"Possibly. By now Grant knows we didn't go to Paris. He's had plenty of time to make an about-face and fly in someone to keep an eye on us."

"What are we going to do?"

Quin ran his fingers through his hair. "I'm not sure. But you're to stay with me at all times. If things gets rough, we may have to make a fast exit out of here."

Gail threw herself into his arms. "I. . .I don't want anything to happen. Please, Quin, I'm so scared."

"Hey, it will be all right. Remember all that stuff you told me a few days ago on our horseback trip? About the fearless woman ready to tackle the world?"

Gail brushed a tear from her cheek. "Horses are one thing. Strange men hiding in corners are something else. I just don't understand why your father is doing this."

Quin sighed. "Because he doesn't want me to leave."

"Huh?"

"He doesn't want me to leave the business. I'm his heir, or so he says. He wants me to pick up the reins once he leaves this world. I've refused him, and now he's getting desperate. He's putting pressure on me."

"I wish he would leave us alone."

"I wish he would, too."

Chapter 11

I don't think you should go," Gail said in a low voice.
"I need to. I have to."
"Can't you just ignore it?"

Quin shook his head as he ran a comb through his hair. "If I ignore this, Gail, I'll never be rid of him. At least the guy's come out of hiding. Now I can confront him and maybe get him on the next plane so we can continue with our honeymoon." He threw the comb on the table and ventured over to give her a hug. "Don't answer the door for anyone, and don't go out on the balcony, either."

"I wish you wouldn't do this," she whispered. "Please."

"It will be all right." He then added as an afterthought, "I guess you could pray for me."

"I will. I'll pray ever minute you're away."

Quin smiled. "An old heathen like me could use prayer, I'm sure." He left the room, his mind buzzing with the memory of the call from the hotel lobby, in which he was instructed to meet with someone named Andre. Quin could not recall anyone in the business with the name of Andre. When he questioned the man's identity on the phone, the voice gave specific details concerning their dinner the evening before, complete with the roses and the heart necklace. Quin's face colored when he realized his life was an open book to all the spies in the business. *I have to put a stop to this.* He pushed the button for the elevator. *If I don't, Gail and I will find ourselves hounded everywhere we go.*

Quin walked over to some chairs in front of large plate-glass windows, where he found a man dressed in a leather jacket and smoking a cigarette. He pushed down a shiver of anxiety that swept through him and took a seat. "Andre, I presume?"

"I work for Grant," he said in a foreign accent.

"So I figured. What's this all about? I don't appreciate spectators on my honeymoon."

"I have news from Grant today." He flicked ash from the cigarette into a glass tray.

"What news?"

"He say the bossman is gone."

Quin blinked. "What?"

"He say the bossman is gone. Dead. Grant is now the new boss."

"You're lying."

"No. I come here at first to watch you and your wife." Andre's eyes scanned the hotel. "Very nice place you pick. Then Grant calls today to tell me the boss is gone and he is the new boss. So Grant say he has no need of you. You are no longer in the business."

"I. . .I don't believe it." *Pop is dead? How could that be?* "Let me call Grant. I want to speak to him. What's his phone number?"

Andre shook his head. "Can't do it."

"Then I'm calling home." Quin jumped to his feet only to find the hand of Andre on his arm, pulling him back down into the chair. "Don't do it, young Costello," his voice warned. "Best to leave it alone. You wanted out of the business; now you are out. Grant says to stay away."

Quin shook off the hand. "I won't have Grant or you telling me what to do. This is my father we're speaking of, and I'm his son. I deserve to know what's going on, even if you don't have any sense in you to understand the relationship between a father and son. So back off." He strode away, his mind a whirl of emotions. He went straight to the suite, where an anxious Gail paced the carpeted floor, her lips moving in prayer. She stopped short when he entered.

"Quin, what happened?"

He ignored her question and headed for the phone to dial the number of the estate. To his relief, the trusted butler named Charles answered.

"Oh, Master Costello, I'm so glad you called!"

"Charles, is it true? Is my father dead?"

"No, but he is very ill. He has been calling for you."

Quin closed his eyes as his hand gripped the phone. *That slimy snake.* He remembered what Grant told Andre. *He tried to tell me my father was dead!*

"You must come right away. We think he has suffered a heart attack, but he won't go to the hospital. He only wants to see you."

"Tell Pop I'm coming home," Quin said and hung up the phone.

Gail was right behind him, listening to the conversation. "Quin, please tell me what happened. Is it your father?"

"Charles says that Pop has suffered a heart attack. I have to leave for home right away. But I want you to stay here. My father's house is no place for you right now. It's way too dangerous."

"I don't care. I'm going with you."

"Gail, I can't risk your safety. There are men with bad blood in their veins who can't wait to grab hold of the business. You could get hurt. Please stay."

"Quin, all that matters to me is you. I told you once before that I would face the danger just to know who you are. Please let me come with you. I love you."

Quin sighed. "Gail, you can't come. Look, if you don't want to stay here alone, then I'll buy you a plane ticket to your sister's place. Go see your sister in Boston and I'll join you as soon as I get through with this mess. But you must do what I say, if you love me at all."

Gail hesitated. "Well, all right. Promise me you'll come the minute everything is all right at home."

"I promise. Right now I have to get on the horn and make arrangements for the earliest flights possible for the two of us. We'll drive to Calgary tonight, find a hotel room, then catch the first plane home tomorrow. The sooner we get out of here, the better. In the meantime, you'd better let your sister know what's going on."

As his mind churned with these plans, he thought of the man named Andre and how he had tried to stop him from making the call to his father's estate. There was no telling what the man might do if he got wind of his plan to leave for home. *God, please,* he prayed, *please keep that man off our backs.*

✳

Andre promptly followed Quin onto the flight to New York, obtaining a first-class seat across the aisle from him. Quin pretended to immerse himself in magazines, anything to keep his mind off the dark eyes glaring at him from across the aisle. The words on the page became a blur. Not only must he deal with his father's illness but also the corrupt men eager to take over the business should anything happen. Quin glanced over at Andre, wondering how loyal he was to Grant. Perhaps the man was new at the game. Quin stuffed the magazine into the pouch before him. *There's only one way to find out.*

After a few minutes, he watched the passenger next to Andre slip out of his seat to stretch his legs. Heaving a sigh, Quin took advantage of the empty seat and sat down next to the brawny man, still dressed in his leather jacket. The man stared at him in surprise.

"We meet again, Andre."

"You should not go home, young Costello."

"What? I'm not supposed to go home and pay my last respects to my father?"

"That's not what I mean."

Quin caught the hesitancy in the man's voice. "Didn't you have a father, Andre?"

"Yes, but he died when I was a boy."

"You miss him?"

A muscle twitched in the man's ebony-colored cheek.

"I'll bet you paid your last respects, didn't you? You told him how much you loved him, that sort of thing. And he told you how proud he was and to remember that you'll always be his son."

Andre turned toward the window and said nothing. Quin could see he had struck a chord in the man.

"So how did he die?"

Andre shifted in his seat. "You ask too many questions, Costello."

"And you shouldn't be involved in any of this, Andre. I can already see that you're a decent fellow caught up with a bunch of thugs. Hanging around

88

Grant is not good for your health. You know that."

"Grant chose me."

"Yeah. He chooses lots of men, and then they end up on the shallow end of the stick. But stick with me in this game and I'll treat you right."

Andre lifted his eyebrows. "You mean join you?"

"Sure. Grant doesn't know half the details of running the business that I know. Stick with me and you'll be a winner. Isn't that what you want? To be a winner in life? Grant doesn't know anything about winning. He's a follower, a bellboy, a common stooge. He only does what my father tells him to do. He isn't a leader. But Pop, the bossman, made me a leader. I'm his son, after all. He taught me everything." Quin watched the taut lines on the man's face relax, yet the coal black eyes remained wide with interest.

"Stick with you," he repeated.

"Don't stick with losers like Grant. By the way, has he even paid you yet for your work?"

Andre shook his head.

"Well, I pay my men up front because I trust them." Quin pulled out his remaining cash from the pocket of his denim shirt. "Here. This should buy you some new clothes. Leather can smell after awhile if you don't change regularly."

Andre's eyes nearly popped out of his head as he counted the cash.

"So we understand each other now?"

He nodded. "I understand. You're the bossman's son. I understand everything."

"Fine and dandy. Now just keep this under your hat. In other words, keep quiet about this to Grant. He might throw a tantrum if he finds out you've switched sides."

Andre nodded as he stuffed the money in his pocket, just as the passenger returned from his jaunt down the aisle.

"Oh, excuse me," Quin said to the man, displaying a roguish smile as he patted Andre on the back. "An old friend of mine. He and I were just discussing how much we miss our fathers. Isn't that right, Andre?"

Andre smiled weakly. Quin returned to his seat and exhaled a sigh of relief, hoping he had just foiled Grant's ambitious plans.

❋

Quin dreaded the meeting to come. Out of the countless conversations he'd had with his father, he knew this one would prove the most difficult. He drove straight from Albany Airport to the family estate with Andre by his side. It amazed him how helpful the giant man had been at the airport—retrieving his luggage and arranging for a rental car. Perhaps money did talk when it came right down to it.

Inside the huge manor house of the Costello estate, all of the help gathered in the hallway in a silent vigil. Solemn expressions marked their faces. In the library sat many of the men Quin had come to know in the business—the hard faces and gnarled hands of men who had spent years in criminal activity. Quin knew that with his father's illness came the likelihood that men like Grant would jump at the chance to take control of the empire and squelch any opposition.

During the drive to the estate, Quin thought about the miraculous transformation that had occurred within Gail. He wondered about this God who changed lives and if there was any way God might make room to help him out a little. With everything about to blow up, he desperately needed some kind of supreme being to watch over him. Prayer now stirred within his heart as he asked for guidance and wisdom.

After a few anxious minutes spent pacing in the hall, Quin saw the family physician emerge from the master suite. He led Quin into the spare bedroom that Gail had occupied the night they were brought in by Grant. Quin could tell by the expression on the physician's face that the situation was grim. "How bad is it?"

"Unless you can convince your father to go immediately to the hospital, he has no chance of recovery. More than likely, his heart has been severely damaged by blocked coronary arteries. His heart is irregular and he is weakening by the hour. He needs immediate medical attention before it's too late, if it's not too late already."

"Then I'll tell him he has to go. Call the rescue squad right now."

The physician shook his head. "You know your father, Quintin. He's a stubborn man."

"Well, I can be stubborn, too. We're related in that way." Quin marched out of the room and into the master bedroom, where his father lay beneath the covers. He paused to watch the man's labored breathing. Perspiration trickled down the pale face as his father fought for his life. Sweat droplets on the tips of his mustache glistened like beads in the light of a lamp sitting on a nightstand.

"Pop?" Quin said softly.

The patriarch turned his head and offered a faint smile. "Quintin. I knew you would come. Stand here beside me."

Quin came closer, fighting to suppress the wave of distress within him. "Pop, you've got to go to the hospital right now. I had Charles send for the rescue squad."

Anton Costello shook his head. "No. . .no, I can't."

"Pop, are you crazy? You'll die! Why are you doing this?"

"It is for the best. I make one final plea to you, Quintin. You must hear me. All my life I have trained you to take over when I am gone. I have seen this past year how you did not want anything more to do with my work. But you must reconsider." He coughed loudly, clutching his chest.

Quin stared at his father. "Pop."

"I'm dying, Quintin. Will you carry on my work or not?"

"Pop, you know I can't. You're leaving me an empire built on greed and corruption. You have used thousands of lives for all of this." He waved his hand at the finely appointed room where his father lay dying.

Anton Costello stirred in his bed. "I knew you would refuse. I. . .I am glad I made my decision."

"What decision?"

"I gave the business to Grant."

Quin stood beside the bed, stone-faced.

"I signed over to him the house, the lands, everything. You will have nothing."

He shook his head and looked away. "Pop, I can't believe you're telling me this. Don't you know that Grant is a slimy. . ."

"He is faithful. You used to be, but something changed in you."

"Yeah, you're right, Pop. Something did change in me. I've seen the light. Hasn't it ever occurred to you that all this activity you've been involved in is wrong? That to persuade these gangs in the inner cities to steal and kill for you is wrong?"

Anton Costello only coughed and turned his head away. After several painful minutes, he said, "I knew you would refuse me. Deep down I knew. I could see that you were not the same devoted son I once loved. You became like Archie, a w—weakling with no sense of getting ahead in the world. I was hoping you would change, but I knew you wouldn't. So I took the necessary steps to prepare." He closed his eyes and appeared to drift off into a restless sleep.

Quin gently shook his father's shoulder. "What? What did you do? Pop, tell me."

"I have already placed Grant in charge of my operations. Even now he has begun the work, starting in Boston. I sent him a few hours ago."

"You sent him to Boston to do what?" Quin again shook his father's shoulder.

"He. . .he will see the Vultures and tell them of the changes." Again his father appeared to have passed out, only to flick his eyes open for a moment. "I trusted you once, but I can't anymore. Another love rules your heart." After this, his father lapsed into a deep sleep.

Quin stared for a moment before leaving the room. At the far end of the hallway, he caught sight of the trusted butler, Charles, who had been with the family since he was little. Quin stopped the older man and asked him about Grant.

"Yes, Master Costello, Grant is on his way to Boston as we speak. Your father was extremely angry when he heard you had not gone to Paris on your honeymoon. When Grant returned from France, Mr. Costello signed over the business holdings to him in the event of his death. Then just yesterday he was stricken with this illness."

"So Pop knew all along what my answer would be, even when he begged me to reconsider." Quin shook his head, glancing back at the closed doors of the master bedroom. "Even when he's dying he tries to manipulate me, only I find out he has already gone behind my back and arranged everything with that buzzard." After thanking the butler for sharing this information, Quin headed down the stairs and out to the patio. He fell into a wicker chair, suddenly overcome with exhaustion.

Everything in his life appeared to be rapidly fading into oblivion. He knew he still had Gail for the time being, but if she were to leave him, he would have nothing left but bitter memories of a corrupt life and a love he could never have.

After a time, he heard footsteps approach, and the butler gave him a mournful look.

"Pop's dead?"

"I'm very sorry. If there's anything I can do. . ."

Quin sighed and closed his eyes. For a fleeting moment, he felt grief well up within him, only to be replaced by anger at the final words shared between them. He asked if his father had left arrangements for the funeral.

"He wished to be cremated, Master Costello, and his ashes buried next to your mother without a formal ceremony."

A knot formed in Quin's throat as he choked out a feeble, "Thank you." Now more than ever he wanted to talk to Gail and feel the comfort of her arms around him. When he called to tell Gail what had happened, her sympathy warmed his heart. She asked about the funeral arrangements. Quin responded in a choking voice that his father wished to be cremated without a funeral.

"Oh, Quin, I'm so sorry! Please come here to Boston and be with us. I've been talking to Dorrie. She and Mick really want to meet you."

"I don't know if I can take any religious bombshells right now," he mumbled. "I hurt enough inside as it is."

"They won't do anything like that. They'll just pour out their love. I think it would be good for you. Who knows, maybe you can even go with Mick when he works the streets. He could use a helping hand at the soup kitchen."

Quin suddenly jumped at the sound of the words. "The soup kitchen? You mean his work with the gangs?"

"Yes. In fact Dorrie was just telling me how he's developing relationships with several gang members, particularly with one of the tougher gangs. It's just amazing to see the love Mick has for them after all that's happened."

Quin paced back and forth as his thoughts began to spin. "This gang he's gotten tight with—do you know the name?"

"I think Dorrie called them the Vultures."

His face paled as he withdrew the receiver from his ear. The Vultures. . .the very gang involved with the business, and Grant is there at this moment! "Gail, I'm sorry but I've got to go."

"Go where? Quin, what is it? What's the matter?"

Quin threw the phone on the cradle and hastened for his car parked on the circular drive. He heard footsteps pattering on the pavement behind him and whirled to find Andre.

"Sorry, Pal, but I have to go," Quin told the hulking figure, still clad in his leather jacket.

"I go, too. We're partners."

Quin shook his head. "Sorry to disappoint you, Andre, but you were right. Grant is in charge of the business now."

Andre's face fell. "You mean he is the boss?"

"Yep, he's the boss all right. Pop turned everything over to him. So I guess you'd better hang out here and wait for Grant to return. Like you told me in Canada, I'm out and he's in."

Andre stared at Quin.

"Look, I gotta run. You take care and don't take any wooden nickels, especially any that Grant gives you. I wouldn't trust him now."

Andre pulled out the cash that Quin had given to him on the plane. "No need for the money now. Maybe you need it for your wife?"

Quin stared at the bundle of money in surprise. "Wow, I never thought you had it in you to give me back my money. What are you doing in this sad business anyway? It's only for the scum of the earth. Get out while you still can. I should be on my knees thanking God that He got me out of it. But right now I've got big problems to deal with." He jumped into the car and started the engine, oblivious to the man's somber reaction until the passenger door opened and Andre peered inside.

"What problems?"

"Andre, I have to get going. I have urgent business in Boston."

"Boston? Can I help?"

Quin shook his head. "No, but thanks anyway. I never thought I'd be thanking a big bully in leather. Now I mean it, get out of here while you still can. Things may blow up, and I don't want to see you caught in the middle of it. Do it for your father's memory, if for nothing else."

Andre blinked. "You speak all about fathers. My father was a good man." He then added softly, "He would be angry at what I do. He maybe look down from heaven and say that I am a bad son."

"So you wanna do something good for your pop?"

Andre nodded.

"Maybe I can use you after all. If you really want to help me, get in. I suppose two are better than one in this game." Once Andre was seated, Quin hit the accelerator and sped off.

"I thought you were out of the game?" Andre asked.

"I am. But Grant is deep into it, and there are family members close to my wife who could get hurt. If there's one thing you can do for your pop's memory, Andre, you can help me keep others from getting hurt."

Andre nodded his head. His dark lips curved into a smile. "Yes, this a good thing. I will help others."

Chapter 12

I can't believe you already have three new members for your Bible study!" Dorrie said happily as she and Gail served chicken salad and croissants for a light supper before Mick left for the evening.

Mick nodded. "Isn't it amazing? Just a week ago I was moaning to the Lord about my work, and now He suddenly opens heaven's gates. I owe a lot to Corky. He was able to convince some of the Vultures to come and begged me to hold another study this evening after last night's success."

"Two gatherings in a row!" Dorrie marveled. "It looks like this might turn out to be a fruitful summer for you after all, Mick."

"It sure does," Gail added. When she arrived in Boston, she had been overwhelmed by the love and acceptance poured out by both Dorrie and Mick. She spent long hours conversing with them about everything that had happened since she was married, after which they prayed for Quin and his circumstances.

Mick broke a croissant in two and began eating. "You know, those guys are really hungry for the Word. I have to feed them while their mouths are open— like a big mother bird, I guess you could say."

"I hope you can feed Quin when he comes," Gail said wistfully. "He needs a man to speak to about his life, especially now that his father is gone. He has no family left." She watched Dorrie produce Jamie's dinner from the microwave. The little boy sat in his highchair, pitching cereal onto the linoleum. Gail bent over and picked up the pieces to toss into the garbage. Jamie gurgled and tossed another piece of cereal onto the floor, watching with wide eyes as Gail again picked up the cereal and threw it into the trash. "You aren't going to have anything left to eat if you keep this game up," she remarked to her little nephew. When Dorrie came over with the baby's dinner, Gail whisked the dish from her hands. "Let me try feeding him."

"You sure? I mean, this is baby care, Gail. Are you ready for it?"

"I want to. I have to learn sometime, don't I?" She watched a warm glow of approval cross her sister's face. Picking up the spoon, Gail attempted to place it in Jamie's mouth. The food dribbled down his chin and onto the bib. "Oops."

"It takes some getting used to," Dorrie said. "Keep trying and you'll get the hang of it."

Biting her lip in concentration, Gail spooned up some more food and succeeded in placing it inside Jamie's tiny mouth. "Hurrah! It went in."

"She's already a pro," Mick observed, rising from his seat to stuff his Bible into a day pack. "Well, sorry to eat and run, but I'm already late." He dropped a kiss on Dorrie's cheek before swinging the pack over one shoulder. "Don't wait up for me."

"Have a great time," Dorrie said.

After spooning in the last mouthful of food, Gail wiped off Jamie's mouth with the end of the terry cloth bib and sighed. "There, what do you think of that, Mom?"

"Very good," Dorrie said approvingly. "You have passed a major test in the area of baby nutritional skills."

Jamie giggled in glee before his face scrunched up. After a few minutes, the room filled with the odor of a dirty diaper.

"Well, Gail, are you ready for the next step?" Dorrie inquired with a chuckle.

"You mean changing him? Oh, no, I couldn't."

"Sure you can. Nothing to it." Dorrie plucked Jamie out of the highchair. "Let's head upstairs for the next session of motherhood."

"I don't know about this," Gail answered dubiously, following her sister up the stairs. "I've seen those movies where inexperienced people have tried to put on diapers, only to have the things fall off and the baby doo-doo go all over the place."

Dorrie laughed. "Well, I will teach you how to do it so that won't happen." She went right to work with the baby wipes. "See? You clean him like this," she instructed. "Now here's the diaper. Be sure you put the part of the diaper with the sticky tabs in the back so they wrap around like this."

Gail had fastened one sticky tab when the doorbell rang.

"I'd better go answer the door," Dorrie said as she quickly finished fastening Jamie's diaper before handing him to Gail.

Gail nestled the small boy close to her. In return, he rewarded her with sticky drool on her cheek. "You're such a cute kid," Gail gushed as she slowly walked down the stairs. "Maybe one day I'll have one just like you." She stopped short and gasped at the two men standing in the small foyer of the townhouse. "Quin!"

"When did we get the baby?" he joked, grinning.

Dorrie quickly took the baby before Gail ran to hug Quin. "I missed you so much. How did you know where to find this place?"

"Well," he began, stealing a glance at Dorrie, "I talked to your sister while you were occupied." He stepped back. "I'd like you to meet our bodyguard. This is Andre."

Gail gazed at the huge figure—dressed in a leather jacket, who stood beside Quin. "Our bodyguard?"

"It's a long story."

"I'm so glad I finally get to meet you, Quin!" Dorrie said in glee as she showed the way to the living room. "Unfortunately my husband, Mick, isn't here right now."

95

"He's out working the streets," Gail added.

Quin sucked in a breath, glancing at Andre before returning his attention to the two sisters. "Do you know where he went?"

"Sure. He usually goes to the soup kitchen," Dorrie said, supplementing the information with directions to the establishment. "He told me he's going to have a Bible study with some of the gang members tonight."

"Which gang members are these?"

"The Vultures."

"Then we don't have any time to lose." Quin rose to his feet, motioning to Andre. "Let's go."

"Where are you going, Quin?" Gail asked, her face showing a mixture of confusion and concern.

"Uh, I really want to meet Mick," Quin said, trying to maintain his composure despite his racing heart. "I've heard so much about him, I feel like I know him already. I'm kind of interested in seeing what he does."

"But you just got here."

"Oh, let him go if he wants," Dorrie said, her eyes sparkling at Quin's interest. "I think it's great that Quin wants to check out what Mick's doing with the gangs. And Mick will think God has really opened up some doors."

"Yeah. . .well, we'd better get going." Quin sidestepped his way to the door. "Nice meeting you, Dorrie."

"We'll see you later," she said with a wave.

Once outside, Quin ran to the car, followed by Andre.

"You tell them nothing," Andre observed.

"You're right, I didn't. I wasn't about to tell Dorrie that her husband may be in danger. That's all I need, two sisters in a state of panic. No, it's better that they think Mick's gonna convert me or something."

A few minutes later, Quin and Andre arrived at the soup kitchen in Boston's inner city. They saw a huge man with ebony-colored skin and wearing a stained apron, working in the kitchen. The man whistled a hymn as he wiped down the stoves and countertops with a sponge. Upon their entrance, he peered through a large open window between the kitchen and the serving area.

"Hey, the kitchen ain't open now."

"We're looking for Mick," Quin said. "Who are you?"

"I'm Harry. Are you dudes here for the Bible study?"

"We really need to find Mick."

"He's at the Vultures' headquarters," the man said matter-of-factly. "Two of them Vultures came here about twenty minutes ago, saying that Mick's friend Corky was out on his feet at the headquarters. Guess he also wants to recruit some more of the brothers to come to our Bible study. You can come, too, you know."

"Do you know where the Vultures' headquarters is located?" asked Quin. "I haven't been there in a long time."

The man eyed him curiously. "So you know them Vultures, eh? Man, they're somethin' else, especially the leader of 'em—Odysseus. Man, one time he came in here and showed Mick his switchblade. If that wasn't a scene! Good thing the big man kept his head about it. That's what I like about Mick. He keeps his head in bad situations, and you gotta be able to do that, runnin' a soup kitchen in this 'hood."

Good, Quin thought. *He'll need his head and more if he finds himself tangling with Grant.*

"Anyway," the man continued, "you go down about five blocks, turn left. Look for two black wings spray-painted on the door. Can't miss it."

"Okay, thanks."

Quin and Andre hustled down the dark street. Young people loitered everywhere, on street corners and in dark alleyways. Memories of the times Quin and his father had come here to conduct business haunted Quin. He recalled the eager faces and wide eyes as his father handed the gang members envelopes full of money for the shipments of goods they had confiscated. He knew the young men would run to the nearest drug dealers to spend the money on crack or other illegal drugs. Seeing the empty faces all around him now, Quin could not help but feel a stab of guilt. He and his father had used these kids mercilessly. They had fed the young people's insatiable appetite for drugs and liquor by offering them a deal too good to pass up. As he walked by them, he felt responsible for what they had become— shells of humanity with nothing to live for but the next high or fix.

They arrived at the door with a pair of black wings spray-painted on the rotting wood—the Vultures' lair. Quin motioned to Andre. They scooted down a narrow alleyway running between the buildings until they came to the rear of the structure. At their feet was a milky window, looking in on a room inside the basement. Quin bent down and stared through the dirty glass. A single light bulb, swaying from a frayed cord, illuminated the room. Members of the gang were gathered in small groups. Each one wore the customary black leather vest with a vulture embroidered on the back. Most of them were smoking cigarettes or sipping beer from cans.

All at once the Vultures came to attention when a large man entered the main room. He wore a red scarf around his bald head and a sleeveless Vultures jacket that displayed his brawny muscular frame. His fist held a youth by the shirt front. In the rear of the room, like a dark statue, stood a man with raven black hair and a scarred face. A smoking cigarette rested between his fingers. *Grant!*

"You lookin' fer yer brother Corky, Reverend?" the huge man sneered.

Quin stared over at the man they called Reverend. He had a head of blond hair and clutched a book in his hands. *That must be Mick, Gail's brother-in-law. And he's got himself caught right in the middle of everything. . .just like his father.*

"Please let Corky go, Odysseus," Mick pleaded.

97

Corky trembled in the leader's grip. "I. . .I didn't say nuthin'," his voice quivered.

"Shut up!" the man named Odysseus snarled. "It's bad enough you go leavin' the gang, only to rat on us to the reverend here! Man, you got the guts of a jelly-fish, you know that?"

"I ain't got the guts of no jellyfish!" Corky responded, only to have the leader shake him.

"Stop it!" Mick cried. "Look, Odysseus, we're only trying to help you and your brothers."

"Help me, huh?" He eyed the group of men in the room and began to laugh. All at once the entire room erupted into raucous laughter. "The reverend here wants to help me? You should have stayed in your church. Guess you ain't never learned the lesson from your old man, huh? You see, we know your old man. He tried to help us, too, and look how he ended up."

"My father cared for your well-being, like I do," Mick said in a quiet voice. He held out the book he carried. "You don't need to keep living like this. Jesus can change your lives. It says so right here in the Bible."

"I don't want to hear no fool talk about Jesus, Reverend! You're just like your old man. You don't know when to quit. You gotta stick your nose where it ain't wanted. That's a real pity."

"Look, I've got the truth in my hand. Read it for yourself. The truth in here can set you free from drugs, from the pain in your past. . . ."

Odysseus marched up and stuck his face into Mick's. "And I'm tellin' you, I don't want to hear no jive truth from you or anyone else." Odysseus clamped a firm hand on Mick's shoulder and spun him around to face the rest of the gang. "You see here? We got ourselves one big problem, brothers. That's this reverend. Man, we gotta do something about this Bible thumpin'." He ripped the Bible from Mick's grasp and began tossing it up in the air like a ball.

"Open it and read what it says, Odysseus," Mick said. "Read and find out for yourself how God loved you enough to—"

The gang leader took the Bible and rammed it into Mick's stomach, send-ing him reeling to the cement floor. Several of the men gripped his arms and thrust him into a wooden chair.

Quin glanced helplessly at Andre. "We've got to do something," he whispered.

"Look, Boss, there's Grant," Andre said, pointing. The two men watched as Grant ventured forward, flicking ash from his cigarette onto the cement floor. All the gang members gave him a wide berth as he walked up and surveyed Mick with dark, malevolent eyes.

Grant elbowed Mick. "So this is the son of that preacher who was shot six years ago?"

"Yeah, that's him all right," Odysseus said. "The high-and-mighty reverend who quotes the Bible jus' like his old man. Two peas in a pod."

Grant paced back and forth before Mick. "I hear you know all about the business of the Vultures, thanks to that foolish kid. Eh?" Grant whirled, fixing his gaze on Corky.

"I. . .I'm sorry," Corky said.

"Sorry doesn't repair the damage, though, does it?" Grant drew a pistol from beneath his jacket. He circled behind the chair, jamming the muzzle of the weapon into Mick's head. "Just like your daddy," he murmured. "Sticking your nose in other people's business."

Quin jumped to his feet when he saw what was about to happen. Andre did the same and slammed his boot through the basement window, shattering it to pieces. The noise sent everyone in the basement whirling around in fear.

"Drop the gun, Grant," Quin ordered as he slid down to the floor, followed by Andre.

Grant lowered the weapon. "Well, well, what a dramatic entrance, young Costello. Back from your honeymoon so soon?" He then eyed Andre, who followed Quin to the floor. "And I see that Andre has brought you. You realize, of course, that you're interfering with important business here."

"You're right, I am." Quin turned to face Odysseus and the Vultures gang. "Look, I'm the son of the big bossman. Some of you brothers will remember me from when my father came to conduct business here in this 'hood."

"You mean your old man is the big boss we hack all them goods for?" Odysseus asked incredulously. "The one who gave us the cash?"

"That's right."

"You're not in charge anymore, Costello," Grant snarled. "You forfeited your inheritance. Anton Costello placed me in charge. The entire Costello empire is now mine."

"I'm afraid you're mistaken. I'm still the boss's son, right? The legitimate heir to the throne?" He eyed the members of the gang, who nodded in agreement.

"Yeah, we know him. He's the bossman's son, all right," several of the members murmured. "We've seen him around plenty."

"And I told you that I'm in charge!" Grant repeated, his voice rising above the murmuring of the Vultures. He rammed his pistol into Mick's skull. Mick winced, then became rigid in the chair as Grant cocked the trigger.

"Now, Costello, you will kindly inform the Vultures here that I am in charge of the business as your father directed, or your wife's brother-in-law dies."

Quin only glared at him. "Yeah, you're in charge all right. And while we're at it, why don't you tell the Vultures who was in charge six years ago when their former leader took the rap for shooting Mick's father. Tell them who really fired the pistol that day."

"I give the explanations, Costello, not you. Don't you realize that everything you worked for your whole life, everything you ever loved, all belongs to me?"

"Hey now, hold on here," Odysseus interrupted as he came forward. "Just what are you sayin' here, man? You mean Ace didn't shoot that preacher years ago?"

"No," Quin said. "Tell these guys the truth, Grant. Tell them it was you who pulled the trigger, but their brother Ace rots in jail to pay for your crime."

"I don't need to, Costello, because your time is up." Grant aimed his weapon at Quin. Andre lunged for Grant, firmly grasping the wrist that held the gun. The two men struggled. As they did, a shot rang out. Grant fell to the ground, gasping as a crimson stain spread across his shirt. A wisp of smoke curled out of the weapon Andre held in his hand. Shock enveloped the man's face as he hurled the weapon to the ground and bolted for the door.

Quin stood over his dying enemy, watching the man heave for air. As he did, he heard a choked whisper. "Y—you think you have won the...the game. You...you don't know who it was who destroyed the Costellos, one by one." Grant squeezed his eyes shut, then flicked them open to stare at the ceiling above.

Quin's eyes widened. "What are you saying, Grant? That you're responsible?"

"All of them," Grant whispered. "Archie, Treva...the big man h—himself... The proud Costellos...gone." He smiled faintly. "All but you. I almost had you, too. But I have my reward." With his last breath, he sputtered, "You will live with this for the rest of your life."

"No!" Quin collapsed next to his enemy, shaking the dead form. "No!"

Suddenly the headquarters was swarming with uniformed police officers and detectives, their sidearms drawn. The Vultures who did not escape the authorities were quickly handcuffed. A detective drew Quin up by his arm, hurling questions into his face. Quin never heard the voice barking at him as he stood frozen in place, staring at the face of his enemy while his confession reverberated in Quin's mind. *Grant killed my family. Grant is responsible for everything.*

The officer searched Quin's pockets, and finding a license bearing his name, pushed Quin to the wall. "Spread them right now, Pal. Hands behind your head."

Hands frisked him quickly before his wrists were forced into a pair of steel handcuffs. Another officer rattled off his rights.

At that moment Mick came forward. "You don't need to arrest him, Officer," Mick stated. "He and this man here...," he pointed to Andre, who had already been handcuffed outside the building, "they saved my life."

"Even if they did do one good thing," the officer responded, "it doesn't erase years of criminal activity. We've been looking to bust up this syndicate for a long time. And this one," the detective ruffled Quin's shirt, "is a ring leader in the operation. He's wanted in at least five other states. Aren't you, Pal?"

Quin said nothing. Mick stared at Quin, who looked straight back without flinching. Mick opened his mouth as if about to say something but never had the opportunity as the police pushed Quin out the door.

Chapter 13

I still can't believe this happened," Dorrie said softly as she sat with Gail and Mick around the kitchen table late that night. "I mean, this type of thing only happens in the movies."

Gail had sat in silence since hearing the news of Quin's arrest. While it pained her to know that Quin and his father were involved in a huge crime syndicate that used gangs in the inner cities to make money, her heart nevertheless was drawn to the man now sitting in some lonely cell. She listened, numb, as Mick and Dorrie rehashed the events of the evening while she twisted the wedding rings around and around on her left hand.

"I tell you, I owe both those men my life," Mick said, his blue eyes acknowledging the somber Gail. "Of course at the time of the incident, I had no idea he was your husband."

"He's not. . .not really," Gail said quietly.

"What do you mean he's not?" asked Dorrie. "Of course he is."

"Dorrie, I don't even know who he is. I thought I did, but he hid himself behind this mask of Keith Hampton, a man I thought I loved. I told him in Canada that I married Keith Hampton, not Quintin Costello." She sniffed as tears rolled down her cheeks. "Now I find out he's a criminal, involved in some syndicate run by his father! Oh, how I wish I could have my sweet Keith back again. I'd do anything! He is the man I love with all my heart."

Dorrie placed an arm around Gail, who had begun to cry for the umpteenth time since discovering what had been concealed from her until this night. Despite the pain, she realized why Quin hid the circumstances surrounding his family. He had warned her countless times of the danger, but she never fully understood what he had meant until now.

A strong hand suddenly gripped Gail's hand. She looked up to see Mick staring at her. "Gail, I know you've been hurt by Quin. But I believe God is trying to change his heart. Don't you see? If he was so wrapped up in his father's lucrative business, why would he risk everything to save someone like me? I was a threat to all of them after Corky told me about their shady business. That man called Grant would have killed me and possibly Corky, too, if Quin and the other man had not shown up when they did."

Gail sniffed as Dorrie pressed a tissue into her hand. She smiled her thanks before blowing her nose.

"Yeah, he's blown it big-time," Mick continued, "but so have the rest of us in one way or another. You remember how I turned my back on God after what happened to my father? In God's eyes, what Quin has done is no worse than what I did. But what's truly amazing is that God can redeem us through what His Son did on the cross. I think it would be wrong for you or me to write Quin off just because he's in jail."

Gail dabbed her eyes with the tissue. "Do you think I should try calling him?"

"I'm going to find out if he has a lawyer and see if there's a way we can communicate with him as soon as possible. I owe Quin my life, but more importantly, I want him to know that someone also gave His life for him. I want to see him made whole. I want him to receive the gift of salvation that we all have."

Gail nodded. "Maybe God can still perform a miracle in his heart, especially after everything that's happened. I know he hurts inside. I've seen his pain. I guess it would be wrong not to be there for him."

"The Bible talks about going to see those who are in prison," Dorrie agreed. "We should be willing to do all we can to see this man set free, not only from jail but from sin as well."

✳

Quin sat in the small holding cell, waiting for something to happen. The family lawyer, George Rawlings, had been by to see him earlier that morning but did not offer him much hope. "We'll first have to see what happens at your arraignment later today and then the preliminary hearing," the lawyer had said matter-of-factly as he stuffed a file folder into his leather briefcase. "With your father dead, it's likely the district attorney will seek to place the blame on you, painting you as a dangerous criminal requiring incarceration."

"If I'm denied bond, that means I'm stuck here?"

"Afraid so. The preliminary hearing will be to determine if there is enough evidence to certify the charges to a grand jury. If the grand jury indicts you, which is likely, then you're looking at a trial in a year, maybe two. The delay will be due to your involvement in other states. It's going to take time to gather all the evidence. I'm hoping to have everything take place here in Boston rather than have you extradited all over the country."

Quin paced back and forth before the wealthy lawyer dressed in a pinstriped suit. "Okay, so lay it on me straight. What are my chances in all of this?"

"Our first order of business is to get you out on bail. That will free you for the time being. More than likely, the grand jury will indict you on the charges specified, with the evidence already secured by the district attorney."

"But I'm not guilty of half the charges they've leveled on me, especially that second-degree murder rap. I've never hurt anyone in my life!"

"That may be, but the district attorney's office is gathering evidence of your involvement in your father's operations. I'll be frank with you, Quintin. It will be a long road if you choose to plead not guilty and proceed with a trial."

"What other choice is there but a trial? I mean, look at the murderers who have gotten off. All I know is I'm not guilty of a lot of those charges. I think a trial is my best chance."

"Well, a trial is never set in stone. After what you've told me about your marriage and how you intervened on behalf of your wife's brother-in-law during the scuffle with the Vultures gang, I believe it's possible to sway a jury member. But I'm not optimistic. I believe entering into a plea bargain might be a viable option in your case. There are many others involved in this syndicate that the police would love to get their hands on. You have the information they need to make more arrests."

"I don't know what they want," Quin said glumly. "I can hardly remember who I am anymore."

"Well, you'd better come up with the information they want, because if you're convicted, you're looking at a pretty stiff sentence."

"Okay, so say I plead not guilty and go ahead with a trial. What then?"

"If you are found guilty on all counts, the prosecution will try to impose the maximum sentence."

"Which is what?"

Rawlings sighed, his face serious. "It's entirely possible you're looking at a life sentence. Possible parole after thirty years."

✷

Life in prison. Life behind bars. The words echoed over and over in his mind as he rested on the hard bed in the corner of the cell. His hands ran through his hair. *Me, Quintin Costello—a jailbird at twenty-eight.* He thought of Gail then as he felt his left ring finger, which no longer wore the wedding band they had purchased together in Poughkeepsie only a few weeks ago. *Gail will never forgive me for all the lies, the deceit, and the pain I caused her.* Again he brushed back strands of his dark hair. *It's probably better for her if I stay locked up. I might as well plead guilty and get the sentencing over with. Gail will not want anything more to do with me. My family's gone. There's no one waiting for me outside these concrete walls.* He slumped his head into his hands when he thought of Grant's dying words about the death of Quin's family members. Anger welled up in him, directed toward his deceased father for hiring such a despicable man. *How could you have done this to us, Pop? To me, to our family? How could you have allowed our family to be destroyed by Grant, all for the sake of your empire?*

Quin lifted his head at the sound of a security officer unlocking his cell. "C'mon, Costello, you have a phone call."

His eyes widened as he followed the officer through the hallways. *Who could possibly want to talk to me?*

✷

Gail sat nervously at the kitchen table, trying to steady her jittery knees. *Why am*

103

I doing this? she thought lamely. The notion of calling a place where criminals were housed felt like something she should be watching on a television drama. Never would she have guessed she would so much as talk with a man arrested for serious crimes, let alone be married to such a man. Yet she could not help but call Quin after watching the news footage of police guiding him into the station, his wrists handcuffed behind his back. His face appeared mournful, his shoulders hunched over as if he carried the weight of the world on them. When Gail saw him, she knew she still loved him, no matter what he had done.

Gail grew rigid in her seat when a soft hello came over the phone. Her heart flipped within her.

"You have five minutes," she heard the guard say.

Gail moaned softly. Five minutes to tell Quin everything that was brewing within her heart. "Hi, Quin. How are you?"

Quin cleared his throat and mumbled, "I don't know."

"Well, I'm calling to tell you I still love you, despite what's happened."

Quin chuckled. "Right. Ol' Jailbird Costello."

"No, I love Quintin Costello. And I'm going to do everything I can to help you." She heard a soft sigh. "Look, Gail, I'm really sorry about all this. I never should have talked you into marrying me. I was selfish. I knew from the beginning it was a mistake. I wanted to make you mine and I didn't care if you got hurt in the process. So you might as well take the rings off and sell them. It's over between us."

"I can't take them off."

"Yes, you can. I'm a hardened criminal. My lawyer says there's no hope. I could get life behind bars after all is said and done."

The weight of that statement caught her off guard. She wrestled with the idea of him in prison for the rest of his life until the reason for her call overshadowed her apprehension. "I want to tell you what I've been thinking." Gail inhaled a deep breath. "I won't lie to you. This whole situation has really shaken me. I know you dropped hints about your family but wouldn't tell me the truth. And I realize that if I did know about your family, it might have put me in danger. You were only trying to protect me, like what you and that bodyguard did for Mick."

She was met with silence. She went on. "You have a lot of love in you, Quin, and a heart that wants to do the right things. But I found out that we really don't have the strength to do what's right. We need God to help us. Inside all of us are bad thoughts, selfishness, pride. All of us should be in jail cells right now."

"Yeah, but you're not," he said pointedly. "You're free."

"You can't really be free unless you have Jesus inside you. In this world you will always do wrong. But I found out something while we were on our honeymoon. I found out that with God in my heart, my old self really did pass away and a new self has been born. When I stared at those mountains, I felt like I was actually seeing them for the first time. It really felt like I had been born all over again. We talked about that, remember?"

"Yeah, I remember."

"Well, that's what it means to be a Christian, Quin. You're born again into the kingdom of God where He forgives all your past mistakes. You really feel new on the inside."

"So is that why you called, to clean me up?"

"No. I called to say I love you and I want to know what is happening. Do you have a trial or something coming up?"

"My arraignment is this afternoon."

"What does that mean?"

"Well, if the judge agrees to set bond and I post it, then I'm out of here until the preliminary hearing."

"And if he doesn't?"

"Then I'll rot in jail for the rest of my life and you'll never have to deal with me again."

The phone clicked in her ear, the line dead. Gail sat still, numbed by his callous response. She replaced the receiver and stood. Bright sunshine filtered through the kitchen window on a crystal-clear day. "No, you're not going to rot in jail, Quintin Costello. Even though you don't believe me, I do still love you and somehow, with God's help, we're going to pray you out of that place."

※

Mick, Dorrie, and Gail arrived at the courthouse where the arraignment had already concluded. Reporters swarmed about them like a flock of seagulls after a bucket of fish, looking for anything they could splash across the tabloids and television screen. Mick provided a quick statement to the press before ushering the sisters into the building. As Gail climbed the last set of steps, she heard a woman reporter ask her why she decided to marry a corrupt man who was part of a crime operation that had stayed ahead of the authorities for years. Gail's face burned with embarrassment as Dorrie shielded her with her arm.

"Dorrie, how can I get through this?" Gail whispered in fear. She clung to Dorrie's hand, heaving quick breaths while trying to maintain her composure. She knew the time of reckoning had passed. Either she would have Quin in her arms very soon, or she would only glimpse his sad face as he sat in a dreary prison.

"It's going to be okay," Dorrie assured her. "God is with us. He will never forsake us."

In the hallway before the wide oak doors leading into the courtroom, Gail noticed a lawyer conversing with court officials. The man glanced up, then nodded his head to the officials before striding over to shake Mick's hand. "I recognize your face from the newspaper. We've talked on the phone," he said, introducing himself as Quin's lawyer, George Rawlings.

"Thank you, Sir. This is my wife, Dorrie, and Quin's wife, Gail."

"Glad to see you all here. I know Quintin values your support. The going won't be easy for him. I am happy to report, however, that we were successful in getting the judge to set bail."

Gail turned and gave Dorrie a hug. Mick was all smiles as he wrapped his arms around the celebrating sisters. "God can perform miracles," Mick told the lawyer. "While we believe in justice, we also believe that Quin's heart has changed. His activities during the last year prove that he knew his father's business dealings were wrong. He risked his life to try and stop it. We prayed for leniency. Thank you, Lord."

"So what happened, Mr. Rawlings?" Gail asked.

"Well, the charges were brought before the judge. The district attorney tried his best to deny Quintin bond, citing the family's history of extensive travel and their criminal activity. It was heavy going there for awhile. The judge heard about what happened last evening with the gang and Quintin's involvement. I believe that swayed him to set the bond at two hundred and fifty thousand dollars."

"Wow, that's a lot of money," Mick whistled. "Can Quin come up with it?"

"He has a trust fund worth over a million that I will access immediately. But this is the first of many steps in a long legal battle, I'm afraid. I wish I could convince him to enter into a plea bargain agreement that might prove better for him than standing trial. I'm sure I can count on all of you to help Quintin. I will need your sworn testimonies in future proceedings."

"You can count on us, Sir," Mick assured him. "All of us will help in any way we can. We'll take it one step at a time. Thank you for your efforts, Mr. Rawlings."

"Well, I must say, this young man is fortunate to have you three. I was saddened to hear about the tragedy concerning his family. It's good to know that he has friends waiting for him when he gets out. I'll be in touch." Rawlings shook their hands before glancing at his watch. "I'd better get over to the bank and arrange for the bail money. We'll have Quintin out by the end of the day."

Gail hugged both Dorrie and Mick, thankful for this small victory in the shadow of greater battles yet to be fought.

Chapter 14

W hy do you want to go through with this?" Quin asked Gail after she returned from running her errands to various shops scattered around the small Massachusetts town.

She smiled as she displayed her purchases of garland, crepe wedding bells, plates, cups, and napkins. "It won't be much," she confessed, "but I'm thankful that everything seems to be falling into place."

Quin shook his head and thrust his hands into his pockets before strolling over to a window to look at the scenery. He was grateful for the small apartment Mick and Dorrie had secured for them in a small New England town outside of Boston, away from all the publicity surrounding his arrest. Quin could not help but marvel at Gail's love and devotion to him since his release. Internally he felt burdened by the guilt of his past, but Gail proceeded with life's activities as if nothing adverse had happened.

"So do your parents plan on attending?" Quin asked.

"Of course. Dad has to give me away, you know."

"I don't believe it. Why are they allowing their daughter to go through with a church wedding to a dangerous criminal? I mean, you heard what the district attorney said on television—I'm a detriment to society."

Gail reached over and placed a warm hand on his arm. "Quin, my folks know we have said our vows to one another before the justice of the peace. They're glad we want to be married in a church before witnesses and especially before God."

"Yeah, but that doesn't erase who I am or the kind of life I once led."

"No, it doesn't. But you know who can erase the wrongs in your past and leave you with peace, Quin."

He continued to stare out the window, watching a robin flutter down to the small patch of grass outside the apartment. The bird hopped along on its clawed feet, searching for worms among the fallen leaves. Soon the robin would fly south to avoid the cold winter that would blanket the ground with freshly fallen snow. As each day passed, Quin wrestled with his own winter and the raw conviction hanging over him. Mick spent time showing him the Scriptures and dealing with his heart, but somehow Quin felt beyond repair. There was still the preliminary hearing and an eventual trial ahead, even though his lawyer continually badgered him to make a plea bargain. Now as Gail happily pounced on the plan to have a real wedding ceremony, he held to his reservations.

"Look, Gail, I can't do this to you and your family," he finally said. "You should just forget about me and find someone else who won't become a jailbird in a year or two."

To his surprise, Gail came and laid her curly head against his shoulder. "Quin, there isn't anyone else. There never will be."

"But how can you marry me, knowing I'll likely be serving time behind bars? You can't have a marriage like that."

"I can because I love you and I know that love is greater than any jail cell. I'll be thankful to God for any time I can spend with you. Now I have to go pick up something at Dorrie's. I'll be back in a little bit."

After Gail departed, Quin replayed the conversation in his mind. He wished he had the same peace and confidence that strengthened her. He found that turmoil, doubt, and anger, combined with his faults, had poisoned his soul. Yet he had witnessed how Gail changed dramatically under the hand of God. She accepted him unconditionally, despite his criminal wrongdoing. He picked up the phone to dial Mick's number, wondering if he might find a similar peace in the midst of his difficulties.

✳

Dorrie came into the living area where Gail lay on the floor bouncing a little clown in front of Jamie, who giggled with delight. "I thought you told me you couldn't handle kids," she commented with a chuckle.

Gail glanced up and smiled. "This is a cute kid you've got, Dorrie. I'm a lucky aunt."

"And he's a blessed nephew," Dorrie said, scooping Jamie into her arms and cuddling him close. "I think you'll be even more blessed when I tell you the news."

"What?"

"Mick's been on the phone upstairs for over an hour, talking to—"

"Quin?" Gail leapt to her feet, ready to dash to the kitchen where the extension phone rested in its cradle on the wall. "I have to talk to him!"

"Hey, now wait a minute," Dorrie called to her. "It's better to leave them alone and let God work on Quin's heart."

"Oh, Dorrie, do you think. . . ?"

Her sister winked. "It looks real good. Praise the Lord!"

Just then Mick came bounding down the stairs, his face beaming as he gave each sister a hug. "I am pleased to announce that the Holy Spirit has just birthed a bouncing new baby Christian."

"Oh, Mick!" Gail cried. "Quin gave his life to the Lord?"

"Every bit of it. Other than myself, I never heard a man cry like he did. He laid everything on the altar tonight—his family, his past, and the whole trial next year. I know something special happened in his heart."

"I have to go see him!" Gail announced, racing for the front door.

"Gail, wait a minute," Dorrie hollered before Mick caught her arm and shook his head.

"Let them celebrate, Dorrie. This is their time to rejoice."

She sighed. "You're right. This is a night to celebrate a new life born into the kingdom of God. Right, little Jamie?"

The baby stared at her with his dark brown eyes, then laughed along with his parents.

❋

Gail drove up the street, her heart bursting with joy. For weeks she had held Quin up in prayer, and now her prayers had been answered. Autumn leaves swirled in a frenzy as the automobile drove by trees painted bright orange and red. She stopped before the brick apartment building, jumped out of the car, and raced for the door. She paused when she heard footsteps approaching from the sidewalk.

"Looking for someone?" a deep voice inquired.

She whirled to find Quin there with a grin on his face.

Gail threw her arms around him. "Oh, Quin! Mick told me what happened."

"Yeah," he said, nuzzling his face into her curls. "I just had to take a walk around the block. Like you told me at Lake Louise, everything looks so new and different—the trees, the birds, the way the clouds move across the sky. I see everything in a new and different way now. I guess this is what it's like to be born again."

Gail stepped back to see the joy radiating in his face. Impulsively, she leaned over and kissed him. The contact startled him before he responded with enthusiasm. When they parted, Gail asked if he now felt comfortable proceeding with the wedding plans.

"With everything that is in me and more," he told her. He went on to share his conversation with Mick. "The greatest revelation came to me after I shared my thoughts about being a criminal. I told Mick that God wouldn't have anything to do with a criminal. Mick said that wasn't true. Jesus knew criminals well. He was crucified with two of them. One ridiculed him, but the other was promised a place in Paradise. He said if Jesus could find a place in Paradise for a criminal, he could certainly find a place for me in His kingdom."

"That's great! I knew Mick would say the right things."

"He really does have a gift for reaching the needy," Quin agreed as they walked down a side street arm in arm, watching the leaves dance about in the breeze. "And it looks like you're going to get your fall wedding after all. I just wish. . ." He paused and closed his eyes.

"What?"

"You know we won't have a lot of time together, Gail. I'll soon be hip deep in all the legal troubles related to the trial, and then. . .well, who knows what will happen. I could be in jail for a long time."

109

"Have you considered this plea bargaining that the lawyer suggested?"

Quin shrugged as he scuffed up a few leaves lying on the pavement. "I've thought about it. But it means mandatory jail time, no matter what. At least with a jury trial I have the chance of an acquittal."

"But you know that won't happen."

Quin nodded. "There's plenty of evidence stacked up against me and some angry people who'll say anything to get me locked up for good."

"Then it looks like a plea bargain may be your only choice, Quin," she said softly.

He turned and gathered her into his arms, holding her as if he never wanted to let go. "Then I will be away from you. If there's any chance I can keep that from happening. . ."

"You'll never be away from my heart. Even if prison bars separate us, it will only be for a time. Meanwhile, we're together right now. So let's make the most of it."

"Okay," he said softly before kissing her lips, which tasted sweeter than clover honey.

※

Gail stood nervously in front of the mirror as Dorrie adjusted the veil on her head and pinned it into place with several bobby pins. "Gail, you keep jumping around, and this thing will be sitting crooked on your little head."

"It's bridal shakes."

"Isn't it funny that there is such a thing as bridal shakes?" Dorrie slid the last pin into place, then stepped back to observe the effect. "Perfect. You look lovely."

Gail examined the long white dress in the mirror, marveling that her mother had decided to hold on to the dress she had originally picked out at the bridal shop. The beadwork glistened in the lights of the room. "I'm so thankful your pastor decided to officiate, Dorrie."

"He was quite touched when Mick explained everything. When he had the chance to meet you and Quin in that private counseling session, he knew that God had placed you two together for a special purpose."

Gail again looked at her reflection in the mirror before ordering her sister to find her a tube of lipstick.

"Just don't get any of it on your dress," Dorrie laughed, handing her a tube.

Gail traced the color along her lips. "There!" she said. "That's something I didn't give up after becoming a Christian. I still like my makeup."

"I think God will overlook that minor quirk in your life," Dorrie joked with a laugh before picking up her bouquet. At that moment Mick entered, dressed in his tuxedo, to stand as Quin's best man. In his arms he held little Jamie, decked out in a blue velvet suit and matching blue bow tie.

"Are you ready?" Mick asked.

"She's ready and she looks lovely," Dorrie answered before Gail could open her mouth.

"So do you," Mick told Dorrie, giving her a quick peck on the lips. "I like seeing you in a fancy dress."

"Well, get yourself a high-paying faculty job at school, then you can buy me loads of party dresses."

"Maybe I will," he said with a grin. "I like the effect it's having on me."

Dorrie shook her head. "No, Mick. God's called you to a higher purpose. He's looking for men willing to throw caution to the wind to reach those in need. I'm so glad you decided to go on with your work at the soup kitchen."

"Yeah," he said softly. "We've had quite a rise in attendance since the whole escapade."

Gail glanced over. "Really?"

"You should see the guys strutting in now, wanting to catch a glimpse of the man who faced the Vultures gang. All the news coverage has increased our contributions to the soup kitchen, both in donated food and money. Believe it or not, the whole thing opened up the ministry like never before."

They walked out to the foyer together. The open doors of the sanctuary revealed an arrangement of carnations sitting in front of the podium and pews decorated with white satin bows. "Well, Mick, if God has opened the door, then you would be foolish not to enter, right?" Dorrie gestured inside the church. "Look what awaits you. Heaven's glory. The sanctuary of God. 'For a day in Your courts is better than a thousand,' " she concluded, quoting from Psalms.

He gave her a loving squeeze. "That's what I love about you. You have a unique grasp on God and His Word that always amazes me. It amazed me even when my heart was far from Him."

"God amazes me how He can take people like us and use us to do His will."

"Amen."

"And I second that," Gail said with a smile. She inhaled a deep breath to steady her nervous tremors and turned to see her father enter the foyer, dressed in his tuxedo. He stood still and silent, staring at her, until he came forward to bestow a hug.

"Your mother is still trying to pin on her corsage without crying," he chuckled. "But you look perfect."

"That's what Dorrie said," Gail noted. "I told her once that you and she are both alike in many ways."

"Well, I'm very proud of my daughter."

Gail stared into her father's eyes. "Are you, Dad? You're not upset about Quin, especially after all that's happened?"

"Well, it was a struggle for me at first," he admitted. "The idea of my little girl running off with a criminal is not the sort of thing a father wishes for his daughter. But after talking with Dorrie and Mick and seeing the big picture for myself, your young man is willing to try to overcome his mistakes. I'm sad that you two will be apart for so long, but you know the saying—absence makes the heart grow fonder." He hugged her once more. "I'm only glad you finally decided to go through with this ceremony. I'll have to admit, it does make me consider what you two girls have done by giving your lives to God. I see changes in both of you that would have never come about unless something greater than you was at work." He added with chuckle, "It wasn't just your upbringing, either."

"Hey, Dad? Mick is wonderful at helping men understand about God."

Her father winked. "Ah-ha, I knew you would say something like that. Well, we'll talk about it after the ceremony." He offered her his arm. "Right now I think you have an anxious groom waiting for you."

Gail smiled and tucked her hand in the crook of his elbow, breathing deeply to calm her jitters. Her dream of a wedding had finally come true. Gail and her father walked down the aisle before the well-wishers gathered together as witnesses. The wedding dress and long train swept the floor while organ music played the processional. Her eyes rose to meet the warm smile on Quin's face as he stood ready to receive her as his wife before the eyes of God.

Afterward there were cheese and fruit trays at the simple reception along with a wedding cake. Gail relished every minute of the festivities as she clung to Quin's arm while mingling with the guests. She enjoyed the moment when they took up the knife in both their hands and slowly cut a piece of the cake. The simple wedding wasn't the elaborate creation she had once envisioned, but she was thankful for all that God had done in bringing her together with the one man who occupied her thoughts every moment of the day.

❋

Quin and Gail rode back to the apartment in his car, which was painted up with the words "Just Married." The ride was made all the more interesting by the tinkling of tin cans fastened beneath the bumper. Quin jumped out and yanked open the passenger door.

"I wish we were leaving on our honeymoon tomorrow," he announced as they walked up to the apartment door. He shook his head. "Life is sure different now, isn't it?"

Gail looked at him and the sudden sadness overshadowing him. "Quin, what's the matter?"

"I'm just thinking about all the things I could have given you if my family and I had made honest money like normal people. Now all I have to look forward to is a criminal trial and lawyers' fees. There's no money for that trip to Europe like you wanted."

"I'm just thankful to finally have the real you."

"Are you?"

"Quin, we're now real people. We aren't pretending anymore or living double lives. We can be the people God meant for us to be and enjoy each other while we have time."

"It was all pretty confusing," he said, stepping up to the apartment door and unlocking it. He looked over at her and extended his arms. "Now that the confusion has passed, we can take the next step."

"What do you mean? What are you doing?"

"We've never had the chance to perform this custom. Come here."

Gail looked at him quizzically until he scooped her up in his arms.

"Quin!" she shouted, batting him playfully on his chest. "Put me down!"

"I'm supposed to carry you over the threshold, Mrs. Costello."

"I just hope no one's looking," she mumbled in embarrassment as he carried her into the apartment.

Once inside, she gasped at the huge bouquet of long-stemmed red roses waiting for her on the table, accompanied by a pair of candlesticks that he lit with a match. "Oh, it's beautiful!"

"Just like you."

Gail stared at the man with whom she had exchanged her heartfelt vows, watching the candlelight illuminate his features and his eyes reflect the flame. His entire face glowed with the eternal light of Christ in his heart and with a deep abiding love for her. Now as they came together to share in a kiss, Gail was thankful to finally know the real man she had married.

Epilogue

The wind swept across his face, blowing his fine brown hair. The sky appeared unnaturally bright with an expanse of turquoise blue stretching from one horizon to the other. He had not seen so much sky in years. Birds clinging to tree limbs sang songs of welcome. Flowers scented the air. Freedom never felt so good to his weary bones as he slowly walked across the pavement toward a set of benches shaded by a large maple tree.

Suddenly he heard a sound rise up as the wind. It was soft at first, like a whisper, then grew louder as he walked.

"Daddy! Oh, Daddy!"

He squinted. A young girl raced toward him, her arms outstretched. Her cheeks were rosy red, her smile radiant. *Could it be?*

"Daddy!" the young girl cried again before her tiny arms looped around his thin form in a fierce hug.

He nuzzled his face into her curly brown hair. "Grace," he whispered. "How I missed you. I. . .I missed everything—your first bite of cereal, your first steps, your first words. Now look at you." He stepped back to survey the pretty young thing with deep brown eyes like her parents. "Why, you're nine years old."

She clasped his hand in hers, swinging it back and forth.

Tears welled up in his eyes and dribbled down his cheeks. "I missed out on so much because of all my mistakes. Oh, Lord, how can You redeem the time I have lost?"

A vision of beauty in the distance caught his attention. It was a vision like so many he had imagined while living day after day in a concrete cell, thinking of all he was missing in life. Only this time the vision of a beautiful woman with curly hair that whipped in the wind was real. A smile appeared on the soft oval face as she approached.

"You're real," he said out loud. "You're not just a dream."

"Yes, I'm real." She came forward and kissed him tenderly. "I'm very real. God heard our prayers. He set my captive free."

"Yes." He ran his fingers through the curly hair he could only dream about while in his cell. The hair felt like silk to his touch. "Thank You, God. . .for my family," he managed to say, his voice choking with emotion.

"Grace, you hold Daddy's hand and I'll hold the other one. We have a nice welcome-home dinner planned, just the three of us."

He smiled as his family led him to a waiting car. After ten long years, Quintin Costello walked away from the huge brick buildings and barbed-wire fencing of the correctional facility, grateful for the power of love that had set him free.

LAURALEE BLISS

Lauralee is a multi-published author of inspirational fiction. She enjoys writing novels that are reminiscent of a roller coaster ride for the reader. Her desire is that readers will come away with both an entertaining story and a lesson that ministers to the heart. Besides writing, Lauralee enjoys gardening, roaming yard sales, visiting historical sites, and hiking a trail. Visit her Web site at www.lauraleebliss.com.

Yesteryear

Gloria Brandt

To Dad and Mom...
for being patient with all my scribblings then—
and supportive of them now.
Thank you.

Prologue

15 August 1853

The woods are beautiful. Deep. Lonely. Isolated.

The last plank of floor was laid today. My sense of "lost" is only over-shadowed when encompassed by the newness and excitement of the pending school year. The odor of fresh wood is such a heady aroma. It smells of. . . future. Truly, each step through my new classroom fills me with anticipation. . .and more than a fraction of doubt. Thoughts of my father's warning flutter through my mind. . . . "Is one of such a tender age capable of this task?" But my resolution returns—with each dazzling sunset, with each songbird's trill.

No, in spite of the vastness of this new land, I am convinced that the Almighty placed me here for a purpose. It is that thought that keeps me from shivering in complete cowardice when the noisy coyotes howl in their nighttime ritual.

How shall I ever bear the following weeks? How shall I ever endure the solitude? My resolve set aside, I cannot help but wonder. . .is the molding and teaching of young minds to be my only life's calling? Or is there more?

Thank you so kindly, Mr. Longfellow, for leaving that ponderous gap. . . .

"No one is so accurst by fate,
    No one so utterly desolate,
But some heart, though unknown,
    Responds unto his own."

I pray it might be so. . . .

—Madeline Whitcomb

Chapter 1

The fly buzzed noisily through the stifling air in the cramped office. Jack Tate swung at it impatiently with the brown felt hat still clutched in his hands.

"Are you sure you won't reconsider?" Bob Feldman leaned across the small, cluttered desk, inadvertently shifting a pile of papers askew.

Jack shook his head without hesitation.

Bob tilted back in the creaking chair that seemed entirely too small for his ample frame. His graying brows rose a fraction. . .then he nodded. "All right. I still think you might be selling yourself short, though."

A dubious stare was all Jack returned, followed by a lopsided grin.

"Okay, okay," Bob chuckled. "Have it your way. What do I know? I only run the place." He twisted around to look at the quickly filling calendar on the wall. "When's the first group scheduled to arrive?"

Jack squinted at the dates. "I. . .uh. . .next Monday."

The older man scribbled something undecipherable on a pad in front of him. "Good enough. And everything's set for supplies?"

A nod.

"You've checked in with Paul? He has all the blacksmithing materials he needs?"

"Mm hm."

"Looks like you've done your job well. . .as usual." He offered Jack a smile of encouragement. "Just wish—well, that you could be more involved."

Jack promptly placed the dusty hat back on his head. "This. . .is fine." With a departing smile, he yanked open the door that always determined to stick and stepped into the hot, early June sunshine—an intense load off of his mind.

✹

She picked dejectedly at the fraying threads hanging from the knee of her tattered jeans. How long had they been out there anyway? She flopped backwards on her bed, wishing she could just go to sleep. But even that seemed to elude her lately.

From outside her closed bedroom door, she heard the voices. Talking quietly, hushed. Afraid she might hear. No matter. She already knew what they were saying anyway. The same thing they'd been saying for the last few weeks. Since the funeral—

No. She would not go there. *Think of something else, anything.* . . .

Soft footsteps approached down the hall.

She quickly assumed a more natural sleeping position on her small bed and took a deep breath before the knock came.

"Carillon?"

Mom.

She didn't move.

"Honey?" The door creaked open, and the sliver of light from the hall barged its way into her self-made dungeon of darkness.

"Lon?" Dad that time.

She released a silent sigh. If they were both here, there was no getting around it. Stretching, she rolled over and squinted at them in mock sleepiness.

Approaching with a cautious air, her parents stood next to the bed. Her mother finally settled lightly on the edge, the concern in her blue eyes evident. Carillon looked away. She didn't want to see it. She didn't deserve it.

"Lon," her dad started, "Pastor Jim is here. He'd like to see you if—"

She shook her head adamantly. "No, I don't want to talk to your holy roller pastor!"

This time the sigh belonged to her father.

She took the sign of disapproval as the cue to roll back over.

From behind her, she felt her mother's hand brush gently across her arm. Carillon didn't pull away as she might have several months ago, but the contact didn't strike any chord within her, either. She was empty. Always would be. She was an awful human being—no, a monster.

"Honey," Mom started, "we're worried about you. It's not. . .natural to stay in here like this. Cloistered."

She remained motionless. Silent.

"Rachel," her father said quietly, "let me."

She felt her mother slowly move off the bed, only to be replaced by her father's slightly larger and heavier form.

"Lon." He cleared his throat somewhat nervously. "We've been talking to Pastor Jim. We think we've found something, or rather someplace, that might help you."

For the first time in a long, long while, Carillon felt something. The quick surge of panic rushed through her veins as her clouded mind raced with a host of unthinkable outcomes of this conversation. They'd stick her in a mental institution or some hospital. Or maybe jail. After all, it had been her fault that—

"Lon, do you hear me?"

She tried not to shiver.

"Turn around, please."

For once, she didn't have the courage to brush the request aside. There was an earnestness in his voice she'd not heard—not lately. She gingerly maneuvered herself over. But she still couldn't meet his eyes.

"This isn't healthy," he began. "And your holing up in here isn't helping you, us, or anyone else."

"So. . .what?" she replied edgily. "You want me to throw a party? Have all my friends whom you love so much over here?"

"That's not what we meant."

"Of course, it isn't. Nothing I do would be right anyway."

He seemed to ignore her last comment and forged on. "We think you need to get away for awhile."

Here it came. What hospital would it be? And how long would it take her to break out of it?

He laid a pamphlet down on her comforter. "We've gone ahead and made the arrangements for your arrival. You can pack tonight. The bus leaves tomorrow morning."

Bus? Tomorrow? Every part of her being wanted to jolt upright and scream, "What!" But she did nothing. Said nothing. It was routine now—trouble caught up with her, consequences around the corner. Until she found her way out.

But this time. . . This time it was different. She might just deserve it. Or at least need to rid her parents of her lifetime of mistakes that tarnished their lily-white name.

Apparently her parents were waiting for some sort of reaction from her. Why, she didn't know. They ought to know by now. . . .

Her father fingered the pamphlet one last time, then tentatively reached over to stroke her hair. But he stopped a few inches from her head.

Keeping her gaze glued to the cotton comforter, Carillon watched his arm fall in resignation before the two of them left the room in silence, pulling the door shut behind them. She collapsed back onto the bed, letting the now-welcome darkness envelop her once more. She heard the slip of paper slide to the floor. She hadn't the energy to retrieve it, much less flick on a lamp to see what it might say.

No, all she wanted right now was the darkness. So no one could see her. Even herself.

※

The long walk back to Jack's "quarters" was quiet, pleasant. It gave him a chance to be pensive without the occasional distractions of work—and visitors. Only the varied chorus of birds provided the background for his welcome solitude.

Underneath the lacy canopy of giant evergreens and maples, he trudged along the well-worn path, finding his destination purely by instinct. He could have walked this in the pitch black of night—indeed, he had. More than a few times. Recently. . .and long ago. An involuntary shiver skittered down his back.

Sloughing off the latter portion of that thought, he came to the clearing that marked his home. Stopping, he assessed it with a critical eye, trying to see it as one would for the first time.

The small, sturdy log cabin sat peaceably beside a stand of pine trees. Behind the white chinked structure stood the weatherworn barn; a chicken coop, complete with cackling guineas; and the building least liked by any employee of Yesteryear. . .the outhouse. He smiled, remembering the arguments that seemed to ensue every year among the staff: Couldn't they just put hidden "modern" bathrooms in the various locales?

Resuming his study, he wondered. . .was everything in place? Anything missing? All miscellaneous, unnecessary items properly put away? It just wouldn't work to have a visitor stumble across a stash of old Pepsi cans while traipsing around the one-hundred-year-old barn's manger.

Removing his hat and once more assessing his plain brown trousers and light-colored work shirt, he nodded to himself. From here on out it was the fifties.

The 1850s.

✳

Nighttime had finally come. For real. Carillon could pull up the shades in her room and let the natural blackness invade the space. Time seemed irrelevant anymore. She couldn't measure hours, days, weeks. Even months and years were fast congealing into an abyss of bad memories and guilt. She found it preferable not to dwell on it at all. The continual hum of the digital clock and the rustling of her bedclothes were the only sounds she knew now. On occasion when she had to go into her small, adjoining bathroom, she ignored the light switch. She wanted no reminder of herself appearing in the bathroom mirror. The ghostly hush was broken only by the sound of splashing water.

Tonight there were a few stars. Faint little pinpricks of brightness in the vast expanse above. For some unknown reason, Carillon reached out and pushed open the window—just this once. Just to let a little bit of the cool night air blow on her face.

It nipped at her cheeks ever so slightly, its dampness settling around her.

She closed her eyes and inhaled deeply.

At least tonight there was no moon. Nothing to illuminate the reminders of her own stupidity, carelessness, selfishness. . .

No wind. No movement to bring even the sounds to her—

"*Carillon. . .*"

Her lids flew open. Her heart stalled for a split second.

Silence.

She stood from the window seat and stumbled backwards.

"*Carillon. . .*"

Around the enormous lump in her throat, she managed a breath. "Evie?" she whispered.

No response.

A different, new courage overtook her. She lunged at the window and flung it open wider. "Evie?" she called desperately into the evening breeze.

Down the street, a lone dog barked out a warning. All else was still.

But she'd heard her. She knew she had.

Plucking her pillow from the bed, she propped it up against one end of the window seat and settled in. If Carillon heard her again—she'd be ready.

Chapter 2

The bus jostled and swayed along the curved, tree-lined road. Carillon knew that out the rear window the last telltale remainders of the city had slipped away. . .somewhere between the suburbs and the increasing rolling hills. If she'd a mind to, she could have turned around and watched as all she knew stayed behind on some paved street while the rest of her was whisked away. Each bone-rattling bounce from the gravel path's potholes made it more than apparent. She'd never been one to lament much of anything. That would have entailed giving a rip about something, and she didn't. Not anymore.

It was clear why her parents hadn't told her of their plans until last night. With such short notice, there was no opportunity for her to run away—hide. Finally she was at the mercy of their "do good" ideals. She didn't want it. She didn't need it.

Facing a span of hours with nothing else to do, Carillon finally relented and pulled out the pamphlet from her duffel. *Yesteryear. A place of history and healing.*

She frowned. *A place of. . .what?*

The little paper was overloaded with Bible verses and photos of ancient-looking buildings. In and around them were people of all ages, apparently dressed to match the surroundings. This was where she was going? And what did they expect her to accomplish there?

She read on and discovered it was a tourist-type place. Apparently the "workers" were people such as herself. And during the summer months, people came to visit the living history museum—to see life as it might have been lived more than one hundred years ago.

Carillon's frown deepened. She was going to have to be Laura Ingalls for the summer?

No, she reminded herself—*only for a little while.*

Shoving the leaflet back into the pocket of her duffel, she tried to doze as the eternal stretch of hours, which might as well have been days, finally ended and the aging vehicle ground to a stop. With the roar of the engine now quieted, the slow patter of the persistent drizzle made itself known against the dusty windows. She knew some of the others aboard, probably filled with equal amounts of curiosity and dread, were straining to see through the watery streaks what would be their "home" for the next three and a half months.

Three and a half months. . .

She still couldn't believe her parents had pawned her off for that long. No matter. It just gave her more time to plan and execute her escape. Then she wouldn't have to trouble her family or anyone else ever again.

In spite of her resolve not to care, she couldn't keep her eyes from straying upward and outward, just for that initial glance.

Before she could take in much at all, a fresh-faced, college-aged girl covered in a bright orange slicker stepped up into the bus. "Good afternoon!" she said cheerily. "Welcome to Yesteryear. If you'll all just grab your bags and things and follow me, I'll take you into the main meeting hall, where we'll go through the orientation material. There are snacks and beverages there as well, so come on in and relax."

Carillon studied the girl. She looked young, in a carefree sort of way. Like she hadn't a care in the world. And why would she? She obviously wasn't there for any reason close to Carillon's. What did these people know about real life when they were stuck out here in the middle of la-la land?

For the first time, Carillon looked around her at the hodgepodge group trailing off the bus. She wondered why they were here.

Waiting until the last passenger had disembarked, she flung her khaki duffel over her shoulder and stepped down the aisle and out into the light rain that covered everything in a gray mist.

Her eyes settled on Yesteryear. Amid the drizzle, four log buildings of varied sizes were situated in a rectangular shape, the one long, open end of a neatly mowed courtyard facing the parking lot where she now stood. Behind all of the white chinked structures stood a continuous row of huge, towering pines.

Out of all the overgrown cabins, the only two clearly labeled were a restaurant and a gift shop. The other two, she guessed, were the non-tourist buildings. Most likely where she'd be staying.

None of them looked genuinely old, but they'd obviously been built to seem that way. Rustic, to say the least. And not exactly what she'd had in mind for her summer months, even before Evie had—

Squeezing her eyes shut and shaking her head adamantly, she bid the thoughts away. . .for the moment. It was only a matter of time until they came back.

For now she had another job to do. Another person to become. . .just until it was all done.

❊

Jack wrapped the slicker closer about his neck as he peered up from under the brim of his hat. Cold rain. The crops were never going to grow if they didn't get any decent warm weather for more than one day at a time. The rain-slicked grass on the path had already turned his boots a moist dark brown. . .and most likely his socks as well. He'd have to remember to put more oil on the boots when he got back home later.

As he neared the building compound that housed the offices, gift shop, restaurant, and sleeping quarters for some of the staff, he heard the roar of the bus driving away, the spittle of gravel being showered back upon the road.

So, they'd made it. The first group was here.

For some reason he'd not yet been able to define, that same sense of apprehension, nervousness, and disquiet nagged at him. The same as the last five years. He'd tried to sort it out. He'd prayed about it. He knew why he was here and that he believed in what Yesteryear was doing. But it still came. Maybe not so much apprehension—more discontent. Thus far he'd been able to brush it aside as he immersed himself in the ever-present duties that needed his overseeing. It was enough—for now. Later. . . ? He'd trained himself not to worry about later. What would come would come. One day at a time.

As he rounded the last stand of giant pines that lined the compound's perimeter, he saw a lone figure standing in the middle of the self-made courtyard among all the buildings. Minus any sort of coat or hat, her long dark hair hung limply down her back, clinging to the equally soaked shirt she wore with a rather tight mini-skirt. She faced the other direction, not seeming to be looking at anything in particular.

She was small, slight. And for a brief moment Jack wondered just how young they were taking these people anymore. But he also knew that physical build could be deceptive. In spite of his own twenty-five years—and at least a dozen of those being spent at muscle-building farm labor—he'd more than once been mistaken for a teen himself. It had bothered him at first, but he'd gotten over it. Wasn't much he could do about it anyway.

As he approached the building, he debated about whether or not to issue an invitation in—and quickly thought better of it. But maybe if she saw him going in, he could at least hold the door open or offer some nonverbal suggestion for entrance.

Making a point of walking rather noisily past her quiet spot, he was halfway to the wooden steps of the restaurant when her smooth voice stopped him.

"Do you have a cigarette?"

He halted in his tracks. Then slowly turned around. The look on her chiseled face was fairly unreadable. No hint of a smile tweaked the wide, full lips.

"N—no. . .smoking allowed," he stammered, suddenly embarrassed.

A quiet, albeit troubled, smile lifted her high cheekbones. Jack quickly realized he'd been an idiot to have thought her a child. Looking at her face-to-face more than told him this was no kid. Pretty obvious. In a lot of ways.

"I know," she said simply.

He looked at her quizzically.

"The no-smoking rule," she clarified. "I knew." She gave a small shrug. "Just tryin' to break the ice."

The rush of warmth flew up his neck and into his face. This girl was getting the best of him and he'd not even met her yet. With a resigned chuckle, he threw a glance at the ground before remeeting those knowing eyes. He noticed her twitch with an involuntary shiver.

Berating himself for being dense, he whipped off his slicker and tentatively held it out to her.

She blinked at it, almost in confusion, before raising her wet lashes and staring at him. Jack saw that familiar flicker of distrust. . .then something else. A brief softening? Too quickly it vanished. And with an equally hesitant hand, she grasped the proffered article and shrugged into it, looking uncomfortable. "Thanks," she said softly.

Turning around, he motioned with his head for her to follow as he started toward the stairs once again. At the door, he held open the heavy wood portal and waited for her to enter. She paused at the threshold and eyed him more carefully. That same disconcerting scrutiny that made his ears burn. He shifted his gaze to the sign just above her head on the door.

"You're shy." The mirth in her voice, obvious.

He returned her direct look and tilted his head in possible acquiescence.

"Do you have a name, Mr. Shy Gentleman?"

"Hey, Jack!" the voice carried across the restaurant's foyer with ear-ringing clarity. He swung his head in the direction of Paul, the blacksmith, and gave him an informal salute. "Bob's waiting for you in the office. Something about the bulk food order."

With a nod, he closed the door carefully behind the young woman whose name he did not yet know. He wished he could ask.

She held out a slender hand and shook his warmly. "Nice to meet you, Jack. Think I'll go and change clothes." She unwrapped herself from the abundant leather slicker and started to hand it back to him.

He shook his head and took a deep breath. "You. . .k–keep it." With a quick glance out the window, he indicated the continuing rain.

Her lips drew into a private smile. "Thanks again." Without another word, she moved gracefully across the empty dining room toward the far hall. And Jack tried to remember the last time his pulse had pounded that loudly in his brain.

※

"Here's the list." Bob handed over the clipboard with a pen. "Not as large a group this time. Should be easier to assign without so much doubling up."

Jack nodded as his eyes roved down the paper. Of the twenty-some names before him, more than half were female. He wondered which one belonged to her.

". . .And the last of the animals were supposed to be delivered this morning."

Lifting his eyes from the sheet, Jack realized he'd just missed half of what had been said. "Really?" He tried to wing it from there.

"They took 'em over to the usual barn at the Hanson place."

"G–good. I'll run over. . .and check on them. . .r–right away."

Bob looked up from his disorganized desk for a moment, concern on his round face. "You okay, Jack?"

He made a point of restudying the names in front of him and let out a breath. "Sure. W—why?"

The older man lifted his shoulders. "Your. . .speech seems a little more choppy today. Everything all right?"

Embarrassment mingled with gratitude as the man's concern made his face flame—again. How many times was that today? With a self-deprecating chuckle, Jack tilted his head. "F–first day. . .I guess. I–I. . .gonna be. . .okay."

Bob gave him an understanding grin and a hearty slap on the shoulder. "Alrighty then. We'll see you tomorrow morning. I'll be anxious to see what you work out for those interpreter positions. Everybody's file with age and experience is in there."

Jack tapped the sheet. "Tomorrow."

✳

"Hi, I'm Lydia. What's your name?" the slightly plump girl with incredibly thick glasses asked cheerily.

Carillon sighed and shifted her attention from the trees outside the window back into the crowded room where they were all seated, waiting to get their first overview of Yesteryear and some preliminary instructions. "Carillon. Carillon DeVries."

"What an interesting name. However did you get it?"

She threw her a placating look. "My parents were poor spellers."

Her antisocial answer must have sufficed. The curly black head nodded in a moment of confusion before turning to the person on her opposite side—with much better results probably.

Yeah, well, friends she didn't need. Not here. All she needed to do was get ahold of Leslie. If they ever got this ridiculous meeting over and done with. She glanced at the clock one more time.

With her chatty neighbor's attention shifted elsewhere, Carillon made it a point to peruse the room. She hadn't seen him again. This. . .Jack guy. Not since she'd first come in. Cute enough—even if he was a little on the scrawny side. But more than that, he'd made her initial job easy. By the look in his eyes and his quiet manner, he seemed like the soft type who was more than willing to. . ."help."

But from somewhere inside, she felt an uncomfortable pang. There was something else about the guy. . . . Something that reminded her of someone else. That softness, that openness—wanting to trust.

The look could have been Evie all over again.

Evie.

The pounding in her head returned, and she pushed her fingers against her temples. *Oh no. Not now. Not here.* She was away from that now. This was where it was supposed to end—

"Okay," the businesslike voice echoed from the front.

130

Thankfully it broke the game her mind was trying to play.

"Welcome to Yesteryear. For those of you who aren't familiar with our facility, I'll give you a brief introduction. This land, all seven hundred acres of it, was purchased by a private party in 1992. Since that time, careful selection of numerous historical sites, buildings, and farms has been made. And each, in turn, has been disassembled, moved here, and carefully reconstructed as a permanent part of Yesteryear.

"We do a fantastic tourist business in the summer months, and the inclusion of people, such as yourselves, helps us out in the summer season when we especially need the extra staffing.

"There is, however, a bigger reason for Yesteryear's existence. Due to the philanthropy of a caring, Christian man, this place has become something of a haven for those who need a healing touch. You're all from different circumstances and backgrounds. But we're all here to work together, support one another, and ultimately let God touch us in a way that happens only when we totally surrender ourselves to Him.

"We hope you find that surrender while you're here—and that Jesus Christ will meet you in a very profound and lasting way."

Carillon began to squirm under the religion this guy was spouting. She should have known the place would be some "churchy" thing. . .the idea coming from her parents' new pastor. Ever since they'd gotten involved in that bizarre place several years ago, she'd seen them take on some pretty peculiar habits. Bibles lying all over the house. Different music coming out of the CD player. She'd even caught each of them, at various times, on their knees, praying. Sometimes right in the middle of the living room. Just weird.

But what made it worse was that they'd gotten Evie mixed up in it. She was just a kid. How was she supposed to defend herself against that at her young age?

"Today's session," the man continued, "will entail our ground rules, including conduct, etc. Tomorrow there will be a tour of the whole facility—every farm and house and store that's a part of what we call Yesteryear. From there, your job assignments will be given out. You might all expect to be 'tour guides,' or what we call 'interpreters,' but that may or may not be the case. There are positions as wait staff in the restaurant, checkers in the gift shop, and so on.

"So, if you'll all turn to the second page in your booklet we handed out, I'll point out the first items we'll need to discuss before. . ."

His voice droned into monotony as Carillon listened with half-open ears. Listening only for anything that might give her more information. Anything inside. All the while, keeping her eye out for Mr. Shy Jack—her possible ticket out of here.

Chapter 3

I was told we got to make phone calls." Whether or not Carillon had a grip on her current, raging frustration and anger, she didn't know. Nor did she care. All she knew was that this perky little college grad in front of her was messing up her plans in a major way.

"I'm sorry. . . ." The young woman glanced quickly at Carillon's name tag. "Miss DeVries, phone privileges aren't extended until everyone's finished the week-long orientation. If there's some sort of emergency, of course, we'd be happy to—"

With a scathing glare, Carillon cut her off. "Fantastic. I'll see what I can do to come up with an emergency. Thanks. . ." She looked just as pointedly at the small badge on the employee's chest. "Miss Zahn. You've been a big help." Stalking away, she ripped her own identification tag from her T-shirt and tossed it into the nearest trash can. These people didn't have any clue what they were dealing with here. How hard could it be to escape from the middle of nowhere? No bars. No walls. No one standing guard.

But she needed to get hold of Leslie. Somehow. Fast.

The narrow hall that lined the perimeter of the restaurant angled off into a deeper corridor. A quick glance around told her no one seemed to be in the vicinity. The majority of the group had stayed in the main conference room during the break, chatting. She had better things to do.

Taking a determined step down the hall, she listened carefully for voices. She heard an occasional muffled conversation behind the several closed doors she passed on either side. At the turn of a corner, the hall ended abruptly with one door leading outside. The small window framed the dismal day and the offices of Yesteryear that lay fifty feet or so across the compound. On her immediate left, a door stood ajar several inches. Peering around the entrance, she noted a room flanked with shelves holding a variety of food stuffs. In the center was a small desk. With a phone.

Carillon bit her lower lip in concentration and slipped into the empty office, quietly closing the door behind her. Stealing over to the corner of the desk, she cautiously picked up the receiver and listened for the dial tone. With one more glance at the door, she punched in a rapid sequence of numbers, chewing on her thumbnail while each ring intensified her paranoia.

Someone picked up and fumbled briefly with the phone. "Hello?" a groggy female voice mumbled.

Carillon frowned. "Leslie?" she whispered.

132

"Hello?" the young woman said, following it with a yawn. "Who's this?"

The pulse points near Carillon's temples began pounding in aggravating rhythm. She felt her senses tightening along with her grip on the receiver. "It's Carillon," she returned caustically, then cringed, remembering to keep her voice down.

"Lon?" Leslie's voice sounded surprised.

Great! She'd been gone how many hours now? And her best friend had already forgotten?

"Where are you?" Leslie mumbled. It was pretty obvious her brain was in no mode for thinking.

"You know where I am!"

"Oh. . .yeah."

Carillon's grip on the phone tightened, her nails digging into the palm of her hand. She suddenly wished desperately that it was Leslie's neck in her grasp. "Have you and Kari got ahold of a car yet?"

"Oh. . .no. I guess not."

"Les!" She bit her lips together, inwardly reminding herself to hush up. "Forget it," she breathed in exasperation as she slid her hand through her hair. Yet again, she'd have to rely on herself. As usual.

"Lon, hold up!"

Carillon slammed the phone down and took several deep breaths while the dull thud in her head intensified into a piercing ache.

Outside the door, distant footsteps echoed down the narrow hall. Her breath catching in her throat, Carillon slipped to the door and gently latched it, engaging the small lock. Then she turned and made a quick assessment of her surroundings.

Behind her, a hand tried the door knob.

Skittering behind a stack of flour bags, she crouched between the huge sacks and the wall, just as a set of keys jingled from outside and one found its way into the lock. She hoped whoever it was didn't need any flour.

With her back against the wood-planked wall, her chest heaving in silent breaths, she waited. There was shuffling through some papers on the desk. And a clipboard suddenly plunked on the stack of flour, right near her head. Unable to completely stifle the quick intake of breath, Carillon held it deep in her lungs. Clenching her eyes shut, she waited. . . .

Some minutes later, after some canned goods had been removed from one of the shelves, the person plucked up the clipboard and, from the sounds of it, exited the office and closed the door.

Hardly daring to release a breath, she peered over the wall of white bags and waited again. Just in case.

Confident she'd let enough time elapse, she slid out from her hiding place and padded toward the door. With a careful hand, she twisted the knob and peered around the jamb. Empty. Leaving the door ajar, as she'd found it, she walked briskly down the hall and stepped back into the common hallway that led back toward the conference room.

"Do you need help finding something?" A man's authoritative voice stopped her short.

"Just looking for the rest rooms," she answered after a moment's hesitation. She glanced over to find a large, round-faced man holding a slew of papers.

"They're the other way." He indicated with his free hand. "Opposite side of the restaurant."

"Thanks." She gave him a half smile and continued on her way.

She'd made it.

And now, apparently, the rest of it was up to her as well. Why she thought she could ever rely on Leslie or Kari for anything. . . She cut off her own thoughts, not ready to bring to the surface those betrayed feelings again. She could do this on her own. Like before. Only one thing she needed. . .just a little more information on the layout of this place. And she knew exactly where to get that.

❋

Jack sat at the rough wood table, bent over the collection of papers before him. The kerosene lamp's flickering flame cast dancing shadows over the vellum sheets. With a heavy sigh, he grabbed the large mug and took one last swig of the cooled coffee. Outside, a particularly brisk shot of wind slammed against the log cabin, making the front door shudder on its broad hinges.

Shoving the file away, he leaned back in the wooden chair, balancing on its rear legs. Done. Everybody had a job to do. Barring any unforeseen personality or ability conflicts, the assignments should work out well. Having a chance to see each person's background drastically increased his insight as to which jobs should be given where.

But for the first time in his five years working at Yesteryear, he'd found his line of concentration broken more often than not. Riffling through all of the women's portfolios first, he tried in vain to discover who the girl he'd seen earlier might be. He wondered why it should matter anyway. He'd learned a long time ago that girls like that were meant for a definite type of guy. And he definitely wasn't it. *Like it's of any consequence,* he railed inwardly. *Do your job, Jack. Remember, you and she are here for completely different reasons.*

But her expressive eyes refused to leave his memory. And he found himself searching for clues again. He really didn't have any idea as to her age—and the records covered everyone from fifteen to forty-four. Even the names were no help, really.

Although, one name had stuck out. . .simply because he'd not heard the word in so long—Carillon.

He'd done a double take at that, then had chuckled. One of his mother's favorite words. "Listen," she'd say as the summer dusk settled around their farmhouse

134

porch. "They're ringing the carillons." To Alice Tate, an incurable romantic, the carillons were the steeple bells from the small country church several miles over the rolling farmland. They announced the twelve and six o'clock hours more faithfully than any practical clock radio.

As a child, Jack had wondered just who had the incredible task of getting to the church well ahead of time and climbing up those narrow tower steps to ring that monstrous bell. Something straight out of *The Hunchback of Notre Dame.*

His own fanciful notions, surely fueled by his mother's own love of literature, had been dashed when his older brother, Jon, had laughingly explained they were on a timer. No one rang them by hand. Not anymore. Jack found that thought sad. He always thought that ringing those bells would be an awesome thing.

But as always, Jon would bring him back to earth, reminding him that any-one with his build would have an impossible time even keeping a grip on the thick rope. Jack had bristled at his brawnier brother's assessment but knew it most likely was true. Still, he spent many a night out in the garage, trying to lift the weights that his brother so effortlessly used to sculpt his thick arms and chest. He knew he got stronger. . .but not much bigger.

But back to the name—Carillon. Carillon. Her exquisite beauty could be worthy of such a title, but he'd also learned long ago not to get too wrapped up in the thoughts of the imaginary. They didn't get one too far. . .especially men, it seemed. Unless one really craved ridicule and scorn.

With a long breath, he eased up from his chair and took the lantern with him toward the sleeping quarters in the loft. One goofy name was sending him back on all sorts of past roads in his memory—ones he didn't need to travel down again. Once had been more than enough. From there, he'd given them over to God, almost imagining the "Road Closed" signs his heavenly Father had erected. No, there was no reason to dwell on things that he couldn't change. Even if he was left with painful reminders—

Shaking his head in annoyance, he deftly stepped up the homemade log lad-der and set the lantern near his thick pallet on the beam floor. The loft was high, adding nearly another story to the one-room cabin, so standing near the peak was no problem. He hung his clothes on the nearby pegs, crossed over to the stash of food and smoked meats that hung on one end, and took down a slab of bacon for his morning breakfast. Placing the meat near the ladder, he settled himself down next to his Bible, once again grateful for the privacy his loft bedroom afforded. Most of the other interpreters had theirs on the main floor of their residences, but considering the number of tourists who traipsed through the cabin, day in and day out, he desired slightly more privacy. For his rest. For his things.

For his memories.

He opened the yellow, worn pages of the well-used Bible and leaned on one elbow as he reclined. "Ok–kay, Lord," he murmured with a half-smile. "W–what do You have. . .for me. . .today?"

Chapter 4

Jack stared out at the group before him, trying not to let his knees quake in total cowardice. The last eternity had really only been approximately eight and a half minutes. Approximately. It might as well have been a year. Trying to simultaneously look official and at ease (something he wasn't sure was working), he shuffled the papers in front of him and glanced at the clock once more. Bob had said he'd be back before nine. It was almost ten after now. The small gathering was getting louder as they passed the time, talking among themselves.

Jack threw one more look back at Steve at the rear of the room. His friend shrugged and gave him a "go for it" nod.

Jack cleared his throat.

"G–g–good. . .morning." That got their attention. But it was pretty obvious for the wrong reasons.

He shifted his weight and frowned at the papers in his hands. "I'm here. . . t–to as–s–s–ign you t–t–to your jobs." He blew out a long breath and tried to ignore some of the curious faces staring straight at him. *Help me, Father. Make this ridiculous tongue work.*

"John. . .Wilson." That was better. He just needed to slow down. "You'll b–b–be working. . .with P–p–p—" He stopped and took another subtle breath. "With. . .Paul. The black. . .smith." One down. Twenty-three more to go. His brain went dizzy.

At that moment, Bob sauntered into the room, looking harried, red-faced, and winded. "Sorry," he panted as his large form moved to the front. "I got a call at the last minute." He reached Jack's side and indicated the sheets before him. "You wanna finish up?"

Jack shook his head and gratefully handed the stack to his boss, trying not to run to the nearest chair before collapsing into it.

Bob took over with the professionalism he'd gained over the years. His booming voice resonated through the room, and there were no whispers, no chitchat, only rapt attention. Jack sat in amazement—only wishing he could command such a presence.

He sat slightly slumped over, his arms leaning across his knees, trying to get his heart rate back down. It was racing not just from his attempt to speak to the crowd, but in anticipation. Somewhere down in the middle of that list was the

136

name Carillon DeVries. And he was dying to know if it was her. And if not, who exactly she was.

But much to his disappointment, the name and assignment came and went with no indication of the person's identity. No, he'd just have to make his rounds of the place and see where she might be. He still had an inkling that name belonged to her, so he'd try the gift shop first. That's where he'd assigned Carillon—whoever she was.

When Bob had finished going through the list, he dismissed the group to head to their new locations to start training immediately. Jack stood and tried to nonchalantly look in that girl's direction. She was near the back, sitting with a couple of the other younger members of the group—ones who looked to be less than thrilled to be here. There were always those in the group. Not all came voluntarily.

When he saw them making small talk, he casually started for the back of the room. Maybe he'd overhear her name in the conversation. A couple of times, he even saw her smile. It was a beautiful smile. . .if somewhat subdued.

Shouldering his way past a small clump of employees, he managed to slip through the door just behind the young women. With their attention ahead of them, he could follow undetected. Instead he concentrated on what their voices were saying.

"I'm in the restaurant," one girl mentioned, seeming apathetic to the placement.

"I got stuck at some farmhouse," another complained.

Then she spoke. "I guess mine isn't too bad. Clerking in the gift shop."

His heart lifted a fraction. He'd been right. It was her.

"Or," she continued with a light laugh, "should I say 'the g–g–g–gift sh–sh–shop.' "

Her two companions laughed with her as they streamed through the front door out onto the grassy compound.

Jack sank against a nearby wall and frowned, trying to swallow the hardness in his throat. Why the comment should matter, he didn't know. He was used to it. But for some reason, the words hurt a little more today.

※

Jack spent the remainder of the morning and a good part of the afternoon doing the animal chores at his own farmstead. It normally didn't take that long, but it was a way to kill his day. There was a lot to be done, what with the tourists beginning to arrive in less than a week. But even he couldn't fool himself out of the real reason for throwing himself into the consuming tasks. Each pitchfork full of straw, each wheelbarrow full of grain, each swing of the hammer on the split rail fence did nothing to relieve the ache in his mind—and his heart.

He was so stupid.

He'd done it again.

He'd let himself get caught up in a foolish notion. . .a dumb dream. Just like Jon always said he did. It seemed like one burning disappointment was enough to teach him a lesson for awhile. But sooner or later, his heart would run away with itself again. Letting him think he was things he was not. Things he would never be. Places he would never go. Dreams he would never accomplish.

It must have been awhile since the last time, because that one stupid comment from that unknown young woman was sending him reeling farther than he had in quite some time.

Well, buck up, Jack. You asked for it. Letting a silly name grab you and running with it. You're still the same. Always will be.

He sank one last spike into the fence, trying to release some of the pent up frustration. He knew he'd need some extra time with the Lord that night. It was the only soothing balm that ever eased the hurts—even the physical ones.

He shook his head. *Don't even go there. You don't need that on top of everything else.*

He strode toward the small barn, hammer in hand, when he saw a familiar form emerging from the trees. It was Steve. And he looked concerned.

Tossing the tool in the doorway, Jack met him halfway across the lawn with a friendly smile. "Hi. Everything. . .all. . .right?"

Steve shook his head. "It's the usual, Bud. It's just happened a little sooner than normal."

Jack nodded in understanding. Every year, without fail, there were one or two new people who invariably caused problems during their stay at Yesteryear—usually at the onset of the summer. But it ordinarily took a few days, at least.

"S–s–so who's. . .the t–troublemaker. . .this t–time?"

Steve pulled out a file and handed it to him. "A Carillon DeVries."

Jack swallowed a little hard.

"She's at the gift shop. Apparently her performance today has already proven to Ruth that she'd be less than 'ideal' in the customer relations department."

Jack glanced at the file and kneaded his temple.

"Ruth is already talking to her about it. Seeing if that would help."

He nodded as he continued to flip through the pages.

"But," Steve added, "I got the distinct impression she'd be more than a little relieved if you assigned our guest elsewhere."

Jack nodded again and released a long breath. "Okay. I–I–I'll see. . .what I–I can do."

Steve gave him a sympathetic smile and patted him on the shoulder. "Better your job than mine." He grinned and threw a wave over his shoulder as he disappeared into the thick stand of pines.

Striding toward the house, Jack tossed the papers on the table and paused at the washbasin to rinse off some of the afternoon's dust and sweat from his face and neck. He poured a glass of water from the nearby pitcher and finally realized how hungry he was. He'd worked straight through the day, not stopping for breakfast or lunch. And judging from the sinking sun, it was late afternoon.

He grabbed a thick slice of bread from the bread box and absentmindedly ripped off a bite as he plopped down on a chair, carefully spreading out the papers before him. There wasn't a lot here on Miss DeVries. It looked like it had been collected in a hurry with a lot of obvious gaps.

She was twenty years old and apparently had had a few run-ins with the law as well. Though nothing too serious was listed, it was readily apparent this was one troubled young lady. He looked for the obvious clues first.

Divorced parents? Nope. They were both listed here. Curtis and Rachel DeVries.

History of past abuse? Nothing was indicated.

Spiritual background? Ah—here might be something. According to the forms filled out by her parents, they'd accepted Jesus Christ as their Savior only about four or five years ago. He digested that for a moment. It wouldn't have been the first time he'd seen a kid who rebelled at the sudden change in their house when their parents "found God." A definite maybe there.

Siblings? Listed was one sister. Yvonne. Didn't list an age. He flipped through more of the sheets. Curiously absent was any other information regarding the sister—however old she was. Older? Younger?

He looked again.

Nope. There were pages on Curtis. Rachel. The brief one on Carillon.

No Yvonne anywhere else.

Maybe she was married and gone or something.

A sudden knock at his door made him jump. Straightening the papers, he rose and pulled open the heavy door. In the growing twilight stood Steve again, this time accompanied by Bob and a few others of the full-time staff of Yesteryear. Their faces were far from comfortable.

"W—what is it?" Jack asked.

Steve was the first to respond. "Remember that girl you were working on reassigning? Carillon DeVries?"

He nodded.

"Well," his friend continued, "Ruth had that talk with her. I guess it didn't go too well."

That didn't sound too unusual. Ordinarily those types were prone to argue. "And?" Jack prompted.

"We need your help." He threw Jack a flashlight. "She's come up missing."

✳

Carillon kept walking. Trying to ignore the mosquitos that were conveniently making her their supper. Trying to ignore the odd noises that ricocheted through the dense trees. Trying to ignore the growing dark and the fact that she had no clue where she was—much less any experience about guiding herself through the middle of nowhere. To call her a city girl would have been an understatement.

There were some things she did know, however. Namely that these people here, these "God" people, were no different from her parents and all their flaky friends from their church. In their eyes she could do no right. Ever.

She'd been stupid to stay even one night. She should have left yesterday—right away. When she'd had more time. When she could still see. The ever-growing darkness was getting more than intimidating now. She was afraid.

"Come on, Carillon," she whispered. "You can get out of here. You can find someplace. Some sort of road. Anything."

But it seemed that each step took her only deeper into unforgiving thickets of briars and branches that held all their secrets silent. The woods weren't going to tell her anything.

Then a new thought captured her and took her hostage.

This was it. This was the end.

This was her punishment. For what she'd done to Evie.

Backing herself against the rough bark of a tree, she leaned against it, her chest heaving with each ragged, painful breath. There was nowhere to go. Nowhere to hide.

Part of her wanted to sit down right there—to just give up. Give in. It was what she deserved.

But another part, unknown to her until now, urged her stumbling feet forward, willing her self-preservation. She gasped and charged blindly through the wicked branches that left their bloody mark across her face and neck and arms. And she ran. From herself. And from the demons she'd learned would never leave her alone—until they had her for themselves.

Chapter 5

They were getting close. Jack could tell. This part of the woods would never be foreign to him. It held too many memories. Too many ghosts.

For tonight he was thankful to have another reason to be out here. A different reason to trail through the darkened, tree-studded, and overgrown paths.

In the distance, he could hear the others' faint voices. "Carillon!" Her name echoed through the branches and across the night sky. Jack knew it was useless for him to try and call out anything. He'd have to rely on other means.

Father. . .You see her. You know exactly where she is. Keep her safe, Lord. And lead me to her.

That prayer internally voiced, he forged on, trying to be sensitive to the Holy Spirit's leading.

❋

Carillon sat in utter fear and misery, the damp, cold ground stealing her warmth, her security.

Her eyes shut tightly, she could hear nothing. She could see nothing. Nothing but the memories that kept swaying across her memory in a haunting waltz. . . .

"Tony, stop it," she heard herself laughing.

His disarming grin was all he needed. "Come on, your parents aren't home yet." His lips reclaimed her neck, making her squirm in pleasure.

"Knock it off." She pushed him away halfheartedly. "They aren't home. But my little sister's upstairs."

"Asleep," he reminded her as his hands started their familiar foray again.

"Tony," she murmured, fully enjoying the whole forbidden aspect of his being there.

That's when he stopped.

"Did you hear that?" he asked, frowning in concentration.

Carillon laughed. "Hear what?" She listened for a moment, then giggled once more. "Now you're paranoid, Mister. Come on. . . ." She invited his attentions, enjoying baiting him again and again.

He kissed her somewhat distractedly.

She slumped against the back of the couch and glared at him. "What is your problem?"

"Lon, I'm serious. I think I heard something."

"My parents are not home."

141

"Not that. Something else."

She slid him a look out of the corner of her eye and smiled slyly. "All right. Fine. I'll go up and see if Evie is spying on us if you're so convinced." She heaved herself up from the leather sofa and straightened her rumpled T-shirt before heading toward the stairs. "But you'd better still be here when I come back down."

"Oh, I will." His seductive smile promised nothing less than that.

Carillon took the stairs two at a time, the sound of her footsteps lost in the plush carpet. She was in a hurry. Check on Evie, close her door tighter, and get back down to Tony before her parents got home.

As she approached the end of the hall, she saw her sister's door was open a crack, just as she'd left it after tucking her in. She started to turn around, certain that nothing or no one had moved since her last trip upstairs.

But something made her decide to peek in—just to make sure.

Easing the door open, she let her eyes wander across the six-year-old's room, the floor strewn with a jungle of stuffed animals, each creature subtly illuminated by the bedside nightlight.

A familiar lump was buried under the pale pink comforter. Carillon smiled. How the kid could sleep with her head totally covered was beyond her. She slipped into the room, just to adjust the blankets around the sleeping form.

She gently pulled back the hem of the comforter, anticipating her baby sister's angelic face reposed in sleep.

Two large, black, unblinking eyes stared back.

Carillon gasped and jumped back.

Then laughed.

Stealthily waiting under the covers was none other than Riley—Evie's over-grown, overstuffed, over-loved brown teddy bear. She tossed him aside and felt around the bed clothes for her sister.

Nothing.

Great. She was supposed to be sleeping. . .and she was probably hiding out in her walk-in closet playing with Barbies—as usual. "Evie?" She started toward the closet door. "Come on, Bug. You're supposed to be asleep."

The door was shut fast.

She yanked on the knob, awaiting her sister's shocked look upon discovery.

The closet was black.

Carillon reached over and flicked on the switch.

Nothing.

Every blouse, every toy was in its place. None telling any secrets.

An uncontrollable panic seized Carillon. She ran back into the hallway and yelled down the stairs. "Tony! Tony, get up here!"

His tall, broad form lumbered into view, the confusion evident on his handsome face. "Yeah, what?"

She gulped. "She's not here. Evie's gone."

✳

The cold was back again. At least she could feel it. Hugging her legs to her chest, Carillon edged herself closer to the tree trunk and rocked slowly back and forth. Trying to stay warm. Trying to forget. Trying to pretend she was somewhere else—someone else. Away from all the things that haunted her no matter where she went. Even here. . .in the middle of nowhere.

They were all around. She could hear them taunting her. It was only a matter of time before they reached out to take her. Only when her resolve was just weak enough.

"Oh, Evie," she whispered through numb lips. "I'm so sorry. . . ."

The lightest of sensations brushed across her arm.

With a petrified scream, she tried to leap to her feet, only to find herself tangled up with some wicked vine. It sent her crashing to the soggy earth again.

Then the light hit her, blinding her momentarily before it slid away.

Still trying to adjust to the spots in her eyes and her erratic breathing, she shielded her eyes from glare and watched as the beam swung up and around.

It illuminated those eyes. The kind eyes. The ones like Evie's.

"Are y–y–you. . .all. . .right?" His voice was barely above a whisper, but it echoed through the stillness around her. And she felt them flee—all the things that had been hounding her and haunting her.

She nodded slowly, wiping her sleeve under her nose.

His hand reached out to her. Sure. Unthreatening.

Hesitating for a split second, she finally relented and grasped it in turn. It's warmth and strength surprised her. He helped pull her to her feet and, once again, slid his own warm wraps around her shoulders.

Without another word, he led her through the maze of tangled limbs and branches. Leaving Carillon to wonder what on earth she had done to deserve being saved.

✳

He hadn't seen her since that night. Well, only in passing. She seemed to be avoiding him—if he was guessing right. Why? That he didn't know. There was a lot more to Miss Carillon DeVries than she was letting on—of that he was sure. But in the end, he reminded himself, it wasn't really his concern or his business. He'd not let himself get wrapped up in any fantasy like that again. He'd just do his job.

The last aspect of his job, relating to her anyway, was her new placement at the Mitchell House, the historic home located in the little section of Yesteryear called Liberty Town. It was, without question, the largest and most well-appointed house on the grounds. The gentleman, Ambrose Mitchell, who'd founded the sawmill, had built the place in the mid-1800s. Not much was spared in its construction.

143

And while by today's standards of a mansion, it wasn't a huge place, it was large enough—with enough antiques to make even the most experienced collector a little green with envy.

Miss DeVries's new job as a "maid" at the Mitchell House seemed like a suitable match. It didn't require her to deal with the public in any sort of interactive way; it kept her in a place where there were a lot of people, lest she try and run off again. And it kept her busy with light duties of cleaning and other appropriate tasks suited to the era of the home.

It was three days into the placement, and so far, so good. Everything else at Yesteryear seemed to be running like a well-oiled machine. Jack was in Bob's office, going over the plans for the annual employee picnic they held at the lake the beginning of every summer. They were just about to discuss the merits of renting some rowboats when the door flew open.

Betty Haskins, the older woman in charge of collecting, cataloging, and caring for the numerous antiques at the variety of sites, pushed into the room, her eyes ablaze. "I tried to overlook it for awhile, Bob. Thought it might have been coincidence. But no longer. She has got to go!"

Bob raised his brows and exchanged a look with Jack. "Uh, have a seat, Betty."

She lowered her reed-slim frame into the wooden chair, her back stiff as a ramrod.

"What seems to be the problem?"

"That DeVries girl! She's robbing us blind!"

Jack felt his heart sink, and he released a slow breath, trying to ignore Bob's second glance at him.

"Slow down, Betty. Why don't you start from the beginning?"

"Well, as you know, we have that wonderful set of Spode china in the Mitchells' cabinet. In addition to the silver service and place setting that are under the glass case."

Bob nodded.

"There are pieces missing."

"How many?"

"Three cups and saucers, the sugar and creamer set, and at least half a dozen of the utensils." She threw an accusatory glare at Jack. "And it's been since she's been there."

"You can't go accusing people until we know for sure," Bob patiently reminded the pinched-faced woman. "Are you sure they haven't simply been misplaced?"

She looked highly offended. "They are nowhere to be found. They are gone. Only I have the key to those cupboards. And only the maid staff has access to my office." She nodded as if that settled the whole issue. Her attention fell back on Jack, and her eyes all but dared him with the unspoken question: *What are you going to do about it?*

"All right, Betty," Bob said on a sigh. "Thank you for bringing this to our attention. We'll look into it."

She rose abruptly from her chair. "Shall I begin filling out the insurance paperwork?"

Bob and Jack exchanged looks again.

"No," the older man said. "Let's hold off awhile. Just to see if anything turns up."

She still didn't leave. After a long silence, she piped up again. "And what about her?"

Bob tried to look busy with paperwork. "Jack will look into it."

She looked doubtful, but turned and whisked out the door with her usual efficiency, closing it tightly behind her.

Jack slunk back against the wall and rubbed his suddenly tired eyes.

Bob looked at him with raised brows. He didn't need to ask.

"I–I–I'll go. . .t–t–talk to. . .her."

Bob nodded. "Let me know how it goes." He returned his attention to his desk, obviously relieved not to have to deal with these sticky personnel issues.

The walk from Bob's office to Liberty Town took Jack only about five minutes—not nearly enough time for him to compile any sort of plan as to what he would say or ask of the young woman.

The familiar clangs of iron upon iron came from Paul's blacksmith shop, the smell of hot metal wafting out on the early summer breeze. Jack wished he had a moment to stop and talk to his friend—he was always full of good, godly counsel. But based on Betty's present state of mind, he thought he'd better get this done.

He marched past the small church, the general store, the inn, and a variety of other houses, slowly approaching the Mitchell House, which lay at the end of the short, dusty main street. Out in the yard, he saw Carla hanging the feather pillows on the line, beating them with the iron tool designed for the task of airing and cleaning the plump, white bags. She smiled warmly at Jack. "Morning," she said.

He nodded in return. "D–do you know. . .where I–I—can. . . fffind—"

"Miss DeVries?" she finished for him.

Jack nodded. It wasn't unusual for people to try and finish his sentences for him. In the beginning it had irritated him. But as he grew older, he realized they were only trying to help. The only time it caused problems was when they totally guessed wrong at the outcome of the sentence he was trying to utter. But he usually managed to get his point across.

Today, Carla already knew.

He nodded again.

"She's upstairs, making the beds, I think."

145

He smiled a thank-you and headed toward the rear entrance of the two-story white house. It was unusually quiet in the kitchen. Lynette, the house cook, who was normally in a bubbly mood, merely nodded at him over the pot of soup she was stirring as he passed through. He guessed that the whole house was in a state of discomfort due to the current circumstances.

With another sigh, he ascended the servant's steep stairs leading from the kitchen to the upstairs bedrooms. In the main hallway, he noticed the breeze wafting in, airing out the stale smell of the old house. From down the corridor, he heard the shuffling sounds of feet on the hardwood floor.

Breathing a quick prayer for wisdom and direction, he started down the hall. She was in the second bedroom, carefully making the bed. Really carefully.

He wasn't sure what it was, but something made him stop, unnoticed, and just watch her for a time.

As she stood in the middle of the bedroom that had belonged to Ambrose Mitchell's young daughter, surrounded by a wooden rocking horse and an assortment of faded china dolls, she almost looked like a little girl herself.

Moving around with a quiet air, she tucked each corner of the intricately stitched quilt firmly into place around the sleigh bed's ornate head and footboard. Then she scooped up a handful of crude stuffed animals made from old flannel with spare buttons for eyes and gently, but methodically, placed them at the head of the bed, right in front of the recently fluffed pillows.

She stepped back and stared at them for a time. Silent.

Her face wasn't visible. . .and he wished he could see some sort of expression. Some reason for her unlikely attention to this little detail.

Finally, his conscience got the better of him. Before she turned around and actually caught him staring, he thought he'd better make his presence known.

Shuffling his feet, he cleared his throat as though he'd just happened upon the scene.

She whirled around a little too quickly. Like she'd been caught at something. And then her expression changed—like she'd just seen a ghost. Almost the way she'd looked when he'd found her that night in the woods.

But the look disappeared quickly. Just as it had that night once they'd come back to the compound. There'd been no thank-you. No gratitude. No words at all. She'd simply walked into her room and shut the door.

"Yes?" she asked him, the hesitation in her voice obvious.

"C–could I–I–I sssp—Could. . .I–I–. . .talk. . .to you?"

A hardness fell across her delicate features. Her back stiffened. Smoothing out the black skirt of her maid's uniform, she stepped purposefully toward the door, brushed past him, and headed down the stairs.

At first he thought she was just leaving. Period. He double-timed it down the steps after her but slowed when he saw her out the kitchen window, waiting in the corner of the yard by the white-picket fence.

Lynette, the cook, gave him another odd look as he passed by the stove. He ignored it this time and headed straight for Carillon. Her back was toward him, as she faced the small village's freshly planted fields just beyond them.

"They think I took them, don't they?" Her voice was quiet and strong all at the same time.

Jack dug the toe of his work boot into the dusty dirt beneath the grass. "I–i–it ssseems. . .that. . .way."

She turned around. Jack was surprised to find a hint of redness in her deep-set blue eyes. "I know. I've heard the other girls talking." She crossed her arms and let out a long, frustrated breath.

"D–d–did. . .you?" He knew he had to ask, in spite of the discomfort it caused him.

She leveled a disdainful glare at him. "No."

Jack nodded and cleared his throat, wondering how to go about this next part.

"But," she jumped in instead, almost as if reading his thoughts, "that doesn't matter, does it?"

He slowly shook his head. "I–I–I'm afraid not. F–f–for now. . .I'll h–h–have to. . .move you. . .ssssomeplace. . .else."

She began to untie the lacy white apron covering her skirt, yanking the strings more forcefully than necessary. "Fine." She threw the apron over the nearby fence. "Where do I get banished to now?"

Jack ran his hand through his hair. Man, this was a lot harder than usual. "I–I'll have t–to get. . .back t–t–to you."

"Why?" she yelled, seeming to suddenly explode. "Why am I even here? No one likes me. No one wants me here. No one believes me! What do I have to do or say to make you understand?"

He rubbed uncomfortably at his jaw, unsure how to handle this little outburst.

"Don't you understand?" she asked again. She moved in closer. "Here, decipher this." Her eyes took on a hard edginess. "I–I–I," she stammered, "d–d–didn't. . . t–t–take the ssssstupid c–c–c–cups!"

Jack knew he willed his face not to change expression. He'd had enough practice at that. All the way through school as a kid. Even into adulthood. But he also knew he couldn't will away the fraction of his soul that wilted every time it happened. And this time especially. What was it about this woman that made him so sensitive. . . ? *God, give me patience. Give me Your patience. Your grace.*

He stood his ground and waited for her tirade to end.

Nothing else came.

"I–I–I'll. . .meet you. . .at the m–m–main office. One hour."

He turned and walked away, wondering if she'd even show up.

Chapter 6

Well, she surprised him. She actually showed up.

Her face was still unreadable, and Jack couldn't help but assume that she'd made it her life's work perfecting that nonchalance. But he also knew there was something else there. Something of which he'd seen only a glimpse—but it was there nonetheless.

Still smarting somewhat from her earlier imitation, he found it a little easier to erect a more objective frame of mind and a professional attitude. Now, if only his ridiculous speech would allow him some reprieve. . . .

They were in Bob's office, Carillon seated haphazardly in the small chair in front of the desk. Jack stood off to one side of the overloaded desk of papers—preferring not to take the seat in any "authoritative, dictatorial" position. And as long as he had the papers in his hands, he might as well get this done.

"Th–th–there is. . .one p–p–position left. . . ."

"Cleaning toilets?" she asked smartly.

He ignored the comment.

"A ssssschool. Y–you. . .w–w–would be. . .the. . .t–t–t–teacher."

"A teacher?" The level of surprise in her voice nearly matched the arch of her back as she straightened up quickly. "Like, with kids?"

"Sssssort of."

Her head shook vehemently. "I don't think that's such a good—"

He halted her protest with an upraised index finger. "Not. . .k–kids all. . . th–th–the. . .time. Only. . .sssspecial days."

She settled back in the chair slightly, but the frown didn't leave her heart-shaped face.

"Y–y–you'll m–mostly. . .give. . .t–t–tours of. . .the. . .sssssschool to. . .visitors." He hoped that was clear enough. In addition, he'd written out what the expectations were for the role of the small town's "schoolmarm." It was easier than his trying to stutter through the whole scenario. He handed her the papers. . .and waited.

Was it his imagination, or did her hands shake ever so slightly as she took them?

"Where is the school?" she asked after a long silence. "I don't recall seeing it in the town."

"I–it's a. . .ways. . .out. P–p–past the. . .fff–farm. . .fields."

Again, she sat in obvious mute misery.

He felt like he needed to say something. But what?

With a long sigh, she stood from the chair and turned toward the door. "Well, thanks so much." The derision in her tone was less than subtle.

"I–I–I'm. . .sssssssorry. Ab–bout. . .the. . .l–l–last job."

She turned back toward him. "Are you?" She huffed in disbelief. "I find that a little hard to believe. It seems everyone around here is just glad to be rid of me. Why should you be any different?"

Jack swallowed and glanced at his boots before returning a concerned look. He shrugged. "I. . .hope I. . .am."

"Right." She leaned toward the awaiting door again.

Say something, an unprompted voice urged him. *Go ahead. . .mention it.* He frowned at the odd direction, but delved in anyway.

"Ssssssome. . .day," he interrupted her escape, "I–I'd like. . .t–t–to hear about. . . y–your ssssister."

She froze in her tracks.

It was some time before she actually turned back toward him.

When she finally did, her face was a mixture of shock, anger, and. . .guilt?

"How did you know about my sister?" she asked, her voice barely above a whisper.

He nodded toward the file on the desk. "Y–y–your. . .file."

Her eyes narrowed as she threw a penetrating gaze toward the brown case. "What did it say?"

He picked up the papers and flipped through them. "Just. . .th–th–that you. . . have a ssssssister." He looked at the sheet again. "Yvonne?"

Her face paled at the mention of the name.

Something inside of Jack clicked with realization.

This was it.

This was the reason for her being here. For her surliness. For that tough facade that she'd managed to create over. . .whatever it was.

Gripping her handful of papers until her knuckles turned white, she wrenched open the door and purposefully walked out of the office, leaving the door agape behind her.

And leaving Jack to wonder all the more. What was that pain behind her clouded eyes?

Without a moment's hesitation, he scanned the file once more and found it. Phone number. He sat down at Bob's desk and lifted the receiver from the cradle.

✳

Carillon took her time walking from the office back through Liberty Town. Indeed, it seemed as if her feet were on autopilot. They had to have been because her mind was certainly nowhere on her surroundings.

He knew about Evie. But how much? And how many others knew?

No wonder they wanted her out of every place he tried to place her. . . . She was a danger—out and out.

She'd already passed by the majority of the places on Main Street when she began to round the corner around Mitchell House. Her thoughts temporarily withdrawn from the past, she noticed several of the maids trying not to peer too obviously in her direction. They were doing a lousy job at it. The only one who seemed to be paying her absolutely no mind at all was the cook—she busily kept digging around in the fenced garden, her head never lifting once.

Carillon was secretly grateful.

Once she'd passed the perimeter of the yard, she gathered herself together enough to glance at the papers Jack had given her. There was supposed to be a map marking the spot of the school in relation to Liberty Town.

Jack.

If her mind had not been in such an upheaval, she might have laughed at the thought of him. Of her. Here she'd gone and pinned her hopes of escape on that young man. How far had that gotten her? Walking from Liberty Town to a remote schoolhouse—that's where.

Training her mind away from the disturbing mention of her sister, she tried to formulate a new plan. A new plan for getting out of here. Maybe this new posting was her unencumbered escape in hiding.

No people around.

Plenty of time to scout out the surrounding area—so she'd not be caught in the woods like the last time.

No, this could well be it. All she had to do was be patient. Be patient—and think. Think hard. She could—no, she would get herself out of this. Once and for all.

※

Jack didn't hear him enter.

He still sat at the desk. His head in his hands. The folder in front of him. His thoughts in an unusual mess.

"Jack?"

Bob's low voice startled him back to reality. He jerked up his head and dropped his hands onto the papers before him.

"Everything all right?" The older man's whiskered face registered immediate concern as he hung up his hat and sat in the remaining small chair.

Jack jumped up, pushing the papers quickly together. "Ssssssorry. Here's. . . your. . .ch–ch–chair."

Bob waved it off, but the worry didn't leave his eyes. "What's up?"

Jack finished collecting the file and tapped it smartly against the metal desk. "I–I–I'm not. . .sure."

His boss remained pensive. "Does it have something to do with Miss DeVries?"

A nod.

"She didn't take the news well?"

He shrugged. "About. . .h–h–h–how I. . .g–guessed. . .she would."

"But?"

Jack frowned and bit on his lower lip for a moment, trying to form some sort of response. One that might make sense. . .even when none of it did to him yet. "Th–th–there's ssssomething. . .else. Why. . .she's. . .here." He let out a long breath. "I. . .almost. . .c–c–called her. . .p–p–parents. To. . .ffff–find out. . .ssssome. . . things."

"Almost?"

He shook his head. "Couldn't. Ssssomething. . .told me. . .n–not to."

"Something?" Bob cocked his head in curiosity. "Or Someone?"

Jack gave him a halfhearted grin. "Rrrr–right."

The older man eased up from the chair and rounded the desk, clapping a huge supportive hand on Jack's shoulder. "Well, then, Jack, I'd say you're on the right track. You usually have a pretty keen sense about these things."

He shot him a doubtful look.

"Well. . .you with some help from the Lord then."

This time he nodded.

As Bob took his seat, Jack headed for the door, beginning again to try to sort out the whole situation.

"Jack?"

He turned back, brows raised in question.

Bob's large, round fingers kneaded his glistening forehead for a second or two. "There is some concern—among the other staff members."

Jack turned fully around.

"They're questioning the wisdom of placing Miss DeVries in such a remote spot."

"W–w–well. . .they. . .d–didn't want. . .her w–w–w–with others."

"True, true. But they're worrying more about another escape attempt. Or her trying to stash more things she might have taken."

Unaccountably, Jack bristled. "Sh–sh–she d–didn't. . .take. . .those."

The man's eyebrows rose a fraction. "Are you sure?"

Shuffling his feet, Jack swallowed hard. "No. . .proof. B–but I. . .j–j–just know."

"I see." He folded his hands together patiently. "Any idea where those things disappeared to then?"

Jack shook his head miserably.

"What about the other concern? Her possible future attempts to run off? Do you have any 'feelings' along that line?"

Again, he had to indicate that he didn't know.

"Jack," Bob began—he was using that professional voice he got when he was overly concerned about something. "I'm going to give this about a week. If she can prove that she can stick to this and doesn't cause any more problems, I'll let her stay. Otherwise, you know what our choices are."

This time Jack nodded. He knew. He'd seen it done. Not often, but done nonetheless.

He just hated to think of Carillon as being that kind of troublemaker. There was a definite reason she was supposed to be here. He knew it. He could feel it. If only he could help her find it.

"That's it," Bob said quietly.

Shaking himself out of his reverie, Jack shifted the file in his arms and nodded. He turned and left. His heart. . .heavy.

✳

Her legs were already tired, and the mosquitoes were starting to get downright vicious. Carillon kept trudging through the knee-high grasses, the path to wherever she was going long since lost in the disuse of the place.

Several minutes later, she saw it.

A small clearing amid a stand of trees. Two small, white buildings looking lonely and forlorn. Brushing a strand of hair out of her eyes, she looked on in chagrin. Then she turned and looked behind her. Liberty Town was out of sight, the path disappearing around the stand of woods curving off to her right.

With a long sigh, she faced the bleak-looking picture before her. The schoolhouse was obviously the bigger of the two. . .a large set of double doors fronting the entrance. The other, smaller, square construction sat fifty feet or so from the school. And this was. . . ?

Carillon glanced through the papers Jack had given her once more. Where was that map? The directions? Nearly losing her grip as she simultaneously sorted papers and swatted at persistent mosquitoes, she at last found the page.

Sure enough. Two buildings were indicated.

One schoolhouse.

One teacherage.

Teacherage?

What on earth was a teacherage. . . ?

A sudden yip and howl from somewhere entirely too close echoed in her ear, sending a blood-chilling shiver down her spine.

Tripping over her own feet in clumsy fear, Carillon ran to the smaller of the two outposts.

Another yip, from somewhere slightly farther off, answered the first.

By the time she reached the small door, she was completely out of breath and her heart was racing so fast it hurt. Knowing no greater relief than when the knob turned under her hand, she slipped into the little house and slammed the door behind her.

152

The next few eternal seconds were spent trying to catch her breath, slow down her racing pulse, and carefully listening for any more unfamiliar and unwelcome sounds from outside.

None seemed to come.

Allowing herself a slight breath of respite, she took a moment to take in the decor of the one-room building.

It was obviously a living quarters.

And it had obviously been visited recently. Funny she hadn't noticed any tracks through that long grass. . . .

Even so, the small bed was crisply made with a rustic quilt and fresh white sheets. On one side of the bed stood an old ladder-back chair. Above it were several hooks hanging at different intervals on the rough planked wall—apparently her closet.

She turned and assessed the remainder of the small room. Two windows flanked the east and west walls. In the opposite corner stood an old woodstove, a fresh pile of firewood stacked neatly by its side. A small sideboard that must have done double duty as a cupboard and a sink with the graniteware tub on top of it. Closer to her, a rather rickety-looking table, recently laden with fresh bread, cheese, and a pitcher of water, and two more ladder-back chairs completed the furnishings. In their entirety.

No bathroom.

She'd kind of expected that. But to have to trek to an outhouse when she was way out—

The high-pitched yipping ricocheted about her again.

Suddenly overcome with fear and complete misery, Carillon sat on the edge of the bed, her nails digging into the thin mattress. She'd never felt so alone. . . . In a split second her tortured thoughts flew to Evie. Was this how she had felt? Had she been this afraid? Felt this alone?

Unbidden, the tears began to trail down her cheeks, the first in a long, long time. "Oh, Evie," she whispered to the silence. "I'm so sorry. I'm so sorry I wasn't there for you. . .when I should have been." The sobs caught in her throat, making it ache in a way it never had before.

All Carillon could do was to lie down on the wind-dried quilt and let the consuming tears keep flowing. There was no stopping them. No stopping the pain.

All she knew was that she wanted to die.

Chapter 7

Sutter's Lake was really more of a glorified pond. But it was cold, and wet, and welcome on humid summer days like this one. Jack helped unload the last of the canoes, setting them along the sandy edge of the brownish water. The June day was shaping up into a hot one already, and he was finally beginning to have hope that the crops might be all right.

In between all those thoughts and his own chores at the farmstead where he stayed, his mind kept racing back to Carillon DeVries. On the guise of readying the schoolhouse for the next week's visitors, he trekked over to her area almost daily. In truth there was a lot that needed doing on the old building.

But in all his trips and work around it, he'd yet to see her.

Well, up close anyway.

On a few occasions he'd get the distinct feeling that he was being watched. He'd nonchalantly step back down the ladder to retrieve more nails for his pouch or something and casually slide a glance toward the teacherage. A flicker of movement at the window was all he'd glimpse. She never came out. Never spoke to him. Nothing.

But she'd also not caused any more problems. . .that he'd heard about. Bob seemed to have forgotten about the threatening prospect of sending her away. Inwardly Jack was relieved—he still sensed that urgency from within. She needed to be here. But mingled with that relief was trepidation—a feeling his flesh knew too well by now. That part of him still ached at the bitterness and resentment she seemed to harbor toward him. And he was at a loss as to why. . . or what to do about it.

In the end, he did all he knew to do. He gave it to God and prayed that even if he never uncovered the reason, she'd know His peace. Somehow. Sometime.

"Jack!" A voice carried across the small body of water.

He glanced up from straightening the last canoe and waved at Carla, the Mitchell House maid.

"Save me a ride, okay?"

He grinned and sent her an informal salute. It had become a yearly tradition since Carla had started working at Yesteryear. They'd trek out in the water one last time before the boats were all loaded up. He wasn't sure how it started or why. . .but they always had a nice time. Sometimes chatting amiably, other times just sitting in companionable silence.

Of all the young women at Yesteryear, Carla was the only one with whom Jack felt somewhat comfortable. Maybe it was because she'd looked past his stutter from the first moment they'd met, whereas with the others, they took on that familiar discomfort until they'd gotten to know him well.

She was also, as a fellow farm kid, one of the few people who understood his frustrations that seemed to resurface regularly—especially in the springtime. It never failed. As soon as the spring sunshine would hit the black earth, sending the lingering aroma wafting around on the light breezes, it would come. That old desire.

To turn over the earth and plant a new seed. To begin anew.

To see it grow, green and proud.

To harvest it at its fruition.

To take the bounty from God's creation and make it a living.

Even now he sighed at the memory. In spite of the fact that it had been nearly ten years since he'd actively farmed, he could remember every nuance, every chore, every sensation related to each aspect of the life.

It wasn't a place he usually dwelt on long, though. For with those fond memories came also the not so fond. The pain. The loneliness. The despair. The sheer disappointment. . .in himself and in his family.

"Hey, Jack!" Paul was headed in his direction.

Jack looked up, grateful for the mental intrusion, and smiled at his friend. He fought another pang of temporary envy as he watched the towering, muscular form of the blacksmith striding toward him, clad only in his swim trunks.

He had no reason to harbor grudging feelings toward the man. Paul had never lorded his size over Jack or anyone else. It was just one more issue that seemed to creep up when Jack's memories were centered on his past.

He tried not to think about his feelings as he straightened his T-shirt over his own slim frame and clasped Paul's hand in a friendly grip. "Rrrr–ready. . .for a. . .sssswim I. . .see."

"You got it! Where's everybody else?"

Jack shrugged. "Ssssstill b–b–bringing the. . .food. . .I guess."

"Awesome! I'm starved." Paul grinned and immediately began slipping off his tennis shoes. Two seconds later, the tall blond was cavorting in the water, yelling for some of the others approaching to join him.

It wasn't long before the entire assembly of Yesteryear's workers and employees joined each other around the quietly lapping shores of Sutter's Lake. The gathering marked the beginning of their summer season—one filled with hard work, new beginnings, new friendships, and a lot of growth for many of those in attendance.

Jack couldn't help but smile as he watched several of the newcomers laughing around the smattering of picnic tables. Already healing had begun. It was the primary purpose of Yesteryear, one in which he couldn't deny his pride. If it could help only a few. . .just to keep those hurts from sprouting into long-term hardships. And ending in a tragic situation like that of his older brother, Jon.

The mere thought of his brother brought back a host of different visions, none of which were too appealing. He shook his head. If only there'd been a place like Yesteryear for Jon. And his father.

※

Carillon had gotten brave enough over the past few days to actually leave the front door of her little house open. The stifling air swarming around its small interior was too overwhelming without some fresh breeze. But there was no question as to when it got shut. As soon as dusk threatened on the western horizon, the wood-paneled door would be latched securely—heat and humidity or not. No wolves were going to get her.

She'd already lost count of the days while being in this isolated spot. The only things that seemed to divide her awareness of the times were Jack's regular, daily visits to the schoolhouse. To her surprise, he never approached her new little home, instead keeping himself busy hammering, nailing, repairing, and cleaning up in general around the little school.

An unaccountable shyness had prevented her from saying anything to him, either. She couldn't quite place her finger on it. At first, she thought it was merely the anger and frustration she'd felt toward all the people who seemed determined to get her.

But if she were to be totally honest with herself, she somehow knew she couldn't blame him for any of that. He'd just been doing his job when he'd reassigned her here.

Then there was the issue of those eyes. Those golden brown pools of emotion that held the uncanny ability to look straight through her. Too scary.

She knew her plan to figure out the layout of this place and all its surrounding land needed to be dealt with soon—before she lost her nerve. But realizing that in Jack Tate lay the only accessible resource for doing so, she found herself putting it off. She needed to steel herself.

So while she waited for that to happen, she took some opportunities to poke around in the schoolhouse when he'd left after his few hours' work. The wood floor, swept clean, supported a handful of simple wooden benches and crude desks. An oversized map of the state of Wisconsin hung on the otherwise sparsely occupied wall. A meager blackboard flanked it on one side, her own small teacher's desk on the other.

The outstanding feature in the one-room school was the huge wood-burning stove, its long black pipe snaking upward and then across the length of the rectangular room. Carillon, more than once, was incredibly grateful that it wasn't the season where she needed to feed the thing. She'd already discovered that nuisance in her own dwelling. After countless burned fingers and nearly smoking herself out of the place, she decided she could live on sandwich makings alone. Hot food, at the moment, was overrated.

But the most unusual find didn't come until the second or third day. And she hadn't even been looking for it.

She'd gone to hang up one of her new "schoolteacher" dresses on the hooks beside her bed. To her amazement, it fell to the floor. Not just the dress, but the whole hook—and a small portion of the paneling behind it.

Berating herself for having already made a mess that would need repair, probably by Jack, she picked up the chunk of wood, determined to refasten it somehow on her own.

That's when she saw them.

Between the inner and outer walls, lying snugly against a board, were two very old, very dusty, leather-bound books.

Curious, she slid her hand into the thin opening, wrinkling her nose when a handful of cobwebs followed. Gently cleaning off the covers, she stared at the ancient volumes, intrigued.

Easing open one of the fragile covers, she squinted at the faded blue script:

Madeline Whitcomb
15 August 1853

Obviously some sort of journal. Carillon flipped through the pages. A good many of them were filled. August, into September. . .she scanned the end. The last entry was from the beginning of June of the next year.

Laying it aside, she picked up the second little book. The cracked and faded black leather felt rough under her fingertips. Aged gold lettering centered the front cover: Holy Bible.

With a frown, she laid it back on the table. And stared at it for awhile. The old feelings of anger and inadequacy surfaced.

If it hadn't been such a ridiculous notion, she might have attributed its presence there to her parents. But that was ridiculous. They hadn't known where she was going. Where she'd be.

Nonetheless, she pushed the book farther back on the table and picked up the journal. With nothing else to fill her time, this looked the more interesting of the two volumes.

But if Carillon thought she was going to get away from God or religion, she was mistaken. Apparently, Miss Whitcomb, whom she discovered to have been the teacher at this very school in 1853, proved to be more than religious herself. More often than not, her entries were feelings, thoughts, poetry, and prayers all mingled together.

Carillon might have set it aside were it not for the intriguing manner of the woman's observations on other matters.

The teacher, whatever her age might have been, obviously had been lonely. To deal with her feelings of isolation, Madeline had listed several Scripture verses. Tempted to skip over the words initially, Carillon found herself going back and reading them anyway—simply because of the soothing effect they seemed to have had on Miss Whitcomb's later entries:

> *He shall not be afraid of evil tidings: his heart is fixed, trusting in the Lord.* (Psalm 112:7)
> *Fear thou not; for I am with thee: be not dismayed; for I am thy God; I will strengthen thee; yea, I will help thee; yea, I will uphold thee with the right hand of my righteousness.* (Isaiah 41:10)
> *The Lord is my strength and my shield; my heart trusted in Him, and I am helped: therefore my heart greatly rejoiceth; and with my song will I praise Him.* (Psalm 28:7)

Carillon read the words with a distant, skeptical interest. Partially because of the sheer engaging personality of the woman who wrote it. . .and partially because, for some weird reason, it made Carillon think of Evie.

Even more strange, her fear of the loneliness that had enveloped her the first day or so had gradually given way to some bizarre form of exhaustion. She found herself sleeping more often than not. And while the nightmares and visions of Evie still floated through her mind, she was able to awaken and for the first time in a long time differentiate between her present surroundings and the awful places of the past.

Yet it was one of those places that kept her at the teacherage today—when she knew full well the others were having their picnic at a nearby lake. That was a place where she needn't go. Ever. No matter what Madeline Whitcomb said about her "strength."

※

"I'll just wait here," Carla offered.

Jack turned back from his trek through the tall grass, his look questioning. "You. . .sure?"

She nodded as she glanced over his shoulder at the schoolhouse. "I don't think she likes me much."

Jack had to chuckle, in spite of it all. "Sh–sh–she. . .doesn't. . .l–like me. . . much. . .either."

Carla still shrugged. "You go ahead. I'll wait here until you get back."

He tilted his head in acquiescence and proceeded toward the small building. He wasn't looking forward to this. At all. It had been Bob's idea to send him over to check on Miss DeVries, since she'd flatly declined the invitation to join the others this afternoon.

Expecting the door might be slammed in his face—if she opened it at all— he took a deep breath and stepped onto the small stoop. He rapped his knuckles on the door frame and tried to think of what he might say if she answered.

He didn't have much time.

The door squeaked open fairly quickly, and her blue eyes peered out at him, full of questions and curiosity. "Yes?"

He swallowed. "J–j–just. . .sssseeing how. . .you're. . .d–d–d–doing."

"Why?"

That threw him. "Uh. . .it's. . .m–my. . .job."

Her unblinking eyes assessed his for a moment before quickly turning away. "I didn't feel much like picnicking."

"O. . .kay."

The mute, discomforting silence stood between them like a solid brick wall.

"Any. . .th–th–thing. . .you. . .need?" he asked, trying to ignore the feeling of total failure that was squeezing him from every side.

"I don't believe so."

He gave her a perfunctory nod and stepped off the stoop. Guess that about ended it then.

She shut the door.

Turning, he trekked back to where Carla stood waiting in the growing shadow of the tall pines.

"Social thing, isn't she?" Carla asked.

Jack threw her a sad sort of smile. "C–c–come on. L–let's. . .get. . .going. M–mosquitoes will. . .be. . .out ssssoon."

Any other comments were lost in the quiet, but Jack couldn't shake the awful feeling that he was missing something about that girl. . .they were all missing something.

※

Standing a good distance from the window pane, Carillon watched them walk away. Wondering why she'd never find her place in the world. And wondering why she should even care. . .especially since Evie's death rested on her shoulders.

She was where she should be. Alone.

Just as her sister had been at the end.

Chapter 8

C arillon reread the entry she'd already read several times:

What a shock to find such a haven.

I'd not even been looking for it. But there it sat. At the edge of the woods, its long, fertile fields wrapped around a quaint white house and barn.

Why hadn't I known that this place even existed? Do they have children who attend school? Is there a wife here whom I could befriend? It's so close—it would be a shame not to strike up some sort of friendship with the owners. I wonder who they are?

Such a lovely place. And it suddenly makes my solitude here seem a little less daunting. So near. . .

Carillon lifted her eyes to watch her footing on the somewhat overgrown path trailing through the lush, deep woods.

It had been days now. Days since she'd seen anyone, including Mr. Tate. She knew the visitors had already begun arriving at Yesteryear. But she'd yet to see any make their way to her schoolhouse.

There were only two possible reasons for this that she knew of.

Either they felt the school building wasn't ready. Or she, herself, wasn't ready.

Well, she'd surprise them when they came. Unaccountably, she'd delved into the historical materials with a fervor fueled by the personal documentation in Miss Whitcomb's journal. Were a group to come through, she was confident that she could walk them through a very typical school day in 1850. And part of her longed to do that. To prove to these people that she could succeed.

With her intense interest had come another benefit. . .one that had initially escaped her notice. Her thoughts of Evie had lessened.

Oh, she still had them. But when they surfaced, they weren't accompanied by that feeling of utter despair. The guilt was still there, though. So she tried to push thoughts of Evie out of her mind and refocus her attention on the musings of Madeline Whitcomb.

Musings. . .It was the latest of those musings that had Carillon traipsing through this dense forest, trying to find a little set of farm buildings that, in all probability, were no longer standing. Something spurred her on anyway.

Clutching the journal in one hand and brushing aside insistent branches with the other, she kept walking, her eyes peeled for any clearing that might be on the horizon.

When it seemed she'd been battling the shrubs and overhanging branches for too long and that perhaps the place no longer existed, she stopped and took a deep breath. Smoothing a wayward strand of hair that had escaped from the combs holding it back, she glanced once more at Madeline's description, then turned and did a full scan of the area around her.

She couldn't see anything beyond the brambles and trees.

Then something flashed in the corner of her vision.

Pivoting in its direction, she strained to see it again. Nothing.

She shifted her weight and leaned to one side.

There it was again. A faint flicker. Like the sunshine reflecting off an object.

She strode in that direction.

Amazingly, in just a few steps, she found herself face-to-face with a large open area. One that had been totally disguised by the dense overgrowth and the waist-high grasses covering the small meadow.

A short distance past the waving blades of grass and heads of wildflowers they stood. A small white house. A larger white barn. Each looking regal amid the wild beauty of the woods but also seeming pathetic and worn from the unforgiving elements of time and weather.

This was it. It had to be.

The journal temporarily forgotten, Carillon waded through the quiet rustling weeds, the birds the only accompaniment to the otherwise bright summer afternoon. When she'd come within fifty feet or so of the house, she stopped, hesitant.

Insistent curiosity propelled her feet closer until she was maybe fifteen or twenty feet from the front door.

The covered porch sagged at one corner, and several of the spindles lining the rail were missing. Only traces of its previous white clung in stubborn patches to the gray, weather-beaten wood. Several windows were broken or missing altogether. She cast a glance at the second-story panes and realized it had been the sun's reflection against the dirty glass that had caught her attention.

Suddenly she felt extremely ill at ease—as if she were peering into someone's home, someone's privacy, even though it was more than obvious that no one had lived here for quite some time.

She almost felt as though eyes were watching her. From somewhere. . .

Carillon slowly turned and glanced back at the barn. The only movement was the constant wave of the grass and the occasional swoop of a bird as it dove from the roof onto the summer breeze.

Hesitantly, she turned back toward the now imposing house.

Part of her ached with curiosity to perhaps just step up the front stairs and peek in the front door.

But a definite sense of foreboding held her back. A sense that she wasn't supposed to be here. Wasn't welcome.

And the longer she stayed, the stronger the feeling became. Until it became overpowering. Overwhelming. Smothering. Terrifying.

Taking breaths in little gasps, Carillon turned and began walking as fast as her feet would take her through the tangle of grassy stems. She looked back just once.

Then she ran.

❈

The late afternoon sun sparked a relieved feeling in Jack. The day was done. He'd almost forgotten how much he looked forward to the end of a day here. True, he enjoyed the visitors. And working with and getting to know the staff. But there was something about completing chores at the end of the day that left him satisfied, tired—in a good way. He distinctly remembered the sensation from when his family had farmed. Granted, they got in from the barn a lot later than most people who worked a normal nine-to-five job, but with that came the distinct feeling of having really accomplished something.

He felt that here at Yesteryear—to a point. But it was never quite the same.

It was with that very feeling that he approached his small cabin, eagerly looking forward to a quiet supper and perhaps some time with a good book before falling into bed.

"Jack."

The voice startled him. He spun around to find Bob puffing his way up the path.

Jack smiled. But his face changed as Bob's expression became clear the closer he came.

Jack held open the door to his cabin and ushered his boss in silently. Whatever the problem, Jack wouldn't have to ask. Bob was never one for beating around the bush.

He took a moment to scrub up at the washbasin before taking a seat at the small table. Bob had already made himself as comfortable as his obviously troubled position allowed.

"Have you seen the DeVries girl lately?"

Jack's heart sunk a foot or two.

"No."

Bob nodded, looking pensive. "We'd thought about opening up the schoolhouse this next week as part of the tour."

Jack nodded. He'd been aware of that.

"We'll have to postpone that for awhile. . .if not indefinitely."

A painful jolt seared through Jack, though it wasn't unexpected. "W–why?"

An equally pained look covered Bob's round face. "There's more things come up missing from the Mitchell House."

Jack sighed and raked a hand through his hair. "Sh–sh–she's. . .not even. . . th–th–there. . .any. . .more."

The older man nodded. "I know. But she knows what's there." He paused and kneaded his brow. "And Betty reminded me that the day of the employee picnic, Miss DeVries declined coming. The house was empty for several hours."

Jack closed his eyes at the horrendous sound of it all. "W–weren't. . .there. . . o–o–others who. . .d–didn't. . .come?"

"Not very many. And the few who didn't were away from Yesteryear, busy with other engagements."

He released another long breath. He had to admit, it didn't sound good.

Bob leaned his weighty arms on the table. "Now, I'm not as gung-ho to jump all over this as Betty is, but I am concerned."

Jack nodded.

"Since you're the closest to her new post, I'd like you to just watch her for a few days. Okay? Keep tabs on what she does. Where she might go."

"F–f–from what. . .I–I've. . .sssseen. . .she. . .d–doesn't. . .go. . .out much."

He shrugged. "Just keep an eye out."

A nod of disturbed agreement was all Jack could muster.

"We've set up a few precautionary measures at the Mitchell place, just in case." Bob hesitated, as if carefully choosing his words. "Just in case whoever is doing this tries it again."

The two men sat in mute silence for a moment or two. Finally Bob scraped the legs of the chair across the wood plank floor, easing up in a tired, weary sort of way. "Guess I'd better go."

Again, Jack could only nod. Part of him ached too much to do anything else. He opened the door and followed the big fellow's frame out into the fast-turning twilight.

"Ssssee you. . .t–tomorrow. . .then."

Bob nodded and started down the path.

Halfway across the small yard, he turned back. "Jack?"

Jack inclined his chin in question.

"You don't think she did it. Do you?" It wasn't a question.

Throwing a look at his boots, Jack shuffled them slightly against the dusty planks of the porch. Then shook his head. "No. I. . .don't."

Bob cast his own gaze to the ground then. His broad shoulders heaved in a sigh. "I sure hope you're right."

✳

Carillon had never intended to stand there that long. She'd never even intended to come to this place. But in her rush to flee from the unknown eeriness at the

163

abandoned homestead, she'd found herself smack dab behind Jack Tate's little cabin.

She could see the light from the lantern flickering in his window, and sheer curiosity had made her keep her place. Just for a moment. Just to see what he might be doing.

But she'd never expected him to come out. And certainly not with Bob Feldman.

Stepping back behind the cover of a nearby oak, she flattened herself against the trunk and listened carefully, trying to hear over the growing chirp of the crickets.

No conversation came.

Frustrated, she leaned back around, trying to catch a glimpse of the two. From her vantage point, all she could see was Bob's large frame going down the path and Jack's thin one leaning against the post of his porch. Just from his stance, she could see he was troubled. And some undefined part of her knew that she was the reason.

She'd been about to flutter off into a host of miserable memories—wondering why she always seemed to have this effect on people—when Bob broke the evening's quiet.

"Jack?"

Startled, Carillon peered out from behind the trunk and sought out Jack's dejected form on the porch.

"You don't think she did it. Do you?"

In the awful silence following the question, she closed her eyes. She'd been right. This was about her. One more thing had happened. One more thing for which she would take the blame. Maybe she wouldn't have to worry about being here for long anyway. . . .

But it was the words that followed that startled her more than anything else. "No. I. . .don't."

That was it. Plain and simple. Jack, in his quiet, yet confident manner, had just exonerated her. Part of her warmed in a way she'd never experienced before.

She glanced in Bob's direction. Waiting. . .

"I sure hope you're right." With that, he walked away, leaving Jack to stand alone in the growing darkness.

From behind Carillon, somewhere in the deep of the forest, it came. That sound. That horrible yipping and howling.

Fear skittered up her spine, paralyzing her. What on earth was she supposed to do now?

Jack remained motionless on the front porch for a few more endless minutes, seemingly oblivious to the horrid sounds echoing through the trees.

Torn between wanting to run for the safety of his cabin and the need to keep her identity hidden, she opted for the latter. How could she explain her presence? How could she make it look like it truly was—her stumbling upon his place—as opposed to her sitting in wait. . .spying.

No. She must stay put. No matter what it meant.

How many minutes ticked by, she didn't know. With some measure of relief, she heard what sounded like the howls growing more faint. And in between her bouts of fear came the intense curiosity. She watched as Jack continued to stand, looking out into the darkness. In the very direction she needed to run in order to get to her own teacherage.

Finally, before complete blackness had fallen over the woods, Jack turned and slipped through the door of the cabin, closing it slowly behind him.

Carillon shut her eyes tight, waiting for a second or two longer.

Then, with a strength fueled only by a stronger fear, she sprinted across the grass. . .hoping. . .praying that she'd make it home.

Chapter 9

Tracking down Carillon DeVries proved to be more of a challenge than Jack anticipated. Not that she had disappeared. . .not by a long shot. Every time he unobtrusively strode by the teacherage and schoolhouse, she could be found. Sitting in the yard reading, walking around the empty classroom, shifting and rearranging miscellaneous items, or somewhere behind the door to her tiny home, the entry open to the winds of summer. But there were other times. Times when her absence was curious.

At first Jack had promptly headed for Liberty Town—Mitchell House to be precise—even though he still had that certainty in his heart that she was innocent of the accusations brought against her. But neither had she been there nor had anyone seen her.

The only one who seemed to have caught any glimpse of her was Lynette, the cook. And Jack couldn't help but notice that the woman seemed more than a little nervous discussing her.

For a split second, he wrestled with doubts—maybe Lynette had seen her take something. Maybe she was trying to protect her. But when it came to any specifics, the middle-aged blond couldn't be of much help. She'd only seen Miss DeVries "at a distance" lately. And she always seemed "in a hurry."

"Except the day of the picnic," Lynette remembered.

Jack eyed her carefully. "W—what. . .do. . .you m—m—mean?"

"Well," she continued, rubbing her tired eyes habitually, "I saw her around the house here that day."

Again, Jack felt a knot grow in the pit of his stomach. "W—w—where. . . ex. . .actly?"

Lynette cleared her throat. "She. . .She was. . ." She kneaded her creased brow. "She was coming out the back door."

"Are. . .you. . .certain?"

She nodded emphatically. But her weary face still looked troubled.

"All. . .r—r—right. Th—thanks, L—Lynette." He tried to give her a reassuring smile. It didn't work out very well. He started toward Bob's office at the main compound.

"What will happen to her?" Lynette's small voice came from behind him.

He turned back, his eyebrows knit in concern. "I. . .d—don't know. W—w—we're. . .not sure. . .sh—she t—t—took. . .anything."

166

"Do you have any other. . .suspects?" It seemed an awkward word to use, and her face showed her embarrassment.

He shook his head.

"Oh." She brushed a wisp of hair from her face. "Good luck."

With a nod, he continued toward Bob's office, wishing and hoping and praying that all the signs that were so clearly pointing to Carillon were somehow wrong.

✳

Day three.

What on earth am I doing here again? Carillon asked herself. Settled in the grass, which now waved over her head from her seated position, she was at least a safe distance from it.

It.

You idiot. It's a house, for crying out loud. It's not like it's alive.

Her head knew it. Her skittery conscience told her something else.

Alternately she delved into Madeline's journal and kept watch over the house. Yet each day she settled a little nearer to it. A little nearer because Madeline's writings urged her to. Or at the very least, took away some of the fear and dread.

The months of 1853 unfolded like some sort of novel under Madeline Whitcomb's pen and ink. And with that unfolding came new discoveries. For Madeline and for Carillon.

Well, I've met him, the entry stated.

William Henrikson. He's the farmer. The occupant of the charming little place I stumbled upon. He happened to be out choring one time when I "happened" by. Quite embarrassing, I must admit. But he didn't seem put out or startled by my appearance.

He seemed a jovial enough fellow. Polite, at least. He has an attractive face (I'm ashamed to even admit I noticed, but it's something I've always taken note of—faces) in spite of the beard he's obviously growing out for the upcoming cold weather.

And he has very kind eyes.

I felt comfortable around him immediately.

Like any well-bred lady, I introduced myself as Miss Whitcomb, the new schoolteacher, and politely made mention that I didn't think I had any students by the name of Henrikson in my class.

With a slightly reddish face, he assured me that, no, I wouldn't. He didn't have any children.

He smiled cordially, and I continued on like a complete ninny, I suppose. "Perhaps your wife is at home," I mentioned. "I'd like to invite her over for tea."

This time a smile crept across his face. Then he informed me that, no, he didn't have a wife, either.

167

Now it was my turn to blush maddeningly.

Unsure of what else to say, I'm sure I made a perfect fool of myself. I vaguely remember saying that it had been very nice to meet him and that perhaps I'd see him at one of the community functions.

I think he nodded and agreed in a quiet sort of way.

Then I left and berated myself all the way home for being such a forward goose. But then, how was I to know he lived there all by himself?

I just pray that the school board doesn't hear of my silly behavior. That would be one way to lose my post quickly—cavorting with and seeking attention from area bachelors.

Carillon had to chuckle at the description. How different life had been 150 years ago. Different. . .and simpler. In spite of the fact that the times and customs seemed archaic to her way of thinking, she again found herself drawn in. Knowing she shared a common thread with this woman—even for the short amount of time she was at the teacherage. It was easier to imagine it. . .to believe it truly happened when she was living right there. So with each page, Carillon found herself drawn into the story of Madeline and her attraction to and interest in the area farmer.

The months in the journal flew along. Christmas came and went with a lonesome Madeline lamenting her station. Bad snows made it impossible for her to return to her family's home out east for the holidays.

Some kind neighbors had graciously invited her to spend the day with them. So Madeline had carefully dug through her stash of scrap material and made each of the children in the family (in addition to their mother and father) some quaint homemade ornaments to hang on their Christmas tree.

She'd been more than a little embarrassed when she'd arrived to find that they had no Christmas tree. Apparently it wasn't a tradition that had caught on yet. Or more likely, the farm schedule just didn't leave time for such frivolities.

But to her further horror, another guest had been invited to the family's get-together. Mr. William Henrikson.

Savoring each description of their encounters, Carillon couldn't help but compare her own encounters with men to this.

Oh, how they paled in comparison.

There'd been more than just a few, Tony being the most recent. She tried to remember back to when she'd met him. It had been at a party—somewhere.

Had she noticed his handsome face? Probably. Definitely his body.

Carillon reviewed Madeline's thoughts. Had she noticed his "kind eyes"?

That was a gimme. Not a chance. She'd seen things in Tony's eyes, but kindness wasn't top on the list. Try excitement. Desire. And more than a little danger.

Kind eyes. . .

The only person she'd ever known who'd had kind eyes was her sister.

"Evie," she whispered.

Closing her own eyes, Carillon let a dance of memories sway across her consciousness. She could see Evie's sweet face that last night. Her impish little smile, so full of life. Hope. Love. . .

"I love you, Carillon."

She tucked the sheets tighter around Evie's little, skinny body and gave her the usual Eskimo kisses. "I love you, too, Ev. Now get to sleep."

"Is Tony still here?" she asked.

Carillon sighed. "Yes. Good night." She flicked on the nightlight and started for the door.

"I'm scared."

With a slump of her shoulders, she turned around. "What?" She trudged back to the six-year-old's bed. "You're never scared." She plopped down next to her and began running her fingers up and down her ribs. "You afraid the tickle monster is going to get you?"

Evie's shrieks of laughter cut the tension of the moment, her blond locks bobbing all over as she tried to squirm out of Carillon's reach. After a few moments, the tickling ceased, the laughter died down, and Carillon smiled down at Evie. "I'm going downstairs now. Good night."

"I'm scared for you," the small voice came.

Frowning, Carillon sought out the wide blue eyes. "Why are you scared for me?"

"Because. I don't think Tony's good for you."

Stifling a smile, Carillon smoothed back a damp curl from the little girl's forehead. "You've been listening in on Mom and Dad's conversations, haven't you?"

She shrugged her slim shoulders.

"Don't worry about me or Tony," Carillon whispered. "We'll be fine." She gave the comforter one last pat and stood up.

"But he doesn't know Jesus."

Closing her eyes for a long moment, Carillon turned around and let out a long breath. "Honey, not everyone. . .'knows' Jesus. Not everyone. . .needs to." She needed to be careful here. Her parents would kill her if she tried to undo all they'd plugged into Evie.

Her sister bolted upright. "Yes, they do!" she declared emphatically. "If they don't, they won't go to heaven when they die. They won't get to see Jesus. They won't be with everyone else who loves Him."

Rolling her eyes, Carillon, yet again, took a seat on the edge of the small bed. "Look, Angel. Sometimes there are people who aren't. . .going to. . .agree with that."

"Why?"

She swallowed and thought hard. "Because they have other things to think about, I guess."

The thin, blond brows knit together in worry. "Tony needs to know Jesus."

Carillon suppressed a smile. "Why?"

" 'Cause then you both could."

This brought a frown. "What makes you think that I know Jesus?"

The sweet little face scrunched up in concern. "He knows you."

"Who does?"

"Jesus."

"And how do you know that?"

"He told me."

"He told you."

"Mm hm. And then you could know Him forever. And I'd see you in heaven someday."

"Bug," she said softly, "you don't need to see me in heaven. You'll see me tomorrow. Right here."

Judging from the little girl's face, it was obvious Evie realized she wasn't having much of an impact on her older sister. The thought must have disturbed her greatly, because she started to cry—quietly.

"Oh come on, Ev." She wrapped her in a hug. "Don't cry."

"I can't help it. I want you to be in heaven, too. I want you to see Jesus, too."

Oh, this was frustrating. How was she supposed to cope with all this nonsense her parents had infected her sister with since they'd gotten "saved"? With a muted growl of frustration, she grabbed Evie's shoulders and held her away from herself. "Listen, Evie. You talk to Jesus, okay? If He wants me to know Him, tell Him to let me know. All right?"

The little girl sniffled and wiped her nose, nodding somewhat morosely.

There. Maybe that would settle this for now. She moved toward the door again.

"Carillon?"

This time she stayed at the door. "Yes?"

"I'd give anything for you to have Jesus in your heart."

"Okay, Doll." She tugged on the knob.

"I would. I'd even die. . .if I knew you'd meet Him and be in heaven with me later."

Carillon whirled around. "Shut up!" The words were out of her mouth before she could stop them. "Just shut your mouth, Evie! Don't you ever say anything like that again. Do you hear me?" She marched over to the twin bed and stared at her sister long and hard.

The little face before her showed no remorse or fear, however. Just the same sad insistence it had held before.

Rubbing her hands across her face, Carillon blew out a long, ragged breath. "I'm sorry, Hon. I didn't mean to snap at you."

Evie nodded.

"I just. . .don't want to hear you talking like that. Okay?"

Another sober nod.

"Good." She placed one last kiss on the silky, blond head. "Good night, Yvonne Laurel DeVries. I love you."

The little smile returned. "Good night, Carillon Brooke DeVries. I love you, too."

Satisfied, Carillon made it all the way to the door and actually into the hallway before she heard her sister's last words.

"And Jesus loves you, too."

The sharp taste of saltwater brought Carillon back to the present and the pain she could never escape. Tears fell unheeded to the leather-bound journal on her lap.

"Oh, Evie. What did you say to Him?" She sniffled as her voice got lost in the ensuing sobs. "What did you tell your Jesus?"

※

"Wait a minute," Bob clarified. He replaced the small reading glasses he'd discarded earlier and looked over the employee schedule sheets that Jack had brought along. "You're saying that there's a possibility that she might not have taken these things?"

Jack nodded. "I–I've. . .known. . .it all. . .al–long. B–b–but . . .I needed. . . p–proof."

"And you have it?"

"M–maybe."

The older man sat back in his chair, patiently waiting for the explanation.

Jack leaned forward and indicated the date of the picnic on the employee roster. "Th–these are. . .the p–p–people. . .who. . .came."

Bob nodded.

"These. . .didn't." He jabbed his finger to a short list of names, among them, Carillon DeVries.

"And?"

"W–where. . .w–were they?"

Bob frowned in concentration as he went down the list. "Ed and Linda were out of town at a family reunion."

Jack pointed to the next name.

"Kent was at his sister's wedding."

Next.

"Margo and Julie weren't here yet. . .still coming home from college."

Next.

171

"Lynette was out of town at her husband's folks."

Next.

"Miss DeVries. . ." Bob let the name hang in the air. "She was supposedly at her cabin."

Jack nodded.

Bob looked a trifle frustrated. "Jack, I'm not following you here. Everyone seems to have an alibi except your Miss DeVries."

Your Miss DeVries? The wording wasn't lost on Jack. Ignoring the strange feeling that accompanied the phrase, he moved his finger back up the list to Lynette Pierce.

"Lynette?" Bob asked skeptically.

"Sh–she ssssaid. . .she. . .ssssaw. . .Carillon. . .the day of. . .th–the picnic. C–c–coming out. . .of Mitchell. . .House. H–how. . .could. . .sh–she. . .if she. . . wasn't. . .here?"

Bob didn't look convinced or impressed. "Betty already told me this. She'd come back to pick up her check before leaving. Simple as that."

"Before. . .leaving," Jack reiterated. "T–to. . .go. . .to. . . ?"

"Her husband's folks." Bob actually looked like he was growing impatient.

And Jack could feel the steel growing in his conviction and in his backbone. "Didn't. . .her h–husband's f–f–folks. . .pass away. Last. . .year?"

A startling look of comprehension washed across the older man's face. He glanced up at Jack with curiously raised brows. "Uh, Jack. Would you mind tracking down Mrs. Pierce? I'd like to speak to her."

Jack nodded and was out the door.

Chapter 10

Lynette Pierce looked less than comfortable.

Betty Haskins looked mortified.

"Bob," Betty began, her face in a troubled pinch, "I certainly didn't come here to point accusations at longtime employees—"

Bob stayed her protest with an upraised hand.

"Nor did we. And we didn't meet to hurl accusations at anyone. Merely to find out the truth."

Mrs. Haskins sighed heavily and backed rigidly into her chair.

Lynette continued to rub her deeply circled eyes.

Jack tried to stay unobtrusively in the background. He knew he was already involved, but he was more than grateful that Bob was handling this. He watched in amazement as his boss's face took on a compassionate look as he turned toward Lynette.

"Are you feeling well, Lynette?"

She shot her head up abruptly, seeming surprised at the question. A quick nod. "I guess so."

"I was curious," Bob continued, "how your trip went."

Lynette looked over at Mrs. Haskins, then at her hand sitting quietly in her lap. "My trip?"

"The day of the picnic," he reminded her. "You weren't able to attend."

"Oh. Right. Yes. Uh, the trip was fine."

Bob nodded and shuffled some papers around in front of him as if he were the most relaxed person in the world. "How are Ken's folks anyway?"

"Fine." She almost met his eyes.

He settled his ample frame back into his office chair, quiet for a moment.

Jack held his breath. The tension in the room was unbearable.

"Betty," Bob began, "I just thought of something. Could you head down to the stock room? I believe there were some donations dropped off the other day and I'd like you to take a look at them."

Mrs. Haskins's thin brows hiked at least an inch. "But I thought—"

"I'd really appreciate it if you could look them over now."

Her reed-slim figure rose from the chair and whisked out the door.

"Jack," Bob addressed him without even turning around. "Could you go and ask Darlene if the new stocks have arrived yet?"

Without a word, Jack strode from the office and shut the door silently behind him. As he trekked to the business offices, he continued reviewing Bob's handling of the situation. He wondered if he'd ever garner such finesse when it came to dealing with people.

He knew he could read them. . .that was a gift he'd long been able to utilize. But to take it further than that. . . Jack sighed. Serious doubts plagued his mind—fueled by the insistent memories.

By the time Jack had seen Darlene and been waylaid by several of the chattier members of the staff whom he seldom saw, a good forty-five minutes had passed. The door to Bob's office was shut tight. Subdued voices could barely be discerned from the hall.

Not eager to intrude on the meeting, Jack leaned against the wall and waited. And prayed. In his heart he knew there were hurting souls involved here, and he hated to jump to conclusions, but when the Lord pressed something on his spirit, how could he ignore it?

Several minutes later, the door creaked open. The first one out was Betty Haskins. Her thin face looked more strained than usual. She didn't acknowledge Jack's presence as she whipped past.

Next came Lynette. Her eyes were puffy and red, her face blotchy from the tears that were still running down her cheeks. Bob was close behind her, assuming an almost fatherly role as he stayed near, but not too close.

Wiping her face with her fingers once more, Lynette paused before Jack and gave him a shaky smile.

He tried to return it. "You. . .all. . .right?"

She shrugged her shoulders and sniffed. "I have some things to work out."

Jack threw a glance at Bob. The older man's face remained unreadable.

"I'll be praying for you," Jack assured her.

Again, the wobbly smile. "I know you will." She ran another palm over her cheek. "Good-bye, Jack."

She started down the hall, Jack looking after her. Bob caught his attention with a nod of his head, indicating Jack should wait in his office.

Closing the door behind himself, he took a chair and waited, passing the time alternately thinking, praying, and wondering. Several minutes later, Bob returned. He sat heavily into his chair, looking weary.

Jack didn't have to ask. He knew Bob would tell him in his way, in his time. "I guess we should pay a visit to Miss DeVries," the older man finally said.

A wave of relief flowed over Jack. He raised a silent prayer of thanks.

Bob rubbed his tired eyes and then leaned his arms against the desk. "How did you know? How do you always know?"

It was a rhetorical question. Jack only returned his gaze and waited for the explanation.

174

"It seems that when Lynette's husband, Ken, lost his parents, they gave him and Lynette a modest inheritance. Nothing grand, but enough where they could have paid off a few things. Unfortunately, and unbeknownst to Lynette, Ken had already picked up an unhealthy liking for gambling."

Jack winced, sensing where this was heading.

"Yeah. Seems he thought the little chunk would grow if put on the right numbers at the casino. Obviously. . .it didn't. It left him farther in the hole than before. According to Lynette, she started getting telephone calls from creditors wondering where their payments were. She thought Ken had been paying the bills."

Jack nodded, understanding. "S–s–so. . .the. . .antiques. . .were a. . .way t–to. . . make. . .m–money."

Bob shook his head. "You know how awful it is to find out something like this?"

Jack could only agree by acknowledging the growing lump in his stomach.

"Betty was absolutely mortified. She didn't know what to say. I did ask her to issue an apology to Miss DeVries, though."

Bringing a hand to the back of his neck, Jack rubbed it habitually. "W–w–what do. . .we. . .do about. . .Miss. . .DeVries?"

The older man steepled his index fingers to his chin pensively. "I think she ought to stay where she is. There's still the issue of her inability to deal with the public."

Jack shrugged. "M–maybe she's. . .c–c–calmed. . .down ssssome."

"I'll leave that to your discretion." The large man rose from his chair.

Jack followed suit, turning to leave.

"Jack."

He turned and met Bob's earnest eyes.

"Thank you." He reached out a huge hand.

Jack took it and warmed under the profound simplicity of the gesture.

"You're a good man, Jack Tate."

※

The words rang in his ears all the way through Liberty Town and on his trek toward the little schoolhouse. Was he? Was he truly a "good man"? And what did that mean?

When he compared himself to Christ, the only man he could think of whom he wanted to emulate, he knew he fell far, far short.

Yet when the obvious comparisons came between him and his brother. . .his father—

Jack halted that train of thought. *You don't need to go there. Don't even start.*

Before his mind could continue on the painful path, he found himself in front of the teacherage door. A whole new host of fears and inadequacies stared him down, disguising themselves among the innocent chipped paint and battered wood.

Shoving those doubts aside, he raised his fist and rapped his knuckles smartly against the panel.

No more than a few seconds passed before it opened. He stood face-to-face with the questions and curiosity in Carillon DeVries's deep blue eyes, only deepening his own insecurities.

Yet somehow, the trepidation evident in those azure depths strengthened his resolve. His purpose. His mission.

Taking a deep breath and simultaneously lifting a prayer, he found himself offering her a smile. The first one he could remember ever attempting.

And what was weirder. . .she returned it.

He lost himself for that eternal moment, just enjoying the subtle complexities of this woman before him.

Before too long, he regained his senses and had the wherewithal to refocus himself on the reason for his visit.

Suddenly remembering his hat, he removed the thing from his head and instinctively raked his fingers through his hair. "G–g–good. . .morning."

Carillon tilted her head, the faintest traces of the smile lingering at the corners of her full lips. "Afternoon," she corrected.

He smiled again and tossed a quick glance at the toes of his boots.

"I–I've come. . .for. . .a. . .rrr–reason."

Her eyes widened slightly in anticipation, but her manner indicated no anxiety. No hurriedness.

He appreciated it.

Licking his lips, he delved in. "I'm ssssent. . .t–to offer an. . .a–pology."

The stare widened more.

"F–f–from. . .all. . .of us." He nodded in hopes that she'd get his meaning.

Tucking a thumbnail between her teeth, she looked uncertain. "You've found out something then?"

He nodded. "Th–th–they know. . .now. Th–that. . .you d–didn't. . .do. . .it."

She gave a slight nod. But her expression changed little.

Jack wasn't sure what he had expected. It certainly hadn't been silence. He shifted his weight and passed his poor crumpled hat from one hand to the other, wondering what on earth to do next.

"Well, then." She finally broke the uncomfortable silence. "Thank you."

He inclined his head and habitually replaced the brown felt hat.

Well. . .that must be it. Chewing at one corner of his lip and turning around, he started down the worn pathway.

"Jack."

The tenderness in her voice did more to halt his steps than any other tone could have possibly hoped to accomplish.

Slowly, he turned, waiting.

Her fair complexion seemed to be reddening suddenly. "I just wanted to say. . .thank you."

He nodded again.

Her slim shoulders heaved up and down. "Not just for. . .this. But for believing in me. No one's ever really bothered to do that before."

"Believe. . .in y–you?"

Carillon shook her head. "That you did means a lot. Well. . .thank you."

A quiet smile played with his lips. "You're. . .welcome."

"Wait," she threw out suddenly, as if she were afraid he might quickly leave. "I have something else to say."

He turned toward her fully and tilted back the brim of his hat.

This time she rubbed her slender fingers across her frowning forehead. "I want to apologize."

A little lump rose in Jack's throat.

"I'm sorry that I. . .made fun of you. I don't know what was wrong with me."

Jack took a deep breath and looked at the ground. Again, he found himself nodding. "It's. . .all. . .right. I–it's hhh–happened. . .before." He tried to give her an understanding smile.

Quiet warmth crept into her eyes. "It shouldn't."

A new and different warmth crept across Jack. One that felt good. Hopeful. Promising.

And with it came a new sensation. A new direction. And now, now that some of those barriers were gone, it was a lot easier to act upon it. "D–do. . .you— W–w–would you. . .have. . .t–time for. . .a. . .walk?"

She looked at him curiously. "A walk?"

"Y–yes. I–I'd. . .like t–to. . .show you. . .ssssomething."

Those intense, deep-set eyes studied him for more than a few seconds. In his heart he knew that she was asking herself if she could trust him, believe him.

He returned the unspoken questions with a confident eye and reached out a hand toward her. "Come. . .w–with. . .me?"

She hesitated for the briefest of moments, then stepped down from the threshold. "Okay."

Chapter 11

Where Carillon expected Jack to take her, she didn't know. She honestly didn't really care. For some strange reason, she just wanted to be with him. Near him. He was the first person in a long, long time to have made an effort to befriend her, in spite of her hostility. Why? She needed to know. There couldn't be anything in it for him personally, could there?

He kept ahead of her, only by a few feet, periodically turning around to see if she was still following. Each time he gave her a smile that she'd come to recognize as only his. Shy. One side of his small mouth curled up hesitantly as if asking permission to be friendly.

When he turned back toward the path, she took the moments she could steal without his observation to study the rest of him. Maybe five or six inches taller than she, he wasn't any giant, that was sure. And in spite of his slight weight, he was strong. She'd seen him as he'd been working around the schoolhouse. What he lacked in brawn, he seemed to make up for with sheer determination and grit.

His light brown hair, normally stuffed beneath that hat, was cropped short, leaving the crown to spike up in a way that stood in sharp contrast to his mild personality.

He suddenly turned around again, leaving Carillon to hide a blush at a perusal she couldn't deny. She tossed her glance to the side of the path, trying to ignore the odd sensation racing through her heart.

But she didn't have to concentrate on her discomfort for long. Within a matter of seconds, she regained her bearings and realized exactly where they were.

Her head shot up and she tried to peer over his shoulder. They couldn't be headed to—

No. It was impossible. Why on earth would he be going there?

Yet that was exactly where they ended up—the same farm she'd been courting for the last week. The house seemed more "quiet" today. Less troubled.

Or did it?

She stared at the dark windows that made the empty eyes of the house. For how long, she wasn't sure. Before long, she felt him staring at her.

Rubbing her fingers across her forehead, she squinted in the afternoon sunshine and dared a glance in his direction. His golden brown eyes were indeed studying her. Waiting. Watching.

"What is this place?" she finally asked. It was a question she'd long wanted to ask, but there'd been no one to field it. Carillon knew what it once had been— Madeline had detailed all of that in her journal.

But what had happened to turn it into this?

Jack's broodish brow wrinkled as he turned toward the building. "Th–this. . . is. . .home."

His voice was so quiet she thought she'd not heard him correctly. But a small catch in her heart made her maintain her silence, waiting.

He tilted his head as he regarded the dilapidated structure. "Home." That time he wasn't talking to her.

Nor did he seem to remember her presence.

She watched as his boots carried him through the waist-high grasses, bringing him closer to the sagging front porch. He didn't slow, instead continuing up the half-rotted steps onto the faded boards of the decking.

"Jack." Her plea was none too confident, and it got lost in the wind that pulled and teased at her hair.

The front door creaked open under his grasp, and she watched as he disappeared into the darkness of the building's interior.

"Jack." She was more insistent this time. Her feet propelled her after him. Not for concern about him, but for herself. She didn't want to be left alone. Several quick steps got her to the porch, and she had to take several deep breaths before drawing the courage to actually follow his lead.

Steeling that resolve, Carillon yanked open the screen door and entered the dimly lit kitchen. The darkened maple cupboards, stained laminate counters, and faded linoleum seemed out of place in the emptiness of it all. There were no appliances. No furnishings. No decorations to make the house a home.

Had she expected there to be? It was vacant after all. But what about the feelings she'd had while being near it before?

A sinister chill tried to wrap itself around her, and she shivered in its wake. "Jack?" Her voice seemed little more than a whisper.

A creak from above made her jump.

"I–I'm. . .up. . .here." His tone sounded quiet, yet assuring.

Releasing a breath of relief, she rounded a corner, grimacing as she brushed aside the host of cobwebs framing the doorway into what had obviously been a living room. The center of the wood plank floor wasn't darkened like the outer edges, a sign of whatever rug had warmed the floors in years gone by.

"Here." Jack's voice floated down from her side.

She turned and gazed up a narrow, steep flight of stairs. His open, fresh face was at the top of the landing. He beckoned her with a hand.

She eyed the painted steps hesitantly. "Is it safe?"

He nodded and descended a few of them, as if to allay her concerns.

Again, squashing her growing fears, she carefully placed one toe at a time on the treads, making her way toward him. He waited patiently for her at the top, but it was evident that his mind was elsewhere. He kept looking down the hall—obviously at one of the several open doors flanking the sides of the constricted passage.

Reaching the second floor, Carillon stifled a sneeze as the dust flew up in little clouds under her feet. Amid the dust, scattered bird droppings and other remainders of small rodents and animals littered the darkly stained wooden planks.

She quickened her pace when Jack disappeared into the room at the farthest end of the hall. Continually brushing aside the spider webs, she tentatively stepped into the small, dormered room, which barely appeared big enough to hold a bed, much less anything else.

More interesting to her was watching Jack.

He walked the small perimeter of the space, touched a series of nail holes in the plaster, and spent more than a few minutes simply standing at the broken window, his thoughts somewhere out in the wild fields beyond.

Carillon stepped back against a wall, leaned against the rough, cracking plaster, and waited.

"I. . .hhh–haven't b–b–been. . .here. . .in. . .t–ten years." He almost sounded remorseful.

Feeling prompted to say something—anything—Carillon found her voice. "Was this your room?"

Almost seeming startled at her question—or perhaps her intrusion into his thoughts—he released a deep breath and turned toward her. "No. Mmm–my. . . b–brother's."

She nodded. "What's his name?"

His intense eyes covered hers. "Jon."

Then he looked away again. Back to the out-of-doors.

"Small," she remarked, eyeing the limited space again. "Is he your younger brother?"

He shook his head. "Older."

Beginning to feel uncomfortable, with not much else to say or ask, she raised her eyebrows and slowly turned, taking in the nuances of the empty room. In one corner, a small door, evidently an added closet, piqued her interest. She started toward it and reached for the tarnished brass knob.

"Don't!"

The sudden strength of his voice made her jump. Instinctively, she took a step back as he crossed the floor.

Within the seriousness marking his features, she saw a sudden added softness. "I d–didn't mmm–mean. . .t–to startle. . .you." He dipped his head in apology.

"Just. . .lct. . .mmm–me." He indicated the knob with a tilt of his head.

Carillon retreated another step and watched with renewed interest as he tentatively gripped the handle. Curious. He almost seemed to hesitate, just for the briefest of seconds. Then, as if anticipating some wild occupant, he flung the door wide open, taking a step back as it thumped haphazardly against the blank wall behind it.

Empty.

Save the dust and dirt that accumulate in time's vacancy.

Shifting her attention to Jack, she watched as he yet again seemed transported to another time, another place. His normally kind, albeit intense, eyes narrowed. And his hand found its way to the back of his neck, unconsciously rubbing up and down through his sandy brown hair.

Then, as quick as he'd been to target this room upon their arrival, he seemed just as eager to leave it. Carefully and deliberately, he pushed the closet door back into the closed position, letting his hand rest on the knob as the latch clicked in the eerie silence of the room. "Are. . .you. . .rrr–ready t–to. . .go. . .then?" He plopped his hat back on his head and didn't wait for her answer.

She followed him back down the hall, daring a quick glimpse into each room they passed, wishing one of them would hold some answers. They held nothing. Nothing for her, anyway.

In less than a minute, they were back outside, their backs to the proud structure as they strode toward the woods ahead. Carillon found herself almost having to run to keep up with Jack's surprisingly long, fast strides.

"Jack." She tried to catch her breath as she stumbled through the tangling grasses at her feet.

Just short of the woods' edge, he stopped, turned, and looked back at her. The apologetic half-smile returned. "Sss–sorry."

But he offered no further comment. While he slowed for her to keep stride with him, the words between them were lost elsewhere. And in truth, she didn't feel much like breaking the silence. She knew too well the necessity of silence. Ofttimes there were no words that could take away the pain, and it was more than obvious that there was pain associated with that house. She'd seen it written on Jack's face.

Never one to wish anguish on anyone, Carillon somehow felt justified, or at least vindicated. There was a certain relief in knowing that someone like Jack Tate, who seemingly had "everything all together," might have issues in his past to deal with as well. But what were they?

They'd reached the corner of the open area where Jack's cabin stood. The same corner in which she'd found herself on that night, hiding behind the tree, listening to a near-perfect stranger stand up for her. She warmed under the memory as she studied Jack again, glad that this time she could be nearer to him.

As if he abruptly realized where he was, he turned toward her and nodded toward his porch. "D–do. . .you like. . .coffee?"

She nodded and followed him up to the quaint porch, flanked with two homemade rockers. Shyly taking a seat in one, she unobtrusively tried to sneak a peek into the little cabin. She couldn't see much more than the roughly hewn table and chairs. In the background she could hear him puttering around with cups and the coffeepot.

By the time he returned with the warm beverages, the sun was just beginning to sink behind the overwhelming stand of trees on the western edge of the lot. As the sky darkened, the cooler evening air took its cue and began instilling a nip in the faint breeze.

She took the mug gratefully, letting the warmth seep through her fingers and hands, willing some of it into her bare arms.

Jack placed his own mug near the opposite rocker before disappearing into the cabin once more. He came back several moments later with a fuzzy, striped blanket, which he unfolded and somewhat awkwardly draped around her shoulders.

Noting the charming reddening of his ears, Carillon felt the warmth she'd been wanting in her arms rising to her face instead. "Thank you." She tugged the edges around her and settled back against the comfortable chair. "You seem to come to my rescue quite often."

He let out a quiet breath of amusement as he shrugged his shoulders and eased into the other rocker.

The night birds were their conversation for a time as each sipped their coffee and occasionally stole glances at the other.

Jack drained the last of his beverage and set the cup on the floor. "M–may I. . .ask. . .y–y–you. . .ssssomething?" He leaned his forearms on his knees.

Carillon tucked her feet up on the chair, wrapping the expansive blanket around her legs as well. "I guess."

With a shy grin, he threw his gaze at the floor. "Where. . .d–did you. . .get. . . your. . .name?"

"From my parents."

He shot her a "touché" look and let out a quiet laugh. The first she'd ever heard. Subtle and masculine all at the same time.

She liked it. And she liked that she'd made him do it.

"Well," she continued, "it's kind of a weird story."

He eased back and waited, his face expectant and interested.

"My parents were somewhat a part of the leftover 'hippie' generation. They were actually a little behind the times." She smiled. "I think they wished they'd been old enough to participate more in the sixties thing.

"Anyway, they spent a year over in France, just knocking around, getting odd jobs here and there, walking wherever they might end up. At one point they were staying around the area of Provence, camping in some farmer's field, and off in the distance was this bell tower. . . ." She stopped as she watched his face. A most unusual smile was creeping across it. "What?"

He shook his head. "N–nothing. Go. . .on."

She shrugged. "You can probably guess the rest. They heard these bells tolling, I happened to be conceived while they were there, and voilà—my name was suddenly Carillon." She took a sip of her coffee. "Pretty weird, huh?"

"No. I. . .like it."

She looked at him askance. "You do? Why?"

"It's. . .d–different."

"Well, you've got that right. Anything else might have been better. Amy. Megan. Jill. And it's not like I can go by my middle name. . .Brooke isn't much better."

She was rewarded with his light laughter again.

"Well, I've spilled mine. What's your name?"

He raised his brows, surprised. "Jack."

"Just Jack?"

Half smile. "Jack. . .W–William. . .Tate."

"Jack William."

He nodded.

Then she went out on a limb. "Jack and Jon."

His head snapped up.

"Do you have any other brothers or sisters?"

Slowly, he shook his head no.

"Is Jon nearby?"

Again, no.

With each little question, Carillon watched his face grow a little more miserable, his frame sink a fraction or two more. She stopped, suddenly wishing she'd kept her questions to herself. How would she feel if he were to press her about Evie?

"W–would. . .you. . .l–like t–t–to. . .hear. . .mmm–my story?"

She sought his face, and for some odd reason the misery she'd seen only moments ago was gone. He looked serious and perhaps a little melancholy, but at the same time, he was peaceful.

"I don't want to hear anything that you're uncomfortable—"

He shook his head. "It's. . .all. . .right. I fff–feel. . .like. . .I–I'm supposed. . . t–to share. . .this."

"Why?"

His shoulders heaved up and down. "I. . .d–don't know." Those brown eyes pierced hers once more. "Mmm–maybe. . .you'll. . .know. . .why."

Chapter 12

Jack closed his eyes, prayed silently, and hesitated for the briefest of seconds. Was he doing the right thing here? Was there truly a good reason for him to share this? But with each doubt came the internal affirmation. *Go ahead. Tell her.*

He settled back into the chair and tried not to let the intimidation take over. "My b–b–brother. . .Jon," he started, "is fff–four. . .years older. . .th–than I. And in about. . .every. . .w–way possible. . .w–w–we're totally. . .d–different.

"He. . .liked ssssports—I liked. . .reading. He. . .hated. . .the fff–farm—I. . . loved it. He's over. . .ssssix feet. . .t–tall—I'm. . .n–not." He tried to offer an ironic smile to lighten the mood, then shifted slightly in his rocker. "He had. . .n–no time. . .for God." A long gaze was sent in Carillon's direction. "I w–wanted. . .nothing. . .but Him."

That last pronouncement brought an uncomfortable silence as she stared into the depths of her coffee cup. So here was where it began. This was where he began to strike nerves.

And for some stupid and bizarre reason, Jack panicked. All the stories he'd been going to tell, all the fears and hurts he'd been somewhat ready to share— they all flew straight out into the cold night sky. Because he'd let his own fear take control again.

After several moments, Carillon broke the awful quiet. "So he was not kind to you—Jon."

Jack shook his head. If this girl only knew. . .

"Where is he now?"

A hard lump rose in his throat. "He's. . .he's. . .a fff–few. . .hours. . .from here."

"And you never see him?"

Another shake of the head.

"That's kind of. . .sad."

Inwardly, he had to agree. But how could he explain it otherwise? Especially when it had been Jack himself who'd made sure that their visits were virtually nonexistent. Jon hated him. He made no effort to conceal that fact. In spite of Jack's knowledge that he'd done the right thing, there would always be a part of him that grieved. Grieved over the fact that he'd lost his brother.

"Are your parents nearby?" she asked.

"N–no. They're b–both. . .gone." The lump intensified.

"I'm sorry." She gingerly placed the mug on the floorboards and pulled the

184

blanket around her more tightly. "I know how it is to. . .lose someone."

Jack thought back to what he'd read in her minuscule folder. According to it, both parents were still alive. But what about—what about that sister? Before he could voice a question however, she spoke again.

"How long have you lived here?"

"Here?" He hiked a thumb at the cabin.

"Mm hm."

"Ab—bout. . .eight or. . .nine y—years."

"Almost since the time you left home then?"

He shot her a quick glance.

"Well, you said—back at that farm—it had been almost ten years since you'd been there."

Slowly, he nodded his head. "Right."

"What happened to it? The farm?"

He inclined his head in question.

"Was it sold?"

With a slight hesitation, he finally agreed. "Yes. It. . .was sold."

"Who owns it now?"

Now it was Jack's turn to begin to squirm. Wasn't this line of questioning supposed to be directed from him to her? Suddenly he was finding himself being backed into a corner. "Yesteryear. . .owns it," he admitted, taking the last slurp of the now nearly cold coffee. "But wh—what. . .about y—you? Where. . .d—do you. . .live?"

Carillon looked thoughtful for a moment, then smiled. "The teacherage."

He smiled back and set his own mug down.

"My parents live in a suburb of Minneapolis. Edina."

"Heard. . .of it. D—d—does. . .your ssssister. . .live there. . .too?"

The previous stillness was nothing compared to the frigid reaction that his question received.

Carillon took a deep breath and abruptly stood. "I like your cabin, Jack. It's very. . .cozy." She peeled the blanket from her shoulders, carefully and deliberately folded it, and placed it over the rocker. "But I should head back."

Jack floundered to his feet, taken aback at her sudden urgency to leave. *Dumb, dumb,* he berated himself. *Way to push too far, Jack.* Would he ever learn to do it right?

She'd already started for the steps when she froze suddenly.

Studying her carefully, he tried to discern what could have made her face blanch in visible fear. Then she did it again.

This time he figured it out.

Somewhere in the distance of the woods, he heard them. A sound so commonplace to him that he scarcely noticed anymore. Their high-pitched yips and howls pierced the summer evening as they called back and forth. "N—noisy tonight. . .aren't th—they?" He stepped next to her at the top of the stairs and shoved his hands in his pockets, listening.

Carillon nodded nervously.

"H—hard to b—believe. . .ssssuch a. . .small. . .animal can m—make. . .ssssuch a ruckus."

Her wary gaze sought his. "Small?"

"Sure. C—coyotes. No b—bigger. . .than a ssssmall. . .dog. Scared. . .of their sh—shadows, too. They. . .ssssee people. . .and rrr—run in. . .the o—o—other direction."

"Coyotes?" Her blue eyes were barely discernable in the near-blackness of the evening.

"W—wait a. . .second." He retreated into the cabin, lit one of his lanterns, and returned to the porch with it. "Y—you. . .ready then?"

"What. . .why?"

"I'll w—walk you. . .home."

"That's not necessary. I know the way."

"It's d—dark."

"I'm sure I can make it just fine."

He wasn't going to win this battle, Jack conceded to himself. "Here. T—take this." He handed her the lantern.

She appeared both grateful and uncomfortable. "Thank you." She began to step down carefully.

"Carillon." Her name jumped out of his mouth before he could stop it. What was he supposed to say now? He wasn't sure. But her leaving—like this. It just didn't feel right. Shuffling his feet self-consciously, he gave it his best shot. "I'm ssssorry. . .if I. . .said anything. . .th—that offended. . .you."

She studied him for a long moment, then shook her head. "You didn't offend me."

Partial relief. But the barrier still existed.

"Good night, Jack." She turned, holding the lantern up, its whitish flame casting swirling circles of light on the path in front of her. He watched until she was out of sight, the glow of the lantern disappearing in the thickness of the dark trees. And he turned and ambled into the cabin, feeling like more of a failure than ever before.

❋

Carillon stared at the journal in front of her. Her normal fascination with Madeline Whitcomb's postings kept getting lost. . .lost in the memory of the evening's events or, more truthfully, in the memory of the conversation.

Every time she tried to picture the farm as described in Madeline's diary, it instead became the place she'd seen today. The emptiness. The loneliness. The isolation. And the troubled look in Jack's eyes.

Compounded by the things he'd tried to share at his cabin. His life. At least a portion of it. That he had stopped well short of anything truly revealing had been very clear. But why?

She knew there was more. Much more. But it seemed as if Mr. Tate had walls erected as well.

It might have been a lead-in, or so she thought initially. Something to get her to talk about her own reasons for being at Yesteryear. To get her to talk about Evie. But as she watched him, as she listened to him stammer his way through his memories, she realized it was something else—something much, much greater.

Jack Tate had shared—or at least had tried to share—a piece of himself with her, and she had a feeling it was a piece that not many others had seen, a piece that he didn't let show often. . .if ever.

The thought warmed her. And scared her.

She relished the warmth.

And fought it.

The last time she'd felt that way, it had built toward a "need" for companionship. For someone to share with.

No, she didn't want that.

She didn't want to be vulnerable.

Carillon stared down at the journal and flipped it shut. Unlike Miss Whitcomb, she didn't desire to find that "heart to respond unto her own."

But what else could she call it when she saw portions of Jack opening up to her. . .and felt her own walls trembling slightly at the prospect of being torn down?

The accompanying Bible that had befriended the journal all these years still sat desolately on the ledge of the small table near her bed.

That there were secrets in it, Carillon did not doubt. That they were waiting for her, she did not doubt, either.

But that her fear of letting go was still too great—that she knew.

No, if God was somewhere behind all of her walls, He was going to have to stay there.

And if Jack Tate thought it was his job to help tear them down. . .then, somehow, it was her job to keep him at a safe distance.

❋

Jack cowered in the corner of the barn, hoping the bales of hay covered him. It was only a matter of time until Jon unearthed his hiding place. He always did.

Short, shallow breaths didn't do much to fill his lungs, and he felt himself getting a little light-headed.

Then he heard it.

The scuff of Jon's work boots on the hay. No other noise. Just the imminent peril.

The shuffling of those boots stopped—just above his head. He didn't have to look up. He already knew what was there. A face so full of hate and contempt that it hurt just to look at it.

Instead, he picked at the green leaves poking out from a nearby bale.

"You had to do it, didn't ya?" Jon snarled. "You just couldn't keep your big mouth shut."

Jack started to shake his head, but it was no use. Jon wouldn't listen to him. He never did.

"I had those magazines hidden. There's no way Mom could have found them." He jumped into the narrow opening between the bales, leaving him almost on top of Jack. Grabbing Jack by the collar of his sweatshirt, Jon yanked him to his feet until his steely eyes were boring directly into Jack's. "You stupid, little rat."

The stomach punch came swiftly.

Jack gasped for breath while he struggled to stay on his feet.

But Jon never let him drop. Each blow, each kick, every fist hit its mark, without a moment's hesitation between. The only thing between them now was the volley of Jon's wicked anger.

After a time, when Jon was breathing hard with his effort, he let him go.

Jack crumpled to the hay, gagging, coughing, and gasping. Every inch of his body screamed in pain. Every inch but his head and face. Jon had long since learned where to place hits to avoid notice by either parent.

As Jon clambered up and out of the hole, he turned around and glared down. "It won't be the last time if you don't learn to shut up." He followed up the threat with a string of profane adjectives.

And Jack sat trying to breathe. . .and trying not to cry.

Then he was somewhere else.

The hay became hard, cold wood. And the dimly lit barn became the pitch black stifling air of a space entirely too small for comfort.

He reached out, groping for the knob. Desperately trying to find the door. "Jon?" he croaked out. The panic started to rise. "Jon, Ill—let. . .m–m–me. . . out!"

Finally, the handle fell under his grasp. Wrenching on the frigid knob, he turned it with all his strength—only to find himself crawling into a dimly lit sanctuary.

Meager light diffused by the stained-glass windows cast a cranberry glow across the vacant church. Vacant—except for the solitary casket fronting the dais ahead of him. Clumsily scrambling to his knees, Jack habitually brushed off his jacket and pants and ran a hand over his hair.

Feeling as if someone had tied leaden weights to his feet, he lagged down the center aisle, trying to catch a glimpse of the casket's occupant. Too soon he saw. The dark hair, the fragile features. The unwelcome look of death on her face.

Grief stole the majority of his breath as he tripped continually closer. "M–m–mom."

By the time he reached her side, the church was no longer empty. From all around him came the shuffling, quiet noises of a congregation. The old wheezing organ pumped out a muted hymn while uncomfortable silence lingered over the place.

Jack turned and watched as all eyes focused on him. Some filled with compassion and concern. Some filled with grief of their own. And one particular set that would not face him.

Sensing the end of whatever this was, Jack stole down the aisle, trying to ignore the burning in his eyes, the ache in his heart. The hopelessness that was trying to pervade his soul.

The heavy wooden doors at the rear of the building creaked open under the weight of his push and he stepped into. . .the barn.

Panic returned, infused with an overwhelming feeling of inadequacy. He shifted into work mode and instantly sprinted for the nearest milker, which was squawking noisily under the cow. He'd just gotten the machine off when another one started its protest. . .then another. . .and another.

Whirling around in confusion, he saw every cow had a milker on. And there were at least a hundred cows—maybe more. Where had all of them come from?

All were bellowing to be fed. But where was the feed? A quick glance in the feed room showed nothing. No corn. No feed bags. Nothing.

"Jack!"

He shuddered as the voice thundered from somewhere outside.

The noise around him fled into the background; he watched his father storm through the barn's side entrance, a heavy concrete block of some sort in his arms. His steps were staggered, his eyes bloodshot and watery, his speech slurred.

Jack closed his eyes and willed the vision to go away.

"Jack!"

The man was closer now, lifting the huge stone in his massive arms, a volley of curses shooting from his mouth like poisonous arrows.

Jack caught a glimpse of the writing on the huge stone in the man's grip:

Alice Marie Tate
1949–1989
Beloved wife and mother

He stared at the tombstone, terror-stricken. "Dad!"

"Don't call me that, you lazy little. . ." More adjectives followed—Jack wincing with each one, but his eyes never left the engraved letters on the stone.

Until he saw it rising higher and higher.

He found his father's reddened, enraged face once more and hit the cement floor of the barn's alley just before the thing smashed into pieces around him.

189

And he ran. Like he'd never run before. Wondering if this time he would ever come back. . .

He sat upright. . .gasping. Wheezing. All the pains hurting all over again. In the darkness of the night, he couldn't see where he was, he couldn't remember. Fumbling to his knees, he felt the hard wooden floor boards. Where was he?

The closet?

He groped for the door. It wasn't there.

His foot struck something. Something solid.

Crawling toward it, he ran his hands over the smoothness of a blanket. The rough edges of his cot.

Relief washed over him.

Inching toward the opposite end, Jack felt for the lantern and box of matches and lit the wick with somewhat shaky fingers. Growing, orange light flooded his sleeping loft. He flopped his head back on the edge of the rumpled bed and took several deep breaths. *Thank You, Jesus.* The silent words were said from more than habit when he realized how close he'd come to tumbling off the edge of his ten-foot loft to the unforgiving floor below.

"Oh. . .Father," he whispered, his heart just beginning to slow from its adrenaline-fueled tempo. "W–when? When. . .w–will. . .it b–be. . .done?"

Chapter 13

"Y ou know the rules," Bob informed him with a grin. "Get yourself out of here today."

Jack tried to smile back.

"And happy birthday." His boss waved over his shoulder as he tromped back down the grassy path, which was fast turning yellowish as the end of summer stole the green of nature.

August 20.

A date he couldn't forget—for a lot of reasons. Never being able to forget one's own birthday was one thing. Compiled with the anniversary of losing one's family farm made it downright impossible.

Now Jack had another reminder for that date: Carillon DeVries. According to her folder, they shared the same birthday. Ironic. Because thus far, they'd shared little else.

He sighed as he pitched another forkful of hay down into the barn's manger below. What he'd do with this day, he had no idea. He'd run out of ideas long ago. Weeks—no, months ago—when it seemed Miss DeVries's attentions toward him turned polite, downright professional, at best.

Granted, she was doing her job. Very well. The schoolhouse tour was proving to be one of the more popular stops among the tourists. Jack, himself, had even snuck in the back of the building several times during her intriguing discourse of an 1850s' schoolmarm. He wondered where she'd obtained so much in-depth information that went well beyond the topical notes she'd received from Yesteryear.

Once or twice she'd caught his eye. He'd mutely moved toward the door as if to leave. But each time something made him stay.

Even Bob couldn't deny that she was causing absolutely no more problems. But she did not make any sort of attempts at befriending any of the other workers, either. And any closeness Jack might have felt or even presumed to exist that last night they'd spoken seemed to be all but nonexistent.

That had been almost six weeks ago.

He couldn't figure it out.

Had he done something to offend her? Said something to offend her? Maybe the sharing of his memories had been a huge mistake. 'Course, he hadn't shared that much.

Whatever it was, the frustration on his part mounted continually. On more than one occasion, he'd found himself poring over her folder again and again—trying to find some vestige of what had brought Carillon DeVries here. What had made her so hard. And alternately, what at times had suddenly made her so soft.

She was a puzzle. An intriguing one at that.

And along with those frustrations were the other emotions he tried so hard to ignore. The feelings he'd long suppressed but was having a harder time continuing to do so.

Guilt often accompanied his frustrations because he ranked them among desires as opposed to much of anything else. True, he wanted nothing more than to see Carillon DeVries free from whatever it was that haunted her, but for what reason? So he might have her? He couldn't deny the thought had crossed his mind more than once.

So he prayed. He thought. He repented. He prayed some more.

He was stumped.

Whatever past experiences he might have had with boyhood crushes, they paled in comparison. There simply was something about Carillon DeVries that made his senses take leave.

And he was not accustomed to that.

Where he tried to make God and His Word the center of his thoughts and mind, for some reason he found himself spending what he felt was too much time dwelling on this new visitor to Yesteryear.

Thoughts of her interrupted his praying, working, reading, everything. He couldn't enjoy the mental imagery, either. Not when he found it an intrusion.

Determined to keep such thoughts at bay, Jack decided to spend the majority of his day down at Sutter's Lake. Maybe take a book, hang out in the rowboat anchored along the grassy shoreline.

Something.

Anything to keep his twenty-sixth birthday from being a completely miserable experience. He'd just have to realign his thinking—remember where he had been and where God had taken him. And be grateful.

※

Carillon lifted her eyes from the journal. She'd been reading in it for the last several hours—engrossed in the unfolding drama of Madeline Whitcomb's growing relationship with the local farmer William Henrikson. Her initial internal sneering at the antiquated protocol of the time quickly abated when she reminded herself that this was no dime-store novel. This was written under the hand of a real young woman. A lonely, yet brave, young woman. One whom Carillon recognized as having far more courage than she ever would have hoped to possess.

Courage.

Or what did Madeline call it?

Faith.

Having now lost count of the times she'd tentatively picked up the worn Bible, Carillon found herself flipping through it and trying to find the passages Miss Whitcomb had detailed in her personal entries. They seemed so applicable to the struggles and feelings that the schoolteacher had been battling. Was it possible that this ancient book had anything to say to Carillon?

Noting that Psalms seemed to be a favorite of the author, Carillon paged through the thin sheets until she found the recognizable heading and began reading the passages that had been underlined at random:

> The Lord is my light and my salvation; whom shall I fear? The Lord is the strength of my life; of whom shall I be afraid? . . .
> Wait on the Lord: be of good courage, and He shall strengthen thine heart: wait, I say, on the Lord. . .
> He shall not be afraid of evil tidings: his heart is fixed, trusting in the Lord. . .
> The Lord is my strength and my shield; my heart trusted in Him, and I am helped: therefore my heart greatly rejoiceth; and with my song I will praise Him.

Frowning in concentration and trying to understand. . .comprehend. . . Carillon closed the book and thought. How was it that Madeline could draw such strength from this book? How was it that these words could dissuade her doubts and fears?

She didn't understand.

With a heavy sigh, she placed the Bible back on the chair next to her bed and stared out the window. In spite of the fact that she had the day off, she'd thus far managed to stay cooped up in the teacherage. There wasn't any particular place she wanted to go.

Lie.

There wasn't any particular place where she felt she could go.

Jack Tate's cabin ranked high on the list.

She knew she'd resolved to steer clear of it, of the abandoned farm, of all of it. But as the weeks passed, she found herself growing more restless, almost like some internal force was trying to make her go out. Seek out. . .something. But what? She was sure Jack might know the answer to those questions. But could she could face him? That was another story all together.

While she debated, the warm rays of sunshine streamed through the glass panes, silently urging her to leave her self-made cell.

With a sigh, she plucked up Madeline's journal and walked out into the early afternoon breezes, debating which way to go. An urge sent her gaze toward a trail on which she'd not yet set foot. Not sure where it led but confident she could find her way back all right, Carillon gripped the little book in her hand and started down the leaf-canopied path.

It meandered and twisted its way through the lush green woods, flanked by smaller trees, assorted berry bushes, and the intermittent fallen log. By the time she reached its end, she was surprised to find a rather large pond taking up the majority of a meadow area. The sun glinted off the bluish-green water while the tender wind pushed little wavelets toward the grassy edges. All else was still, save the bobbing of a small dory anchored near the shore.

Carillon's initial response to the scene was favorable. It seemed quiet, quaint. . .almost out of a picture book.

Until the memories crashed in.

Water.

The last place she wanted to be.

Whirling around on one foot, she started back in the direction of the path. But somewhere in the distance, she heard the muffled voices of a group of people. Tourists.

Closing her eyes in frustration, she threw another look over her shoulder at the offensive body of water. Which one?

She didn't feel much like playing tourist guide today—and it was her day off. That it was her birthday as well, she tried not to dwell on. In truth, she really didn't care.

But to stay here? Next to this. . .place?

The voices grew somewhat louder as the group traversed an intersecting path nearby.

Letting loose a long breath of resolution, Carillon picked her way through the wavering grasses and plopped herself down several yards from the shoreline.

There. Not too close. But still plenty of room for privacy.

Letting the warm beams of sun splay across her shoulders, she flipped open Madeline's journal and tried to find where she'd left off.

Until the loud splash startled her.

Jumping in the wake of the sound, she peered around, trying to find its source.

Other than the ripples fanning out near the shore, she saw nothing.

Fear getting the best of her, she scrambled to her feet, wondering if perhaps a bear or some other equally dangerous animal had somehow caused the commotion.

Then she saw it. Closer toward the middle of the pond. Someone bobbing along at a leisurely stroke.

Her heart contracted.

Instinctively, she knew exactly who it was.

Before she could hide, his head flipped around, flinging a short spray of water from his wet hair as he suddenly faced her direction.

He stopped.

For several moments all they did was stare at one another.

Afraid he'd think she'd been spying on him, she nonchalantly raised her hand in an informal wave.

He nodded his head in return and began swimming back in the direction from which he'd come.

Chewing on a thumbnail, Carillon watched as he expertly paddled toward that little boat she'd seen earlier. Unable to keep her eyes completely busy elsewhere, she couldn't help but notice his dripping form as he emerged from the water. Clad in swim trunks, she was surprised to see there was more to Jack Tate than she realized. Despite his small appearance, it was obvious that hidden underneath his chore clothes lay well-defined muscles. She'd seen his strength and felt it that night she'd been lost in the woods. Here was proof.

Feeling herself blush, she nearly had to stifle a smile. When was the last time she had blushed? Had she ever?

Picking at the binding of the old book, she kept her eyes down until she heard him approaching. Tentatively lifting her gaze, she saw that he'd thrown on a T-shirt and another pair of shorts atop his swimsuit.

"Good afternoon," she said quietly.

He nodded with that endearing half-smile of his. "And. . .you." He stopped within several feet of her and ran a hand through his sopping hair, casting another glance out over the water. "Feels. . .great. Y–you wanna. . .sssswim?"

She shook her head. "No. Thanks."

He hiked his thumbs into the front pockets of his cutoffs and assessed her. She tried to ignore the disquiet that brought on.

"Haven't. . .sssseen you. . .in. . .awhile."

With a shrug, she forced her gaze back out over the water. "Been busy, I guess. Lots of people coming through now."

He nodded. "Yeah. I. . .n–noticed that." Her gave her a little smile. "Y–you're doing. . .a g g great. . .job."

"Thank you." Again the maddening blush tried to overtake her face.

As if suddenly remembering something, Jack swung around and then back. "Hey. You w–wanna. . .go. . .for a b–boat. . .ride?"

She shook her head adamantly. "No, thank you."

"Really?" He nodded toward the little conveyance. "It's no. . .c–cruise ship. But. . .it's k–k–kind of. . .fun."

"I really don't think—"

"C–come on," he urged with a charming grin. "F–for. . .your birthday."

She stopped short and stared at him.

His grin retreated into a quiet smile. "I. . .get to ssssee. . .the records. . . on. . .everybody."

That inner urge was prompting her again. She was trying her level best to ignore it. "It doesn't look very big," she said, eyeing the boat skeptically.

"It's n–not an. . .ocean-going. . .vessel. B–but it. . .works. . .for here."

"Are you sure it's safe?"

He cocked his head and smiled again. "I've n–never lost. . .any p–passengers . . .yet."

"I don't know. . . ."

He reached out his hand.

Carillon stared at it. So strong and capable-looking. She lifted her eyes to his face. Once again she saw that peace in the depths of his golden eyes.

Fighting every cautionary urge she'd spent years to erect, she stretched out her hand and placed it in his.

It was warm. Solid. It felt right.

Without another word, he led her, hand-in-hand, to the shore.

Chapter 14

Well, she'd managed to get into the boat without too much incident. She tried to ignore the fact that shortly it would be taking her out over the open water. She also tried to ignore the fact that her heart trip-hammered when Jack assisted her into the little rowboat. What was it about his touch—his mere presence—that unsettled her so? Unsettled her. . .and gave her a profound sense of safety. An odd dichotomy.

Whatever it was, she tried to get over the next hurdle—swallowing her fear as Jack pushed the craft out into the water, deftly manning the oars in smooth succession. For some odd reason, it wasn't as hard as she anticipated. From across the wind came the trill of the late summer songbirds. The wooden paddles slapped the water quietly as the boat streamed across the calm pond. All else was still. And Carillon was grateful. Quiet was what she needed right now.

Feeling herself relax in the caress of the sun, she actually dared to drop an arm over the side, letting her fingers trail in the surprisingly warm water.

"Feels good. . .d–doesn't it?"

She let her eyes find his and slowly nodded.

"You. . .sure? N–n–no. . .swimming?"

Immediately she shook her head. "No. I don't care much for. . .swimming."

He shrugged his shoulders and kept heaving against the oars.

For a long time they simply sat, basking in the stillness of the afternoon, both of them seemingly unsure of how to break the reverie or even if there was a good reason to. Occasionally a slight catch of an eye or a timid smile would interrupt the serenity.

After a time, Jack finally found his voice. "Your. . .tour," he started, "it's. . . r–really. . .impressive."

She smiled shyly and tipped her head in a thank-you.

"I'm. . .curious." He tugged on the oars one last time before tipping them up and resting them on the gunwales, letting the boat drift lazily on the subtle current. "W–where did. . .you get sssso. . .much. . .information?"

Carillon shifted a bit and swallowed. "What do you mean?"

"Well, we. . .had a sssschool. . .teacher. . .before. Her t–talks weren't. . .nearly as. . .interesting." He grinned at the confession.

Biting back a smile of her own, Carillon shrugged. "Actually, I ran across a journal. It's helped a lot."

He nodded and proceeded to lean back against the bow of the little boat, propping his feet comfortably on the side. "Must be. . .quite a. . .read."

She agreed silently.

In the far corner of the pond, a small fish jumped, temporarily shattering the mirrorlike surface. Carillon looked over at Jack, who now had his head leaned back as well, his eyes closed against the glare of the sun, its rays picking up the golden highlights in his hair—casting shadows under his chiseled cheekbones and well-defined jaw. He almost looked sculpted. Perfect. Why had she not noticed it before? Not a drop-dead gorgeous face. . .but fine. Full of character.

But was it truly only the physical that exuded that character?

Carillon knew better.

She'd seen it. In his eyes. In his walk. In his words. In everything about him. Had he drawn strength from the Bible as Madeline Whitcomb had?

Or had his past experiences, whatever they entailed, made up that portion of him that defied definition?

The curiosity burned at her. Glancing at his resting form warily, she drew in a deep, silent breath. "Jack?"

He opened one eye, peering at her under the sun's brightness. "Yeah?"

Shifting her gaze to her hands, she fidgeted with them. "Where does your brother live?"

Both eyes opened.

"I mean, you said he lives a few hours from here, right?"

Jack's sneakered feet plopped into the bottom of the boat as he straightened back up, his face looking more sober. "Yes. He. . .lives a few. . .hours away. Th–that's. . .right."

"Where?" Amazed, and somewhat embarrassed, at her sudden boldness, Carillon watched him carefully.

Letting out a long sigh, Jack picked up the oars again and plopped them back into the water with an unrefined splash. He began tugging on them with renewed energy.

Great, she berated herself, *let's just alienate him right off the bat.*

"How. . .much time d–do. . .you have?" he suddenly asked.

The question startled her. "Um, all day, I guess." She tried to throw in a meager attempt at a smile.

He nodded and gave a halfhearted attempt back. "It m–m–might take. . . that long."

"All right," she replied quietly.

As Jack continued to pull against the wooden paddles, the story unfolded. "M–my brother. . .Jon, is in. . .prison."

She tried to quell the sharp intake of breath.

"He'll b–be there. . .fff–for a. . .long time." A profound look of sadness swept across his face.

"Why?"

Not even meeting her eyes, but losing his gaze somewhere out over the tall treetops lining the lake, he began again. "He. . .killed a. . .girl."

If she'd been shocked before, her heart positively froze now. "What?"

He nodded miserably before finally finding her face. "Over. . .t–ten years ago now."

"What—in some sort of accident?"

He shook his head. "No." His eyes narrowed as he scanned the horizon again. "He raped. . .her. Then sssstrangled her."

Carillon felt that iciness creep into her gut as she looked down at the water, not knowing what to say—and wishing she'd not said anything.

"It sssstarted a. . .long time. . .b–before that. He'd. . .always k–kind of. . . been. . .in and out. . .of t–trouble." He kneaded his forehead as if trying to remember. "I d–don't know. . .what age he. . .sssstarted buying. . .the m–magazines." He shook his head. "It. . .w–went downhill. . .from there."

"How old was he. . .when it happened?"

"Nineteen."

"And the girl?"

"F–fifteen."

Nausea crept into her.

Two distinct pools formed in Jack's eyes. "Nice. . .girl, t–too."

"You knew her?" she whispered.

He nodded. "Sh–she was. . .our neighbor." Wiping at his eyes with his palms, he dropped the oars with a thunk back into the boat and raked his fingers through his hair. "By. . .the time th–they. . .found her b–body, I. . .knew." He rubbed at his jaw thoughtfully. "I. . .just knew."

"What happened then?"

"The t–trial. P–pretty short. D–didn't take them. . .long. . .to l–look at. . .the obvious. . .evidence."

Her heart constricting a fraction more, she studied him carefully. "And you had to testify, didn't you?"

"Yep." He cast his gaze back over the scenery. "I p–put my. . .own brother . . .in jail."

Without a moment's hesitation, Carillon carefully slid off her seat and moved one closer to him. "No, you didn't," she said. "No, you didn't."

He sought her face as she inched closer to him.

"His own actions put him there. What if you hadn't said anything? What if he'd gotten away with it? What might he have done later?"

Behind the golden depths, a moment of clarity resurfaced as he stared at her.

Carillon reached out and took one of his hands. "Jack, you did what was right. Responsible."

He remained silent.

For some unknown reason, she forged on. "There's more to this, isn't there? It doesn't end or begin with this whole ordeal—the trial?"

His full lips pursed momentarily. He shook his head.

"That closet upstairs in your house. . ."

The nod finished her sentence.

"And that was the least of it, wasn't it?" Suddenly, somehow, she knew. Her grip tightened on his. "You did the right thing," she repeated.

He kept staring at their clutched hands. "He's. . .still m—my. . .brother."

"Yes." She swallowed hard. "And you still love him—in spite of it all. Don't you?" It wasn't a question.

He took a deep breath. "I l—looked up. . .t—to him. Fff—for so. . .long."

"And now?"

He finally looked into her eyes. "I. . .found out—you c—can't. . .look to. . .men. Only. . .Jesus." He smiled somewhat shakily.

Carillon retreated a fraction at his pronouncement. Now she was totally at a loss as to what to say.

"Th—thank you," he said quietly.

"For what?"

"For. . .listening. And. . .understanding."

Slowly, she withdrew her hand. "For listening. . .? Sure." She tried to smile, but failed miserably. "But don't ever blame yourself, Jack." A painful lump rose in her throat. "I know what it's like to be responsible for someone's—for someone. And to blow it. You are not one of those people."

Now it was Jack's turn to look confused. But if he held questions, he was gracious enough to silence them—for now. Carillon was eternally grateful.

Off on the skyline, a distant roll of thunder rumbled.

Both of them cast their eyes in that direction. A long ways off yet, but steadily moving in, a long, wide band of black clouds was eating up the blue sky.

Jack slowly pulled his fingers away from hers, and Carillon was surprised at the keen disappointment that flooded her soul. Plucking up the oars, he began heading back toward the shore. "G—guess we'd better. . .get in."

She nodded in agreement while her heart railed at the coming storm. For having started the day desiring to be totally alone, now she found herself wishing she could remain in Jack's company.

The quiet of the slapping paddles seemed a good interlude between their ride and the reality that lay awaiting them at shore. Carillon tried to sort out her feelings as they approached, finding it difficult to do so while in his presence. One question came into view.

"Jack?"

He raised his chin and waited.

"You—" She cleared her throat. "You read your Bible, right?"

He nodded without hesitation. "I'd never. . .have b–been able. . .to m–make it. . .without."

"Why?"

He looked at her curiously.

"I mean, what's in it? Well—I know what's in it. . .but what do you get out of it?"

His face softened. "Life. Strength. Hope. . .w–when all hope. . .is gone."

Carillon bit her lip as she contemplated his answer. "All just from those pages? Those words?"

This time he shook his head. "Not. . .the words. From the. . .author of. . .those words."

"God."

He nodded and smiled a little. "If I. . .sssstruggle at. . .t–times, all I. . .have t–to. . .do is. . .go back. B–back to. . .the beginning."

She nodded as if she understood. She didn't, though. *The author? God? How could Jack find Him in there?* She'd read Madeline's similar thoughts along those lines and had been just as confused.

Carillon had read the words, too. And that's just what they were. Words on a page. Nothing more.

She started to ask one more question and then thought better of it. She didn't want to appear totally ignorant. So she merely nodded a thank-you for his answer and waited until they pulled up on shore, her head swimming in confusion and curiosity.

❈

The darkening sky had as yet to spill any of its threatened rain, but it kept getting more sinister by the minute. Jack kept one eye heavenward as he jogged along the path cutting through the woods toward the compound. If his clock had been right, he still had time to make it there.

As his steps took him nearer, he reflected on the afternoon. What could have been a miserable, lonely day had surprised him. Doubly.

That Carillon had even approached him had been enough of a shock. That she'd agreed to spend some time with him had been a pleasurable bonus. Until the subject matter had grown serious.

But amazingly, God, in His goodness, had used that as well. Normally such reminiscence would have put Jack into a funk for days, but this time telling his story had been only a sweet release. An understanding heart had listened. He thanked God for that.

But alternately, he felt a tugging at his soul—an urgency about Carillon's own heart and his own feelings of inadequacy. . .whatever the reasoning behind them all. He thought this gesture, as small as it might be, would be appropriate.

With a confident stride, he entered the door of the gift shop, waving at the two young women behind the counter.

"Hi, Jack," they chorused in unison.

He smiled back and headed in their direction.

"Need something?" Karen, the younger of the two, asked.

"Yeah." He cleared his throat. "D–do you. . .have any. . .journals?"

"Like diary-type journals?"

He nodded.

"Sure. We have a really nice selection back here." She beckoned him to follow her to the rear of the store where a long shelf stood, filled with an assortment of bound books. She pulled off a few plain, leather-bound varieties for him to peruse. "Like these?"

He glanced at the offerings, then studied the shelf again, his gaze shifting toward a different one. A cream-colored fabric encased the volume, the center a showcase for a few delicate, pressed-and-dried wildflowers lying behind a protective plastic window. He picked it off the ledge and smiled. "This. . .one. Please."

Karen inclined her head in deference to his choice. "Alrighty."

"And c–could you. . .wrap it for. . .me?"

She agreed and headed back up to the counter.

Jack followed her all the way, smiling.

Chapter 15

Carillon settled back onto her small bed, rereading Madeline's entry one more time:

> *It seems the more time I spend with Mr. Henrikson, the more he becomes "William" to me—though I'd never dream of calling him that to his face. In my heart, I already have. And unless I'm under completely false assumptions, I think he must feel something for me as well. But here we are—the guidelines for my occupation and good society requiring us to keep our distance.*
>
> *Frustrating.*
>
> *How can two hearts connect with all the barriers between?*

Carillon released a long breath and glanced out at the growing darkness of the impending stormy afternoon. How indeed?

Barriers? She had them. Jack had them.

But perhaps she, too, was being presumptuous. Had Jack really indicated that he'd shown more than a passing interest in her? Anything more than any other person at Yesteryear? Jack Tate was a caring person. He seemed to love everybody. And everyone loved him right back.

Love.

Carillon swallowed hard around the mere thought of the word. She couldn't let herself even close to that. She wouldn't. The last person she'd loved was gone. Evie was gone forever—and it was all Carillon's fault.

No, she wouldn't wish her love on anyone—assuming she could even muster the emotion anymore.

But as vainly as she tried to deny her feelings, every facet of Jack flooded her mind. Every movement, every compassionate glance, every touch. Each sweet, stammered word.

Frustration mounted that she'd allowed herself to become so soft. What had happened to her walls? To her fortress she'd erected so perfectly? Tony hadn't come close to it. Nor had any of the others. How could Jack, this person she'd known for such a short time, knock down such a vital protection with his first glance at her?

Her eyes trailed back to the diary:

I know all sense of propriety is lost when my mind succumbs to these fanciful notions. But I've simply never met anyone like William. All the dandies from the cities east do not hold a candle to him. Where they're fine and regal, he's strong and steadfast. Where they simper and complain, he frowns in concentration and is diligent. Where they blatantly feast their eyes upon a woman's beauty, he makes me feel one hundred times more beautiful simply by treating me like a lady—even though the times we've shared together are so few.

Running a hand through her hair in amazement, Carillon couldn't stifle the smile. This man sounded so much like Jack.

I pray that my thoughts and emotions won't supercede God's plans for me. But I'm reminded so much of Solomon's wisdom in trying to understand the complexities of this scenario:

"There be three things which are too wonderful for me,
yea, four which I know not:
The way of an eagle in the air;
the way of a serpent upon a rock;
the way of a ship in the midst of the sea;
and the way of a man with a maid."
. . .the way of a man with a maid.

Father, You've created us to be this way. To interact this way. To love this way. Guide me in Your will.

Carillon read the words again. How could she not agree? The effect that Jack had on her resisted any definition. Any understanding.

Her thoughts were broken by a strange sensation. From her front door, a subtle shuffling could be discerned. Then silence.

Remaining on her bed, she glanced out the small side window but saw nothing. Curiosity getting the best of her, she rose and crossed to the door, letting it creak open on its rusty hinges.

The meadow before her was quiet, not giving up any secrets. Perhaps it had just been a small animal nosing around.

She started to shut the door, but then she saw it.

A small parcel lying on the top step, propped against the threshold. Wrapped in a muted yellow paper, a simple length of lace gracing the front. And a little envelope taped alongside it.

A lump rose in her throat as she stared at the gift. No question who'd delivered it. With shaking hands, she bent down to retrieve the package and looked once more out across the waving grasses. Nothing.

Retreating into her cabin, she hesitantly detached the envelope and pulled out the card. A pen-and-ink sketch of an aged barn surrounded by tall wildflowers and prairie grasses graced the cover. Biting her lips, she eased the card open and slowly drank in the words written in Jack's hand. A deliberate, masculine scrawl that seemed. . .him:

> *No one should have to celebrate a birthday alone. I'm glad you were here to share mine. And whether you wanted company on your own day or not, I'm equally glad I was the one to be with you.*

Her heart stalled for a moment at the pronouncement—then she warmed under its ardor.

> *You mentioned the journal you'd been reading. Journals can be powerful tools in helping us understand ourselves—especially as we look back at all God has done for us and through us. I've kept one for a number of years. And hoping I'm not being too presumptuous, I thought you might be interested in one, too.*

> *Happy Birthday, Carillon.*
> *Jack*

Laying aside the card, she unceremoniously tore into the paper and pulled out the simple but elegant little book. And for an uncomfortable, emotional moment, her eyes filled with tears. Cracking it open, she saw her name written carefully on the inside cover. She was overwhelmed with the thoughtfulness, the generosity—and the memories. . . .

"Happy Birthday, Lon!" her little voice chirped in its normal four-year-old exuberance.

Carillon grinned and hugged Evie to her. "Thanks, Bug."

"I have something for you!"

"Oh, Honey, that's all right. You don't have to give me anything—"

"I want to. Wait here!" She sprinted around the corner while Carillon smiled and returned to her bowl of breakfast cereal.

It wasn't two seconds before the little imp was back, her arms held awkwardly behind her back. In a fumbling of fingers and arms, she produced the very crudely wrapped gift, covered with probably more than twice the wrapping paper needed and three times that amount of tape.

Stifling a laugh, Carillon took the thing and proceeded to rip away at the inch-thick barrier of transparent adhesive. "What do we have here?" she asked, her eyebrows rising expectantly.

Evie just stood with her arms clasped behind her back, twisting back and forth in anxious anticipation, the grin covering her little face.

By the time Carillon reached the interior, a small fuzzy leg covered in black-and-white spots stuck out from the paper.

Immediately she knew what the gift was, and her fingers stalled as she looked at her little sister.

Evie jumped up and down. "Open it! Open it!"

Carillon finished peeling back the paper to reveal exactly what she'd guessed. A small Beanie Baby dalmatian—Evie's favorite. The one she had to have when going to bed, going on trips, even just to the grocery store. The little dog was never separated from her.

"Evie," she started, "this is—"

"Dean!" the little girl proclaimed gleefully.

Carillon smiled. "Dean" had been toddler Evie's attempts at saying "Beanie." "He's. . .great." She stared at her sister. "But I can't take Dean."

The face fell a fraction. "Why?"

"Well. . .he's your special dog. I wouldn't want him to get lonely without you."

A frown started across the little girl's face. "He won't be lonely. I know you'll take good care of him. And you'll love him as much as I do."

"Sure, Hon. But don't you think—"

"Lon, I want to give him to you. It's all I have to give you."

Carillon fought back a few tears as she grabbed Evie in a fierce embrace. "You don't have to get me anything, Bug. You are more than enough." She pulled back and ruffled the curly mop of hair. "But if you really want me to have Dean. . ."

"I do! I do!" The jumping began again.

"Okay." Carillon nestled the little dog next to her face and smiled. "But you'll have to promise to take care of him for me while I'm at school and stuff."

Evie nodded earnestly.

Carillon's heart swelled at the memory. Was there nothing that Evie wouldn't have done for her? Clutching Jack's gift, she stroked the smooth cover and frowned. So giving. There were more and more similarities that she saw between Evie and Jack all the time. Why?

Releasing a long breath, Carillon placed the book on the table. Well, she wasn't going to let this opportunity go by. She'd been nurturing her selfish side for most of her life. . .now it was time to learn some lessons from her little sister. To give back while she still could. Because she'd missed the chance once, she wouldn't let it happen again.

Heading back to the door, she peeked her head outside. No rain yet. Just the smell of it soon to come. Good enough. A little rain never hurt her. And she had a mission to accomplish.

Pulling the door shut behind her, she started in the direction of the compound.

There had to be something she could find for him. Something that would show her appreciation.

Something that would make Evie proud of her.

✳

Jack had a hard time containing his grin as he strode back to his cabin. He'd struggled with the option of handing her the gift himself or just leaving it. He opted for the latter—not wanting to push her. Intimidate her. It was better this way.

And it felt great.

By the time he reached his porch, he noticed something unusual. What? Stealing a glance around the barnyard, he noticed all was quiet. Too quiet. The guinea hens who normally fussed and cackled around the perimeter of the small farm were nowhere to be seen.

He trudged toward the small building that housed the chickens and poked his head in. No, they were all there. Sitting in their boxes, albeit nervously. Their uncomfortable shifting and turning not lost on him, Jack pulled his head back outside and noticed for the first time the complete stillness in the air.

The breeze that had played through the trees all afternoon had died away. No birds sang. Even the insects were silent. It was eerie.

Casting an eye at the sky, he felt his stomach roil up. The blackness was much nearer now. But worse was the sky fronting the inky clouds. It held a bizarre greenish glow—one that Jack remembered only a few times from his childhood.

Sprinting toward the cabin, he took the steps in one leap and stormed through the door. He dug the battery-powered weather radio from one of the cupboards and flicked the thing on. He was immediately greeted by the attention-grabbing monotone beeps of the weather alert system.

Waiting a few seconds more, he listened for the announcer's voice, the crackling of the airwaves distorting the words every so often. "A severe thunderstorm is moving in a wide band across the west-central portion of the state. Be alerted that this storm could contain heavy rains, hail, and damaging winds. If you're out of doors, seek shelter immediately."

The station crackled again, and Jack picked up the radio, fiddling with the antenna and shaking it impatiently.

From outside the still-open front door, Jack heard the wind pick up as the leaves on the trees began to rustle—first slowly, then more forcefully.

The radio voice returned.

"We have several reports of funnel clouds sighted along the border of Minnesota and Wisconsin—and more sightings east."

Outside, the wind intensified, whipping the tall pines ferociously, their slender trunks bowing down to the strength of the force moving in.

Jack ran to the door and looked at the sky. It was a churning, turbulent

207

mixture of green and gray and black. It looked anything but good. Across the yard, one of the shed doors began banging haphazardly back and forth.

All Jack could think of was Carillon. Out in the middle of that open meadow—the teacherage hardly in any condition to withstand strong winds. Without a second thought, he dashed out, just as the first fat drops of rain began pelting the ground.

He had to get to her—get her to Liberty Town, where they'd be safe. Just until this thing blew over. He ran, the wind at his back propelling him along, the scent of something ominous hanging in its crest.

And in the now-vacant kitchen, the weather radio blared out its warning to no one. "Seek shelter immediately in a basement or sturdy interior room with no windows. Do not go outside."

Chapter 16

While it looked at first like it might hold off for a time, instead the inclement weather barged onto the scene like the snapping of a whip. By the time Carillon reached Liberty Town, the wind was buffeting her so fiercely she could scarcely push her way through it. The wicked drops of water bombarded her like so many arrows. She was having a hard enough time just trying to catch her breath. Realizing she couldn't continue toward the compound, she stood in the middle of the main street, vainly peering against the sheets of water blurring her vision.

From somewhere under the howl of the wind, she heard a voice. Faintly.

"Carillon!"

Shielding her eyes against the torrential rain, she searched for the source of the voice.

"Carillon! Over here! The house!"

She turned and made out the form of Paul, the blacksmith, battling his way toward her. Never so grateful to see another human being, she didn't hesitate when he offered his hand and arm to help her across the yard toward the Mitchell House. As they walked, a section of the white picket fence uprooted and went cartwheeling in front of them. Paul shielded her with an arm and glanced around, looking for any more debris.

Finally, all but dragging her to the side door at the house's foundation, Paul helped her down the wet, slick stone steps and pushed through the heavy wooden door. While he grunted as he tried to slam the thing closed, Carillon's eyes adjusted to the dim light flickering in the center of the small, dank-smelling room. All the residents of Liberty Town were huddling against the far wall, blankets and other miscellaneous wraps scattered among them.

Carillon released a long breath, realizing that she'd probably been holding it since the wind had kicked up so suddenly. Paul had managed to latch the door and stood at her side, his hair plastered against his head, his white work shirt almost transparent with moisture.

"You okay?" he asked breathlessly.

She nodded and realized she, too, was soaking. Carla came over with a blanket and tossed it around her shoulders. Carillon accepted it gratefully, trying to wring some of the excess moisture from her hair. "Some storm."

The others looked at her soberly. A few nodded.

"When do you think it will blow over?" she asked.

Paul looked the most morose. "I don't know," he breathed, reaching for another blanket someone was handing him. "I don't like the looks of this one."

Before the words were completely out of his mouth, an excruciatingly loud *Pop!* thundered from outside. Everyone jumped in its aftermath.

"What was that?" one of the men asked.

He was answered by a load creaky groan, a dull thud, and the unmistakable shattering of glass.

"Come on," Paul urged Carillon and everyone else. "Let's back up against the far wall as much as we can."

Dumbly shuffling along with the others, Carillon looked over her shoulder and watched the plank door shudder on its heavy hinges, the invisible monster outside trying its best to break in.

Huddled with the others in a tightly knit clump, Carillon watched the anxious faces and suddenly wished that Jack were here. She always felt better when Jack was nearby.

Jack!

Her arm shot out, grabbing Paul's shoulder. "What about Jack?"

A serious frown creased his brow, but he didn't hesitate in giving his answer. "Jack'll be fine. All the farms have root cellars. He'll know what to do."

"Are you sure?"

Paul nodded again in reassurance.

Before a remnant of peace could soothe her, she heard it. So did the others apparently. Their faces turned toward the door, their eyes wide. . .anxious.

From somewhere beyond, and moving steadily nearer, a distant hum. . .then a rumble.

"Oh, sweet Jesus. . . ," someone behind Carillon prayed.

The rumble fast grew into a roar, and had she not known better, Carillon would have guessed that they were immediately under a train track.

"All right, everybody," Paul said in an authoritative voice, "heads down. Cover up as much as possible!" The order turned into a yell as the clamor outside evolved into a deafening cacophony that defied comparison. All Carillon knew was that for as long as she lived, she never wanted to hear it again. "And pray!" Paul yelled again. "Pray hard!"

For the first time in her life, she had no problem with that. "Please, God," she whispered, her voice lost even to her own ears in the din. "Please be with Jack. Please. . ."

❊

Jack couldn't see anymore.

He fought and struggled and gasped for breath in what suddenly seemed to be a vacuum.

He knew the teacherage was just ahead. Occasionally he'd catch a glimpse of the white frame before him. Then it would be eaten up again in the fury of the elements. Accumulating as much breath as he could, he shouted for all he was worth. "Carillon!"

Stupid. He couldn't even hear himself. How was she going to hear? No, he'd just have to get there and get her out.

From behind him, a snap and pop prompted his feet to propel him forward just as a medium-sized pine crashed to the ground. Then the roar approached, shaking the ground, the air, and the sky as it ate up all in its path.

Squinting against the dismal gray and into the yawning black beyond, Jack's heart stalled. The wide funnel was weaving and twisting and dancing its way toward him, oblivious to the trees and other landmarks in its way.

Adrenaline his guide, aided by pure instinct, Jack stumbled forward, half running, half crawling toward the doomed building. "Carillon!" he screamed, his voice now hoarse with the effort.

Then his breath was gone.

He couldn't move.

Splaying himself out onto the ground, he tried to lift his head, but branches, chunks of wood, and other items he couldn't even identify kept hurtling past him. He ducked his head, dodged a piece, and lifted it up once more, watching helplessly as the sinister cloud advanced.

One more time. He lifted a knee, trying to get into a hands-and-knees position—and was knocked flat with a wicked slap to his side. Grimacing at the sharp pain in his ribs, he turned and watched a substantial beam flying end over end. With a groan, he flattened himself on the ground once more. "Father," he croaked, "again. . .You kn–know where. . .she is." Even the effort to speak hurt. He closed his eyes. *Wrap Your arms around her. Protect her, Lord. Draw her close to You.*

At that moment, an earsplitting explosion of wood, glass, and other material showered the tense air around him.

Barely able to lift his head, he looked up and ahead.

The teacherage was gone. Gone.

A lump grew in his throat and he buried his head back in the wet grass. But the grief was quickly taken over by panic as he felt himself rising off the ground. Battling for what he knew could very well be his life, he thrashed against the force trying to suck him from the earth. Each movement brought the same stabbing pain to his side and somewhere deeper inside his chest.

Trying to inch, crawl, scramble—anything. Anything to escape from the invisible clutches of the tornado's talons.

In a split second, he felt himself drop back to the unforgiving dirt below, the cavernous suction still stealing his breath. *It must be moving away—in the other direction.* That was his last thought before a chunk of debris slammed viciously against his skull.

For the briefest of seconds, he felt no more pain. Only a dizzying warmth. A muted comfort. A stillness. Then everything became blackness.

✳

How long they'd been in the root cellar, Carillon couldn't begin to guess. Ten minutes? Ten years?

The resounding roar had abated quite awhile ago, and now the only discernible sound from the other side of the door was the subtle patter of rain. Paul was the first to stand up. None of the others seemed eager to join him. Taking his leadership role seriously, he headed to the door, slowly unlatched it, and peered hesitantly up from the bottom of the steps. After a second or two, he started up, his legs then his feet disappearing as he went higher. Everyone else was silent. Anxious.

After a minute or two had passed, some of them started to squirm. "Paul?" one of the guys called out. "Paul, what's out there?"

After a moment, Paul's feet reappeared on the stairs. Each person eagerly watched as his face came into view. Their eagerness fell into subtle despair when they saw his countenance.

"You can come out now," he said quietly. "It's over."

Their legs wobbly from fear and from sitting so long, the small group rose to its feet, timidly following the blacksmith out and up into the slowly abating rain.

The first thing that met them was the huge oak, sprawled literally only feet away from the house like some felled giant. Under its mass of crushed leaves and branches lay what remained of the carriage house.

A few gasps were heard behind Carillon—along with a few whispers of thanks to God that the tree hadn't hit the house proper.

But then their eyes shifted to take in the entire town.

Or rather, what was left of it.

The general store had shifted off its foundation, its sides bent at an awkward angle, looking like a toy building made of matchsticks that had been stepped on by a child. The boardinghouse had no windows intact, and the roof looked like someone had peeled off most of the shingles. But the worst site was the blacksmith shop and livery stable.

They were gone.

All that remained was the erect stone chimney of Paul's fireplace.

Carillon heard several sniffles behind her. She, herself, was still too stunned to register much of any emotion.

"Look!" someone cried.

All the others turned to where they were pointing. There, at the far end of the main street, unscathed by the battle that had just occurred, stood the church.

212

Proud and patrician. Graceful and resolute.

Several in the crowd headed in its direction. More began to follow.

But Carillon hesitated, her eyes wanting to turn the other way—over the field and through the battered woods.

Paul must have sensed her hesitation. She found him standing at her side looking down at her, his eyes full of understanding. "Shall we go and check things out?"

Taking a deep breath, Carillon nodded. "I just want to make sure he's okay."

He tossed off the blanket still hanging over his shoulders. "All right. You head to his cabin. I'll go and see about your place."

Giving him a weak smile, she threw off her own wrap and started down the gravel road, the only sound between them, the crunch of their feet on the wet stones. She found herself praying again. *Please. . .please let him be all right.*

By the time she and Paul split up to take the separate paths, Carillon was nearly at Jack's cabin. Unconsciously holding her breath, she rounded the corner to the clearing. Never before had she felt such relief.

The barn stood strong. All the other buildings remained intact. The cabin had not been bothered an iota. Closing her eyes in thankfulness, her steps quickened as she approached the cabin. "Jack!"

The front door gaped open. Skittering up the steps, she stood in the kitchen, noticing the floor was wet. Apparently the door had blown open during the storm. "Jack? Are you in here?"

No answer.

Sense coming to her, she realized exactly where he'd be. Outside. Checking the buildings. The animals.

She raced to the barn. "Jack?"

Only the nervously twitching cows and horses stared at her.

The chicken house? Not there, either.

She stood in the middle of the yard and slowly turned around. "Jack?" Why she kept calling, she didn't know. It was obvious he wasn't there.

The only other place he might be— Of course, he'd have headed to the compound. . .or even Liberty Town to survey the damage everywhere else. It's what he would do.

Taking a relaxing breath, she started back toward the path that led toward the town again. Halfway there, curiosity got the better of her. What about the school? The teacherage?

Frowning, she looked from the one trail to the other. She could just check on it quickly, then head back.

Before her mind had completely made itself up, she saw a figure approaching under the shadow of the trees from the path leading to her place. Ready to call out Jack's name, she held her tongue when she realized it wasn't him.

213

Paul emerged, his face an ashen white.

Carillon scurried over to him. "What? Is it the school?"

He shook his head. "The school is. . .beat up. But okay."

"The teacherage?"

"Gone," he said hoarsely.

"Gone?" Her mind refused to grasp the immensity of the statement. "Gone?" She looked past his shoulder and started to walk around him.

He grabbed her arm and held it fast.

Surprised at his sudden grip, she met his eyes and frowned. "I want to see. I can handle it—"

Paul shook his head again. "Jack's back there." His voice was barely above a whisper.

"What?"

A surprising pool of tears welled up in the young man's eyes.

"What?" Her eyes darted to the path again. "What do you mean, Jack's back there?" She started forward again.

He tightened his grip on her arm.

"Paul! What do you mean? Is he okay? Is he hurt? What. . ." Her words died away as she watched his face contort in an effort to control a sob.

Hot tears sprang to her own eyes, spilling down her cheeks maddeningly. "What's the matter?" she demanded angrily. She didn't understand her anger or who it might be directed at. She just knew she was overwhelmed with rage. "What's happened?"

Paul could only shake his head as his lower lip quivered.

Carillon grabbed his immense shoulders and shook them with all her strength. "Where is Jack? Is he all right?"

He sniffed and swiped a large palm over his eyes. "I don't know. Bob and some of the other guys were already there. They've called for an ambulance."

"An ambulance?" Horror squeezed her lungs and her heart. "Paul, tell me."

Paul gazed off toward the teacherage. "He wasn't moving. He was on the ground, and he wasn't moving."

The words buzzed around in her head—around and around and around. They were making her dizzy. Sick.

She, too, looked down the seemingly peaceful trail, fraudulently disguised under the now calm trees. It became a tunnel—the edges getting fuzzier and fuzzier, fading to black. To black.

To nothingness. . .

Chapter 17

Complete and total exhaustion drained the life from her body in a way Carillon had never experienced before. If the events of the last twenty-four hours weren't enough, their staggering repercussions were.

Reeling in shock, along with everyone else at Yesteryear, she'd taken the trek to the hospital with a small group of people. Yet when she'd walked into Jack's room, for some ridiculous reason, she was totally unprepared for what she saw.

The myriad of tubes and wires taped to his pale, still frame nearly sent her over the edge. It was too much. Flickering in and out of her wavering consciousness as she stared at him were images of Evie. . . .

A flurry of doctors and nurses surrounded Carillon's little sister. Orders being called out—the tone direct, but quiet.

Her parents finally at her side. Carillon feeling a world away from them—and wishing she were twice that far away physically if only to escape the intense guilt and shame smothering her.

Back at Jack's room, someone had the presence of mind to grab a chair and usher her into it.

Everything else seemed so surreal. This couldn't be happening, could it? What seemed only hours ago, they'd been together on the little boat. Now here he was unconscious in a hospital bed. His future? None of the doctors seemed to want to speculate. The terms "possible brain injury" and "further tests" kept coming around, but nothing more definite than that.

In her hands, Carillon clutched the few things she'd brought with her, the only things that seemed of any importance anymore. Amazingly, in the midst of the rubble surrounding what had been the teacherage, she'd found Madeline's journal and Bible intact, as well as the journal from Jack.

She stared down at the volumes now.

Everyone else had vacated the room. Why, she wasn't sure, but she suspected that Paul's prompting had something to do with it. So other than the beep and hiss of machines floating amid the subdued aura of the ICU, it remained quiet. She wondered what on earth to do. To say. The nurses had encouraged them all to talk to Jack, reminding them that often those in a coma can still hear, still comprehend.

She had planned to read some of Madeline's entries to him because she couldn't come up with any words of her own. Not any that wouldn't cause excruciating pain—or more guilt. In the back of her mind, Carillon couldn't forget that the reason Jack Tate was lying in this hospital room, vacillating between life and death, was because of her. Plain and simple.

Here it was all over again.

The same reason Evie had slipped away from her. . .it was all her fault.

By the time Bob came to tell her it was time to go, she'd spent the entire fifteen minutes saying nothing, barely able to keep her eyes focused on his face. Occasionally she had reached over and tentatively touched his hand, his fingers. They felt so cold. So unlike him. . .

It had been the ride home in the large van that put the quintessential cap on this day. In the midst of the chaos surrounding Yesteryear's sudden need for closure, the employees and visitors found themselves faced with the question of where to go next—and when. For the majority of them, their only choice was returning home.

Carillon couldn't comprehend their eagerness. Each, in spite of the disappointment of a short season and the worry surrounding Jack, seemed relieved at the prospect of heading for home.

Was that her only choice? Would her parents show up to retrieve her? To take her back to wherever they lived now? During the few months Carillon had been gone, her parents had managed to sell their house—the one with so many bad memories—and locate elsewhere. Closer to church, they'd said. Carillon hadn't responded. Did it really matter where they lived? It would change nothing. Undo nothing.

If that possible scenario wasn't enough to keep her brain busy, Bob had blown her out of the water with his own request—to look after Jack's cabin until he came back. Carillon didn't miss the hopeful optimism in his voice. Nor did he seem to miss what must have been obvious doubt flickering in her eyes.

"Are you sure?" she stammered. "I mean, Paul. . .or somebody else could—"

"Paul has agreed to do the outside chores. But he's staying at the compound, helping tally the lists for replacement and repair costs." The large man's face looked anxious. "If you wouldn't mind?"

Carillon tried not to sigh too loudly as she directed her gaze out at the drizzly day. "All right," she agreed quietly. "I'll try."

Bob clapped a large hand over hers in gratitude. "Thank you, Carillon."

Now here she was.

And it was the worst mistake she'd made thus far in her short life.

Sliding her arms across the wooden table, she let her head flop down on them, the painful lump in her throat so thick it burned with every swallow. "What are you doing?" she whispered to the silence in the little cabin. The little place that personified Jack.

She'd managed to clean up the kitchen and living area mechanically, washing, drying, stacking, sweeping—grateful for how quickly it made the time pass. But now. . .now the sun had sunk behind the horizon, the flicker of the lantern cast wavering shadows across the log walls, and the doubts and fears and inadequacies were finding her again.

Lifting her chin wearily, she stared at the sturdily made ladder that led up to Jack's sleeping area. His own personal place. The yawning black space above gaped down at her, almost daring her to invade it.

Closing her eyes, she rested her forehead against the table again. She'd made a stupid, stupid mistake. Again. She'd promised to do something more than she could. Another hollow word to add to her list.

But where else could she go?

Trying to will her nerves into some sort of resolve, she stood and gripped the handle of the lantern in one hand and placed a somewhat shaky grip on the rung of the ladder.

Boosting herself up, she climbed. Step after step, rung after rung, as the orangish light slowly ate up the darkness above her.

Reaching the top, she stepped onto the loft's platform, surprised at the generous-sized room. Bookcases dominated one whole side of the loft. In spite of herself, Carillon couldn't contain the little smile. Of course. Jack would have scads of books.

The end, under the steep dormer, housed a small window looking to the woods beyond. The wall opposite the bookshelves left enough room for a goodly sized cot and a small bedside table and chair.

Carillon stared at the small bed, its sheets and blankets still mussed from the last night of sleep. Jack's sleep. Inching toward it, she hesitantly reached out a hand, smoothing the edge of the thick blanket. Easing to her knees, she straightened the bedclothes and finally grabbed the feather pillow, fluffing it gently as she replaced it at the head. With each movement, each tuck, the subtle scent of Jack greeted her senses. A soulful combination of fresh air, wood smoke, and soap.

The choking lump in her throat grew larger still, and her eyes burned with threatening tears. Turning her back on the bunk, she focused her attention instead on the books. Read. Maybe that would help. She must get her mind focused on something else—anything else—until she was ready to drop off to sleep immediately. But even then, she had no clue how she was going to manage sliding into Jack Tate's bed and sleeping peacefully.

For the moment, she concentrated on the stacks and stacks of volumes before her. Lots of classics. Lots. But nothing that really grabbed her attention. Her finger trailed along the worn edges of the leather spines, hesitating every few titles.

Then she came to the end of the top shelf. The huge book had to be at least four inches thick. Hefting it from its place, she blinked at the cover.

Holy Bible.

Settling onto the floor, she tugged it onto her lap and peeled open the crackling cover. Within the first few thick, yellowed pages were a myriad of handwritten words in aged, blue ink. Obviously in some other language—German, from the look of it.

Intrigued, she continued. She came to a series of pages with a distinct pattern of neat, heavy lines. Each one held a name, a date, sometimes a note.

A family tree of sorts.

Glancing at the first entry she came to, she sobered. *Byron Alvin Tate, died March 4, 1992.* She swallowed. Jack had mentioned that his parents had died, but reading it in Jack's neat hand somehow made it harder to think about.

Alice Marie Tate, died July 7, 1989. His mother. Her heart ached for him.

Then, smiling a little shakily, she touched the following words: *Jack William Tate, born August 20, 1974.* They were written in a neat, feminine script she assumed to belong to Jack's mother. She went on.

Jonathon Byron Tate, born November 17, 1969. Her heart chilled for a fraction, until she reread it and imagined the posting being entered by a new mother on the birth of her firstborn son. What hopes and dreams had she had for her sons?

Byron Alvin Tate and Alice Marie Henrikson, married June 30, 1968. Jack's parents. Byron and Alice.

Carillon started to move on—then looked back. Zeroing in on Alice's name. Henrikson. Odd. She remembered Madeline Whitcomb's farmer. . .William Henrikson. It had to be coincidence. Henrikson was a common enough name.

Even if Jack's middle name was William also?

Her breath quickening, she slid her finger down the continuing list of names, through WWII, through the Great Depression, through the turn of the century. The name Henrikson remained a mainstay in the genealogy from Jack's mother back.

The list grew shorter and shorter as she flipped through the pages of birth dates, children, marriages, deaths. Then she came to the final entry among the pages, the one that signaled the beginning of the record keeping. Her heart stalled.

William Peder Henrikson and Madeline Sarah Whitcomb, married August 3, 1854. No way. This was not possible. It just couldn't—

Carillon shoved the book off her lap and scrambled back down the ladder to where she'd left the journals on the table. Scooping them up and trotting up the rungs again, she plopped next to the still-open Bible and began flipping through Madeline's journal. She'd almost read the entire thing. Almost.

But for now, she flipped straight to the end, finding the last few entries. Eighteen fifty-four.. Spring, spring, end of school year. . .here it was—summer.

8 June 1854
    The school year is finished. I survived!
    The children brought me an assortment of lovely wildflowers and miscellaneous candies and baked goodies today. On several occasions I had to

rein myself in so as not to show too much emotion in front of them. It was both a good and rather difficult day.

I received a letter from Mother and Father today. Even Father seems surprised at my success in having completed the year "unscathed." I penned them a letter back almost immediately. Partially to tell them of my final day at this charming little school—that thought still brings tears to my eyes at times. I think I could stay. . .if there were not future plans with which to contend.

As my parents will make their trek out here to help retrieve some of my things, I think—no, I know—they will be much surprised when we pick them up at the station. . .William and I.

For William has a particular question he wants to ask of my father.

And it's that thought alone that thrills me. . .and makes the giving up of this teaching position a rather small thing to bear. For if our plans go as we hope, within a few short months, I will be Mrs. William Henrikson— and quite possibly the most blessed and happy woman on this earth.

Carillon let the diary slip from her hands to the floor, landing next to the family Bible.

Somewhere in the lineage, Madeline was Jack's however-many-great-grandmother. All the treks Carillon had made from that same teacherage to that same farm to see a descendant of the Henrikson name. . .

It was too unreal. What kind of fate would allow this to happen? And with such a cruel ending?

Whatever the reason Carillon had ended up here, she knew it was no longer her place to stay. She could not stay and dare to hope that her future lay anywhere in the same vicinity as people like the faithful Madeline Whitcomb or the equally righteous Jack Tate.

Probably, she'd already stayed too long. She'd already messed things up. She'd taken away whatever good life Jack might have had. All because of her.

Taking labored breaths, she glanced around the cabin, feeling the age-old oppression ever creeping in on her.

Leaving the Bible, the journal. . .even Jack's gift, she grabbed the lantern, descended quietly to the kitchen, and strode out the door.

Shirking her responsibility to Bob? Probably.

But in the long run, he'd thank her. No one needed her kind of help around. The kind that only seems to take, take, take.

Evie was gone.

Jack was going.

And Carillon wasn't going to be there to watch it. Not this time.

Chapter 18

Two months later

J ack reached up and ruffled the short, spiky hair that had grown back after they'd shaved his head. . .or so he'd been told. Along with everything else in his immediate past, the memory of that event was gone. He relied on the reports of doctors, nurses, friends—and the disjointed memories. The last thing he remembered was running toward the teacherage, calling her name.

His heart panged. Even the briefest reminder brought a piercing to his gut.

Fairly unaware when he'd finally come out of his coma, it had taken him some time to orient himself. A regular flow of visitors eased the transition as he watched the faces from his past float into his present. All but that one.

He could only assume that she'd gone. That left the greatest hollowness within him. No one mentioned her. At all. Other than to assure him, somewhat hesitantly, that Carillon was all right. . .she'd not been injured in the storm. Then the subject quickly shifted to the repairs and rebuilding being done at Yesteryear. With some frustration, Jack had listened, unable to voice his further questions, concerns.

It seemed the shocking blow given his brain had produced a few changes. To his amazement, the stutter was gone. But in its place, giving him equal, if not more frustration, was his occasional inability to properly voice his thoughts. Where before the words had stumbled around on his tongue in an effort to get out, now they were elusive—hiding in some secret, locked part of his mind that gave no rhyme or reason to when and where it would act up.

The doctor assured him this was normal and that most likely, with time, his language skills would return.

In the meantime, he sat in the stiff hospital bed, counting the days until he might be released, eager to get back to the little cabin. And wondering what the future might hold now.

His thoughts were in that very place the afternoon that Bob Feldman came to see him. Jack had been busy studying the changing leaves outside the window, the last of the colored remnants stubbornly clinging to otherwise bare branches.

"Jack!"

He turned with a smile and greeted the jovial man. "Hi, Bob."

Shrugging out of his ample jacket, Bob grinned as he plopped down a new set of books to occupy Jack. "Maybe by the time you finish these, they'll let you out of here."

"We can only hope," Jack muttered, perusing the titles.

"Well, that and guests should keep you busy."

Jack inclined his head. "Yeah? I've actually been tempted to start watching Oprah." He nodded at the television mounted to the wall.

Bob let out a low breath. "I'll talk to the doctor today."

They smiled at one another as Jack adjusted himself in the propped-up bed, grabbing the stack of books.

"Uh. . .Jack?"

He kept rummaging through the volumes. "Yeah?"

"There's someone here to see you."

Jack lifted his eyes and studied his ill-at-ease friend. Maybe it was Bob's tone. Or his hesitancy. Whatever, it grabbed him, causing him to struggle to continue suppressing the hopes he'd been harboring since he woke up those many weeks ago.

"They've come a ways."

They?

From the corner of his eye, Jack saw subtle movement beyond the glass window of his room's door. "Who is it?"

Bob slowly cracked the knuckles of his short, thick fingers. "Mr. and Mrs. DeVries."

Boom. Just like that. And not at all what he'd expected, if he'd expected anything. "They want to see me?"

Bob nodded and shot a look over his shoulder at the closed door.

Suddenly self-conscious, Jack ran a hand across his head again, hoping to smooth down any errant cowlicks. Bob didn't say that Carillon was with them. But what if. . .

"Is that all right?"

Jack nodded and pulled himself straighter in the bed, smoothing the wrinkled sheets.

Bob rose from the low chair, crossed to the door, and opened it a fraction, sticking his head out into the hall and beckoning with his arm. Within a matter of seconds, Jack found himself face-to-face with Carillon's parents.

Stunned, he immediately recognized that she'd been a perfect composite of the older couple, with her mother's small build and coloring and her father's regal features. Jack suddenly realized that he was staring.

Thankfully, Bob broke the somewhat uncomfortable silence. "Mr. and Mrs. DeVries, this is Jack Tate. Jack, Mr. and Mrs. DeVries."

They nodded at one another as each of them reached forward and cordially shook hands.

"Curtis," her father corrected with a friendly smile.

"And Rachel," his wife added.

"Nice to meet you."

"Here," Bob interjected. "You two have a seat." He pushed up another chair. "I'm gonna go see what's for lunch today." With a broad smile, he waved and backed out of the room, pulling the door shut behind him.

Jack nodded after him.

For several seconds, the two parties simply looked at one another, the discomfort and uneasiness palpable. Curtis finally broke it. "I understand you were trying to save Carillon when the tornado hit."

Studying his hands with a slight frown, Jack shrugged his shoulders. "I didn't know she wasn't there."

"We appreciate your efforts," Rachel added. "All of them."

His gaze snapped up to theirs.

"Mr. Feldman has told us some of what you did. . .and what you tried to do for our daughter," Curtis said. "We really can't express our gratitude."

With a quiet smile, Jack felt his heart soften. "She's. . .all right then?"

The couple looked at one another. Curtis spoke again. "We don't know."

Jack was puzzled by his response.

"We haven't seen her since she left for Yesteryear."

"What?" He sat up straight again, momentarily wincing at the pain that surged through his ribs now and again. "But I thought—"

Rachel shook her head. "She never came home. We don't know where she is."

With a long breath, Jack flopped back against the pillows and shut his eyes. Where on earth had she gone? What was she doing? Was she all right? Somewhere in the midst of his selfish concerns, he remembered whom he was sitting next to. He peeled open his eyes and found them looking at him. "I'm sorry," he murmured. "It must be very. . .painful to not know where your daughter is."

Rachel DeVries's eyes clouded with tears. "I'm afraid we haven't known where our daughter has been for a number of years."

Jack studied them, confused.

Curtis grabbed his wife's hand and squeezed it tightly. "Did Carillon mention anything to you? Anything at all?"

"About?"

"Us?"

Jack shook his head. "Nothing other than how she got her name."

"Her sister?"

Again, he shook his head. "She didn't seem eager to share much of anything."

Curtis sighed heavily. "I'm afraid that's probably our fault. You see, we haven't exactly been the best. . .example."

"Of. . . ?"

"Christians."

"Both of us were saved about five years ago," Rachel explained, seeming to have gotten the tears under control. "We were ecstatic in this new hope we found in Jesus. Our pasts wiped clean, our futures bright with His promise."

Jack nodded in understanding.

"Carillon, though, was less than thrilled with our newfound faith. She was fifteen, full of a bit of normal teenage rebellion, and not real eager to be attending church every night of the week. It seems we did find something to keep us at the church almost every night. She didn't understand it. And we didn't understand her hesitancy."

"We see now," Curtis offered, "that we neglected our responsibilities as parents in lieu of trying to do everything with our new family at the church. Given Carillon's age and mind-set, we needed wisdom and patience in how to show her our faith without totally ramrodding it down her throat. We could have done far more by simply loving her, rather than pointing out all of her shortcomings when stacked up against our new expectations."

Jack sighed, finally understanding the young woman's attitude, fear, and seeming callousness. But at the same time he felt genuine regret and compassion for the couple before him. He knew the last thing they'd wanted to do was lose their daughter. By the looks of things, it seemed that's exactly what had happened. His mind turning over past events and memories, one question shot to the forefront. "What happened to your other daughter?" he asked quietly, carefully.

"Evie?" Rachel inquired.

Again, they sought one another's eyes before Curtis took the cue. "Last May, just before Carillon came here to Yesteryear, Evie drowned in our swimming pool."

The ache in Jack's heart settled into a sickening lump in his stomach. "How old was she?"

"Six."

Feeling the profound sorrow emanating from these parents, he simply waited, realizing their need for space, time.

"What made it worse," Curtis continued, his voice husky with emotion, "was that Carillon was home, baby-sitting her." He again squeezed Rachel's hand, as the tears freely fell down her fair cheeks. "We know that Carillon blames herself. She didn't ever say much to us, but it seemed. . .it seemed as though she felt that anyone she would get close to. . .would die."

Jack nodded, the final pieces fitting together. Her self-made walls. Her animosity used to fortify those walls. Her distance fueled by the fear of getting close to anyone. And now—now she was gone.

"Jack?" Rachel sniffled.

Trying to ignore the tightness pressing against his chest, he turned toward the woman.

"Do you know," she pleaded, "do you have any idea where she might have gone? Did she ever say anything to you about leaving?"

With the most severe case of regret he'd ever felt, Jack slowly shook his head. "No. She never did."

Unable to stifle the sob, Rachel shook under its quiet intensity. Her husband wrapped his arm around her shoulders, trying to console her while his own face held the most piteous look of grief that Jack had seen in a long, long while.

Lost in the discomfort of the moment, Jack sank into the background until that inner urge spurred him to action. He studied the couple before him, then swallowed hard. "Uh. . .would you mind. . ."

The two faces peered up at him.

"If we prayed?" he finished the question.

Nodding, they gripped each others' hands, stood, and took Jack's outstretched ones.

Jack closed his eyes, released a deep breath, and settled in. "Father, You know why we're here today. . . ."

❋

The warmth of the Ozark sun permeated the cab of the huge semi, the rolling landscape temporarily lost on Carillon as she stared out the window, seeing nothing and feeling everything. The roar of the air-conditioning and quiet banter of the radio filled in the otherwise quiet space. That was fine with her. She'd had a hard enough time deciding whether or not to take this particular ride—scintillating conversation she didn't need.

But glancing again at Ralph—whom she'd known for about, oh, three hours now—she realized for once she had nothing to fear. Other than fear itself. She smiled inwardly at the irony.

If her mind had been a whirling vortex of confusion the last couple of months, the last few hours would have to top it all. She tried to piece together the avenues that had gotten her here. . .sitting in this strange rig with a man who defied all stereotypes of truckers she'd ever heard about.

Her night-covered departure from Yesteryear was somewhat of a blur. All she knew was she'd ended up near an interstate highway, her small duffel of belongings slung over her shoulder. Somehow, between good-hearted citizens who probably thought she was a mere kid scraping together enough fare for a long, bumpy bus ride, Carillon had found herself traveling farther and farther away from that place. From home. From all that she no longer wanted—nor wanted to remember.

Two months. Eight and a half solid weeks had elapsed when she ended up near Branson, Missouri, and then found her way to a YWCA where she could at least shower, change clothes, and sleep for a pittance. But after a time she questioned what she was doing. What kind of a life was this? And for how long could it last? She needed to at least find a job. Anything.

After having grown accustomed to the peacefulness of Yesteryear, she began hiking out of the city of Branson to the outskirts—some of the smaller towns that lay in the highway's path. Seeing a large truck stop, she gratefully went in, counted out the money she had, bought a meager meal, and inquired about possible positions available for waitressing—or anything else.

Needing help, they hired her on the spot. Carillon felt good that she was on her way to independence, and she concentrated on her job. Doing it well. Doing it constantly. Working double shifts whenever possible just to avoid the time alone, the time for her thoughts to revert back to people and places she had no right to be dwelling on.

But more than once she'd almost dropped her platter of dishes when, from across the dining room, she'd spotted that golden-brown hair. . .the slight build. Her heart lodged in her throat when he turned around to reveal a face entirely too different—disappointingly so.

And in the aftermath that always occurred, she found herself battling bizarre longings. Desires to go home. To head back to the upper Midwest. To what she knew. To what might have been—even if it would never be.

But the desires disappeared as she counted out her skimpy tips, realizing there was no way she would get back to Wisconsin or Minnesota on this wage. Then the bitterness and misery set in. She knew she had no one to blame but herself, as always. But she was also beginning to wonder if God had a personal vendetta against her.

What made it worse was the realization that she'd landed right smack dab on the buckle of the Bible belt. On more than one occasion, she'd have to endure invitations from her coworkers to attend their church. She always found excuses—even if they weren't particularly imaginative.

But God never let her go. She could feel it. And she chafed under the discomfort. She wanted to be left alone. What had started as a relieving cry of freedom had now turned into a continual ache. One that wouldn't go away. If she'd been miserable before, each day took Carillon well past that edge, making her wonder how she'd hang on.

It had been today's lunch rush that had harried her the most. It seemed a zillion people came and went. Hundreds of seniors on their way to their southern winter homes and twice that many headed for the entertainment capital of Branson kept the place packed. And of course there were the usual hosts of truck drivers.

When the final flow had ebbed a bit, Carillon had taken two seconds to sit in an empty booth, grab a sandwich, and rub her aching legs. Letting her gaze follow the continuous maze of traffic to the restaurant and gas pumps outside, she felt a chunk of the sandwich lodge funnily in her throat.

From across the crowded lot, a truck barreled into a parking stall. And into her brain.

The front grill of the huge Peterbilt was adorned with the most unusual ornament she'd seen—and she'd seen some unusual ones. But this one. . .

The neon blue light glowing to beat the bright sunshine, the shape unmistakably fashioned into a cross.

Carillon frowned at the image.

She watched as a middle-aged, normal-looking guy hopped down from the cab, waved at a couple of truckers who were fueling up, and proceeded into the restaurant. Unable to take her eyes off him because of her curiosity, she jumped when Charlotte had nudged her elbow.

"Hey, Doll," she'd said with a weary smile. "You mind taking over for me for a bit? I have to pick up Billy from his dad's all of a sudden and take him to the sitter's."

Carillon nodded, cleared her basket, and smoothed her apron. She watched as the cross guy settled into Charlotte's section.

"Thanks," her coworker mumbled, digging her keys out of her purse and striding out the door.

Feeling an odd sense of apprehension, Carillon snatched up a menu from the holder and strode over to the man. "Good afternoon," she offered.

He smiled at her. "It is that. Nice day today."

No accent. She noticed that right away. Nodding with a polite smile, she placed the menu in front of him and ran off to fetch him a hot cup of coffee.

By the time she returned, he rattled off his order quickly and efficiently.

"Boy, that was fast," she admitted, scribbling down the order. "You must be in a hurry today."

He grinned and took a sip of the steaming liquid. "Sure am. Heading home tonight."

"Ah." She knew that was always a cause for good-spirited truckers. "Where's home?" she asked by way of conversation.

"St. Paul."

Her pencil ground to a stop on the little pad, snapping the lead.

She was sure he had noticed her reaction when he eyed her and asked, "Heard of it?"

Keeping her eyes glued on the writing in front of her, she nodded. "Sure." With that, she stuck the order slip on the merry-go-round for the cooks and went to check on any other jobs she might be able to accomplish—if only to avoid the unsettled feeling she got while around this new customer. Maybe Annie needed help refilling the ketchup bottles.

"Got it covered," she informed Carillon.

There weren't many options left. Other than ones right around Mr. Cross.

Steeling herself against her ridiculous nerves, Carillon returned and began wiping down the counters around his stool. She saw him watching her. Not leering, but studying.

When his order came up, she placed it in front of him with her usual smile.

"Looks terrific." He smiled in return. Then he bowed his head and prayed silently.

Unable to tear her eyes from him, Carillon watched his silent conversation with God.

When he'd finished, he lifted his head. . .and noticed her staring. He tilted his head slightly in question, his brows lifted.

Feeling her face heat in embarrassment, Carillon tried to think of something to say just to break the awkwardness of the moment. "Why do you have a cross on your truck?" she blurted out.

He smiled. "I'd love to tell you about it."

The remainder of the day was a blur now. An obscure cacophony of memories, feelings of homesickness, the unusual story of this man's ministry, Truckers for Christ, and the shocking question this complete stranger had posed before he'd left.

"I feel like I'm supposed to ask you something," he said while paying his bill.

"What's that?" Carillon asked with more than a little apprehension.

"I feel like I'm supposed to ask you if—" He broke off with a huff of amusement. Or maybe it was his own hesitation. He cleared his throat. "I'm supposed to ask you if you want to go home."

Carillon didn't remember her reaction—or how long it took. She just remembered the dizzying, overwhelming feeling that came over her as she placed her apron on the back counter and told Joe, the cook, that she wouldn't be back tomorrow. Or again.

As she sat in the cab of the truck, reviewing her day, Carillon felt an overpowering sense of fear, apprehension. . .and peace.

Somehow, deep inside, she knew. It was time to go home.

Chapter 19

Jack stared out at the drizzly day, the wet road beneath him, and the choppy Mississippi lining his route. He'd been on the road for several hours now, yet each mile that brought him closer to his destination increasingly filled him with trepidation. That he was doing the right thing, he had no doubt. Doubt was one issue he didn't seem to struggle with much anymore. He'd been shown that in quick order over these last weeks and months. Life was too short. And he knew now, when God directed—you went.

That had brought Jack to his first decision.

After his release from the hospital, he'd reveled in walking the paths of Yesteryear again, even though things had changed subtly. He'd watched Paul and some of the others lending a hand when the carpenters came in to start rebuilding the lost and damaged property. And entering his own cabin. . .it had been bittersweet. Full of good memories, comfortable. Yet filled with painful reminders as well. Namely, Carillon's journal still lying in his loft. Unopened. Blank. Next to it, the family Bible and his distant relative's own journal— amazing that they had survived not only the tornado but also all those years in waiting. Perhaps waiting for someone to find it? Someone. . .

He prayed for her constantly. Wherever she might be. And hoped that those simple prayers would be enough not only to sustain her, but to sustain him, as well, and fill the emptiness left by her departure.

His trek to the old farmstead had probably given him the biggest shock, though. Stepping into the clearing, he'd blinked. . .then blinked again at the gaping space.

The house was gone. The barn, gone. Not a trace of anything save the debris littering the rain-beaten grasses. In that instant of sorrow and relief, Jack knew. He knew without a doubt what he was supposed to do both immediately and long-term.

It was the immediate directive that found him now driving in Bob's truck, heading down the highway to a place he'd never been. A river town called Prairie du Chien.

By the time he'd passed all the locks and dams dotting the Mississippi's long descent along Wisconsin's western border and found himself rolling into the quaint but busy place, he pulled into a gas station, refueling the small pickup. He paid for his purchases and cleared his throat, eyeing the attendant.

"Could you tell me how to get to the prison?"

The lady's carefully penciled-in brows lifted a fraction. "The max one?"

He nodded.

She leaned over the counter, pointing out the window, rattling off street names and numbers of blocks.

He nodded his thanks and stepped out into the cold, rainy October day. Easing into the cab, he took a deep breath, let it out slowly, and closed his eyes. "Okay, Father. Here we go. I can't do this without You." Twisting the key in the ignition, he popped the truck into gear and set out down the road.

❋

"Are you sure?" he'd asked for the hundredth time. "I know Deb wouldn't mind if you stayed with us—even for just a few days."

Carillon nodded, reassuring him. "I'll be fine." She hoisted the duffel farther up on her shoulder and reached out a hand. "Thank you, Ralph. For everything."

He gripped hers in return and smiled. "Jesus will be at your side, Carillon, every step of the way."

She nodded, trying not to let the tears choke her up again. "I think I kind of know that now," she whispered. "Someone else told me that quite awhile ago. I just need to find Him."

"No," Ralph answered, "He's already here. Don't go looking. Just meet Him where you are."

She frowned a little, but nodded anyway. "Good-bye. And thanks again."

He released her hand and gave her a confident smile. "We'll be praying for you."

She waved over her shoulder and started toward the nearest bus stop. With the little money she'd managed to bring, along with a hefty chunk of Ralph's he had insisted she keep, she could afford a few short fares. After that? She didn't know. She guessed she'd cross that bridge later.

The huge city bus hissed to a stop in front of her, its door sliding open to allow her refuge from the damp day. She plopped the required fare into the box and found a seat near the back, settling onto the cold vinyl bench as the roar of the engine inched the vehicle forward, taking Carillon to a different place and time. To a place where she hoped to find. . .something. Peace? Closure? That part was unclear yet. And it scared her more than a little.

❋

They let him in quickly enough. He'd had the foresight to call several days before and set up an appointment. After the guard at the front verified who he was, Jack found himself following another armed guard through a maze of hallways, double-thick steel doors, and security gates. Some corridors were eerily quiet; others ricocheted with the voices of men in the midst of some activity or another.

After several minutes, Jack was led to a small room with a table and a few chairs. Heavy, black iron bars girded the few windows letting in the meager light from the gray day.

"Have a seat, Mr. Tate," the guard informed him. "I'll let 'em know you're ready."

He nodded and opted to stay standing, crossing to the windows, clutching his Bible with renewed intensity. Staring down at the courtyard, he felt that sick feeling rise from the pit of his stomach again. The space outdoors was empty in the inclement weather. But the grass was nicely trimmed. The paved area showed no immediate signs of disrepair. Several basketball hoops flanked the ends of the yard. It looked like an overgrown playground, minus the equipment.

Until one looked at its perimeters.

Lining the seemingly pristine grounds, huge chain-link fences rose to towering heights. Not one, but two fences followed each other in a parallel pattern, completely encasing the area surrounding all of the prison. If the height of the fences alone wasn't enough deterrent against escape attempts, several feet of wicked razor wire twisted and coiled sharply in an intimidating cap on the barrier. The mere sight of it chilled him. It brought back memories of pictures he'd seen of the concentration camps during World War II. Only this time the barriers weren't to keep people in because of one sick man's desire to rid the earth of all he deemed inferior. These barriers protected those on the outside from the sickness and sin that permeated the people held in this place.

The door latch clicked open behind him. Jack jumped and turned around to see two guards leading a man in.

Jon.

Jack felt that lump rising in his throat, and he battled to swallow it again. He needed to be strong.

It had been many, many years. He was still big. Jack didn't have to guess that he probably made use of the weight room. But his muscular arms and legs were somewhat hidden under the required uniform he wore. His ankles were cuffed and chained, his arms secured tightly behind his back as well. It was odd to see him so. . .subdued. His hair was still the same shade as Jack's, albeit with a few gray strands poking through. His face. . .Jack couldn't see. So far Jon kept his head toward the floor.

The guards assisted Jon to a chair, and Jack released a breath, slowly approaching the opposite side of the table. "About fifteen minutes," one of them said as they retreated through the door.

"Wait."

They turned, eyeing Jack expectantly.

He nodded toward his brother. "Could you at least take off his handcuffs?"

They looked at one another. "I don't think so," the shorter man replied. "He's not been on his best behavior lately. Have you, Tate?"

Jon snorted and shuffled his feet, the chain jangling noisily.

230

"Just for a few minutes?" Jack tried again.

Neither of the employees looked at all comfortable with the request. "I don't know," the taller man muttered. "Can you behave yourself, Jon?"

"Sure, sure," came the mumbled reply.

They started to unlock the cuffs, looking pointedly at Jack. "We'll be right outside this door, all right?"

He got the drift. "Thanks."

The door shut behind them, and Jack stared at his brother, losing himself in a host of emotions.

Jon's gaze finally rose to meet his. Jack pitied what he saw. The eyes were hard. The mouth even more so. The beginning of wrinkles lined the creases of his face. For being a mere thirty-one, Jon looked like he'd lived through three times that many years.

Rubbing at his wrists, he stared at Jack. "Well. . .sit down." He nodded at the chair across from him. "Sorry I don't have any tea to offer you."

Ignoring the sarcasm that apparently had only intensified since Jon's incarceration, Jack took the seat and set his Bible in front of him.

Jon's face took on a surly grin. "Are we having Bible study today?" He ran his fingers through his mop of hair and leaned back in the plastic chair, his eyes full of as much daring and bravado as always.

Jack felt himself sinking under the strain. The intimidation. *Jesus, You have to help me out here. It's happening already.* He shifted in his own seat and chewed on his lip in thought. "I know you're not thrilled to see me," he began.

"No," his brother's voice chortled in mock defense. "I'm always glad to see my baby brother! Especially since the rest of my family is dead."

The snideness of Jon's tone couldn't be ignored. But Jon forged on before Jack had a chance to reply.

"So. . .what did you bring me? Cigarettes? Maybe some of Dad's favorite whiskey? A woman? Man, do you know how long it's been since—"

"Jon, I came here for a reason."

The meaty arms leaned on the table, bringing his haggard face closer. "Really."

Jack met the challenge, unflinching. "Really."

"And that would be?"

Frowning in concentration, Jack stared right into the depths of Jon's gray eyes—looking through the past. Mentally flying over every word, every fist, every hurt, every intent for evil, and staring them in the face at the same time. At that exact moment, Jack felt an incredible peace flood his whole being, his strength renewed by a Source far beyond his own. "I came here to tell you. . .I love you."

※

The wet grass below was fast soaking through her meager little canvas shoes. But she didn't notice.

Instead, Carillon concentrated on searching the myriad of headstones standing like little sentinels in the rain. The months since she'd been here last seemed like years ago. And it was still too soon.

But that inner urge propelled her feet through the maze of faceless names chiseled in granite and marble until she finally found it. The little rectangular stone, lying serenely amid the perfectly manicured grass. In one corner, a small etched image carved into the pink granite—Jesus holding a little girl tightly, her hair cascading over His encircling arms, the look on His face a heart-wrenching mixture of grief and joy.

The tears started before Carillon could even try to stop them. "Hi, Evie," she murmured through her chilled lips. "I miss you." She clamped her mouth shut, wondering what on earth to say next. She knelt down on the damp sod and began picking out the errant blades and weeds invading her sister's place. "I know you probably can't hear me," she continued as she weeded. "You're with your Jesus now. And I'm glad. He can take care of you far better than anyone here." She swallowed. "Especially me."

Feeling the control starting to leave her, Carillon shifted her conversation. "I met someone, Evie. Someone who reminds me a lot of you." Her eyes lifted to the gray skies. "Who knows—maybe you already know him. Maybe he's there with you.

"You would have liked him. And I know he would have loved you."

That feeling was coming again. The loss of control. The panicked sensation of facing the unknown. She fought it for all she was worth.

"Evie. I'm trying really hard to understand why all of this happened." She sniffled as the tears began to take over her voice. "I couldn't understand why God would take you away from me. For awhile. But then. . .then I realized the truth. God didn't take you away. I let you go."

Her voice wavered. She slumped back onto the grass, the rain trailing down her cheeks, mingling with the hot tears.

"Excuse me?"

Carillon jumped. Whipping her head around, she saw an elderly man, covered with a pale yellow slicker, studying her thoughtfully.

Swiping her palms across her cheeks, she scrambled to her feet, trying to avoid the pointed stare of the old gentleman.

"I'm very sorry," he said quietly, nodding at the stone before them. "Sister?"

Carillon nodded.

He stuffed his gnarled hands in his pockets. "I'm here visiting my wife's grave. She passed away nine years ago today."

"I'm sorry," Carillon mumbled.

"Some days I am, too," he admitted, "but only because I'm anxious to join her." A little smile broke the heaviness of the moment.

She studied him incredulously. "You want to die?"

"No. I want to live. Forever. And when I get to heaven and see her face next to my Savior's. . ." He beamed again. "Nothing will compare."

To that, she nodded miserably. "That's nice. That you'll be able to see her again." Carillon balked slightly at her words. She didn't even know this guy. Why on earth was she choosing to get involved in a conversation—especially one like this—with a perfect stranger?

The old man looked at Evie's stone. "Your sister, is she. . . ?"

She looked hard at the aged face beside her. "I'm more than certain she is."

He smiled. "Then you have every reason to harbor the same hope that I do."

Right. If this man only knew. Stinging tears blurred her vision again. "I'm afraid not."

"Why not?"

"There's a reason why people like Evie go there. And there are more reasons why people like me—" She halted, letting him figure out the remainder.

He was silent for a long moment, which kind of surprised Carillon. But not as much as his next words. "John 3:16–17."

"What?" She glanced at him.

He pointed to Evie's marker. Sure enough, those Bible verses were carved right below the image of Jesus. "It's not meant just for her." He smiled. "It's truth."

With that, he walked slowly away through the rows of headstones and monuments, leaving Carillon to stare at the words. The raindrops glistened in the tiny crevices, giving the letters an almost lifelike quality. "Hey, wait!" she called after him.

Only he was no longer there. Anywhere.

Carillon spun around, searching the large cemetery. No one.

Shrugging off a little shiver, not entirely from the chill of the day, she dropped to her knees, rummaging through her bag, looking, desperately searching.

There. Her fingers curled around the little book Ralph had given her before she'd left. A small New Testament, wasn't that what he'd called it? She flipped through the pages, looking for the book of John. Her cold fingers fumbled through the thin pages until she found the spot.

For God so loved the world, that He gave His only begotten Son, that whosoever believeth in Him should not perish, but have everlasting life. For God sent not His Son into the world to condemn the world; but that the world through Him might be saved.

Overpowering feelings of losing control again surged through her. But for some reason, this time it wasn't as terrifying, just overwhelming. Because she had no other recourse, because she'd tried everything else that she'd known to try, Carillon let herself go. Let it take over.

Not to condemn. . .God so loved the world. . .He gave his only Son. . .not to condemn. . .so the world might be saved. . .

The Truth enveloped her as the words she'd read rang with clarity. Jesus. He wasn't just Evie's Jesus. Or Jack's Jesus. He was hers. And He was waiting for her.

Letting the tears roll freely, she laid down on the grass, oblivious to the rain and cold. For the first time, she only felt warmth and peace that she couldn't fathom. Peace that she never, ever wanted to let go.

❀

Jack wiped the spittle from his eye. But not before it was replaced with another deftly aimed splat.

Jon rose out of the chair, his face a contorted mask of seething anger. He threw out a volley of curses—using a few more than he had as a kid.

Hearing the sounds of disturbance in the room, the guards burst through the door before Jack could get to his feet. A very brief struggle ensued as the two prison officials overpowered the adrenaline-charged inmate, clapping the cuffs back on his hands and wrestling him out the door. His oaths echoed down the hall, growing more distant until the slam of a door bit off the final intense word.

Wiping his face with his sleeve, Jack lifted his eyes to see the guard who had accompanied him to the room standing there, waiting.

"Sorry about that," he offered.

Jack shrugged and picked up his Bible, wiping the stray flecks of spit from its cover.

"You ready to go then?" the guard asked.

Jack released a deep breath and nodded.

As they stepped down the now quiet hall, Jack kept staring at the worn book in his hands. "Could you. . ." He hesitated as the guard looked over at him. "Could you possibly give this to my brother?" He held out the Bible.

The young man couldn't hide the surprise on his face. "You want to give him that?"

He nodded.

The guard stopped, seeming hesitant to accept it. "Um, no offense. . .but I don't think he'd take it."

Jack lifted his shoulders. "If he doesn't take it, then give it to someone who you think might. . .use it."

A flicker of understanding flashed in the man's eyes as he reached out for the offering. "Okay." He shifted the book under his arm. "Yeah, I could probably find somebody."

Jack gave him a smile, then threw one last look down the corridor.

Chapter 20

Seven months later

J ack turned loose the last of the cows, their slow gait taking them out of the barn door and up to the promising green pasture on the hill. The surrounding oaks and maples were just starting to get that fuzzy look as their buds poked out from dormancy, eager to be caressed by the warming sun.

Jack leaned against the door frame, watching the scene unfolding before him. He couldn't help but swell with pride. Not a pride that could become the ruin of him—no, this feeling was a God-ordained sensation. For it had truly been His hand that had gotten Jack here. Of that, he had no doubt.

Christmas had come and gone after last year's harrowing autumn. Jack had stayed on at Yesteryear until that time. Partially out of obligation, partially out of sentiment. If he were honest, he'd admit that he also held a thread of hope that perhaps, just maybe, certain people might return for the Christmas reunion they housed each year. The Lamplight Tour proved popular with locals and a few tourists brave enough to battle Wisconsin's winter elements. Each cabin and home was lit up with candles, the smells of an old world Christmas lingering in the air, the tours being led by guides with lanterns, each guest tucked cozily into one of the many horse-drawn sleighs.

They'd had a fair crowd, Jack had to admit.

But no anticipated face had been among the many he studied. And this time Jack couldn't ignore the disappointment. Several times he'd caught himself just before phoning her parents' home. What if she hadn't returned? What if she'd never come home? Did he want to be the one to bring such a painful reminder to people who had already lost so much?

But what if she was reunited with her parents? His finger paused countless times over the keypad.

No. He put the receiver down. If she had any reasons to want to see Yesteryear. . .or him. . .she'd have made it known by now.

So he prayed a little harder and forced himself to get on with his life.

God rewarded his obedience. Within a matter of months, a series of hoops that shouldn't have been so easy to jump through were history. With some help from Bob and a first-time farmer loan, Jack was the proud owner of a one-hundred-acre dairy just twenty minutes or so north of Yesteryear.

In April he'd added his modest herd of thirty-eight Holsteins, hoping it would grow a little in the next year or two. Judging by the number of heifer calves they'd been turning out the last month, it didn't look like growth would be a problem.

With a smile, Jack shooed the remaining lazy animals from the barnyard out into the fast-growing grass and shut the gate behind them. As he finished the last few chores in the barn and shut off the lights, he glanced at his watch. He had a little over half an hour. He'd better get moving if he were going to squeeze in a shower before he left.

Bob had called him last night—caught him in the middle of milking, actually. He'd informed Jack that the new group of employees was starting their training tomorrow and asked if Jack wanted to come and visit with them to share some of his experiences at Yesteryear.

Hesitating at first, Jack finally consented. He knew he'd get an opportunity to see Paul, Bob, Karen, and some of the other mainstays. For that reason alone, he sprinted to the little ranch-style house, kicked off his boots on the stoop, and barged through the door.

Showered and changed with a couple of minutes to spare, he hopped into his truck and honked the horn as his black Lab, Ranger, chased him out the long gravel driveway. He might even get there a little early.

The sun was illuminating the clear blue spring sky, and Jack found himself humming as the truck zoomed down the back roads toward Yesteryear. By the time he reached the parking lot, he was astounded. The thing was packed. Completely. Buses and cars lined every available stall.

With a sigh, he cranked the wheel and turned down a dirt road usually reserved for trucks making deliveries. He didn't think Bob would mind. It got him right in front of the buildings that made up the main compound. Groups of people were milling about, looking like little clusters of bees.

Jack noted the expanded structures. He'd known about Bob's plan to rebuild and add a little more, but this—it looked huge. He smiled just thinking of how many more people would come, how many more would be helped.

The tornado that had come to destroy had had the opposite effect. The media had grabbed the tragic story, complete with Jack's coma recovery, and plastered it all over the television and newspapers. Suddenly the demand for Yesteryear both as a haven and as a tourist attraction skyrocketed. God had taken what was meant for evil and made it good.

Slipping down from the cab, Jack shut the door and leaned against his truck, hanging back for awhile to observe. The chaos of the large numbers of people left him wanting some solitude.

Slowly, Jack saw leaders emerge, rally their individual groups, and head through the doors toward the orientation room. The numbers dwindled. Maybe now he'd have a chance to find Bob or Paul.

He started to take a step toward Bob's office.

"Can I have everyone's attention?" A voice rang out over the remaining people.

Jack's heart trip-hammered.

Squinting into the sun, he shielded his brow and watched as a young woman hopped unceremoniously onto a picnic table, forcing everyone's attention on her.

As if Jack's needed forcing. . .

Her long brown hair hung simply down her shoulders, catching the sun's rays. Her heart-shaped face was still fair, still fine-featured, and still the most beautiful thing he'd ever laid eyes on. Maybe more so because there was something different about it now. That softness it had lacked. . .

Jack shook his head, afraid what he was seeing was only a dream, a mirage. Dared he hope that all his prayers for her safety had been answered? To find her here? Working here?

She continued talking to the crowd around her, self-assured, calm, confident. But whatever words she might have been saying Jack couldn't hear or comprehend. He was gone.

Several blissful minutes ticked by while Jack stood, content in just watching her. He was not too eager to disrupt the scene, especially not knowing how she might react or respond to him anyway. No, for the moment he simply reveled in the fact that she was there.

Until the inevitable happened.

Her deep eyes scanned the crowd, then suddenly lifted. Right to his.

Jack straightened, wondering what to do or say.

He needn't have worried. Before he could collect himself enough to at least wave, her slim form stepped down from the table and walked deliberately toward him until she stopped, a mere three feet from him. If he'd thought she'd been beautiful from a distance, close up he could see that her face positively glowed.

All Jack could muster was a somewhat nervous smile. "Hello, Carillon," he said, as if they were the only two people in sight. His hand reached up to his hair, unconsciously combing it into place.

"Hello, Jack," she murmured back. "It's. . .good to see you."

He nodded. Then his eyes began to fill with tears. Amazed, embarrassed, and everything in between, he tossed his gaze to the ground, hoping to quell the emotions he'd been totally unprepared for.

From behind Carillon, he heard Paul's familiar low voice taking charge. "Okay! If everyone in Miss DeVries's group would just follow me through this door, we'll get you squared away for orientation." The bustle of the crowd faded as the group entered the nearby building.

Jack stared fixedly at the ground, desperate to regain some sort of composure.

"Jack?" Her quiet voice floated over to him.

He still couldn't look up at her. Not yet.

He heard her step closer. "Jack, I'm sorry. I'm so sorry for everything. I know I should have stayed. I should have let you know I was all right." She hesitated, her own voice sounding like it was choking up. "When I heard that you'd recovered from—" Apparently that did it. She quit, too.

Realizing he wasn't going to get the flood to stop anytime soon, Jack dared to raise his head, only to find her eyes brimming as well. "You're okay," he managed to croak out.

She gave him a wavering, watery smile. "In every way imaginable."

He nodded, trying to smile back, feeling his chin quiver in the process. "I'm just. . .I'm glad—"

Her feet took two steps closer. Her hand reached out, hesitantly.

Jack grasped it with one hand. Then both. Then before he could even think, he pulled her fiercely to his chest, letting his arms wrap around her petite body, relishing the warmth, the comfort. The overwhelming desire to protect this woman for life surged through every part of his being. He stroked her long, silky hair once more before easing her away a few inches. "Carillon—"

She put a finger to his lips, the look in her fathomless blue eyes silencing anything he might have hoped to say. Then she leaned closer, her forehead almost touching his. "I love you, Jack Tate."

It was all he needed to hear, all he'd ever wanted to hear.

Closing his eyes, he brushed a kiss across her full lips. . .trying to remember when he'd ever felt such joy, when he'd ever felt so complete. He seriously doubted that anything in the remainder of his life would come close to a moment as sweet as this.

Epilogue

Carillon floated down the leaf-strewn white runner, her simple empire-waisted dress blowing in the gentle September breeze. A hundred times today she'd thanked God for the perfect weather, the friends lingering outside in Yesteryear's courtyard. . .and even for her mother, who'd nervously fluffed and fidgeted with Carillon's simple wedding gown. Their relationship was growing. Both women knew they had a lot of time to make up, but they also knew that it would be easier now that they had both apologized for past wrongs and shared the healing power of forgiveness.

But the most perfect thing Carillon could give thanks for on this fall day was standing at the end of the runner. Behind the smattering of chairs housing their friends. Just beyond the little trellis intertwined with climbing blossoms.

Jack.

His hair was slicked back in an attempt to tame the cowlicks. His new sport coat hung snugly on his shoulders. And his eyes held a sparkle of promise that took Carillon's breath away.

Gripping her father's arm, she tried to concentrate, tried to focus. She didn't want to forget one single portion of this day. No music accompanied their short stroll. The birds sang a simple prelude, keeping time with the melody soaring in her heart.

As they approached the front, the minister smiling eagerly, Carillon's gaze fell to a small white chair standing next to Karen, her attendant. Surprised at its appearance, she noted its adorning ribbons, bows, a little porcelain doll—and a tiny little crown of laurel, delicately hung over one corner of the back. Tears started to blur her vision, and she had to force her feet to keep walking. Her father must have noticed her misstep. He, too, studied the little chair and looked at Carillon. She sought his eyes. "Jack?" she whispered.

He nodded and smiled through a few glistening tears of his own.

She looked again at the small seat set up in honor of her sister. If it were possible, her heart swelled with twice as much love for her husband-to-be, thanking God that He had brought such a wonderful man into her life.

When she kissed her father and accepted Jack's arm, she clung to it tightly, looking directly into his eyes—his kind eyes. "Thank you," she mouthed silently.

He placed a tender kiss on her hand and gave her that little half-smile that always sent her heart flipping.

"Jack and Carillon," the minister began, "God's Holy Word tells us that there is no fear in love; but perfect love casts out fear, because fear involves punishment, and the one who fears is not perfected in love." He smiled at them both. "We love, because He first loved us."

GLORIA BRANDT
Gloria resides in Wisconsin with her husband and four daughters, who keep her non-writing time occupied with homeschooling and life in general.

Love in Pursuit

DiAnn Mills

Many thanks to Troy and Kari Marrs for all of their help.

"So do not fear, for I am with you; do not be dismayed,
for I am your God. I will strengthen you and help you;
I will uphold you with My righteous right hand."
ISAIAH: 41:10

Chapter 1

Allison Reynolds's first customer of the day at the local Budget Builder's Store smelled of strong coffee and stale tobacco and had a disposition to match.

"Did you find everything you need, Sir?" Allison asked, flashing the middle-aged, balding man a warm smile in hopes it might melt his icy demeanor.

"I guess so," he muttered, avoiding eye contact. "I really needed a paint stirrer. Wasn't anybody back there to shake up the paint or give me something to mix it with. Don't know why ya'll have that fancy machine if nobody's gonna use it."

"I'm sorry, Sir." Allison produced three wooden paint stirrers from underneath her checkout counter. "Is there anything else, or would you like for me to call someone from the paint department?"

"Naw, just ring me up." He swiped at his nose. Allison proceeded to scan the brushes, paint cans, and paint thinner.

"Is this the best paint you got?" the customer asked. His brows lowered as though he relished the opportunity to pounce on her.

Allison recognized the brand name and knew the various types and grades. "What kind of job are you doing?"

"Rent house," he said, staring at a crumpled piece of paper. "I'd have asked back there if anybody had been around."

"Well, Sir," she began, "this is a good, medium-grade, latex paint. It's not our best but certainly not the bottom of the line."

"It'll do." He opened his wallet. "How can you be so happy this time of the morning?" He handed her the cash for his purchases, and she inhaled a heavy dose of his breath.

Allison managed another smile. "I'm a morning person." She wanted to say her joy came from the Lord, but the last time she made mention of God to a customer, she almost got fired.

"Well, good for you." His tone rang with sarcasm. "I'm not. Ain't gonna be, either."

She hefted several paint cans into a cart and sacked up his supplies. "You have a wonderful day," she said, and he nodded sourly with a token grin.

Allison stifled a laugh. Some customers challenged her more than others, but she always tried to coax a smile from the cranky ones.

She yawned and stretched. Her watch read seven-ten, and her body ached to claim more rest. Thank goodness no other customers mingled about the front of the store. She welcomed the reprieve before it grew busy. This morning came much too early after spending half the night helping her sister, Susan, nurse her twin sons through a case of flu. Unfortunately, Susan couldn't handle cleaning up vomit and called on Nurse Allison for the job.

Taking a deep breath, Allison glanced about her. The air felt heavy, and for some reason, the hair on her nape bristled. Something bothered her—something she couldn't name or figure out. She neither felt ill nor stressed, but a strange sensation hung like a pendulum between her heart and her mind. *Lord, are You trying to tell me something?*

A moment later, she greeted another customer, a familiar, elderly contractor who handed her a ticket for a load of lumber. It amazed her how a man of his age could work so hard every day, but he appeared to love it. His regular visits and habitual manner of seeking her out at the checkout made him one of her favorites.

"Good morning," the older gentleman said, "and how is my green-eyed brunette today?"

"Just fine, Mr. Billings," she replied, taking his ticket. "I see you have your day cut out for you."

"Hard work keeps a man young, I always say." Mr. Billings's gray eyes twinkled. "You know, I wouldn't recognize you without your cap and work shirt." He proceeded to pull a checkbook from his shirt pocket.

"Probably not, but one day soon I'll replace these with a nurse's uniform." They'd talked about her plans for a nursing career in earlier conversations, and Mr. Billings always encouraged her. Sometimes she had to pinch herself just to make sure she wasn't dreaming. This time next year she'd be working in a hospital.

"When do you start your last semester?" Mr. Billings asked, once she gave him the total and he scribbled out his check.

"In three months—at the end of August. I would have been done in May, but I couldn't complete my clinical work at the hospital when I broke my ankle. I love my job here, but I'm excited about finishing my education."

"This store will lose a smart and pretty employee. And if some sensible young man persuades you to marry him, I want first bids on building you a house."

She laughed and took his check. "You have a deal."

He leaned a little closer her way and whispered, "I'll keep praying for you, too."

Waving good-bye, Allison knew she'd see him in a week or two. Customers like Mr. Billings made her job worthwhile. She'd miss him once she began her nursing career. It was a long time coming. She'd be twenty-six by the time she received her degree.

"Good morning, Allison," the store manager greeted, rushing past her. "I see you're staying busy. Keep it up. I like to see industrious employees."

"Yes, Sir," she replied, amused. The manager never walked at a normal pace or spoke to any of the employees directly. He always hurried and scurried about, but no one knew where. His short, chubby frame and constant movement reminded Allison of the White Rabbit in *Alice in Wonderland.* He even owned a pocket watch.

A couple pushed a cart into her aisle, and Allison turned to assist them. Behind the pair, a man caught her attention. He smiled, and she returned the gesture. Good-looking, with gorgeous eyes, but he wore a hideous, heavy metal T-shirt.

❊

Officer Beau Oliver backed his truck from his garage onto the driveway. With a huff, he shifted the truck into park and exited the vehicle to manually lower the garage door. Yesterday he'd disconnected the automatic opener when it refused to respond to his remote. After a lengthy examination of his garage door, he discovered the problem lay in the remote attached to his key chain and not the unit in the garage. What a pain.

His whole body cried out for sleep. Working all night, then heading home in time to shower and change before a meeting with the sarge irritated him. *Not all of us are day-baggers,* he inwardly moaned.

A quick glimpse at his watch revealed he had time to stop at the Budget Builder nearby and replace the remote or purchase a new battery before heading downtown. The day's agenda rolled across his mind. Working undercover for the Houston Police Department demanded every minute of his life. Right now, a huge drug case blasted at his senses. He'd been working on it for months, and every turn in the investigation met with a dead end.

As he drove out of the driveway, he caught sight of his neighbors' recycling bins lining the curb for pickup. "Great," he muttered.

Moments later, after another bout with the garage door, he retrieved his own recycle bins from the garage, set them at the curb, and hurried to the store. Perspiration trickled down his temples, and aggravation seeped from the pores of his skin. Already the humidity proved suffocating, and this early May morning promised a long, grueling summer.

Once on the road, he expelled a heavy breath as traffic slowed to a crawl. Some days the idea of driving a patrol car and wearing a uniform sounded appealing. He eased his truck around to the right shoulder and sped past several cars. *I need to call Mom and Dad tonight. I'm so involved with this case, I've neglected them.* Lately, he couldn't think without deliberating who stood behind a huge narcotics ring.

At the Budget Builder, Beau slipped his pickup into a parking space near the store's exit so he could make a quick escape after checking out. He hesitated. His month-old, green-and-tan truck might get scratched, but he'd have to chance it. Realizing he had thirty minutes to spare, Beau vowed to find a new remote with a battery and be rid of his problem in short order. He stuffed his keys into his pocket, stepped out into the morning sun, and headed for the entrance. Dressed in cutoffs and a heavy metal T-shirt, he looked more like a blue-collar worker than a police officer.

A certain uneasiness swept over him. Some cops called it instinct, but he'd never bothered to label the feeling. He had, however, always taken heed and kept his eyes open.

Cool air greeted him from inside the huge warehouse-type store. The smell of fresh lumber reminded him of the deck he planned to build on the back of his house. So many projects and so little time. . .He studied the overhead signs to find which aisle contained garage door materials. *Aisle 8*, he read and walked briskly to the area.

"Can I help you?" a teenage boy wearing one of the light blue Budget Builder's shirts and caps asked.

Beau smiled and shook his head. *I wonder how many speeding tickets you have.* Immediately guilt hit him head-on for his unkind thoughts. "No thanks, I believe I can find everything myself."

Once he located the garage door openers, he spent five minutes looking for a possible solution to his existing problem. Frustrated and losing patience with the whole matter, Beau reverted to his original thought and decided to purchase a new remote. Before long he wished he'd utilized the young man's offer. There were too many types and options for him, and he was pressed for time. Beau snatched up a small remote similar to the one dangling from his key chain and headed for the checkout.

He'd forgotten a battery, but luckily a display of them in every size and brand stood in front of one of the registers. Instantly Beau spied the correct size and stepped behind the next customer. He glanced up at a young woman behind the checkout and allowed himself a few indulging moments to appreciate the captivating peach-kissed brunette. He liked the way she smiled, and she talked with her eyes—huge, green, endless pools that sparkled when she spoke. They reminded him of the sun glistening atop the water at his favorite fishing lake. He envisioned little flecks of gold dancing off their light.

I wonder if she likes to fish, he mused, imagining the beauty seated next to him in his bass boat. Beau noticed when she laughed, her ponytail bounced. Not every girl looked good in a ponytail, but on her, the no-frills-or-curls approach had an innocent and charming appeal. This way, he could see her entire face framed in caramel-colored hair, and he liked it. He read her nametag. *Hmm, Allison. I wonder if she has a boyfriend. Dream on, big guy. In your line of work, there's no time for a relationship.*

"Good morning," Allison said with a flash of another generous smile. "Did you find everything you needed today?"

"Sure did."

A bearded, greasy-looking man in his midtwenties suddenly caught Beau's attention, and all thoughts escaped him except for the alarm going off inside his head. The man approached the young woman and shouted a string of obscenities. She dampened her lips and attempted politeness, but his voice grew louder.

Beau's every nerve reacted to the scene before him. From the looks of the man's eyes and his erratic behavior, he was either drunk or on drugs—or both.

"Sir, can I get someone to help you?" Allison asked. Her hands trembled.

"No! You're the one I want to see," the man said. "I'm tired of this. Every day I wait for you to come home, and every day you ignore me. Now you're going to pay."

"I believe you have me confused with someone else," she said. "Would you like to talk to the manager?"

Beau quickly laid aside his purchases and stepped forward. "Hey, Man, can we talk about this outside? I've had my fill of trouble with women, too." His voice rang calm and controlled while his gaze swept over the man's loose clothing looking for a possible weapon.

The man bellowed another string of curses and claimed his dislike for anyone interfering in his business. From the corner of his eye, Beau saw the other customers move away from the scene, but Allison didn't budge. She looked scared—too scared to move.

"Miss, step away from here," he directed, not once taking his sights off the man. "You know, Man, we can work this out," he continued. "Why don't you tell me all about it in the parking lot?"

"You stay right where you are," the man ordered when Allison attempted to move away from the register. His slurred words convinced Beau of the suspected substance abuse. "And you, get away from me. You ain't stopping me from what I came here to do." The man waved his hands with every word he spoke.

Wishing he had his revolver, Beau cautiously moved toward the assailant in an effort to overpower him. The man clumsily pulled a pistol from inside his shirt, still shouting meaningless threats. Concern for the young woman caused Beau to position himself in front of her. The man aimed and fired repeatedly, pumping bullets into Beau's body. He counted six shots before he slumped to the floor. White-hot pain surged through his side and leg. He tasted the acrid air. Warm blood oozed through his fingers where he clutched his side, and he heard the screams of those around him as he fell prey to utter blackness.

Chapter 2

The shrill call of the ambulance's siren wailed through Allison's ears, and her heart hammered furiously against her chest. Panic seized her in its grip, choking out her once-comfortable world. An eerie wind whistled around the doors as though a demon encircled the racing vehicle. And the rattle—why did every piece of equipment have to shake? Her mind spun in fear and disbelief. How could this be happening? Surely she'd awaken soon and find her world safe and secure, but the bandaged wound in her left shoulder and the vivid memories of gunshots and blood told her the nightmare had been real.

A paramedic released the blood pressure cuff from around her uninjured arm and called in the reading to a hospital. Hearing the numbers, she cringed. The bottom one disturbed her.

"It's always low," Allison mumbled.

"Your blood pressure?"

"Yes, Sir." Allison opened her eyes and focused her attention on the paramedic adjusting her IV. Brown eyes relayed warmth and compassion.

The hideous bloodstains on her shirt nudged her into another dilemma. *How do I get this out of my shirt? Soak it in cold water and hydrogen peroxide like Mom does? She'll help me. Mom, Dad, I know I'm an adult, but I'm frightened.*

"You're going to be all right, Miss," the paramedic assured her. "We'll have you at the hospital very soon."

Allison moistened her lips, then bit back the pain searing from her shoulder to her wrist. She tried to concentrate on the muffled voices from the ambulance radio, but instead, tears rolled down her cheeks. She was trained to help those hurting, not deal with her own injuries.

"I know it hurts. I'm sorry, but the doctors don't want you to have anything yet." He adjusted the flow of liquid into the IV. "Just a little while longer. We're headed to Northwest Medical."

She managed a deep breath for courage and strength. Questions bannered across her mind, unanswered fears about her shattered world. "What happened to the man with the gun?" Her gaze darted around the ambulance as though he might be lurking inside.

"You don't need to worry about him," the paramedic said.

Allison closed her eyes. "Yes, I remember. He turned the gun on himself." She didn't think he could have possibly survived. Gritting her teeth, she relived the man firing the weapon into the side of his head. Horror gripped her in a strangling hold.

"The man who tried to help me—" She swallowed the bile rising in her throat. "Is he alive?"

The paramedic took her hand. "He's holding his own."

Allison felt another stab of pain race through her arm. "Thank you," she whispered. "He saved my life."

The fiery wound in her shoulder throbbed incessantly, as though her heart pounded in its place. She refused to give in to the overwhelming sensation to settle into unconsciousness. Not yet. She prayed for the brave man, the frightened people at the store, and the family of the man who shot her. What a waste of human life.

Allison searched the recesses of her mind. She had never seen the gunman before today, and his ravings about her made no sense. Perhaps she should have been kinder, more sympathetic. A sob rose in her throat. Maybe she could have said or done something differently to change the outcome. Except now it didn't matter.

The memories pierced, fresh and gruesome. She again saw the puddles of blood draining life from both men. She remembered staring at her arm, watching the same vital fluid flow from her shoulder, through her clothes, and onto the floor. Now the white bandage seeped crimson.

"Hey, we're almost at the hospital," the paramedic whispered. Still holding her hand, he reached for a tissue and dabbed the wetness from her cheeks.

But you didn't see the hideous, twisted flesh of both men or hear the ghastly screams of the people as they fell to the floor, she wanted to shout, but he had witnessed the scene. He'd been the first paramedic inside the store. The pungent taste of bile again rose and fell in her throat.

"It was so horrible," she said. "I'll never forget it—no never." *Oh, God, why? I don't understand any of this. I know You're with me; I believe You're here. Oh, sweet Jesus, I'm scared. . . . And the man who was shot trying to help me, spare his life, please.*

Allison felt the ambulance slow to a grinding halt, and for the first time, she felt safe.

The hiss of the automatic doors leading into the emergency room and the sterile, antiseptic air jarred her senses. The sights and sounds worried her, because she knew from her nursing education what would happen next. Like a child, she dreaded the procedures. Closing her eyes, Allison sought refuge behind darkness.

"Can you give me some information?" she heard a woman ask crisply.

Allison nodded and felt more tears stream down her cheeks. A burst of agony exploded from her shoulder, and she cried out.

"The young woman's parents have given us enough for now," another female voice stated firmly. "She can sign later."

"Mom, Dad?" Allison questioned weakly. She opened her eyes to look for them, but the paramedics quickly wheeled her through a set of double doors and past several more doctors and nurses all in a haze of colored scrubs. She heard someone bark orders to move out of the way.

A flash of light blinded and momentarily disoriented her, then she realized someone had taken her picture. She closed her eyes to the lights and activity whirling around her, but she couldn't stop the throbbing pain.

"Get away from my daughter!" Allison heard her father shout. The words he spat startled her. She'd never heard him sound so angry.

"Allison," her mother called. Instantly, her parents raced alongside the gurney. Her mother grabbed her uninjured hand, and Allison attempted a feeble smile.

"I'm all right," she whispered, mustering the strength to keep from crying. "I'm fine, knowing you're here with me."

"That's right, Baby," Dad said, his voice cracking with emotion. She saw his lips quiver and his green eyes soften. "You rest, and the doctors will fix you up right away."

Allison wanted to say she didn't hurt—that she'd be going home to her apartment in a little while, but she knew better. Her mind continued to spin with concern over the injured man. "A man was shot trying to help me." She bit her lip against the pain. "Dad, make sure he's okay."

"I will; I promise. The doctors are working on him."

She opened her eyes and searched the round face of the balding father she loved so dearly.

"Hush," Mom said, her blue eyes cloudy with tears. She tucked a strand of silver hair behind her ear and patted her daughter's hand. "Save your strength, Sweetheart. We can talk later."

A nurse stepped forward. "We'll take care of her from here," she said gently. "You folks will have to stay in the waiting room. We'll notify you as soon as we can."

Allison's agony suddenly overpowered her, and she drifted into blackness.

※

Allison's whole body felt numb. Could this be death? Had it all ended at the hospital? What about the injured man? Her parents? Questions zipped in and around her mind, none with answers. She opened her eyes and, through blurry vision, focused on a woman's face. Forcing her eyes to focus, she saw the woman was dressed in green scrubs.

"Allison, are you awake?" the nurse asked, pronouncing every word distinctly. She nodded and blinked. "I can't feel anything. Am I paralyzed?"

"No, Honey." The nurse smiled and provided in a soothing voice, "You've had surgery, and you're in recovery."

Allison's lips felt powdery dry, and her throat hurt. "I'm thirsty."

The nurse glanced up at the IV while checking her pulse. "I can get you some ice chips. That will help. Are you hurting?"

"No." Allison sobbed. "I feel like such a baby, but I can't feel my arm."

The nurse gingerly lifted Allison's uninjured hand and rested it on the opposite arm. "See, it's all there, only bandaged."

Relief flowed through her veins and left a sense of humiliation in its wake. "Thank you. Do you know what happened to the man who was shot?"

"I really don't know. Would you like to see your parents? They're waiting outside, and I know they're anxious."

Allison nodded. *They must be worried sick.* She remembered their tears and Dad shouting at someone taking her picture.

The nurse stepped to the door. "Mr. and Mrs. Reynolds, you can see your daughter for a few minutes."

Allison attempted a brave smile. She detested the lines of obvious grief and worry etched across their drawn faces. She expected to see Mom's eyes red and puffy from crying but not Dad's. He was always the strong one. "I'm sorry," she whispered. "I've put you through a lot."

"It's not your fault, Baby," Dad replied. She saw his eyes well up, and huge droplets rolled down his cheeks.

"Dad, don't cry. I'm fine." She felt so tired, and although she willed her eyes to stay open, they closed. "Mom, tell him I'm fine. I don't want ya'll upset."

"I'll tell him, Allison. I'll tell him."

✻

Beau battled with the pain raging through his body, a tormenting abyss, as though he battled with Satan and all of his diabolical forces. He begged God for release. In one breath he pleaded for God to take him home, and in the next he wanted to live.

He should have reacted faster to the scene at the store. Maybe that young woman wouldn't have been hurt. . .or worse. He wished he knew, and he summoned a prayer for her and the poor soul who shot them both. Amid the black, swirling confusion, he heard voices and the clatter of metal. Slowly, he felt his body succumbing to peaceful numbness, and he eagerly embraced it.

✻

Hours later, Allison woke in a darkened room. She focused on two shadowy figures seated at her bedside. Relief flowed through her as she recognized her parents. "Mom, Dad, I'm awake," she whispered and dragged her tongue over her dry lips.

Instantly the two rose to her bedside. "Are you feeling better?" Mom anxiously adjusted the sheet and thin coverlet around her neck.

"Yes, but I'm thirsty," she replied hoarsely.

Her mother spooned ice into Allison's mouth, then took a separate piece to moisten her lips.

"Thank you," she murmured. "I never thought ice could taste so good." She opened her mouth for another spoonful.

"You look like a little bird," Dad said with a chuckle.

"No worms, please. I don't think they'd set well on my stomach." She took a deep breath. "Dad, I felt you and Mom praying for me."

He laid his hand upon her forehead. "We have a lot to be thankful for tonight."

"God was with me, wasn't He?" She swallowed the lump in her throat before turning her attention to her mother. "Tell me about my shoulder. What did they do to it?"

Mom held her hand lightly. "They removed the bullet and closed the wound."

"Sounds simple enough." Allison forced a faint smile. Time and rehabilitation would mend it just fine.

"You've got an excellent doctor. He took extra care, so the healing should leave a minimum of scarring."

"Good," she breathed. "When can I go home?"

"Whoa, Girl," Dad said. "The doctor wants to keep you a few days for observation. You've lost a lot of blood, and he wants to run some routine tests."

"Sounds expensive," Allison said with a sigh. "Good thing I have insurance. Oh, great," she moaned. "I bet Susan is fit to be tied."

"Why?" her mother asked.

"Remember? I agreed to watch Chad and Christopher while she and Tad went out tonight."

"Oh, they went out all right," Dad said. "Your brothers and sisters are all here at the hospital. They just headed to the cafeteria for coffee."

Allison felt strangely comforted in knowing her siblings had been there. From the initial looks on her parents' faces, they needed support. Oh, how she treasured her family. Without warning, the morning's happenings traversed her mind.

"Dad, how is the man who tried to help? Did he make it?"

He brushed a loose strand of hair from her cheek and took a deep breath. "He's critical. In fact, they transported him to Hermann Hospital, but he's fighting, and we're praying for him."

She closed her eyes. Without warning, exhaustion swept over her, and her arm throbbed. "I'll never forget what he did for me. I want to see him as soon as I can."

Chapter 3

Two days later, the doctors discharged Allison from the hospital. With her left arm bandaged and in a sling and the doctor's orders tucked inside Dad's planner, she stubbornly stood from a wheelchair and walked through the hospital doors with the aid of her parents.

She couldn't remember the sun reflecting so brightly or the sky such a deep shade of azure. The birds sang sweeter, their song soothing her troubled mind, but what she noticed the most was the hint of spring flowers and fresh air teasing her nostrils. The busy sounds of city life buzzed about, and it left a disturbing sadness deep inside her.

"What's wrong, Honey?" Mom searched Allison's face through blue eyes. "Are you in pain?"

"No." She hesitated. "Everything seems so. . .normal, like no one cares about what happened to the man who helped me or the man who died."

"Does the reality of this world frighten you?" Mom asked, placing a comforting arm around her shoulders.

Allison tilted her head thoughtfully. Mom had a way of putting emotions into words. "I think so," she said. "See those construction workers over there?" She pointed to a group of men across the street working on the hospital addition.

Both parents glanced in their direction but said nothing.

"The newspaper said Joe Lopez, the man who did the shooting, worked on a construction crew. I know it sounds silly, but I'm afraid of those men. That's prejudiced and wrong, but I still feel shaky. My nurse's training did not prepare me for this."

Dad opened the rear car door and helped her slide inside. "It's not silly or wrong, Alli. You've been through a traumatic experience, and it'll take awhile to get over it."

"I've got a horrible feeling other people are going to be asking me questions and gawking at me like I'm a sideshow freak."

He reached in to fasten her seatbelt and planted a kiss on her cheek. "They may," he replied with a sigh. "Folks are naturally curious, and most of them don't think before they ask. Well-meaning friends will want to hear the story, and it'll be up to you to discourage their questions. I'm going to do my best to protect you from newspaper reporters and the like, but I can't be with you all of the time."

Allison smiled sadly, wishing she hadn't voiced her apprehensions. "I'm nearly twenty-six years old, Dad, and I'm sure I'll be fine in a few days. I should be going home to my own apartment instead of staying with you."

"You're not getting out of my sight until I'm positive you're okay," Mom said in her don't-question-me voice.

Allison's mind wandered to the injured man, Beau Oliver. She needed to see him, thank him for saving her life. She'd read the newspaper accounts about the shooting. The pastor at his church had initiated a twenty-four-hour prayer vigil, and his parents pleaded for Christians to pray for their son. Praise God, this morning he'd been taken off the critical list.

But the additional news broadcasts sickened Allison. Reporters made it sound like she was some lowlife who had led the assailant to his demise and the man who helped her to his near death. Dad had phoned the TV station and newspaper office in protest, but it didn't do any good. Joe Lopez might have lived in her apartment complex, but it was huge, and she didn't remember ever seeing him.

Mom's voice broke her thoughts. "Remember how you wanted all of this to be a testimony of God's provision? I have faith God will give you the strength and the words during trying times."

Allison nodded. As much as the memory of the shooting sent a surge of terror to her very being, she refused to bother her parents with all of her fears and disillusionment about the media and what other people thought. Her parents would only fret about her state of mind. She'd handle the gossip, or rather, she'd let it rest in God's hands. Last night she asked Him to take the burden from her mind and to turn the whole thing into something good. God had a purpose, but for now, Allison desperately needed the nightmare haunting her to end.

"I want to see Beau Oliver," she announced several minutes later. When she didn't hear a response, she added, "Dad, nothing is going to change my mind."

"There's something you need to know," he replied, "something the press cannot find out. Beau Oliver is an undercover policeman—off duty at the time of the shooting."

※

"Okay, Alli. I've pulled some strings to get you here," Dad said as they linked arms in the parking garage of Hermann Hospital. "But you won't have much time." His voice sounded chipper, but Allison heard the uneasiness.

"I realize he's in bad shape, but I can handle it. I'm going to be a nurse, remember?" She smiled up into his warm green eyes and wished she could see the familiar glimmer of laughter.

"I wondered about your career choice after this nasty business." He pointed toward the elevator.

"The Lord has reaffirmed my calling to be a nurse," she assured him, with a lift of her chin. "I'm at an advantage because now I know what it feels like to be a patient."

If only she could convince herself so easily. Her first night home from the hospital had been spent tossing and turning, reliving every hideous moment of the shooting. The doctor had prescribed sleeping medication, but Allison refused to give in to synthetic sleep. Her parents suggested counseling, and she'd agreed that speaking with her pastor might help—but shouldn't her faith in God be enough to sustain her through this?

Dad pushed the UP arrow and teetered back on his heels. "If I were you, I wouldn't want to ever see the inside of a hospital again."

She wrinkled her nose at him, and for the first time, he laughed heartily. His paunchy stomach jiggled, and she relished the knowledge that she'd caused his mirth.

Once on the elevator, she watched the numbers rise to each floor. Her mind spun with what she needed to say. As of yesterday, Officer Oliver had not regained consciousness. It didn't matter; she simply wanted to see him and possibly relate her gratitude for saving her life to his family.

All too soon, the doors opened, and they were at the nurses' station. A pleasant male nurse confirmed the unconscious state of the patient before authorizing her visit.

"His parents are with him. In fact, I'll walk with you down to Mr. Oliver's room."

Allison suddenly wondered why she had felt so compelled to come. She trembled slightly, and Dad patted her hand. Exchanging reassuring glances, they followed the nurse.

Inside the hospital room, she studied the middle-aged couple seated near the bed. From the looks of the woman's wrinkled blouse and the man's crumpled shirt, they must have been there all night. The nurse spoke quietly to them and both glanced her way. Reluctantly, they rose from their chairs and ambled toward the door. Taking a deep breath, Allison approached them.

"I'm Allison Reynolds," she said quietly. "I want to tell you how sorry I am about what happened. Is there anything I can do?"

The couple glared at her. "I don't think so." Mrs. Oliver peered down her nose. "The doctors are doing all they can."

Mr. Oliver wrapped his arm around his wife. "He doesn't need any help from the likes of you. You're wasting your time."

Allison refused to allow their icy demeanor to stop her. Dad had already warned her about hostile feelings.

"I'll only be five minutes," she said. "And I'm praying for your son, too."

"Go ahead," the nurse said to Allison with a kind smile. "Mr. and Mrs. Oliver, let me show you where you can get some fresh coffee."

Grateful for the nurse's control of the situation, Allison slipped into a chair next to Beau Oliver's bed. Outwardly he looked stable, but one look at the two IV poles holding six bags of fluids, antibiotics, and precious blood told more of the story.

Dad reached for the hand extending from her sling. She knew his thoughts; the officer had taken her place.

Her gaze took in the policeman's well-chiseled features and strong, firm jaw. Thick, dark brown hair swept back to reveal a widow's peak and hung loosely about his shoulders, and below his high forehead were deep-set almond-shaped eyes and high cheekbones. *I wonder, what color are your eyes?*

A slight ridge formed across the bridge of his nose as though it had once been broken, and she resisted the urge to touch a tiny half-inch scar resting on his right cheek. She envisioned his full lips formed into a smile. Beau's TV picture had not done justice to his handsome features.

"Mr. Oliver," she began and leaned closer to him, "I don't know if you can hear me, but I'm Allison Reynolds from the Budget Builder's Store. I just want to thank you for saving my life. I'll always remember what you did for me, and my whole family is praying for you. In fact, lots of people are praying." Allison swallowed her tears. What else could she say or do for this courageous man?

"He's a big fellow," Dad whispered. "Muscular. His size will help him fight the injuries."

She nodded. "I want to come here every day until he's well."

Her father squeezed her hand lightly. "I understand, but right now we need to go. Our time is up, and his parents should be returning. Shall we pray for him first?"

She felt the familiar calluses from Dad's years of hard work. Somehow, she'd always thought God's hands would feel the same way.

Dad's deep voice broke the silence. "Heavenly Father, we praise Your holy name and humbly ask that You give the doctors wisdom and guard the life of this brave man. In Jesus' precious name, amen."

She stood and studied the face of the heroic police officer who fought for his life. If only she could do something else for him. Prayer didn't seem to be enough when she ached to do more. Struggling with the emotion burning in her throat, she said, "I want to do whatever I can to help him recover."

"He might not want your help, Alli, and his condition is not your fault."

Allison took a deep breath. Her arm throbbed, and she wished she'd taken the pain medication, but it made her drowsy. "Dad, maybe I do blame myself for this, but I don't have a choice in the matter. He took my place, and I'm determined to help him recuperate."

❊

Through the murky cloud of a pain-infested world, Beau crept through the shadows to grasp a ray of life. No longer did he wonder if he hovered between earth and eternity; heaven promised no pain. And the fire branding his body had only one origin.

He felt as though his flesh had been ripped from his body. For that matter, maybe it had. He couldn't summon the strength to move his arms or open his eyes to find out.

"Mr. Oliver. Mr. Oliver," a woman's gentle voice said. "Are you awake?"

He stirred. He fought the overwhelming desire to float back into obscurity, a blissful existence.

"Can you open your eyes?"

He felt himself climbing, struggling to reach the top of a bottomless pit. Clinging to the voice of the woman, he grappled with the force sealing his eyes shut. At last he managed to let a slit of light enter his darkness. He opened his eyes to greet a lovely, Asian woman, her voice sweeter than honey.

"Are you in much pain?"

He nodded and watched her adjust an IV. "This will help. You have a couple of people here who are anxious to see you."

He tried to move his head, but the fierce pounding stopped any movement.

"Lie still, Son," his mother whispered. "Your dad and I will be waiting when you awake."

He wanted to convince her he felt okay, but he couldn't rally the strength. Instead, he managed what he believed resembled a smile.

"The doctors say you're going to be just fine," his dad said. "Good as new in no time at all."

Beau closed his eyes. In no time at all. God had brought him this far; He wouldn't abandon him now. He wanted to ask about the condition of the young woman at the Budget Builder. Her face had swept across his mind even while his body erupted in agony—or could it be he'd seen an angel?

How much time had elapsed? Would he recover completely? Was he paralyzed? Had he lost a limb? Questions. . .and no answers. Beau felt himself fading into a peaceful state of sleep. Already the torment had subsided.

✳

Allison stopped by the hospital every afternoon, although Mr. and Mrs. Oliver clearly disliked her. Her stays were but a few minutes, and she realized those visits were vital to her own healing. Guilt riddled her for the injured officer. Sleepless nights and weary days often reduced her to tears.

The thought of telling Mr. and Mrs. Oliver and the media her version of the story tugged at her, but in light of Beau's undercover work, she refrained from exonerating herself. The fact remained, the shooting looked like it had been partially her fault. Since the assailant died, she shouldered the blame.

On this afternoon visit, Allison learned Beau had regained consciousness early in the morning. He'd been comatose since the incident occurred five days ago, and his pale, emotionless face haunted her day and night. All the way down the hall to his room, she thanked God.

She stole into his room and watched his parents hover over his bed. Standing back, she heard him stir, waited in hopes of hearing him speak, and felt a deep longing inside to know him personally. She believed him to be Christian like his parents, for a green leather Bible with his name imprinted in gold lay on his nightstand.

Still she wondered, what kind of man did undercover work? Were his parents aware? Did he thrive on the adrenalin rush?

Mrs. Oliver's glare, as usual, made her wish she'd stayed home.

"Our son is conscious now," she said. "There's no need for you to continue your visits."

"Who is it?" Beau asked, his voice barely audible.

His mother cleared her throat. "The young woman from the building supply store."

"I. . .I'd like to talk to her."

His mother sized up Allison as though trying to decide what variety of rotten fruit existed in human flesh. Mrs. Oliver gave her a steely gaze, and Allison timidly stepped to the bedside.

Seeing Beau alert and conscious was an answered prayer. Her eyes pooled as prayers of thanksgiving spun through her mind.

"Don't cry," he said, each word an effort for him to speak.

She blinked and swallowed. Every day she'd come here waiting for this moment. "I'm Allison Reynolds, and I want to thank you for saving my life—for taking those bullets meant for me. I'm available to do anything you might ever need as you recover."

"It's not necessary. . .really." Perspiration beaded his brow, and his eyes narrowed.

"Son, you don't need to talk to this woman," his mother said. "You're too weak."

"Yes, I do," he whispered and moved his head slightly toward Allison. "Go ahead, please."

"I need you to know it's important for me to do whatever I can, and I want to tell you that my church, my family, and friends have been praying for you."

He offered a faint smile and cringed as an obvious wave of pain swept over his rugged features. "I. . .felt them; God worked a miracle." He attempted to lift his head, but the strain eased him back onto the pillow. "Your arm. . .is it okay?"

She nodded, willing her tears to cease. Glancing about, she prayed for the courage to say what her heart truly felt. "I know your family needs to visit with you, so I'll be leaving, but I hope you don't mind if I continue to stop by." She paused to find her words. "Mr. Oliver, I didn't know that gunman. I'd never seen him before in my life, and although he did live in my apartment complex, I'd never met him." She gazed into his hazel eyes. "I do have one more thing to tell you. What you did for me is like what Jesus did for us all, and I praise Him for sparing your life. I will forever be indebted to you for your selfless act of bravery." She bent and brushed his cheek with a kiss. "Thank you."

❋

Beau watched Allison leave, an angel in disguise. How refreshing to meet someone sweet and gentle, especially when he encountered so many shoddy characters in his line of work. He'd spent too many hours pretending to be one of them.

His mom followed her outside into the hall. No doubt to thank Allison for her daily visits; however, he didn't understand Mom's apparent rudeness.

"That young lady lives her faith," Dad said, staring after his wife. "I'm afraid I misjudged her." His gaze trailed back to Beau. "Son, you look exhausted. Get some sleep now."

Beau could only close his eyes in agreement. Strange how a few words of conversation had worn him out. Allison. . .his own angel. Too bad his life held no room for a woman. He remembered his first impression of her and how he wondered if she'd like fishing. Fat chance. He didn't have time to fish himself. His life was too dangerous. . .too easy to get killed.

Chapter 4

"**M**iss Reynolds."

Allison whirled around in the hallway to see Mrs. Oliver hurrying after her. She cringed. What would the woman say now? She'd threatened a restraining order before.

"Can I talk to you for just a minute?" One of Mrs. Oliver's eyes twitched as she rubbed her palms together.

"Sure." Allison stepped aside to avoid colliding with a technician who carried supplies to draw blood. The needles reminded her of Mrs. Oliver's dagger-like glares.

"I owe you an apology." The older woman's hazel eyes brimmed with tears, and she unapologetically let them flow. "I'm so ashamed of the way my husband and I have treated you. You've been faithful in visiting Beau every day since your hospital release, and we've made your stays miserable. I'm very sorry."

Allison viewed the sincerity in Mrs. Oliver's lined face, and compassion seized her heart. "I never intended to upset you or your husband. I simply had to do something for your son to let him see my gratitude." She adjusted the shoulder strap of her purse. "The media reports have been brutal. Given the same circumstances, I would have probably reacted the same way."

"You're too kind, Dear. I hope you continue to visit our son and forgive this foolish mother and father. We've been selfish, unable to see your good heart. We're a Christian family, but we failed to act like one."

Allison's body relaxed, and she felt a smile tug at her lips. "Of course I forgive you, and thanks. Your apology means a lot to me."

※

Days passed, and Allison continued to make her daily trek to Hermann Hospital to spend a few moments with Beau. After the first few times, she drove herself, freeing her father from the drive. Oddly enough, each visit grew longer and longer. She enjoyed Beau's company and loved the sound of his hearty laugh. No longer did his parents condemn her with seething glares but welcomed her. Now, if they were present when she arrived, they excused themselves and allowed her time alone with him.

"Tell me about yourself besides your work at the Budget Builder," Beau said one afternoon. He inched down the hallway with a walker, his third time, and the creases across his brow plus the heavy droplets of perspiration indicated the toll taken on his mending body.

"I have one semester left to finish nursing school, which will start in late August. I'm a bit of a late bloomer when it comes to career, but I'm nearly there." She stopped with him while he took a breath. "By the way, you're doing a terrific job with the walker."

"Thanks. It's whipping me," he said, with a grim smile. "What else about yourself?"

"Hmm. I'm the youngest of five. We're a close family and all live within the Houston area. Our parents are great; they've raised us to love Jesus and instilled strong values of right and wrong. What else. . .I have an apartment on the northwest side of town."

He took another deep breath.

"Don't overdo it," she said, her heart filled with compassion. "This is important to your healing, but your strength has to be built gradually."

He forced a smile. "Thanks, Nurse. If I don't get out of here soon, I'm going to climb the walls." He continued slowly down the hallway. "I live in the northwest area, too, and I'm a Christian."

"I thought so when I saw your Bible on the nightstand."

"Do you have a boyfriend?"

She laughed. What an odd question to ask. "Don't have the time or the desire to keep up with one of those. Maybe someday, when I'm settled into my career. What about your life?"

"Boring, and I'm a solo man, one of those married-to-my-job types." By this time they'd reached the end of the hall, where a window brimming with sunlight warmed them. "Must be hot outside." He maneuvered his walker around to retrace his steps.

"Tell me more," she said. "Why is your life boring?"

He chuckled. "I work and I putter around the house."

She avoided asking what he did for a living. She feared it might build a wedge in their new, fragile friendship, and truthfully, she wanted him to tell her. "Any pets?"

"Nope. My crazy schedule wouldn't allow it, but sometimes a big old drooling dog sounds good. What about you?"

She could drown in his hazel eyes, and for a moment those pools distracted her. "Apartment living doesn't lend itself to animals, although I do have a betta fish living in a large glass vase with a plant."

"What is a betta?"

"It's a Siamese fighting fish. Mine's blue and turquoise, really pretty. The odd thing about bettas is, they don't get all their source of oxygen from water and must occasionally rise to the surface for air."

"So the lady likes fighting fish? Is that supposed to indicate something about your personality?" He laughed and she joined him.

"Not really. It was a gift."

"I see. What about sports?" he asked, and she knew their conversation kept him from dwelling on his obvious pain.

"Absolutely. I play softball with my church league, and I dearly love watching baseball and football."

"I'm an Astros and Texan fan myself."

By now they were back to his room. He clearly looked like a nap was in order. "Beau, you're tired. I think I'd better go."

He pressed his lips together, then said, "You don't have to baby-sit me."

His tone stung, but she knew patients often developed depression in their recuperation, making them tense and irritable. "I'm not baby-sitting you, simply visiting."

"It's not necessary." He stiffened.

"You're right; it's not, but I enjoy our afternoons together." She refused to cater to his bad mood.

"Don't bother. You have your life, and I have mine."

"All right," she said, drawing her keys from her purse. "Take care." Allison walked away without glancing back.

✳

Dinner came and remained untouched while Beau brooded over his parting comments to Allison. If he meant to deter her from visiting every day, why did he feel so crummy? She'd done absolutely nothing to deserve his bad mood—nothing except spread sweetness into his life. She drove to the hospital each afternoon to visit him, and he looked forward to seeing her. Her laughter rippled over him like a gurgling creek, and those sea green eyes caused funny feelings in his heart.

He could easily fall for a woman like Allison, but as he told her earlier, he lived a solo life. No time for a woman. He'd been there, and relationships didn't work. He'd tell her he was an undercover cop, and as soon as the newness wore off, he'd hear the "can't handle your job" story. She'd cry and say good-bye, like they'd all done before.

He'd be left bitter and disillusioned about the whole love business. Broken hearts never got easier to mend, and he'd decided God didn't want a woman in his life.

Feeling even more sorry for himself, he flipped on the TV, but the sitcoms only increased his sour disposition. Allison's fresh optimism about life intrigued and irritated him at the same time. He'd hate to be the one to burst her Pollyanna bubble with a heavy dose of street life.

If they were together, both of them would have to lie about his job, and she wouldn't know his whereabouts for hours on end—certainly not a fair situation in a relationship.

What am I doing thinking about Allison as though we were involved? I've known her for a handful of days. Must be this hospital and nothing to do is clogging my good sense.

Staring at the phone, he realized he owed her a call. Knowing she wouldn't be back to see him didn't set well, and already he missed her. Beau opened his Bible where he'd placed her number. Apologies were not his forte, but she deserved his best.

She answered on the third ring. "Allison, this is Beau. I. . .a. . .I'm sorry about this afternoon. I acted like a real jerk." For a moment, he thought she wouldn't reply.

"I understand you're bored and want to get out of there, but yeah, you were rude."

He smiled. Hearing her voice made him feel better, even if she did agree about his behavior. Telling him the truth without hesitation gave her another bonus point. . .not that he was keeping count of her attributes. "I'd like to see you tomorrow—that is, if you haven't filled my slot with someone else."

"Not yet. I'd be glad to come, but not unless you want me there. I'm not a doormat."

She didn't make it easy for him. "Guess I had that coming. I would like your company," he said. "And thanks for not hanging up on me."

Replacing the phone, Beau remembered he hadn't eaten dinner. The food still sat on his tray, covered in cellophane and stainless steel. He lifted the lid cautiously and took a whiff of beef stew. Immediately his taste buds swung into gear.

✳

"I can't believe I'm playing Monopoly," Beau moaned, "and getting beat, too."

"Relax, the game's not over yet," Allison said with a laugh. She couldn't help noticing the way a lock of his dark hair fell across his forehead. "Besides, you've won every game of Clue."

He jiggled the die for his throw. "I'm supposed to; I'm a cop."

"What's that got to do with detective work?"

"Closely related." He paused. "Did anyone tell you about me being an undercover cop?"

She nodded. "My dad told me when I was dismissed from the hospital. He also said the information wasn't to leak out to the press. I haven't told anyone."

"Thanks. I'd hate to have my cover blown. I'm surprised you haven't mentioned it."

"I didn't know how you might react after the shooting—and the sensitive nature of your work."

He chuckled. "I was off-duty then—no gun."

Allison scrambled for something to say. The incident still lay fresh in her mind, raw and painful.

Compassion spread across his face. "I see you're having a rough time dealing with it. Might be a good idea to seek some counseling."

"My pastor," she replied simply and forced a smile. "He's helping me work through the—" She swallowed a lump in her throat, "the memories. I'm sure they must be worse for you."

He shook his head. "No worse than any of the other messes I've gotten myself into."

She shook the die and rolled it across the middle of the board. The number landed her on the Pennsylvania Railroad, which she owned. "I've lived a pretty sheltered life. Your world is what I've seen on TV and the movie screen."

"So are you into cop shows?" he asked with a wry grin.

"Not in the least. I want to be entertained, not scared to death."

He moved his little racecar forward five spaces, which sent him straight to Jail. "At least that's someplace I've been before," he said. "Can I make one call?"

"No. It's pay up or stay put."

"How about bail?"

She shook her head and tried not to laugh. "Remember the old TV show with the detective who said, 'Don't do the crime if you can't do the time'?"

"I remember, but this is Monopoly, and I'm an injured man."

"The law doesn't accept excuses." She snatched up the die and counted the spaces, landing her in the Jail square. "Pay up, Sister," he growled. "This city runs a tight force."

Chapter 5

Allison stepped through the door of Beau's hospital room. Every day he grew stronger. . .and more impatient to be released. The afternoon sun highlighted his handsome profile and danced off his dark brown hair, giving it a reddish cast. If she had a notion to be interested, she'd look no further, but she neither welcomed the thought of romance nor had need for it.

He laughed and talked with a sandy-haired man who had his back to her. She paused in the doorway and listened to the guy-talk.

"I remember those impersonations you did of our high school teachers," Beau said with a chuckle. "Got you a regular seat in the principal's office."

"I couldn't help myself," the man replied. "I needed some kind of excitement. What about the time we duct-taped the legs of the star quarterback?"

Allison cringed. She could only imagine the pain of pulling off that tape. What made guys do bizarre things to each other?

"Yeah, I remember," Beau replied. "We picked on him all of the time. Now, I feel a bit guilty about it. Do you know what he does now?"

"Not a clue. All I remember is we called him Duct."

"He writes and arranges Christian music," Beau said. "He performed at my church a few months ago, and he has six kids. I meant to tell you but forgot."

"Six! I can't believe you forgot to tell me. You were probably on a stakeout and had other things on your mind."

Beau nodded. "Imagine so."

Suddenly Allison felt heat creep up her neck and face. She had no business eavesdropping on their conversation and invading Beau's privacy. Deciding to head to the cafeteria, she turned to leave.

"Allison, wait a minute," Beau said, waving her inside.

The sandy-haired man whirled in his chair and greeted her with a broad smile, dimples and all. "So this is Allison," he said, standing and taking giant strides her way. He extended his hand. "I'm Kieron Bates, and Beau didn't tell me you were this gorgeous."

She laughed. "Pleased to meet you. Sorry to interrupt. I think I'll grab a soda and come back later."

"Not on my account," Kieron said. He had the clearest violet eyes. "I've been here way too long; time I headed home." He swung his gaze back to Beau. "I'll continue to get your mail and stash it in a bag until you get out of this hotel."

"Thanks," Beau replied. "I appreciate you looking after my place. I owe you for this one."

"A steak will do when you're up to it." Flashing Allison another smile, Kieron left with a promise to return.

"I didn't mean to run him off," she said, still feeling the color warm her cheeks.

"Not at all. He'd been here over an hour," Beau replied, clasping his fingers behind his head. "Kieron and I go back to high school days. Lost touch in college, then when I bought my house, I found out he lived across the street."

"He seems very nice, and we all need lots of friends."

Beau's brows narrowed. "Got to be careful in my line of work. Sometimes friends are a luxury."

His words moved her to compassion. "I'm sorry. I never realized your job could be so lonely."

"Hey, sorry to intrude," Kieron said, hurrying into the room. "Did I leave my cap?"

Allison picked up an Astros cap on the nightstand and handed it to him. Kieron snatched it up and sprinted toward the door. He reminded her of a comic strip scarecrow after a flock of crows, and she laughed. As Beau joined her, his gaze captured hers. A warm tingling sent little shivers up and down her arms. *Where did this come from?*

The phone rang, breaking the magic, and he reached to answer it. She couldn't decide if she welcomed the diversion or regretted it.

"For you." He handed her the receiver.

When she grasped it, his fingers touched hers, igniting an unexpected flame. Taking a deep breath to calm her peculiar reaction to him, she attempted to concentrate on the caller. The person had to be Mom or Dad.

"Allison, I'm not finished with you yet," a low, raspy voice said. "It's only a matter of time."

"What?" she asked, confused at not recognizing the male voice.

"I see you're driving alone these days. Daddy let his little girl out? How sweet of him."

Allison felt her stomach churn and her body shudder. "Who is this? What do you want?"

"Our friend did a lousy job. Bad aim. Next time, your boyfriend won't be around to save you."

Allison dropped the phone, horrified, physically ill. Had the nightmare begun again?

"What's wrong?" Beau asked, sitting straighter in the bed. "Are you all right?"

She studied the tiny lines etched at the corners of his eyes, hoping the concentration relieved the gut-wrenching fear that ravished her senses. "A man just threatened me," she whispered.

Beau grabbed the phone, but the caller had hung up. "What did he say?"

She eased down onto the chair beside his bed. Fright gripped her as though the gunman had stepped into the hospital room and pointed a gun at her.

"Give me your hand," Beau urged. "Talk to me."

Allison opened her mouth to speak, but couldn't utter a word. She held out her clammy hand and allowed his strength to flow through her. She took several deep breaths while her sights flitted from the doorway back to Beau's face.

"I've got to know exactly what he said."

She took another deep breath. At last, she repeated the man's words.

Beau squeezed her hand lightly, then released it to pick up the phone. Wearing a frown, he pressed the numbers in rapid succession. His hazel gaze captured hers, and again he wrapped his fingers around her trembling hand.

"Sarge, this is Beau. Got a problem down here at the hospital."

"Not me. Allison Reynolds. While she was visiting, she received a threatening phone call." He paused. "No, it came into the hospital room."

A moment later, he replaced the phone and studied her face. "You are to stay right here until my sergeant arrives. He'll need to ask you some questions."

"I've done it again." Chills soared down her arms. "I've put you in danger."

"Allison," he began, much more calmly than she felt. "You have obviously seen something that worries these guys. Can you remember anything?"

"No, nothing," she replied, lifting her chin. She prided herself in being strong and self-reliant and refused to be utterly shattered. "I'd never seen Joe Lopez before he pulled his gun at the store, and I've never been involved with anything or anyone who shaded the law. My life is so routine—I work, go home, attend church, and in late summer, I'll finish nurse's training." She combed her fingers through her hair and whirled to face the window. "Could the man who just called be friends or family of the gunman?"

"Possibly," he said thoughtfully, his tone neither agreeing nor disagreeing.

She stared at the world outside, quiet and peaceful with no hint of turmoil. "How did I get involved with such violent men?" She turned back to him, desperately craving answers.

The firm set of his jaw convinced her she wouldn't hear any of his thoughts about the matter. "I need to get out of the hospital," he said. "Being chained to the bed like a helpless invalid won't let me get to the bottom of this."

"What have I done to anger these people?" Hot tears stung her eyes, and she felt as though she'd fallen into a frenzied whirlpool. What happened to her resolve? She felt weak and angry at the same time.

"Would you like to pray?" Beau reached for her free hand again. "We may not understand what is going on, but God does. And we need His peace here."

"Yes, please," she said through quivering lips.

"Heavenly Father God, we have a big problem with the shooting and now this phone call. Allison is frightened, and I'm angry. Guide us supernaturally, and give us Your peace."

In less than thirty minutes, a tall man sporting thick, prematurely white hair strode into the room.

"Sarge, this is Allison Reynolds," Beau said, reaching out to shake his hand. "Allison, meet Sergeant Jason Landow."

She saw the strain tug at Beau's facial muscles. He needed to rest, not deal with this upheaval. Once the introductions were completed, Sergeant Landow shed his navy blue sports jacket and veered his attention to her. He asked her to repeat the conversation, word for word.

"And you have no idea who this guy was or his reasons for threatening you?" he asked when she finished. He crossed his arms over a barrel chest.

She shook her head. "No, Sir. I lead a pretty dull life. I've spent hours wondering why the shooting took place, and today's call confuses me even more."

"What about your family?"

His question made her bristle. What did her family have to do with anything? "I'm the youngest of five children. Dad owns a printing business. My oldest brother is a pastor, the other brother works with my dad, one sister is a teacher, and the other is a housewife. We're all boring. Besides," she paused to control her rising anger, "I imagine you investigated me thoroughly after the shooting."

Sergeant Landow chuckled, but she didn't find him amusing. He studied her a minute, causing a flow of self-conscious emotions to snake its way through her.

"Can I have your car keys?" he finally asked.

"Why? I'm quite capable of driving."

"I want an officer to search your vehicle before he follows you home."

She fumbled for her keys and handed them to him. At least her bandaged arm was the left one, and he couldn't complain about her driving ability. "It's parked on level three." She pulled a small notepad from her purse and jotted down her license number along with a description of her blue car. Tearing off the piece of paper, she handed it to the sergeant. She shouldn't be angry with him; he had a job to do—one of protecting her against crime.

Sergeant Landow held the car information while he spoke. "Once you're home, the officer will go through your apartment. This is not an invasion of your privacy, but an opportunity to make certain no one is, or has been, there."

She moistened her lips, wondering if her life had turned into a sick movie. "Then what?"

"We wait and see. In the meantime, do you have caller ID?"

"No, just an answering machine."

"I suggest you don't answer the phone unless you know who it is."

She shivered. "I understand. What about my cell phone? Only my family and close friends know the number."

"That should be safe," Sergeant Landow said. He jammed a hand into his khaki pockets and pulled out a business card. "Keep your cell with you at all times, and if you suspect anything out of the ordinary, call me. You can reach me day or night at that number."

He offered the card, but she couldn't bring herself to touch it.

"Allison, take his card," Beau said. "He can't help unless you follow his directions."

Slowly, she reached for the card, although accepting it meant admitting to impending danger. "I don't plan to tell my family or anyone about this," she said. "They'd only worry."

"Are you sure you don't want to stay with your parents awhile?" Beau asked. "I'm wondering if living alone is wise."

"No," she responded a bit too sharply. "Enough people have been hurt because of me. My apartment is in a good area with a gated entry and constant security. I'll be fine."

"If they want in, security systems won't stop them," Beau said, capturing her gaze. "Be careful, and don't open your door unless you're positive who's on the other side."

Sergeant Landow summoned an officer, who took her keys and car information. A short while later, the officer radioed the sergeant that her vehicle was okay.

"I'll walk you to the parking garage," the sergeant said. He turned to Beau. "I'll be back in a few minutes."

"Allison," Beau urged. "Call me when you get home."

"You might be sleeping."

His eyes narrowed. "Call me."

Too exhausted to argue, she merely nodded and joined the sergeant in the hallway. She wanted to ask questions, nail him down for when her world would be safe again, but the words climbed to the top of her throat and slid back down.

"Miss Reynolds, we're working diligently on the investigation, and we'll do all we can to find the answers to today's threat," the sergeant said, as though reading her thoughts.

"I don't want answers; I want it all stopped and someone thrown in jail." She heard the desperation in her voice, as though someone else uttered the words.

He spoke to a passing nurse pleasantly, as though nothing could possibly be wrong. Allison clenched her fists with a strong desire to scream and beat her fists into his face. *I'm so scared. I can't even find the right words to pray. I thought the nightmare had ended. Instead, it has started again.*

All the way to her car, her mind spun with the threatening call and Sergeant Landow's questioning. She didn't care for the tactics of either one. At her car, the police officer returned her keys.

"Thank you," she said, still shaken.

Sergeant Landow opened her car door, then patted her arm. "I know all of this has been difficult, but I'm sure today must have been a prank call."

Allison refused to acknowledge his utterly ludicrous explanation. She knew better, and so did he.

Chapter 6

I don't care what it takes," Beau said, once the sergeant returned from the parking garage. He balled his fist and slammed it into his palm. "Allison needs police protection until this is resolved. I don't believe Joe Lopez simply walked into the Budget Builder's and shot her because he was high any more than you do. The threat today proves she's in a lot of danger."

Sarge paced the floor in front of the window. "Aren't you overreacting? Today's caller was just some idiot trying to scare her. He saw the media reports and jumped in on the hype."

"Well, it worked, didn't it? And you and I know he had to put out a little effort to follow her here." He heard his voice rise. "I'm not stupid enough to swallow the prankster excuse."

"I'll get to the bottom of it. We already closed the shooting case, but today's business opens it up again."

"Brilliant," Beau growled.

"Looks to me like you're involved with this girl."

Beau rose on his elbows. "Whether I am or not is not the issue. She's in trouble, and you're blowing it off!"

Sarge rubbed the back of his neck, the lines on his face speaking volumes.

"What are you not telling me about this case?" Beau asked, reaching to his nightstand and pouring a glass of water.

"It's still under investigation."

"I'm not a rookie, so don't give me that stuff."

Sarge hesitated. "We haven't turned up a thing. The investigation shows the gunman mistook her for another woman when he shot both of you. What happened today is another matter."

Beau's anger was rapidly reaching its peak. "A coincidence? I don't think so. Now, what are you really thinking?"

"The little lady obviously made somebody good and mad, or she lied to us."

※

Three hours later, Allison had yet to call Beau. The wait gave him plenty of time to repeatedly go over the phone call. He had a gut feeling she hadn't lied. She'd have to be a good actress to pull off the terror he'd seen on her face. What little he knew about her didn't indicate anything suspicious. Innocent and naïve more closely resembled his angel, a dynamic Christian woman who had gotten caught up in the middle of a vicious crime.

The more he spent time with Allison, the more he liked her. Lately his thoughts were consumed by all the little things about her that intrigued him—the fresh sweetness about her, the intelligence behind those endless pools of green, and her giving heart. Every day she brought light and laughter into the dull world of hospital routine. With Allison, he masked his irritation over the lack of progress in his rehabilitation. His leg hurt constantly, and the wounds in his side weren't healing fast enough for his liking.

He wanted to pack up his few belongings and walk out of that sterile environment and back onto the filthy streets. Strange, he craved clean streets for the citizens of Houston, but he wanted to do the cleaning.

Allison symbolized hope for all those who had ever suffered from a senseless crime. Maybe that's what attracted him to her.

Of course, once the doctor released him and he got back to work, things would change. She wouldn't occupy his thoughts night and day, and he could focus on his case.

Beau glanced at the clock. She'd been home long enough for the cop to go through her apartment several times. Fuming, he snatched up the phone and a slip of paper with her phone numbers.

After the third ring, the answering machine picked up. Good, she'd listened to Sarge. "Allison, this is Beau. If you're there, I'd like to talk to you."

The phone clicked. "Hi. I hadn't called because you looked so tired this afternoon."

"How could I sleep, worried about you?" He bit his tongue to keep from lashing out at her.

"Don't concern yourself with me. Everything here is fine. The officer checked out every nook and cranny."

"This is not a laughing matter."

Silence reigned on the other end of the phone.

"I know," she said, her voice weak. "I'm afraid to leave my apartment and afraid to stay. Next Monday, I'm supposed to go back to work."

"I'm really sorry. I forget you don't live with this stuff like I do, and I'm not being very sympathetic."

"How long do investigations like this last? Maybe if I could mark it on my calendar and see progress—" She stopped talking. "I'm a fool, Beau. I know this could drag out and get very nasty before it's all over."

Beau hated putting her through this, and he couldn't lie to her. Already his feelings for her soared beyond what he believed safe for his solitary world.

"You don't have to say a word," she said. "That man is after me, and I don't know why. The sad part about this whole thing is you've already taken several bullets on account of me, and now he's threatening you. I can't visit you at the hospital anymore. It's too dangerous. The next time, you could be killed."

Beau couldn't believe the absurdity of Allison's statement. "Not a chance," he said with a wry laugh. "I'm the cop here, and we're in this together."

"You must have hit your head during the shooting," she replied. "I don't know how many times I need to repeat this, but your vacation in the hospital is my fault. Remember?"

He'd seen the feisty, independent side of Allison a few times, and he rather liked it, even though her conclusions were ridiculous. "You are the nursing student, and I'm the cop. I'm trained to handle jerks. If that guy was serious, then you don't have a chance without me."

"You're awfully sure of yourself," she said, her voice a level below shouting. "I put my faith and trust in God, not a wounded cop who can't get out of bed."

"Ouch."

"You asked for it."

"So what's your plan, Miss Nurse Detective?"

"That wasn't nice, either." She sighed. "I'm sorry. I don't want to argue. Can we call a truce?"

He clenched his fist. Stubborn woman. "As long as you understand one thing. Your specialty is nursing, and mine is police work. And for the record. . . my source of help is God."

"I know."

She sighed, and he seized the opportunity to continue with his lecture. "The truth is, you're scared, and you have every right to be. I'm going to do all I can to find the lunatic who called you today, but I can't be worrying about you not following safety precautions. Are you going to comply?"

"All right," she replied meekly. "I'm listening."

Finally she'd come to her senses. "Number One: I'm working on police protection, but in case Sarge refuses, you don't go anywhere unless I know about it— nowhere alone at night, and your cell phone is to be with you at all times. I mean sleep with it, shower with it. Agreed?" When she failed to reply, he repeated his question.

"Okay. I'll do my best."

"Better than your best. Any more calls like today, and I want to know about them immediately."

"Doesn't sound like I have much of a life," she said. Resistance punctuated every word.

"For right now, no. And one more thing: Keep the blinds and drapes closed in your apartment."

"Do you enjoy giving orders?"

"Yes, especially when it involves saving people's lives. One last request—don't come to the hospital tomorrow."

"Just tomorrow?" she echoed, her tone laced with sarcasm.

"Yes, I plan to get out of here. Enough is enough."

"You're not ready. The doctor won't release you."

Her words stung. "Watch me. You're talking to a determined man, and I will leave in the morning."

✳

Allison considered hurling the phone against the wall and irreparably shattering it. Then no one could harass her. What right did Beau or Sergeant Landow have to dictate her every move? She thought the police would have solved this case by now. Instead, her life had become more complicated and completely out of control. She, the confident, clear-headed one, had exchanged her cool demeanor for a dose of debilitating panic.

Someone wanted to kill her, and she didn't know why.

The policeman had searched through every corner and closet and declared her apartment safe. How little he knew. Haunting whispers wafted about the rooms, taunting her with cruel laughter and odious memories. Always she saw the blood, and in her nightmares the crimson pools flooded until she swam in a river of red.

Oh, God, help me. I'm so afraid. I can't remember any Scripture, and when I try to read Your Word, nothing makes sense. My mind is paralyzed with fear. What am I to do?

Allison rubbed her shoulders in an effort to dispel the terror surging through her veins. Peace. She craved God's tranquility like a newborn craving his mother's milk. The tears were always a breath away, those uncontrollable moments when she weakened to emotion. Always she feared weeping would push her past the brink of sanity, and she'd never be able to step back into a rational world.

Closing her eyes, she tried to pray, but all she managed was a pitiful cry for it all to end. A single drop slipped from one of her eyes, and she hastily wiped it away. Shaking her head, she glanced about the apartment, dreading the shadows ushering in the night. Light—she needed to see. Frantically, she flipped on switches and lamps throughout the rooms.

Remembering her promise to Beau, she closed the blinds in her living room and bedroom. Normally when evening approached, she closed them, except this time the act meant survival. Shutting out the impending sunset and night diminished her chances to be seen by him—whoever he was.

Could she have seen a crime in progress and not realized it? Perhaps the caller had been a friend or family member of Joe Lopez or a man who merely wanted to scare her. Whatever the reason, his tactics worked.

Allison swallowed. She heard a rumble in her stomach and ignored it. Food took a backseat to the problems raging through her mind. Right now she wanted to think. Until two weeks ago, she'd never heard of Beau Oliver. Now her life revolved around him. She dare not breathe or take a step outside her apartment without informing him. A few hours ago, the future looked more optimistic than the present. Now she wanted to crawl into a cave and stay there.

When Beau had held her hand today, she had felt an inkling of something forbidden, a hint of things shoved to another time and place. Her life didn't have room for a man. She had enough complications, and the thought of falling in love made her a bit angry. Yet, if she allowed herself to dwell on Beau, he more than attracted her. His rugged, good looks accompanied by the way he lifted his right brow when he talked, his low, throaty chuckle, and his heart for the Lord all persuaded her to bend just a little. But she couldn't. Once HPD resolved the shooting and the phone call, she'd go back to her world, and he'd venture back to his.

Allison crossed her arms and settled down onto her sofa. After all, her changing emotions could merely reflect her dependence on him. God, not a policeman, was her bodyguard.

Over and over, her thoughts revisited the events over the past month. She stared into a lit candle, now and then inhaling the vanilla pear scent waltzing about the room. The phone rang, echoing around the apartment like a banshee. She jumped and waited for the answering machine to pick up the message. Two rings. Three rings. "Hi, Allison. This is your mother, wondering about—"

Allison snatched up the phone. "Hi, Mom. What can I do for you?"

"Your dad and I have been talking about your policeman. How is he doing?"

My policeman? When did this happen? "He's not mine, Mom, and he's doing very well."

"Good. I only referred to him that way because he saved your life. Nothing more."

Allison relaxed and leaned onto a pillow on the sofa. "Oh, I know. Sorry if I sounded sharp. He's wanting to get released, tired of being cooped up in a hospital."

"Honey, are you all right? You sound stressed."

Allison caught her breath. Mom couldn't hear a word of what happened today. "I'm fine. A little tired is all."

"Maybe making the drive to Hermann Hospital every day is taking its toll. After all, you need recovery time, too."

Allison forced a smile into her response. "You're probably right, and I don't plan to go tomorrow."

"Would you like to have lunch? What about your favorite tearoom?"

Allison squeezed her eyes shut. She refused to risk her mother's safety. She needed to ask Beau about such ventures. "I'm not sure. Haven't gotten my appetite back yet."

"If you change your mind, call me in the morning."

"Thanks, Mom, I will. Thanks for calling, and I love you." Allison laid the phone back into the charger. She hated deceiving her mother, but what choice did she have?

The evening dragged on. More and more, her thoughts turned to Beau. She remembered the warmth in his eyes and his gentle touch earlier in the day. Before this afternoon, they'd laughed and talked about fun things they'd done in their younger years, the awkward awareness of the teens, and the sudden realization of adulthood.

"Rebellion was my middle name," Beau had said. "I spent my high school days sitting in the principal's office and the nights roaming the streets, looking for trouble."

"And you were friends with Kieron then?" she asked, finding it difficult to believe Beau had been a problem teen.

"Oh, yes. We were a pair. Then, one night, a friend of mine met up with a couple of guys who wanted his tennis shoes. They were high on drugs, and my buddy died from their beating."

Shock and disbelief ruled her reply. Although she'd heard about such things on the news, it hadn't happened to anyone close to her. "I'm so sorry. How tragic."

Beau nodded grimly. "God began to move in me, and on the day of Dave's funeral, I cried my eyes out to my dad. He led me to Jesus Christ as my personal Savior. Before graduating, I felt God wanting me to dedicate my life to ending crime on the streets."

Allison nibbled on her lower lip, remembering the sincerity in Beau's eyes. Tomorrow she'd call and apologize for venting her fear and anger on him. Glancing at her watch, she saw a few minutes left before visiting hours ended. She could call and apologize now.

The sound of his voice soothed her frazzled nerves. "Hi, I just wanted to apologize for earlier this evening. I took out my frustrations on you." Suddenly she felt incredibly foolish.

"You already did, remember?"

"Yeah, but I don't think I really meant it."

He chuckled, and she felt the same tingling as when he'd held her hand. "What makes now any different?"

"I'm feeling more gracious." She laughed and looped the phone cord around her fingers. *Am I flirting with this guy?*

"Truth is I'm glad you called. Real glad."

She shifted uncomfortably, realizing she felt more for him than good judgment dictated. She couldn't allow emotions to jeopardize her carefully laid plans for the future.

Confusion tore at her senses. If she hadn't met Beau under tragic circumstances, would she be losing her heart now?

Chapter 7

Beau observed his tall, thin mother meticulously place his few belongings into a duffle bag. He had just shoved the stuff in there, but Mom needed to make sure each item had a perfect spot. She'd bought him a new shirt and jean shorts to replace the bloodstained ones from the shooting, although she chose a colorful sports shirt with a button-down collar rather than a T-shirt more reflective of his undercover work. He'd already given one of the nurses his bloody clothes to throw away before his parents arrived. No point in upsetting them all over again. They already had serious doubts about his ability to maneuver about his house and wanted him to stay with them. That would cramp his investigative spirit, and he didn't handle smothering well.

"Hey, Dad, you want to go fishing Saturday?" He picked up a rubber band and pulled his hair back into a ponytail. "My boat's in good shape."

His towering dad glanced up from searching through the drawers one more time to make sure Beau had all of his things. "You gonna feel up to it? I heard the doctor cautioning you about doing too much too soon."

"Sure. I may walk with a limp, but I can still balance myself in a boat and toss out a line. What better way to relax?" He reached across the bed for his cane. "If the fish aren't biting, I can always hit 'em over the head."

His parents laughed. He started to comment about his mother frying up the fish, but the phone interrupted him in midsentence. He snatched it up, savoring the idea of spending time with his mom and dad.

"You want us to lay off your girlfriend?" a male voice asked.

Beau whirled away from his parents, nearly losing his balance, to face the window. Lightning whipped across the sky, followed by a low rumble of thunder. "Glad you called," he replied, "I'm listening."

"Then stop the investigation."

"I don't know what you're talking about." He tore through the recesses of his mind for a clue to the caller.

"So you want to play games?"

"No, just tell it to me straight. I'm confused."

The man cursed. "We leave Miss Reynolds alone in exchange for you backing off your case."

"So that's what this is all about?"

"Exactly. Are you going to play, or do we continue to shake up the little lady?

278

I'd hate to see the pretty woman hurt again because of you. Next time she might not be so lucky."

"Did you have anything to do with that?" Beau asked as he watched the wind bend the trees and toss debris.

"The ex-boyfriend lunatic? Come on. I'm smarter than you give me credit for."

"I've got to think about this."

"Humph. Don't take too long. I'm an impatient man."

Click. Beau took a deep breath and expelled it slowly. Were the two incidents connected or not?

"Problems, Son?" Concern etched lines around his father's nut brown eyes.

Beau gave him a feigned smile. "Naw. Some guy wondering when I'd be back to work. Can't seem to let a fella rest."

"Well, you need time to recuperate. Can't chase bad guys with a limp," his mother pointed out. She snatched up a tissue and dabbed her eyes. "I sure am praying for you to give up this line of work. Every time I hear a siren, I cringe."

Beau kissed her cheek. "Oh, Mom, you want me to pass up the excitement? What would I do with my time?"

She stiffened her five-feet-ten frame and wagged a finger in his face. "You were nearly killed a few weeks ago. That's not excitement; it's simply pure stupidity. And if you're looking for something to do, why not see more of Allison? I really like her. Besides, I don't think she'd take your bossiness."

"I'm praying about it all, too," he said. *Looks like my cover is blown, anyway.*

✳

After Beau's parents settled him in at home, he bid them good-bye at the door. He waited for their car to disappear down the wet street, then called a taxi to take him downtown to meet with Sarge. The latest phone call held priority over everything for Beau—including his health.

His boss eased back in his chair and tapped a pen on the top of his paper-laden desk. "We've got a problem here, Beau. Someone knows who you are and what you've been doing."

"And believes Allison and I are involved."

"I told you that yesterday."

A muscle twitched in Beau's jaw. "I haven't known her very long. She's not the issue here; it's the joker making the phone calls."

Sarge lowered his eyebrows. "You must have stumbled onto something incriminating, and they're worried. Scaring the girl is insurance to keep you quiet."

"Nice thought, if I knew who to arrest. All I have is what I've heard on the streets. The dealers sell exclusively to those who've worked for them a long time."

"Do you think it's an inside job?"

"The thought's crossed my mind." Beau stretched out his leg. It burned from the day's abuse. He should have popped a pain pill.

"Any idea who?"

"I have a few suspects, but nothing concrete."

"I want a list of names." Sarge pushed a tablet of paper toward him. "In the meantime, you're off the case and taking a lengthy medical leave of absence. That should get our friends off your back and give Allison a little peace of mind. Does she know about today's call?"

"Course not. I want to leave her out of it as much as I can." Beau hesitated. "I know the other day you didn't think there was a connection between the shooting and the threats, but have you changed your mind?"

Sarge shook his head and tapped his pencil faster. "Not sure. The gunman had a record of dabbling in a list of crimes, but nothing that would indicate a key position in trafficking narcotics. Naturally, he could have taken his orders from someone else, but it doesn't make sense. Remember, he targeted Allison with his wild accusations, not you."

"Are you sticking to separate incidents? Because I sure don't believe they are." Beau shifted his leg again and frowned. He wanted the answers now.

"There's no connection. Besides, the caller just denied it. You know the type. If they've done something, they want the credit."

The longer he discussed the two situations, the more Beau felt his temper rising, or maybe the pain in his leg had attacked his logic. "Between you and me, I'm still on the case."

Sarge gave him a wry smile and dropped the pen. "As I said, you're off the case due to a medical leave of absence; but if you unofficially stumble onto something, keep me informed. I can always arrange for backup. Just be careful and keep an eye out for that girl of yours."

"Friend," Beau said, feeling the strain of his first day out of the hospital. "She's a friend."

※

The following morning found Allison bored and irritable. Sleep had evaded her, and she'd ended up watching a late movie. Unfortunately, the mystery thriller succeeded in frightening her so that she couldn't fall asleep until nearly five o'clock. At eight, she awoke to the sound of a storm raging outside. Lightning seared the sky, and thunder crashed like a myriad of kettledrums. The same thing had happened in the movie.

While the roar and flashes of nature surrounded her, she attempted to get some food into her stomach. She poured a glass of orange juice and stuck two slices of stale bread into the toaster. Before it finished toasting, she lost power. Drinking the orange juice, she settled for a speckled banana and a handful of dry cereal. The pitiful breakfast suited her mood, and she conducted her own pity-party right on her sofa.

With the drapes and blinds still closed, she lit a candle and placed it on her coffee table. Its meager flicker looked like a tribute to her depression. She wished Beau would call and let her know if he'd been released.

Staring at her Bible and understanding her comfort lay beneath its pages, she thumbed all the way through from Genesis to Revelation. Every verse she had ever underlined held new clarity and meaning. She turned back to Isaiah, where a verse captured her attention—chapter two, verse twenty-two. "Stop trusting in man, who has but a breath in his nostrils. Of what account is he?"

Okay, Lord, my faith is in You and in Your deliverance.

Chapter seven, verse nine she'd memorized her first year in nursing school when other students pressured her to join them in drinking and partying. Now, the words held even more meaning. " 'If you do not stand firm in your faith, you will not stand at all.' "

I understand, Lord. You are in control.

On she read as the prophet Isaiah recorded the words of God in His message to the people of Judah. The Scripture soothed her troubled spirit and assured her of God's provision.

Chapter forty-one, verse ten calmed her the most. " 'Do not fear, for I am with you; do not be dismayed, for I am your God. I will strengthen you and help you; I will uphold you with My righteous right hand.' "

Allison realized God had not forgotten her. In this precious book of the Old Testament, He had penned the words to comfort her today. He knew why she'd been shot, even if she might never discover the reason why. And He knew who had threatened her. No matter what the future held, He had it all under control. Beau and Sergeant Landow had given her precautions and instructions to keep her safe. They were trained officers who had her well-being in mind, so she intended to abide by their wishes.

What a blessing to have a Christian policeman like Beau concerned about her! She'd much rather have him on her side than a whole force relying solely on themselves.

The weather subsided, and Sandy, a girlfriend from church, stopped by to visit. "We need a shopping day before you head back to work," Sandy said. She stood and whirled her whole five-feet-two-inch frame. "I've lost ten pounds, and I'm ready for a summer wardrobe."

Allison laughed. "I noticed as soon as you came in. How does Saturday sound?"

"Wonderful." Her gaze darted about the room, then back to Allison's face. "Why do you have it so dark in here?"

"The storm earlier bothered me, so I shut all the drapes and blinds." Allison detested the lie.

Sandy strolled to the living room window and pushed back the drapes. "The bad weather passed an hour ago, and this place looks like a tomb. You're pale, too. A burst of sunshine is just what you need."

Allison held her breath. She couldn't do a thing about Sandy's gesture of friendship. "Thanks. I tend to hibernate since the accident."

Sandy offered her a smile. "I don't want to bring up an unpleasant topic, but do you need to talk?"

Boy, do I. "I'm fine, really. The pastor is counseling me."

"How is the man who was shot helping you?"

A wave of peace swept over her as though Beau sat in the same room with them. "He's doing quite well. In fact, he may have gotten to go home from the hospital today."

"Good. Now he can put his life back together. So, is he married?" Sandy's eyes twinkled.

"No." Allison laughed. "I'm not interested, and he's pretty dedicated to his work."

"What does he do?"

Allison paused to think a moment. She didn't dare tell the truth. Beau hadn't discussed this with her, and she'd already lied to Sandy about the drapes. The term "undercover cop" now left a nasty taste in her mouth. "He assists people in finding new purposes for their lives."

"Oh, like social work, or is he involved in a ministry?"

"I think a little of both."

After Sandy left, she grilled a cheese sandwich and peeled an orange. For certain, she had to start eating better.

At two-thirty, she wished she'd accepted her mother's invitation to lunch, as much for the company as for a good meal. She couldn't avoid her family until the police department determined the problem, nor did she want to. Beau and Sergeant Landow said to keep them informed—not to isolate herself. It might be too late to have lunch with Mom, but a good chat seemed in order.

"Are you feeling better?" her mother asked when Allison called. "You've been on my mind all morning."

"Yes, I am. During the power outage, I had a good prayer time, and God has given me a sense of peace about all of this."

"Wonderful. I nearly came over."

"Oh, Mom, I wish you had. I was terribly lonely, but Sandy stopped by, and we planned a shopping trip for Saturday."

"Things are on their way back to normal. Once you start work on Monday, that nightmare will soon be forgotten. I'm certain of it because my friends and I have been praying."

I only wish it was over. "Thanks, and tell your friends I appreciate their prayers."

Her mother sighed, obviously relieved. "I'm making vegetable beef soup and herb bread tonight. Would you like to join this old couple for dinner? I might add a strawberry pie."

"Love it," Allison replied. She had plenty of time to contact Beau and relay her plans. "And Mom, about last night—I was rude, and you're the last person I want to catch the brunt of my bad moods."

"Don't worry a thing about it. In your shoes, I'd be a basket case. You just keep your chin up and let us love you."

Allison replaced the phone. Spending time with family and friends had been the highlight of her day. What a real blessing. Scrutinizing her living room, she saw dust and a week's accumulation of newspapers. Perfect. She'd clean before phoning Beau and taking off to her parents' house.

After taking on the job of disinfecting her bathroom with one hand, she pulled down her shower curtain and tossed it into the washing machine. Due to her bandaged arm, the job took longer than she expected. She vacuumed the entire one-bedroom apartment and changed the sheets on her bed. Snatching up a cloth and a bottle of lemon oil from her utility cabinet, she tackled the mounds of dust.

Allison glanced at the answering machine. It flashed a new message. She hadn't heard the phone and guessed it rang while she ran the vacuum. Depressing the PLAY button, she waited in hopes Beau had called.

"Allison." She felt the hair bristle on her neck. "I see you didn't get much sleep last night. I saw the light through the blinds of your bedroom until nearly five o'clock." He chuckled. "You can't run from me; I'm everywhere. You know, like God. You want this to stop? Maybe you need to talk to your boyfriend. We spoke today, and he knows exactly what he's supposed to do."

Chapter 8

Allison struggled to punch in the numbers to Beau's cell phone. She could barely read them on the slip of paper he'd given her, for the stinging tears blurring her vision. Twice, she had to start over.

"Calm down, calm down," she whispered. "God's in control." She trembled and glanced out the window where the drapes were still open. She felt violated.

Beau answered on the second ring.

"Beau, this is Allison." She caught her breath and covered her mouth in an effort to stop the hysteria.

"What's happened? Talk to me."

"He just called again," she managed and repeated the conversation.

"Did you erase it from your answering machine?"

She glanced at the flashing light. "No. I thought you'd need it."

"Good girl. I might be able to detect something in his voice that I missed this morning."

Allison swallowed the lump in her throat. "What did he mean, saying he talked to you earlier?"

Beau expelled a breath so heavy she could feel his fury. "He contacted me at the hospital. Right now, I'm downtown talking to the sarge. Do you mind if I stop over? If that guy's watching your apartment, he might even call again while I'm there."

Allison heard his urgency. "My parents are expecting me for dinner."

"No problem. I won't stay but a few minutes."

"Are you feeling up to this? I mean, you shouldn't be driving in your condition."

"I'm taking a taxi."

She hung up the phone and checked the time. After putting in a call to her mother about being a few minutes late due to Beau's visit, Allison eased back onto the sofa and waited. Her mother insisted Beau join them, and Allison didn't have the heart to tell her the truth. No point in upsetting her parents—anxiety didn't solve a thing.

What had her nursing classes said about the value of cool, clear thinking in the middle of an emergency? Those instructions hadn't applied when the nurse was the one knee-deep in trouble.

She sat on the sofa, staring out the window, until early evening shadows crept across her apartment, casting in dappled shades of the western sun. Another day soon to be done. No hint of violence or threats, only streams of light. She needed to close the drapes and blinds, but she felt cemented to the sofa. In the heat of summer, her living room became nearly unbearable, but the cooler months were cozy. At another time, she'd have welcomed the light and hint of summer, but not with the thought of a stalker observing her from some point outside.

Uneasiness crept over her, as though every move was being filmed. She stood and closed the drapes, chastising herself for not doing it earlier. She couldn't bring herself to switch on a lamp but instead lit the candle again. The monster had invaded her privacy, violated the sanctity of her home, and threatened more. Now she had a clearer understanding of the trauma of rape. All the nursing classes in the world hadn't prepared her for this piercing terror. Who was this man, and what had she done to anger him?

An hour later her doorbell rang. Staring at the door, she tried to rise, but her legs refused to move.

"Who's there?" She hoped she sounded braver than the fear pounding against her chest.

"Beau. The taxi followed another car through the security gate."

The sound of his voice brought a mixture of cleansing tears and relief. Her limbs responded, and she fumbled through releasing the deadbolt lock. Seeing him in the doorway brought a new realization, accompanied with overwhelming guilt.

"Beau, you shouldn't have climbed those two flights of stairs!" She gasped at his pallor as he leaned heavily on a steel cane. How had he climbed those stairs?

"Hey, Sunshine," he said, his narrowed eyes and the wrinkling of the side of his nose indicating his pronounced pain.

Allison reached for him. "Why didn't you call up here, and I'd have come to you? You're going to end up back in the hospital at this rate."

"Naw." He grimaced. "I'm a strong healthy male. . .good shape."

She helped him to the sofa. "In good shape as compared to what?"

"Funny," he replied, grabbing the arm of the sofa before allowing himself to sink into the cushions. "If nursing doesn't work out, you can always be a comedian."

She poured him a glass of water and wrung out a washcloth to wipe the perspiration beaded on his forehead. He protested as she dabbed at his face.

"Don't smother me, Nurse Reynolds," he said. "I can do it myself."

"Hush. When you're feeling better, you can handle it all. Until then, let me practice my skills on you."

He closed his eyes and swallowed hard. "You're stubborn, you know that?"

She smiled. "Thank you. I find some forms of stubbornness highly desirable."

After a few minutes, his breathing slowed, and he reached for her hand. "Aren't you supposed to be somewhere for dinner?"

"Mom knows I'll be late, and you're invited."

He rubbed his chin. "How much do they know?"

"Nothing. The information would be too much for them."

He nodded as if in agreement. "I should go home, but I don't want to. We could talk on the way."

She combed her fingers through her hair. "You're an inch from passing out, and you're ready to tackle the stairs again?"

"I'm hungry." He grinned, but the tightening of the muscles around his eyes told her of his discomfort.

"When did you last take a pain pill?"

"Haven't since leaving the hospital. I had things to do and didn't want my senses dulled."

"That's the idea behind them—mask the pain and put you to sleep. You should have stayed in the hospital."

He leaned his head back. "I'd worn out the welcome mat. What's your mom cooking?"

She hid her amusement with his change of subject. "Vegetable soup and homemade bread. I suppose you haven't eaten since breakfast, either."

"Right. I'm a man on the move."

She didn't like his color, and for a moment she wondered if he would pass out. "Perhaps you should rest a bit more."

"We need to go, but first, I want to hear the recording."

"Beau, this is senseless. You're not a well man."

"Don't argue with a cop," he growled, "but I'll make a deal. You can drug me once we get to your parents'."

He listened to the answering machine tape three times, ejected it from the machine, and put it in his pocket before he appeared satisfied and announced his readiness to leave. Although he protested, Allison helped him down the steps and into her car. In her concern over his condition, she nearly forgot about being watched until she closed the door on the passenger side. Glancing about, she neither saw an unfamiliar vehicle nor any strangers.

Once they pulled onto the street, she broached the subject of the phone calls. "I want to know what he said to you," she said, "all of it—not the Cliff Notes version."

"You're awfully pretty," he replied, "but demanding."

"Comes with being the youngest. Please tell me what he said."

Beau turned his attention to the side window before he spoke. "He'll leave you alone in exchange for me stepping back from a narcotics case I've been working on."

"How is this connected to the shooting?"

"According to him, it's not."

She rolled her eyes. "I'm smarter than that."

"So am I, but Sarge believes they're separate incidents. The problem is, I can't seem to connect them."

She slowed at a stoplight and willed her trembling hands to stop while toying with her next question. "What did you tell him you'd do?"

He lifted a brow. "Worried, are you?"

Her insides crumbled, and her lips quivered. He touched her shoulder. "Hey, I'm teasing here. I'm off the case and taking a ninety-day leave of absence. That should give Sarge time to get to the bottom of this."

Her shoulders relaxed slightly, but with his decision came another realm of questions. "You're walking away from a case?"

"Would you rather continue to live in fear?"

She wished she could see his hazel eyes, but in the evening shadows she could only imagine them. "No. My concern is what you're giving up to accommodate me."

"Just because I said I'm off the case and taking a leave doesn't necessarily mean I'm going to sit at home and watch TV."

She understood exactly what Beau implied and didn't know if she found any comfort in his words.

※

"What are the odds of an off-duty, undercover cop getting shot up like you did?" Lucas Reynolds asked.

"Lucas," Marge Reynolds said, dropping her knife onto her plate with a clink. "You shouldn't ask Beau such a question. Why, he doesn't even know we found out about his. . .position."

Beau chuckled at Allison's parents' squabbling. "I don't mind you knowing, as long as you keep the information to yourselves."

"Oh, we have," Marge replied, her eyes widening. "We haven't told a soul—not even our kids."

"Good." Beau raised a soupspoon loaded with beef and vegetables to his lips and remembered Lucas's question.

"I guess the odds are rare."

"I hear you don't wear a bullet-proof vest when you're working," Lucas added.

Beau caught the shock on Allison's face. "Right. Hard to hide one of them under a T-shirt."

"In any event, we owe you for our little Alli," Lucas said.

Beau took a sideways glance at Allison and saw a slow rise of red. Amused, he reached for his glass of iced tea to drown the laughter gurgling inside him. He liked this family; they reminded him a lot of his own. Someday he might have a wife and a few kids but not anytime soon. When it happened, he'd work a day job, then spend tons of time as a Christian husband and father—not the double life he led now.

Sleep crept over him like a sneaky cat. He'd put off taking the pain medication until they arrived for dinner, and the effects were taking over. His leg and side didn't ache, and he wanted to curl up somewhere and not wake up for three days, but he'd been trained in staying alert and concentrated on the conversation around him.

"Beau," Allison said, her voice gentle as a summer breeze off his favorite lake. "You have to get home before you keel over."

"She's right," Marge said. "Honey, why don't you take him home? He looks a fright and pale, too. I'll pack up a piece of the pie and some of dinner so he'll have food for lunch."

Beau's mind registered an alarm. "I don't want her running around at night. As soon as we get back to her apartment, I'll call a cab."

"I won't hear of it," Lucas said. "I'll run you home as soon as you're ready."

Beau pushed aside any muddled thoughts. "Sir, I appreciate your offer, but I want to see Allison home safely first. It's a thing with me—you don't take advantage of a lady inviting you to dinner."

Lucas slowly nodded. "For a minute I forgot about what happened. I'll follow you two over, escort my little girl to her apartment, and take you home."

Beau smiled. Not the optimum solution, but it served his purpose. At least he'd have a few moments alone with Allison in the car. He thanked Marge for the delicious meal and stood, ready to finish up the evening and crawl into bed. If he sat there much longer, he might fall face-first into his soup bowl. He hadn't done that since he was a kid, and he had no intentions of doing so now.

"I'm sorry," he whispered once he and Allison were on their way. "I didn't mean to spoil your evening."

"You need to be in bed, and I'm a poor nurse to allow all this activity."

"You see, I had to see this beautiful lady."

"Pleeeze," she said. "You're under the influence, remember?"

He wet his lips and took a few deep breaths. For now the annoying urge to sleep would have to wait. He hated the way medicine affected him. "I'll call you in the morning and make sure everything is okay." His cell phone rang, interrupting his broken train of thought. Yanking it out of his pants pocket, he saw "caller ID unavailable." Beau mumbled a hello.

"Good work, Cop. You follow orders better than most."

"So you found out I'm off the case and taking a leave of absence."

Allison stiffened, but he needed to concentrate on the caller.

"Oughta give you lots of time with your pretty girlfriend. Oh, by the way, you had a hard time making it up her steps tonight. Thought for a minute you might need some help." He laughed low.

"Glad you're amused at my expense."

"Just remember. One slipup, and Miss Allison will pay. Got it?"

"Sure. I'm keeping my end of the deal." Beau slid the phone back into his pocket. He reached across the seat and laid his hand on her shoulder. "Relax. He won't be bothering you anymore."

She breathed sharply, and he heard a sob. "But you didn't tell him you'd unofficially work at home, did you?"

"The secret is to let them think you are doing exactly what they want."

Chapter 9

Allison took in a deep breath before she unleashed her anger and fright. "You're playing with my life. How can you do that with a clear conscience?"

"It'll be all right," Beau said, much too kind to her liking. "Only the sarge will know I'm tinkering with the case at home. Another cop has already been assigned to the streets."

She stopped at a yellow light and stared into the dark surroundings as though the faceless man with the raspy voice might try to pull her from the car. "I hate this," she said, banging her palm against the steering wheel. "Everything I once took for granted has exploded in my face. I'm afraid for myself and those I care about."

"Allison, you're no longer in danger," Beau said. "I gave them what they wanted. They were trying to get to me, not you."

"Right," she said. They sat in silence until the light changed, and she stepped on the gas a little harder than she intended. The car sped away, tires squealing and most likely leaving a patch of rubber behind them.

Two more turns, and she pulled up to the security gate of her apartment complex. Punching in her code, she crept through the entrance to her building. Her dad's convertible wasn't behind them, but he knew her security numbers. She swung into her parking slot and turned off the engine.

"Dad drives slower than I do," she said, avoiding his piercing stare.

"Most people do," he replied, but she didn't appreciate his dry sense of humor at her expense.

"I'm nervous, okay?" She leaned her head on her hands against the steering wheel. The sobs started, and she couldn't stop them.

Beau's hand caressed her shoulder, and as angry as she felt at him for duping the man who had frightened her beyond imagination, his touch felt comforting.

"Scoot over here by me," he whispered.

"I can't," she said. "I might not be able to stop crying, and Dad will be here any minute."

"And he won't understand you're upset after all you've been through?"

"He and Mom think I'm the pillar of strength," she said, sniffing.

"I imagine he knows the real you—his little girl." He massaged her tight neck muscles, reducing the stress ripping through her.

She shook her head and felt her nose dripping over her upper lip like a four year old. She yanked a tissue from a box between them and wiped her nose while more tears flooded her eyes. Beau wrapped his arm around her shoulders and urged her to lay her head against his chest. She wanted his embrace to cease the flow of tears, but it even made her cry harder. Finally the weeping subsided, and she glanced up at the silhouette of his rugged features. She mentally traced the outline of his square jaw, remembering how close to death he'd been because of her. Of course he needed to find those drug dealers. Undercover work was his life, his calling.

He lifted her chin with his finger and pressed a kiss against her forehead. She stared up into his eyes and envisioned the mixture of gold, brown, and green swirled into one. Slowly his head descended until their lips barely met. She couldn't allow this to happen. Her life didn't have room for romantic involvement and certainly not with a man who lived every moment in the foothills of crisis. She pulled away—not really wanting to, but believing that nestling next to him would spur her heart in a dangerous direction.

"I wouldn't do anything to hurt you," he whispered, toying with a strand of her hair. "You're too important to me."

She hesitated, then leaned back into his embrace, the lure of his kiss too powerful for her to refuse. He lowered his head and gently tasted the lips she timidly offered. His intensity deepened, nearly frightening her, and he released her.

"I should apologize, but I've wanted to kiss you for days."

Before she could respond, headlights flashed behind them, and her father pulled into the parking space beside her car. She eased back to the driver's side and opened the door.

"I'll call you tomorrow," Beau said. "I want to make sure you're okay."

She chose not to respond. Tumultuous emotions caused by his kiss and his intentions to continue with his undercover work frightened her. She wished sleep would dull her senses and bring relief.

"Sorry I'm late," her father said, holding up a plastic container. "Your mom wanted to make sure Beau had plenty of tonight's soup."

"Thanks," Beau replied. "It'll be gone in no time."

"Come on, Alli," her father said. "Let me walk you up those stairs. Your bodyguard needs time to recuperate."

※

Beau slept soundly past noon the following day until he woke from the dull ache in his leg. *Those stairs at Allison's apartment.* A moment later he remembered his trip downtown to see the sarge and admitted he'd overdone it. Great. And he had so many things to accomplish today.

How did the caller get his cell number? Unless one of Beau's informants had turned on him. . .The whole mess could be an inside job, or someone had gone through his trash. The latter was impossible, because he shredded every piece of mail. The conclusion stunk: nothing worse than losing a good informant or a cop going bad. He didn't want to think who it might be.

In the course of considering the past weeks and attempting to put some sense to his case, Beau struggled with the fact that Allison danced across his mind and ruined any good deliberation. From the first moment he saw her, she'd consumed his thoughts, and if he didn't watch it, she'd possess his heart. Last night he'd kissed her, and now guilt riddled him.

He didn't lead women on. Period. In fact, he avoided them. His experiences in the past had been disappointing at best. The women he'd considered had a tendency to wrap their arms around him and beg for him to quit his undercover work. Beau expected God to make it perfectly clear when to find another vocation, and he felt sure it wouldn't come in the form of a woman who didn't understand his need to make the city a better place to live.

But Allison had goals and ambitions of her own. She'd started late in pursuing a nursing career, and her plans were centered on finishing school and paying off the debts incurred to complete her education. She appeared perfectly independent and in no need of a husband. Perhaps a good, solid friendship was in order—one without any threat of the relationship heading into treacherous territory. Like his heart.

Who am I fooling? Allison is perfect for me.

He wanted to spend every spare minute with her, and his defenses were fast losing their resolve. He hated seeing her frightened, especially when this new problem originated with his continuing the case. She'd been through enough with the shooting, and now some thug thought he could get to Beau through a woman. And it worked. That's why he couldn't consider getting involved. Then why did he kiss her? Caution ruled every decision he made, and a woman complicated the ever-present danger. Once he nailed the guy threatening her and had him in jail where he belonged, they'd part company. Until then, they could be friends. He simply had to put his heart in check.

Beau glanced at the clock: twelve-thirty. He needed to check in with Sarge about the latest findings and his thoughts about the caller.

He also needed to call Allison—make sure she'd not received anymore phone threats. The climb out of bed to retrieve her number from his pants pocket nearly sent him sprawling to the floor. Grabbing the edge of his nightstand, he steadied himself until he could maneuver. Today would be the pits, but that's what he got for not minding the doctor's or the nurse's advice.

Her phone rang three times before it rolled over to the answering machine. "Hi, Allison, this is Beau. Are you there to pick up?"

Her sweet voice sent a tingle to his toes. "Good afternoon. How are you feeling?"

"Like I just got run over by a truck," he said with a chuckle. "You doing all right?"

"Yes, no calls today. I've been wondering, how long before you feel I'm okay to come and go as I please?"

He despised the anxiety in her voice. "You can now, just not at night. All I want is for you to be careful and let me know where you're going and when you expect to return. Make sure you always have your cell phone with you."

"I see. Life is a little strange when you're always looking over your shoulder." Beau sighed. "Not when you know who's in control."

"Always the optimist, but I appreciate your attitude."

He glanced around his bedroom. Normally a whole day without demands was welcome, but not when he hurt and couldn't do all the things he wanted. "Are you busy right now?"

"No. I've cleaned, written out bills, and talked to long-lost girlfriends. What did you have in mind?"

"I've got a prescription to fill, and I'm hungry. Are you interested in taxiing around a decrepit old man?"

"Sure." She laughed. "I'd welcome the change of scenery. My apartment is driving me crazy. When do you want to leave?"

"Truthfully, I just woke up. I need to make a few calls and get a shower, which will take a little while with this battered body. How about an hour?" He gave her directions and hung up the phone.

Beau remembered a term his grandmother used to use: fickle. He'd just given himself all the reasons why he shouldn't be anything more than a friend to Allison, and now his heart betrayed him.

Lord, if she is not for me, close the doors. I really like this girl, and despite all the arguments against becoming involved, I want to know her more.

※

Allison laughed until her sides hurt. "If you don't stop, they're going to throw us out of here." She leaned across the restaurant's table in their booth. "You weren't this funny in the hospital."

He bent as though to tell her a secret. "I didn't have this freedom."

She smiled and glanced down at her salad. Refusing to put a damper on their jovial mood, she pushed aside the ugliness that had brought them together. "I didn't think picking up a prescription and heading to lunch would be such entertainment."

"It's the company you're keeping," Beau replied, stabbing a slice of tomato in his salad.

She caught his gaze and saw fire smoldering in those warm eyes. He hastily glanced away. Could he feel as uncomfortable as she about the two of them together?

"Allison," he began and reached for his water glass, "sometimes when two people share a crisis or danger, they're bound forever by a strange magnetic force that other people seldom understand."

"I do understand a little. I've heard my dad talk about the Vietnam War and the special bond of the vets."

"Exactly." He replaced his glass and reached across the table to grasp her hand. "You and I have one of those relationships. We're friends, but with more of a sensitivity than those who experience more good times than bad ones."

"As though woven in a peculiar tapestry?"

"Yes. Part of it is our Christian faith and our certainty of the hereafter. We are more aware of purpose and meaning in our lives."

"Beau, what are you trying to tell me?"

He propped his other elbow on the table and rested his chin on his hand. "I feel I've known you forever. You're driving me crazy. No matter how many times I've tried to logically say you're just a woman with whom I've shared danger, I find myself thinking about you again, then I'm angry for doing so."

All morning, she'd tried to convince herself she didn't need an undercover policeman in her life. She had a career ahead of her in the field of medicine, one she felt God had ordained for her life. Yet, the attraction for Beau—everything about him—beckoned her.

She shivered, but not from the air-conditioning in the restaurant. He stated exactly how she felt. She placed her fork beside the salad, willing the appropriate words to flow from her tongue.

"Strangely enough, I feel the same way. I wish you weren't so likeable—it would make things much easier." She hesitated at the risk of sounding bold. "What do you want to do about us?"

"That's my dilemma. I should pick up my cane, go home, and forget I ever met you, but I can't. This whole thing is not fair to you. You know my line of work and the danger involved."

"Yes, and I respect your commitment."

He rubbed his chin. "I've never had much luck in the romance department."

"Did other women ask you to give up your police work?" She offered a faint smile.

"Exactly. Ultimatums of their so-called love."

"I really understand how a woman could care for you and want to make sure you're safe. From what you've told me, your job is a lonely proposition and involves a lot of hours where no one can contact you. Those circumstances could be difficult."

"How would you feel? I mean. . ." He shifted in the booth. "We've known each other so short a time. But if. . .if we were together, would you be able to handle the stress and pressure?"

Allison stared into his face, knowing she was losing her heart to the man before her. "I don't know, Beau."

Chapter 10

I have to be honest," Allison continued. "Up until a few weeks ago, my life looked pretty ho-hum. Then I was shot by a stranger who thought I was his ex-girlfriend, and now I'm threatened by a guy who believes I'm your girlfriend. Tell me, what would you think?"

Beau's mouth formed a grim line, and he released her hand. He reached into his pocket for his wallet and slapped a twenty-dollar bill on the table. "I'll call a taxi for a ride home. You don't need one more minute of this. I don't know what I was thinking."

"No, wait." She reached across the table for his hand. "I said I was being honest, and I'm not finished."

He lifted a brow, but waited with one hand on his cane and the other resting beneath her grasp.

"I don't believe anyone meets by chance, but rather God places people in our lives for a reason. At first, I thought you were there to save my life. Later I wondered if you were to help me through those threats. Now, I honestly don't know. I've told myself repeatedly that you and I have nothing in common, and I'm too busy right now for a man in my life. But. . .my emotions are telling me not to let go."

She saw a flicker of something in his eyes. By his own admission, he wrestled with the same thoughts.

He chewed on his lower lip and glanced down at the hand she'd placed over his. "I should walk away and never bother you again, but I don't want to. Something about you has handcuffed my heart." He offered a faint smile, and she felt her lips tug upward.

Before they could say another word, the server stopped to refill their iced teas.

"Are you staying?" Allison asked, hoping he understood she meant their friendship and not the meal. Odd, she thought she wanted to go back to her own comfortable lifestyle; but when presented with the choice, she changed her mind.

"Some days are tough," he said, neither moving toward his food nor leaning on the cane to stand. "And I've already told you how frustrating my schedule is."

"And dangerous," she added.

"That, too. It's probably not a decision to make on the spur of the moment."

"Is that what you're asking?"

He shook his head. "I'd be a fool to force the issue. Like you, I'm confused about us."

"I've seen tough days," she said, wanting him to see she could hold her own in a relationship if necessary.

"Some days, you might not hear from me at all. When you do, I can't tell you where I've been or what I've done."

She nodded. "My dad retired from the navy. He worked Intelligence, and sometimes he was gone for weeks."

He slowly swung his body back to the table and caught her gaze with his. "God has a plan for our lives. Trouble is, He hasn't told me yet if you and I are in it together." He took a long drink of his iced tea. "Whether we decide to continue seeing each other or go our separate ways, I won't discuss this case with anyone but Sarge. Those on both sides of the law have been told I'm on a leave of absence, maybe permanent. I'm still questioning the connection between the shooting and the threats, and there's a lot of investigation to be done."

"I understand. It's scary—all of it."

"So, with that in mind, are we still buds?"

She instantly prayed for guidance. "How about blossoming buds, taking one day at a time?"

❋

An hour later, Allison parked her little blue car in front of Beau's house. Like tin soldiers, three towering pines kept guard of the door, and their stance amused her. When she'd picked him up earlier, he'd been waiting on the driveway for her. She'd assessed his house, thinking the brick two-story looked more like a family home than a single man's domain.

"I know I said this before, but you have a beautiful home and yard. Looks as manicured as a woman's nails."

He laughed. "Thanks. I enjoy gardening and landscaping, but there are times when I have to call on a service to keep it mowed and the weeds pulled," he said. "What saves me are the perennials adding color. The rest is maintenance."

"I've just discovered your hobby," she said, admiring the neatly trimmed shrubbery intermingled with Shasta daisies, hibiscus, which hadn't yet bloomed, pink pentas, golden lantana, Mexican heather, and what her mother called "hummingbird plants."

"Oh, I have another sideline, but you have to come inside to see those projects." He tossed her a grin.

"Are you a man of many talents?" She turned off the engine.

"Not really. My dad tinkered in a bit of everything, and I tagged along, learning a few things along the way."

They exited the car and walked up a winding sidewalk leading to an oak-stained door. As soon as Beau's key turned the lock, the alarm signaled. He hobbled into another room and disarmed it.

She glanced about, impressed by the exquisite, detailed furniture, some hand-painted and others finished in a rich cherry. She detected the faint scent of a man's citrusy fragrance, a hint of Beau's private realm.

"Gorgeous furniture."

"I like building things," he said simply, "and Dad enjoys painting and staining them."

Her eyes widened. "You built these pieces?" She stepped closer to a small, three-drawer chest that was painted a cream color and trimmed in gold. A green vine stretched across the top and trickled down the sides. "This is lovely. I'm surprised you and your dad haven't gone into the furniture-making business."

He shrugged. "We both enjoy it as a hobby, not a vocation. Personally, I don't want people telling me how they want something constructed. Let me show you the bookcases in the den."

She followed him into a kitchen overlooking a sunny breakfast nook and an open TV area. A wall-length, cherry bookcase and entertainment center captured her attention.

"Oh, the scrollwork on this is perfect." She noted the mantel above the fireplace held the same wood and scroll design. "I am really impressed." Glancing down at the hardwood floors, she shook her head, knowing the homes in this neighborhood most generally contained carpet. "Did you install the floors, too?"

He leaned against the kitchen counter. "Sure did. When my head's spinning about a case, I take to the yard or to the garage. Works like a charm."

Allison saw the perspiration beads mount on his wrinkled forehead. Again he'd overdone it. "Beau, you really should lie down, or you'll be right back in the hospital."

"Aw, Nurse," he said, stuffing his hands into his jeans pocket and scuffing the toe of his tennis shoe across the floor, imitating a little boy. "I don't wanna much."

"And what did you plan to do instead of take care of the body God gave you?" She folded her arms across her chest in an effort to imitate a stern disciplinarian.

He frowned. "Did you learn that technique in nursing school?"

"No." She laughed. "It's my own."

He eased himself down on a recliner and pointed to a paper grocery sack on the table. "I'd like a nap, but Kieron brought over my mail, and I need to go through it this afternoon and pay bills."

"Nice guy to take care of it for you."

"I feel sorry for him, especially since his wife left him. I keep talking to him about the Lord, but nothing's registered."

"How sad. Do they have children?"

A mass of dark hair fell across his forehead. "No. They were high school sweethearts—never dated anyone else. He caught her running around on him, and when he wanted to make it work, she left." He shook his head. "She never came across to me as the type. Guess I misjudged her."

Not knowing how to reply, Allison decided to head home and hopefully he would rest. "If you don't have any more errands for me, I'm going home," she said with a tilt of her head. "I hope you get some sleep."

"I will think about it," he said without an ounce of commitment.

She sighed and took another quick look around the room. "I have a difficult time picturing you as an undercover cop."

He chuckled and narrowed his eyes. "Do I look mean enough for you now?"

"As compared to what? You don't scare me. Besides, you look more like a teddy bear." She grinned and groped through her purse for her keys until she tightened her fingers around them. "Thanks for lunch."

"Thanks for hauling me around." He tried to stand, but she protested. "I can at least walk you to the door."

"Another time." She wondered if a daylight kiss would affect her like last night. Feeling herself grow warm, she whirled around for the door and jingled her keys. "Bye. Have a wonderful nap."

She heard him laugh. "I'll call you later."

Once at her car, Allison slid onto the extra-warm seat and stuck her key into the ignition. Pressing the air-conditioning button, although she knew there wouldn't be any cold air just yet, she paused to take one last glimpse at his house. What a great guy and talented, too. Not at all what she envisioned for a man in his line of work. She swung her gaze across the street to where Beau indicated Kieron lived. How sad that his wife had abandoned him. She must remember to pray for the couple.

As her car left the curb, the familiar cloud of gloom settled upon her. For a little while, she'd forgotten the ugliness of what really brought her and Beau together. She prayed the worst had passed, but in the back of her mind a shadow of doubt gripped her.

❋

Beau woke three hours later at the sound of his doorbell. Swinging his legs over the bed, he attempted to stand, but a surge of pain broke huge beads of sweat down the sides of his face. Groaning, he grabbed the cane and limped to the door, wanting to verbally terrorize whoever stood on the opposite side.

Kieron greeted him with a broad smile. "Hey, Beau, how are you feelin'?"

Beau raked his fingers through his hair and forced a greeting he didn't really mean. "Better. Just tired and ready to move on." He stepped back from the door. "Come on in."

"Ah, can't stay but a minute," he said, ducking his head in the doorway. "Just wanted to see how you were doing and if you needed anything."

"No, thanks. Allison stopped over earlier, and we picked up a prescription at the drugstore. Come on in." He leaned on his cane and maneuvered around so

297

Kieron could step inside. His leg hurt something awful after jumping out of bed and putting all of his weight on it. If the stupid thing didn't stop throbbing soon, he'd be under the mercy of another pain pill.

"What about dinner?" Kieron asked. "I could grill us a couple of steaks."

"Allison's mother gave me some soup, and Mom dropped off fried chicken and potato salad. My appetite isn't quite ready to handle a lot of food yet."

"Looks like your pretty little girlfriend is taking good care of you," Kieron said, leaning against the side of the door.

Beau grinned and nodded. "She's a friend, nothing more, but that part of getting better makes it almost worth getting shot."

"So, when are you heading back to work? All those bad guys need you settin' them straight."

"I'm not, at least for a good while. Maybe never. I'm off my current case, and I've taken a ninety-day leave of absence."

Kieron whistled. "That'll be the day when Beau Oliver stuffs his undercover work aside. I bet you intend to stay on cases at home, just not let anybody know."

Beau shook his head. He didn't like lying to people, but Allison's well-being was more important. "The shooting slowed me down. I'm facing rehab three times a week and a pile of projects around here to last all summer. If and when I go back, I don't know what I'll be doing. The way this body of mine looks like a battleground, a desk job sounds good." His last statement held more truth than he cared to admit.

Kieron turned and grasped the doorknob. "You let me know if I can be of help. You certainly were there for me when I cried the blues over Lori leaving."

"No problem. Never know, during this time off, I might finally get you to church."

His friend shook his head. "Don't think so, but I appreciate the offer." He patted his jeans pocket. "I forgot your house key. Do you want me to run it back over?"

"Keep it for now. The way my head has been spinning the last few weeks, I might lock myself out and need it."

"Okay. Get rested up." Kieron turned the knob and let himself out.

Beau didn't waste any time plodding back to bed. A burst of fire-hot pain raced up and down his leg. What did he expect with the doctors removing two bullets in his upper thigh and two more in his stomach? At the moment, pushing a pencil had more appeal than hanging out with the likes of the man who tried to kill him. Allison would agree with him on that observation.

Allison. She'd been honest with him this afternoon, and he respected her candid reply to his question. He'd been lied to enough by women to know the signs. . .first the wheedling into his heart, followed by the poignant remarks of fear and the inevitable crying, and finally the severing of the relationship.

Pretense didn't equate to Allison's personality, and although she held the characteristics of a nurse who might tend to smother him, she knew when to give him room. Perhaps God had given him an angel.

He'd rest awhile, call Allison, and tackle the bag of mail. The bottle of pain medication resting on his nightstand alongside a glass of water captured his attention. He knew he needed it; he simply hated to give in. With a sigh, he screwed off the lid and downed a tablet with the water. As his mind grew fuzzy and the pain subsided, he thought about Kieron and how miserable he must feel without the Lord. What Lori had done to him surprised Beau as much as Kieron. She'd always been devoted to him. For certain, Beau didn't intend to give up on his old friends, and he knew the Lord didn't, either.

Chapter 11

Beau slumped into his leather recliner and expelled an exhilarating, exhausted sigh. Lethargic, and loving it, he leaned back and launched the footrest into smooth sailing. His leg ached, but he didn't care. Fishing all morning with his dad ranked an inch short of heaven. They'd talked about things from when he was a kid—things he'd nearly forgotten—but once they got started, all those memories rolled fast and furious.

He chuckled. The two hadn't caught a single fish, probably because they hadn't stopped talking long enough for the fish to take a nibble. Beneath a brilliant sunrise and on to the sweltering heat of noon, the sparkling waters lifted his spirits and healed the ache inside him for days gone by. He felt closer to his dad than in years. They'd eaten salami and sharp cheese on rye with gobs of hot mustard, munched on a whole bag of barbecue potato chips, crunched on huge dill pickles, and washed it all down with a gallon of sweetened iced tea. Once they returned home, Mom served a fresh blackberry cobbler and ice cream. What an indulging lifestyle. He could get used to it real fast, even if he had to get himself nearly killed to value the great outdoors and the blessings of terrific parents.

Allison had spent the morning with a girlfriend shopping. They'd both been busy, just apart. She told him yesterday she enjoyed fly fishing and often went with her dad.

How could he be so lucky to find such a wonderful woman?

He glanced at the phone across the room, wishing it sat right beside him so he could call her without subjecting his bruised body to more torture. He refused to take another pain pill and waste the rest of the day sleeping.

"I'm getting old," he told himself. "Can't even dodge speeding bullets anymore." No wonder they hadn't hooked any fish this morning.

His own thoughts caught up with him. A couple of matters had cropped up since he'd found more time to think about his old case, the shooting, and the phone threats. The phone. . .Attributing his suspicions to his wary mind or preferably his moxie, he wondered if his house could be bugged. Sarge would most likely get a hoot out of this one, so he'd keep his ungrounded suspicions to himself. No one knew where he lived. . .but how else would someone know he'd almost figured out who stood behind the narcotics ring?

Since he'd decided to continue with the case, he'd keep his deliberations to himself and make his calls away from home until he purchased a new cell phone. Beau shook his head. He was either getting smarter or senile. Time would tell.

Forcing himself from the easy chair, he limped across the room to the cell phone. He turned it over in his hands and slid out the plastic flap housing the battery. Nothing out of the ordinary there. He took a moment to study the handset before disassembling it. After finding it perfectly intact, he laughed at himself and put it back together. Good thing he hadn't mentioned this aspect of the case to Sarge. He'd have ordered a psychological workup.

Maneuvering back to his easy chair, he punched in Allison's number while glancing at his watch: two o'clock. A smile tugged at his mouth as he anticipated the mellifluous sound of her voice.

"Hi, this is Allison. I'm not at home right now, but if you'll leave a message, I'll get right back with you."

"Hey, Nurse Allison, this is your decrepit bodyguard. Give me—"

"Good afternoon," she said, and he envisioned her sea green eyes dancing with an impish twinkle. "Are you laden down with fish?"

"Not exactly." He laughed and went on to explain the glorious hours with his dad. "And did you buy out the mall?"

"Oh, I found a shoe sale, but I limited myself to one pair of totally awesome, comfortable sandals. My budget wouldn't allow any more."

"How's your budget on gas?" he asked, once again leaning back in his recliner.

"Full tank, all ready for work on Monday morning."

He didn't want to convey his worries about her heading back to the Budget Builder. God could handle his apprehensions much better. "Do you think you might consider transporting a gnarled old man to the grocery?"

"Gnarled?" she laughed. "My amiable side would consider it a worthy cause—you know, help the needy."

"I definitely fall under the title of 'needy.' I'd like to take you to dinner and possibly a movie for your trouble, if you don't already have plans."

"Hmm, Officer Oliver, you drive a hard bargain. How about if I cook dinner and we rent a movie? You're recuperating, or have you forgotten?"

He frowned and let out a feigned sigh. "My first weekend home, and you want me to resign myself to taking it easy. Unfortunately, I'm at your mercy."

"You have a deal."

"I need to shower and wash off the smell of sweat and the lake. Wouldn't want to scare away my taxi driver."

She laughed, and he thought how much he missed her.

"Everything quiet today?"

Silence pelted his senses. Finally she answered. "No problems, and I'm obeying you and Sergeant Landow."

"Good girl," he whispered. "Soon it will all be over."

They agreed on a time, and he limped from his chair to the shower. Odd, how he suddenly found more energy in knowing he'd see Allison soon.

At the grocery, she teased him unmercifully about squeezing the tomatoes and picking through a whole bin of purple onions for just the right one to make his prize-winning roast and potatoes.

"Now that I'm home, I might as well be a gourmet chef," he said, holding up an onion to the light. "By the way, I'm cooking tonight."

"I don't think so," she replied, examining two good-sized potatoes and placing them in the cart.

"I asked to take you to dinner, not for you to wait on me hand and foot. I might be a bit slow on my feet, but I'm still a prideful man." He attempted to scowl but couldn't hold the pose.

"Okay, let's make a deal," she said. "You sit on your patio and grill the chicken breasts while I bake the potatoes, make a salad, and throw together something for dessert."

"I hear a 'not fair' in all that."

She shrugged and gave him a flirty smile. "Of course it's a fair deal. I simply don't want my chicken burned."

He grabbed a loaf of the grocery's fresh, hot bread and inhaled deeply, allowing its delectable aroma to drive him to distraction while Allison picked through plump, juicy strawberries. For a moment, he felt guilty about refusing Kieron's offer for dinner the night before.

En route to the dairy aisle for whipped cream, Beau found himself face-to-face with Lori Bates—a very pregnant Lori Bates.

"Hi, Beau," she said with a fragile smile. "I haven't seen you in months."

Who's fault is that, since you walked out on Kieron? He didn't want to debate her obvious infidelity. "Been busy, working."

"I'd heard you'd been hurt. Are you mending okay?"

"Sure. I'll be running in no time at all. I'd like you to meet somebody." He turned to Allison and introduced the two women.

Lori's hand covered her protruding stomach, and her gaze flitted about the dairy section, then back to him. "I'm sorry I didn't talk to you before I left. Frankly, I didn't know if you could help or not."

"I wish you had," he replied, thinking about how Kieron had cried for weeks about his wife. "Maybe I could have helped—recommended counseling or something."

"It may not be too late," she said wistfully. "I miss Kieron, but the baby's welfare is more important."

Confused, Beau waited for her to say more.

"You don't know what I'm talking about, do you?" She continued to look uneasy.

He shook his head. "Not really." Kieron wouldn't hurt her or a baby, even if the child didn't belong to him.

Her eyes pooled with tears, and she brushed back a strand of auburn hair. "He's addicted to cocaine," she whispered. "I discovered it months before I moved out, although I suspected the abuse for a long time. When I found out about the baby and Kieron still refused to get help, I had no choice but to move out. Wishful thinking, I guess, but I hoped he loved me and the baby enough to leave it alone."

"What? Kieron, a user?" Beau asked, his heart pounding like a sledgehammer. "There's got to be a mistake."

She shook her head. "No, it's true. Kieron never came near you when he was high. I assumed he feared with your line of work and all, you'd catch on in a heartbeat."

A million thoughts raced through Beau's mind. Never, not ever, had he detected drug abuse from Kieron. In fact, he doubted it now.

"I can only imagine what he told you about my leaving," Lori said. "I phone him regularly, but he either hangs up or doesn't return my calls. As his friend, perhaps you can stop in unexpectedly. He has a lot of respect for you, and I know he'd listen." She reached into her purse and ripped off a square of paper from a notebook and jotted down something. "Here are my home and work phone numbers. I'm with my parents until I can get on my feet. I. . .I am attending church again." She glanced around him to Allison. "Nice to meet you, Allison. You have a great guy here."

She pushed her cart past them while Beau fumbled through his recollections of all Kieron had told him about finding Lori with another man, all those sordid facts that Beau didn't want to hear at the time, but his friend had needed to tell him. Kieron had spent hours with Beau, shedding buckets of tears over his high school sweetheart, the love of his life.

Beau turned to Allison, the revulsion for Lori Bates causing him to tremble. "I don't believe a word of it," he said. "Kieron may have bent the law in his younger days, just like I did, but he'd never lower himself to the degradation of drugs." He clenched his fists. "I'm a cop. I'd have seen it in his eyes, and he knows how I feel about users and pushers. Lori must think I'm a complete fool."

Allison shrugged. "Even if Kieron hid it from you? Even if he's so addicted that he couldn't quit?"

He swung his gaze at her, then to Lori pushing her cart away down the aisle. "Impossible. I know the classic signs. He's clean. She should have realized I'd see through her story."

Allison reached into the dairy case and pulled out a carton of whipped cream. Her lips pressed firmly together, and her silence spoke volumes about her impression of Lori Bates.

"You believe her, don't you?" Irritation rippled up his spine.

Allison paused, her doubts vivid in a thin-lipped smile. "I don't know either of them, Beau. They're your friends, and I'm an outsider. But I can't help wondering which one is telling the truth."

Chapter 12

Allison felt Beau's hand slip over hers as the choir sang a final refrain to Sunday's special music. As the organ completed its portion, the melodious harmony touched her soul with the peace she so desperately needed. How refreshing to spend this morning at Beau's church! She'd accompanied him when he mentioned driving himself to the worship service—a feat he didn't need to attempt just yet. She admired his church, the expanse of oak evident in the many rows of pews, the stairways curving up to the balcony, and detailed trim. The deep green carpet gave the illusion of walking in a thick forest. Definitely a beautiful sanctuary.

She focused on the cross behind the choir loft and considered how she depended on Jesus to get her through each day. The threats had stopped, but the fear remained, and the idea of being followed made her nauseous. What if the caller continued to spy on her as he'd done before? Beau said she could relax, but his reassurance didn't help the uneasiness or queasiness. She believed he knew more than he admitted about the case, but he wasn't offering any information, and she didn't know what specific questions to ask.

Deep in the recesses of her heart, she thought all the happenings of this last month were connected, but where did all the pieces fit? Repeatedly, she wondered if she'd seen or heard something illegal at the Budget Builder. Nothing flashed across her mind, while frustration and terror twisted at her heart.

Beau wasn't invincible; the shooting proved his vulnerability. He could tease and refer to himself as her bodyguard, but the unseen enemy had already dealt a nasty blow. God, and God alone, held their destiny.

Destiny. She wondered if this fragile thread of love tying her heart to Beau's would be strong enough to keep them together. She fully understood how a woman could abandon a relationship with him. The ever-present danger easily provided a multitude of sleepless nights. Yet, if Beau's undercover work resulted from God's plan, he must continue, for being out of His will meant a spiritual death more tragic than anything man could do.

She had agreed to deepen their friendship, fully aware of the hazards and equally unable to say no. Whatever the reasons for them being together, she intended to stay until God guided them apart.

Beau squeezed her hand, and she realized she trembled in the wake of her own thoughts. He knew what assaulted her ponderings, although they didn't speak of it. If she stared into his hazel eyes, he might see her honest uncertainties. He lived in a different world from hers, and as much as she wanted to be there, the thought petrified her.

"Thanks for the taxi service," he whispered. "I like having you sit next to me."

She could feel him studying her. "You're welcome, and I like being here, too."

"We've come a long way in such a short time," he went on. "Don't be afraid."

"But I am," she replied, keeping her attention fixed on the choir. "I want to be this tower of strength, but I'm not."

"Do you want to call it quits? It might be easier if we weren't together."

She stiffened. "No. That's the crazy part. I want to be right here beside you."

※

Beau felt Allison's clammy hand firmly within his grasp. Was he fooling himself? With all of his thoughts and prayers heading skyward for God to shelter his angel, had he selfishly overlooked the real problem? In his desire to protect her, had he put her into a more perilous position? Would the joker truly not harass her anymore? Questions and more questions, all without answers. Each time he gave the matter to God, he yanked it back and tried to tell Him how to go about His business. How unlike a Christian. *How like me.*

In his undercover work, he played with people's minds. He lived among the bad guys, talked their talk, did what they did, got arrested with them, deceived whomever he could, and then looked for the big opportunities to throw them in jail. Granted, he had a calling and a ministry, but too often he didn't feel any better than the guys he arrested. Sometimes he felt like an actor on stage instead of a lowly man bent on cleaning up the streets from drug dealers and users. There were times when the tacky clothes, the trashed-out cars, and those he associated with made him question if he was any better than those he exposed.

He believed God knew his heart, but sometimes Beau doubted himself. He thrived on the adrenaline rush and excitement surrounding his work. The thrill of danger put him into deeper and more dangerous situations. Had it all moved from God's ministry to Beau's private entertainment center? He hoped not; he prayed not.

In thinking about Allison and how his heart had taken a huge plunge, he once again considered a desk job. Other undercover cops were just as good, most of them better, but they didn't know the Lord. They didn't pray over the young and old roaming the streets in search of a fast buck or a way to escape their depressing worlds. He did, and often while talking with them.

Am I in Your will, Lord? Am I being a humble servant, or have I gravitated to becoming a self-seeker? Oh, Father, I pray my motives are pure. I don't want to wake up one morning and despise myself. Please, Lord, protect my Allison. If it means letting her go, then I will. I want to be obedient.

Beau knew her life and his rested in the Father's hands. He pushed aside his apprehensions and turned his attention to the pastor and worshipping the Lord.

✳

On Monday morning, Allison collected her courage and arrived at the Budget Builder ten minutes before it opened. The extra time provided an opportunity to pray before taking the leap from her car to the employees' entrance.

She anticipated curious and often insensitive onlookers would hurl questions like a rock avalanche, and she didn't particularly want to relive the shooting for the sake of lacing someone's mind with gory details. In fact, she'd like to wear a sign saying "Don't ask, 'cause I don't want to talk about it." Although that attitude best described her feelings, it sounded a bit immature.

Lord, help me to be sweet to everyone, not only the ones who are sincere and mean well, but also those who have a tendency to glorify crime.

Allison took a deep breath and opened the car door. The security guard stood by the entrance, but his presence didn't alleviate her anxiety. His presence didn't help one bit the morning of the shooting. Only God gave her peace of mind.

Soon her fears diminished and, for the most part, she easily swung back into her old routine. Even her friend, Mr. Billings, stopped in a little after seven o'clock.

"Hey, Sunshine. Good to see you," he said with his familiar smile. "I prayed for you and the people involved in that nasty business. How is the man who tried to help you?"

"Thanks. He's home from the hospital," she replied, appreciating his discretion. She glanced about them. "This is my first day back, and I'm a little nervous."

Mr. Billings grasped the plastic Budget Builder's bag and leaned over the counter. "Before you know it, that business will be behind you, like a pesky nightmare. Me and the missus pray for you regularly."

She watched him stride away, thinking how much she'd miss his charm and encouragement once she completed her education.

At noon, she munched on a turkey sandwich and soda in the employees' break room. Allison talked freely with two women, but they seemed uncomfortable. Finally, the situation had grated at her nerves long enough.

"Okay, what's the problem? You two act like I have the plague."

The older woman, near her mother's age, cleared her throat. "We're not sure what to say, Allison. You went through a terrible ordeal, and we're both afraid of saying the wrong thing and upsetting you."

Heaviness rested on Allison's shoulders. "Look, I'm still me. Nothing's changed for you to act differently. I had a horrible experience, and it's over. The idea of talking about it turns my stomach, but we had plenty to talk about before the shooting. Please, relax and be my friends again."

The older woman pulled a sleeve of crackers from her lunch sack. "Deal," she said, "and since I'm the mama here, I'll spread the word."

Allison gave her and the younger African American woman a hug. She noticed her friend's lunch. "Tricia, did your mom make a strawberry pie?"

Tricia beamed. "Yeah, and there's enough for you, Mama Grayson, and me."

Once they finished dessert and chatted about the store, Mrs. Grayson and Tricia decided to take a stroll outside before heading back to work. Allison picked up her cell phone and punched in Beau's number. She knew he had rehab scheduled for late morning, but she wanted to leave a message. She laughed at his greeting.

"Hey, this is Beau. Not here. Gone fishing. Throw me a line, and I'll hook up with you when I get back."

"Hi, this is Allison. I wanted to tell you that work has been just fine, and my jitters have nearly vanished. Hope the therapist hasn't overworked you today."

Allison headed back to work, and for the first time she felt like nothing had ever happened. Later in the afternoon, she heard someone call her name, looked up, and saw Kieron in her cashier's line. She smiled and waved, but a huge lump settled in the bottom of her stomach. Ever since she'd met his wife at the grocery and listened to her conversation with Beau, something about the man bothered her. Normally she didn't prejudge a person, but to be blunt, Kieron Bates made her skin crawl.

Lord, help me. I'm not thinking Christlike thoughts here. Kieron is Beau's friend, and he should know his friend better than I.

"Kieron is a great guy," Beau had said. "I don't know what I would have done without him while I was stuck in the hospital."

By the time she checked out three customers ahead of Kieron, she'd convinced herself that she'd misjudged him.

"How are you doing?" she asked as he handed her a bag of roofing nails. His fingers wrapped around her hand, but she pretended not to notice and pulled back.

"Great. Even better now that I have you ringing me up," he said low.

"Seen your neighbor today?" *Is it me, or is Kieron coming on to me?*

"Naw. I left at the crack of dawn. Doubt if he was stirring then." He produced a credit card, and she swiped it through a machine beside her register.

Feeling his gaze upon her, she glanced up. His violet eyes met hers with a lusty sheen, and it angered her.

"Want to take in a movie tonight?" he asked.

"No, thanks."

"Why? Got plans?"

"Yes, with Beau." The nerve of him.

"Cancel them. I can show you a better time. I'll throw in dinner at a nice place and anything else you want."

She paused, forming the right words to let him know exactly what she thought of his crude behavior. "I'm not interested," she replied, "not now or ever."

"Aw, aren't you tired of the cop yet?"

She glared straight into Kieron's eyes. Disgust raced through her body. "I wonder what he'd think of this conversation, especially coming from his best friend."

Kieron chuckled. "He wouldn't believe you. I'm his bud."

"Don't be too sure of that."

She tore off the signature portion of the register slip and set it on the counter with a pen. He scribbled his name and grabbed his bag.

"I bet you're a great kisser," he said for only her ears. "I'll find out soon enough."

Allison crossed her arms. "I don't think so."

"I'm only teasing," he said with a grin that unnerved her. "No hard feelings?"

"Of course not." *I'll just consider the source.*

Chapter 13

Beau limped into the waiting room to inform his dad he'd been released from rehab jail. The session had been gruesome, and he ached all over. After complaining to the male therapist during the entire hour with no results, Beau wanted to tear apart something or someone in retaliation. Instead, he pasted on a smile, realizing his dad didn't need to face a surly son.

"Ready for lunch?" Beau asked, while pain washed over his body.

"Of course. Were they hard on you in there?"

Beau gritted his teeth. "Like a torture chamber."

His dad chuckled. "I can tell by the look on your face. What about some red-hot chili to add a little color?"

"And add indigestion to my whipped body?" He shrugged. "Why not? Gotta get this man back into shape."

At the restaurant, he decided to check his messages at home and give Sarge a call from the pay phone. He still suspected someone had leaked vital police information, and the thought lingered like a dull headache. Right now, Beau's head pounded. He swallowed two headache tablets and gave the waitress his order for chili with a side of jalapenos.

He punched in his number and listened to Allison's angelic voice leave an upbeat message about her first day back at work. Grinning like a kid, he phoned her home number.

"Hey, Angel, glad your first day is a success. I know I'm whining, but this rehab is going to make an old man out of me. I'll call you later."

Before contacting Sarge, he studied the area about him—a habit he didn't feel safe to give up. His boss answered on the second ring.

"Sarge, just checking in. Can you tell me who's working with Ace on my case?"

"GW. I believe you've worked with him a few times."

"Yeah, great guy. Both of them are looking at spending a lot of days hanging out with those guys. It took me months to build up their trust, and even when I bought a couple of pounds of dope, I never found out who was supplying." He hesitated. "I take that back. I must have stumbled onto something because of the threats Allison and I received."

"Any new developments?

"Not a thing I can pass on," Beau replied. "The street's pretty quiet."

"You be careful, and call me day or night when you put it all together. You're the best I've got Beau, and I'm counting on you."

"Not much pressure there," Beau said. "You'll be the first to know, which brings me to another matter. Until I get a new cell, don't call me at home or on my other cell phone."

Sarge chuckled. "Suspicious, are you? Probably a good idea, since we don't know where the leak is."

"And I'm becoming more and more convinced that the shooting and my case are linked. I still need a few more pieces. I'd like more info on the gunman: any family members involved with the police, including his wife, who else lived in his apartment complex, and if Lopez had any other arrests. Put the word out on the streets, and keep me posted."

Beau replaced the receiver and joined his dad. The waitress had set steamy bowls of chili before them along with generous slices of jalapeno cornbread plus an additional bowl of jalapenos. His dad wasted no time in blessing their lunch and digging in.

"Your mother would have a fit if she knew I was eating this," his dad said with a grin and lifted the spoon to his lips. "Of course, I'll have a hard time explaining the heartburn."

"We'll get some antacid before going home," Beau replied, thinking he'd need some, too. One disadvantage of working undercover was that the greasy, spicy food had a habit of coming back to haunt him.

His dad rubbed his nose, a prerequisite to whatever he planned to say. "We—your mom and I—really like Allison."

"Good," Beau replied, taking a generous bite of the cornbread.

"Uh, is there anything else in the making?" He rubbed his nose again and reached for his soupspoon.

"Like what?" Beau asked, inwardly amused. "Oh, you mean are Allison and I seeing each other?"

His dad reached for his glass of water. "You could make this a little easier for your old man."

"And spoil the fun?" Beau took a generous bite of the chili and let it slide down his throat before replying. He pointed his spoon at his dad. "If anyone else asked me about Allison, I'd say we're just friends, and don't be repeating what I'm going to say, especially to Mom—at least not yet. But I like Allison. She's intelligent, strong, independent, drop-dead gorgeous, honest, and a pretty good cook. On top of that, she doesn't smother me, speaks her mind—in fact, I like the way she strings her thoughts together—and most importantly, she's a Christian."

His dad tilted his head back and laughed. "Is there anything about her you don't like?"

Beau joined him. "Not yet." The fact that she questioned Kieron's story about Lori bothered him a little, but not enough to dissuade him. After all, she spoke her mind, and he didn't want a woman to always agree with him, just sometimes.

"I think you have a winner there," his dad said.

"And I think you're right."

Later on that evening, he called Allison at home to hear more about her day.

"Some of the employees didn't know what to say to me at first," she said. "But by the close of the shift, it was like I hadn't been gone."

"Good. I don't want my girl overdoing it. What hours do you work during school?"

"Depends on which hospital I do my clinical rotation at."

Beau detected something amiss in her voice. "Is there anything wrong?"

Silence.

"Alli?"

She expelled a heavy sigh. "Kieron came into the store this afternoon. He asked me out, Beau, and he didn't mince words about it, either."

Beau chuckled. "I'm sure he was teasing. You just need to get to know him."

"No, thanks. I have better things to do." Agitation edged her words.

"I'm sorry you're upset," he said, once more regretting Allison's view of his friend. "I'll speak to him about it, and I'm sure he'll apologize."

"No, leave the matter alone. I'll deal with him myself. I'm a big girl."

Her words stung. "I know you can take care of yourself, but he insulted you, which means I'm involved."

"Beau, the last thing I want to do is come between friends. Just forget about it unless it happens again."

"Are you sure?" Somehow he didn't believe her.

"Yes. And you're right: I don't know Kieron. I probably misinterpreted what he said."

But he didn't believe her for a moment.

✳

"I can't believe I'm spending my day off helping you pull weeds," Allison moaned, wiping the perspiration dripping from her nose. "I've worked six days a week for three weeks straight. I should be resting or stretching out by the pool at my apartment."

"Oh, but you look so adorable with dirt sprinkled across your cheeks," Beau said. "And hard work is good for the soul."

She stood and feigned exasperation. "Show me the chapter and verse."

"Oh, it's in there. I think Genesis. . .something about the sweat of your brow."

She picked up the hose and aimed it in his direction. "This lady packs a thirty-eight," she said, scrunching her eyes in an effort to look tough.

"Won't work. That's a fifty-foot hose, not a thirty-eight." He eased closer, tossing her a huge grin. "You don't want to use that on me."

"Watch it, Fella. I've been out in this heat for three hours. The ice in the water has melted, along with my makeup, and you said we were going to plant flowers—not pull weeds. Besides, you promised lunch, which means I'm hot, tired, thirsty, hungry, and grouchy, and that means you're in trouble."

"I'm going to take good care of you. We're merely clearing the way for those zinnias and marigolds," he said gently.

"Right. I think you got yourself some free labor. Besides, those flowers are annuals not perennials."

He tilted his head and stepped closer. "Thought since I had time on my hands at home, I'd add a little color to the beds." He clamped his foot down on the hose.

Allison pressed on the nozzle handle, but only a dribble of water made its way to the ground. "You cheated," she cried.

"Don't mess with a cop," he said. "We have our ways—secret, cunning, and definitely clever." He reached for the hose.

"Not so fast." She jerked her hand from his grasp, no longer able to control her laughter. "I've watched a few police shows in my time, and you're a leg short of being as fast as I am."

Worry lines creased his forehead. "Are you taking advantage of a wounded man? A man who risked his life for you?"

"Absolutely." She wished she could see his eyes, but his sunglasses stopped her.

He groaned, and his injured leg buckled beneath him. She dropped the hose and rushed to his aid. Instantly he snatched up the nozzle and turned it on her, full blast. Water showered her from head to toe, but it felt wonderful.

"How could you do that to me?" she screamed, using her hands to shield her face. "Me, a defenseless female."

She took off running, realizing his leg would slow him.

"You can run, but you can't hide," he called after her, as she raced down the driveway. She remembered another hose at the rear of the house and quickly turned on the water. Snatching up the nozzle, she met him in the driveway—armed and dangerous. She sprayed him unmercifully, despite his protests, but he returned her fire with vigor. Every inch of her dripped.

"Okay, I give," she finally said, holding her aching side as she laughed.

"Oh, but you gave a great fight," he said in between his own laughter. He dropped his hose and headed her way wearing the look of a properly chided little boy. "My poor baby is soaking wet," he said. "I think she needs someone to hold her."

"Don't you pull that sweet stuff on me." She held him back with an outstretched arm. "I'm on to your games."

He slipped off his sunglasses. "See, I'm truly sorry."

"Then, get me a towel so I can dry off and head home."

"But we were going to have lunch." His sad voice melted her resolve to find a way to get even.

"I'll bring some back. We can finish pulling weeds and plant your flowers this afternoon."

After he produced a towel, she borrowed it to sit on for the ride home. No matter she looked a sight, she'd had fun, but they always did.

Over an hour later, she pulled up in front of his house with a deli bag full of sandwiches, chips, and drinks. He'd finished the weeding, and some of the flowers filled in the bare spots. The added color did look good.

She smiled. Like a little boy, he couldn't wait to get started on his project. Snatching up her purse and the food bag, she exited her car and spotted what her dad called a junk car parked on the other side of Beau's driveway. The vehicle hadn't been there when she left. It must belong to a neighbor kid. She made her way up the sidewalk to Beau's front door and pressed the doorbell. The sound of deep laughter rose from inside his house. He must have company. Perhaps she should have phoned first. Too late—Beau opened the door.

"Hi," he greeted, "come on in." He took the bag. "Hmm, this smells great, and I'm starved. I've got some friends I'd like for you to meet."

Feeling like she just walked into a male bonding project, Allison started to protest, but he insisted.

"These guys have heard all about you." He motioned her inside.

She allowed him to usher her to the kitchen. Three of the worst characters she'd ever seen sat around his kitchen table drinking sodas. One wore an orange bandana tied around his head, two earrings, a white, sleeveless T-shirt, and jeans with a huge hole at the knee. To top it off, he sported a three-day-old beard. Another had bleached blond hair longer than hers and looked just as grimy as the first. The third man, an African American fellow with a huge, round face, didn't have a hair on his shiny head and was dressed in black. He wore more earrings on one ear than she owned. These were Beau's friends! She swallowed hard and managed a fragile smile.

"Guys, this is Allison." They all raised their hands and waved. He pointed to the earring man. "That's Ace. Orange bandana-man is Freddie, and blondie is GW."

"I think I might get myself all shot up for a girl as pretty as you," Freddie commented.

"Yeah, me, too," GW said. "You always get all the breaks, Beau—long vacations, someone to bring you lunch, and you were always the first one out of jail."

Beau laughed and turned to her. "It's okay, really. You can relax. These guys work undercover with me."

Allison felt as though someone had lifted a ton of bricks from her shoulders. "I see," she said and glanced from one of his friends to the other. Did Beau look like this when he worked? She remembered his offensive T-shirt. "Well, you certainly had me fooled."

Freddie chuckled. "One look at your face was enough to shake the devil. Has Beau ever told you about his exploits as Superman?"

She stared at him blankly, not sure if she wanted to hear or not.

313

"Don't believe a word," Beau replied. "They haven't slept since yesterday, and they're punchy."

Ace finished his soda and set the can on the table. "Normally, we're sleeping now, but we had big business this morning. Then, Freddie here thought it would be a good idea to see Superman. There he was, sitting in the grass planting flowers. Wish I'd had my camera."

"I'm glad you came by, even if you saw me taking life easy," Beau said. "Want another soda?"

"No thanks," Ace said. "We've got to get home. Besides, the lady brought you lunch."

The three rose from the table and made their way to the back door.

"Good to meet you," Ace called, and the other two men echoed him. After a few minutes of tossing barbs back and forth with Beau, they left.

He closed the door and hobbled back into the kitchen. Wrapping his arms around her, he grinned. "The look on your face was priceless. I should have called to warn you, so I apologize for that—and for drowning you earlier."

She hesitated. So many things about him surprised her. "You're forgiven." She played with the collar of his clean shirt and asked wistfully, "Superman, huh? Will I ever really know Beau Oliver, undercover cop, gardener, friend, and bodyguard?"

He drew her to him tighter and hugged her close. "I'm not complex. Time is all it takes." He cupped her chin and planted a light kiss on her lips. "I'd spill my guts to you for a sandwich and some chips."

"I should have brought steak. Bet I could have learned a world of things about Superman's wildest adventures."

"I don't think you'd recognize me in action," he whispered, nuzzling her neck. "Sometimes I look pretty bad."

An image of Ace, GW, and Freddie rose in her mind. She had a choice of her old, quiet, comfortable life—or marching on with Beau. With a sigh, she leaned against his chest. No matter the outcome, this was where she wanted to be.

She swallowed her emotion. "I remember back in May when a local Christian radio station hosted a month-long prayer vigil for National Policeman Month."

"Yes, and the station distributed blue bracelets engraved with the names of officers to remind the wearer to pray for them."

She nodded. "I had one of those bracelets, and at the end of that month I stuck mine in my prayer journal so I'd continue praying. At the time, I didn't know any officers personally, other than a few acquaintances at church. Now I see the real sacrifice necessary for those who choose to protect and serve our city. I know I'll never look at an officer again without appreciating his commitment, or," and she smiled, "wondering if some strange character is really working undercover."

Chapter 14

Beau limped to a pay phone at the grocery store. After he'd spent another morning in his yard, his leg had begun to ache. He wondered if it would ever be back to normal. The therapist said yes, but Beau's patience ran thin with the prognosis. He'd run five miles a day before the shooting, and now he couldn't stand on it for very long without a burst of fire racing up and down his body.

I should be glad I'm alive. Thank You, Lord. Sometimes I lose track of all the blessings You've given me.

His mind lingered on Allison—her face, her smile, her delightful perspective on things, that mischievous sparkle in her eyes when she teased him. Guess his dad had been right. He had it bad. Beau wanted to tell her he loved her, but not yet. His confession could scare her away. First things first, which meant nailing the guy who threatened her. With no evidence to prove his gut feeling, he knew the shooting and the threats were part of the same scheme.

He glanced about and picked up the phone outside the store, punching in Sarge's number.

"Hey, the fellas stopped by to see me around noon. Said they had an earlier meeting with you, but that's all. I know they believe I'm off the case and didn't want to tell me more."

"Right. Seems like they get one lousy lead after another. They've made some buys but can't get enough trust to make a bigger one."

"My informant says our man is close to home," Beau said.

"So, you're still thinking it's from the inside?"

"I'm leaning in that direction. I know the cops on my list all checked out—and don't say a word about the fellas working on the case. I've known them for a lot of years."

"Beau, it could be anybody, and the person we're looking for is probably the last one any of us would suspect."

He raked his fingers through his hair. Freddie, Ace, and GW's faces and their commitment stood foremost in his thoughts. The idea one of them might be behind the calls churned his stomach. They'd been in some tight places together, and he refused to even consider them.

"I'll keep digging," Beau said.

"Keep in touch."

He hung up the phone and started for his car when his pager sounded. Exhaling a heavy breath, he saw the callback number came from Ace. Retracing his steps, he contacted his old friend. They'd worked together for seven years.

"Beau," Ace began. "I didn't want to tell you this in front of GW and Freddie, but I heard you found out too much when you were working the streets."

"Yeah, I heard the same thing. Sure wish I knew what it was. I've racked my brain trying to find out. Yet, nothing."

"Be careful, okay? Lately Superman hasn't done too good in dodging bullets. I know you're into religion and all, so light a candle or whatever it is you do."

"I pray, Ace." Beau chuckled. "And I appreciate your concern. How about sitting down and talking about Jesus sometime?"

"Not today, but one day soon. I promise."

※

Frustrated, Beau kicked the right rear tire of his truck, the one slashed identical to the left rear tire. That's what he got for leaving his vehicle parked on the driveway last night instead of putting it in the garage. He'd talked to Alli on the phone until after midnight, then rolled over and went to sleep. Laziness. Pure laziness had caused this.

Beau walked to the end of the driveway. Frustration riddled his senses. He scanned the houses up and down his street. While his neighbors took their safety for granted, he and other fellow police officers risked their lives to keep them secure.

Possibly those foiling his case could have initiated the tire slashing to let Beau know they lurked in the shadows. The suspicion brought a nasty taste to his mouth. Never, absolutely never, had a case plagued him so. While he played cat-and-mouse with these guys, more drug deals went down, and Allison lived in constant fear. Oh, she didn't admit it, but he knew the truth. She thought she masked her trepidation, but her eyes told it all.

I live and breathe undercover. First these guys get my phone numbers and now they have my address. Last night was just their way of letting me know my cover's blown. Well, I take that personal, real personal. I wasn't being paranoid when I wondered if my place is bugged—they really do know where I live.

Palming his fist into his other hand, Beau ambled back up the driveway. What a great way to start a day. He dreaded calling Allison. Last week, she spent her day off helping him weed his flowerbeds, and in recompense he wanted to take her to the beach today. He glanced at his watch; he was supposed to pick her up in fifteen minutes. Some boyfriend he turned out to be. Now, he had to cancel their plans of spending the day in Galveston.

※

Allison tossed her beach bag into the trunk of her car. Poor Beau. He sounded so pitiful in explaining what happened to his truck—pitiful and angry. She couldn't blame him. Probably kids, he'd said, but she wondered if it was a stunt from the man who insisted upon making their lives miserable.

"I'm sorry, Alli," he'd said. "I wanted you to have this great day at the beach, but now we're stuck here."

"No, we're not," she'd replied, determination taking over. "We can take my car."

"Absolutely not. You've hauled me around long enough. I'll see about renting a truck."

"Don't argue with me," she said pointedly. "Besides, I'm on my way, and you can drive my car if it makes you feel any better. I'm not letting a little matter about whose vehicle we take stop our plans. Just go ahead and call the towing service to get your truck taken care of, and I'll be there before you know it." She hung up before he could spout all his arguments that indicated his pride had been damaged.

Thirty minutes later, Beau drove south on I-45 en route to Galveston. The day promised to be glorious, not a cloud in the sky, and Allison imagined a balmy breeze blowing in off the ocean and the rhythmic lull of the waves crashing against the shore. She'd tucked stale bread inside her bag to feed the seagulls, along with plenty of sunscreen—more for Beau than herself.

"You have a nice car," Beau said, sounding as though he'd dealt with not driving his truck. "Handles well."

"Thank you. Dad found it for me when I entered nursing school and needed something reliable."

"When did you get interested in nursing?" He turned down the volume on the car stereo.

"I suppose I was born with this need to care for hurting people. Right from the start, I bandaged my dolls, my brothers, and my sisters—anything that would hold still long enough for me to play nurse." She flashed him a smile. "Note, I said care, not smother."

He grinned and nodded. "Point well taken."

"We moved a lot with Dad in the navy, and I tended to be shy, so my friends were my patched-up dolls."

"Sounds rather sad." He envisioned a lonely little girl with her family of bandage-covered dolls. "I would have thought you played with all your brothers and sisters."

She laughed. "I'm the youngest, remember? And a whiny, spoiled pain. They usually hid from me."

"A brat? You?"

"Exactly." But she wanted to punch him. "In fact my childish attitude is why I'm late in completing my education. I played all during junior high and high school, thinking if God intended for me to be a nurse, then He'd give me the willingness to study. Obviously, my excuse didn't work."

"Ouch! Learned things the hard way, huh? Well, I'm proud of you, and I know you'll be a perfect nurse. Look how well you've taken care of me. I've never felt a single shot—they all felt like kisses."

"Charmer," she accused and laughed with him.

"Where are you headed with your career? Pediatrics? Working in a doctor's office?"

She tilted her head and tried to picture his response. "Inner city hospital. I want my faith and my nursing skills to make a difference."

He raised a brow. "Wow, I'm impressed, but that'll be tough. I've met a few unfortunate characters there—victims and villains."

"Maybe, but I do speak fluent Spanish."

His eyes widened. "So do I. We could be quite an undercover team, but then we already are."

"Right, Officer Oliver. You and I are servants of the people—as long as we don't get killed in the process."

Chapter 15

Y ou're burned," Allison claimed, pressing a finger into Beau's shoulder and noting the white print. "You should have used sunscreen."

Beau lifted his sunglasses to look up at her. "Are you kidding? A tough guy like me? I don't need that stuff."

"Would you like a lecture about the dangers of too much sun?" She glanced down at his chest, the way the muscles molded around his ribs and narrowed into his waist.

"No, thank you, Ma'am. I may be a little pink today, but tomorrow I'll be nice and brown." He replaced his glasses. "By the way, are you admiring my physique?"

Embarrassed, she searched frantically for a rebuttal.

"Thought so." He chuckled. "I may be full of holes, but I can still turn a lady's head."

"Beau!"

He propped himself on his elbows. "Are you denying it?"

She wrinkled her nose at him. "Not exactly."

When he finished laughing, he reached for her hand. "Honestly, I'm the lucky one here. I have the most beautiful woman in the whole world right beside me."

Allison glanced around at a few scantily clad females whose suits left little to the imagination. Not that she wanted to be in anything else but a one-piece suit, but she still felt self-conscious.

"I'm serious," he said, as if reading her mind. "You're gorgeous, intelligent, witty—"

"Keep going," she coaxed.

"And you put up with me."

"There's the clincher."

He planted a kiss on her cheek. "How about a walk along the beach?"

Against the sounds of the waves crashing against the shore and the call of the seagulls, Beau lightly squeezed her hand as they sunk their toes into the sand. She loved the feel of it squishing between her toes.

"We can imagine we're on a desert isle," Beau said, "surrounded by coconut palms and thick green foliage. The water's blue instead of brown, and we don't have to step around the oil spots in the sand." He waved toward the horizon. "In the distance white sails flap in the ocean breeze, and we can taste the salty air."

"Do I detect a bit of a poet in you?" she asked, curiosity gaining the best of her.

"Possibly. I'm a fan of Emerson."

By the rude bridge that arched the flood
    Their flag to April's breeze unfurled
Here once the embattled farmers stood
    And fired the shot heard round the world.

"You constantly amaze me."

He laughed low. "Someday I'll give you a complete recital."

A twist of a breeze danced off their faces, so refreshing in the sultry sun. She felt absolutely relaxed: no cares or fears. On they walked while she dreamed of the Caribbean.

"You never said. What do you think of my island paradise?" he asked, breaking the silence.

She laughed. "Wonderful. And where is this place?"

He stopped and gazed in the direction of a shrimp boat. "I suppose off the coast of Florida."

"Good. I spent six years in Puerto Rico, and the beaches are exactly as you described. That's where I learned to speak Spanish."

"I learned the hard way, in school."

He released her hand to pick up a seashell, perfectly shaped without a flaw. *"Usted recoge conchas?"* Do you collect shells? he asked in Spanish.

She studied it as he brushed the sand away. *"Solamente los inusuales."* Only the unusual ones.

"What makes them unusual?" he asked in English.

"When they remind me of people."

He picked up a shell and tossed it back into the sand. "Explain your theory."

She bent and picked up the same one he'd just discarded. Holding it in her palm, she began, "I like the irregular-shaped kind, the ones that are rough with ridges and holes, the type you have to wash away the dirt and sand to really see what they look like."

He nodded and grinned. "I see, like people who don't look the part? Like policemen who wear ponytails and earrings?"

"Exactly. It's their heart that makes the difference."

He wrapped his hand around her waist. "Yours definitely has captured mine," he said softly.

Allison felt a delicious tingle race up her spine as he planted a kiss on her neck. Admittedly, she had fallen for this wonderful, unusual, rough-around-the-edges man.

"Hey, what do you say we head home after our walk?" he asked a moment later. "I think I'm burned."

※

Allison stretched and yawned. The clock on the wall of the Budget Builder read

320

eleven o'clock. One more hour before she could call it a day—or rather a night. In order to take the Fourth of July off this coming week, she agreed to work not only her own day shift from seven to three, but also the afternoon hours from four to twelve tonight.

She stifled another yawn. The extra shift was worth any number of hours. Of course, she might be a bit crabby in the morning, but she'd be spending the entire holiday with Beau and her family.

The Fourth had traditionally been a freedom celebration at her parents' home. Her mom decorated the inside and outside of the house in red, white, and blue banners, streamers, and balloons. She even purchased a trio of petunias to match and planted them by the front door beneath the US flag. She and Dad served foot-long hotdogs, baked beans, potato salad, chips, and whatever else suited their fancy. Homemade ice cream complete with strawberry, chocolate, and blueberry topping hit the dessert line. At the end of the day, they all piled into their cars and headed for a fireworks display.

The last hour dragged by, but finally Allison clocked out and walked from the building with a few other women.

"You ladies want an escort?" the security guard asked.

"No, thanks," one of the women replied. "I think we're all parked together."

"Okay, but I'm here if you need me," he called.

As they ventured across the parking lot, Allison spotted an unfamiliar truck parked beside her car. "Do any of you own that truck?" she asked.

When no one responded, she stopped and studied it. Enough weird things had happened to her lately to risk making a foolish mistake.

"Let's go ask the manager who owns it," Allison said, straining to read the license plate.

"Why not just get the security guard? I think you're overreacting," the first woman said.

Allison shrugged. "Maybe so, but unless any of you have been shot lately, then you probably don't understand my precautions." She turned and retraced her steps while the others followed.

"What's the problem?" the guard asked as the women approached him.

"Strange truck parked over there," Allison replied. "Has the manager left yet?"

"He's still inside. You mean the one driving away?" The guard pointed to a truck leaving the parking lot.

Allison nodded and watched the vehicle speed onto the road and race out of sight. It sounded like a diesel. Maybe she'd acted hastily and paranoid. . .then maybe not.

※

July Fourth dawned with a downpour predicted for the entire day. Gray clouds rolled across the sky, echoing a low rumble and dumping buckets of water on the dry earth as Beau and Allison pulled his truck next to the curb in front of her

321

parents' home. Earlier in the week, Beau accepted their invitation to join them and their brood for a hotdog extravaganza and homemade ice cream. If the rain stopped, they all planned to attend a fireworks display near an elementary school.

Beau viewed Allison's four siblings with a twinge of curiosity—two brothers and two sisters, but he hadn't met any of them before today. She often talked about her family, especially the years her father served in the navy.

With the grandchildren unable to play outside, Allison's mother had set up games and toys on the enclosed porch to keep the children entertained. Their parents mingled with each other and kept an eye on the boisterous group of seven, who longed to be in the sunshine.

Beau found himself assisting a pair of lively, eight-year-old twins, Chad and Christopher, build a space station out of interconnecting, plastic pieces. He thought the project looked easy, especially when he recalled how he used to play with a similar set, but the boys were pros.

"Mr. Beau, try this piece," Chad suggested while Beau struggled through the many shapes and sizes of the building set.

He noted the boy's crystal blue eyes and took the piece, which fit exactly.

The boys' father, Allison's brother-in-law, Tad, joined them on the floor. "Susan and I are grateful for what you did for Allison," he said.

"What did you do, Mr. Beau?" Chad asked, rubbing his freckled nose.

Beau ruffled the boy's hair. "Oh, I helped your aunt Allison when she hurt her arm."

"Oh, yeah, we know about her accident," the boy continued, snapping a wheel into place. "She fell at work and had to go to the hospital for a couple of days."

"She was 'posed to baby-sit us that night but didn't," said Christopher, the mirror of his brother.

Beau glanced up at Tad, who had passed on many of his physical characteristics to his sons. "Allison is a great lady, and you're welcome. Looks like you have a couple of fine sons."

"We think so," Tad replied with a smile. He turned to his sons. "Boys, I'm going to borrow Mr. Beau for a few minutes. We're going to get something to drink."

As Beau struggled to his feet, nearly losing his balance, Tad offered to give him a hand, but he refused. Pride had a lot to do with his independence, although Beau hated to admit it. Once in the kitchen, they poured huge glasses of iced tea.

Tad added sugar to his drink. "Every time I think about the shooting, it makes me angry all over again," he said. "I wonder what happened to the security guard or where Houston's finest were when you and Allison needed them."

"Who knows," Beau replied after a huge gulp of the cold drink. "I'm just glad God allowed me to be there when she needed the help."

Tad pointed to Beau's leg. "How are you doing?"

He chuckled. "All right by the therapist's standards, but mighty slow according to mine."

"How long you off from work?"

"Until the doctor releases me. Probably September."

"What line of work are you in?"

This guy asks as many questions as I do. "Oh, I work for the city."

Tad chuckled and added another spoonful of sugar to his tea. "So, my tax money is supporting you for the rest of the summer?"

Beau grinned. Ordinarily a comment like Tad's would make him bristle, but Allison had said her brother-in-law was blunt. "I'd rather call the cash disability."

He felt an arm slip around his waist and give him a gentle squeeze. The light floral fragrance of his Allison greeted him.

"Is my brother-in-law giving you a bad time?" She snuggled against Beau's shoulder.

"Of course," Tad replied. "I was about to ask him where he went to church, where he worked, his portfolio, and if he made a six-figure income."

Allison's laughter rippled through Beau's spirit. "Good thing I rescued him. Brian and Justin are as bad as you."

Amused, Beau listened to the two banter back and forth. Her brothers hadn't asked many questions at all; neither had her sisters, Susan and Dixie.

"Are you surviving this?" she whispered in his ear once the twins called for their dad. Her warm breath sent crazy messages to his brain.

"You bet. Reminds me of being a kid at family gatherings. I envied my hoards of fun-loving cousins, and they were jealous of me because I didn't have to share my stuff."

"I've always had my brothers and sisters," she said. "Of course, as I said before, I was spoiled rotten, and they didn't want to play with me."

"Spoiled or not, you're my angel," he said, wishing they were alone so he could kiss her.

She grinned. "Thanks for coming today. If this rain doesn't stop, we can leave whenever you want. I don't want the kids—or Tad—to drive you nuts."

He shook his head. "I'm seeing this party through to the end, even if I get stuck cleaning up."

She sighed deeply and tilted her head, her caramel-colored hair draping like layers of silk on her shoulders. "What will things be like when you go back to work?" Everyone else appeared busy and couldn't overhear their quiet conversation.

"I work nights," he said simply, "and I'm off in the middle of the week. The action happens late and on the weekends."

"I'm used to seeing you almost every day. Your hours will be an adjustment."

He caught her gaze and the sad reflection in her green eyes. "Can you handle my schedule? Not knowing where I am or what I'm doing?"

She lifted her chin. "Yes. I'm not a quitter. I can make the changes. Besides, I'll be starting school a few weeks before you head back to work."

He welcomed the opportunity to change the topic of conversation. Today he didn't want to discuss the business in the weeks to come, although he needed to face it. "What's involved in your last semester?"

"Hard work," she replied. "The only thing I have left to do is a clinical rotation where I take on a full patient assignment with a staff nurse as my mentor."

"And you'll graduate in December?" he asked, mentally calculating how long they'd be forced to endure each other's hectic pace.

"Uh huh." She laughed. "My first job will most likely be at a hospital, working nights."

He wrapped his arms around her waist. "This will all work out. I promise."

She nodded, but said nothing. More than ever, Beau wanted to find out who had harassed her. Allison had enough going on in her life without some guy making threatening phone calls.

※

The following Saturday morning, Allison invited Beau to attend Chad and Christopher's soccer game. Under a sweltering blanket of humidity, the twins' team lost, but a pizza buffet soothed their temporary disappointment. Amid the video games and seeing friends from school, the little boys' spirits rose to a deafening roar. Allison questioned her sanity in having Beau tag along with the gruesome twosome, as she referred to Chad and Christopher.

"They're heading this way," she whispered to Beau.

"Who? The twins?" He laughed. "I've handled some pretty shady characters. These two are nothing."

"We'll see." She glanced behind them at the advancing troop of eight year olds. "They've brought reinforcements."

"What could they possibly want but a grown-up to play with them?" he asked, downing his soda.

"Mr. Oliver, would you play some video games with us?" Chad asked.

Beau winked at Allison. "See, harmless little boys who are looking for a role model." He turned his attention to the pint-sized soccer team. "Sure, guys, I'll even buy the first couple of games."

Allison shook her head. He'd be singing another tune before the boys were finished with him. The twins, alone, were a handful, and they had half of their team tugging on Mr. Beau.

An hour later, he plopped onto a chair beside her. "I should have listened to you. They wore me out."

She giggled. "Told you. Chad and Christopher are impossible to keep up with, without adding the energy level of a half dozen more."

He raised a brow. "I think I could use them on my next stakeout."

"With or without pepperoni?"

"Without so much energy."

Afterwards, Beau and Allison stopped by his house for a newspaper to see what movies were playing at the theater. Just when they'd decided on a comedy, the doorbell rang.

"It's Kieron," Beau said, as he unlocked the front door.

She instantly recalled his rude mannerisms at the Budget Builder. Call it stubbornness, but Allison couldn't accept Kieron's side of the marriage breakup story. She had nothing to base her opinion on but a feeling, and how could she expect Beau to understand a woman's intuition?

For Beau's sake, she'd be pleasant and try to find something likeable about his neighbor.

"Come in," Beau said, opening wide the door. "Allison and I are heading out to a movie in a few minutes, but we always have time for you."

Kieron flashed his violet gaze at her. She saw a look no decent man should give a woman, and she wanted to sail her hand across his face.

Am I overreacting? Selfish of Beau's time? Jealous of his friends? Lord, help me here. I know I had a bad first impression of Beau's undercover buddies, but not when he explained them to me.

"Hi, Allison. This guy being good to you?" Kieron stepped a bit too close for comfort.

"The best," she replied and hooked arms with Beau.

"I'll only be a minute," Kieron went on, giving Beau his attention. "My TV blew last night, and I wondered if you would tape this afternoon's baseball game. I'm heading out now to get a new TV, but I also need to check some things at the construction site."

Beau waved a hand in protest. "Why don't you watch the game here? No one will be around anyway. Just lock up and set the alarm when you leave."

Kieron glanced away, then back to Beau. "Are you sure?"

"After all those days you picked up my mail and kept an eye on the place? My home is yours. Help yourself to a soda in the fridge or whatever else you can find."

Kieron pressed his lips together as though he found Beau's offer incredible. "Great. Let me run over to the house and lock up. The game starts in thirty minutes."

Allison watched Kieron dash across the street. Dare she tell Beau about the licentious look he tossed her way? Beau's naïve attitude about his friend irked her. She took a deep breath and walked back into the kitchen. No point in Beau seeing her obvious disgust with his best friend. Besides, her attitude didn't sound very Christian, and she wasn't proud of her thoughts—even if she believed they were true.

"You don't like him at all," Beau stated behind her.

Allison whirled around. He'd jammed his hands into his jeans pocket, his usual sign of frustration. She bit back all the curt remarks she wanted to say about Kieron and swallowed them along with her anger. "Be careful, Beau," she said as gently as possible. "Something about him is not right."

Chapter 16

Allison left Wednesday night choir rehearsal exhilarated with the music they'd practiced for Sunday and the realization she and Beau were sharing a fabulous summer. Each time they met confirmed their relationship, and even their few squabbles resulted in a stronger bond. The one issue they failed to agree upon was Kieron Bates.

She didn't like him. She didn't trust him. Something about the man was evil, but Beau refused to consider that his old friend might have made improper advances to Allison or lied about his wife. To Allison, if a man lied about one thing, he'd lie about another.

Pulling her car onto the main street, she drove toward home, but a sudden urge for a cold drink and fries caused her to swing into a fast food restaurant and head for the drive-thru. A late model truck eased in behind her—no doubt, the munchies had hit that driver, too.

After giving her order, she moved ahead to the cashier window, handed the young man her money, and grabbed her fries and drink. Odd, the truck behind her didn't pick up any food. She glanced in her rearview mirror but couldn't see the driver because he wore a cowboy hat.

She shrugged and headed home. The truck followed her.

A moment later, he turned the same way she did. He must live in her neighborhood. Still, she didn't like the way he rode her bumper. Feeling a bit apprehensive, she signaled a right turn and drove down a street away from her general direction. He followed.

Suddenly she remembered the truck parked at the Budget Builder when she pulled a late shift. Could it be the same?

Allison's pulse rose, and her mouth felt dry. She jammed the straw into her soda and took a drink. All the while, she noted the truck trailing behind her.

She signaled left, and he turned with her. Allison's body trembled. The shooting and the phone threats rose like an erupting volcano in front of her eyes. Clumsily, she locked her doors and yanked the cell phone from her purse. Using speed dial, she punched in Beau's home number.

It rang once, twice. *Please, Beau, pick up.* Three times. The answering machine started to play his message. She swallowed hard, biting back the tears and yet feeling the panic seize her quivering body. At least he had caller ID and would recognize her number.

Oh, Lord, help me. I don't know what to do!

Allison stepped on the gas and sped through the residential area, but the truck stayed right behind her. Once she tried to capture a look of his face, but the cowboy hat hid any visible features. Frightened and uncertain of what to do, she searched the area for a police car. At least if an officer stopped her for speeding, she'd be safe.

If only she'd taken the time to program Beau's new cell number into her phone. In the darkness, accompanied with her rather reckless driving, she couldn't pull the number from her purse or dial it in the dark. For certain she needed to get out of the neighborhood before she hit something or someone.

At the next stop sign, she turned onto a major thoroughfare while the truck rode her bumper. Pressing ahead to the next corner, she turned right onto a four-lane street. Surely she could lose him now. Her phone rang, rattling her senses, and she hastily picked it up.

"Hi, Baby, sorry I missed your call; I was outside with Kieron."

She burst into tears, barely able to speak. "A truck is following me," she finally managed through chattering teeth.

"Are you sure?" he asked, his tone filled with concern.

"Oh, yes. Since I left the church, he's been on my bumper. I've even wound through a subdivision, but he's still behind me. Now, I'm on Louetta, just before 249, and I don't even see a police car to help me. There aren't any at the gas stations, the convenience stores, nothing."

"Listen, head my way. I'll be standing outside." His voice sounded calm against the roaring of her frenzied mind.

"Okay. I'm not that far." She swerved into the next lane to miss a car. Perspiration trickled down the side of her face, but she couldn't swipe it with the phone in one hand and the steering wheel in the other. Praise God, she no longer wore the sling, yet the arm grasping the steering wheel ached.

"Don't hang up the phone. Lay it on the seat if you need to, but keep me on the line. How close are you now?"

She took a deep breath and blinked her eyes to clear her vision. "About ten minutes or so at the speed I'm going."

"Can you see his face?"

She snatched another glimpse. "No, he's wearing a hat and driving a big pickup. And he's too close for me to read his license plates."

"Don't worry about that, Allison. Just continue to drive my way," he said without a hint of apprehension.

"Please, keep talking to me. I'm afraid I'll lose it if you don't." She shivered while her hands felt clammy.

"You can do this," he went on. His gentleness was a blessing as she battled her hysteria.

"It has a diesel engine," she managed through chattering teeth.

"Good girl. That will help us later in filing a police report. Ignore him and simply concentrate on the road."

A thought plunged into her mind. "Do you. . .do you think he's the man who threatened me? Or someone from the shooting?" She sucked in her breath. Control. She had to find control.

"Honey, he's probably some kid who saw a good-looking girl and is all caught up in the chase. He's banking on you being scared and wrecking your little blue car."

His evaluation didn't soothe her nerves or stop the truck behind her. "I don't believe your lame explanation for one minute. I know this whole thing is connected—the shooting, the phone threats—and I know you're hiding things from me." Her rise of tone startled her. "I'm sorry. This is not your fault."

"Honey, I don't have any more information than when I left the hospital," he replied. "But I promise I'll get to the bottom of this—"

"If we live through it."

"Allison, don't even think such a thing. God is looking out for us."

She bit back a sob. "I'm sorry, and I know God's protecting both of us."

"Now I hear your spunk. Where are you?"

"Turning into your subdivision." She heard him sigh. "He's right behind me." She sped on, but when she took a left at Beau's street, the truck raced past her. "He's gone," she whispered.

"The rat knew where you were headed," Beau muttered.

Once in his driveway, she flung aside the seatbelt and jumped from her car into the comfort of his arms. All the while she cried, repeatedly telling herself to calm down. God had protected her. The ordeal was over, at least for the moment.

As her tears subsided, she relaxed until she could pull herself from Beau's embrace. Fright and anger coursed through her veins at the man who bullied her. She desperately wanted answers and the assurance that those who had made her life and Beau's a living nightmare had been apprehended. Then she wrapped her arms around him and felt it—a gun tucked into his belt at the small of his back.

Allison shuddered. As though Beau read her thoughts, he drew her back into his arms.

"I'm a cop," he said, reaching for her hand hanging limply at her side. "He could have stopped in front of the house and opened fire."

This part of his life sounded so foreign to her. She'd never seen him in a police uniform or with a gun, and he didn't even wear a bullet-proof vest when on the streets. He'd told her about his job: the endless waiting, the getting to know people, and how he and Ace often worked together until they built up enough trust to buy narcotics.

Beau, as an undercover cop, had a lifestyle far from her realm of understanding. Reality hit her hard. She recoiled at his touch, the memory of the shooting, and the crimson pools of blood vivid in her mind.

He's a trained officer. He knows how to use a gun. This is what he does while the rest of the world sleeps, and soon he'll return to it.

"Are you all right?" he asked against the sound of singing crickets and the canopy of a star-studded sky.

"I. . .I think so. I just want to wake up and find out this horrible nightmare is over." She wanted to find reassurance on his face, but she couldn't forget the touch of cold metal against her fingertips.

Lord, help me overcome this fear. I don't want to shut Beau out because of my inability to handle his using a gun.

Slowly her gaze moved upward to his face. The faint glow from the streetlight outlined his rugged features, and she slowly brought her hand to his cheek. "You are the last one I want to take out my frustrations on," she whispered.

"I understand," he said and kissed the hand caressing him. "Let's go inside. I'll put the gun away and call Sarge."

She nibbled at her lip. "I never told you this, but the night I worked until midnight, a strange truck was parked next to my car when I left. When I walked back to talk to the manager and security guard about it, the truck left. I think it might have been the same one. Beau, I want us to pray about tonight. . .and everything else."

He retrieved the gun from the small of his back before taking a long look up and down the street. He slipped one arm around her waist and gave her a slight squeeze. Gently, he shepherded her to the back door, to light, and safety.

Inside the house, he set his gun on top of the refrigerator and grasped her hands with his. "We need to pray before we do another thing." When she agreed, he began, "Lord, we aren't sure what happened here tonight, if it's connected to my old case or the shooting. But we know You do, and we're giving all our fears and questions to You in faith and trust. We are clinging to the cross and Your promise to never forsake us in times of want and need. Give us wisdom and strength to meet each day with the supernatural joy that comes only from You. In Jesus' precious and holy name, amen."

She stepped into his arms and basked in the strength of the godly man sheltering her. She felt God's presence whispering His peace and offering hope for a victory won on the cross. "Thank you," she said. "Lately I forget God has a purpose in all of this. I needed the reminder."

He weaved his fingers through her hair, resting his head atop hers. "Sometimes I think I shouldn't see you anymore—that my involvement with you invited those threats. Except, now I believe we've been thrown into some sort of crucible, and we're bound by another force to stick it out."

She feigned a smile. "I wish I had your bravery."

He kissed the top of her head. "I'm not so brave."

She felt the rise and fall of his even breathing and heard his heart pounding in her ears.

"When those guys are in jail and you have absolutely nothing to fear, I want to talk to you about another matter. Right now, I have a case to solve," he said.

"We," she reminded him, "we're in this together."

"Of course. Just remember the bodyguard in me wants to protect you from all of this, and I'm not doing a very good job."

"And the independent side of me says I don't need you risking your life for my sake."

He hugged her close. "What we both need is to rely on the one and only protector. The invincible." He brushed his finger across her lips. "As much as I like holding you, I'd better call Sarge and see if he has a clue about the road hog."

She glanced at the phone and saw the answering machine flashed a message. He reached across the kitchen counter and depressed the PLAY button.

"Pretty little Allison okay?" The man laughed low. "I just needed to make sure you were keeping your end of the bargain. Beau, if you value Allison's lovely little neck, don't double-cross me."

Chapter 17

Will it ever end?" Allison uttered. "What more could they want?"

Anger surged through Beau's body as he quickly checked his caller-ID. Naturally the caller had the number blocked. He clenched his fists and gritted his teeth. He wanted to curse like the street people he normally kept company with, to run his fist through a window—all the things contrary to his faith. He wanted nothing more than to get his hands on the source of her fear and tear him apart. Nothing had changed. He'd gone through the motions of abandoning the case, but it hadn't stopped the culprits from frightening an innocent young woman.

Who were these guys? If he'd been so close to uncovering them, he should have a lead. Instead, he looked like an idiot, while the woman he loved stood before him, trembling. He'd cracked harder cases than this—one involving a member of city council and another where a woman laundered her money through a mission.

Oh, Lord, You gave me a mind and a heart for police work. Am I not listening? What am I doing wrong?

"I hate what this is doing to you," he finally said, viewing the tension through the stiffened muscles in her body. "I promise you, I will find out who is responsible for this."

She shook her head and swallowed. "If I'm terrified, imagine how others feel who don't have the Lord. Beau, I want you to do whatever is necessary to stop these horrible men."

Her declaration irritated him. "Don't you think I am? I'm on this case night and day."

"But what about your old contacts? Have your friends been able to get information from them?" She crossed her arms as though she could hide the viciousness plaguing her.

"You've been watching too many police shows," he said, releasing her to pick up his new cell phone and call Sarge.

"I'm simply thinking about what you've already told me about your job. You said it took a long time to win people's trust. Those cops assigned to your case haven't had time to develop friendships, and you and I know the drug guys are far too clever to risk getting caught."

He frowned, his anger threatening to go out of control. "What do you want

331

me to do? If I'm officially on the case, don't you understand I may as well invite them to put a bullet in your head?"

"No! I'm simply saying what you're doing is not enough. Protecting me has become an obsession rather than doing your job." She glared at him as though waiting for his reaction before she exploded.

He threw the phone down and grabbed her shoulders. "Don't you know I love you? I can't let anything happen to you."

Her eyes widened, and she paled. He'd frightened her with his fury. Instantly, he released her arms. "Alli, I'm sorry. I had no right to grab you."

She rubbed her flesh where he'd squeezed much too hard. "What did you say?" she asked slowly.

"I said I'm sorry." He sighed heavily. "I care about you; I love you. Nothing matters to me except your safety."

A tear trickled from her eye. "And I love you." She wiped away the wetness. "I'm no help to you at all. In fact, I'm in the way of everything you're trying to do. If not for me, those guys would be in jail." She hesitated, her sea green pools filled with emotion. "And because I love you, I can't stand idly by, helpless and scared like some rabbit. Beau, you have a job to do, and it's not being my bodyguard."

"Honey, these guys play for keeps. I can't do any more than what I'm doing now. So help me, I'll find out who they are and get them put where they belong."

Hours later, after Allison had received a police escort home, Beau paced the living room. Alone in the dark, he played and replayed every word, every scene surrounding the drug case. Whatever the answer, it had to be something so obvious that he ignored it. He felt so stupid, so insignificant, totally broken.

First thing in the morning, he'd call Sarge and request another criminal history check on Joe Lopez. This time he wouldn't let anything slip by him. He knew a link existed, something he had repeatedly missed.

He glanced across the street at Kieron's dark house. Snippets of their times together in high school flashed across his mind. Kieron had gotten into a little more trouble than Beau, but nothing serious. Then he remembered the car theft. Odd he'd forgotten, but it happened after Beau had come to know the Lord. Kieron wasn't interested in Jesus, and they'd started to go their separate ways. Kieron's dad had gotten him out of the trouble, but later Beau saw his old friend still kept bad company. After graduation, he'd lost track.

Beau shook his head. Those old recollections of Kieron bothered him—his friend, his neighbor, the guy who watched his house and got his mail while he recuperated in the hospital, the same man who cried buckets when his wife left him for another man. His bud.

The one person who knew his job as an undercover cop.

A twist of uneasiness settled upon him like the deadly calm before a twister. Allison didn't care for Kieron, although she tried to mask her real feelings for

Beau's sake. He saw the words unsaid and her obvious dislike and distrust. Plus she believed Lori's story. Maybe he ought to talk to Lori again and make sure her reasons for leaving matched Kieron's.

Oh, Lord, what if I've been wrong? I hate the thought of making excuses for a man who lives on the wrong side of the law. Forgive me, Lord. Give me wisdom to end this thing.

Nine o'clock the next morning, Beau searched through the junk drawer in his kitchen for Lori's parents' number. She'd given it to him at the grocery, and he'd stuck it on the side of the refrigerator, but somehow her number had disappeared.

Lori, Kieron, and Beau had all gone to high school together, but Beau could not remember her maiden name. Finally he gave up and dragged down his school annual from the attic. Just when he thought his leg had healed nicely, he attempted something to prove otherwise. Climbing up and down the attic ladder highlighted one of those moments.

He dialed the Hayley number with a mixture of curiosity and regret. The last thing he wanted to find out was his old friend had lied.

An hour later, he pulled up in front of Lori's parents' home. The huge New Orleans–style home brought back a flood of memories from high school days. Her parents had opened their doors to every teenager who needed a listening ear, a meal, or someplace to stay for a night. Mr. and Mrs. Hayley had one standing rule: If you stayed over on Saturday, you attended church on Sunday. No excuse. Beau had almost forgotten their hospitality and Christian beliefs.

He chuckled and opened his car door. It would be nice to see Lori's parents again. Too bad the visit couldn't be under more pleasant circumstances.

Lori greeted him at the door. She looked even bigger than before, like a balloon ready to pop. "Mom and Dad just left for an appointment," she said. "They wanted to see you, but perhaps another time. Come on in."

"Tell them I said hello," Beau said, feeling a bit awkward. "When's the baby due?"

"Two weeks," she said with a smile. She patted her rounded stomach. "She's kicking me to pieces today. Most likely wanting to get out of there."

Beau laughed. "I suppose you have a name picked out."

With her hand resting on her stomach, she said, "Sure do. Bethany Lynn."

"That's a pretty name. Let me know when she gets here." He detected the tantalizing aroma of cookies. "Does your mother still bake like she used to?"

"Always," Lori replied, smiling. "It doesn't help my waistline. Grab some cookies on your way through the kitchen." She gestured toward the family room. The old, denim sofa had been replaced with a cream-colored leather one, and the chipped and scratched tables were now chrome and glass. Even the food stains on the carpet had vanished. "Sit down and tell me what brings you here today."

He sunk down on the sofa. "To talk about Kieron."

Lori frowned. "I hope you're not here to persuade me to move back with him."

"Not at all." Suddenly he felt uncomfortable with the questions probing his mind.

"Would you like something to drink?"

"Don't think so, but thanks." The cookies had lost their appeal with what he needed to find out. He watched her move awkwardly toward an easy chair and wondered if she needed help.

"Glad I don't have much more of this waiting left," she said. "Beau, why are you so nervous?"

He leaned forward and folded his hands. "I've some serious questions about Kieron."

"Is he all right?" Her forehead wrinkled.

"Sure, as far as I know." *You're not being truthful.*

She placed a hand on her bulging stomach, like she'd done at the grocery store as though protecting her baby from what she needed to say. Taking a deep breath, she began, "Remember all the fun we had in school? College days were great, but not like being young with all our friends."

Beau smiled. "Great times. I think in college we all had different agendas; I did, anyway. I always thought I could go back to those old high school days, but they're gone forever."

Lori closed her eyes. "Kieron always had such wild ideas, and he was incredibly funny. I used to love his impersonations. He could do anyone, facial contortions and all."

"Yeah. He had us all in stitches most of the time," Beau said, then nodded. "He had all the teachers pegged."

An uncomfortable silence followed.

"Have you seen him high?" Lori finally asked.

He shook his head. "Never an indication, which bothers me. What you told me at the grocery sounded. . .rather bizarre."

"Kieron hid his habit from me for a long time, but I found out for sure after getting pregnant—or I wouldn't have risked a baby's health. I have no idea how long he's been a user—probably about three years."

"Three years?"

"That's when I first started noticing the mood swings and money disappearing. I thought his roofing business was doing badly, but when I checked into the records, I found out the opposite."

"Did you ask him about the missing money?"

"Yes, and he exploded. Then we started having more cash again, and I felt better for a long time. I ignored the mood swings and thought he felt trapped in our marriage. He mentioned starting a family, so I assumed a baby would take care of the problems."

"So then you caught him high?" Beau asked.

"Several times." Her gaze flitted about the room. "Something else, too. One day, as a surprise, I cleaned out his office. You can't imagine how messy a contractor's office can be. Anyway I found a huge amount of money in the back of a drawer."

"How much?"

"One hundred thousand dollars," she whispered, as though someone in the house might hear. "Took me a long time to ask him about it. Frankly, I was scared."

A strange feeling curled in the pit of his stomach. "What did he say?"

"He very calmly said he'd been saving the money for a new home for us and the baby. I wanted to know why he hadn't deposited it into a bank, and he said he didn't trust them." Lori swallowed hard. "I didn't believe him and told him so. I demanded to know where the cash came from, but he lost his temper and told me never to go through his private things again. He stormed out. Several hours later he returned home, apologized, and left again. When he came back this time, he was high."

"Did you two talk then?"

"No. I waited until a few days later. I gave him an ultimatum—the drugs or me and the baby. You know the rest."

Beau took a deep breath. "Do you have any idea where the cash came from?"

She hesitated, and a tear rolled down her cheek. "I have my suspicions, Beau, but they're too awful to even say."

He nodded, understanding completely. He didn't want to believe it, either. "Have any shady-looking characters ever been to see him?"

She took a deep breath, and he waited for her to respond. "No, but some of his employees look like he scraped the bottom of the barrel to find them," she replied. "Beau, I need to know why he said I left."

"Does it matter?"

"I still love him. He has a substance abuse problem, and because of that I won't subject our baby to his mood swings or his illegal habit." She stared at her hands, then lifted her head. "What he's told people is important to me."

Beau hesitated a moment longer. "He said you left him for another man."

Lori didn't flinch. "I'm not surprised. He accused me of an affair whenever we quarreled. He even suggested the baby belonged to you." Her gaze bore into his. "I've never been unfaithful. Kieron has been my life."

The look in her eyes told him she'd spoken the truth. "I understand, Lori. I'm sorry to have upset you, but I needed to know the truth."

Her eyes pooled with tears. "It's the law, isn't it? Kieron is in terrible trouble. I just feel it."

Chapter 18

Allison nervously flipped on her turn signal and whipped her car into the left lane. The beat-up vehicle behind her followed. Her stomach churned with the memory of the last time a truck trailed her. The car stayed on her bumper as it had for the past several minutes, ever since she finished her shift at the Budget Builder. Up ahead she needed to turn left and swerved into that lane. A yellow light quickly flashed red, bringing her to a halt. Beau had therapy this afternoon, or she'd head in his direction. She glanced into her rearview mirror and saw the other car had swung in behind her. She also grabbed a glimpse of the driver and passengers: a carload of teens laughing and pointing at her.

Relieved, she relaxed slightly and focused her attention on the traffic light. Kids. They must have just gotten out of school and were in a hurry. For a few moments, she thought she'd been followed again. When had she become so paranoid? And this wasn't the first time she'd panicked in traffic. Lately, every vehicle seemed to represent danger. She wanted this nightmare ended now.

At times she feared her attraction to Beau centered around the danger they faced together. He'd mentioned that facet of their relationship before, but when she thought of not having him in her life, a deep sense of loss pierced her heart. And it had nothing to do with police work. Her feelings had everything to do with love, the kind God intended for a man and a woman.

Her thoughts drifted back to the night Beau told her he loved her.

"When this is all over," he'd said, "I'd like for you and me to sit down and talk."

"You've said this before. What are we going to discuss?" she'd asked.

"The future—and what it might hold for us." The earnest look on his face had told her he wanted God's best.

"We can discuss it anytime," she had replied.

He had shaken his head and drawn her into his arms. "No. I don't want you making a decision until those guys are in jail. Right now I'd be afraid you were thinking in terms of the danger we've shared rather than what God intends for us. In the meantime, don't forget I love you."

Allison touched her lips, remembering the kiss sealing his words. They'd known each other for a little more than four months, but she couldn't imagine her life without him. She let her thoughts dance with the years ahead, Beau continuing in his police work and she fulfilling her own ministry as a nurse.

The love swelling in her heart brought an errant tear.

She snatched up her cell phone and punched in the code to his house.

"Hi, it's Allison. I'm checking in to see how you're doing. Hope today's session went well. I'll be home until seven o'clock. This is choir night. I'll give you a call around nine-fifteen from my cell—depends on how long I talk afterwards. Oh, Mom called and invited us to dinner Friday night. Check your schedule and let me know. Bye, love you."

The mention of her mother left a path of regret. She and Allison had always been extremely close, but since the shooting, their conversations wavered between deceit and superficial. She couldn't tell her about the threats, at least not until arrests were made.

※

Beau examined the criminal history check and the additional data put together about Joe Lopez. By using the man's social security number, the police department could secure a wealth of information. Although Beau had read most of the background material before, he needed to refresh his memory.

Born and raised on the southeast side of town. In and out of trouble since the age of fifteen. Arrested twice for possession. Done time for theft. Sister lives in San Antonio. Parents deceased. He'd worked construction with a string of companies, one of them, Bates Roofing, until about eighteen months ago.

Bingo.

Finally he saw a connection between the shooting and the narcotics case. Kieron's involvement with Lopez infuriated him. No doubt with Beau's house key, he had access to everything: Beau's phone numbers, laptop files, his undercover buds stopping by, the ability to watch him come and go. Everything Kieron needed to continue dodging the system lay right there at his fingertips. Beau felt like a rookie cop, more so a fool. But why had Lopez come after Allison? That part still didn't make sense. But Lopez had been high—confused and disoriented.

Unless Joe Lopez had been after Beau and not Allison.

Snatching up his cell phone, Beau punched in Sarge's number.

"I think I've figured out most of it," he said and proceeded to tell him about the connection between Joe Lopez and Kieron Bates, including Lori's reasons for leaving her husband.

"Your best friend?" Sarge said. "We knew it had to be someone on the inside."

Guilt washed over Beau. "I'm going over to see him tonight. Try to talk some sense into his thick skull. I have no idea how deep he's in with this—hate to even speculate."

"You're going to need backup," Sarge said.

"Right. But give me lots of time. He doesn't get home until seven-thirty or after, and I want to ease into this, hopefully get a confession."

He heard Sarge tap his pen against the desk. "All right, we'll keep a surveillance on the house, starting about eight. It's your call, but if we don't hear anything from you by nine-thirty, we're coming in."

Beau hung up and punched in Allison's number. He waited for the answering machine to pick up.

"Alli, it's Beau. Are you there?"

"Hi. Did you have a good day?" The musical lilt of her voice temporarily erased what he needed to do that evening.

"I think so. Listen, Honey, I may have this case wrapped up tonight."

"You're kidding. Oh, Beau, what wonderful news. I can't believe it. What has happened?"

"I'll tell you all about it later, but for right now I could use a few prayers."

"Beau," she said slowly, "this is dangerous, isn't it?"

He heard the panic. "Not for a veteran like me."

Silence met him. "What time are you leaving? I might stay home from choir rehearsal tonight."

"No, please go on to church. Remember, this is my life, what I do every day. In about a month, I'll be back on the streets again."

She paused. "I understand, and I'll be praying while I'm singing."

"It'll be late before I can get back to you," he said.

"I don't care. I won't be able to sleep, anyway."

Beau laid his phone on the kitchen counter. *Lord, this is going to be tough, and I need You with me. I pray for Kieron. He needs You. I pray for a clear head and Your words in my mouth. Protect me from evil and let me represent You. In Jesus' name, amen.*

Shortly before eight o'clock, Beau stood outside Kieron's door and contemplated the reality of his best friend being knee-deep in drugs. Anger coursed through him as he considered the death of Joe Lopez, the phone calls to Allison, and the countless other people who were dead or addicted to drugs. No matter what Beau's past or present relationship might be with Kieron, the drug ring had to be stopped.

The cop side of him felt decisively stupid for not detecting the warning signals. Allison had been on to Kieron from the beginning, while Beau tossed the obvious aside. He didn't like his suspicions about a few other things, either. He didn't want to believe any of it, but if Kieron had money hidden about his office, then he knew way too much about the narcotics game.

Beau rang Kieron's doorbell. He glanced at the untrimmed shrubbery and weed-infested flowerbeds. Last summer Beau and Lori competed with yard work and flowers, which probably led Kieron to accuse her of infidelity. The idea disgusted him. He knew a time when they were like brothers, but brothers didn't do what Kieron suspected of Beau.

"Hey. Come on in." Kieron hosted a wide grin. "Want to join me for a couple of burgers?"

"Sure." Beau limped along behind him to the kitchen. The house looked like no one had done anything to it in months—probably since Lori left. Clothes were strewn everywhere along with fast-food bags, drinking glasses, and newspapers. All of the blinds and drapes were drawn, and the smell of spoiled food and filth lingered in the air like a bad omen.

"What have you been up to?" Kieron asked, opening the refrigerator and removing a package of hamburger patties.

Beau feigned a chuckle and eased into a chair at the kitchen table. "Looking after my yard, driving to therapy, and slowly working on building a new patio."

"Such a life. While I'm working in the hot sun, you're in air-conditioned comfort, living an easy life." He smiled easily: Kieron, the charmer.

"Not all the time. I did see Lori today," Beau said casually.

"Oh?" Kieron asked, lifting a brow. "How is she?"

"Very pregnant. Of course she told me you already knew."

Kieron nodded and turned his back. "The brat has to belong to her new boyfriend."

"Lori said the baby is yours. She's living with her parents and claimed she never had a boyfriend."

Kieron shrugged. "He must have booted her out."

"Whatever. She said a few other interesting things, too. She said you two had some serious problems that you refused to face." Beau felt calm, amazingly calm, the kind of peace only God orchestrated.

"Like what?" Kieron asked, pulling a bottle of Worcestershire sauce from a cabinet. He twisted off the lid and doused the patties.

"She said you had a drug problem and refused to get help. That's why she moved out."

He whirled around to face Beau, his features strained. "Women. You give them the best you have, and they make up garbage. Leave 'em alone—that's my advice. Even your pretty little Allison will turn on you. Wait and see."

Beau felt his stomach curdle. The way Kieron spit out "pretty little Allison" triggered an alarm. He'd heard the voice before—at the other end of the phone. Kieron's impersonations.

"So you're the one," Beau said as evenly as discussing the weather. "You made the phone calls to Alli."

Kieron forced a laugh. "What phone calls are you talking about? First you come over here with some wild accusations you heard from Lori, and now you accuse me of threatening your girlfriend."

Beau stood, his fists clenched. "I never said the calls were threatening."

A slow smile spread over Kieron's face, and he stepped over to a drawer. "Right you are. Looks like you and I are finished with our little conversation." He whipped out a revolver and pointed it at Beau. "I think you'll be staying awhile."

"You don't want to do this," Beau said, staring straight into Kieron's violet eyes. "It's not too late to turn this thing around. I can help you."

He sneered. "Why would I want to go to jail when I'm making a small fortune?"

"Supplying narcotics to kids and users?" Beau asked. The truth cut him like a knife. He never wanted to believe Kieron was capable of destroying lives.

"You bet. Easy bucks when you're smart. I thought I'd died and gone to heaven when you moved in. What a stupid cop. You played into my every move—giving me a key to your place and letting me know where and when you went on duty."

Beau took a step forward. He needed to shorten the distance between them.

"Don't move." Kieron's tone took on a deadly sound.

"I've got a backup team outside. They're coming in whether you give yourself up or not."

"Liar," Kieron said. He pulled a roll of duct tape from the drawer. "Have a seat. You're not going anywhere."

Beau settled back into the chair; no point in pushing Kieron into pulling the trigger. Backups didn't do a dead man a bit of good.

Kieron whipped Beau's hands behind the chair and wrapped the tape tightly around his wrists, chest, and feet. He pulled Beau's phone from his pocket and tossed it on the table. "Good old duct tape," he said, with a sneer, "has a million uses."

"You're already caught, Kieron. I'm telling you, it's only a matter of time before they move in. You can give yourself up, and things will go easier."

"Not hardly. I suppose you want me to pray about it?" He snorted. "Think about it. Your God doesn't have much clout with me, and all He's done for you is make sure you were filled with lead and made to look like a fool."

"There's more to God than that."

Kieron waved the gun in front of his face. "I've heard enough."

"What about Lori and the baby? You're throwing away your future with a woman who loves you," Beau said, stalling for time. "Think about it. What good is the money without your family?"

A flicker of compassion spread over Kieron's face. He did love his wife. "She made her choice," he said gruffly, as though denying his feelings. "Her loss."

"Lori still loves you."

"She has a strange way of showing it. I'm moving on to bigger things." Kieron's face hardened. "Does Allison know about your coming over here tonight?"

Beau shook his head, disgust filling his senses. "Don't drag her into this."

"She's been involved all along. I can't have her running around with information, now can I?"

"She doesn't know a thing," Beau said, fighting to control his voice. "Leave her alone."

Kieron rubbed his chin. "You're not in any position to tell me what to do, but I do need to have the latest on your case."

"There isn't anything to tell," Beau said, wishing he'd asked for the backup sooner.

"Maybe I haven't made myself clear. Either you tell me, or Allison is dead. Then we'll talk about your parents. I have a business to run, standards to maintain."

"So you're the one heading up the whole thing." The realization made Beau feel even more stupid—and angry.

"Right, Buddy. I'm your man."

Beau tugged at the tape binding his hands. "I've been off the case for weeks. You know that."

"I know you, and you don't give up on anything." Kieron set a frying pan on the stove and switched on the gas burner. "I'll give you time to think while I cook up these burgers."

"I hate to disappoint you, but there's nothing to tell."

Long moments passed in silence. Beau's wrists grew numb with the tape cutting deep into his wrists. He struggled, but the binding held him tight against the chair.

The frying meat spit and splattered while the aroma wafted across the kitchen. Time was running out. Beau needed to think of something to appease Kieron.

"You waited too long." Kieron scooped up the burgers and dumped them onto a couple of open buns. He reached inside the fridge and pulled out a bottle of ketchup.

"I already said I'm off the case." Beau gritted his teeth to keep from lashing out. *Oh, Lord, help me.*

Picking up a burger, Kieron licked the thick, red ketchup oozing from the bun. He picked up his cell phone and punched in a number. "Yeah, she's at the church until nine. Set it up, and call me back."

Beau watched Kieron greedily devour both burgers. He tore into the sandwich like a wild animal devouring the flesh of a lesser creature.

Repulsion for his old friend snaked through Beau's body. How could Kieron be so evil and Beau have not recognized the warning signs? At that moment, Beau despised himself. He knew Kieron had arranged something for Allison's demise. *God help her. Stop him before anyone else is killed.*

Kieron's cell rang, and he snatched it up. "Good," he said. "Go on home, and I'll call you later." He set the phone on the counter and tossed Beau a triumphant smile. "A bomb's been planted in Allison's car. I told you I meant business."

Chapter 19

Allison placed her sheet music into the allotted slot for Sunday morning. She glanced at her watch: eight forty-five. The music minister had let them out early. She'd prayed for Beau all evening, finding it difficult to concentrate on choir rehearsal. The sooner she got home the better, and this was not a night to stay and visit. The drive home took ten minutes, but she wanted to be there now.

The thought of the past four months' nightmare nearly being over filled her with a mixture of joy and panic. Whatever Beau was doing had to be risky, because he'd called and asked specifically for prayer.

This part of Beau's life plagued her. Before the shooting, she hadn't met an undercover policeman. They existed in news reports and thriller movies, but not in her perfectly contented world. It wasn't until the night she saw his gun that she understood the gravity of his work. He lived in danger due to reality; she lived safely because of his commitment. The world could be an ugly place if given over to the degradation of men's minds without the Lord. Beau had been trained to protect and serve the innocent and rid the streets of crime. God forbid if she ever took him or any other police officer for granted.

She knew for certain her love for Beau didn't stem from gratitude. Those misgivings faded into obscurity when she learned his heart. He had a ministry as valid as her pastor, her Sunday school teacher, or the missionary sent to a Third World country. She couldn't ever ask him to quit; neither did she want to. She loved Beau—who he was and what he viewed as his life calling. She must learn to trust God for his safety, but in times like these, that aspect was so hard.

She moved through the crowd of choir members toward the exit, greeting them, but hardly making any small talk. Preoccupied with Beau, she found socializing nearly impossible. After all, she couldn't tell any of them about it.

"Are you okay?" Sandy asked, with a tilt of her head.

"Oh, sure. I'm just tired and have a ton of things on my mind." *Now I've lied to my best friend.*

"Do you want to grab a cup of coffee and talk?"

Allison forced a smile. "No, thanks. I think I'll head home and get to bed early."

Walking toward the front door, Allison dug through her purse for her keys. She gripped them tightly and checked her cell phone: no messages. Within ten feet of her car, she stood ready to disarm the security system and suddenly had an urge to go back inside the church to pray for Beau. She paused for a moment, then retraced her steps. She entered the worship center and slipped into a pew. A muted light shone above the choir loft, illuminating a purple banner that read, "He is Lord." Sunday the area would be filled with two hundred voices praising God in song, but right now, she needed the solace of His peace.

For the next few minutes, she read from a Bible inserted on the back of the pew. She leafed through the Psalms and prayed many of them. Tears welled her eyes and a sense of urgency needled at her heart.

Lord, I've repeatedly asked You what You desire of my relationship with Beau. Ever since he's entered my life, I've felt Your hand in all we do. The danger has been devastating, but I've never felt alone. You were there with me then, just as You are here with me now. I pray for Your protection over Beau. Give him a clear mind and courage to do the tasks You have placed before him. Lord, I need courage and stamina to stand beside him. He's a soldier in a war zone, but You are his light.

Suddenly the sound of an explosion startled her. She jumped up, nearly dropping the Bible. At first she thought the noise came from another part of the church, then she realized it had to be outside. Not sure how long she'd prayed, Allison feared for the safety of her friends. She hurried from the worship center into the large atrium where glass doors led to the parking lot.

Allison caught her breath, too frightened to scream. Her car had burst into flames. A moment later, another explosion shattered what little remained of it.

✳

Beau twisted his wrists in an effort to loosen the tape binding his numbed hands. Although he'd succeeded in gaining more mobility, he still was nowhere near freeing himself. Every moment ticking by increased his anxiety. Every thought became a prayer for Allison's life. Some bodyguard he'd turned out to be. He'd led his precious Alli right to the grave, and he couldn't do anything about it. His gaze wandered about the kitchen for a clock. The microwave read two o'clock, the oven below it read six. The actual time had to be nearly nine.

Lord, I don't care about me. It's Allison I'm begging for. Please, stop them from planting that bomb in her car. If only my backup would step in sooner. Oh, Lord, I'm rambling. I'm scared. I'm trusting in Your mighty power and deliverance.

"Can't you leave Allison out of this?"

"Don't think so," Kieron said. "She got in the way of things when Joe followed you into the Budget Builder."

"So he was after me." Being right didn't stop the ache in his heart for Allison.

Kieron nodded and swallowed hard. "You got it. Remember the last buy you made the night before? They nearly led you to my door. Couldn't have them give away my cover, could I?"

"But why involve her in the first place?"

Kieron shrugged. "I found out Joe took a hit before he entered the store. Seeing her must have confused him."

"You nearly killed an innocent woman." Beau clenched his jaw. "How many others, Kieron?"

"Not sure. I tried to get you once, but Joe blew it," Kieron replied, leaning against the counter. "This time there won't be any mistake."

"Doesn't murder bother you?"

"Naw. I've done it before; I'll do it again."

Beau wrestled with the raging thoughts threatening to push him over the brink of sanity. If given the opportunity, he'd tear Kieron apart piece by piece.

Allison, his precious angel. How could anyone want to hurt her? He loved her innocence, her total abandonment to God. How often he envied her child-like faith. And she loved him—the limping cop who thought he could shield her from harm. *God, forgive me for ever placing myself in Your position of the one true protector. My arrogance has cost Allison's life.*

Beau bit back the sobs threatening to surface. *Oh, Father, forgive me for not being Your humble servant. Keep my Allison safe. Stop this madman.*

Kieron glanced at the clock. "Looks like choir is over. One of my guys had a good time following her home one night. Sorry, Pal, your pretty little girlfriend is about to meet her maker."

"I don't believe you," Beau said, masking his rage like the calmness in the eye of a storm.

"Suit yourself, but a bomb was set inside her car to explode at nine fifteen."

✷

Allison's breath caught in her throat. Someone had tried to kill her. She stepped back from the glass doors to a wall. Whoever had put the bomb in her car could be out there watching. They didn't need to see she'd survived. Could this really be happening?

Her knees weakened, and her mind spun. She couldn't faint, not when she needed to think. Leaning against the wall, she slid to the floor and closed her eyes. *I'm safe in the shelter of God's house. But for how long?*

Forcing her eyes open, she glanced around at the dimly lit foyer. A floor-to-ceiling cross with a huge crown of thorns caught her attention. Several yards of royal purple cloth draped around the crown and down both sides of the structure. Jesus had suffered and died for her so that she might live one day with Him—be it in the next few minutes or at another time when God saw fit to take her from this world. She could make it through what lay ahead. But what of Beau? What had happened to him?

She cringed at the thought of how he'd feel once he learned about the car bombing. He'd blame himself. Maybe she'd try calling him on his cell phone, although he probably had it turned off. And her parents. The news would devastate them. She had to make it back into the worship center and retrieve her phone.

"Allison?"

Her gaze flew to the janitor, Tom Vorder.

"What's wrong?" he asked, wobbling toward her. His eyes widened. "What is burning outside? I. . .I need to call the fire department. Has everyone gone home?" His gaze searched her face.

"Don't look at me," she said hoarsely. "Talk to me while you're staring outside at my car."

Tom paled. "Your car? Are you all right? What happened?"

"Somebody put a bomb in my car. It. . .it exploded while I was inside the worship center."

He shook his head and kept his gaze fixed outside. "I was setting up chairs for tomorrow's ladies' Bible study. With all the clanging, I didn't hear a thing."

She moistened her dry lips. "I'm so glad you're here. Look, Tom, I need to get my purse and make a couple of calls. Please keep your eyes focused on something else."

He moved toward the doors and locked them. "That ought to keep them out there."

She managed to stand on wobbly legs, using the wall for support.

"Let me get your purse," Tom said. "You don't look like you'd make it, but I'm calling the fire department and the police first. You just stay put."

"Thanks," she whispered and slid back to the floor. "My legs feel like jelly." Her heart pounded so hard it hurt.

Tom pulled out his phone and headed toward the worship center. As soon as he returned with her purse, she yanked out her phone and punched in Beau's number. Voice mail met her ears.

"Beau, somebody just blew up my car, but I'm okay."

She glanced up at Tom for reassurance. "I believe the fire department and police are on their way." The older man nodded. If the pallor in his skin was any indication of how she looked, they both were in trouble.

Trembling, she called her parents. Thankfully, Dad answered.

"Dad, don't panic, but my car's just been blown up. I'm safe and at church, locked inside with the janitor. The police are on their way, but I'm staying put."

"I'm coming up there!"

"No, please don't. It might be better if whoever has done this thinks I blew up with the car."

"What do you mean? What is going on?" he demanded. She heard the shaking in his voice.

"Oh, Dad, I'm not sure, but I'll explain it all to you as soon as I can. Right now I need to make another call."

"Where's Beau?" Dad asked. "Are you two in some kind of trouble? What can I do?"

"Later, Dad, please." She wanted to cry, but if she broke down, Dad would be at the church within five minutes. He'd probably come anyway. "I've got to go; I'll call you back in a little while. Just pray, okay?"

She took a deep breath and realized Tom had positioned his portly frame beside her.

"Are you going to be okay?" he asked, his face filled with concern.

She nodded. "I'm better." She offered a faint smile, and he patted her shoulder.

Allison needed to call Sergeant Landow, and with shaking fingers she found his card and phone number. He answered on the first ring.

"Sergeant Landow? This is Allison Reynolds."

"What can I do for you?" he asked, and she shakily explained what had happened. "Anyone hurt?"

"No." In the distance she could hear sirens. "The police and fire department are almost here."

"Good. I want you to stay with the officers until you hear from me or Beau. Have the officer in charge call me when he gets there."

"Yes, Sir. Is Beau all right?"

"I'm sure he is." He hung up.

She sucked in her breath, realizing the man had no idea about Beau, either.

Chapter 20

Beau's mouth tasted like cotton. Visions of Allison sped like fast-rolling film across his mind. His ears roared, and his stomach threatened to convulse. She couldn't be gone; he refused to believe it. Again, a wave of guilt and accusing whispers tore at his conscious. God forgive him. He'd killed her by his negligence, his all-consuming pride.

Gritting his teeth, he fought the despairing thoughts of Allison and what he'd done. For the moment, his attention needed to be focused on Kieron. Beau had to find a way to stop him.

A twisted smile spread over Kieron's face. He'd validated murder as if bidding on a roofing job. The head of one of the most difficult narcotics cases in Beau's history with the police department had been his neighbor and longtime friend.

Beau licked his dry lips and vowed to keep his mind alert, but every inch of him fought the desire to snap. Like billowing waves crashing against a rocky shore, adrenaline bubbled through his veins. His hands would not budge from the tape binding him, and although his backup stood outside waiting for the designated time, he wanted freedom now. His life meant nothing. All that mattered centered around stopping the animal he once called his friend.

Kieron wiped his mouth with a dirty towel. "I'm fixin' to retire," he said. "With what I've built here, I'm set for life. No one will ever suspect me. I'm just a poor guy who couldn't stand living in the big city without his precious wife."

"What are your plans?" Beau asked, twisting his wrists.

"Get rid of you. Grieve your death and bide my time before heading to South America." He waved his hand around the room. "I won't ever have to live like this again." He picked up his phone and punched in a number. A moment later Kieron spoke to someone. "Yeah, I'm ready to bring the goods. We'll dispose of him north of town. See you in a few minutes."

"You don't have a chance, Kieron," Beau stated firmly. "The police are outside waiting."

"I doubt it. My bet goes that you kept this to yourself in hopes of prying a confession out of me," he replied, picking up the roll of duct tape. He tore a strip and wrapped it across Beau's mouth. Pulling a pocketknife from his jeans pocket, he flipped open the blade. "We're going for a little ride, but don't try anything heroic."

Beau heard the tape rip as the pocketknife sliced through to free his ankles, then around his chest where he'd been bound to the chair. With his keys in hand,

Kieron opened the door leading into the garage. "I'm right behind you," he said. "Walk through that door easylike."

Beau slowly complied, but a quick shove sent him sprawling through to blackness. Whipping around, he kicked the door shut, slamming it into Kieron's face. He dashed around to the opposite side of the car. Gunfire exploded. Kieron cursed and flung open the door. Crouching by the right front wheel, Beau waited—nowhere to go.

A split moment later, the police burst through the house. Beau heard another gunshot and then the sounds of the officers handcuffing Kieron.

Beau leaned against the tire, memories of Allison tearing at his heart.

Ace shouted his name and snapped on the garage light. "Are you okay? Need some help?"

He slowly stood and emerged from the side of the car. He ignored a surge of pain in his leg and stumbled toward Ace.

"Beau's out here," he called and opened his pocketknife to free his hands and mouth. Ace shook his head. "Superman, you had us all worried."

Beau winced as the tape ripped out pieces of his hair and tore across his face, taking a layer of skin with it. "Allison," he breathed as soon as he could speak. "Kieron said he bombed her car. Is she safe?"

"I don't know, Man," Ace said, crumbling the tape into a ball and tossing it across the garage. "But we'll find out."

Sarge appeared in the doorway. "Great job. We got him and have a lead on his buddies." He tossed Beau his cell phone. "Call Allison. She's worried sick about you. Poor lady's been through enough for one night."

"Her car?" Beau gasped.

"It's destroyed, but she was inside her church when it exploded."

"Allison's into this God thing, too?" Ace asked, furrowing his brow.

"You bet. Prayer works, Ace."

He shook his head. "Maybe it's time I listened, because working with you can be dangerous."

Beau clumsily pressed in Allison's number, shedding unashamed tears of relief. He gripped Ace's shoulder, silently thanking God for all of the night's miracles.

"You're all right," he blurted when she answered.

"Only by the grace of God," Allison said, stifling a sob. "And you? You're okay? Is it finally over?"

"Yes, Baby. I'm fine. Kieron was behind the whole thing, right from the start. The police have him in custody."

She sighed. "Kieron, your friend. I'm sorry, really I am."

"I'm the one who should be apologizing. Look at what I caused by my own stupidity."

"It doesn't matter," she said, emotion filling her words. "We can finally live again. No more threats."

He needed to see her, touch her, and make sure she hadn't been harmed. "Where are you?"

"At the church. I never left."

❋

Allison ventured up Beau's driveway and massaged her arms and shoulders. For March, the temperatures were much too cool. Spring couldn't come soon enough. She smiled, envisioning Beau's gorgeous display of flowers soon to blossom with warmer temperatures. He'd promised to give her garden tips if she kept his weeds pulled.

"Beau, where are you?" she asked, opening the gate leading to his backyard. She noted his scheferela looked healthy, and the English ivy had weathered the winter nicely.

She glanced around. He said he'd be on his patio when she arrived. She whirled around and rang his doorbell.

A pointed object poked her in the back. "You're under arrest for possession," a familiar voice muttered.

Allison laughed. "Possession of what?"

"My heart," Beau said gruffly.

"Oops. Guess I'm caught."

"Don't take this too lightly, Ma'am. This is serious business. Are you sure you want to confess to anything without an attorney? Anything you say can and will be used against you."

"I'm guilty as charged." She tried to control the laughing but gave up.

"Any last words before I handcuff you?"

"No, don't think so." She placed her hands behind her back. "Lock me up, Officer."

Beau pinned both arms behind her, making it impossible to wiggle free. Allison felt him grasp her left hand and slip something over her finger.

"This is a life sentence, you know," he whispered in her ear. His warm breath on her neck sent ripples through her body. He brushed a kiss across her shoulder, and she shivered.

"No plea-bargaining?" she whispered. "I thought undercover policemen could work special deals?"

"Absolutely not." He released her arms and turned her to face him. Before she had a chance to look at what had been placed on her finger, he wrapped his arms around her. With a deep smile, he bent and kissed her deeply. "I love you, Allison. Will you marry me and accept a life sentence with a man who desperately needs you?"

Her heart did a double flip. "Yes, a million times yes. Without a doubt, I'm shackled to you forever."

DIANN MILLS

DiAnn believes in "Writing on the Edge" when it comes to sharing her Christian faith through her writing. She is the author of twenty-six novels and novellas, as well as nonfiction, numerous short stories, articles, devotions, and the contributor to several nonfiction compilations.

She wrote from the time she could hold a pencil, but not seriously until God made it clear that she should write for Him. Three of her anthologies have appeared on the CBA Best-Seller List. Two of her books have won the distinction of best historical of the year by **Heartsong Presents'** readers, and she is also a favorite author by **Heartsong Presents'** readers. She is a founding board member for American Christian Romance Writers and a member of Inspirational Writers Alive. She speaks for various groups and conducts writing workshops.

DiAnn and her husband are members of Metropolitan Baptist Church, Houston, Texas, where they both serve in the choir and she volunteers as church librarian and teaches ladies' Bible study.

Visit her Web site: www.diannmills.com.

Escape

Kathleen Paul

To Richard V., who, through a myriad of minor computer glitches
and major crashes, always managed to delve into the memory
of a confused PC and find my manuscript.
And to his wife, Debby, who had confidence in me
that I could finish this story and confidence
that Richard could find it one more time.
God bless good friends!

Chapter 1

The gate stood open. It was the delivery gate, less ornate than the heavy black iron grating in the front gate. Its locked bars usually served to keep the inmates in. Today it stood wide open.

A solemn young woman paused in her aimless walk across the expansive lawn. She stood rooted to the spot, staring at the open gate. A prayer formed in her mind, side by side with a wild hope. With deliberate nonchalance, she turned her head to survey the scene behind her. No one was close. The nearest attendant pushed old Mrs. Donaldson's wheelchair down the paved garden path on the other side of the rose hedge.

The girl's brown eyes scanned the windows of the mansion, an old plantation house, or rather, a replica of one. The Texas panhandle had not come by this impressive structure legitimately, for a Southern plantation was not in keeping with true Texas history. Instead, in the twenties, a businessman had built this extravagant layout.

The girl looked at its stately white columns lining the front verandah. No matter how elegant the house appeared, it was still a prison.

No one watched from the windows. No one on the immaculate lawn looked her way. She was just yards from the gate, the open gate.

With agonizing self-control, the slim figure strolled toward freedom. When the distance was but a few feet, she made a dash, rounded the corner, and dropped behind one of the brick pillars that held up the heavy iron gate. She was out.

Three years. She'd been inside for three years. Her heart pounded in her chest. Her thoughts jumbled with countless prayers. One surfaced above the others. She prayed for order. She must think clearly. She must be calm.

She knew exactly what she needed to do. She had planned her escape a thousand times. At the barred windows of her richly comfortable room, she had stared out over the wall. She had memorized the terrain beyond. Then, she had prayed for the opportunity. Now, prayers for strength and courage rose to her heavenly Father.

Every tree and bush to use as a screen was mapped out in her mind. Her goal was the riverbed. She had seen it from the elevated position of her window, though it was hidden from view now. No matter. She knew the way. She knew exactly what she would do. She had been planning and waiting and praying for two years. The first year didn't count. The first year was lost.

Her eyes darted down the dirt road and off to the highway. She was on the outside. The impossible had happened. "Nothing is impossible with God." Little did her captors know that over the past years, they had allowed her the one means to remain sane. She smiled cautiously with the knowledge that they had not been clever enough to keep the Bible out of her hands.

She must move. She had made the first step. She must not remain frozen. Three years, and she was out. If she was going to stay out, she must move.

She took a deep breath and ran the length of the wall to the place where she had planned to cross the road. With a quick look around to see if anyone was in sight, she crossed the highway and dropped behind a bush. With her eyes always on the next spot to hide, she crossed the field with amazing speed. Much sooner than seemed possible, she lowered herself over the embankment.

The riverbed was almost dry. A muddy stream coursed down the middle. She plucked off her shoes and stepped into the middle. The murky brown water was only ankle deep. She had expected it to be cool, but under the hot Texas sun, it had become tepid.

The riverbed cut deep into the land. When she stood, her head was well below the rim; she wouldn't be seen from a distance. She ran all out now, putting as much distance between herself and the last three years as she could. The trickling stream did little to impede her speed. The sandy bottom was hard enough to run on and smooth enough not to hurt her feet.

In her imagination, she had run like this. But in her daydreams, the atmosphere was sunny and bursting with life. Wildflowers, not the carefully cultivated blooms of the estate, but riotous wild blooms nodding their heads in the breeze, lined every path in her fantasy of escape. Birds rejoiced at her freedom with trilling spurts of song. That was fantasy, and this was real. The day was gray and still.

She ran fast, heedless of the noise she made. She didn't fear detection. No one would overhear her splashing through the trickle of water, for she knew the area to be practically forsaken. She rarely even saw cattle out in this scrubby wasteland. Birds, jackrabbits, once a coyote, but never cows, horses, people. Beyond where the sprinklers gave life to the estate's lawns, the land was little more than a desert.

The heavy fall air stung her lungs as she gasped. The northern sky held dreary clouds. A low rumble of thunder drew her attention, and she paused for a moment with her hands on her knees, bent over to draw deep breaths into her aching lungs.

She heard no sound other than her own ragged breathing. Those clouds meant trouble. An unexpected gust of chilling wind foretold the coming cold. A Blue Norther it was called; she'd been imprisoned long enough in this area to recognize the signs.

She ran. She ran to get away. She ran until she couldn't, then she trudged along until she caught her breath and began to run again.

At first her prayers had surfaced merely in reiteration of all the last two years' prayers. The pleas were a litany born of desperate repetition. Soon, they simplified to the essential issues: "Lord, give me strength. Lord, protect me. Help me, Lord. Hide me. Don't let them find me." The water splashed warm against her legs, soaking the hem of her uniform's skirt.

Eventually, the stream widened and deepened. Small tributaries added to its strength. She looked again over her shoulder and supposed those heavy clouds were dumping water some miles away. The steep banks on either side of the creek began to worry her. She knew the water could rampage through these gullies with a force sufficient to carve away the heavy dirt. Was she safe? Would she hear a flash flood in time to scramble up the sides? Was the mental hospital far enough behind to chance walking in the open? "Oh God, guide me."

The stream became a lazy river. What river was this? How far did it go? In the three years that she had browsed through the extensive library at the hospital, she had never found a book containing maps of the area. No histories for the Texas panhandle to give her a clue. But she had a plan. Getting to the stream was only her first goal.

She slowed to a walk as the water rose above her knees, then edged over to the side, where it was ankle deep. Something moved in the water ahead, and she stopped to wait for it to pass. The stout body of a water snake glided lazily toward a patch of sun from a shady spot under a tree. His copper back bore wide, dark, ragged-edged crossbands. She held her breath, never taking her eyes off the snake until he was far enough away to be only a ripple in the water. Clouds gathered and less warmth radiated from the sun as it appeared and disappeared in a game of hide and seek.

The girl slipped from the water and collapsed under the tree, cold and shivering. Had the snake been a water moccasin? She didn't know one snake from another. She caught a sob as it rose to her throat, and she prayed she wouldn't fall apart. Three years of her life gone, and now she was out. She had to stay out. Clutching her shoes to her chest, she went back into the water.

Her mind pictured the activities on the estate. She had made her escape right after they had eaten lunch, so if she was lucky, they wouldn't notice she was missing until dinner. Would they use dogs to track her? Would they look for her at all? Of course, they would. They weren't paid to let her go. They were paid to keep her locked away.

She would not go back.

How long had she been out? She'd been in three years. Had she been out three hours?

It started to rain. *This is good after all,* she told herself. She was cold and wet, but the rain would shield her from curious eyes. She praised God for the rain even as she shivered. Perhaps the sheets of rain would obscure any footprints she'd left. Could dogs track in the rain? How long had she been out?

She came to a highway that crossed the river with a bridge. She sat under the bridge, out of the rain, resting. It was important to think clearly and stick to the plan. She had made the plan when she had plenty of time to weigh alternatives. Being wet and grimy might prove awkward. She'd have a hard time explaining what had happened.

She'd stick to her story as closely as she could, however. Her name was Daisy Madden. Daisy because of the beautiful wild appearance of the blossoms on the estate that contrasted with the otherwise pruned and cultivated gardens. The daisies had never seemed to fit into their surroundings, just as she had never fit. And "Madden" because she was mad to think she would ever escape. But she was out, and she was going to stay out.

The rain subsided. Daisy Madden climbed the embankment to the road and started another phase of her journey. Always with a prayer, she moved forward. Praying had become a habit. God was the only One with Whom she had felt comfortable talking during her years of captivity. She had no idea if she was going east, west, north, or south. She was just going, but God was going with her.

By now they had discovered she was gone. Would they call the police?

Daisy dodged to the side of the road every time she heard a car. The rain stopped, leaving the air wet and cold. The sun was down. This highway had few travelers.

She came to a rest stop beside the road. It had two picnic tables, a cement grill with rusted-out grating, and two terrible, smelly rest rooms. She ducked inside the door marked WOMEN to get out of the sharp wind. Exhausted, Daisy couldn't bring herself to sit on the cold, slimy floor. Fatigue compelled her to find some other shelter.

She slipped back outside and huddled behind the building out of the wind. She pulled the bulky sweater she wore close about her, covering more of the patient's uniform dress. The dress was a somber blue, like gray and blue that had been polished together. The resultant color made the cotton polyester material have a sheen to it. It was a simple shirtwaist, cut with a pocket on the bodice and in each side of the skirt. It didn't have a belt. Patients were not allowed to have belts.

Both the navy blue sweater and the dress were wet, but Daisy was beyond caring. Hunched against the cold concrete, she slowly slid to the ground. Her chin dropped to her chest. She fell into an exhausted sleep.

A noise woke her—but what? She stared into the darkness and thought she saw a movement. Some animal scurried between bushes, and she sighed her relief. Another noise beyond the building caught her ear. With cold and stiff muscles, she carefully crept to the corner. If she had to get up and run, they'd catch her.

Someone started whistling. The cheerful tune came clearly through the night air, and she peeked around the corner. A man crouched beside his car, changing a tire. He had a four-door sedan of a light shade; she couldn't tell what color in the dark of the night, for his car was at the edge of the pool of light coming from the top of one towering pole. The large man wore a heavy coat, wrapped warmly against the cold.

The thought crossed Daisy's mind that she had never been so cold. She shivered and her eye settled on the blanket he had thrown on the wet pavement to protect his clothing. Obviously it was an old, tattered thing. Surely he didn't value it.

He finished and threw the tools in the trunk, slamming the lid. The blanket still lay on the ground. He gathered something from the front seat of the car and carried it to the trash container. She heard him make some mild exclamation as he turned back to the car. He walked over and jerked up the blanket, then threw it in the backseat of the car.

His tall, solid form moved toward the building, and Daisy held her breath. He passed her and went to the opposite end, where he entered the door marked MEN.

She made a dash for the car and opened the back door. It was warm inside and smelled of tuna fish. Half a sandwich lay on the console between the two front seats. Without thinking, she reached out and took it. She was as hungry as she was cold. Her intention had been to snatch the blanket, but instead she unwrapped the sandwich and devoured it.

Whistling alerted her to the man's return. She'd been too slow, and now she had no shelter to hide her between the car and the building. Quickly, she got in and closed the door, but it didn't latch. She frantically scrunched down on the floorboard and drew the blanket over her.

The whistling stopped. What was he doing? The door to the back opened. She held her breath. She felt the blanket move around her ankles as he poked the end of the blanket in and slammed the door.

He hadn't seen her. He got in the car, turned the key in the ignition, and started down the road. At least he was going the right direction, away from the estate. He'd have to stop for gas or something, and she'd slip out.

She prayed. She had prayed at the estate to get out. She had prayed running in the river that she'd make it. She had prayed sitting under the bridge for a clear mind and protection. Now, she prayed this man was half-blind and perhaps a bit stupid.

He turned on the radio and switched through the stations until he found one he liked. He sang with the music and crunched on something that was in a bag next to him. Once, he rolled down his window. Daisy guessed he was trying to stay awake, and she prayed he wouldn't fall asleep at the wheel. An accident was not part of her plans.

Chapter 2

A heavy hand dragged her back from a pleasant dream. She wanted to sleep. Persistent nudging against her shoulder would not go away. She shrugged and tried to burrow farther down into the covers. A voice called, "Hey, come on. Wake up."

She came awake all at once and struggled hopelessly to get out of the car. She was wedged in an awkward position between the seats, and the blanket had wrapped around her legs to further impede her.

"Take it easy." A pleasant voice. The man! She looked up into the face of the car's driver. He stooped beside the open back door so that his face was almost level with hers, the light in the car's ceiling illuminating his strong features. Green eyes flecked with brown looked darker than they really were. Dark brown hair curled thick and disorderly around his rugged face. Lines crossed his brow in furrows as a small smile tugged at the corners of his mouth. He looked puzzled.

He was seeing a remarkably disheveled young woman. She wore no makeup, but her dark frightened eyes, fringed with ample dark lashes, scarcely needed it. She was probably pretty, but her hair was wet and clinging to her muddied face.

"Let me help you get out." Without waiting for a response, he grabbed her below the arms and, with no apparent effort, pulled her up toward him. He didn't drag her out of the car, but allowed her to arrange herself in a more dignified position on the backseat.

"I gather I picked you up when I changed the tire." His tone was conversational. She nodded her head.

"You ate the rest of my sandwich."

She nodded again. He seemed more amused than angry.

"I thought I must have thrown it away with the trash, but I could have sworn I left it in the car."

"I'm sorry," she managed to whisper.

"The lost sandwich doesn't matter." He grinned at her with a lopsided smile. "I was concerned I'd lost my mind. Then I began to hear noises in the backseat. I've been driving a long time, and I thought it was getting to me."

She looked down at her hands. Three years had passed since she had talked to anyone but an attendant or Dr. French. Should she tell him her made-up tale now or wait for questions? She decided to wait. She began to shiver.

"You're cold," he said. "Climb in the front seat, and we'll get moving again."

He gave her his hand to get out and walked her around to the passenger door in front.

"You're soaked. Take the sweater off and put my coat on."

He proceeded to remove her sweater and throw it on the backseat. He wrapped his coat around her and pushed her into the car, then pulled the blanket out of the back to wrap around her legs and over her lap. Whistling, he returned to his side of the car, slammed the back door shut, got in, and started the car.

The warmth of his coat enveloped her, but instead of shivering less, she seemed to be shivering more.

"Why did you get in?" he asked.

"I was cold." Her voice sounded small and she couldn't hide the trembling.

"You sure are shivering. Maybe I should take you to a hospital. You may be suffering from exposure."

"No!" The word came out in a little gasp.

He studied her. She tried to look stony-faced, not revealing any emotion. The false mask accentuated her fear.

"Okay. No hospital." He saw her relax, but the shivering turned to shuddering. "You may be running a fever."

He reached out a hand, and she ducked.

"It's okay. I was only going to feel your forehead." Slowly this time, he reached out to touch the back of his fingers lightly to her forehead. "Well, I'm not much of a judge, but I don't think you have a temperature."

He paused and looked with unconcealed curiosity at his stowaway. "What's your name?"

"Daisy Madden."

"Hello." He extended a hand for a friendly handshake. "My name's Peter Hudson. I'm a rancher."

"You don't look like a rancher." She observed his college grad sweater and slacks.

"Well, Ma'am," he drawled, "seems I forgot my horse and Stetson back at the ranch."

She smiled at him, the first time she had smiled in a long time. Even the feel of it was strange to her face.

"What were you doing, soaked through and out in the middle of nowhere?"

He was direct, and she liked that. She was ready with her half-truth, half-lie story.

"I'm running away."

"What from and where to?"

"Where to doesn't matter." She purposely looked into his eyes, hoping to dispel any suspicion that her story was fabrication. "I have to find a job because I don't have any relatives to run to. What from is home. My mother is dead and my father drinks. Dad's not very pleasant when he drinks." She deliberately turned her head, staring out the side window, hoping to end the discussion. She'd decided over the two years of preparing her "history" that it was better to put forth an outline and let the listener fill in the details. She hadn't expected to feel like such a liar uttering the words out loud.

"The next town should pop up pretty soon. I'll have to stop and get gas." His voice was noncommittal. She had no way of knowing whether he believed her or not. The miles slipped away in silent darkness with only the radio commenting on the passage of time.

They pulled into an all-night convenience store. She would slip out here. She hadn't stopped shaking, though, and she wondered if something was wrong with her. He finished pumping the gas and stepped inside to pay. Now was her chance to find someplace to hide. Huge trash containers lurked behind the building. Beyond that, a parking lot sprawled around a shabby apartment complex.

He took longer than she expected, and still, she hadn't moved. She was out of her prison; if she blew it now, she'd have to go back. What would he do when he came back and found her gone? Would he look for her? Probably not. Would he call the police? She'd only stolen a sandwich. Maybe he was calling the police now. Not for the sandwich, but because she was a runaway.

She leaned forward and strained to peek around the pumps and inside the store. No, he was talking to the cashier. He was joking. She could see him laugh. If she could only stop shaking, she'd get out.

Too late. He pushed open the double glass doors and started toward the car. She'd have to make her escape at the next gas stop. She'd be warmer then, more rested. And there would be that many more miles between her and the estate.

As soon as he sat down behind the wheel, he handed her a warm sandwich and a cup of something hot.

"Put the hot chocolate down here until it cools a little. You'll scald your tongue. There's a special drink holder down here. See. The sandwich is just one of those microwave jobbies."

She had already unwrapped it.

"Slow down," he said, watching her first bites. "When you're that hungry, you can get sick eating too fast."

She dutifully tried to eat more slowly, and he started the car again. When she was finished, she sipped on the chocolate. Finally, the shivering subsided.

"Thank you." She belatedly remembered her manners. He didn't answer, and she stole a look at him. He looked very serious as he gazed out at the road before them. Half asleep, she thought it was a shame that she had to slip away the next chance she got. He was not part of her plan. Now that she wasn't shivering anymore, though, she'd be able to think and make good her escape.

When she awoke, it was daylight. The car was stopped. The trunk slammed shut, and she twisted around to see Peter Hudson come around to her window. He opened the door.

"Good, you're awake. See if you can clean up your face a bit." He handed her one of those containers out of which you could pull a wet paper towel.

She scrubbed and looked up at him. He shook his head woefully.

"It's not going to work." He sounded disappointed. "You're still too messy to take in anywhere. People would notice you and wonder what happened, and that would make them remember you. I take it you'd rather not be noticed?"

It was a rhetorical question. He seemed to scarcely take note of her shaking head.

"Well, I had half a notion to drive straight through, but I'm more tired than I expected." He gazed off at the clouds, seemingly more concerned about the weather than his rider. "It still looks stormy and if I hole up for the day, it'll have a chance to clear.

"I'm going to get a motel room and get some shut-eye. You're welcome to take a shower and then do whatever you want. I'm not proposing anything indecent. I'm just going to sleep."

He saw the look of uncertainty on her face. She looked at him and she looked at her clothes.

"I'll never get a job looking like this." She wavered. "Are you sure?" She looked at him, wanting to trust.

He put his hand up in mock pledge. "You'll be as safe as my old maiden aunt."

"What's her name?" Daisy Madden asked.

He laughed. "You got me. I can't think of one." He turned serious. "It's all right, Daisy. You've had a rough deal and I'm not going to add to it."

His earnestness made her feel guilty, and she lowered her gaze from his honest eyes to stare at her hands.

"Okay," she said. *God, protect me,* she prayed.

Chapter 3

"You're a mess," Peter whistled in astonishment.

They were inside her motel room. He had gone into the office and secured two rooms while she waited in the car. He took some luggage in, and when the coast was clear, she got out and ran in. Rather, she started to run in, but she found that her legs had turned to spaghetti. If Peter had not been beside her, she would have hit the pavement. He swooped her into his arms and carried her across the threshold, put her on her feet, and quickly closed the door behind them.

"Are you sure I don't need to take you to a hospital?" She heard real concern in his voice and the sympathy nearly broke Daisy's resolve. His hands were on her elbows, supporting her, or she would have turned away.

Somehow his honest gaze made her feel more like a liar. Contemplating the lies as she plotted her escape was different from actually living the falsehoods.

"No," she said, unable to look him straight in the eye. "I'm all right."

"If he. . .hurt you just before you left, maybe a doctor should look at you."

Again, she felt the lump rise in her throat. She shook her head and took a deep breath, forcing herself to look up at him.

"It wasn't like that." Her voice broke under that steady look. Her eyes shifted away, and she tried again. "He. . ." She gave up and shrugged. One more lie wouldn't matter but still she could not utter it.

There was a moment's pause. His hands loosened their grip on her elbows, and since she didn't fall, he let go and stepped away from her.

He was still silent. She'd make one more try, as close to the truth as she could get. "I don't think the law can do anything to him for what he did. There's no proof."

Again, silence. She looked down at herself and had to agree she was a mess. Mud splattered her legs and dress. Scraggly hair hung around her thin shoulders. She looked in the mirror over the dresser and was feminine enough to be shocked. With no makeup and hair that had just grown with no trims, perms, or styling for three years, she looked bad. Add fatigue and fear and mud, and she looked horrible. Rather hopelessly, she began to pluck at the drying mud on her dress.

"We're going to have to do a complete overhaul," Peter acknowledged. "Here's some shampoo from my bag and a sweater that should swallow you up sufficiently. You go in the bathroom and hand out all your clothes. I'll take them to a Laundromat. Take a nice long bath or whatever, and crawl into bed when you get out. I'll lock the door and take the key."

"But you were going to sleep."

"I'm not the one who looks like the creature from the slimy lagoon or Swamp Man's sister."

His lack of gallantry comforted her and even brought a small smile tugging at the corner of her mouth. She followed his instructions.

❊

He tiptoed in when he returned. His passenger was curled in the bed and never moved as he walked quietly around the room. Now he put the clothes on the end of her bed. He also placed a new toothbrush, a tube of toothpaste, a brush, and a comb there.

Peter Hudson stood staring at the girl who called herself Daisy Madden. Was that much of her story true? He'd had three little sisters and had been in the habit of taking care of them. That was ancient history, though. Since then, he'd been to college and done a hitch in the Marines. He had, for all practical purposes, taken over running the family ranch. His sisters were grown and married. They no longer needed him to look after them, and he looked after cattle instead. He shook his head, bewildered by his own behavior of the past few hours. *Well, Lord,* he prayed, *it looks like I've picked up a stray. What am I going to do with her?*

Resigned to the fact that he was not going to get an immediate answer, he put himself to the tasks that would keep "the old horse ready." His mother had impressed upon him that his job was to be prepared for battle. Taking a moment to grab the Gideons' Bible and locate the verse, he looked at it with reassurance. The battle was the Lord's.

He put aside the problem of a frightened young lady under his protection. He wanted some sleep. He went to his own room and took a shower, but he dressed again before he lay down on the bed. He slept immediately.

A stealthy noise awoke him. He lay perfectly still for the minute it took him to orient himself, then he got up and put his head out the door. The girl was fully dressed and tiptoeing away. That was the slight noise he had heard.

"You don't have to sneak out. You're free to go."

She jumped. "You were asleep."

"Have I done anything to make you treat me like the bogeyman?" His calm voice filled her again with guilt. Or maybe it just resurfaced. This lying wasn't as easy as she thought it would be. If only he weren't so nice.

"I'm sorry."

He held the door open with one hand and stepped back. After a moment, she went into his room.

Peter sat down on the edge of the bed.

363

"I was planning to eat dinner and then get back on the road. You're welcome to join me. I thought we'd talk a bit about finding you a job, Daisy."

She studied his face, but she saw nothing there but honesty. Maybe she could trust him a little, if she didn't forget to be careful. She nodded at him and was rewarded with a warm smile. He stood up and began gathering things together. Daisy just watched; she was wearing all her possessions.

The crowded restaurant was not conducive to a heart-to-heart chat. They didn't try. Peter watched her look at the menu, and then her eyes darted around the room. Was she wondering what to order? Maybe he should reassure her that he could afford anything she might want. He ordered for both of them, but he decided the menu wasn't the problem when she still showed signs of nervousness after the waitress had gone off with their order.

"What's wrong? Are you afraid you'll get spotted? I'll bet we're two hundred and fifty miles from where we joined courses."

Daisy gave him a quick, unsteady smile. "I haven't been around people much lately. I'd forgotten what it felt like to be in a crowd."

A question sprang to his lips and he suppressed it. He knew from his experience raising sisters that the best confidant asked few questions.

※

When the meal came, she bowed her head for a moment. In a quick, silent prayer, she thanked God for protecting her and giving her unexpected help. She asked for blessings upon Peter Hudson for his generous spirit. Raising her head, she caught him watching her.

"You were praying?"

"Yes," she answered.

Again, he looked bewildered. "Daisy, you are the most peculiar runaway I've ever heard of."

Confused by the remark, she chose to ignore it and concentrated on the food before her. She found that she was starving. Nothing inside had ever tasted as fine as the things she had eaten on the outside, even though the menus at the estate were always a fine bill of fare. Daisy cleaned up every morsel on her plate and sighed with contentment.

As she looked across the table at her companion, she noticed that Peter was only halfway through his meal. She must have wolfed down her food. A blush stained her cheeks. Her three years inside the hospital had apparently washed away good manners. She ducked her head, hoping to avoid the penetrating observation of her rescuer. Peter noticed.

"Didn't that drunken father ever feed you?" he asked, a smile hovering around the corners of his mouth. Daisy glanced up to see the humor with which he viewed her distress. She blushed a deeper red. She wanted desperately to have him as a friend, but she'd started by lying to him, and she had to ditch him as soon as possible. He was not a part of her plan! She couldn't afford a friend.

"Do you want another roll?" He offered her the basket.

Now she had the impression he was teasing her. In her strange upbringing, there had never been anyone to tease her in this gentle, brotherly way. She wasn't quite sure what he was up to.

"If you'll wait a minute until I catch up, I'll order us some pie with ice cream."

Was it the mention of the pie on top of everything else? Or was it the chaotic atmosphere of the restaurant that suddenly seemed to swell in her ears with its noise and push in all around her? Was she somehow sick from the exposure or the fear? She only knew her head was swimming.

"What's wrong?" His voice was sharp.

"I feel faint. No," she said as a new sensation flooded through her, "I'm going to throw up."

He was curt. "The rest room's by the door we came in, behind the register. Move." His military command underlined the words.

He sat quietly, watching her push through the crowd, praying she'd make it. When she was out of sight, he returned to the few bites left of his dinner.

Shaking his head, he wondered what he was going to do with the little heifer. One of his sisters might befriend her. That would be an option he would put to her. They each lived in larger towns where she could possibly get a job. He wondered offhand what she could do. So far he knew she could sleep and eat— and she might have just flunked eating.

Another thought occurred to him that made his brows draw together in a sharp frown. It was time they did some real talking. A few minutes after he'd finished, Daisy returned. She was pale, but no longer green.

"I suppose you'll be hungry again in a hundred miles." He rose to greet her and grabbed the check. He looked up to see her swaying and grabbed her around the waist. "Come on, Puny. We'll stick you in the backseat of the car. You can lie down and close your eyes."

They drove a hundred miles while the night blackened the surrounding countryside. Here and there lights glowed, indicating the presence of houses and farms. Peter's thoughts drifted through a series of business affairs and the order and manner that must be used to deal with them. Persistently, the stray thought of the homeless waif in the backseat interrupted his tidy business dealings.

Where had she been that she was no longer used to crowds and wore dresses that looked like institutional issue? She certainly had not been treated kindly. Was the exhaustion physical, emotional, or both?

He heard a movement, and then he felt her warm breath on his cheek. She was peeking over his shoulder.

"I feel better now. May I sit in the front seat?"

He pulled the car over to the side of the road, and she hopped out of the backseat, opened the door to the front, and slid in beside him. He reached over the back of the seat and pulled the blanket to the front, draping it over her legs.

He turned off the engine, and her head came up quickly. He saw her startled eyes searching the darkness, trying to see his face. The light came from a highway lamp behind him. He could see the concern and fear flicker in her eyes. "Don't be so afraid. I just want to talk to you." Peter cleared his throat. Whatever had scared this child had scared her through and through. He looked out into the night. It was a lonely stretch of road. The stupid kid could be out here with a mad rapist. Thank God their paths had crossed. He proceeded carefully. "I want you to trust me. I want to help you, but I can only do that if you're truthful."

Involuntarily, not realizing how much she gave away by the gesture, Daisy winced and abruptly turned away.

"Daisy, are you pregnant?" He put the question to her bluntly.

Her gaze came back to his face, a genuine smile on her lips. Her eyes danced merrily as she shook her head vigorously. "No."

"Why is that amusing?" Given the circumstances, the question was legitimate. She was running away. Physically, she was tired beyond what would be considered normal. And she was experiencing nausea.

Peter watched her carefully, hoping to gain more information from her expressions and movements than from her words. Obviously, she would willingly disclose only so much.

"I can't be pregnant. I wasn't allowed to date." Her voice cut off abruptly. The smile vanished and she again preferred to look out the window rather than at her inquisitor. She did not see the look of exasperation pass over his features.

"What kind of work are you going to do?"

"Waitress."

"All right, when we get to Dooley, I'll introduce you to the right people."

"Where's Dooley?"

"It's a small south Texas town. I was raised there, and I know most everybody. Or I've got sisters in Corpus Christi, Victoria, and Houston. I'm sure one of them would take you in and help you get started."

"No." She whispered the word, but it sounded definite. "I have a plan. I must stick to my plan. It's already been muddled some, and if I get too far from it, I'll. . . mess up. I can't afford to mess up."

Daisy turned pleading eyes to his darkened form. She could not see his face, could not read his reaction. She reached out and clutched his arm. "Please," she said, her voice trembling.

He laid a strong hand across hers and discovered hers shaking. *God*, he prayed, *what is the right thing to do for this girl?*

Chapter 4

A car pulled to a stop behind them, and its headlights filled Peter's car with light. Peter twisted around to look.

"It's the state patrol. Don't lose your head. He probably just wants to know if we've got car trouble."

"Do we?"

"No, stick to the truth. You've been nauseated. We stopped for awhile."

"That's not all true," she objected. "We didn't stop because I was sick."

"I must say I'm surprised to hear you objecting to such a little prevarication." Peter chuckled. "It's true enough." He turned his head and rolled down the window as he greeted the officer.

So, thought Daisy, *he isn't as stupid as I had prayed for. He knows I'm hiding at least part of the truth*. She had no more time to think over his statement.

"You folks having trouble?" The patrolman's tone was friendly as he briefly shone his flashlight in their faces.

Peter answered, nodding toward his passenger. "She gets carsick. We just stopped to rest a little."

The officer interrupted. "It's not exactly safe to sit on the highway at night. There's an all-night diner about twelve miles down the road. Perhaps your Mrs. could get a soft drink to settle her stomach."

"Thanks, Officer." Peter began rolling up the window and the uniformed man walked away.

Peter turned on the engine and directed the car out onto the road.

"How old are you?" he asked.

"Twenty-one."

He let out a muffled whistle.

"That officer has better perception than I do. I thought you were about sixteen. I was going to pass you off as my daughter."

"You're not that old," she protested.

"I'm twenty-nine, and I was going to glower to put a few extra years on my countenance."

Her ripple of laughter touched his heart. This child was made to laugh, and someone had stripped all the joy from her life, crushing her spirit. Well, if they wanted to get to her again, they'd have to go through him.

He didn't stop to think about it, but his protective feelings were not quite the same as the brotherly surveillance he'd kept on his sisters. Somehow, knowing her true age had changed something. Unconsciously, he forgot about getting this child under some protective custody, some organization that dealt with abused children.

After a few miles of silence, Peter flicked on the radio and searched for some music. He zeroed in on a station and let it play. After several songs, Daisy spoke up.

"Last night you sang along."

"I didn't know I had an audience." Peter laughed. "If I remember, I was singing loudly to help keep myself awake."

They listened without comment for awhile.

"Tell me about your sisters," Daisy requested.

Peter gladly jumped on the topic. Since Daisy wasn't going to go back to sleep, maybe she would reveal a little more of her background through conversation.

"My sisters are all younger than I am. The youngest is Midge—or Margaret. She's the brainy one. She's in Houston with her husband, Mike. Mike is a computer processor instructor at the university, and Midge is studying law. We have an uncle on my father's side who is a lawyer.

"The middle sister is Scram. Her real name is Sarah. Sarah is twenty-five and lives in Victoria with her engineering husband, Joe. They have two kids, Tiger and Tabitha. Tiger is three and Tabitha is five.

"Lisa is twenty-seven, married to a teacher. She works in the museum in Corpus Christi part-time. They have no children, but they are trying to adopt."

"Do you like having a family?"

"Yes, don't you?"

"I haven't got any."

"How about your drunken father?"

Quietly, she said, "Would you count a drunken father as family?"

Peter could see the logic in this. He didn't contest the point.

"You haven't any sisters or brothers?"

"I have an uncle, but I'm not much use to him. I haven't seen him in three years, and he made it very plain when we parted that he would like to never see me again."

"Is this your father's brother? They sound like they are cut out of the same cloth."

Peter wondered what sort of callous cad could turn his back on Daisy. He'd met many families where the familial characteristics were not a Roman nose and wide-set eyes, but a nasty temper and sharp sarcastic tongues. If Daisy was raised in an environment of selfishness and abuse, why did she seem so utterly defenseless and pure? And where had she been brushed with religion? Not many people prayed over their food in a restaurant.

"Yes," she answered Peter's question. "But I've never been around him much."

❋

Memories flooded through her mind. She was little Julie again, laughing as she raced with her carefree daddy across the lawn of their farmhouse home. The impressive old home had been purchased by her dad for her mom as a wedding present. Together they had completely renovated and furnished it with the exquisite taste and lavishness that much money allows. Antiques crowded each room. Handcrafted decorations that her mother had ferreted out of bazaars and craft shows all over the country covered the walls and tables.

A swimming pool and a stable graced the back acreage. Her daddy had taught her to swim and ride almost before she was walking. Julie spent hours of almost every day in her father's company. His fortune had been passed down through several generations, growing with each succession. Her father's business philosophy was to keep in touch and in control, but hire someone else to do the work.

Julie's fondest memories, and the most tragic, were associated with the fun shopping trips to country fairs and bazaars, rummaging around antique stores. She and her mother would take off in a fancy red pickup and "scrounge," as her mother called it, in every old furniture store they could find. Or they'd fly to some special event such as a state craft show. Sometimes her daddy would come along, and then the trip was more fun. Worn out from spending money, Mom would rest in the hotel, and Julie and her daddy would explore whatever town they were in.

When she was eight, they had planned a minor excursion to visit a craft show in Iowa. They were going in a friend's small private plane. Julie, however, came down with a bad cold and an ear infection, and she was left at home with the housekeeper. The plane crashed, and Julie was a very rich and lonely orphan.

Uncle Jacob swooped into her life.

Uncle Jacob was the opposite of his brother, her father. He inherited all the lust for power, the drive to achieve that had benefited the fortunes of the family ancestors. He scorned his older brother's lifestyle and resented the disinterested brother who controlled the interests of the family business. With great relish, Uncle Jacob took over. His joy was hampered by the presence of a sprightly heiress-in-waiting, Julie Jones.

He developed a plan of action. For years Julie attended fine boarding schools all over Europe. She never stayed long at any one because she was "to have a taste of many different cultures." As a result, she never formed any deep and lasting friendships that would complicate things for the uncle whose main interest was his own profit.

Uncle Jacob handled vacations and holidays much the same way. He hired different companions to escort her as she traveled. She never had the same one twice, and they were carefully selected to discourage comradeship. Julie was never allowed to visit a school chum's home during the school breaks but was trudged off for more exposure to culture under a carefully screened dour dame's un-friendly escort.

Fortunately, one of these caretakers was Frances Belvedere, a religious fanatic. Mrs. Belvedere's creed didn't impress Julie, but during the course of their summer together, the older woman hauled Julie to evangelistic meetings in various countries. Memories of sitting in her mother's lap and hearing Bible stories resurfaced. Julie remembered the contentment associated with these cozy times. The message of hope reached her, and she easily gave over a life of despair to the One Who saves.

"You've been quiet a long time." Peter interrupted her memories. "I thought you'd gone to sleep again."

She shook her head.

"Would you like to drive? I could use a break."

She shook her head again. "I don't have a license."

She'd been welcomed "home" when she was eighteen with the gift of a beautiful, sleek little red sports car. She had not seen her uncle in years; he had only sent her short business letters, telling her where she was going, what she would be doing, and who was coming to do it with her. Consequently, she felt no affection for her uncle. She met her aunt for the first time and immediately felt sorry for her. Maria Jones clearly feared her husband.

Two weeks later, Julie knew the woman had good reason to be afraid of this man. Kind Uncle Jacob who smiled with his lips but never with his hard, cold eyes, slipped Julie a drug that knocked her out. Uncle Jacob then secreted his niece away to Dr. French's estate, where she was to undergo an unneeded recovery program for drug abuse. The charlatan doctor got a handsome recompense for keeping her drugged for six months. By then, a very confused Julie was physically ill.

For six months after that, she had daily sessions with Dr. French in which she tried to tell him the truth. One day she realized he knew the truth and was paid well not to help her. Since Dr. French wasn't interested in losing a high-paying patient, she tried talking to the attendants and finding one who would help her. They were used to crazy talk from the patients. After all, wasn't this where the extremely rich sent their mentally unbalanced?

Quite abruptly, she gave in. All outward appearances indicated she had resigned herself to her fate. She continued to see Dr. French for an hour of "therapy" three mornings a week. He sat and read, or he did paperwork (a crossword puzzle) or sometimes played solitaire. Occasionally, he'd notice her and say, "Miss Jones, anytime you feel like it, we'll discuss your problems." She never felt like it.

At first she was bent on revenge. Her uncle had done this to have control over the inheritance. She would get out and prove she was healthy and of a sound mind. As her thinking cooled down and became more rational, she could see the things he had done over the years to make sure no one knew her well, so no one would come to her aid. He had reckoned without God, though. God, her powerful ally, would have to be given full reign to make right the horrible wrong. Her dilemma was beyond the powers of any human she could call on.

At first she had hoped that something would come to the notice of the authorities, and her situation would be rectified. State health inspectors came and went, though, and no irregularities came to light.

As the months passed, gaining freedom became more important than seeking revenge. To say she could bring about justice was pointless.

If she got out, she realized, she would concentrate only on staying out. If she fought her powerful uncle, he would know where she was and throw her back in the estate. If she continued to be a problem, she had no doubt that Julie Jones would unfortunately succeed in a suicide attempt. She decided that she would turn justice over to God and take care of living on her own.

Planning a new life was her best option. She'd already seen half the world, and her curiosity over what living a normal life would be like was intense. She had never been grocery shopping, for instance, or made her own dentist appointment. She began to like the idea of shedding the person of Julie Jones and becoming someone who mopped floors and shopped for bargains.

Time passed within the confines of the French Estate Private Hospital. Julie Jones became a model resident, quiet, not demanding, never bothersome.

Chapter 5

Peter sang quite vigorously with the radio. Daisy reluctantly opened her eyes and became aware of her surroundings. The road stretched before them and disappeared into darkness.

"Where are we?" she asked.

"South of San Antonio," Peter answered cheerfully. "We'll get to Dooley in the morning, probably around nine o'clock. But, I've got to get some coffee and my dinner is all gone. Are you in the least bit hungry?"

In fact, she was once again starving, but she answered demurely, "I am."

"I'm trying to remember what's along this road that might be open all night. That is, something other than a beer hall. Keep your eyes open for a truck stop."

Two hours later, they came to something Peter thought was suitable. Meanwhile, he had bought them chips and soda when he stopped for gas. Daisy had drifted off to sleep again.

Peter parked the car outside the diner, thinking he'd get out and stroll around in the cold air before waking Daisy. He gazed at his sleeping rider and gently pushed back a lock of hair that had fallen across her face. Suddenly he withdrew his hand. He had not liked the sensation that had flashed through him. Her eyelashes were too long, and he knew they covered eyes that were too innocent for their own good. Her tiny nose was no longer red from cold and crying. Her lips were tender and pink.

She was not strikingly beautiful, but her sweetness attracted him. This would not do. Taking care of a girl like he would one of his sisters was one thing. Getting romantic and sentimental was another.

He cleared his throat gruffly and put a firm hand on her shoulder. "Let's eat." He promptly got out of the car.

She was getting out of her door rather slowly, not quite awake.

"Lock your side, Daisy." He glanced up to see if she had heard him. Two police came out of the restaurant door. One was chewing absently on a toothpick until he turned and caught sight of Peter and Daisy. His attention was arrested and he seemed to be weighing something in his mind.

Peter felt a stab of uneasiness. He quickly came around the front of the car and impatiently locked the door for Daisy, then shut it with a thud.

He whispered, "Fight with me, Daisy." He answered the questioning look she threw him. "There are policemen just a few feet behind you."

She jumped in without losing a second to thinking. "Why are you so grumpy? I'm not the one who decided to drive all night."

"I'm grumpy because I don't like visiting your relatives, and if we drive all night, I can sleep through one whole day of the abominable visit."

"I don't make such a fuss when we visit your folks."

"My folks don't serve a noodle casserole at every meal and listen to twangy country music at full volume twenty-four hours a day," Peter complained bitterly.

He took hold of her arm and started toward the restaurant door, staying between her and the officers as they passed. He hoped the men hadn't gotten a good look at her in the shadowy light. He also hoped he and Daisy sounded natural in their roles as a bickering couple.

When they got inside, he told her to go to the rest room immediately and stay five minutes. He didn't want them to get a better look at her in the bright fluorescent lighting.

He took a booth in the almost-empty diner and ordered for both of them. Peter sighed his relief as the policemen got in their black-and-white car. He froze as he watched an officer talk for a minute on his car radio.

Finally they rolled out. They hadn't looked too anxious to catch any desperate criminals. Man, he was getting nervous. How much of what Daisy had told him was true? He guessed about half. Now he wondered which half was true? And what was the real story to fill in the false half?

The waitress brought his cup of coffee, saying something about the weather and the pain of being up when normal people were in bed. He responded as he should, but he felt a growing uneasiness. Nervously, he kept checking the door marked WOMEN at the end of the room, waiting for it to open.

The waitress returned with the two plates.

"Would you mind checking the ladies' room for me? My wife has been ill, and she's taking a long time."

"Sure thing. What's her name?" The waitress glanced toward the closed door.

"Daisy," he answered.

He watched as she went down the length of the room. Suppose the little idiot had slipped out, thinking she would make it on her own? He held his breath as the waitress disappeared. Immediately, the door reopened, and she came out, looked at him with a frown, and shook her head. Peter jumped up and started for the door.

"Maybe she went to the car," he threw over his shoulder.

Outside he looked around. He knew she wouldn't be in the car, but he looked anyway. He walked quickly to the back of the building. Where would she go?

If I were foolish and scared, without an ounce of sense, where would I run to? he asked himself.

He surveyed the area. *I'd head for town to get a job as a waitress.* He took giant strides toward the lights of the small sleeping town. *Now, where would I hide until morning?*

About half a mile down the road was a school bus shelter. *Dear God, let the little idiot be there.*

She was. She heard him coming and nearly died before she realized it was him. When she saw his familiar frame in the doorway of the shelter, she leaped up and grabbed him, burying her face in his coat. His arms came around her, and he rocked her comfortingly back and forth. She cried softly.

"Come on, pull yourself together. They've gone, and they weren't the least bit interested in us."

She sniffed loudly, and he pulled a handkerchief out of his pocket. She blew her nose.

"Now, you're going to have red, puffy eyes again," he chided her. "I told the waitress you'd been ill, so she'll just think you're having a bad time of it. Let's go back before you get too cold."

They walked back to the truck stop. He kept his arm around her shoulders, saying nothing.

The waitress greeted them with concern. "Are you okay, Honey?"

Daisy managed to nod.

"She wanted some fresh night air. Now, let's see if we can persuade her to eat a little."

"That's the right idea. I'll get your plates. I put them back in the kitchen to keep them warm."

She bustled away, and Peter leaned over to whisper in Daisy's ear, "For Pete's sake, eat like you're sick, not like a wolfhound."

She grinned up at him. "Can we take a doggie bag?"

"Yes, and I'll buy you breakfast by the gulf in Corpus Christi if you'll behave yourself for what's left of tonight."

Chapter 6

They reached Corpus Christi at seven in the morning and ate in a little café next to the beach.

Peter smiled at her. "I thought I'd picked up a truck driver by the way you've been eating." His good-natured teasing brought a smile to her lips. "Do you feel as tired as you were?"

"No, much better," she answered.

"Good. Your body is at least recovering from your ordeal. Now, tell me how you are doing otherwise."

"What do you mean?"

"Emotionally?"

"I'm okay. I know I've just got to do what's got to be done. I'm not so panicky feeling."

"Spiritually?"

"I trust God. He got me out of there. It took three years, but if I'd left a day before, I wouldn't have had you to help me." She smiled at him shyly. "Thank you. You really did rescue me."

"Bring on the dragons, fair lady. I haven't had so much fun since Scram accidentally sold Dad's prize stallion at an auction for fifty bucks, and I had to get him back before Dad found out."

"Did you do it?"

"Yes, Ma'am," he drawled, grinning at her.

"It would be so wonderful to have family. I'm going to get married and have lots of children so they can play with each other and not be lonely and always have each other to run to." She was staring out at the gulf. Peter thought she didn't even realize she had expressed her dream out loud.

"We're going to be later than I thought getting to Dooley. Come on."

Daisy hesitated.

"Maybe I shouldn't go with you to Dooley."

Peter held his breath. He had feared they would have to cross this bridge. He had prepared some mighty good arguments.

"You see," she continued, "my plan is that at every place I stop, nobody from where I was will know where I've gone. That way I won't be linked from one place to the next. I'll change my name and work at a different occupation so they won't always look for a waitress."

"Daisy, even if your drunken father files a missing person report, you're twenty-one; you don't have to go back to him."

Daisy stared down at her empty plate. This was going to be hard. She had thought that the lies she had practiced would flow from her mouth. The last thing she wanted to do was lie again to Peter. The glib tales stuck in her throat.

"You don't know him," she said simply.

"If you tell the law your reason for being afraid, they will protect you."

"Forever, Peter? They can't watch one person forever, and he would wait."

Her eyes met his, and he saw the fear there.

"Come on," he said abruptly. He stood up and reached for her arm. "We'll talk in the car."

They were five miles out of town before he spoke again.

"Daisy, I just can't let you go off by yourself. You come to Dooley and get a job, and I can keep my eye on you. Wouldn't you like to know there is someone to come to if your father shows up?"

"Yes," she answered truthfully. The prospect of facing Uncle Jacob, or even Dr. French, left her breathless.

"I'll pretend I don't even know you, so no one will know that I brought you to town, and no one will know where you came from."

"Just for a little while," she conceded and did not notice the slow smile that spread across Peter's face. "My plan is to only stay two or three months in one place."

"Are you going to do that for the rest of your life?"

"No, just until I change enough. I have to gain weight and change the color of my hair. And, I have to figure out what kind of clothes I'm going to wear. Before I would have picked soft pastel colors. I like ruffles and lace. But I thought I'd try bold colors now. And, when I change my hair color, that will affect the colors I should wear."

Peter grinned. There were times when Daisy could have been voicing the thoughts of any of his three sisters, except he never heard one of them wanting to gain weight.

"It seems like you're going to a lot of trouble. If there is a description of you, the police will only be interested for a few weeks," Peter pointed out. "Then their minds will be filled with the latest happenings, and you'll be history."

"He'll send out a private detective, maybe a lot of them. And there might be a reward."

Peter raised his eyebrows.

"He's got a lot of money," she explained, not mentioning that a great deal of it was really hers.

"Daisy, did you take anything with you when you left? Something that he could claim you stole?"

"No, I didn't take anything."

"Then I still say you are safe. He can't kidnap you."

Silence met his proclamation. He looked over at her. She stared out the front window, and he could only see her profile. Clearly, kidnapping was exactly what she thought her drunken father would do.

In his dealings with his sisters, he had learned some procedures that guaranteed cooperation. He decided to call upon his old expertise.

"Well, we'll stop at the next town, and I'll get you the hair dye. What color do you want?"

She turned unbelieving eyes to him.

He continued, "I'd better get a scarf to cover your head until you've had a chance to dye it. I can't think how we could get it dyed before we get there. It's a shame we didn't think of it while we were in the motel."

"Thank you," she whispered, her eyes still filled with disbelief.

"You just remember to get in touch with me if you're in trouble. I'll give you several numbers where you can reach me or leave a message." He took a hand off the steering wheel and covered one of hers, giving it a squeeze. "Promise?"

"I promise."

"And, you won't take off without telling me good-bye, no matter what?"

She didn't respond, and he squeezed her hand again. "Promise?" he demanded.

"I promise."

"Good. There's a drugstore up here in the next town that should be open."

※

They parked about a mile outside of Dooley.

"Now when you get to town, go to Rio Street. It'll be right after the bank. Turn left and go to the third block. There's a big white house on the corner. That's the McKays'. They have two pieces of rental property behind their place, and the little servants' quarters house has been for rent since the beginning of summer. If that rented while I was out of town, Mrs. McKay will help you find a place.

"Go there first and dye your hair. Put on that new dress and get out and find a job."

He reached in his rear pant pocket to pull out his wallet. He took three one-hundred-dollar bills out of it and handed them to Daisy. She gasped.

"I don't like traveler's checks," he explained.

"I can't take this," Daisy objected.

"It's already in your hand, and I'm not taking it back. We'll call it a loan. If you don't get a chance to pay it back to me, you can give it to someone in trouble years from now, and we'll consider it even."

"You've been so good to me. I've thanked God a hundred times for you."

"We sit here much longer and it'll blow the whole thing. Someone will drive by and recognize my car. Now, hop out."

She did and got the suitcase out of the back. Peter had explained to her that she had to have luggage and a purse to avoid suspicion. The suitcase only had one dress in it. He had bought it and brought it back to the car with the suitcase, purse, and hair dye. He instructed her to buy more clothes in Dooley, and he told her the two cheapest stores to go to.

"Wait," he called just as she turned to leave. "Tuck your hair in the front. It's showing again."

She obeyed.

"See you later, Daisy."

"Remember, you don't know me," she warned.

"I'll remember." He turned the key in the ignition and left her trudging down the road. He glanced in the rearview mirror. Not know her? He'd never be able to forget her.

Chapter 7

Peter Hudson warded off the enthusiastic greeting of his hound, Sidney, and went straight to the phone. The dog persisted in demanding a proper greeting, and Peter's vague words and absentminded pats did little to satisfy him. Sidney sat at Peter's feet as he perched on the edge of his desk and fumbled through a rolling address gadget. It took him a minute to find the Dallas number he wanted. Impatiently, he dialed it and fumed when he had to leave a message to have the call returned.

Sidney sighed heavily, and Peter looked down at his faithful and momentarily disgruntled companion. Disappointment dragged at the basset's already woebegone expression. Mournful eyes gazed up at him, and the long droopy ears limply hung beside the melancholy expression. The fleeting joy of greeting, the exuberance of his welcome were past. Old Sidney was now in his regular hangdog mode. Peter slipped into his leather chair and reached down to caress the dog's ears and neck with the proper affection due to man's best friend.

"Old boy," commented Peter, "I've got a problem and the problem is female. And the female has a problem."

Sidney leaned into the massaging hand and offered a deep-throated rumble that sounded very much like sympathy.

"Our uncomplicated bachelor life may undergo some severe trials."

Mail had piled up on Peter's desk, and he sorted through it, finding it hard to keep his mind on the mundane business. In an effort to get his mind off the multitude of questions, he called his office to get a rundown from his secretary on what had transpired since she contacted him the day he left Denver.

"It sure took you a long time to get home, Mr. Hudson," Mrs. Wilson complained. "If you hadn't shown up today, I was going to contact the state troopers to look for you."

"That would have complicated matters," he said under his breath.

"Pardon?" said Mrs. Wilson.

"Oh, nothing. I just ran into some hitches." Was Daisy technically a hitchhiker or a stowaway? Was one land and one water? Or was it determined by how you got on board?

"Mr. Hudson, I asked you if you had car trouble." Mrs. Wilson's querulous voice came over the line.

"No, just a flat tire. But things like that can lead to complications." He smiled, then decided to leave the subject. "Come by the house on your way to lunch and pick up these papers from Denver to type. You can bring me the Henderson deal to look over."

"Yes, Sir."

As soon as he hung up, Peter knew he was still at the mercy of his chaotic thoughts. He sat back in his leather desk chair and stared for a moment at the ceiling. He had only one recourse under the circumstances. If he could not control his thinking, he'd better turn it over to Someone more capable. He grinned as he bowed his head to submit his will to his Maker and ask for guidance.

✻

The expected phone call finally came.

"Hello, Uncle Henry, I'm in need of your help."

"Sure, Peter, anything I can do."

"I want someone investigated, and I want it done quietly."

"This sounds very interesting, Peter. You don't usually get involved in this sort of thing. Do you suspect one of your business contacts has gotten into something shady?"

"No, Uncle Henry. I've fallen in love, and I think the girl is in big trouble, but I can't get her to tell me everything yet."

There was dead silence on the other end. Peter waited. Finally, his uncle's calm Texas drawl came back on the line.

"You better give me some details, Son. We'll see what we can do."

"I can't tell you her name. I'm pretty sure she lied to me about that. I picked her up in the panhandle about twenty miles north of Dalhart, on Highway 385. She was at a rest stop there. She was wearing a dress that looks like she'd been in some kind of institution, a uniform of some sort. Good quality, not what you would expect from a prison. And she's too old to have been in a private school, although that was the quality of the dress. It had a name stamped on the inside collar, but it was blurred. The middle word was Estate with a capital 'E.' The first word started with 'Fr' and had four more letters I couldn't make out. The next two words were a disaster. I couldn't make out the third one, and as to the last word, I'd guess eight or nine letters and the last one looked like an 'l,' or the number one."

"Okay, I've got that down. Now, are you going to satisfy your favorite uncle's curiosity?"

Peter complied, telling all, even to the point of the moment when he knew he loved her, in the school bus shelter.

"Uncle Henry, she is a naïve idiot. If someone doesn't take care of her, I swear the big bad wolf will come out of the woods and carry her off."

"But why do you have to be the one to protect her?"

"Because I've gone swimming in those big, sad eyes," Peter answered matter-of-factly. "If I'm wrong about her, I'll eat my hat and pull myself together. I don't

380

intend to be made a chump of by a pretty little thing who's got a real good act." Peter paused, contemplating his own words. "I can't convince myself that she's not on the level, and I'm willing to go out on a limb to find out. See what you can find out on solid ground, and be ready to throw me the lifeline if I fall out of the tree into a lake of lament." His voice had lightened as he expressed his serious feelings under the guise of humor.

"Okay, Son," answered the lawyer. "I'm convinced you've got it bad when you start spouting bad poetic dribble. You've always been a sensible fellow. I don't know many young scalawags who manage to lose their hearts and keep their heads. I'll put a private detective who is very discreet on this one and call as soon as I have news." Peter heard the old man sigh. "I guess I just have to say it, even though your words sound like you're standing firm. Pray this one through, Peter. Don't leave God out of this most important decision of your life. We both know how many miserable unions there are out there. Love and marriage are more crucial than any executive decision you'll ever make in your entire illustrious business career."

"I know, Uncle Henry," Peter agreed with a wry grin. "Your sermon also reminds me that I have other people who care enough about me to be praying I make the right moves."

"You're right there, Boy. You know I'll share all this with your beautiful aunt."

"I didn't think you'd even try to keep it from your wife. That would be impossible—and we leave the impossible to God, right?"

"Right." His uncle's rich chuckle came over the line.

Peter hung up feeling relieved. He wondered how long the investigation would take. He wondered how Daisy looked in her dark auburn hair. Had she found a job? Did she go shopping for bold colors or pastels? What was she going to eat for dinner? Did that little servants' quarters come with pots and pans? What if she skipped town on him? He knew the answer to that one. He grinned. He'd be sending out more private detectives to track down one idiotic waif.

Chapter 8

Finding the McKay residence was no problem. But Mrs. McKay was the mothering sort, and she wanted very much to take this shy young thing under her wing. She would have liked to know all of Daisy's troubles.

Daisy merely said, "I was unhappy at home, so I ran away. I want to find a job and be my own boss."

Mrs. McKay nodded wisely. "There's a position open at the café."

"A waitress?" Daisy could not believe her good fortune.

"Yes. Do you have experience?"

Daisy's face fell. "No, none."

"Well, you go down and ask anyway." Mrs. McKay gave her an encouraging pat on the shoulder.

Daisy let Mrs. McKay's pleasant voice wash over her as she turned her attention to the servants' quarters. The small white house looked like an elaborate playhouse built for a rich child. There were two rooms, the bathroom and the front room. The bathroom had a shower and no tub. This small room also held a tiny closet with a row of shelves down one of the inside walls. It was fortunate Daisy had very little clothing to store in the cubbyhole.

The front room had a hide-a-bed sofa, and Mrs. McKay showed Daisy how to pull it out. The fabric on it was not new, but it was clean and comfortable, even if the odd shade of yellow did clash with the golden rug.

A small metal table with one painted navy blue wooden chair sat in the kitchen area. One counter had a sink. The other had an abbreviated refrigerator under it that wasn't even three feet tall. The "stove" was a hot plate and a toaster oven.

Cream-colored lace curtains covered the windows, and cheap pictures hung on the walls. Daisy, who had visited the finest art galleries and museums in Europe, thought the roses and kittens were adorable. Pots and pans and dishes nestled in the cupboards; towels and sheets sat on the shelves in the bathroom closet. Daisy was enchanted, and Mrs. McKay was happy to have a new tenant, even a noncommunicative one.

Mrs. McKay wanted to stay and talk, but Daisy was just as determined to get the scarf off her head and a new color in her hair. She told Mrs. McKay that she wanted to get settled in and go after that job at the café as soon as possible. The friendly landlady reluctantly gave up and left cross-examining her new tenant for another day.

Daisy liked the way her hair turned out. The new color seemed to add some body along with the rich, warm, reddish brown tint. She put on the new dress and admired herself in the full-length mirror on the bathroom door. Peter had chosen a soft flower print with a gathered skirt. The narrow belt fastened with a big gold buckle. Daisy smiled to herself. This was the first belt she'd had in three years; patients at the Estate were not allowed to have belts, since belts could be used for a suicide attempt. The dress was finished off with a broad white collar edged in lace and sleeves that came to just above the elbows, ending in a white cuff with the same edging of lace.

She was pleased with what she saw and wished she could show Peter. Daisy firmly reminded herself that she could not see Mr. Hudson. She didn't know him and she was supposed to be on her own.

She still wanted to do a few more things. The variety store was the closest of her stops, so she went there first. She bought makeup, underthings, two skirts, and three blouses. A sweater and a pair of jeans seemed necessary and a flannel nightgown.

Her next stop was her little house to fix up her face and put away her purchases. She hung up the clothes in the bathroom closet. *I ought to get rid of the Estate dress,* she thought, but she didn't know what to do with it. She hung it in the back of the closet and headed out to find the café.

Daisy walked through the café's door a little after four o'clock. A HELP WANTED sign still hung in the window. Daisy asked the waitress standing by the register about the job.

"My name's Polly," the friendly woman greeted her. "I'll take you to O'Brien. He's the owner and he's the cook, too. He's an old grouch. Don't let him scare you."

O'Brien glared at her and asked a few questions, but he didn't seem much interested in the answers.

At last, he turned to Polly. "Show her the ropes and get her a couple of uniforms."

She had the job, and she could start with the dinner crowd.

The gray uniform had maroon piping. One uniform was too big, but it would pass. The other fit well, but the girl who had worn it before had shortened the skirt considerably. Daisy chose to wear the one that was too big.

Polly steered her through the first scary night with lots of advice and encouragement. Daisy tried not to let her nervousness show. At ten o'clock, O'Brien sent her home with Roy, the busboy. Daisy sat back on the cracked vinyl seat of the old wreck of a car and happily let him escort her. This big and enthusiastic high school kid gabbed on about everything. Not only did his size dwarf the petite new waitress, but his monologue bowled her over. He talked all six blocks to the McKays'. By the time they pulled in the drive, Daisy knew about his girlfriend and her age and ambitions, his age—sixteen—his new driver's license, and his madness for basketball. She liked him and enjoyed his engaging foolishness.

※

The days went by and Daisy did not see Peter. She did learn about him from Polly.

"I saw Peter Hudson's back from Denver," she heard Polly tell a customer.

"He didn't bring back a bride like his father, did he?" the lady laughed.

"No, he's as single as ever, and after his daddy's big boo-boo, he may stay single forever," answered Polly.

When the woman was gone, Daisy found a chance to ask, "Who's Peter Hudson?"

"He runs the Bar 26 Ranch now that his father is retired. It's a huge spread. I forget how many thousands and thousands of acres. It's a real old ranch, goes back to a Spanish grant or something. Anyway, he's okay, pretty nice guy. They say he has other interests besides cattle, and that worries some folks. If he goes running around after all that other business stuff, he might neglect the ranch and let it fail. Not likely, though—family tradition and honor and all that kind of thing are big with the Hudsons. He's clever enough to keep the place going while juggling all the other business. He's smart."

"Why did that lady say that about bringing a bride back from Denver?"

"She was joking about the second Mrs. Ray Hudson. The first one, the mother of all the kids, died fifteen years ago, just when I was getting out of high school. Three years ago, Mr. Hudson went to Denver for a week of business and came back married to a girl younger than his son and his oldest daughter. Now, those two gallivant all over the world, and Peter runs the ranch. Folks say Mr. Ray is ashamed to be seen with her in his own town. She's spoiled and demanding and can throw some real fits."

That was all Daisy was to learn about her benefactor or his family for awhile. If Peter Hudson was keeping an eye on her, he was staying true to his word and not allowing anyone to know.

The first week of work was hard. At the Estate, she had done little but walk aimlessly about. Daisy found that she was exhausted every night when Roy took her home.

Chapter 9

Peter intended to wait until he'd heard from his uncle before he made contact with Daisy again. He hoped he'd bring her good news, that everything was not as black as she imagined, and his lawyer uncle had figured out a way to help her.

One night as he drove through town late, he noticed the lights of the diner. He had heard they had a new waitress there, and he knew it must be Daisy. At a quarter before ten, it would be closed soon. He fought the urge to see her right now, talk with her right now, and hear all that she had been through since he had left her on the road. He could go in for a cup of coffee, only that would be strange, since he had never done such a thing before. Peter told himself there was time enough later, and she'd be mad at him for trying to see her. It was foolish, an unnecessary risk. He parked down the road to wait and watch.

He had purposely kept away. He had hoped if he didn't see her, he could dispel the strong emotion that drove him to protect her. It hadn't worked. Now, he waited in his dark car, lurking in the shadows, of all things. He just wanted to see that she was all right, though. He wouldn't offer her a lift or anything so foolhardy. This was a very small town, and someone would be bound to see them. Nobody did anything without it going through the grapevine. He'd just sit and wait. . .and maybe there would be an opportunity.

A couple of minutes before closing, Roy came out with Daisy right behind. They walked to the kid's car and got in. Peter followed them to the McKays' and again parked down the street, this time in the shadows of a huge old weeping willow. Still, he worried that someone would spot his familiar car.

Roy left as soon as Daisy was in the little house. Peter assumed from the direction he was going that he was on his way back to the café. The big McKay house was dark. The neighborhood was quiet.

Peter decided he couldn't chance a visit to Daisy. He turned on his ignition and drove home. Inside, Sidney leaped up to greet him, delightfully surprised when his master grabbed the leash and took him out for a late walk. They walked the ten blocks back to the McKays'.

Peter allowed Sidney to snuffle under the bushes as they passed. The deserted road probably had no witnesses to his nocturnal rambling, but if anyone did see him, they would just think he was out for a stroll with his dog.

Daisy was going to be irritated to see him, but he'd deal with that as it came.

Man and dog crept up the driveway of the McKays' silent home and went through the backyard.

"Well, Sidney, you're a better watchdog than Mrs. McKay's old hound," Peter told his companion, thanking God that the other dog must be sound asleep.

He knocked softly on the door of the little white house.

She opened the door almost immediately. "Peter," she exclaimed. Her voice was surprised, and the door held firmly in place was unfriendly. "I thought it was Roy. That I'd forgotten something, or he wanted to tell me one more time that everything would be okay."

"Let me in before someone sees me," Peter urged.

"No," she said. "Why are you here?"

"Because I want to talk to you, and you haven't got a phone."

"Go away."

"No," he returned. "I'm not going away until I talk to you. You'd better let me in."

She opened the door, and he stepped in, bringing a curious Sidney with him. Daisy looked down at the dog but made no comment. She walked over to the other side of the tiny room and fiddled with the curtain on the window.

Peter realized that she wasn't behaving as she ought. She was nervous. What worried him more was she kept sneaking looks at him as if she expected him to pounce on her. She seemed to think she had to keep an eye on him. Dear Lord, what's the matter? How could he help her if she'd decided he was the bogeyman?

In the light of the small living room, he saw how pale and distraught she was. She'd probably been crying earlier, though her eyes were dry now.

"What's the matter?" he asked abruptly.

"Why are you here?" She threw him a look of distrust.

"I thought we were friends. Why are you acting this way?"

"How am I acting?" she countered petulantly.

"Like I'm going to attack you."

"Men are beastly," she said emphatically. Her angry eyes met his puzzled ones.

Peter nodded as if in full agreement with Daisy's assessment of his fellow-man. He willingly condemned all of his gender. "Why don't you tell me what happened?"

"Polly says to just keep the target well out of range, so I've been trying to stand farther away from the tables when I'm serving male customers. O'Brien says I'm too sensitive. You've just got to expect that sort of thing and not make a federal case out of it."

Daisy paced up and down in front of the kitchen area now. She wrapped her arms tightly across her chest as if she were cold.

Peter silently wondered if he were picking up the clues properly and deciphering correctly the message she was sending.

"The pinches and pats I've learned to avoid now, but the first few days were terrible." She stopped by the couch and picked up a fringed throw pillow. She hugged it, avoiding Peter's eyes. "Tonight there were two guys left in the diner. I was cleaning up tables, and they called me over for their check. I had a pitcher of ice water in my hand. I was standing there talking to one of them, when the other one dropped his napkin. He leaned over to pick it up, only he put his hand on the inside of my ankle and came up my leg and under my skirt."

"What did you do?" Peter kept his voice remarkably calm in light of the rage bolting through him. Sidney responded to the underlying emotion in Peter's voice and came to his feet.

"I screamed and dumped the ice water over his head. Then I ran for the kitchen. Only I threw the pitcher up in the air, and when it came down, it landed on the tray of glasses I'd collected, and they went everywhere. I'd put the tray down on their table to tear out their check. There were broken glass and ice cubes and water all over the place."

"What did O'Brien do?"

"He went out and apologized to them! He mopped them up himself. The men were all wet and he was wiping them up and agreeing with them that I was a stupid female. He took them to the register and checked them out himself. Then he came back to the kitchen and told me I was a fool, and if I ever created such a scene when the diner was crowded, or for that matter, ever again, I'd be canned. Polly yelled at him, and Roy said it wasn't fair, so they both got yelled at, too."

"What did you do?"

"I cried. O'Brien said it was obvious I wasn't going to be any more help tonight. He yelled at Roy to take me home."

Sidney shuffled over to sit at the distressed girl's feet. She bent over and placed a hand on his silken head. His truly sympathetic gaze met hers. No one can offer as much sympathy with a look as a well-bred basset.

"I like your hair," Peter said.

"What?" Daisy looked up.

"Your hair. The color is nice. I like the way you fixed it, too."

Unconsciously, she reached up a hand to touch the soft braid in the back.

"It's called a French braid. Polly helped me do it, and she cut the bangs. I've never had hair this long, and I've never had bangs. I'm thinking about getting a permanent," she added.

"No, don't do that," he said. "When you leave here, you ought to have some money in your pocket, so you can lay over a day someplace to work on changing your identity. That's when you should do things like permanents." She listened intently. Seeing her absorbed in this possibility, he went on. "Also, you should chuck the clothes you wore the most, your favorite blouse, things like that."

"That's a good idea."

"Did you get some new clothes?"

Her face brightened with enthusiasm, and Peter once again thanked God for all the tactical training he had had, not in the Marines, but in dealing with his sisters.

"Yes, but I've hardly had a chance to wear them. I wear the uniform mostly. One is way too short."

"Mrs. McKay sews. See if she will help you take the hem out or something. Let me see what you bought."

"How do you know Mrs. McKay sews?" she asked as she went into the bathroom to the closet.

Peter sat down on the couch. Sidney settled at his feet.

"She made prom dresses for my sisters."

Daisy came out with a skirt and two blouses. The broomstick skirt had vibrant colors, a floral print. The blouses were soft and feminine. One was white with big, billowy sleeves and a broad collar. The other was pink with a tight little collar and straight sleeves that buttoned at the cuffs. Both the collar and the cuffs were trimmed neatly with a thin band of lace.

"I can wear both of these with the skirt."

Peter nodded agreeably. "They're very pretty. Were you able to get anything else?"

That sent her back to fetch another outfit. It was a denim skirt with a peach, country-cut blouse. She'd bought a matching peach scarf to tie around her waist.

Peter approved again and asked her if she had anything to drink. She offered tea. Peter said he'd take a cup if she didn't mind. Daisy saw the smile quirk the corner of his mouth and she knew he'd manipulated her, but she found she didn't care.

While she was fixing the tea, Peter stewed. Obviously, she was not capable of fending for herself. She was too trusting. Even after her scare at the diner, she had let him in. Of course, she should trust him, but it showed a too gullible nature that she just let him talk his way in the door. The more he thought about it, the more he could see that an unscrupulous fellow would be in seventh heaven with her. He couldn't let her fall into the hands of one of the local Don Juans.

When she sat beside him on the couch, he played for time by introducing his dog.

"My sisters gave him to me as a puppy when I returned from my hitch with the Marines. They felt the responsibility of owning a dog would keep me closer to home. That's what they said, anyway. I think they fell in love with him first and then thought of an excuse to keep him."

Daisy smiled down at the likable dog and reached to rub his ears. Sidney rewarded her by leaning against her leg.

Peter decided the time was right to lay out the plan he had just conceived.

"Daisy, you are going to become my girl."

She turned those wide dark eyes to his face. She wore a trace of makeup, and her hair glimmered in the light of the lamp behind the couch. He caught his breath at the sight and took a sip of the hot tea to distract himself.

"What do you mean?"

"Tomorrow I am going to come to the diner and 'meet' you for the first time. We'll take it from there. But this is the point of this maneuver—if I'm chasing you, that will put off some of the local yokels. At least, as big brother to the three gorgeous Hudson girls, I served the purpose of cooling some of their unwanted suitors. It could work in this situation."

"You don't mind?" she asked.

Peter nearly groaned out loud. She needed to be locked up for her safety.

To the best of his ability, he answered in a serious tone. "No, not a bit."

When he and Sidney left her, he promised to see her in the afternoon at the café. She told him where to sit so that it would be one of the tables she covered.

❋

At two-thirty, Peter Hudson walked into Dooley's only eatery. He said he was waiting for someone, but he'd take a cup of coffee. He seemed to ignore Daisy, and she went about her business.

Polly grabbed her arm behind the counter and whispered, "That's Peter Hudson."

Daisy lifted her eyebrows in mock surprise. "I thought rich ranchers were older and a little bald."

Polly giggled. "Well, his father is, and he has a slightly rounder belly, too. But so far, Rich Cattleman Jr. is holding up all right."

"How old do you think he is?" asked Daisy.

"I know he's twenty-nine because he graduated two years after I did from high school."

Mr. Hudson, rich cattle rancher, called her back to the table and asked her for a piece of pie. He scarcely looked up from the papers he was studying. Daisy filled up his coffee cup without being asked.

A little after three, he waved her over, asking for his check.

"Look," he said, "I was supposed to meet a man here, and he didn't show. Maybe he had car trouble. Anyway, his name is Mick Bigelow. I don't know what he looks like, but if someone comes in looking for me, would you ask his name and send this Bigelow fellow down to my office?"

"Sure," answered Daisy. "Where's your office?"

Peter looked up at her, somewhat surprised. "It's down the street on the left. The sign says Hudson Bar 26. It's next to the barber shop."

"Oh, I've seen it," Daisy acknowledged.

"You aren't from around here, are you?"

She shook her head.

"What's your name?"

"Daisy Madden."

"Welcome to Dooley, Daisy," Peter said smoothly, his smile charming and his eyes friendly. "I'm Peter Hudson."

"Thank you, Sir." She walked away.

Peter strolled to the end of the diner and spoke for a few minutes to a couple of men who were enjoying a coffee break. When he went to the register, Polly took his check and rang him up. They exchanged a few pleasant words. He started to leave as Daisy came out of the back, her hands full with a huge tray that carried five dinner plates. She was on the way to the family seated in the corner booth.

He caught her eye and spoke, "It was nice to meet you, Dixie."

He left abruptly as if he had business to attend to. Polly laughed, "Well, at least he noticed you, Dixie. I'd be willing to change my name for one of his smiles."

"I'm not planning to change my name anytime soon," Daisy replied, aware of the irony of the statement. "Daisy has suited me well for as long as I've had it." She hurried to the customers whose baby was beginning to squall.

Later that day, when they were busy with the dinner crowd, O'Brien frowned his fiercest as his three waitresses gathered around the florist box that had been delivered for Daisy.

"The box says Cutter's. That's in Browmere. It's the nearest flower shop with any class," said Gayle.

"Browmere is about twice as big as Dooley," added Polly. "Look at this box. It's straight out of the movies. There should be a dozen long-stemmed red roses in it."

"Hurry up and open it," urged Gayle.

"Yes," bellowed O'Brien. "Hurry up!"

Daisy slipped the blue ribbon and bow to the end of the box and handed it to Polly. She lifted the lid and the two girls exclaimed together, "Daisies!"

"Wow!" said Gayle. "There must be three dozen. Where are you ever going to get a vase that big?"

"Look how gigantic they are. They must be a special kind." Polly started digging around in the folds of the green paper that wrapped the stems. "Here's the card. Read it, Daisy."

Daisy opened the tiny envelope and pulled out the card. She read aloud, "Was halfway down the street when I realized my mistake, Daisy. This is so I won't slip again. Please accept my apology. Peter."

"Wow!" said Gayle.

"I'm going to 'wow' all of you if you don't get on these orders," came O'Brien's rough, angry tones from the kitchen. The girls jumped.

Fifteen minutes later, Daisy saw that someone had put her flowers in one of the diner's huge glass pitchers. They looked rather nice, if a bit crowded, on the counter next to the register.

Polly and Gayle were excited and Daisy was very quiet. Roy was the one who had found time to put the flowers in water, and he persuaded O'Brien to let her take the pitcher home when they left that night.

When he took her home, he said, "I'm going to go to college and get a real job that pays big money. Then, I'm going to send a giant bunch of flowers to whatever girl is the girl of my dreams at the moment. You should have seen your face when you opened that box."

Chapter 10

The telephone rang. Peter put down the papers he was reading and reached across his desk to pick up the receiver.

"Hello," he said.

"Hello, yourself," came the answer.

"Uncle Henry." Peter sat up, shaken from his relaxed attitude. "What did you learn?"

"I'm fine, thank you. And your aunt and cousins are doing well. Little Bobby has had the measles, but he's recovered nicely." Uncle Henry's voice was full of his particular brand of droll humor.

"Uncle Henry," Peter replied sternly, "I have been waiting for almost two weeks. Cut the funny business and tell me what you've found out."

Uncle Henry became serious. "Peter, if your gal is the one we think she is, she has got problems. First, if the background put out about her is true, she's a psychological mess and you wouldn't want to touch her with a ten-foot pole. Then, there's the other side, which is the one I lean toward. She's been given a raw deal. If my suspicions are correct, she is in a very dangerous situation."

"I'll bet it's the second scenario, Uncle Henry." Concern permeated Peter's voice. "Clue me in."

"We think she is Julie Jones. She spent the last three years in a place called the French Estate Private Hospital. She was initially admitted for trying to commit suicide overdosing on sleeping pills. The family had not been aware of a drug problem because she was schooled abroad. She has always been in boarding schools or under escort as she roamed through Europe.

"Our detective romanced an attendant from the hospital and discovered the girl had turned up missing. She was reported to the police, and private detectives were put on the trail. The attendant says the girl was calm and no trouble recently, but the first year she was a wild, hysterical patient. Of course, Dr. French's treatments have helped a lot, but it is still believed that she is highly suicidal.

"Peter, it is my belief that if they find her, she will conveniently die by her own hand."

"Why?" Peter asked in horror.

"She was put in that hospital by her uncle and declared incompetent. He has control of the business left to her. A very lucrative business, by the way. I've had the uncle checked out. His name is Jacob Jones. He is not a nice man either in business or at home."

"Mafia?" Peter questioned.

"He has no compunctions with whom he does business, but he is really a small fish in their eyes and on the outside of their close-knit circle."

"Well, I guess that's something to be thankful for. Where does he live?"

"New York. But the home ground is Indiana."

"I didn't think anybody with really big money came out of Indiana."

Uncle Henry laughed. "Apparently, he doesn't, either. And he wants to be as rich and powerful as they come, so he moved on to more promising ground. He's beginning to have a very strong hand in government. If his niece is found and her inheritance restored, he will lose three-quarters of his wealth."

"What do you suggest?"

"Do you think the girl is crazy?"

"Naïve and gullible, but not crazy," Peter returned.

"If she comes out to claim her inheritance, she's got to have help. They could whip her out of sight and into another hospital. Or she could have another suicide attempt that doesn't fail. The court has awarded her uncle protective custody. We wouldn't have a legal foot to stand on if he opted to take her away. As it is now, he'd be doing it for her own good in the eyes of the law."

"What are we going to do?"

"Well, we're going to have to prove her case before they find her. I'm already working on that. I think I can get enough evidence to unmask that phony hospital. I wonder how many other rich patients are incarcerated there. I'll work on that, and you work on keeping her out of sight and safe."

"Right. How long is this going to take?"

"I've no idea, Peter."

※

Peter had been to the diner twice, but he chose times when he knew Daisy would not be there. This caused the talk he wanted. He'd never been a regular customer of the diner and it was suspicious that he should start popping in. The gossips of the town were speculating, and that suited him fine.

The third trip, he caught her at work, and as he left, he asked her when her day off was.

"Tomorrow," she answered.

"I'm going to Corpus tomorrow. How about going with me, and I'll take you out to dinner?"

"I'd like that," she said demurely. A quizzical little smile played at the corner of her mouth, and her eyes twinkled with secret laughter. He looked at her and wondered what kind of monster would want to hurt her.

"Fine. I'll pick you up at nine-thirty tomorrow morning. Is that too early?

I have to do some business in town."

"That's fine, but don't you want to know where I live?"

He laughed. "You haven't ever lived in a town this small before. I found out where you lived the day after I met you."

He left, and Polly and Gayle descended upon her.

"Wow!" said Gayle. "You play your cards right, Honey," she advised. "He's worth something. Not just money, either. He's a nice guy."

"Why didn't he come to my house to ask me out?" Daisy asked.

Polly shrugged. "Who knows for sure? Maybe because of nosy Mrs. McKay, although they know each other fairly well. Most of us know Mrs. McKay. She taught Sunday school for years. Anyone who grew up in Bayside Church had a couple of years of her, stories and all."

Gayle hadn't attended the Bayside Church so she had a different opinion. "Maybe he thought you'd be spooked if he just showed up at your door. I mean, think how awkward it would be. You couldn't just ask in someone who is practically a stranger."

Polly agreed. "He's never been the rich playboy type. But you wouldn't know that. He could have been thinking of your reputation, too."

"You're going to have the reputation for being out of work if you don't stop jawing and get busy!" A familiar bellow interrupted the girls' conversation.

Daisy continued to think about what the other two had said. What would they think of her adventure on the road when Peter picked her up, fed her, gave her a place to sleep, and gave her money and clothes? Thinking along the lines of not even letting a "stranger" into her little house, Daisy thought perhaps she had been even more blessed by God than she realized. Her story might have been a lot different if a villain had come to her aid instead of a hero.

Chapter 11

Dark clouds and a chilly wind had turned the day dreary when Peter knocked on Daisy's door the next morning. She wore the dress he had picked out for her and the sweater from the Estate.

"Is that all you've got to keep warm?" he asked her gruffly.

"Coats are expensive," she answered.

"Well, we'll look for one in Corpus."

"You can't buy me a coat," Daisy objected.

"I didn't intend to. Do you have your money with you?"

She shook her head.

"Daisy, no woman from Dooley goes to Corpus without her pocketbook as full as she can get it. Go back in and get your money."

She returned shortly, clutching her purse.

"Was it under the mattress?" he asked.

"No, folded in the sheets in the closet. I kept it in the hide-a-bed last week." She looked up at him with that complete lack of duplicity that wrenched his heart. In order to relieve the pain, he bent over, brushing his lips quickly and gently across hers. She gave a small gasp. Her eyes widened and her mouth fell open just a tiny bit, enough to accentuate her attraction.

"Oh," he groaned and grabbed her by the arm, propelling her down the backyard sidewalk to the driveway where he was parked. "Let's get moving. I'm drowning."

"What?" she asked, not sure she heard him right.

"Nothing," he responded. "I'll have my uncle Henry explain it to you someday."

On the way to Corpus Christi, Peter outlined his plans for the day. They'd eat lunch first, since it took about two hours to get there and that would put them in Corpus at lunchtime. Then he had a business meeting at one. He'd called his sister Lisa, and she was going to meet them at the museum. Daisy and Lisa could go shopping together while he worked.

"Is that a good idea?" Daisy wondered aloud.

"I thought shopping was always a good idea." Peter was puzzled.

"I mean meeting your sister. I'm not supposed to make a lot of friends who could accidentally betray me."

"Don't give her any information."

"I've gotten good at that." Daisy grinned with mischief in her eye.

"You have?"

"Yes." Daisy giggled, pleasing Peter's heart. "Mrs. McKay gives me lots of practice. She comes over bound and determined to find out all about me. I ask her one question about one of her kids, though, and I'm safe for an hour and a half. I'll bet I could write that woman's family history."

Peter laughed, too. His knowledge of the dear lady backed up Daisy's claim.

"It works a charm on everyone," Daisy continued. "Polly is always curious, but her boyfriends are more interesting than where I came from and what I used to do."

"The reason I want you to hang around my sister," explained Peter, "is because it ruins the image of a lady with a mysterious past. Would I take you to go shopping with my sister if I had even a suspicion of something shady in your past?"

"Peter." The tone of her voice made him turn to look at her. "How do you know I don't?"

He pulled the car to the side of the road and turned off the engine. He prayed that she was ready to tell him the truth. He sat with his hands on the wheel, giving the moment to God before he turned back to look into those questioning eyes. He had no idea what to tell her. If he told her he knew the truth, he would also have to tell her how much danger she was in. If she took off like a scared rabbit, how was he going to even begin to protect her? He was frightened to think how unguarded she was, even with him watching from a distance.

He put his arm around her shoulders, drawing her closer to him. His hand cupped under her chin, he tilted her head just a little more in order to receive his kiss. It was a soft kiss, but her lips warmed beneath his and responded. He tightened his hold on her and felt the need to always be her guardian. Her arms came around his neck, and he knew she was enjoying the same warmth that he was.

He pulled back and looked at her. Her cheeks were flushed rosy and her eyes had a dreamy, unfocused look.

"Understand?" he asked.

She nodded. Abruptly her expression changed. She sat up, drawing away from him.

"No, I don't understand," she said.

"I trust you because I've opened up my life to you. Without trusting you, I wouldn't have allowed you into the position where you could hurt me. I don't expect you to be perfect or to have a past without a blemish. I do expect you to hold this trust with the care I know you are capable of. I know you would never deliberately hurt me any more than I would hurt you."

"It scares me," she said.

"Why?"

"It's not part of my plan."

396

"Daisy, check that plan out with God. I know you believe in Him, but do you trust Him? Are you giving Him all your troubles, the big ones and the day-to-day ones?"

"Trust again." She sighed.

"Love and trust are bound together."

"I figure God's taking care of anyone looking for me. I think He expects me to take care of myself."

"He expects you to depend on Him in every area. He's a God who takes care of details. Do you know in the Bible it says when the fisherman brought in that unbelievable catch, there were 153 large fish? Mrs. McKay taught me that story— and she said God knew about little boys because every year the boys wanted to know how many fish there were, and God included the information.

"He cares about lost coins, wine at a wedding. Yes, He raised Lazarus from the dead, but He also stopped to be friendly to children. Trust Him with all the little details."

Daisy listened to Peter. She had rarely had anyone with whom to discuss her ideas about Christianity. She wanted time to think about what he had said.

Peter heaved a sigh. He didn't know how well he had expressed his beliefs. Had he reached beyond that fence she had guarding her heart?

"Daisy, let me help with your plans."

"For a little while," she said guardedly.

Peter fought the urge to lay into her with arguments and logic and all the things that lost battles for him when he handled his sisters.

"Okay," he said. He turned on the engine. They continued their journey. He prayed they were on the right path. He prayed they could go through life on one path, so that when one fell, the other would be there to help.

※

They ate at a seafood restaurant. Peter explained that to have all new clothes whenever she turned up someplace would be conspicuous. Shopping at Goodwill or Salvation Army would be cheaper and the clothes from these places would be less noticeable.

Peter left her in his sister's care, instructing both girls to go to Goodwill first. Lisa was a wiry girl with dark, flashing eyes and bouncing brown hair.

"Humph!" said Lisa as her older brother drove away. "He's always like that, Daisy. He orders you around like you couldn't make one decision for yourself."

"No, I need to shop at Goodwill, Lisa," Daisy explained. "I don't have much money and I need a winter coat. He was just telling you where I wanted to go."

"Well, don't let him bully you. He has a big-brother complex. Anything small and feminine ought to be bossed around. He lost more girlfriends that way in college. We were at school together for a few years, but would he listen to advice from a little sister?"

"I'm glad he didn't. He might have been married by now."

"Oh, ho!" exclaimed Lisa with a glimmer of triumph in her eye. She was always happy to ferret out information on her older brother. As much as she liked to tease him, she loved him and was concerned over his perpetual bachelorhood. "Does he have it as bad for you as you do for him?"

"I don't know," answered Daisy truthfully.

"No girl ever does," observed Lisa sagely. "But, I'll tell you that my brother is a good egg even though he comes on strong as the mighty protector of the weak and lowly. He'd make a great husband and father."

"I don't know if it will ever get that far." Daisy had a worried look in her eye. "It would take a miracle to work out all the details. And I don't think I could be weak and lowly for the rest of my life."

"That's a good show of spirit." Lisa laughed and then gave her attention to the traffic for a few minutes as she maneuvered through a narrow street. When she spoke again, she was serious.

"I believe in a God that is still doing miracles, do you?"

"Yes," said Daisy. "Definitely."

"Then He'll take care of those details. Where do you want to shop?"

"Goodwill," answered Daisy.

"All right," Lisa conceded. "Goodwill first, but then we'll go someplace I choose."

They met Peter at the appointed hour and transferred Daisy's purchases to his car trunk.

"Did you buy out the stores?" questioned Peter.

"No, your friend here needs lessons in shopping with abandon," said Lisa.

"And I know the expert who would volunteer to instruct her in the finer arts of blowing a wad," returned Peter.

Lisa laughed. "Why don't you two come home and eat dinner with John and me? It'll make you late getting home, but we'd love to have you."

Peter looked at Daisy and raised his eyebrows, questioning. She nodded.

"Okay, we'll follow you."

It was the first time Daisy had eaten in someone's home since she had been sent away to school. At first, she felt shy, but Lisa lured her into the kitchen and set her to work making the salad. When Lisa next paid attention to what her guest was doing, her eyes popped.

"That's some salad," she exclaimed, looking at the big bowl artistically arranged with flowered radishes, curled carrots, celery frayed at the end to look like wands, bell peppers cut in rings with cherry tomatoes as centers, and cauliflower buds accentuating their colors.

"I went to cooking school once. I really did well in soups, but I almost flunked pastries. I made an apple pie that the senior chef couldn't put his fork through."

"How are you on gravy?"

"Clear or creamed?"

"Clear," said Lisa.

"Let me at it. I finally conquered lumps in the other, but it's been too long. I'd probably produce something that looked akin to dumplings."

The two couples enjoyed the dinner; and when they left, Peter stopped so they could walk on the beach before they went home. Beautiful moonlight did nothing to offset the bone-chilling cold, but Daisy wore her Goodwill coat. The quilted fabric reached down past her knees, and the nylon fabric rustled as she walked. She shivered.

Peter noticed and gathered her into his arms.

"It's crazy to be walking out here tonight, but I just don't want to take you back yet." He kissed her, and when she pulled away from him, he was surprised.

"I don't want to fall in love with you, Peter," she pleaded, as if he could do something about it.

"Isn't it too late?" he asked. She didn't answer. He gave her a little shake. "Answer me. Isn't it too late?"

"Yes," she admitted and threw her arms around his neck.

Chapter 12

The diner would be closed for Thanksgiving. Peter's sisters, by tradition, always tried to be home for the holiday, and Peter had invited Daisy to the feast.

He was happy with the prospect, but he soon detected a note of reserve in Daisy's attitude.

"What's the matter?" he asked. They sat on her couch, and Sidney had persuaded her with his typical woebegone expression to allow him up on the couch as well. He lounged in luxury with his head in her lap.

Peter didn't want to leave Daisy even though the hour was growing late. This was not unusual. The talk of the town was how hard the cattleman had fallen. They had been dating for three weeks, and where he went, she went. He took her to church; he took her grocery shopping; when he could, he ate breakfast, lunch, and dinner at the café. She traveled with him on her days off, riding in the pickup over the range or tagging along as he did business in the neighboring towns. Now Peter Hudson, cattleman, had two faithful companions: the furry beast they were used to seeing and the much more beautiful waitress from O'Brien's diner.

"What do you mean?" she asked.

"Every time I mention Thanksgiving, you get tense," he explained.

"You have so much family." She tried to explain. "The only ones I know are John and Lisa. It's a bit overwhelming to meet so many people at once, and I really don't know much about Thanksgiving."

"You don't know much about Thanksgiving?" Peter sounded incredulous.

"No, I never. . ." She broke off. This was leading to dangerous territory. In Europe, Thanksgiving wasn't celebrated. "We didn't do holidays much in our house." That was certainly true. Daisy hedged further. "There didn't seem much point when there wasn't any love."

Peter remained quiet. Maybe she was ready to tell him the truth.

"There wasn't ever anybody to share that sort of thing. All this is foreign to me as if it were the custom of a different country." Again the many lonely holidays spent abroad grew vivid in her memory. "Does it make sense to tell you it makes me homesick? It makes me homesick for things that happened before I was eight years old, and I really don't have many clear memories of that time."

Peter hugged her to him. "Tell me what it was like. What did you do for holidays?"

She jumped out of his arms. Sidney slid to the floor and gave her a disgusted look; she usually was very polite about removing him from her lap before she got up. Daisy paced the floor.

Peter watched in growing frustration. He wanted to catch her and make her give up all the pretense that stood between them.

"I can't, Peter," she cried.

Her desperation crumbled his resolve. He stood up and intercepted her. She grasped his arms tightly in her hands and looked earnestly into his eyes.

"I can't lie to you anymore, Peter. I just can't tell you even one more lie. So much of what you know about me is half-truths. I can't tell you anything at all."

"Why can't you tell me the truth?" he asked quietly.

"Because I love you."

"That doesn't make sense, Daisy." He tried to keep the irritation out of his voice. "I love you, and taking care of you is a God-given responsibility that comes along with that love."

"You might get in trouble, too."

"I'm a big boy," he said, trying to lighten her mood. "Let me tackle the troubles."

She looked down at the floor and shook her head sadly. He came very close to shaking her. His failure to break through her reluctance to include him in all her life chafed against the patience he knew he must maintain.

He gathered her in his arms and held her fiercely. *God, I need Your control. Tell me what to say, what to do.*

"Peter." Daisy interrupted his silent prayer. "Would you go home now? I can't think when you're here, and I'm all mixed up."

He was silent, not answering. Finally, she looked up to find him watching her.

"Please," she said.

He nodded, his face stern and his jaw set.

"Please don't look like that. I don't know what you're thinking."

"I'm thinking I should spank you."

"I don't think it would help." Her face wore a wistful smile.

"Neither do I, or you'd be across my knee this minute." He kissed her gruffly and grabbed his coat. "Don't do anything foolish, Daisy. Remember your promise. You won't ever leave without saying good-bye."

"I remember."

He left, feeling unsettled.

❋

Thanksgiving Day, he picked Daisy up at ten. She had asked him what to wear, and he had suggested the flowered skirt and a blouse would fit in with what his sisters would be wearing. When they arrived out at the country ranch house, she immediately noted the sisters wore casual clothing, nice but casual.

Lisa took her around to introduce her, and the feeling of being out of place soon passed. A Hudson family trait was hospitality. She felt accepted by the members of Peter's family.

Scram was nearly as tall as Peter. Lisa said she stole all the height in the family, just as she had stolen everybody's makeup or hair curlers or anything else she had needed.

Tiger and Tabitha won her heart.

"If we are really, really good," Tabitha confided, "we get to stay up late and listen to the grown-ups talk."

Tiger nodded solemnly and added, "If we blow it, we get a spanking."

"You got that right," affirmed his father, Joe, good-naturedly.

Lovely and sophisticated Midge spoke with more reserve than her sisters. She had a warm smile and welcomed Daisy generously, but she didn't have that lively sense of humor that bubbled out of the other two sisters. Daisy labeled her serene in her mind. Midge's husband, Mike, was quiet, too.

The surprise was the presence of Uncle Henry and Aunt Harriet, who was often called Aunt Harry. They had their eight-year-old grandson, Bobby, with them. They had decided to join the family gathering because Uncle Henry had some business to discuss with Peter, and it had been too long since he'd seen his future law partner, Midge.

Lisa hauled Daisy into the kitchen of the house where Peter had grown up. Their father's home stood empty most of the time, but the girls had thrown it open for the holiday and brought in a supply of groceries.

"Dad and Suzanne are rarely here anymore," Lisa explained. "And I don't think Suzanne is too keen on cooking when she is here. They were in Florida a week ago. Dad called to say hello. I told him about you."

"About me? What could you tell him about me?" inquired Daisy as she peeled potatoes.

"That Peter had finally found someone who seemed willing enough to be perpetually bossed."

"Peter really doesn't do that," Daisy defended.

"Humph!" replied Lisa. "I think love has put wax in your ears."

"He just knows so much more than I do." Daisy tried another tactic.

"Oh, brother," exclaimed Lisa. "No wonder you've got him wrapped around your little finger."

Lisa caught the look of confusion on Daisy's face and gave her a sisterly hug. "Don't worry, Kid," she said. "I think it's the best thing that could have happened to him."

Scram and Midge soon joined them to help in the food preparation. Frivolous talk and banter bounced around the busy room. The sisters teased and laughed without hurt feelings. Daisy enjoyed listening to their lighthearted bantering.

The atmosphere in the kitchen was entirely new to her, and she loved it. She busied herself with the tasks they gave her and listened, rarely contributing to the conversation.

"Daisy," Scram spoke to her, "Lisa says you went to cooking school. Where was that?"

Daisy had heard, but she feigned absorption in her task and didn't answer.

"Hey, Daisy," Lisa hollered. Daisy turned reluctantly. "Scram has asked you twice where you went to cooking school."

"Oh. . .oh," she stammered and smiled shyly, "I was just thinking about Peter." She made sure her voice was adequately dreamy without going over the edge to ridiculous. A starry look hovered on her face. "Isn't it funny what some men will eat? Peter picks me up after work and takes me home. Almost every night he stays and has scrambled eggs. I've cooked them in so many different ways, I could write an egg cookbook. His cholesterol will be sky-high. You'd think he'd get tired of scrambled eggs."

The sisters exchanged knowing looks. Daisy pretended not to notice. She'd given them two topics of conversation: men and their eating habits, or health and cholesterol. They chose what men will eat and completely forgot about where Daisy went to school. They were still talking about it when they set dinner on the table.

Daisy sat between Uncle Henry and Peter during dinner. When they held hands with the person next to them and bowed heads to pray, she nearly cried, so moved was she by the love that flowed among them. She had heard that where three or more were gathered, Jesus was in their midst, but she had never before experienced that extraordinary warmth of fellowship. She was surprised that Uncle Henry thanked God for her presence and asked for protection and guidance for her. Again she fought the tears; only by thinking how embarrassed she would be to burst into tears among these kind people did she control the flood.

Dinner began in earnest, and Daisy covered her emotional response under the guise of passing and scooping the delicious dishes. She longed to be swallowed up by this family, forever cosseted within their circle of fellowship.

Uncle Henry quietly asked her polite questions that she turned away by encouraging him to talk about himself. This time she hungered for more information about the family because each little tidbit made her feel more connected. She still used her technique to deflect his getting to know anything about her background, but she was aware that she was establishing an affinity that was priceless to her lonely soul.

After dinner, Daisy joined the ladies in the kitchen for cleanup. Uncle Henry and Peter hid themselves away in the study to discuss business. She didn't know she was the business.

Chapter 13

"I don't think she's as dumb as you think," Uncle Henry told Peter.

"Wait, the way I remember the conversation, I particularly told you she is not dumb," he objected.

"Naïve, you said naïve. And I'm examining that adjective as well. I tried to get her to talk about herself, and I found myself telling her about our last vacation, and Bobby's loose tooth, and the Sunday school picnic last July."

Peter laughed. "She's beautiful, isn't she?"

"I assume that is a rhetorical question. She is very pretty, Peter, but she is in a lot of trouble. Is she still not telling you all?"

Peter shook his head.

"That surprises me."

Peter sighed. "I had hoped by now she would trust me."

"Are you sure it is a matter of trust, or does she love you so much she wants to protect you?" Uncle Henry asked.

"Protect me?" Peter sounded astonished by the idea.

"Yes, Peter," chided the older man. "Others in God's kingdom can be inspired by the noble desire to protect the ones they love."

"Have you found out anything useful?" Peter decided to turn down a different path of conversation.

"What we have discovered is indeed interesting."

"So tell me," demanded Peter.

"There are fifteen patients presently at the French Estate. According to our investigations, which are not complete, seven of those poor individuals have a similar history. It is most convenient for someone to have them out of the way. The someone, in each case, just happens to be paying the hefty bill."

"Can you prove it?" was Peter's urgent question.

"Some of it is circumstantial. But there is enough that is solid and too many coincidences to be ignored. By the time we take it to the district attorney, they won't have a chance."

"What about Daisy?"

"You mean Julie. She'll ride along with the others. Jacob Jones will not dare touch her. The scandal alone will protect her from future attempts."

"You don't think we can get him behind bars?"

"That's what I'm aiming for, but I'm realistic enough to know when there is that much power and money involved, things don't always turn out equitably."

"Final justice comes from God, and no one escapes that," stated Peter. He shook his head, thinking about those people dependent on plain old human justice. "Uncle Henry, how in the world do these patients get there? I mean, if I wanted to dispose of one of my darling little sisters, how would I know there was an accommodating private hospital in the panhandle of Texas that would be willing to lock away my problem for that hefty fee you mentioned?"

Uncle Henry's odd sense of humor took over. He raised his bushy eyebrows in a comical questioning attitude. "Do you suppose this man French has an advertisement in the *Wall Street Journal* or the *New York Times*?" Henry turned serious and shrugged off his facetious answer. "I can't tell you. Word of mouth, maybe."

Peter ignored his uncle's humor. "How long before it's over?"

"At least another month, Peter. We don't want to be shorthanded on evidence when we present the case. Remember, these are unscrupulous opponents. If we let them slip through our fingers, the innocent people under their authority will be further victimized.

"And we plan to present the case at several levels simultaneously. That way, if one jurisdiction has been bought out, we have another chance.

"Publicity will help as well. The scandal sheets love this kind of thing. We can use their morbid curiosity to keep things hot for the offenders. In the meantime, we don't want to lose Julie or allow any of the guilty parties to get wise and skip out."

"Uncle Henry, I think I should marry her."

"Why is that, Peter?" the lawyer responded seriously.

Peter grinned. "Well, aside from the obvious reason, I think I'd be in a better position to protect her legally. Wouldn't it be difficult to get protective custody away from a husband?"

"They could always claim you took advantage of her confused state, but, yes, we could have our own doctors examine her and prove her of sound mind."

Peter took in his uncle's cautious demeanor. "But. . ."

"Peter, realistically, you have not known the girl but five weeks." He held up his hand against Peter's retort. "And is it fair to her? You are her knight in shining armor. She led a very sheltered existence in Europe. She's been three years in an insane asylum. She is naïve and gullible. Your words. You've been kind to her. Does she really love you, or is she scared and grateful?"

Peter soberly gazed out of the window.

"I'll wait," he finally said.

When they rejoined the family, they found Tiger curled up asleep on the couch. Scram, Aunt Harry, Midge, and Joe were at work on a jigsaw puzzle with Daisy looking on.

"Peter, would you believe it?" Aunt Harry exclaimed. "Daisy has never done a jigsaw puzzle."

"We've been instructing her," said Scram. She turned to their pupil and intoned with the air of a great pedantic scholar, "Wise people pick out the flat edge pieces first."

"Incorrect," declared Midge in mock outrage, obviously rehashing an old argument. "Those with superior organizational skills separate by color first."

Ignoring their dramatics, Daisy reached down and stuck in a piece.

Scram abandoned the fight to recall, "Do you remember the race we had one Christmas holiday?" She turned to Daisy to explain. "We had two identical puzzles set up on two card tables, Daisy. Peter and Midge made up one team, and Lisa and I were on the other. We started at nine o'clock one morning and vowed we wouldn't leave the tables until a team won."

"Who won?" Daisy asked the obvious question.

"Nobody. Somebody let Scooter in. He was a barn cat and definitely not allowed in the house. Jake, our faithful dog, took after him, and Peter took after Jake because Mom was yelling. Dad came in to see what the trouble was, only we had set one of the tables right in front of the door, and he ran smack into it. Scooter, Jake, and Peter managed to flatten the other. The tables tipped toward each other as they fell, so the pieces were irretrievably mixed."

Tabitha's childish screeches from outside interrupted Scram's story. The little girl came barreling through the front door, her cheeks red from the cold and her face lit up with delight.

"Grandpa's coming down the road. I saw his car at the bend." She turned and raced out again, determined to be the first to greet him.

A subtle change in the room caused Daisy to look from one member of the family to the next. The spirit of joy fizzled out and was replaced by apprehension. Uneasy looks of sufferance passed between several people and others sighed, obviously resigned to the inevitable.

"I'll put some coffee on," said Aunt Harry and left for the kitchen.

"Come on, Daisy. We'll go out and meet them." Peter took her arm and guided her toward the door. He stopped at the wooden pegs on the entryway wall and pulled down her coat from among the others. He slipped it on for her and reached for his own.

"It's my father's wife, Suzanne," Peter explained *sotto voce*. "She's caused quite a few scenes at our family gatherings. No one knows quite what to expect when she arrives."

Daisy nodded. She tucked her arm in his and they went out to greet the unexpected arrivals together.

Daisy froze. The woman was, of course, older. But the remarkably beautiful face, the refined features showing the signs of a storm brewing, all were the exact likeness of the spoiled Suzanne Winthrop, who had attended Madame Melanz's conservatory many years ago. Her cool gray eyes under the streaks of perfectly arched black brows still reflected that thoughtless attitude that had caused many vulnerable girls to steer clear of her. Suzanne Winthrop might be ten years older and Mrs. Ray Hudson, but she was still a pouting brat.

For a fleeting moment, Julie Jones was afraid she would be recognized. She set the fear aside. She had been a lowly eleven-year-old, far beneath the imperious sixteen-year-old beauty's notice. Julie Jones had only been at that conservatory three months. Suzanne Hudson would never be a threat.

Chapter 14

Ray Hudson's attention was claimed by the enthusiastic welcome of his granddaughter, Tabitha. Such a display of childish affection clearly bored Suzanne, and she turned her back on them. Her gaze fell upon Peter and Daisy. Peter, she ignored. She already knew what to expect from him. When her eyes fell on Daisy, they registered surprise. Julie Jones momentarily felt discovered, but she soon recognized the disdain that permeated Suzanne's appraising inspection.

Mrs. Hudson evaluated the new female. She had expected her stepdaughters, but she was obviously surprised to find an unfamiliar rival. Suzanne did not trust any of her own gender; all women were rivals. It was her nature to size up the competition immediately.

One quick glance told her that this female hovering beside the wonderfully attractive Peter was an inferior specimen, of no consequence. Daisy could read the contempt in her eyes.

Daisy, instead of being offended, relaxed under the survey of the scornfully superior Mrs. Hudson. Suzanne did not recognize her former schoolmate and wouldn't be bothered with this "no-account." Daisy was glad to be thought a no-account. She would not have to do anything for this lady's benefit except stay out of her way.

Ray Hudson turned to his son, and they exchanged a hearty hug, somewhat awkwardly since Tabitha still clung to her grandpa's neck.

"Why, who's this little filly?" Ray inquired. Daisy saw Suzanne wince over the colloquialism, and Daisy felt a glimmer of amusement. The high-and-mighty obviously disliked her husband's willingness to pay attention to riffraff.

Peter put his arm around Daisy and pulled her close.

"This is Daisy Madden, Dad. She's the love of my life."

Daisy blushed.

"I'm pleased to meet you, Daisy," Ray said cordially. "This is my wife, Suzanne." Suzanne audibly sighed.

"How do you do?" She arched her eyebrows, and a scene came back to Daisy's mind from her days at Madame Melanz's Conservatory.

One of the ten-year-old girls had heard that the older girls were meeting in the cellar. She persuaded Julie to go with her and spy on them. They had hidden, and sure enough, four older girls had shown up and arranged themselves on the steps, closing the door to the first floor. Julie remembered stifling giggles as Suzanne had descended the steps theatrically and struck a match to a forbidden cigarette. She had then proceeded to promenade before the girls and spout off "wisdom" she had accumulated on men, marriage, wealth, and the running of private schools.

After the older girls had left, Julie and her chum had taken pencils and pretended they were cigarettes. They strutted back and forth in a fair imitation of their worldly wise upperclassman, mockingly imitating Suzanne's speech and facial expressions. It had been a hilarious afternoon at Suzanne Winthrop's expense.

Now clear, cold eyes examined Daisy from head to toe and came back to look in her face with undisguised disdain.

"Yes, I believe Lisa said you were a waitress." She paused for effect, then turned away. "How quaint."

A bubble of laughter rose to Daisy's throat and spilled over. "How quaint" was one of the phrases she and her friend had repeated over and over in imitation of Suzanne's sophistication.

Mrs. Hudson had not expected the girl she had snubbed to burst out in delighted laughter. Her head snapped around and her eyes narrowed as she looked at the impertinent girl.

"I'm sorry." Daisy knew an explanation was in order. "I heard someone say that in a sort of a play once. It was a put-on kind of production and terribly funny. I didn't realize people actually said, 'How quaint.' "

Peter cleared his throat. "Let me help you with the luggage, Dad. There are a couple of able-bodied men hiding in there. Tabby, go get your daddy and tell him his strong arms are needed."

Daisy took the cue to move on to other topics and asked, "You didn't drive from Florida. Isn't that where Lisa said you were?"

"Right," Ray said, relieved that the tense moment had passed. "We flew in to Corpus and drove down. I keep this car in a parking garage there."

"Was it a good trip?" Daisy asked politely.

"Coming home is always a good trip," Ray answered with feeling.

"Shall we discuss the weather next?" Suzanne cut in sarcastically.

Daisy remembered distinctly Suzanne's cutting remarks wounding tender hearts right and left at the conservatory. She sniped with her words, verbally abusing those less witty. Now, her words were not only rude, but they were playing havoc with a family Daisy cared about. Her own temper blazed. Before she made any effort to give the anger over to God, a cold retort formed in her mind.

She turned a mild and unassuming face to Suzanne's. "I don't think we could discuss the weather, Suzanne. It requires pleasantries, and you seem to be a few short."

Suzanne's sharp intake of breath indicated her displeasure, and everyone froze, waiting for her reaction. Daisy plunged ahead. "But you've come to the right place to pick up a few. Pleasantries, you know, kind words spoken for the benefit of someone other than oneself. This family overflows with consideration and kindness."

Joe and Mike shuffled out of the house, unaware they were entering a battle-field. Peter took the opportunity to grab a suitcase in one hand and Daisy's elbow in the other. He propelled her to the house. Once inside, they met up with Lisa. He pushed Daisy at the surprised Lisa and said, "Here, hide her from the vam-pire for awhile. Show her the house. Better yet, show her the barns. Keep her out of sight."

He turned on his heel and went back outside.

Lisa guided Daisy quickly down the hall and toward the back of the house. "What on earth happened?" she asked.

"How could that woman embarrass your wonderful father like that?" Daisy fumed. "She's just a spoiled brat."

"That's the truth. Did she have her fangs out?"

"She's rude. A five year old has better manners."

"Some five year olds, Daisy. I've seen Tabitha display some mighty fierce temper tantrums."

"And I bet she gets spanked for them."

Lisa laughed as she pushed Daisy out the back door.

"You bet she does."

"Maybe Suzanne would benefit from similar instruction," Daisy said emphatically.

That sent Lisa off in a peal of laughter. "I can just see the scene with Dad and that old wooden spoon he used to use on us."

They stopped inside the first barn, which was empty save for some old farm equipment.

"Seriously, Daisy," Lisa began, "we try hard not to ruffle her feathers. I think Dad is very sorry he ever gave her his name, but he never says so. He's too much of a gentleman. Our mom was an extra special lady, and going by her instruction, we try to kill her with kindness. You know. Turn the other cheek. Heap coals upon her head. She hates being with us. I think it's because we're so good to her, it makes her feel rotten."

"I read in a book once that God gave us the law so that we could measure ourselves against it to see how far we fall short. Does that mean that by showing her how one should behave, you are making her look at how badly she behaves?"

"Yeah, in Suzanne's case we can always hope she'll start measuring. Personally, I'm more like Jonah, not wanting the Ninevites to repent. But my mom would want me to be nice to the woman out of respect to my dad."

"I really blew it, didn't I?" asked Daisy.

"I wasn't there, remember?" Lisa smiled warmly at her new friend. "You might not have paused to let God in on the conversation. Mom used to say that counting to ten wasn't good enough. We were supposed to count to five 'One, God loves me. Two, God loves you. Three, God help me. Four, open my heart. Five, give me Your love.' It works most of the time."

"Most of the time?" Daisy tilted her head to one side.

Lisa laughed. "I had trouble counting past four when I was a younger Christian. It takes practice, and I don't think we ever have it down pat."

They found Bobby in the second barn talking to one of the horses.

"I'd sure like to ride one." Bobby perched on the top rail of the stall and stroked the face of the roan horse he visited. The horse pushed forward, almost knocking the young visitor off the board.

"Hold on, Bobby," said Lisa enthusiastically. "He's doing that because he's enjoying your company and he probably would like to go out just as much as you would. I don't see any reason why we can't go riding. Daisy, do you ride?" She turned inquiring eyes to her charge. A glimmer of mischief brightened her eyes. "It'll keep you out of harm's way for awhile."

"Yes, I love to ride." Daisy's face broke into a warm smile at the thought of being astride a horse again, but it fell almost immediately. "I've ridden mostly on English saddles. Actually, I haven't been on a horse at all for three years. My father taught me on a western saddle when I was very young," she admitted. "However, I'm game to try. I'll bet the worst that will happen is that I'll be too sore to walk tomorrow." Her face clouded again after the brief lightening of her mood. "Lisa, I haven't got the right clothes."

"No problem," assured Lisa. "You are about the same size as Midge, and I bet she has something."

"I'm not going to change in the barn, am I? Aren't I to be kept out of sight?"

"Are you in trouble?" asked Bobby.

"I was rude," admitted Daisy.

"I bet it was to Aunt Suzanne," observed Bobby wisely. "She wants me to call her AWWWWWnt, and I always forget. That's why I came out to the barn as soon as I saw she was here. The Bible says to flee temptation."

Lisa giggled, but she redirected the conversation. "When we were kids, we often changed in the barn. Mom didn't like us dragging in all the mud and grime, so she had this old trailer installed in the back of the barn. It was heated and had running water. Let's go see if it's too cold to change in."

Surprisingly, the chilly trailer only had a few cobwebs for them to knock down. Bobby ran off with a message to the house, to be delivered, if at all possible, without disturbing Aunt Suzanne.

Bobby nodded after receiving his tactfully worded instructions. The sharp kid didn't want his temperamental aunt interfering with the proposed horseback

411

ride. He delivered his message with the adeptness of an espionage agent and reported back that many of the house party were going to join them. The atmosphere inside the house since Suzanne's arrival was conducive to outside activity.

In an hour, ten not-quite cowboys hit the trail. Some of the smaller cowboys perched before an adult on the quarter horses. The biting wind forced them to pull their wraps tightly around them. The weak winter sun did little to warm them, but the temperature hovered around forty degrees, and when the wind died down, they unbuttoned their coats.

The girls wanted a bonfire as they had often had in earlier years. Aunt Harry and their dad had volunteered to load up supplies and come along later in the jeep.

Daisy sat her horse like an old cowhand, despite the unfamiliar saddle. She had ridden as a child and had attended a riding school in Europe. Riding stables were often part and parcel of the private schools she had attended.

She gradually relaxed, allowing the rough beauty of the south Texas mesquite, yucca plants, and scrub brush to capture her attention. Nothing out here reminded her of Uncle Jacob's devious plots.

They went across country five miles to a draw protected from the wind. A stream ran through it, and a hollowed-out place collected the water from a small stream into a shallow pond.

Peter explained, "This is a favorite water hole. Keep a sharp lookout, Bobby, you might see deer or a bobcat. Of course, it's more likely that you'll just see more cattle."

Daisy didn't know if he was saying that to pique Bobby's interest or if truly some animals would show up.

"Just so long as there are no snakes," she stated firmly, "I'll be happy."

Peter laughed, "It's time for all good little rattlesnakes to be taking their winter nap."

"Is that meant to reassure me?" Daisy asked with a mocking tone of voice. "What about all the bad big rattlesnakes?"

"Rattlesnakes aren't really that big," said Bobby, entering into the fun of teasing a female. "Not when you think of a boa constrictor or an anaconda. Texas rattlesnakes rarely grow over fifteen feet." He cast a conspirator's grin at Peter.

"He's just saying that to get you rattled, Daisy," Peter said seriously. "I've personally never seen one over twelve feet long."

"Rattled, huh?" Daisy grinned. "You couldn't resist that terrible pun. Totally ruined your credibility."

Peter grinned back, and for a moment they shared the intimacy of good friends sharing a bad joke. Bobby thought it looked pretty mushy and spurred his horse to catch up with better company.

He chose Lisa, and Daisy noted that Peter's sister welcomed the boy's companionship. Once they reached the spot chosen for the bonfire, they dismounted and went off to gather wood.

Daisy wondered how long it would be before Lisa and John would be able to adopt, and the thought spurred a question.

"Peter, why isn't Bobby with his parents?" she asked.

"His parents are divorced. He stays mainly with his dad, Uncle Henry's son. However, he's an engineer and his company sent him to Saudi Arabia. He could be there two years and Robert, Bobby's dad, says it's too tough for an American kid without a mother."

"So, he's staying with your uncle and aunt?"

"Yes, but that's not entirely satisfactory, either. They are doting grandparents, and on the one hand, they don't discipline enough, and on the other, they're too old to enjoy doing eight-year-old activities constantly."

"Why can't he stay with Lisa and John?" Daisy suggested.

Peter looked at her curiously. Turning his head, he looked over to where Lisa and Bobby were piling sticks, joking with John over the quality of work being done. A dispute arose as to whether size was a true measure of ability. They happily laughed over a lot of nonsense.

Peter took Daisy in his arms. "Just today I informed Uncle Henry that you certainly are not dumb."

Daisy's face assumed an expression of astonishment. "You mean to say that dear Uncle Henry said I am dumb?"

Peter laughed. "No, don't go charging after the poor old gentleman. The context of the conversation saves him from any blame."

"I guess I should be grateful that no matter what the context, you leapt to my defense."

"Having appointed myself dragon-slayer and knight in shining armor on your behalf since the day I met you, I am now willing to state that I shall always leap to your defense in any situation that threatens you."

He drew her closer and kissed her.

Chapter 15

Peter and Daisy walked away from the others.

"Uncle Henry mentioned that I should give you some time, that I'm rushing you." Peter sighed. "I'm old and rather settled in my way of thinking, and when I see something I want, I'm pretty sure of it. I know I want you to be my wife. I want to go on loving you forever, taking care of you and providing for you. He advised me to wait. See how good I am at taking my lawyer's advice?"

"Twenty-nine isn't ancient," Daisy commented.

"The point is not how old I am, but how young you are."

"Twenty-one isn't that young," Daisy objected.

"The point is, I love you, but do you love me?"

This didn't sound like Peter. Peter was decisive. Now he was unsure and hesitant in his speech. He looked at her beseechingly.

"I'm the guy who came along when you really needed help. Now you're grateful and perhaps you've mistaken it for love. Or maybe you know you're not in love with me, but you're just too kind to hurt my feelings." He let out an exasperated groan. "Listen to me. I sound like a sixteen-year-old boy with his first girl."

"Peter," she said.

"What?"

"I love you."

He crushed her in his arms and kissed her. "You'd better mean it, Daisy. I'm never going to let you go. Marry me."

"I have to think."

"No." He kissed her again, trying to prevent any thought processes getting started. "Marry me," he demanded between kisses.

"Let me think, Peter." He let her go, and she took a quick step back. She stood looking at him for a minute. Then she sighed as if making a monumental decision. "First, I have to tell you the truth."

Peter nodded.

"My name's not Daisy Madden."

A quizzical smile played at the corner of his mouth. "I guessed," he said.

She smiled back at him.

"Must you stand so far away from me while you tell me the truth?" he asked, his eyes bright with mischief.

"I'm within arm's reach," she responded with the same playful grin. "I'm not running away."

"But it's so much warmer when you stand closer."

"It's an amazingly warm evening for November," she countered.

"You look tired. Wouldn't you like to lean against me?"

"Peter," she exclaimed, "I'm trying to talk to you about something very serious."

"You're right," he apologized, but he could not quite banish the happy smile from his lips. "I'm sorry."

"Sure you are." Her expression clearly said she didn't believe him. Daisy looked away from him for a moment while she gathered her thoughts. Taking a deep breath, she began her explanation.

"My name is Julie Jones. When you found me, I was running away from the French Estate Private Hospital. It's for rich mentally ill patients."

Without batting an eye, he asked, "So why were you there? You're not mentally ill."

She glanced up at him, her eyes reflecting her gratitude at his faith in her. "Because my uncle paid to have me locked up out of his way. I don't have a drunken father. My parents died in a plane crash when I was eight. My uncle runs the business, and I inherited the controlling interest. By having me proven mentally ill and incompetent, my uncle remained in control."

"Come here and let me kiss you."

She obeyed and walked into his arms. Peter kissed her.

"Now, I have to tell you the truth."

She looked up at him inquisitively.

"Don't be mad, but I've known all this for a very long time. I just wanted to know you trusted me enough to tell me yourself." He waited for her response. She was now looking down at the zipper of his coat, hiding her expression. She did not speak, and he could not wait any longer. "Are you angry with me?"

"No," she said, "but if you knew, how did you know? And do others know? How close am I to being caught?"

"Uncle Henry knows, and we are doing everything possible to keep you safe. We had a private detective search out the facts, and Uncle Henry is now working on getting evidence to lock the scoundrels away."

"Uncle Jacob?"

"We hope so. If we can't get him behind bars, you will at least have your fortune back, and he'll be ruined financially. With the loss of his money, he loses power. Without that power, you should be safe."

"Nobody else knows?"

"No, and if there is trouble and I can't help, get to Uncle Henry. I'll give you his phone number and address. Dad would help, too, if he's here. But he doesn't know a thing about it. I'll ask if he's planning to stick around. Or rather if

Suzanne is planning to grace us with her presence. Right now, let's think about our plans. When can we get married?"

"I haven't said yes yet, Peter." Daisy kissed him lightly. "Give me some time."

Peter groaned, "All right. But I can't wait forever. Remember, I'm practically a senior citizen."

※

When they returned, the bonfire blazed. Everyone but Suzanne had come out in the jeep to join the horseback riders. Aunt Harry had brought hot dogs and their fixings, marshmallows for roasting, and hot chocolate. The sun sank below the western horizon and the air turned colder. Peter and Daisy drew close to the fire with the others.

Peter's dad played the guitar and they sat around the fire singing songs that Daisy had never heard before.

"Your education has certainly been neglected," Ray Hudson teased her. "My daughters were singing these standards of Americana when they were just grasshoppers in the hay."

Lisa came to her defense. "Don't be too hard on her, Dad. She rides well, and she cooks well, and she's earning her keep waitressing. Sounds like things you were always trying to get your daughters to do."

"She'll make some young man a good wife," Peter threw in.

"Big brother, are you trying to tell us something?" asked Midge.

"No, I'm still trying to tell Daisy something."

"Well, let us know when she gets the message," put in Scram.

They left late and rode back to the ranch house by a beautiful moon. Daisy got her clothes out of the trailer. When she had changed, Peter steered her past the house to his car.

"We aren't going to say good night?" asked Daisy.

"No, Suzanne is unpleasantly drunk. They don't need us in there."

Chapter 16

A week had passed since Thanksgiving Day. The morning sun graced blue skies, and the crisp air held the briskness of a northerly breeze. Daisy wrapped her coat close about her as she started down the street toward work. She hadn't had to go in for breakfast, but she was expected soon.

A car pulled up beside her and a voice called, "Daisy, get in."

She turned with a start and saw Suzanne at the wheel.

"Why?"

"Hurry, there's been an accident. I'm supposed to take you to Ray."

"Why Ray? Is he hurt?"

"No, it's Peter. Hurry up! I had a hard time finding the street. I don't know this town like the rest of them."

Daisy climbed into the car and anxiously asked, "What happened?"

"I really don't know. I woke up to hear Ray packing a bag. He said Peter had been in an accident. He had me get up to come get you and we're supposed to meet him."

"Where are we supposed to meet him? This isn't the way to the ranch or the hospital."

"The airport. It's out in the country."

"I didn't know there was an airport."

"Well, it hardly qualifies. It's got two hangars and an airstrip about three yards wide."

"But why are we going to the airport? Where is Peter? What's happened to Peter?"

"Don't get hysterical," Suzanne said sharply. "I told you I don't know. His car turned over last night. They flew him to Corpus. Ray wants you to go to Corpus with him. So I was sent to find you and bring you to Ray."

They pulled into the little airport, and Daisy spotted Peter's father right away.

"He's next to that plane." She pointed. Suzanne drove across the field to the plane.

Before she had a chance to turn off the motor, Daisy jumped from the car and ran to Ray.

"What happened? Please, tell me what happened?" Ray Hudson looked twenty years older. He was pale and his mouth was set in a grim frown. His

417

normally cheerful eyes were red-rimmed and distant. "His car was found this morning. He was trapped in it. Apparently, he'd been there most of the night.

"His injuries were too much for our local hospital. They stabilized him and flew him to Corpus. They are going to operate on his legs." Ray's voice broke and he dashed his hand across his eyes. "I've got this plane ready, Daisy. He's been calling your name. He's really hurt bad, really messed up. I don't know if they can save him."

Daisy laid a hand on his arm. There didn't seem to be any words she could say.

"We must get going." Ray turned to climb in the plane.

Daisy looked at the little Cessna. The plane her parents had died in had been just such a personal "bush hopper." Since her parents' death, Julie Jones had never ridden in anything smaller than a commercial airline. She scanned the length of the small craft from nose to tail and found it looked disturbingly fragile. But Peter had called her name. She climbed in.

Ray Hudson was their pilot, and soon they were in the air. Daisy prayed with each thrum of the powerful engine. She only stopped to listen to Ray.

"I called Lisa," the worried father stammered. "She was going to the hospital to meet the helicopter carrying Peter. There will be a taxi waiting for us at the airport. I don't know why we are hurrying. He'll be in surgery for hours."

"We're hurrying because we love him," Daisy stated flatly. "Perhaps to the medical people his injuries won't seem so dangerous as we think. They see trauma patients all the time and they do miraculous things." Daisy stared down at the miniature houses. "We can hope, can't we?" she murmured. Her words were drowned by the roar of the small engine. Realizing Ray couldn't hear her, she repeated her question in a shout.

"I don't know. They said at our hospital that they saw no head injury or damage to his back. He's cut up, but he lived because no main arteries were severed."

"That's something to hold on to. God has protected him so far. He's placed Peter in good hands, I'm sure."

Ray Hudson didn't seem to hear any of her comforting thoughts. He continued as if she had not spoken.

"His left arm is broken in two places and a rib or two as well. They don't know what kind of internal injuries they will find there. We do know his legs are in danger." Ray's voice caught on a sob. "If only he hadn't been out there for so long before they found him."

"Who found him?"

"A couple of the ranch hands. He was on the old river road. And that's strange. Why did he go down that road last night? Why was he out there? When did he leave you?"

"A little before eleven. He didn't say anything unusual. I just thought he was going home."

They were both quiet. After some time, Daisy spoke. "He'll tell us when he wakes up, Mr. Hudson."

Ray nodded but didn't say anything. The possibility was too real that his son might never wake up.

✳

They reached the hospital to find that Peter was not yet in surgery. His condition after the transport had been precarious and he had stabilized just within the last hour. Also, they had had to wait for an orthopedic surgeon to come in.

Lisa and John were waiting for them in the hallway and filled them in on what had been going on.

"He calls for Daisy, but anything else he mumbles," said Lisa.

John tapped her on the shoulder and pointed down the hall.

"Here comes his doctor." He indicated the gentleman who was approaching them in green surgery scrubs.

He came directly to Daisy, who clung to Ray Hudson's arm without realizing it. "Would you be Daisy?"

She nodded.

"Come with me. I want you to speak to him before we put him under. He keeps fighting to consciousness and calling for you. I want him to be reassured that you are here."

Daisy wordlessly left the others and followed the tall, calm man back down the hallway.

"He looks a mess. His nose is broken, and he has many little cuts on his face. What you see will look awful, but it isn't the serious part of his injuries. Try to keep your voice calm. Tell him you're here and that he is going to have surgery, and you will be here when he wakes up. I'm not sure he will hear you, but I believe in giving my patients every extra edge they can get."

Even with the doctor's kind preparation, Daisy gasped when she saw Peter. His head wounds had been cleaned and stitched, but the black and purple bruises, the yellow stain of the antiseptic, and the dried blood across the black stitches combined in an awful visage. He was connected by tubes to oxygen and an IV. His heart rate was being monitored, and the machine's steady monotone blips added to the desperate atmosphere of the scene.

The doctor's arm braced and guided her between the nurses, technicians, and equipment to stand beside Peter. His unbroken arm lay exposed on the bed sheets.

"Go ahead and touch him. It's all right. Speak to him," encouraged the doctor.

Daisy gingerly took Peter's cold, limp hand. She leaned forward. "Peter, Peter." There was no response. She looked imploringly over her shoulder at the doctor. He patted her arm.

"Just talk to him," he instructed and left her side.

"Peter, it's Daisy. I'm here. It's going to be all right. You're going to have surgery. I'm going to be right here. When you wake up, I'll be right here. Peter, please hear me." She caught back a sob. He looked so little like the Peter who was strong and confident, decisive and generous. He was swollen and deathly pale where he wasn't battered with bruises. He looked weak, and Daisy wondered if he would ever open his eyes again, if he would ever smile at her again, or say her name.

"Peter." She continued to speak an endless stream of the same reassurances. At some point her words turned into prayer, and she asked God to intervene for the one she loved, to give him strength and heal him. She thanked God for Peter and the great blessing he had been in her life. She thanked Him for everything in her life that had led her to trust in Him. Her prayer dissolved into encouraging words just for Peter.

He stirred. "Daisy."

"I'm here, Peter," she answered, squeezing his hand. For a second she believed she felt an answering pressure on her hand. Surely, he must have heard her.

They took him away to the operating room.

She followed them as far as she could, and then when he went through the last double doors where she could not follow, she turned to find Ray Hudson behind her. He encircled her with his arms, and she sobbed against his shoulder.

✳

A little after noon, Suzanne appeared in the surgery waiting room. She answered the surprised looks with her usual attitude.

"I wasn't about to stay in Dooley with the rest of the clan in Corpus. Ray darling, I'll go check us into the Sea Castle Hotel. We'll obviously need a place to stay while we're here."

Ray nodded, and Suzanne exited. Daisy noted she hadn't even asked after Peter. It didn't matter.

John found cups of soup in the cafeteria and brought them up. Knowing they had no appetites, he encouraged them to sip the broth.

Periodically, a nurse came from surgery and gave them a progress report. The extent of damage to the legs was completely repairable. There was some nerve damage and months of therapy were likely, but Peter would not lose his legs or the use of them. The team of doctors felt confident that circulation would be unimpeded, and barring complications, they could expect slow, steady progress toward normalcy.

Finally, Peter was returned to an intensive care unit. Each of the members of his family present visited him briefly. He didn't respond to their presence, but they received a measure of comfort just seeing that he was breathing. They nominated Daisy to be the one who stayed with him. Her eyes filled with tears as she realized the generosity of this offer. Again, she felt that she was a part of this family.

Sitting in the huge recliner chair in the corner of the room, she watched Peter's rhythmic breathing. The monitors blipped a steady reassurance that everything was well. Daisy prayed gratefully for this man and his family and for the doctors and nurses who had been there to make a difference. Her mind wandered through a conversation with God, counting her blessings, imploring Him to keep them close, expressing her adoration for His presence in her life until she fell asleep.

The next day they moved him to a regular private room, and close to noon, he began to stir. Daisy talked to him and listened to his mumbling. He wanted to be sure she was there and that she would not leave. She promised every time he asked.

When his eyes opened, she knew he recognized her. He slipped back into unconsciousness, but she praised God, knowing Peter was going to be all right.

Every time Peter awoke, he wanted to see her. The nurses brought in a cot, and Daisy camped in the corner of the room.

Lisa packed a suitcase for her. The brand-new clothes came from a quick trip to the discount superstore.

"I wasn't about to buy you things from the Goodwill, Daisy," Lisa teased. "I had an enormous amount of fun on this shopping spree, and you are not to feel guilty. Daddy handed me his credit card and ordered me to do it. You wouldn't want me to disobey my father, would you?"

Daisy looked down at her waitress uniform, which she had been wearing for fifty-two hours. She nodded numbly and reached out a hand to take the offered suitcase.

"Who's taking care of Sidney?" she asked. The problem had settled in her mind. In all the turmoil of the accident, this was a simple difficulty that popped up again and again, as if by resolving this minor problem, she would have more control over the circumstances.

"The housekeeper," answered Lisa.

Daisy nodded listlessly. She looked at the still figure in the bed. So many tubes seemed to run out from Peter. He would be pleased that someone was taking care of his dog.

The third day, Peter showed much improvement. Each time he awoke more lucid. He still insisted that Daisy be right there beside him, and he would awake agitated until he saw her or heard her voice. Ray, Lisa, and John visited and tried to give Daisy a break. But neither Daisy nor Peter would cooperate.

On the fifth day, Peter got the idea in his head that he must marry Daisy now. He asked Ray to arrange it.

"Peter." His father spoke calmly and reasonably. "There is no hurry. You are going to be all right. There's plenty of time for that when you're stronger. Daisy will be right here."

"No, Dad." Peter was cross and distraught. "There's something I can't remember. I know I was thinking about it while I was under the car, but I can't remember. I've got to tell Uncle Henry."

"Tell him what, Peter?"

"I don't know what," he snapped. "I've got to marry her, Dad. It's important."

Peter would not drop the subject and became more and more anxious as the day went on. While he was resting under the influence of the painkillers, Ray took Daisy aside.

"Daisy, do you intend to marry Peter?" he asked solemnly.

"Yes," was her simple reply.

"Would it upset you to marry him now instead of waiting? Perhaps we could calm Peter down by agreeing to start the wedding preparations. He is improving daily, and tomorrow he might be more reasonable."

Daisy looked at Peter's dad and saw the concern the father held for his son. This man loved Peter and was willing, as she was, to do the unreasonable until he was more rational. "Next time he wakes up," she said, "let's tell him we can do it just as soon as we get the details worked out."

Peter awoke pleading with his dad to get busy and fix things so he could marry Daisy. Ray agreed.

"She needs a blood test. She can do that in the hospital. I don't want her to leave the hospital," Peter commanded.

Daisy smiled. Here was a trace of the take-charge Peter who had rescued her in the middle of her escape.

"And get Uncle Henry here. I have to tell him something."

"What, Peter?" inquired his dad. "Tell me, and I'll call him and tell him right now."

"I can't remember." Peter's surly tone matched the scowl on his disfigured face, and Ray asked no further questions of his son.

❋

"Daisy, I can't feel that this is right." Ray relaxed in the chair while Daisy lay stretched out on her cot. Peter slept, still heavily sedated most of the time. "My girls all had big lovely weddings, and you're going to miss out on that. This is a one-time thing, and you ought to have your pretties to remember."

Daisy laughed outright. "Mr. Hudson, look at my groom."

Ray turned to survey his sleeping son. "I see your point, Daisy. He does look like a cross between *The Mummies Rise Tonight* and *Frankenstein*. In addition to those gruesome black eyes, he hasn't shaved in a week."

"Lisa said she'd pick out a pretty dress. I'm not upset about the ceremony. I just want to marry him. Maybe he'll believe I won't disappear if he sees his ring on my finger."

"I've gotten the rings, Daisy. Peter won't be able to wear his till the swelling goes down in his left hand."

422

"Is Uncle Henry coming?"

Ray nodded. "Peter can tell him the vitally important message he can't remember." He sighed at the mystery.

"Maybe when he sees Uncle Henry's face, it'll come to him."

※

On Peter's tenth day in the hospital, he was sufficiently alert to participate in his wedding. Uncle Henry had arrived to help them get the license, and the minister from their church in Dooley drove up to do the ceremony. Lisa had picked out a knee-length evening gown of cream satin with a lace cape draped across one shoulder and tight lacy cuffs. Rhinestones danced in the light as they nestled in the folds of the cape.

The nurses thought the whole idea was fantastically romantic and joined in the spirit, finding room for Daisy to dress. Lisa arranged her hair in a fancy French braid with ribbons and flowers intertwined with the locks of hair. John shaved the groom, but at Lisa's insistence, he took a before and after picture of her "noble big brother."

The vows were exchanged with all due respect to their meaning. Daisy leaned over to kiss the groom in his bed. They were husband and wife. Peter sighed his relief.

"Now," said Uncle Henry, "I am going to take the bride out to dinner."

The groom looked startled and opened his mouth to object.

"Peter," Uncle Henry cast a stern look at his favorite nephew, "you are to rest. Daisy will be escorted by the entire family, and we will bring her back to you safe and sound. You have kept her a virtual prisoner in this room for ten days."

"Uncle Henry." Peter's strained voiced showed the weakness of his present state. His thinking was getting hazy from the excitement of the day. "There is something I must tell you. I was thinking about it under the car. It's important."

"Yes, Peter," his uncle said patiently. "You've told us that before. You will soon remember what it is and be able to get it off your mind. Rest now. Maybe you will dream of it and be able to tell me when we get back from dinner. Now, don't fret. Just rest."

Chapter 17

Peter's eyes popped open. The hospital room was dark except for the night-light beside the door to the hall. He could hear Daisy's steady breathing from the cot in the corner. He shifted slightly, trying to ease the ache in his hips. How many days had it been since the accident? Eleven? No, twelve. He turned his head to peer through the darkness at Daisy's sleeping form.

"Daisy," he called softly.

She stirred immediately and rose on one elbow. When she saw him awake, she tossed back the covers and quickly rose. She came to the right side of his bed, and he put his arm around her waist.

His own personal angel. The thought warmed him, and Peter thanked God for this blessing. His good hand held her, lest she evaporate like some vision.

"Do you need something?" she asked. "Do you want me to call the nurse?"

"What time is it?"

She looked at the clock. "Three-twenty."

"They won't give me anything for pain for awhile yet. I'll be okay. Lie down with me and talk." He smiled. "My thinking is a bit mystic as it is. I probably should guard against overdoing the drugs, even though the doctors think I'm within the safety range."

"What do you mean?"

"I'm not quite sure you floated to my bedside, but you sure look like an angel to me. My lovely angel, sweet and kind."

"You're right," agreed Daisy with a grin, "you don't need to get any higher."

She eased herself onto the bed, careful not to jostle him, and stretched out slowly. Her head rested on his shoulder with his arm protectively down her back.

"You okay?" she whispered.

"Not exactly," he answered.

"Am I hurting you?"

"No." He enjoyed the feeling of having her close. He noticed how little room she had. "But you can't be comfortable."

"I'm happy even if I'm not comfortable."

"Daisy, why was I out on that road? Where was I going?"

"Nobody knows, Peter. When you left my place, I thought you were going home."

Peter was quiet for a time.

"I was going home. Something happened, and I can't quite put my finger on it. Help me remember."

"How?"

"Tell me what happened before I left you."

"We came home from the diner. You had me fix you a sandwich."

"What kind?"

"Pastrami with cheese and sauerkraut."

"A person should be able to remember that." There was a hint of amusement in his voice, and Daisy smiled in the dark.

"Daisy, I do remember. It was dripping and made a mess on your couch."

"Yes, and I said, 'Thanks a lot. Now, I'll be sleeping with the smell of sauerkraut.'"

"And you objected when I kissed you good night. You said I tasted like an old German. I wanted to know how many old Germans you'd been kissing."

"That's right," she encouraged him.

"Turn your face up here so I can kiss you."

Daisy obliged. He kissed her softly.

"This blasted broken nose ruins my style."

"I'm just glad you weren't turned topsy-turvy in that car. Then your head would have been smashed instead of your legs."

"I think if I wasn't on all this pain stuff, I could think more clearly. There is something that I was thinking under the car that made perfect sense, and it was important, but it's escaped me."

"It'll come back in time."

"That's the problem, Daisy. It feels urgent, as if there isn't any time to waste."

"And it has to do with Uncle Henry?" she prodded.

"Not directly. . ." Peter concentrated, trying to capture the elusive thought. "I need to tell him because he could. . ."

She felt his body tense. She twisted her face up to see his expression.

"I remember. Daisy, call Uncle Henry."

"It's not even four yet, Peter."

"It's important. Call him and get him here."

"I will not, Peter! It can wait until six o'clock. It's waited twelve days, and two more hours won't hurt."

"What if I forget again?"

"Tell me, and I'll remember," she urged.

His arm tightened around her. "No," he said. "But I want Dad and Uncle Henry here as soon as possible in the morning." His lips brushed the top of her head. "I don't think you've ever defied me before."

"Defied you?" she asked, puzzled.

"Didn't you refuse to make one little phone call for me?"

She laughed softly. "I suppose in our married life there will be times I will argue with you. But it is only to give you a chance to refine your wisdom with the benefit of another point of view."

He laughed and then groaned as his muscles reacted in pain from the movement. In a minute, he rubbed his cheek against her hair.

"Julie, I love you."

"Peter, don't call me that. It's not safe," she objected.

"You're my wife now. I am going to keep you safe."

"I love you, Peter."

"It's mighty inconvenient to be bound up like this on your honeymoon," he complained.

"For our second honeymoon let's pick a more secluded resort and leave all the nurses behind."

"Good idea."

❋

Peter's six-o'clock pain medicine helped him to cope not only with his discomfort, but his impatience as well. He would have his dad and uncle by his bed soon. Daisy called both men after six and woke each one with Peter's imperious summons. They arrived around seven-thirty, both anxious to hear what he had to say.

"Dad, I want you to walk Daisy around the hospital while I tell Uncle Henry. Then, after I get his advice, we'll let you two in on it."

"Peter, I want to know now." Julie stood by his bed with no indication that she would oblige and go for a walk.

"Who was it that said a few more hours wouldn't matter? Let me discuss it with Uncle Henry first and get his legal opinion."

She recognized the futility of trying to dissuade him and chose to graciously accept his decision. "I don't think it's fair, but I'll do it." She made a face at him that made him laugh. He winced.

"Dad, watch her."

"Yes, Son," his dad answered seriously, though he thought Peter had been suffering from melodramatics ever since his accident.

As they left, Uncle Henry pulled a chair close to the bed and sat down. He leaned forward, his elbows on his knees, his hands clasped together in a double fist on which he rested his chin. He was at attention and waiting.

Peter took a deep breath and began. "It wasn't an accident. When I got to my house that night, there was a car parked in the street. One man was in the car. Another man approached my car before I got out. He asked directions to Palacio Street. He was referring to a piece of paper in his hand, which he brought over to the car, and he reached through the window to show it to me. He jammed it in my face. It was not paper but cloth, soaked with chloroform or something like it.

"The next thing I knew, I was under the car and hurting." He paused. "Those men wanted to kill me. The only explanation is that Julie's uncle Jacob knows where Julie is and wanted me out of the way so he could get to her. With me out of the picture, there would be no one likely to investigate what happened to her."

"We'll notify the police immediately, Peter. Her esteemed uncle is lying in wait for his next opportunity, and I don't like it. We have enough evidence to draw the noose tight. And if we miss a few culprits because we've had to move more quickly than we wanted, at least we will have Daisy safe and those current inmates freed."

Peter nodded.

"Now, I'm going downtown," said the lawyer. He had a gleam in his eye as if he were a fighter going into a fray. "When Ray and Daisy return, tell them the truth. Ray will be a worthy ally. Daisy must be on her guard. You might hint that she needs to guard you as well. I don't want her running off in the mistaken belief that she will be taking danger away from you. You're helpless, and someone needs to hold your hand."

Uncle Henry grinned at the look of indignation that flared across his nephew's countenance. "Come on, Boy," he chided, "tell me you're ready to take on a couple of hoodlums."

"Don't rub it in, Uncle Henry," Peter growled. "Don't you know how it goes against the grain to know anyone could walk in here and grab my girl? I could shout about it and nothing else."

"We've got it under control, Peter," Uncle Henry assured him. "Nobody's going to snatch her."

He left, and ten minutes later, Daisy and Ray returned.

"We've had a nice little walk," said his dad. "And we've decided to get the truth out of you, one way or another. What's going on, Son?"

"Sit down, Dad," Peter directed. "This is going to be a bit involved. In fact, I really don't feel up to it. Julie, why don't you tell Dad everything about the Estate and your escape. When you get finished, I'll tell him about the accident."

Ray turned curious eyes to his daughter-in-law. "I take it your name is not Daisy. This is an interesting beginning."

Daisy began with her real name and how she was brought up. She even mentioned that she had briefly attended a school where Mrs. Hudson was also a student. Her account of her imprisonment in the Estate Private Hospital was factual. She did not elaborate on the three lonely, desperate years. When she got to her escape, her voice warmed with enthusiasm. It was an adventure worth telling, especially the entrance of Peter, her knight in shining armor. She glowed as she finished her part of the tale.

"God has been so good to me, Mr. Hudson. Through all the bad experiences, He gave me hope. He never left me, and then it all led to good. Without

His guidance, I might never have met Peter. God is so good."

Ray shook his head in wonderment. "How can you say that? Look at the two of you. Peter is broken to pieces, and you're hiding from a thoroughly evil and powerful uncle."

"But are we alone? Even before I met Peter, I knew that God was watching out for me and guiding me."

"It seems to me you've been on your own for the most part. It's just coincidence that you crawled into the backseat of the right car."

"Then I'd say you are on the outside looking in," Julie responded truthfully.

"What does that mean?" Ray was taken aback.

"You aren't a Christian."

"Of course I'm a Christian. Do I look Jewish or Hindu?" The sarcasm that so often riddled his wife's comments touched his words.

"What makes you a Christian?" Julie asked.

"I was born in America and went to a church most of my life."

"What do you believe about Christ?"

"The same thing everybody does."

"I believe my sins would send me to hell, but Christ's death and resurrection gave Him the right to save me. My acceptance of His love gives me the right to go to heaven."

"Peter's mother used to talk about heaven and hell. Pretty old-fashioned concepts, if you ask me."

Julie laughed. "You know, I think God is probably as old-fashioned as He is futuristic. Being eternal, He would kind of have to be."

"Where did you get your faith from, Daisy—I mean, Julie?"

"My mother," she answered directly. "She introduced me to God and Jesus at a very early age. In fact, I don't really remember a time when she didn't talk about Him and pray with me. When she died, I clung to the fact that both my parents had been close to God. Since they were with Him, I could stay close to them by staying close to Him.

"But it was on one of my trips in Europe that I responded to the gospel message. It has sustained me through many lonely times. I've learned a lot by studying God's Word, but I've learned more by witnessing in my own life how faithful He is."

"I'm sure I'll never understand what you are talking about."

"And I'm just as sure you would understand if you truly tried to find out. God is the rewarder of those who seek Him."

Ray gazed at her steadfastly. She met his look without flinching. In her heart, she prayed that her words had somehow been used by God to reach this man she had grown to love as Peter's father.

He turned abruptly away from her, and she knew he had taken in as much as he could for the moment. He chose to put it aside for now. She prayed that the Holy Spirit would draw him closer to the kingdom of God.

"Peter," said Ray. "Are you asleep?"

Peter stirred. "I guess I drifted off while Julie was talking about the Estate. It is so inconvenient to be incapacitated now."

"You promised to tell us about the accident," reminded his dad.

"It wasn't an accident. Someone was deliberately trying to remove me from the scene."

Ray's face went blank with disbelief, and then in quick succession he looked incredulous, sickened, and finally outraged.

"You say this was an attempted murder." His voice held an edge of steel that Julie had never heard before. She scarcely noticed as the full realization of what this meant dawned upon her.

She grabbed Peter's good hand and clung to it. "Peter, because of me?" Her voice was full of anguish.

Peter turned his attention to her, remembering his uncle's warning. "Yes, Julie, because they knew I would do anything to protect you, and if you disappeared, I'd hound them like a dog until I found you."

"It's because of me you're hurt." Still the magnitude of what he was saying enveloped her, causing her to sway under an overwhelming sense of guilt.

"A soldier goes out to war to protect his country but, more specifically, his loved ones. It was a call I would have answered had someone stated it. I would do anything to protect you, Julie. But now, I need you. Until I can get on my feet, I have to depend on you. Don't let me down."

"I won't, Peter," she whispered.

"Remember your promise?" he quizzed her seriously.

She nodded. "I won't ever leave without saying good-bye."

"You must never leave me, Julie. I couldn't make it without you."

Chapter 18

Uncle Henry returned with a detective and a police artist in tow. An additional policeman stationed himself outside the door.

Detective Lieutenant Brock looked gruff and hardened by years on the police force. Sergeant Tina Perez, the artist, was small and feminine with dark hair and happy, friendly eyes. The lieutenant's stout six-foot-four frame filled the room as he entered. Sandy hair strictly groomed to remain in place crowned his otherwise unkempt appearance. Perhaps the control he exercised over every strand of hair was overcompensation for his naturally disheveled figure. The sergeant quickly retired to a corner and was hardly noticeable as an occupant of the room where the lieutenant commanded attention.

Peter fought fatigue in order to answer the policeman's questions. He had not seen the man in the car at all. He was able to give a fairly accurate description of the car, since he had looked at it closely, trying to identify it as belonging to one of his friends. Also, he had looked closely at the man who had approached him, expecting to recognize the late visitor as a neighbor.

Julie listened as Peter described the scene, and again she shuddered to think that these men had attacked Peter because of her. They were vicious and her Peter could be dead. She praised God they had not succeeded in killing him.

Uncle Henry and the detective left, but the artist remained. For the rest of the day, Tina Perez sat with Peter, and when he was awake, they worked on getting an image on paper of the man Peter remembered.

At four o'clock, one of the nurses came in to check Peter's vital signs. The many days in the hospital had increased Peter and Julie's circle of friends. This nurse was Patty, a huge blond who had been divorced three times and was raising three sons by herself. She was interested in what the policewoman and Peter were doing.

"With a policeman posted outside your door, everyone on the floor is curious. Is it true that your accident was attempted murder?" Patty asked outright.

Peter nodded.

"What are you drawing?" she asked Tina.

"These are composite pictures. I have a notebook here with facial features in many different forms. We put them together until we come up with a sketch that looks like the man Mr. Hudson remembers," she explained politely.

"I've seen those in TV shows," said Patty, who made no effort to conceal her curiosity. "May I look?"

Sergeant Perez handed over the latest sketch. The nurse took it with interest and stood gazing at it. A worried frown came across her face. She handed it back.

"Can you give him heavier eyebrows?"

Patty watched intently as Tina wordlessly complied. Watching over the artist's shoulder, the nurse nodded.

"His ears hang down more, kind of floppy, not attached. You know, this earlobe part." She pointed with a large finger.

Again, the artist sketched in the change.

The nurse nodded decisively.

"He's been here."

Sergeant Perez showed the changes to Peter. Peter grimly nodded his head in agreement. The ears and eyebrows looked more like what he remembered.

Immediately, Sergeant Perez arose and took the sketch to the man on duty outside, warning him that this man had been seen in the hospital. She then called her station and left a message for her superior.

"Is there anything else you can add to this picture?" she asked the nurse.

"No," Patty answered, "I don't think so."

"A detective will come to ask you some questions. Try to recall everything about this man. Where he was, what he was doing, even his attitude. I'm going to take this picture downtown and run it through our computer. I'm glad you came along when you did." She smiled as she gathered up her paraphernalia and left the room.

Peter looked over at Julie and saw that she was pale and upset. "Come here, Honey." He beckoned her with his free hand.

She came to him and clasped his one good hand in both of hers. Her eyes were wide with fear. "He's been here," she whispered.

Patty straightened her considerable frame and bristled like a mother hen threatened by an ill-mannered farm dog. "He's not going to get past our nurses and that policeman," she reassured Julie. "We think a lot of you two, and he's going to find we can be a very protective gang."

Peter smiled at the nurse. "I can just see you attacking him with one of those long needles you stick in my hip."

"We've got 'em longer than that. He just better not mess with us." She stormed out of the room.

"I bet she's on the way to alert the troops." Peter grinned. He squeezed Julie's hand. "I've missed you today."

"I've been here all day."

"Ah, but I've gotten used to having you all to myself with no one else around. Today, I had to concentrate on something else, and all I really wanted to do was talk to you and think about our future."

"And sleep, Peter," she teased. "You still sleep more than anything."

"Yes, but when I sleep I dream of you." He became more serious. "I can see some improvement. I am getting better."

"I know you are. You are looking better all the time. Why, the bruises across your nose and eyes have faded to a nice greenish yellow. And the swelling went down enough that I can admire those devilish green eyes."

"Now don't be telling me how handsome I am. It only increases the frustration I feel, knowing how much you appreciate your handsome husband."

"How is that?"

"I want to make love to my wife." He gazed at her sweet face. "And," he continued, "I'm hungry for pizza."

Julie chortled, knowing he was trying to ease her tension. "Now I know where I rank."

"It's a compliment, my dear." Peter joked with her. "Ever since I was in high school, pizza has been very high on my list of priorities. I make a pizza from scratch that we shall one day enjoy."

"Peter, normal living seems so very far away," she sighed.

He removed his hand from hers and laid it against the side of her head, feeling the texture of her soft hair.

"Not so very far away. I promise, Honey. Things will come quickly to a head, and then all this will be behind us. Be strong and of good courage. The Lord our God is with us."

✳

Two days passed with a policeman always guarding the door. Uncle Henry brought news that the Estate was being subjected to a thorough investigation. Outside doctors were reviewing the patient records and interviewing the staff and inmates. Dr. French had tried to disappear but had been arrested in Los Angeles in an airport. Jacob Jones, however, could not be located to answer questions concerning the hospitalization of his niece, Julie Jones.

"There's no question about your having to go back there," Uncle Henry told Julie, his smile confident. "They will be shut down for good."

"What about Uncle Jacob?"

"His spokesman says that he obviously had been duped by Dr. French, and he is very distraught that you have suffered. He is, however, out of the country on business and will gladly talk to the press and investigators as soon as he returns."

Julie was staring down into her lap, where her clasped hands revealed how anxious she was.

"I need your official permission to sue on your behalf." Uncle Henry spoke gently. "Your investments shall be returned to you, I am sure. Whether we can bring him up on criminal charges is still up in the air. I think when French cooperates, we'll have the evidence we need to get a full conviction."

Julie's eyes filled with tears, and she quickly dropped her head.

"What is it?" asked Peter.

Julie looked at him with pain and confusion in her eyes. "He's my father's brother. He's the only family I had for thirteen years. He never loved me, never visited me, or had me to visit him. Yet I always thought of him as my uncle who at least cared enough about me to provide the very best education and all sorts of different vacations. I used to imagine that he was trapped in his office, buried in paperwork, and he would think, 'Where would I like to go to escape it all?' Then, he'd know he couldn't get away and would think, 'I'll send little Julie, instead. She can enjoy it for me.' I know it was just fantasy, but it was pleasant to think someone loved me even if it was in a distant way."

Uncle Henry put his arm around her shoulders. "You've got real family now. When you took on our Peter, you took on all of us from Tiger to Ray's queen Suzanne."

Julie leaned her head against his shoulder and he gave her a comforting hug.

"That reminds me," he continued. "I brought Bobby down here with me. It looks like I'm not going to be allowed to take him back. Lisa and John want to keep him until my son Robert comes home. Bobby is in seventh heaven."

"Oh, that's going to make Lisa so happy."

"I think it will work out just fine. And your affairs are going to work out as well. I wish we could do something for Ray and Suzanne. Their problems defy solution. I could have kicked my brother's backside for bringing that cat home. And I'm sure he's regretted his folly many times over."

"All we can do is support him," sighed Peter.

"We can pray," Julie reminded them.

"But what do we pray for?" asked Uncle Henry bitterly. "I'd like to pray an avalanche on her head the next time she insists they go off to some fancy ski resort. However, I'd be guilt-ridden if that prayer were answered."

"There's only one thing that really changes people," Peter said solemnly. "Nothing is impossible for God. He could heal their hurts and restore their lives."

"I find it hard to imagine Suzanne listening to the gospel." Uncle Henry's tone was scornful.

"But Peter's dad did one day." Both men looked up at Julie's eager face. "Have you ever told him you're a Christian?"

Neither man answered.

"Well?" she insisted.

"No," said Peter. "I've always felt uncomfortable. He's supposed to advise me as to how to live my life. It didn't seem my place to guide him."

"Timothy was a younger man and he was used in the lives of others," said Uncle Henry. "Presumably, some of those under his authority were actually older than he. I can't cast stones, though, since I've avoided the subject myself when it comes to my little brother. I always figured he'd resent it, just as he did when we were growing up and I tried to tell him what to do."

"I think if you just talk about your faith instead of pushing to make it his faith, he'll be interested," Julie proclaimed.

"See, Uncle Henry," Peter beamed, "I told you she wasn't dumb."

Chapter 19

Three weeks passed before the doctors spoke of arrangements to move Peter to a rehabilitation hospital where he would begin therapy. Uncle Henry had returned to Dallas. Suzanne had gone on a shopping trip to New York City. Ray flew back to the ranch and happily took care of things as if he'd never retired.

Dr. French sat in jail waiting for trial. Several of his business associates were also arrested. Most of the staff at the private hospital were not involved. Dr. French had rotated his workers to keep them in the dark. The former patients were out in the world again, though all of them were receiving treatment for drug addiction or therapy just to be able to integrate into real society again.

Uncle Jacob had eluded the law. His wife claimed to have no information as to his whereabouts. The investments that rightfully belonged under Julie's administration were being returned uncontested. Uncle Henry busily worked on legal matters on her behalf.

No further attempts had been made on Peter's life. The police had a name for one of the suspects. He was Leonard Day, a man with a long history of bad dealings. It looked like Uncle Jacob had dropped out of sight to save his neck, and with no one to foot the bills and pay a handsome fee, the criminals were likely to lose interest and disappear.

Julie was reading a book one day when Patty came in with a round of medication for Peter. Julie glanced up, and they exchanged pleasantries about the weather and the few days that were left before Christmas.

Peter took the small paper cup that contained his pills from the nurse. He placed it in the hand that extended from his cast-covered arm. With his right hand, he reached for his glass of water. Patty grinned at his predicament but offered no help. Julie had to laugh as she watched a puzzled look come over his face. With the glass in his good hand, he couldn't hold the pills, nor could he bend the arm in the cast to bring the little paper cup to his mouth. She stood up to help him.

"Do you want me to hold the glass of water or the pills?" she asked.

"The pills," he answered.

Julie dumped them into her hand, and Peter looked at them quizzically.

"My pills are usually orange. Those are gray. Patty, would you check my chart and see if the doctor has changed my meds. He usually tells me everything and he didn't mention it."

Patty scowled, all her teasing vanished. She whisked the gray pills away and returned shortly with the familiar orange ones.

"Mr. Hudson, we didn't make a mistake. A switch was made. We don't have those gray pills in our supply. I gave them to the officer and he's called his boss. I'm sure glad you noticed the difference. No telling what they are, but I'll bet it's not good."

The nurse's prediction was accurate. When the reports came back from the police lab, it was determined that Peter would have been dead had he taken those pills.

Evidently Uncle Jacob had not given up.

✳

Lieutenant Brock came barreling through the hospital door into Peter's room. His usually dour face was split by an incongruous smile. Julie remembered a gargoyle that she had seen on a European castle. The stone image had worn a similar broad smile showing a row of discolored teeth.

"Good news," he boomed. "Leonard Day has been picked up in Houston. So far he's denying everything right and left." The big cop shrugged eloquently. "Would be nice if we had a good set of fingerprints from the car. But some sharp cop down in your neck of the woods got a bug to be a detective and dusted Mrs. Hudson's old living quarters for prints. Bingo! His prints and the fingerprints of a Harry O'Neill were everywhere. Now, if we lay our hands on the second guy, we can play them against each other and get them to talk."

The policeman actually rubbed his hands in glee over the prospect. Julie grinned. Somehow, she was reminded of a little boy playing cops and robbers. The image superimposed over the rugged, formidable lieutenant made it almost impossible for her not to giggle. She pressed her lips firmly together. She didn't think the gentleman would appreciate her sense of humor.

Peter spoke up. "We will be moving to the Dolman Rehabilitation Hospital in a couple of days. I can't expect the local police to provide a bodyguard for me indefinitely. I'd like to hire off-duty officers to fill in, or do you have an idea of a guard service to employ?"

Lieutenant Brock puzzled over the question before answering.

"We have officers who need to pick up the extra money, but you'll find scheduling them is a nuisance. There are several reputable companies that provide guard service, but there you run across screening their employees. It would be awfully easy to slip in an assassin."

"I remember reading in the paper recently about an officer who was shot and would be laid up for six months," Julie interrupted.

"That was Officer Rodriguez," acknowledged Brock.

"Well, couldn't we hire him to organize the off-duty officers? He'd know which ones were available, and he could use the telephone, and do it from his home."

Lieutenant Brock considered the idea. "I'll call him and propose it. It would be good for him as well as you. He was very popular, and the guys would enjoy working with him." The gruff lieutenant nodded abruptly and added so softly that Julie and Peter almost didn't hear him, "Keep his spirits up, too."

❈

The day came for the transfer. Peter went in an ambulance, and Lisa and Bobby came to help Julie collect all the things she had accumulated. It was the first time Julie had been out of the hospital since her wedding dinner. As they drove past the dingy winter beach, Lisa teased her about freedom and the taste of the outside world. She smiled shyly.

Bobby popped off, "We're forgetting she's an old pro at being locked up. She's been in a prison camp for three years."

"Oh, my goodness, Bobby," Julie gasped. "Where did you get that idea?"

"I read all the papers, and Grandpa told me some things after they had it on TV about the crooks being arrested." The boy showed his enthusiasm about the subject.

"Maybe I'd better tell you a little about it," Julie suggested. "Half-truths can be very misleading."

"Yeah," said Bobby. "Tell me."

"First, the French Estate Private Hospital was nothing like a prison camp. We were surrounded by luxury. My room was very elegant, but it included a closed-circuit camera so that I could be monitored while in my room. The food was top-notch cuisine. And there were gardens to walk in and a pool that was opened twice a day, but heavily supervised. There was a grand piano in the living room where I played for hours, and there was a library of maybe three thousand books. We were not allowed to listen to radio or watch TV, but that was because it upset many patients."

"It was like a posh resort?" Bobby's eyes were full of doubt.

"Yes," answered Julie, "but it still was a very unhappy place."

"I don't think I'd like having a camera on me in my bedroom," said Bobby. He turned to Lisa. "I don't do anything bad. It's just kind of a creepy idea."

"I agree," Lisa answered.

"You see," continued Julie, "you weren't supposed to be yourself or think for yourself. God created us to be individuals with minds, and they tried to obliterate that gift from God. God in His infinite wisdom made us cherish our right to choose and make decisions.

"That's an important part of becoming a Christian. People aren't born Christians or automatically made Christians because they go to church. They have the opportunity to learn about God, decide He is wise and good, and choose to follow Him. It is part of our nature to want to make the decision instead of being forced or manipulated into it."

"So you were unhappy 'cause you couldn't follow God?" Bobby tried to understand.

"I couldn't follow Christ freely. Within those walls, there was very limited opportunity to serve Him, worship Him, or tell others about Him. However, I did learn I could do small things. Just being kind to others, playing the piano to His glory, encouraging someone with the Word of God were some of the things that came my way. And praise God, I still had my Bible by my bed. In fact, I'd like to have my Bible. I left it behind."

"Maybe Grandpa can get it for you," Bobby commented.

"Maybe he can," said Julie. "The hard part was not choosing my own clothes or dinnertime or going out to town. I felt very confined. Remember, I had traveled all over Europe and Asia and parts of Africa. I even went to Brazil once. I had rarely stayed anywhere more than six months and to be locked away was entirely different. I needed Jesus to comfort me and be my friend. I knew that He was with me."

"So that's why you didn't go crazy?" Bobby was very serious.

"That's why," Julie answered emphatically.

"Boy, does He stick by me like that?" asked Bobby.

"I have no idea, Bobby. That depends on if you're a Christian," Julie answered honestly.

"How do I know if I'm a Christian?" he asked.

Julie sent up a silent prayer that she would have the right words. "First, you have to know there is a God."

"Sure, there is. My dad's talked about Him ever since I was little. What else do I have to know?" asked Bobby impatiently.

"Next, you have to know who Jesus is."

"That's easy. He was born on Christmas and died on Easter."

"What did He do in between?" Julie asked.

"He grew up and did miracles," Bobby stated simply.

"And taught about God. He was able to do these things because He is God's only Son."

"Yeah," Bobby easily agreed.

"What did He do after He died?"

"Huh?" This was a strange question.

"What did Jesus do after He died?" Julie repeated.

"I don't know," he admitted.

"He got up from the grave and wasn't dead any longer. He did some more miracles. Lots of people saw Him. Then, He went up to heaven to do another kind of job for God the Father, and He left us behind to continue His ministry here on earth until He comes again."

"Okay."

"Now, tell me why He died on the cross, Bobby."

"Because there were some bad men who wanted Him dead, so they rigged up a fake trial and killed Him."

"But He was the Son of God, Bobby, and He could have gotten off that cross anytime He wanted."

"Really?"

"Yes."

"Then why didn't He?"

"Because He wanted to pay our debts for us so we could go to heaven."

"If I know this stuff, can I go to heaven?"

"Yes, and He promises us that we are then His special children and He will never leave us or forsake us here on earth."

"Why did it have to be just Him that could do it?"

"Because He is God's perfect Son who never sinned. When He died, He took on all the sin of every believer."

"You believe all this, don't you?"

Julie nodded.

"And Cousin Peter?"

Julie nodded again.

"And you, Cousin Lisa?"

"Yes, Bobby, I believe." Lisa's soft voice firmly acknowledged her allegiance to God.

"What do I do? Do I have to sign a paper or something?"

"No, Bobby," Julie answered. "Just talk to God in your heart. Tell Him the things you've just figured out. Tell Him about your sins. You don't have to list them all. It is enough to agree with Him that you do wrong things. Thank Him for His Son, Jesus, and ask Him to be the most important friend in your life."

"Right now?"

"Right now is fine. Lisa and I will be quiet so you can think it out."

Silence filled the car, but three people were very involved in prayer.

Some time later, Bobby spoke up. "I think we should stop and get Cousin Peter a pizza. He's going to be tired after the move, and he likes pizza almost as much as I do. He took me to a pizza place in Dallas when he was visiting once, and I only ate one more piece than he did. I had to though, 'cause it was a contest."

Lisa gasped, "Bobby, didn't you do it?"

"Yeah, I won the contest," Bobby explained.

"Not that, Bobby," Lisa was astonished. "Didn't you talk to God?"

"Oh, yeah," said Bobby, "that was miles ago. Now I'm hungry. Can't we get the pizza?"

"Sure, we'll get the pizza. And we'll tell Cousin Peter it is in celebration of something and make him guess what," agreed Lisa.

"Celebration because I believe in Jesus?" Bobby asked in bewilderment.

"Yes," Lisa beamed. "It says in the Bible that the angels rejoice over every saved sinner. If they are going to party, we ought to, too."

Cousin Peter was too exhausted to be enthusiastic about pizza, and he didn't eat much for the rest of the day. However, the news of Bobby's decision delighted him, and he wanted to shake hands with one of the newest members of the Kingdom. He urged Bobby to write his dad as soon as he got home.

Bobby looked at him with big eyes. "This is a big deal, isn't it, Cousin Peter?"

"Yes, Bobby, a very big deal. You're going to find that you will be curious about exactly what the Bible says and how Jesus would act in all sorts of situations. For the rest of your life, you are going to be seeing God working, while other people who don't know Him can't seem to see a thing."

"Doesn't everybody do this?"

"Sad to say, many people never see the light."

"You look awful," Bobby commented bluntly. "Do you feel good about God even when you feel so crummy?"

"Yes," answered Peter. "And when I think of how crummy I'd feel if I had to go through this without His help, it makes me sick to my stomach."

"Let's let Peter rest, Bobby," Lisa said. "You and I need to go home and fix a special dinner and celebrate with Cousin John."

"Why don't we go out for pizza?" he suggested with his mouth full of the pizza they'd brought along.

"Bobby, you'll turn into a pizza," Lisa laughed.

"Cool. Then I'd speak Italian." Bobby's eyes danced, and they all laughed.

Chapter 20

I hear carolers," Peter said as he dipped his spoon in the mandatory red Jell-O on his dinner tray. "This hospital has the same menu as the other. I can't wait to get into our own place and have a bowl of your soup, maybe an omelet, and a homemade pizza, my homemade pizza."

"Soup, omelet, and pizza together?" Julie's eyes crinkled as she questioned her husband's choice of menu. He was often cranky these days and sometimes his ill humor struck her as amusing.

Peter ignored her comment and changed the subject back to the music in the halls.

"Is that a radio or are there really carolers out there?"

"It sounds like real singers," answered Julie. She got up from her own dinner tray and went to open the door to the hall. "What date is it, Peter?"

Peter picked up the menu beside his tray and looked at the handwritten number scratched in the corner.

"December 23. Christmas is the day after tomorrow!"

Julie came back to take his hand.

"I don't have anything for your Christmas present and I'll bet you don't have anything for me," she lamented.

"You're right about that. I suppose I could get Lisa to shop for me. We both know she'd get a kick out of yet another shopping trip."

Julie grinned. Shopping was never a burden to her sister-in-law.

"I can't believe I forgot," complained Peter.

"You have had other things on your mind."

The carolers stopped outside their door. They sang two songs for the benefit of the patients in the rooms nearby, and then with a cheerful "Merry Christmas," they moved down the hall.

"Why don't we wait?" suggested Julie. "We could have our gift exchange in a couple of months."

Peter pushed the tray away with his good arm. "Get in here," he ordered, pulling back the covers.

Julie closed the door and lay down next to Peter, doing her best not to bump him. She carefully snuggled against his good side.

He whispered into her hair, "Ten more days and they'll take this cast off my arm—then I'm going to hug my wife with both arms."

Julie giggled. "You'd better go slow, Mr. Hudson. There is still a lot of you that is temporarily out of commission."

"I'm going to be the best rehab patient they have ever had," Peter bragged. "I have real motivation to get all my abilities back in working order. Meanwhile, I should be grateful my darling wife is satisfied with broken-nose kisses and one-armed hugs, waiting for Christmas, and generally putting our life on hold."

"I'm happy, Peter. I want nothing more than to make you happy, too."

"Loving you makes me happy," he said.

"Loving you makes me happy," she repeated.

※

Peter's therapist's name was Kitty, a name that did not fit her personality at all. She was six-foot-three inches tall, without one particle of fat on her anywhere. Her long blond hair was an overdone mass of curls that she lassoed into a loose ponytail. She probably could have lifted two men Peter's size, and she had as much compassion as a drill sergeant in a marine boot camp. To accentuate the oddities of her character, she had an elaborate mask of makeup with three different shades of eye shadow highlighted with heavy black eyeliner and eyebrows.

Quickly assessing his progress so far, Kitty outlined the program before him. She liked his attitude and said so bluntly. She warned him that she was a bully by nature and fully enjoyed her job.

Her daily visits were swift and effectual. Peter groaned when he heard her coming down the hall, worked diligently for her, and groaned with relief when she departed. Sometimes Julie chose to take her walks during the sessions. She was too softhearted and wanted to brain the taskmaster, even though she was getting excellent results. On one of these walks she met Andrew Skye.

"You're Mrs. Hudson, aren't you?" asked a young man as he stopped before her.

Julie paused and looked at the man warily. He was wearing the blue garb of the therapist, the male version of Kitty's uniform.

"Do I know you?" she asked.

"No." He smiled easily, showing two charming dimples that added to his boyish good looks. "I'm Andrew Skye and I work with Kitty in the children's wing. She speaks very highly of your husband."

Julie nodded, not knowing exactly what she was supposed to say. The man was friendly, but Julie felt she had the right to be cautious these days.

"I've seen you in the gardens often," Andrew said, obviously not concerned by her reticence. "I imagine it's kind of rough being cooped up in rehab when you aren't the patient."

Julie smiled her acknowledgment of the unnecessary sympathy. True, she was often waiting for Peter, waiting for him to wake up, waiting for him to get through with some therapy. But she was contented to be here, to be Mrs. Hudson.

"Mrs. Hudson, do you swim?" he asked.

"Yes, like a fish, and I really enjoy it," answered Julie, for the first time showing some enthusiasm.

"You know there's an indoor swimming pool here that we use for therapy. There are two hours every afternoon when the patients and their families can use it."

"Yes, I just haven't taken advantage of that yet. Maybe when Peter reaches that stage of his therapy."

"I'd like to ask a favor of you," Andrew said.

Julie's eyebrows rose in surprise.

"I'm working," he continued, "with a little girl who needs the water workouts. Usually, I have the mother sit in on the sessions and then it is up to her to repeat the exercises two or three times between my sessions. However, this lady is a real bimbo and deathly afraid of the water. It works against me to even have her anywhere nearby. If you could sit in on the sessions and take over her practice sessions, I'd appreciate it. The girl is ten and a honey to work with if her mother is out of sight. When Mom's around, she reverts to a basket case."

"I'd be willing to try," she answered. Suddenly the idea of interacting with a child and being of some use appealed to her. She admitted to herself that her days were long and rather empty. Of course, being with her husband was wonderful, but too often he was tired from his therapy and irritable. As a honeymoon, it left much to be desired. Perhaps if she had something to occupy her time, she would be better company for Peter.

When she explained to Peter and asked if she could go shopping for a bathing suit, he said, "Sounds all right to me, but you take the guard with you when you go to the mall."

"Yes, Sir." She smiled at his bossy tone.

True to the unfathomable mandates of marketing, the stores were in the midst of January winter coat sales while they stocked their floors with beach attire. Julie went with her escort, Officer Camp, to a nearby mall early in the day when the crowds of shoppers were likely to be thin.

Finding a swimsuit proved an easy task. She also purchased a knee-length purple terry cloth cover-up with matching beach towel. Then, her eye was caught by the coats on clearance, and the thought of her Goodwill coat urged her to browse through the racks of sale items.

Officer Camp patiently hung around as she tried on one coat after another. Shopping in Europe had been a lot different than this, and Julie thoroughly enjoyed herself in a genuine American mall.

"My shift is going to end before we get back, Mrs. Hudson," said Officer Camp many hours later. He privately blessed his own wife for the comparatively short shopping excursions she dragged him on. He had followed Mrs. Hudson up one side of the mall and down the other on all three levels.

"What?" said Julie, looking up from a selection of men's pajamas.

"We need to be heading back. It's getting late."

Julie looked at her wristwatch. "Oh my," she exclaimed, shocked that so much time had slipped by. "Peter will have my head." She grinned at the rather comical caricature of the long-suffering husband whose wife shops till she drops.

The reality she faced when she returned to Peter's room late in the afternoon in no way resembled the lighthearted mental picture she had formed.

✱

Peter glowered, his eyebrows lowered to just above his squinted eyes. He watched without comment as Julie and Officer Camp loaded down the sofa with packages. The policeman took note of the husband's mood and quickly made himself scarce. As soon as the door closed behind him, Julie turned to Peter. Her face reflected confusion and anger.

"Why are you being so rude?" she asked. "Couldn't you have even said a few pleasant words to that man? What on earth is wrong?"

"Nothing's wrong." Peter bit into the words with a petulant tone. "I expected you to be gone an hour, maybe an hour and a half. After two hours, I began to worry. During the third hour, I tried to remind myself that you don't get to shop very often. I couldn't concentrate on my therapy exercises because I wondered where my wife was. For the last hour and a half, I've been wondering who they would send to tell me about the terrible accident or the kidnapping or whatever."

"You were worried," Julie commented, some of the heat having gone out of her anger. She looked at him with narrowed eyes, contemplating how she felt about this rather ridiculous overreaction on her husband's part. It was good that he cared for her. Right? Then how come it felt bad to be harangued like this when she returned unharmed?

She walked over to the sofa and begun rummaging through the packages, putting things away without even showing off the purchases.

The silence in the room became oppressive. Julie carefully avoided looking directly at the ogre in the bed. She came across the pajamas she had taken such pleasure in buying for her husband. He was being unreasonable, but she could have called. She sneaked a peek in the mirror and saw he was staring at the ceiling. He must be tired of being in the bed. She had relished being away from the hospital; lost in her own pleasure, she had never once thought he might be concerned for her safety. She turned slowly to offer him the gift and try to apologize for her lack of consideration.

"I'm sorry, Peter," she spoke softly. She moved over to put her hand on his arm.

"Julie," he whispered, still staring at the ceiling, "I thought you were dead."

"But I promised I wouldn't go away without saying good-bye," she reminded him.

Peter's head turned quickly. He frowned as his eyes searched her face until he saw the gleam of mischief in her own dark eyes.

"I suppose you would have told St. Peter you had an errand to run before you could go through the gates."

Her shoulders relaxed when she heard the light note in his voice. She sat on the edge of the bed and stroked his arm.

"If he had any authority to grant me a favor, I might." She stretched out beside him, carefully adjusting to fit at the side of his body without jostling him. She was getting pretty adept at this maneuver. She laid the pajama package on his stomach.

"I am sorry I was so inconsiderate. You know, I never had to report to anyone when I was off gallivanting around Europe. When I was in school, we had free time and a curfew. There was a set time to be back in the dormitories. But on the excursions, there was only the paid companion who was always at my side. Officer Camp was just like my chaperones, although a good deal less bossy. He was just there while I shopped. I didn't relate to the here and now and the husband waiting for me. Forgive me?"

Peter's arm tightened around her. "I've been a bear lately. I know it. While I was fretting over your disappearance, convinced your uncle had spirited you away, I realized how much I snap at you and order you around. It would have served me right if you had decided to take off to get away from yet another oppressive tyrant."

Julie smiled and hugged him gingerly. Full hugs still caused him to wince, even though those ribs were almost healed.

"We've had a real fight, haven't we?" She seemed pleased.

"I'd say it was more of a misunderstanding," insisted Peter.

"No, Peter," she objected. "I was really mad. I was thinking about what to throw at you that wouldn't hurt you too badly."

"Okay. I was wishing I could get out of this bed on my own power so I could strangle you the moment you came through that door."

"I love you, Peter."

"I love you, too, but I think I've missed something in the natural progression of this conversation."

"Umm?"

"Shouldn't you still be fuming at me? I was acting like a pig."

"Yes, but when couples have a fight. . ."

"Misunderstanding," he interrupted.

"Fight," she insisted. "Then they make up. Let's just skip the rest of the fighting part and get right to the making up."

Peter groaned and kissed the top of her head. "Oh, God," he prayed loud enough for her to hear, "get me out of these clumsy leg casts soon."

445

Chapter 21

"Couldn't you have found a bathing suit that covered more of your body?" The petulant tone was back in Peter's voice and Julie wanted to throttle him. She picked up the purple cover-up and put it on, hoping that it would indeed cover up the offending garment.

"This bathing suit had more material in it than most of the ones I saw at the mall, Peter."

"I just don't like the idea of all those healthy males ogling my wife."

"I am going to the children's exercise class."

"I've got eyes in my head, Julie. Not all the therapists are women like Kitty. Some of them are very healthy young males."

"That's the second time you've emphasized 'healthy,' Peter. Would you get off the 'healthy' kick? You're getting better. I'm patiently waiting for you. I'm not going to fool around with some guy just because he's walking on two legs. Just because he's 'healthy.'"

"I'm not doubting you," Peter protested. "It's just that I suddenly see the virtue of those black bloomers and bulging blouses my great-granny wore to dip in the ocean. Why don't you promise me to get into the water quickly so those 'healthy' male therapists won't get an eyeful?"

She turned to do battle and brought herself up short as she saw the corner of his mouth twitch.

"You're teasing me," she accused.

"Well, yes and no. It is frustrating to be tantalized by seeing you in that lovely but skimpy swimming suit. I confess to having the urge to hide you in the closet until I'm able to walk beside you and glower hideous threats at any male who dares to appreciate your figure."

"Peter, you have to relax a little bit." Julie nervously twisted the beach towel in her hand. She looked up to see that Peter's face had returned to that forbidding scowl.

"When I came home from shopping, you said something about being an oppressive tyrant."

Peter was silent. Julie turned away, bravely plunging on but not brave enough to watch his face.

"Sometimes lately I feel very confined. I do want to escape. I want to escape this room. I want to get away from your bad moods."

446

Peter was still silent.

"I know you aren't grouchy on purpose." Her voice faded away. She waited for him to speak.

"Come here," he said quietly, after what seemed to her a very long moment. She turned to see he had his good hand stretched out to her. Quickly she came across the room to his bed and took the offered hand. He squeezed her fingers gently, but he didn't speak.

"I must not be any good at relationships," she stumbled on. "If you think about it, for thirteen years I haven't had any close ties to anyone. Maybe I just can't be a good wife. I just don't know how."

"That's ridiculous," barked Peter. Immediately his face changed from impatience to concern. He continued in a softer tone of voice. "Julie, you are the most loving individual I have ever met. I thank God for you every day. I love you and I am very sure of your love for me. Please put up with me. I'll try to do better."

The pleading in his voice took her by surprise. She gazed down at the lines of worry on his brow, and with her free hand, she reached out as if to smooth them away. He pulled the hand he held up to his lips and kissed her palm.

"Julie, I love you."

She nodded, unable to speak past the lump in her throat.

"You are fully capable of giving me all the love I need, and I will try to be less of a tyrant. I think we need to include God more in the areas of our marriage that give us trouble. What do you say we spend some of these long evenings in a Bible study? Just you and me."

"Yes," Julie readily agreed, feeling again the rush of happiness that this man brought her.

"And, we could make it a habit to pray together."

She nodded again.

"Forgive me?" he asked.

She hurt him when she threw herself down on his chest, but he suppressed the "Oomph" and hugged her tightly with his good arm.

※

Harry O'Neill was apprehended in Galveston. Between the two suspects, the police came up with a full confession. Each one would reveal something additional, and then the police would use that to their advantage in questioning the other. The pity was that the arrested men had no idea who was the person behind their employment. They had dealt with a middleman. Now police were tracking this criminal.

Uncle Henry flew down to visit Peter and Julie.

"This is a more comfortable setup for Julie," he commented soon after he had walked into the room. The hospital catered to long-term recovery, and the room had the hospital bed for Peter and a regular bed for Julie, since often a parent or spouse would be in residence with the patient. There was also a couch and chair and small desk. Double glass doors opened up to a small patio and a walkway ran down to a central garden. When Peter could use a wheelchair, they would be able to go on walks. Now, Peter insisted she take a walk with each officer as he came on duty. He told her she was going to be pale and puny-looking unless she got out.

Uncle Henry's visit concerned Julie's business interests.

"You're going to need a full-time executive to replace Jacob Jones. That man had a lot of business sense, but no scruples. Some of his dealings bordered on criminal; most of them were ruthless and did damage to a lot of poor people. His methods earned him a rotten reputation and many old business associates harbor a great deal of justified resentment.

"I suggest we send out a letter clarifying the position of the new management. Also, I believe there are many cases where you can make restitution. It means your profits will be down this year and quite possibly for the next two years. But you have it within your ability to do it, and I don't feel right about just letting it slide."

"I agree," Julie readily answered. "What about a business manager?"

"I'm thinking Peter is the logical choice. This is the kind of business he enjoys. He's a good rancher, but his heart is not in it like his dad's. Now that Ray has had to go back to the ranch in order to keep things going, he's a new man. He sounds like he's ten years younger when I've spoken to him on the phone."

"Now you know," said Peter to Julie. "I married you to get controlling interest in your inheritance."

"That's very ignoble of you, but I think you proposed before you knew the extent of my wealth. For that matter, I don't know the whole of it."

Uncle Henry laughed. "I've been involved with it for weeks, and I'm just now beginning to realize what a monumental project we've gotten into."

"Do you really think I can handle it?" asked Peter.

"I have absolutely no doubt," affirmed his lawyer uncle. "I'm so sure, I brought the first set of papers for you to go over and analyze. There is nothing wrong with your mind except you get tired easily. This will give you something to concentrate on in between those torture sessions they call therapy."

"Thanks, Uncle Henry," joked Peter. "You always were a thoughtful relative."

✳

When the cast came off his arm, Peter declared he was half of a new man. From the waist up, he was doing very well. His nose was healed, though tender to the touch. The discoloration, which had gone from black and purple to greenish yellow to yellowish tan, had now faded away to his natural coloring. He was accustomed to more sun, so he still looked pale, and the many little scars from the shattered glass still crisscrossed his skin, mostly across the forehead. The doctors said those would fade with time. Only two were very deep, and those were in the hairline. One doctor joked that he had come very close to being scalped. Julie did not think it was funny.

His broken and cracked ribs were healed and his left arm looked puny next to his strong right arm. Kitty was quick to instigate exercises on behalf of the weakened muscles. She smiled with delight when she came in and saw him unencumbered with plaster. He groaned at her obvious pleasure.

Two days later, they removed the leg casts and replaced them with casts that could be taken on and off with Velcro straps. This also heralded the beginning of his water exercises, which he enjoyed. Soon, Julie, Peter, and their new little friend Katie were spending several hours every afternoon in the pool with other patients and family members.

Although Katie thought Julie was great, she obviously had an overwhelming crush on Peter. He could get her to try almost anything, but most often he was caught up in his own exercises. He rarely bothered with Katie other than to nod when she clamored for his attention. Julie wanted to shake her single-minded husband.

Chapter 22

Peter sighed in exasperation as he looked at the briefcase sitting on the sofa across the room. Where was Julie? He was tired from his morning bout with Killer Kitty, but not tired enough to sleep. If he could go through those papers one more time, they could send them off to Uncle Henry's office with the revisions marked. He didn't want to bother a nurse just to come hand him a briefcase.

Peter reached for the TV remote and switched on the set. He surfed through all fifty-six cable channels and hit the OFF button in disgust.

Perhaps Julie was helping with Katie's exercises, which meant she was also in the company of Andrew Skye. Peter didn't like Andrew Skye. It seemed to Peter that Andrew Skye was just a little too friendly. Whoever heard of a therapist who constantly needed some other patient's wife as an assistant? Killer Kitty never brought in outside help, certainly not help who wasn't on the hospital staff.

Peter reached for the newspaper on the bedside stand and succeeded in knocking it to the floor out of reach. He leaned back against the pillows and glared at the ceiling.

"I'll talk to You about this, God, but I'm warning You, I'm not in a very congenial mood. I'm tired of this whole business. Get me out of here. I'm doing my part. I've never worked so hard in all my life. If I'm supposed to be learning to be humble, I think we marked that one off with the first go-round on the bedpan.

"If we're working on patience, doesn't holding my tongue when that squeaky-clean Andrew Skye comes around winking at Julie and escorting her off to help fix Katie's hair with new pink ribbons count as monumental self-control? Give me a break. Where's the girl's mother? When did Julie become a hairdresser? What business is it of muscle-bulging Andrew if Katie has a new hairdo to cheer her up?

"And pardon me for mentioning it, but it does seem a little unfair to bless me with an extremely attractive wife and then handicap me so I can't enjoy loving her."

Peter heard laughter in the halls and his face hardened. Julie was returning, but she wasn't alone. The door opened, and Peter got a glimpse of Andrew Skye, blue-eyed, blond locks, with muscles straining the blue fabric of his therapist uniform. The man was a caricature of health and goodwill. Peter grimaced and bit off the "bah humbug" that sprang to his lips.

"Thanks for your help, Julie." Andrew reached out and placed a hand on the arm of Peter's wife. "Katie's progress is as much from your encouragement and friendship as from my skill."

"I am proud of her," agreed Julie. "See you tonight."

She turned into the room with a smile on her face that faded when she saw Peter's expression.

"Katie took three steps today," she announced with forced cheerfulness. She saw the paper on the floor and came over to pick it up. She offered it to Peter, and when he didn't take it, laid it back on the bedside table.

"How was your session with Kitty?"

"I stood up from a chair, walked across the room on the crutches, and sat down in another chair," he reported without any enthusiasm.

"That's great, Peter," replied Julie.

"Would you hand me the briefcase?"

"Sure." Julie quickly retrieved it and gave it to Peter. He took it without comment and proceeded to immerse himself in the paperwork.

"Peter, I didn't do anything wrong."

He didn't look up from his papers. "I didn't say you did." Fact was, he was being very careful not to say anything.

"Would you like me to get you a soda from the machine?"

"No, thank you." He'd like her to get rid of the lecherous therapist. There was no use pretending that the man was friendly in any way other than as a single male stalking a vulnerable, beautiful female.

"Are you going to join us for a swim this afternoon?"

"Probably." At least then he could glower at the Adonis therapist.

"I think I'll get a soda." Julie grabbed her change purse and bolted out the door.

Peter groaned. He was being a complete fool, and he couldn't stop himself. He vowed when she came back in, he'd do better. He'd apologize again and try not to be such an overbearing clod. He used to pride himself in his expertise when he dealt with his sisters. Where was that skill now? Hadn't he handled this skittish filly with finesse before they were married? What had turned him into such a heavy-handed hombre? How could she love and respect a man who pored over the Scriptures with her in the evening and browbeat her during the day?

All of his good intentions came to naught. She didn't return until it was time to get into his wheelchair and go down the hall to where the mobile patients ate in a dining room.

Julie pushed him up to the table where Katie and her mother sat. Two other patients would share their table, a teenage boy who had been in a motorcycle wreck and Mr. Gonzales, a stroke victim. As was Julie's custom, she then joined the servers and returned to the table when all the patients had their meals before them.

"Have you already prayed?" she asked.

"We waited for you," said Katie.

"Thanks," she returned with a smile. They reached out to hold hands, and Peter bowed his head, knowing they expected him to give the grace.

"Father, for the bounty of food before us, we thank You. For the bounty of forgiveness we receive through Your Son, we thank You. For the bounty of love we experience through Your Holy Spirit, we thank You. Bless us and strengthen us through this food to do Your will, and through Your wisdom, create in us a desire to do Your will. In Jesus' name, we pray. Amen."

The others dropped hands to pick up their forks, but Peter held on to Julie's until she turned to look at him.

"I've been a boor again," he said quietly, only for her ears. "Forgive me?"

She smiled weakly and nodded, but without much enthusiasm. Peter was often unbearably caustic and then just as earnestly repentant. Julie was getting tired of it. Peter was aware that his apology had only been accepted in a half-hearted way.

Silently Peter prayed for a solution to his problem. *Lord, I am fully aware that I am the one causing all this trauma. Please give me direction. If nothing else, stop up my mouth, tie my hands, keep me from further alienating the woman I love.*

As Peter passed the basket of rolls to Katie, he noticed her cheerful smile. She really was an endearing child. Peter watched and listened as his wife and this young girl interacted. Truly they had a remarkable friendship. Perhaps it would be expedient to his own peace of mind and his relationship with his wife to join their friendship.

It was Julie's involvement with Katie that took her away from his side. Peter had been so immersed in his own therapy that he hadn't really paid much attention to Katie other than to grouse about the time Julie spent with her. Andrew Skye really wasn't the person Julie was interested in. Peter vowed to be more involved in his wife's interests.

Lisa and Bobby showed up right after lunch to join them in the pool during the free swim. Peter welcomed them enthusiastically and his sister tossed him a quizzical look.

In the water, Peter felt much more confident. Without the wheelchair or cumbersome crutches, he could move with relative freedom in the pool.

Julie immediately entered into a game with some children. Soon Peter would begin the exercises he had learned. Peter watched Julie, longing to reestablish the rapport they had once had. For just a moment, he lounged in the water with his sister. With his new awareness of just how self-centered he had become, Peter realized that he had never told Lisa how much he appreciated her taking the time to come visit.

"Thanks for bringing Bobby out and joining us, Lisa. Julie looks forward to your visits."

"Brother," Lisa looked at him askance, "this is the second time today you've surprised me by being aware of something other than your therapy. Have they begun mental health rehabilitation on you in addition to the physical?"

Peter laughed uneasily. "Do you think I need it?"

"I think most people who are going through intensive rehab may be a bit single-minded, but given your rather forceful personality and stubborn streak, you've outdone most."

"You want to spell that out in plain English, little sister?" Peter asked even though he feared forthright Lisa was about to confirm his suspicions.

"You asked for it." Lisa grinned. "You have become a boor, a self-centered boor. You speak abruptly to Julie and give commands without using that pretty little word 'please' that our mother drilled into us. I'd throw a bedpan at you."

Peter looked across the pool to where Julie was playing a beach-ball game with Katie, Bobby, and several other young patients.

"She truly is a gift from God," he murmured.

"Yes," agreed Lisa, "and you've been treating her like your own personal slave."

Peter nodded his head, acknowledging the truth of his sister's words. He decided to join the game instead of repeating the water exercises Kitty had given him. With strong, powerful strokes, he swam to the circle of children and took a position directly across from his wife.

Julie looked startled to see him. Again he was aware that during these times he usually stuck to his self-imposed regimen of work. He avoided the social atmosphere and concentrated on doing even more to accomplish his goal of regaining total use of his legs. His therapy, his goals, his problems. Perhaps his single-mindedness had been to the detriment of his relationship with his wife.

She smiled at him now and he felt a lightheartedness fill his soul. There was more to life than therapy. Thank God there was more!

When the young players went off in different directions to new interests, Peter stayed by Julie. They swam leisurely back and forth across the pool, just enjoying each other's company and chatting about nothing in particular.

Two hours of free swim passed quickly, and soon the pool would be taken over by the scheduled therapy sessions. The patients were beginning to climb out. Julie noticed that Katie clung to the edge of the pool talking to another patient, Hannah, giggling over some of the exercises inflicted upon them by Kitty.

The rest of the afternoon went quickly with a visit from the pastor of Lisa's church. They ate with the crowd in the dining hall and stayed a little longer than usual. An older man was telling stories of his days in vaudeville. Peter felt he made great strides toward relaxing and enjoying his wife's company.

As soon as they got back to the room, Peter was immersed in the long ritual of getting ready to retire for the night. Finally, he was alone with his wife.

"Julie, come here," he called quietly.

Julie came out of their bathroom with a hairbrush in her hand and a guarded expression on her face. She expected Andrew to come by soon. Whatever Peter wanted, she didn't want to get involved right now.

"Yes?" She stood in the doorway, not coming to his side.

"Can we talk?" asked Peter.

"How about in the morning?" she countered.

Instead of the angry, petulant expression she expected on Peter's face, he looked concerned.

"You're going someplace?"

"Only to the dining room. I'm meeting Andrew," she admitted.

Peter nodded, and his face looked so sad, she realized how much she hurt him by being distant.

"He's bringing some material on courses I could take," Julie explained. "He thinks I could be a therapist. He says I'm really good with Katie, and I could specialize on children."

"You want a career?" asked Peter carefully. He felt they had made some progress this afternoon and he didn't want to sound condemning or scornful. He didn't want to cause her to withdraw any further.

Julie remained quiet. She studied the hairbrush in her hand, turning it slowly as if she would find the answer hidden on it.

She sighed. "No, not really. I thought I could help more with your therapy, but I realize it would be two years before I would be of any use to you, and by then you will not need me. I thought you might be proud of me, less angry that I just sit around doing nothing."

"Angry with you?" he asked, incredulous.

She nodded.

"Oh, Julie, no!" He stretched out a hand, hoping she would come to him. After hesitating a moment, she did. He grasped her hand, eager to explain now that he had some inkling of what was going wrong between them. "I'm angry with myself for taking so long to regain my mobility. I'm angry with your uncle for what he did. I'm angry with the police for not getting enough evidence to throw your uncle behind bars. I'm angry with Uncle Henry for how slow the court process takes, as if he could hurry it up. I'm even angry with God for allowing all this to happen. But I'm not angry with you."

"You don't act angry with anyone but me, Peter."

"That's because I trust you. I don't pretend everything is all right when I'm with you. It's hard to explain, Julie, but you're the one that gets the brunt of my anger because you're the one I love."

Julie squeezed his hand and he pulled her down beside him.

"Let me hold you," he begged. She stretched out beside him in the familiar position that lately she had avoided.

"Lisa told me I was being a self-centered boor. I've had my focus on myself and my therapy. I don't even know anything about your little friend, Katie. Why is her mother so uptight?"

"The same fire that burned Katie's legs so severely killed her sister. The mother is convinced the whole thing was her fault. She's paranoid that something else will happen to Katie."

"Doesn't sound like she has any faith in the goodness of God."

"She doesn't have any faith at all. She's had to go through all this without the knowledge that God loves her and her family. She's bitter and fearful." Julie craned her neck to look up into Peter's face. "I know I should be witnessing to her, but I can only think of little things to say once in awhile. In the face of what she's been through, my words of comfort sound trite."

"But we know they aren't trite, Julie. Don't worry about having the right words to say. I'm sure she witnesses your gentleness and peace even if you aren't verbally spouting great doctrine. I believe God uses you just as you are. He's used you in my life. Even today."

"Even today?" she asked.

He nodded emphatically. "Today, God got my attention through you. He told me that I had made out my own list of priorities without regarding His will. I haven't been content with the state I've found myself in, and by concentrating on getting myself out of this state through my own efforts, I have risked losing a great gift He has given me."

"Gift?"

"You."

There was a knock on the door, and Julie sprang off the bed and to her feet just as it opened.

"Hi," said Andrew, beaming. "Did you forget our appointment, Julie?"

"No, she didn't forget." Peter thrust down the immediate annoyance he felt. He must behave with more charity. He continued in a friendly tone. "She just got delayed. But I'm interested in this project of my wife's. Could you stay here and talk it over? I'd like to hear more, and I'm afraid I've been so wrapped up in my own therapy that I've neglected making friends with my wife's friends. I intend to get to know you and Katie."

Peter smiled at his wife. Julie smiled back. Their eyes caught and held, and a new look of understanding passed between them. A sigh of relief escaped Peter before he turned to pay attention to the young therapist's brochures and magazine articles about a career in physical therapy.

Chapter 23

Tom Quidmore escorted Peter and Julie when they went out for a Valentine's Day date. Everything about the lighthearted police officer was thick. He was indubitably short and squat. His frame was solid. His neck was thick like a football player's. His torso was thick. His arms and thighs were thick. He looked like a human block in a uniform with curly, flaming red hair on top.

Tom regaled them with teasing banter as he escorted the finely dressed couple to his jalopy. He made much of the fact that he'd tried to borrow the chief's car, but he wasn't trusted with anyone's vehicle, since he held the record for busting up patrol cars.

"You will drive carefully?" asked Julie, rising to the bait.

"Like I was driving the king and queen of Spain, Ma'am," he answered with a twinkle in his eye.

Julie and Officer Quidmore maneuvered Peter into the backseat, and Tom stowed the wheelchair in the trunk. He opened and shut the door for Mrs. Hudson, putting on a chauffeur's attitude. He gabbled about society celebrities in Corpus Christi while he drove. At the hotel, he helped them out and had the valet park his tin heap. Upstairs in the restaurant, he suddenly melted into the background, where he kept an eagle eye out for any possible trouble.

Peter and Julie sat at a table by the window overlooking the water. They watched the lighted waves wash against the shore.

"Remember we walked along that beach a long time ago?" Peter took her hand and smiled at her.

"I remember. It was cold."

"You were lovely then in that horrendous coat, but you are a vision tonight."

Julie blushed under his praise.

"Let's talk about the future," Peter urged. "By March first, I intend to be released from Dolman."

"Oh, you do?" interrupted Julie with arched eyebrows.

"Yes, I do," said Peter with confidence. "I think that's a reasonable goal. However, I'll remember not to neglect my wife," he promised. "I'll have to go in for therapy, so going back to Dooley is out of the picture for awhile."

"So what are we going to do?"

"Lisa and John are moving to a bigger apartment, and I figure we could move into the same apartment complex."

"Have you already rented the place?" Julie asked, annoyed that he was making all these plans and consulting her after the fact.

"No, but Lisa has two for you to go look at."

The last statement brought Julie up short. She had assumed that he wasn't allowing her to be a part of the decision-making process. She was wrong. How often was she going to be guilty of jumping to the wrong conclusion and causing tension between them?

Peter had disappointed her by being demanding and bossy. She understood that these characteristics had been part of his personality before the accident and were the same, only intensified, during the stressful period of his recovery. Now she realized that not only would she have to be tolerant of this while he was vulnerable, but she would also have to guard against developing bad habits of reaction in herself. She decided she would address this present issue with a light attitude.

"When did you two scheme this up? I thought you were never out of my sight except for therapy sessions in the torture chamber of Killer Kitty."

"You forgot the times you go help with Katie's therapy," Peter reminded her. "Katie's going to be an outpatient herself before too long. She's come a long way. I'm right proud of her. And I'm proud of you."

Julie glowed with happiness.

"I think we ought to venture out as a group and go to church next Sunday. The church Lisa and John attend would be perfect for her. There are a lot of outgoing young people there."

"Okay," agreed Julie. "I see now that you've gotten out once, you will be a hard man to keep behind bars."

"That's right, Honey," Peter joked. "I've had my taste of freedom and I like it." At once, he was serious, squeezing the hand he still held. "You've been terrific, Julie. You don't complain about being so confined. At least you don't if I remember to behave decently. It must bother you a lot after your experience at the Estate."

"Peter, you idiot," she laughed. "It is not the same at all. In the Estate, I chafed to get out to live my life. In the hospital with you, my life was right there to live. You are my life."

"Someday it will be more than just me. We are going to fill a ranch with little ranch hands."

Julie smiled at the prospect. She loved it when he said something particularly "cowboy" to make her laugh.

"But now let's consider the immediate future. You'll have to do some shopping to furnish the apartment."

"Okay," she agreed.

"Have you decided about those courses Andrew outlined?"

She nodded, and Peter held his breath while waiting for her answer. He had decided to support her in any decision she made.

"I would like to try it."

"Well then, that's another reason not to rush back to Dooley. You can take classes in Corpus."

The music had started and couples were moving to the dance floor.

"Next year, we'll be dancing, too," Peter promised.

When they were ready to leave, Officer Tom Quidmore appeared to take them home. He was obviously "on duty" until he had them loaded in the car, and they were on their way back to the hospital. Then he began his stream of cheery banter while Peter and Julie held hands in the backseat. Peter answered with an occasional comment, but the policeman didn't really need any help with his conversation. Peter put his arm around his wife's shoulders, and she cuddled up against him.

An hour later, Peter lay in the dark tucked into his hospital bed, listening to his lovely wife putter around in the bathroom.

"Julie?"

She came to the door and the light from behind her outlined her figure as she stood in a shimmery nightgown.

"Do you need something?"

"Oh, yes, Honey, most definitely."

"A drink?"

"No."

"Do you need to get up to go to the bathroom again?"

"No."

"Are you overtired? Do you need a painkiller?"

"I don't seem to be tired at all, and what's bothering me can't be touched by a painkiller."

"Peter, I am not a mind reader," Julie retorted, annoyed that he seemed to be beating about the bush. "What do you want?"

"You."

"You mean. . ."

"Yes."

Julie stood stunned for a moment.

"Are you sure?" she asked, breathless.

"Honey, this might be a bit of an awkward seduction, but I'm a determined man, and you, my wife, are going to be seduced. Turn off that light and come here."

Julie smiled shyly and turned off the bathroom light. Sometimes she liked the way Peter bossed her around.

✳

They moved into the apartment the weekend after March 1.

Peter took on more of Julie's business affairs. Visitors representing different industries under their control began to call. For the most part, these were pleasant encounters. The executives were happy to have someone more reasonable to deal with than the previous management. Those who were of the same mind as the departed Jacob Jones were being weeded out of the companies owned by Julie Jones Hudson. Uncle Henry was invaluable help and had generated a division in his firm of lawyers just to handle the business Julie's interests brought in.

Policemen continued to keep them company. The off-duty officers wore their uniforms and were with them twenty-four hours a day. All of the men were friendly, but none of them were actual friends. In the interest of performing their duty, they were aloof and alert. Involvement with the family could possibly distract them and cause them to miss a suspicious circumstance.

Peter and Julie had become familiar with them all and had favorite characters among the dozen men who stood guard over them. It was a part of their lives, and they ceased to think of it as anything but normal.

Spring began to make itself felt in the air one day in early April. Julie had had an extra officer that morning to go shopping with her. She'd stopped at a greenhouse and loaded up with plants, some for inside the apartment and some for the patio. This officer left about fifteen minutes before the guard in the apartment was to be relieved by the afternoon duty officer.

Julie bustled around the kitchen fixing lunch. When she realized that Officer Cranz was still there, she was puzzled.

"Weren't you supposed to be relieved at noon?" she asked.

"Yes, Ma'am, but Kroger is late."

"Do you need to go? I'm sure we can manage for a few minutes."

The officer grinned. "Mrs. Hudson, you ought to know better than that. I'll wait ten more minutes and then call Rodriguez."

Julie returned to the kitchen. Minutes later she heard the doorbell ring.

"Sorry I'm late. I had a hard time finding the place," she heard a strange voice explaining.

"Who are you?" asked Cranz.

"I'm new. Kroger couldn't make it, so Rodriguez called me."

"What precinct are you from?"

"Third. Just started. I used to work in Houston. I'm hoping this smaller city will be an easier job."

The telephone rang and Julie left her eavesdropping to answer it.

"Hello?" she said into the receiver.

"Mrs. Hudson, this is Kroger. I've had car trouble and I'm suspicious. I've already phoned for a patrol car to come by your place and check things out. Now, don't let on it's me, but if you think something might be wrong there, just tell me Mr. Hudson can't come to the phone."

Julie felt the skin on the back of her neck crawl. She looked up to see both policemen watching her.

"Maybe later," she said, hoping her voice wouldn't crack. "Peter is resting and can't come to the phone."

"Okay, Mrs. Hudson," returned the reassuring voice of her well-known Officer Kroger. "If there is someone there who shouldn't be, I want you to tell me how many by saying one o'clock for one, two o'clock for two, and so on."

"You could call back at one o'clock," she answered.

"Is Cranz still there?"

"Yes," Julie sighed.

"In case he hasn't caught on, I want you to keep him there. Talk to him about anything, boating, fishing, flowers, anything. The backup unit is on its way. Try to act natural and keep out of reach of the suspect. Don't leave the apartment. There might be an accomplice outside waiting."

"Okay, I'll tell him as soon as he wakes up." Julie hung up the phone.

She started back to the kitchen and then stopped as if she remembered something.

"Bob," she addressed Officer Cranz, whose first name was Bill. "I'll get that recipe for your wife that you wanted." Officer Cranz was also single and enjoyed his bachelorhood immensely. "I've got a backup copy. If I can find it, I'll only take a few minutes. If I have to write it out, it will take longer. Have you got a minute to stay?" she asked. Did he understand a backup unit was coming?

"Sure, Julie," Cranz answered, using her first name when he had never called her anything but Mrs. Hudson or ma'am.

He got the message, she was sure. Julie slipped into the bedroom to sit with Peter. She whispered to him what was going on, even though she knew that the impostor hadn't a chance of overhearing her from the next room.

"I'm going out there." Peter grabbed his crutches.

"You are not." Julie moved between him and the door. "Let them handle it. You'd be something extra for them to worry about when they grab him."

"You're saying I'd be in the way." His tone was angry. The truth was that he would be in the way, and he knew it.

"You stay here and protect me," Julie cried. "If that man gets past the police, who's going to help me?"

"You're good, Julie. That argument will keep me by your side, but I want you to know I recognize it for what it is."

She put her arms around him. He leaned against her slightly and put the arm still holding the crutch around her slender shoulders.

"I'm scared," she said against his shoulder.

"It'll be all right," he reassured.

They stood waiting and praying. Soon they heard the backup policemen arrive. Apparently, the impostor recognized he was outmaneuvered and did not resist arrest. A knock on the bedroom door told them it was all over. Officer Cranz called, "Come on out, folks."

Julie opened the door, and Peter followed her into the room. The policemen were just escorting the criminal in handcuffs out the front door.

"Sorry for the inconvenience." Bill Cranz grinned. "I got to tell you, Mrs. Hudson, you are one cool dame."

"Really! You should have seen me clinging to Peter in the bedroom. That was the longest few minutes I've ever been through."

Peter sniffed the air.

"Julie, I think you're burning lunch."

"Oh, bother." Julie rushed to the kitchen. "It's ruined," she called back.

"Good," Peter proclaimed. "Let's order pizza." He turned to Officer Cranz. "That is one of Julie's major failings. She never thinks to order pizza. I think it comes from being raised in Europe. She's always fixing these delicious, well-balanced meals with things like brussels sprouts and asparagus. Mind you, it is all delectable. But someday I'm going to get in that kitchen and make her a super-Hudson homemade pizza that will knock her socks off. Our children will bless the days old Dad enters the kitchen and takes over."

Cranz smiled at Peter's oratory on Julie and pizza, but something came to his mind and his face became serious.

"By the way—"

Peter held up his hand. "Don't tell me. Lieutenant Brock will be by this afternoon to take our statements."

Cranz grinned again. "Yes, Sir, that's right."

Chapter 24

S he's not coming back, Son," Ray told Peter as the men sat in the living room of the apartment. "I can't say that I blame her. She never was cut out to be a rancher's wife. I should have seen that before I married her."

Peter hung his head, looking at his hands, not knowing how to console his dad.

Ray went on. "She called last night and said she'd had it and was filing for divorce. Ever since I married her, I've felt like I betrayed the memory of your mom. I felt like I'd let you kids down, though you never once said anything. Not one of you blew up and told me what a chump I'd been. I guess that was your mother's training in you. With Suzanne, I constantly felt that I'd failed her. The only way to please her was to be someone I'm not. I tried, but I failed."

Peter prayed silently. His father needed comfort beyond what he could give.

"You know, your mother only asked one thing of me that I wouldn't give her. She wanted me to be an entirely different person, too. But she never made me feel like dirt. She always made me feel like the king in his palace, even though I was too stubborn to change the one thing she asked for. She wanted me to be a Christian. She raised our kids to be Christians. Just before she died, she asked me to join her in heaven." Ray's voice broke with emotion and he dashed his hand across his eyes.

"I can still see her soft, lovely face. Her voice was always so ladylike. She was always a lady, even when she was cooking for twenty cowhands, or scrubbing the floors, or thrashing one of you kids for being ornery. She wanted me to trust her Savior, and I told her it was nonsense. Even when she was dying, I was too stubborn to admit I needed her Savior."

Peter watched the agony his dad was going through and was at a loss as to how to help.

"I should have listened. These past five years have been hell, and all she wanted for me was heaven."

"It's not too late, Dad." Peter spoke softly.

"I'm afraid it is, Peter." He sighed. "I'm an old fool. What kind of a God would take in an old fool at the end of his life?"

"Jesus tells a parable that says our loving God will do just that. Sometimes I've resented the fact that the parable says those who come late will reap the same benefits as those who labored all their lives. But now that it could mean my own dad, I don't care that there appears to be an injustice. I rejoice that you can have it all, too."

"I know all the words, Peter. I've heard the gospel preached all my life, though I've tried to avoid it, resisted its call. Do you think if I pray after all these years of scoffing, He's going to hear me?"

"He'll hear you and believe you and forgive you and accept you. His Word promises you won't be rejected. He can't cast you aside without damaging His own character. He has to fulfill His promises. He can't help it."

"Peter, I can't do it. It is like having to go to the principal's office when you know you deserve to be expelled."

"Are you remembering the time I had to go to the office for painting the lockers purple?"

Ray nodded and grinned.

"I remember that you went with me. I don't think I could have gone down that hall and opened the door if you hadn't been beside me."

"You were as guilty as they come. You bought the paint, and your fingernails were caked with the stuff. You even had a purple streak in your hair," Ray recalled.

"Would you like me to go with you before the throne of God?" Peter asked. "One of the verses in the Bible says that a child of God has the privilege of boldly coming before the throne. I am a child of God, and I'm willing to go with you."

Ray gazed into his son's earnest eyes. After a moment of silence, he nodded his head and slipped from the chair to his knees. He'd seen his wife kneel beside their bed and scoffed at her. Maybe that was why he felt his confession must be made on his knees. Peter knelt beside him.

"Father in heaven," Peter began. "Please comfort my father and give him peace in his heart. Help to loosen his tongue so that he can speak to You. His heart is heavy, Lord, from the burden of rejecting You for so long, but You have drawn him close. Help him to make that last step that will put him in Your kingdom for eternity." Peter fell silent. In the gathering dusk of the day, Ray Hudson finally came before his Maker and confessed his need for a Savior.

When Julie returned from grocery shopping with her cop in tow, she found Peter's cop standing in the hall.

"What's up?" she quizzed.

"Mr. Hudson has a visitor. It's his father, I think."

Julie rushed in to find the two men having coffee.

"Were we expecting you, Mr. Hudson?" she asked.

"I object," said the older Mr. Hudson. "You have been married to my son for five months. Surely you can call me something besides Mr. Hudson."

Julie laughed. "How about Mr. Greenjeans?"

"No." He laughed, too. "How about Dad?"

She put down her bag of groceries and hugged him.

"It would be my honor, Dad," she said. Then with mischief in her eye, she said, "Dad?"

"Yes?"

"Will you go get the rest of the groceries?"

"My honor," he answered with a bow.

Chapter 25

T his makes me nervous," said Aunt Harry as she drove up the highway toward Austin.

"Nothing is going to happen," assured Peter. "The troopers are just a precaution because we're state witnesses. They are escorting us as a mere formality. Nobody expects trouble."

"That's not what I mean," objected Aunt Harry. "Every time I look in the rearview mirror, I think I'm going to be pulled over for speeding." Her eyes once more checked the little mirror and once more she saw the trooper's car.

"Are you speeding?" asked Julie.

"Of course not. I wouldn't dare," answered the flustered driver.

Peter and Julie were expected to testify in the trial against Dr. French. Uncle Henry had assured Julie that it would not be an arduous ordeal. He was right.

The actual time spent on the witness stand for each was less than one hour. The hard part proved to be the reporters who were following the trial and made coming and going to the courthouse miserable. Peter, although up on crutches, could not move fast and that made them prime targets. They spent two days in Austin, and as soon as their testimony was complete, they left by airplane for Corpus.

Peter testified about where he had picked up Julie and her general condition. The lawyer was most interested in whether she had seemed mentally competent at that time. Peter had to phrase his answers carefully, since he had thought from day one that she was incapable of taking care of herself. He said she was obviously intelligent and had thoughtfully planned the details of her escape. He did not say what he thought of those plans. He said she was in a state of near exhaustion, but she had been reasonable to deal with. He did not say that she was like a lost puppy in need of tender loving care. He added that in the months since her escape, she had proven to be a very capable young woman.

Julie's brief testimony was damaging to Dr. French. Her lucid recollections and precise information clearly revealed that she had been the victim, not a patient, in the scheme.

When the Hudsons reached Corpus Christi, Peter returned to therapy three times a week. Katie was gone, though, having returned to her home in Houston. She wrote letters of going back to school. Her letters bubbled with excitement over the news of the trial she'd seen on TV and read in the papers. Julie wrote back and bullied Peter into writing a paragraph, knowing the little girl would be more interested in what Peter had to say.

Julie's business interests and Peter's therapy kept them busy for weeks until Peter announced he couldn't stand the city for another minute, and they were going to go to Dooley for the Fourth of July weekend, and they could have a fireworks display on the ranch like the ones he remembered from his childhood.

Bobby, Lisa, and John jumped at the chance to go along. The private police force that kept surveillance over Peter and Julie seemed a bit excessive on a weekend trip to the country. The Hudsons decided the holiday from Friday to Sunday could be spent without their armed guards. Peter was mobile now and they would stick close together, not giving anyone an opportunity for mischief.

Julie stopped at Lisa's apartment to go over plans for the trip.

"I've packed some snacks for the trip." Bobby grinned as he set down a second brown paper grocery bag filled to the top.

Lisa looked at the two bags on her kitchen table and shook her head. Julie grinned in anticipation; how was Lisa going to handle Bobby's excess diplomatically?

"Bobby," Lisa objected, "it's only a two-hour drive to the ranch, and we'll probably stop at Dillon's Truck Stop for hamburgers."

"Hamburgers?" Bobby was skeptical. "John doesn't like hamburgers."

"He likes these," insisted Lisa. "Haven't you ever been to Dillon's?"

Bobby shook his head.

"They have burgers this big." Lisa held her hands out, indicating a circle as big as a dinner plate, and Bobby's eyes grew big as he imagined the size. "They claim to be the most famous hamburgers in the state, the biggest in the country, and the best in the world. You can also have venison hamburger, buffalo hamburger, or a weird thing they claim is a seaweed hamburger."

Bobby was intrigued by the prospect. "Well. . ." He considered the bag of junk food. "We'll probably need this stuff at Uncle Ray's," he pointed out practically. "You know when we were there at Thanksgiving, there was nothing but rice and powdered milk in the cupboards. And the refrigerator wasn't even turned on."

"You're right," Julie chipped in, "but remember that your uncle Ray has been living there ever since, and he's stocked up by now."

"I wouldn't count on it. Dad took me hunting there once when I was real little, and we ate Vienna sausages more than anything else. There wasn't even any peanut butter." Bobby was close to pouting over the prospect of eating canned meat for a whole weekend.

Lisa thought about what she knew of her dad's eating habits after her mom had died. "You know what, Bobby? I think you have a point. I wonder how much of this stuff we can get in the car and still squeeze in us and the luggage."

Bobby brightened. "You're going to take my stuff?"

"Sure, but let's trade some of these chips for cans of soup, a loaf of bread, a jar of peanut butter, and jelly," Lisa suggested.

"How about breakfast?" Bobby asked. "We might go fishing, but if we don't catch anything. . ."

"I know he has cereal," said Julie.

"Yeah," agreed Bobby with no enthusiasm. "Nature stuff that tastes like straw." Julie laughed out loud.

Lisa cast her a warning look.

"Hey, I'm sorry," she said, "but I don't like straw for breakfast, either!"

"You win," conceded Lisa. "Get a box of ours. We don't want you to turn into one of his cows."

"What is all this junk?" asked John in disbelief when they picked him up from the school where he worked. The others were already in the minivan and they were on their way out of town.

"This isn't junk," said Bobby.

"Yeah," said Lisa defensively. "This is selective stuff. Bobby, Julie, and I spent a lot of time deciding just what should come and what would be left behind."

John climbed into the driver's seat as Lisa moved over. "Did you bring the kitchen sink?"

"No, we had to take it out in order to fit in your fishing gear," she answered smartly.

"I thought," said Peter, "that they had packed for a week-long camping trip in Mexico. But they assured me we are going no farther south than the ranch."

"You guys have no right to fuss," complained Lisa. "We did all the work. Right, Bobby?"

"Right!" he answered with gusto.

Lisa turned to her sister-in-law. "Right, Julie?"

"Right," she said. She unexpectedly leaned over and gave Peter a bear hug. Peter was surprised. "What was that for?"

"I just love your family." She grinned. Peter shook his head in amazement. They seemed pretty ordinary to him.

❋

They reached the truck stop after dark. Bobby eagerly went inside and scrambled into a huge corner booth. He grabbed the menu and gasped when he saw that there was nothing but hamburgers to order on the main-dish column. The establishment boasted of Texas burgers for visitors, which were one-quarter pounders, hamburgers for moderate Texans, which were one-half pounders, and hamburgers for Real Texans that contained a pound of meat on a gigantic handmade bun. Lisa and Julie ordered the hamburgers for visitors. But the three men, Bobby included, ordered the Real Texan burger. The adults were skeptical as to the wisdom of Bobby's order, but not only did Bobby polish it off, he finished before anyone else.

He sat quietly, not interested in the grown-ups' talk, until he began to feel very sleepy.

Julie saw him nodding. "You want to go for a walk with me before we get back in the car?" she asked.

"Sure." Bobby jumped at the chance.

"We'll stay close to the building," Julie told the others, and she and Bobby made good their escape.

They looked at the giant rigs and read some of the names the truck drivers had written on their cabs. A shiny blue one named Heaven's Sent and a red one with gray stripes named George's Buggy sat side by side. There was Spike's Speeder and Simon's Speeder. Julie and Bobby wondered if the two were related.

"What's that noise?" asked Bobby, tilting his head to hear better.

"I don't hear anything," remarked Julie.

"Listen," ordered Bobby.

She heard it then. A puppy was whimpering behind one of the semi-trucks. It yipped as if in pain.

"It's stuck or something." Bobby started around the dark corner.

"Wait, Bobby. We should get the others." But Bobby had already charged off. Julie followed. Around the corner, a little brown puppy pulled at a rope tied to a stake. He wriggled with ecstasy when he saw potential rescuers.

"It's all right, Bobby," said Julie. "Some trucker has tied him while he went in to eat. The puppy is just lonely, not hurt."

Bobby sat on the ground next to the furry, squirming mass of energy. "Isn't he great? I'll bet he's smart."

They jumped as a man came hurrying around the corner. "He's smart all right," he spoke loudly. "Would you like to have him? I thought I'd take him to my grandkids, but my daughter put her foot down when I showed up with the little tail-wagger. No dog. Not now. Not ever."

"That's awful," exclaimed Bobby, truly distressed for the poor kids with such a mean mom. But the prospect of his getting their reject brought a smile to his face. "Can I go in and ask, Julie?"

"We'll both go in." Julie did not like the idea of waiting alone in the dark with this burly truck driver until the others came out.

Bobby began his plea before he even reached the table. To Julie's surprise, John got up and immediately went to investigate. By the time they had paid the bill and left the restaurant, Bobby was the proud owner of a born troublemaker. He had a sack of puppy food to squeeze into the car along with a water dish. John had paid a nominal amount to the driver.

"What are you going to name him?" asked Peter once they were on the road.

"I have to think about it," answered Bobby.

The puppy was wiggling to be free from Bobby's lap, eager to explore his new surroundings.

"I suggest Slugabed," said Julie, laughing at the puppy's antics. "He is obviously lacking in energy."

"How about Rasputin? He looks like a rascal," offered Peter.

Lisa said, "I like Cuddles. If he ever slows down, he'll be such a sweet little bundle to cuddle."

"Only his master will pick the right name," interrupted John. "You guys lay off Bobby and let him get acquainted with his dog."

The dog turned out to be a good traveler. Soon after the car was in motion, he settled on Bobby's lap and went to sleep.

Peter turned to his brother-in-law. "I didn't think you'd be such a pushover, John."

"Oh, Lisa and I have been talking about getting him a dog. We also think we might move to a house. Robert has called and said he would like to stay in Saudi indefinitely. Bobby will go spend a month or more with him this summer, but for most of the year, he'll be with us."

"Sounds like a great arrangement!" Peter was pleased.

Chapter 26

Ray, John, and Bobby shuffled around the ranch house kitchen at dawn. Repeated invitations to those still in bed were ignored. The threesome stomped out for their early morning fishing expedition and brought back a string of fish several hours later.

"I caught the biggest fish," Bobby told Lisa.

"Hey, Buddy," interrupted John. "That's the only fish you caught. I caught the most."

Not to be outdone by this display of manly bragging, Ray put in his bit. "I may not have caught the biggest fish, but all of mine weighed more than John's. John would keep the babies in order to say he had the most."

John started to bluster, but Lisa stepped in. "John knows the smaller fish have the most tender meat."

Her father looked at her in dismay. "Girl, you don't believe that?"

Lisa grinned. "My own father used to tell me the calves had tender meat. Veal, isn't it?"

"What applies to cattle doesn't necessarily apply to fish!"

"If you've cleaned those fish, I'll fry them," said Julie in an effort to divert the conversation. She thought the family was just being silly, but she wasn't quite sure. She was still getting used to their brand of bantering.

Lisa snatched the string of fish from her husband's hand. "They know better than to bring fish to the kitchen before they're cleaned. I'll fry, Julie, if you'll make the biscuits."

"Don't you remember I got a bad grade in pastries?" asked Julie, smiling. "Jesus turned a few fish into a feast for the multitude and my miracle is turning small bits of bread into stone."

Everyone laughed and they got on with the breakfast.

After they ate, Peter took Julie aside for a snuggle before she went horseback riding with the others. "Do you know what you did this morning?"

"Made chewable biscuits?"

"No, you joined in the jesting with my family. That's the first time you've done that." He kissed her. "You're beginning to feel comfortable with them."

"Yes, I am," Julie agreed, pleased with this little bit of evidence that she was really becoming part of her husband's family. She went off for her ride in great spirits.

✳

After lunch, the family played cards until Peter lay down for a nap. Ray sorted through some papers he wanted to show Peter when he woke up, and John and Lisa went to visit some friends. Julie and Bobby went outside to play with the dog.

"I've decided to call him Higgins," said Bobby.

"He looks like a Higgins," said Julie, tilting her head and watching the puppy investigate a pile of rocks. "Where have you heard that name before?"

"There was a boy in my class named Josh Higgins at school a long time ago. He never could sit still in his chair and sometimes the teacher made him stand up 'cause he made so much noise shuffling his chair and the desk around."

Bobby abruptly called, "Hey, Higgins." The dog had taken off down the dirt road. "Come back!"

The little monster looked over his shoulder in a "catch me if you can" challenge and ran faster. Bobby took off after him. Julie followed in a leisurely way. She didn't see how anyone could run in the afternoon sun of a Texas July.

They had gone quite a ways down the road and were almost to the little bridge that forded a small stream.

"Can we go on to the brook?" Bobby called back to Julie.

"Sure," she answered and waved him on.

By the time she got there, Bobby and the puppy were splashing in the slow muddy waters.

"Watch out for water snakes," Julie warned and sat down on the bank under a scrubby mesquite tree, being careful to avoid the long thorns.

The boy and dog tirelessly splashed in and out of the water. Julie figured any snake with an ounce of self-preservation was miles away by now. No breeze moved the hot air. At the Estate she would have spent much of the afternoon in the pool. She thought it would be nice to have a pool when she and Peter settled down after the therapy sessions were over. Perhaps in the backyard of his house in town. She smiled as she imagined him teaching their children to swim much as her father had taught her. She pulled vague memories of her laughing, carefree father from the depths of her mind.

"Julie." Bobby's frantic call brought her out of her musings. "Higgins took off."

Julie jumped to her feet, and the two humans began pursuit of the exasperating puppy.

Bobby scooped tired Higgins into his arms. The dog's long pink tongue hung out as he panted. He had finally stopped scampering just out of their reach and lay down in a little spot of shade.

"You rascal," scolded Bobby. "You're bad. Bad dog!"

"Which way should we go?" asked Julie. The surrounding countryside looked forbidding. As far as they could see, short prickly bushes dotted the barren land. It all looked the same. Julie had no idea which way was east or west, and even if she figured it out from the position of the sun, she still didn't know in which direction the ranch house lay.

Bobby knew.

"See the low place over there?" He pointed and Julie focused on the horizon.

"No," she answered, dismayed.

"See that patch of green?" continued Bobby with patience. "That's treetops. The ground dips down and there is water there. The trees grow and we can see the leafy green stuff on top but it looks like it is just short bushes. That's where we had the bonfire last Thanksgiving."

"You're sure?" It all looked pretty much the same to Julie, various shades of washed-out green with lots of brown and sandy tan.

"Yeah," answered Bobby confidently. "Uncle Ray used to take me out riding before he got married."

"Bobby, that was three years ago! You sure you remember?"

"Relax, Julie. He used to tell me it could be a matter of life or death to know what you were doing in this country. I paid attention."

"Okay," said Julie. "So where are we and which direction do we go?" Julie wasn't sure about relying on Bobby's store of knowledge, but his was bigger than hers, so she might as well trust in him while she sent prayers up to God that he was right.

Bobby sensed her skepticism and decided to show off.

"That's a teddy bear cholla." He pointed at a twelve-inch upright plant densely covered with yellowish gray spines so thick they looked like fuzz. His finger moved to another larger cactus that spread out with platter-type leaves frugally covered with large ugly spikes. "That's a prickly pear, and that's a hedge hog. It has water stored in the barrel."

"I'm impressed," Julie admitted. "So which way do we go?"

"The ranch house is over there."

They stood up and began to walk. Higgins ran ahead and looped back whenever Bobby called.

"Maybe he's learned his lesson," commented Bobby. "It's good to have him with us. If a snake sees him, it's more likely to slither off than challenge him."

"Snakes?"

"Rattlers."

"Bobby, this is not a good time to tease about snakes."

"I'm not teasing. Watch where you step."

Julie prayed again. Surely the God who turned a rod into a snake for Moses would be willing to turn rattlers away from their path.

They walked on in silence, trudging through the sparse underbrush. Higgins got tired and lay down in a small patch of shade under what Bobby said was a soapberry. Julie was too hot and tired to comment. Bobby picked up his puppy and trekked on.

How does he do it? wondered Julie. Her back was wet with sweat. Her throat felt like she had swallowed cotton, and her feet hurt from stepping on rocks, since the soles of her shoes did little to protect her. Her legs weighed a ton and were gaining weight with every step.

"Bobby, I have to rest."

"We're almost there."

"I don't see the house."

"You won't till we get past the hill."

"The hill?" Julie looked out over the flat land and thought maybe Bobby shouldn't be trusted after all. She sunk down and sat without ceremony on the barren soil.

Bobby sat beside her and Higgins jumped out of his arms.

"You should at least sit in the shade."

Julie looked around. "What shade?"

"You're really sunburned."

A sarcastic answer came to Julie's mind, but she was too tired to express it. Besides, Bobby had been a real trooper. She was the whiner. At least she refrained from voicing much of her complaining. Julie brought her knees up and dropped her head down to rest.

"It's not a good idea to stay here," prompted Bobby.

"Just a minute, Bobby, just a minute," whispered Julie.

Bobby sighed.

"I'm tired, too. And thirsty. Really, Julie, it's not much farther."

Julie didn't answer.

"I could go ahead and get help and bring it back," Bobby offered.

Julie lifted her head and gave him a weak smile. "Bobby, you're the greatest. I'm coming."

They stood up and Bobby called to Higgins. He didn't come and Bobby called more urgently. Julie joined in. Had the puppy wandered off again?

"Higgins, Higgins," Bobby yelled.

There was a crashing noise in the underbrush. Higgins bounded through, closely followed by a low-slung, powerfully built basset.

"Sidney," exclaimed Bobby and Julie in unison.

"Where did you come from?" asked Julie as she bent to greet the dog.

"See," said Bobby, "we are close. Come on, Julie. I'm so thirsty, I could croak!"

Bobby started off with renewed vigor and Julie followed. The dogs bounced around their ankles, then darted off into the tangle of weeds and scrub and returned to urge them on. Soon Bobby had outdistanced Julie.

"We're almost to the top of the hill," Bobby called over his shoulder. "I see Peter. He's coming this way. Hurry up, Julie!"

Bobby ran on, and Julie watched as he disappeared over the horizon. There must have been an incline, she realized as she followed, hurrying now that she knew Peter was just ahead.

She was surprised to see the land drop away when she finally got to the high point. Looking back, she saw that the rise had been too gradual to notice. This was the crest of the "hill." Ahead of her, the ground slanted away, and she saw the dirt road coming off of the highway and the house and barns of the main house.

She caught sight of Bobby just as he reached Peter. Suddenly her strength was renewed and she scrambled down through the cactus.

He used a cane now, but knowing that he still toppled easily, she forced herself not to tackle him. He carried a sports bottle, and as soon as Bobby had taken a drink, he handed it to her.

"Peter, I've never been so glad to see anyone." She hugged him.

"I'm glad to see you, too, Honey, but we've got a problem."

"What?" Her face crumpled into a frown.

"Jacob Jones is at the house."

Chapter 27

"U ncle Jacob?" Julie squeaked.

"That's the bad guy, isn't it?" Bobby's eyes grew big.

"Yes," said Peter as he started herding them across the field. "Let me tell you real quick what has been going on. We need to act fast."

"Why are you pushing us away from the house?" asked Julie.

"We're not going in," answered Peter. "We're going to the barn. John and Lisa came back from town and they brought Sidney with them. I took Sidney out to look for you because I was getting worried. I saw a car I didn't recognize come up to the house and three men get out. I didn't have any luck finding you, so I turned back. When I got back to the house, I looked in the window just as I was passing by."

They had reached the barn, and Peter steered them to the back door.

"The men were all together in the front room. One of them held a gun and it was obviously not a cordial visit. That's when I recognized your uncle from pictures my uncle Henry had."

"He's in there with a gun!" Julie's voice came out in a squeaky whisper.

"No, he's just sitting there. It's one of his henchmen who has the gun."

"But your dad, John, and Lisa are in there with henchmen?"

Peter nodded.

"We've got to do something!"

"I'll ride for help on one of the horses," volunteered Bobby.

"No," said Peter, "but I am going to ask you to do something dangerous."

Julie frowned at Bobby's enthusiasm. This was serious.

"What? Do you want me to go in and distract them?"

"No, I want you to sneak in the back way, go up to Lisa's room, and bring back her cellular phone."

Bobby nodded. "Sure."

Julie shuddered and she took hold of his arm. "Bobby, this isn't a game. Those men are criminals."

"I'll be careful, Julie." He patted her hand. "You don't have to worry."

"I can't help but worry," Julie said emphatically.

"You should pray." When she didn't respond, he gave her a big hug and then pulled away. "Okay, here I go."

He slipped out before someone could make another objection and interfere with his adventure.

Peter and Julie stood facing each other in the dim light of the barn. Horses shuffled in their stalls. Higgins and Sidney sniffed around, enjoying the smells of hay and animals that drifted around them.

"I'm scared," said Julie.

"Come here." Peter held his arms open. She walked into them and laid her head against his chest.

"Pray, Peter, pray."

They stood together as Peter said a quick prayer of protection for Bobby as he sneaked through the house and for those who were sitting in the living room with the gunman.

"I'm back," Bobby announced as he came through the door. He held up the cellular.

Peter dialed, reported the situation succinctly, and hung up.

"They say sit tight," he said as he shut the unit. "Man, I don't like this. Somebody is going to get hurt." He rubbed his hand over his chin. "I'm going in."

"No!" said Julie.

"Julie," said Peter. "I'm going in there. You forget that I was a Marine. Not only that, but I was Military Police. I'll hobble a lot on my cane and look unsteady and they'll think I'm no threat."

"No!"

"There is only one man with a gun."

"The other man may have a gun."

"Trust me, Julie. I won't take any unnecessary chances. I don't want to go back into the hospital. If I caused someone to get hurt, it would be on my conscience, and I don't want that, either."

"Peter," begged Julie, but he turned to Bobby.

"Bobby, after I've been in the house three minutes, I want you to put both Sidney and Higgins in the back door. Got it?"

"Three minutes from when you step through the front door. Got it."

"Good." Peter hit his shoulder in approval. "Julie, you go with him and help manage the dogs."

"Peter."

"Go on now and get in position."

Bobby already had a hold of Higgins, and Julie reluctantly went to take Sidney's collar in her hand.

"Be careful," she admonished and followed Bobby out the back door of the barn.

Peter walked in the front door as if he suspected nothing.

"I didn't find them, Dad," he called. "Have we got company?"

"Yes," said Jacob Jones. "I'd say you have company."

Peter stopped in the doorway to the living room and surveyed the scene.

Little had changed since he'd looked in an hour before.

Lisa sat on the couch next to John. The man with the gun stood near the front window. A second man stood beside the chair where his father sat, and Jacob Jones sat in his father's favorite chair. Peter carefully kept his poker face, but he was glad that Julie's uncle was in that chair. The springs were gone out of the seat and even his athletic father had to struggle to get out. Jacob would not jump into the fray when it began. The man next to his father was in a favorable position for their side as well. Peter had no doubt that his father, who had on more than one occasion subdued drunken cowhands, could deal with that character. The man would not expect a senior citizen to be as spry as his dad. That left the man with the gun for Peter.

Peter decided that when he made his move, he would thrust the gun toward the bookcase on the opposite side of the room. If it went off by mistake, no person would be in the path of a stray bullet.

He hobbled in a few steps, leaning heavily on the cane, and he saw his father's eyes widen slightly at the sight of his unsteady progress.

"What is the meaning of this?" Peter said, eyeing the gun. "Who are you people?"

"You haven't guessed?" asked Julie's uncle. "I've come to retrieve something that belongs to me. First, I'll collect my unfortunate niece and then, in due time, the property that is mine, erroneously placed in her hands."

Peter moved awkwardly into a position that put him directly in the line of fire between his family and the gun.

"I don't think you have a realistic grasp of this situation." Peter spoke directly to Jacob Jones, seemingly unaware of the man with a gun at his back. "The courts have proven French's operation was fraudulent. No one will believe that Julie is insane."

"A woman who shoots her family and then turns the gun on herself is hardly sane, Mr. Hudson." Jacob Jones's twisted smile almost caused Peter to lose his concentration.

Peter took a step back as if recoiling in horror. From the deep recesses of the house came a howl. There was a scrabbling noise on the tiled floor of the hall, and two furry cannonballs exploded into the room. At the same moment, Peter body-slammed the rugged individual behind him, being careful to lock on to the arm holding the pistol, guiding it away from the people. Peter easily secured the gun after he had the man on the floor; he looked up to find his dad had a headlock on the other man and John was towering over Jacob Jones. Lisa sat where she had been, both dogs in her lap.

"Lisa," Peter ordered, "go tell Julie and Bobby the mission is accomplished."

❋

"Still want to take those therapy courses?" asked Peter.

Julie looked away from the dust kicked up by the departing police cars.

"To tell you the truth, Peter, I hadn't thought much about it today."

"The reason I ask is that I'm feeling pretty full of myself right now. I subdued a hardened criminal and all, you know."

"Yes, I know," contributed his wife.

"I'd say I am pretty well rehabilitated."

"And. . ."

"And, if it's all the same to you, if you don't have your heart set on starting a career. . .mind you, you can if you want and I'll stand 100 percent behind you."

"Yes. . ."

"I just thought it would be nice to put aside adventure and intrigue for now and. . ."

"And start a family?"

Peter nodded.

"I'm a jump ahead of you, Papa."

Peter searched her face.

"You aren't kidding, are you?"

Julie grinned.

KATHLEEN PAUL
Kathleen lives in Colorado Springs, where life has gotten busier and busier now that she's retired from teaching. She leads weekly writing workshops, volunteers at church and MOPS, does crafts—currently stamping—reads, reads, reads, plays with her grandson, and tries to find time to write every day. Check out her Web site at www.donitakpaul.com.

A Letter to Our Readers

Dear Readers:

In order that we might better contribute to your reading enjoyment, we would appreciate your taking a few minutes to respond to the following questions. When completed, please return to the following: Fiction Editor, Barbour Publishing, Inc., P.O. Box 719, Uhrichsville, OH 44683.

1. Did you enjoy reading *Kaleidoscope?*
   - ❑ Very much—I would like to see more books like this.
   - ❑ Moderately—I would have enjoyed it more if _____
   _____
   _____

2. What influenced your decision to purchase this book? (Check those that apply.)
   - ❑ Cover
   - ❑ Back cover copy
   - ❑ Title
   - ❑ Price
   - ❑ Friends
   - ❑ Publicity
   - ❑ Other

3. Which story was your favorite?
   - ❑ *Behind the Mask*
   - ❑ *Love in Pursuit*
   - ❑ *Yesteryear*
   - ❑ *Escape*

4. Please check your age range:
   - ❑ Under 18
   - ❑ 18–24
   - ❑ 25–34
   - ❑ 35–45
   - ❑ 46–55
   - ❑ Over 55

5. How many hours per week do you read? _____

Name _____

Occupation _____

Address _____

City_____ State_____ Zip_____

E-mail_____

HEARTSONG ♥ PRESENTS

Love Stories
Are Rated G!

That's for godly, gratifying, and of course, great! If you love a thrilling love story but don't appreciate the sordidness of some popular paperback romances, **Heartsong Presents** is for you. In fact, **Heartsong Presents** is the premiere inspirational romance book club featuring love stories where Christian faith is the primary ingredient in a marriage relationship.

Sign up today to receive your first set of four, never-before-published Christian romances. Send no money now; you will receive a bill with the first shipment. You may cancel at any time without obligation, and if you aren't completely satisfied with any selection, you may return the books for an immediate refund!

Imagine. . .four new romances every four weeks—two historical, two contemporary—with men and women like you who long to meet the one God has chosen as the love of their lives. . .all for the low price of $10.99 postpaid.

To join, simply complete the coupon below and mail to the address provided. **Heartsong Presents** romances are rated G for another reason: They'll arrive Godspeed!

YES! Sign me up for Heartsong!

NEW MEMBERSHIPS WILL BE SHIPPED IMMEDIATELY!
Send no money now. We'll bill you only $10.99 postpaid with your first shipment of four books. Or for faster action, call toll free 1-800-847-8270.

NAME _____

ADDRESS _____

CITY _____ STATE_____ ZIP_____

MAIL TO: HEARTSONG PRESENTS, P.O. Box 721, Uhrichsville, Ohio 44683
or visit www.heartsongpresents.com